THE BEEBO
BRINKER
CHRONICLES

TRIANGLE CLASSICS

ILLUMINATING THE GAY AND LESBIAN EXPERIENCE

The Beebo Brinker Chronicles
by Ann Bannon

And the Band Played On
by Randy Shilts

The Autobiography of Alice B. Toklas
by Gertrude Stein

A Boy's Own Story
The Beautiful Room Is Empty
by Edmund White

Brideshead Revisited
by Evelyn Waugh

The Celluloid Closet
by Vito Russo

City of Night
by John Rechy

Dancer from the Dance
by Andrew Holleran

Death in Venice and Seven
Other Stories
by Thomas Mann

Giovanni's Room
by James Baldwin

Orlando
by Virginia Woolf

The Picture of Dorian Gray
by Oscar Wilde

Rubyfruit Jungle
by Rita Mae Brown

Surpassing the Love of Men
by Lillian Faderman

The Well of Loneliness
by Radclyffe Hall

What Is Found There/An Atlas of the Difficult World/
The Fact of a Doorframe
by Adrienne Rich

Zami/Sister Outsider/Undersong
by Audre Lorde

THE BEEBO BRINKER CHRONICLES

ODD GIRL OUT
I AM A WOMAN
WOMEN IN THE SHADOWS
BEEBO BRINKER

ANN BANNON

QUALITY PAPERBACK BOOK CLUB
NEW YORK

ODD
GIRL OUT

ONE

THE BIG HOUSE was still, almost empty. Down the bright halls and in the shadowy rooms everything was quiet. Upstairs a few desk lights burned over pages of homework, but that was all.

There was one room in the sorority house, however, where no reading was going on. It was a big, warm room, meant for sprawling and studying and socializing in, like the others. Three girls shared it and two of them were in it now on this autumn Sunday night.

One was a newcomer. Her name was Laura and she had just finished moving all of her belongings into the room. It was a scene of overstuffed confusion, but at least she had somehow succeeded in squeezing all her things in and now there remained only the job of finding a place for them. Laura sat down to rest and worry about it. She tried to ignore the other girl.

Beth lay sprawled out on the studio couch with her head cushioned on a rambling pile of fat pillows at one end and her feet dangling over the other. She was drinking a Coke, resting the bottle on her stomach and letting it ride the rhythm of her breathing. She wore slim tan pants and a dark green sweatshirt with "Alpha Beta" stamped in white on the front. Her hair was dark, curly, and close-cropped.

Laura sat by choice in the stiff wooden desk chair, as if Beth were too comfortable and she could make amends by being uncomfortable herself. She was nervously aware of Beth's scrutiny, and the sorority pledge manual she was trying to read made no sense to her. The worst of it was that Laura wanted Beth to like her. Beth seemed like all good things to the younger girl's dazzled eyes: sophisti-

5

cated, a senior, a leader, president of the Student Union, and curiously pretty. She had a well-modeled, sensitive face with features not bonily chic like those of a mannequin, but subtle, vital, harmonious. She wasn't fashionably pretty but her beauty was healthy and real and her good nature showed in her face.

Laura flipped nervously through her pledge manual, not even pretending to read any more. Finally Beth saw that she wasn't reading and smiled at the ruse.

"One hundred and thirty-seven pages of crap," she said, nodding at the manual. "All guaranteed to confuse you. I don't know why they don't revise the damn thing. I've passed an exam on it and I still don't understand it."

Her attitude embarrassed Laura, who smiled uncertainly at her new roommate, thinking as she did so how many times she had smiled in the same way at Beth, not sure of how she was expected to react.

She had never known quite how to react to Beth from the first day she had seen her. It had been shortly after Laura's arrival at the university, when everything she saw and felt excited her to a high pitch of nervous awareness. Even the sweet smoke of bonfires in the early-autumn air smelled new and tantalizing.

Laura walked around the university town of Champlain, down streets chapeled with old elms; past the new campus with its clean, striking Georgian buildings and past the old with its mellow moss-covered halls; past that copy of the Pantheon that passed for the auditorium; past the statues; past the students walking down the white strip of the boardwalk, sitting on the steps of buildings, stretching in the grass, and talking . . . always talking.

It thrilled her, and it frightened her a little. Some day she would know all of this as well as her home town; know the campus lore and landmarks, the Greek alphabet, the football heroes, the habits of the campus cops. Some day she wouldn't have to ask the questions—she would be able to answer them. It made her feel a sort of grateful affection for the campus already, just to think of it this way.

She had been in school a week when she went up to the Student Union to join an activity committee. It seemed like a good way to meet people and get into the university's social life. Laura had an appointment for an interview at three o'clock. She sat in the bustling student activities center on the third floor waiting to be called, clearing her throat nervously and sneaking a look at herself in her compact mirror. She had a delicate face shaped like a thin white heart, with startling pale blue eyes and brows and lashes paler still. A face quaint and fine as a Tenniel sketch.

She waited for almost half an hour and the sustained anxiety began to tire her. She stared at her feet and up to the clock, and back to her feet again. It was when she glanced at the clock for the last time that she saw Beth for the first.

Beth was standing halfway across the room, tall and slender and with a magnetic face, talking to a couple of nodding boys. She was taller than one of them and the other acted as if she towered over him, too. Laura watched her with absorbed interest. She tapped the smaller boy on the shoulder with a pencil as she talked to him and then she laughed at them both and Laura heard her say, "Okay, Jack. Thanks." She turned to leave them, coming across the room toward Laura, and Laura looked suddenly down at her shoes again. She told herself angrily that this was silly, but she couldn't look up.

Suddenly she felt the light tap of a sheaf of papers on her head, and looked up in surprise. Beth smiled down at her. "Aren't you new around here?" she said, looking at Laura with wide violet eyes.

"Yes," Laura said. Her throat was dry and she tried to clear it again.

"Are you on a committee?"

She was strangely, compellingly pretty, and she was looking down at Laura with a frank, friendly curiosity that confused the younger girl.

"I'm here for an interview," Laura said in a scratchy voice.

Beth waited for her to say something more and Laura felt her cheeks coloring. A young man thrust his face out of a nearby door and said, "Laura Landon?" looking around him quizzically.

"Here." Laura stood up.

"Oh. Come on in. We're ready for you." He smiled.

Beth smiled, too. "Good luck," she said, and walked away.

Laura looked after her, until the boy said, "Come on in," again.

"Oh," she said, whirling around, and then she smiled at him in embarrassment. "Sorry."

The interview turned out well. Laura joined the Campus Chest committee and turned her efforts toward parting students from their allowances for good causes. Every afternoon she went up to the Union Building and put in an hour or two in the Campus Chest office on the third floor, where most of the major committees had offices.

It had been nearly two weeks later that Beth stopped in the office to talk to the chairman. She sat on his desk and Laura, carefully looking at a paper in front of her, listened to every word they said. It was mostly business: committee work, projects, hopes for success. And then the chairman told her who was doing the best work for Campus Chest. He named three or four names. Beth nodded, only half listening.

"And Laura Landon's done a lot for us," he said.

"Um-hm," said Beth, taking little notice. She was gathering her papers, about to leave.

"Hey, Laura." He waved her over.

Laura got up and came uncertainly toward the desk. Beth straightened her papers against the top of the desk, hitting them sideways the long way and then the short way until all the edges were even.

"Beth, this is Laura Landon," the boy said.

Beth looked up and smiled. And then her smile broadened. "Oh, you're Laura Landon," she said. She held out her hand. "Hi, Laur."

Nobody had ever called her "Laur" before; she wasn't the type to inspire nicknames. But she liked it now. She took Beth's hand. "Hi," she said.

"You know each other?" the chairman said.

"We've never had a formal introduction," Beth said, "but we've had a few words together." Laura remained silent, a little desperate for conversation.

"Well, then," said the chairman gallantly, "Miss Cullison, may I present Miss Landon."

"Will Miss Landon have coffee with Miss Cullison this afternoon?" said Beth.

Laura smiled a little. "She'd be delighted," she said.

They did. And she was. An occasional fifteen- or thirty-minute coffee break was traditional at the Union Building. Beth and Laura went down to the basement coffee shop, and came up two hours later because it was time finally

to go home for dinner. Laura couldn't remember exactly
what they talked about. She recalled telling Beth where
she was living and what she was studying. And she remembered a long monologue from Beth on the Student
Union activities and what they accomplished. And then
suddenly Beth had said, "Are you going to go through
rushing, Laur?"

"Rushing?"

"Yes. To join a sorority. Informal rush opens next week."

"Well, I—I hadn't thought about it."

"Think about it, then. You should, Laura. I'm on Alpha
Beta and, strictly off the record, I think we'd be very interested."

"Why would Alpha Beta want me?" Laura said to her
coffee cup.

"Because I think it's a good idea. And Alpha Beta listens
to Beth Cullison." She laughed a little at herself. "Does
that sound hopelessly egotistical? It does, doesn't it? But
it's true." She paused, waiting until Laura looked at her
again. "Sign up for rushing, Laura," she said, "and I'll
see to it you're pledged."

"I—I will. I certainly will, Beth," Laura said, hardly
daring to believe what she'd heard.

Beth grinned. "My God, it's nearly five-thirty," she said.
"Let's go."

After that it had been easy. Beth spoke the truth; Alpha
Beta did listen to her. Laura had signed up for rush, with
the secret understanding that she would pledge Alpha
Beta. But even at that, it was a thrill when Beth called her
two days after rushing was over and said, "Hi, honey. Pack
your things. You're an Alpha Beta now. Officially."

Laura had cried over the phone, and Beth said, "You
don't have to, you know."

"But I want to!"

Beth laughed. "Okay, Laur, come on over. You just
joined one of the world's most exclusive clubs. And you
have a new roommate. In fact you have two."

"Two?"

"Yes. Me. And Emily."

Emily had spent the day with them, helping Laura bring
things in and put them away. Laura was so tired now she
could hardly recall Emily's face; all she remembered was
a warm, ready laugh and the vague impression that Emily

was fashioned to please the fussiest males: the ones who want perfect looks and perfect compliance in a woman.

Beth had called a halt to their work early in the evening.

"We've done enough, Laura," she had said, dropping down on the studio couch. "We've even done too much."

"It was wonderful of you to help me, Beth."

"Oh, I know. I'm wonderful as all hell. I only did it because I had to." She grinned at Laura, who smiled self-consciously back. Beth liked to tease her for being too polite and it made Laura uncomfortable. She would have gone to almost any length to please Beth, and yet she could not abandon her good manners. They struck her as one of her best features, and it puzzled her that Beth should needle her about them. She knew Beth could carry off a courtesy beautifully at the right moment; Laura had seen her do it. But Beth was much less formal than her new roommate, and furthermore she liked to swear, which Laura thought extremely unmannerly. Beth made Laura squirm with discomfort. And in self-defense Laura tried to build a wall of politeness between them, to admire Beth from faraway.

There was a vague, strange feeling in the younger girl that to get too close to Beth was to worship her, and to worship was to get hurt. As yet, Beth made no sense to her, she fit no mold, and Laura wanted to keep herself at an emotional distance from her. She had never met or read or dreamed a Beth before and until she could understand her she would be afraid of her.

Laura had been thinking about this that afternoon while she filled the drawers of her new dresser with underwear and sweaters and scarves and socks, and had resolved right then that she must always be on her guard with Beth. She didn't know what she was trying to shield herself from; she only felt that she needed protection somehow.

Beth had suddenly put an arm around her shoulders, shaking the thoughts out of her head, and said with a laugh, "For God's sake, Laur, how many pairs of panties do you have? Look at 'em all, Emmy."

And Emily had looked up and laughed pleasantly. Laura couldn't tell if she were laughing at the underwear or at Beth or at the look on Laura's face, for Laura looked as surprised as she was. She stood there for a minute, feeling only the weight and pull of Beth's arm and not the necessity to answer.

In a faint voice Laura answered, "My mother buys all my underwear. She gets it at Field's."

"Well, she must've cleaned them out this time," said Beth, smiling at the luxurious drawerful. "I'll bet they put in an emergency order for undies when she leaves the store."

Emily laughed again and Laura shut the drawer with a smack and cleared her throat. She hated to talk about lingerie. She hated to undress in front of anyone. She even hated to wash her underwear because she had to hang it on the drying racks in the john or in the laundry room where everyone could see it. It was no comfort to her that everybody else did the same thing.

"Of course, I don't believe in underwear myself," said Beth airily. "Never wear any." She swept a stack of sweaters theatrically off the table and handed them to Laura, who gazed at her in dismay, reaching mechanically for the sweaters. Beth laughed. "I'm pretty wicked, Laur."

"Don't you really wear any—any underwear?" Her whole upbringing revolted at this. "You *must* wear some."

Beth shook her head, enjoying Laura's distress and surprised at how little it took to shock her. Laura looked at her with growing outrage until she burst out laughing and Emily intervened sympathetically.

"Beth, you're going to make your poor little roommate think she's fallen in with a couple of queers," she said with a giggle.

Beth grinned at Laura and the younger girl felt strangely as if the bottom had fallen out of her stomach.

"She has," said Beth with emphatic cheerfulness. "She ought to know the dreadful truth. We're characters, Laura. Desirable characters, of course, but still characters. Are you with us?"

Laura wished for a moment that she were all alone in a vacuum. She didn't know whether to take Beth seriously or not; she felt as if Beth were testing her, challenging her, and she didn't know how to meet the challenge. She transferred a sweater nervously from one hand to the other and tried to answer. Nobody was a more rigid conformist, farther from a character, than Laura Landon. But the bothersome need to please Beth prompted her to say weakly, "Yes."

She put the sweater in a drawer, turning away from Beth and Emily as she did so, and silently and secretly scraped the white undersides of her forearms. It was an old gesture. Whenever she was disappointed with herself she bruised herself physically. The sad red lines she raised on her skin were her expiation, a way of squaring with herself.

Beth, who could see she had gone far enough, confined herself for a while to friendly suggestions and answering questions. It was a great relief to Laura. She was almost herself again when Beth suggested a tour of the sorority house.

The two girls went first up to the dormitory on the third floor, where everybody but the housemother and the household help slept.

"Does anyone ever sleep in the rooms?" Laura asked as they mounted the stairs.

"Oh, once in a while. In the winter, when the dorm is really cold, some of the kids sleep in their rooms. The studio couches unfold into double beds. They can sleep two."

They had entered the big quiet dorm with its dozens of iron bunk beds smothered in comforters and down pillows and bright blankets. Laura shivered in the chill while Beth pointed out her unmade bed to her.

"We'll have to come back and make it up later," she said.

Beth had then led Laura down to the basement. She was enjoying this new role of guide and guardian, enjoying even more Laura's unquestioning acceptance of it. They found themselves playing a pleasant little game without ever having to refer to the rules: when they reached the door to the back stairs together, Laura stopped, as if automatically, and let Beth hold the door for her. Laura, who tried almost instinctively to be more polite than anybody else, readily gave up all the small faintly masculine courtesies to Beth, as if it were the most natural thing in the world, as if Beth expected it of her. There was no hint that such an agreeable little game could suddenly turn fast and wild and lawless.

In the basement Beth showed her the luggage room, shelved to the ceiling and crowded with all manner of plaid and plastic and leather cases. In the rear of the room was a closed door.

Beth turned around to go out and bumped softly into Laura, who had been waiting for an explanation of the closed door. Laura jumped back and Beth smiled slowly and said, "I won't eat you, Laur."

Laura felt a crazy wish to turn and run, but she held her ground, unable to answer.

Beth put her hands gently on Laura's shoulders. "Are you afraid of me, Laur?" she said. There was a long, terribly bright and searching silence.

"I—I wondered what the door in back was to," Laura faltered. Her sentence seemed to hang suspended, without a period.

Beth let her hands drop. "That's the chapter room," she said. "Verboten. Until you're initiated, of course."

"Oh," said Laura, and she walked out of the luggage room with Beth's strange smile wreaking havoc in the pit of her stomach.

On the way upstairs they met Mary Lou Baker, the president of Alpha Beta. She came down the stairs toward them, towing a bulging bundle of laundry which bumped dutifully down the stairs behind her. She smiled at them and said, "Hi there. How's the unpacking coming along, Laura?"

"Fine, thank you." Laura watched Mary Lou retreat into the basement, impressed with her importance.

"She likes you," said Beth as they headed back up to their room.

"She does?" Laura smiled, pleasantly surprised.

"Um-hm," Beth answered. "Usually she has nothing to say to newcomers for a few weeks. If she notices you right away it's a good sign. At least it is if you're interested in her approval." She said this rather disparagingly.

Walking down the hall behind her, Laura smiled.

And now here they were in the calm of a Sunday night, alone in their room, curious and shy at the same time. Beth finished her Coke and set the bottle down on a glass-topped coffee table in front of the studio couch. The clack of glass on glass startled Laura and the pledge manual slipped from her hands to the floor.

"Want to go make your bed up now?" Beth said. Her voice was soft, as if she were rather tired.

"Oh, yes. I guess I'd better."

"I'll help you." Beth sat up, swinging her long legs to

the floor. She sat still for a minute as if getting her bearings, looking at her feet. Then she lit a cigarette. "Come on, let's go do it," she said finally with sudden brightness.

"*I'll* do it, Beth," said Laura firmly. "You've done so much for me today, I just hate to have you do any more."

Beth blew smoke over the table top. "Laura, if you don't stop thanking me for everything you're going to wear me out," she said. "Or turn my head." She said this good-naturedly, to tease more than to scold. But then she saw that she had hurt Laura and she wanted instantly to reach out with comfort and reassurance. She was not impatient with Laura's hypersensitivity, only unused to it. She never knew when she might scrape against it and cause pain.

Laura's mouth tightened and she gripped the cover of her pledge manual in an effort to calm herself.

"Laura," said Beth in a gentle voice, and she got up and went over to her. Laura drew back in surprise as Beth dropped to her knees in front of the chair, putting a hand on Laura's knees and smiling up at her. Laura was too startled to pretend composure.

"Laur, have I hurt your feelings, honey? I have, haven't I? Answer me."

Laura said helplessly, "No, Beth, really—"

"I know I have," Beth interrupted her. "I'm sorry, Laur. You mustn't take me so seriously. I'm only teasing. I like to tease, but I don't like to hurt people. You just have to get used to me, that's all. Take me with a grain of salt." She looked earnestly at her with the shade of a smile on her lips and she thought how good it would be to skid her hands hard up Laura's thighs and . . . So she kept talking. It was better to ignore the peculiar feelings Laura awoke in her; she covered her confusion with words.

"Because I want us to be good friends," she went on. "And I'll try not to—to shock you any more. I guess I'm a little crazy—the results of a misspent youth, of course." And she grinned. "But I'm not dangerous, honest to God. Now—" she smacked Laura's knees amiably—"we're over the first crisis. Are we going to be friends, Laur?"

Laura wanted desperately to pull her knees together. "Yes," she said to Beth. "I hope so."

"Good!" said Beth and she bounced to her feet. "Come along, then. Let's make your bed."

It hadn't taken long to make up the austere box bed and Laura found herself back in the room and faced with the humiliating problem of undressing in front of somebody else. Her shyness settled in her cheeks and neck like a heat rash. As soon as she felt the burn, it spread to her shoulders and bosom. She blushed very easily and she despised herself for it. She wanted to scratch at her arms again, but because Beth would notice it she had to content herself with biting the tender flesh of her underlip until she was afraid it would bleed and cause her more grief.

She turned as far from Beth as she could and unbuttoned her blouse, somehow feeling that Beth's bright eyes were doting on every button. But Beth was subtle; she was humming a tune and busy with her pajamas. She saw Laura without seeming to and Laura began to envy her pleasant abandon. After a moment she said, "Laur, do you have a sweatshirt?"

"Yes." Laura eyed her quizzically.

"Better put it on. The dorm is a damn deep freeze."

Laura found the sweatshirt and pulled it over her head, and Beth led her up to the dorm. On the door was posted a wake-up chart with a pencil on a string hanging beside it. Beth signed Laura's name under "6:45."

"Think you can find your bed?" she asked.

"There it is," said Laura, pointing.

"Okay, in you go," said Beth.

Laura studied the upper bunk, which looked unattainable. "How?" she faltered.

Beth laughed quietly. "Well, look," she said. "Put your foot on the rung of the lower bunk—no, no, wait!—that's right," she said, guiding her. "Now, get your knee on the rung of the bed next door. Now, just roll in. Whoops!" she said, catching Laura as she nearly lost her balance. She gave her a push in the right direction. Laura rolled awkwardly onto her bunk, laughing with Beth.

Beth climbed up where she could see her and said, "You'll catch on, Laur. Doesn't take long." She helped Laura under the covers and tucked her in, and it was so lovely to let herself be cared for that Laura lay still, enjoying it like a child. When Beth was about to leave her, Laura reached for her naturally, like a little girl expecting a good-night kiss. Beth bent over her and said, "What is it, honey?"

With a hard shock of realization, Laura stopped herself.

She pulled her hands away from Beth and clutched the covers with them.

"Nothing." It was a small voice.

Beth pushed Laura's hair back and gazed at her and for a heart-stopping moment Laura thought she would lean down and kiss her forehead. But she only said, "Okay. Sleep tight, honey." And climbed down.

Laura raised herself cautiously on one elbow so she could watch her leave the dorm. Beth went out and shut the door and Laura was left to her strange cold bed in the great dark dormitory. She felt cut loose from reality.

It took her a long while to get to sleep. Her nerves were brittle as ice and they all seemed to be snapping from the day's pressure. She lay motionless on her back and studied the luminous checkers on the ceiling, laid there through the window by the light of the fire escape. She thought of Beth: Beth beside her watching her, whispering to her, reaching out to touch her.

The stillness grew and lengthened and Laura lay in it alone with her thoughts. Far away on the campus the clock on the Student Union steeple pulsed twelve times through the waiting night. Laura pulled her covers tight under her chin and tried to sleep. She was just drifting off when she heard someone stop by her bed and she opened her heavy eyes and saw Beth outlined by the night light.

"Still awake?" she whispered.

"I'm sorry. I'm dropping off now." Laura felt guilty; caught with her eyes open when they should have been shut; caught peeking at nothing; caught thinking of Beth.

"Just wanted to make sure you were all right."

"Oh yes, thank you."

"Shhh!" hissed someone from a neighboring bed.

"Sorry!" Beth hissed back, and then turned to Laura again. "Okay, go to sleep now," she said, and she gave Laura's arm a pat.

"I will," Laura whispered.

TWO

A T SIX FORTY-FIVE, Laura heard a soft voice whispering, "Time to get up, Laura." She sat up immediately in her bed as if pulled by a wire, and looked over to see an unusually pretty face staring up at her.

"Thank you," she said.

The face smiled and whispered, "Wow, are you easy to wake up!" and moved away.

Laura had a good morning. She spent a lot of it wondering about her strange desire for a good-night kiss from Beth, and hoping Beth hadn't understood her sudden aborted gesture. At lunchtime she sat with everybody in the big sunny dining room, talking while she ate. She glanced over at Beth, who sat two tables away from her and found Beth returning the look. Laura answered her smile and turned, in confusion, to prospecting for nuggets of hamburger in her chili.

After lunch they studied together for a while. Laura sat down with her book in a large green butterfly chair in the corner and struggled to get comfortable. She was still trying to conform to the incomprehensible chair when Emily ran in from the washroom, grabbed her coat and a notebook, and ran out again. Seconds later she was back.

"Hey Beth, if Bud calls tell him I'll see him at Maxie's at four."

Beth pulled her reading glasses down to the end of her nose and looked over them. "Right," she said.

"Thanks." And Emmy was gone.

Beth stared after her, shaking her head and smiling a little.

"What?" said Laura.

"I just don't get it. Or rather, I get it but I don't like it. He's too crazy for her. Emmy needs a steadying influence." She winked at Laura and turned back to her book.

Laura began to glance furtively at her, half expecting her to be looking back, and she was rather disappointed when Beth kept her nose in the book. After a while Laura gazed

17

openly at her, resentful of the book that claimed all Beth's attention. And then she forgot the book and thought only of Beth. . . .

The two girls walked to their afternoon class together. It was a brisk day, snappy and sunny and invigorating. Beth walked with long, smooth strides. She liked to walk and she walked well, as if she were really enjoying her legs; enjoying the rhythmic cooperation between legs and lungs, crisp weather, space and speed. She had a lusty health that almost intimidated Laura, who was breathless with trying to keep up. And breathless, too, with pleasure at walking beside Beth.

They arrived in class five minutes late, and the instructor had already started his lecture. He interrupted himself to note, while gazing out the window with a wry smile, "Glad you could make it, Miss Cullison."

Beth, slipping out of her coat, looked up at him with a grin. They were friendly enemies, she and the teacher; they liked to catch each other slipping up somewhere.

"I see," he added, "you're leading the innocent astray."

Laura blushed in confusion. It scared her to see someone flirt with authority as Beth did: she expected to see the hallowed rules and traditions crash down on Beth and crush her, and when they didn't she was as surprised as she was relieved. To Laura, the things Beth said and did were daring in the extreme. To Beth, who knew herself and people better, it was just a half-hearted revolt; a small scale protest that was more in fun than in earnest. She didn't want to be an out-and-out character any more than she wanted to be one of the herd, so Beth beat herself a path between the two.

Laura was happy, when she saw the letter was from her father, that Beth and Emily weren't in the room. Her divorced parents were a faraway sorrow she tried to pretend out of existence. She opened the letter slowly.

"Glad to hear you like your new home," she read. "I understand Alpha Beta is a pretty good sorority."

Yes, father. Pretty good. If you say so. She hated the way her father phrased things.

"Anyway," the letter went on, "they had a good house when I was in school. Your roommates sound like nice girls, especially the Cullison girl. That's the kind of friendship you should cultivate, Laura, with people who can really do you some good. This girl sounds like a real go-getter—president of the Student Union and etc. That's quite an honor for a girl, isn't it? She can probably do a lot for you—get you into the right activities and so forth. I'd treat her well, if I were you."

Laura sighed with exasperation over her father's ideas of friendship; if it weren't useful somehow it just wasn't friendship, only a waste of time.

"By the way," he continued, "Cliff Ayers's son Charlie is in school down there. I'd like you to give him a call—he'd like to hear from you, I'm sure."

Sure, thought Laura with futile resentment. He'd like to hear from Marilyn Monroe. But who's Laura Landon? He won't even remember the name.

"Cliff says Charlie looks just like him, which means there's probably a line of girls ahead of you."

Is that supposed to encourage me? Laura wondered bitterly. If Charlie Ayers wants to hear from me, which I doubt, he can call me himself.

"I understand that your mother has found a nice apartment. You will spend half the holidays wth her and half with me, of course. I must say, Laura, you took the divorce pretty well, though of course I expected you to."

Laura crushed the letter with angry hands and threw it into the wastebasket by the desk. Then she put her head down and wept, until she heard Beth and Emily coming down the hall. They found her dusting the already spotless coffee table and smiling at the job.

Beth looked at her oddly for a moment and then picked up a manila envelope and hurried out of the room. She would be at a committee meeting all evening long and left Laura and Emily to study alone in an embarrassed silence. Both of them wished rather uncomfortably that Beth would come back and mediate for them. After a while the dearth of words between them began to pall and they were both suddenly conscious that they would be rooming together for the rest of the year. It seemed an interminable length of time.

Emily could usually chatter easily with people. She was natural with them and they responded naturally to her. But every word and gesture of Laura's seemed to her to be rehearsed, calculated to please, and it threw Emmy completely. She got the feeling that she could smash a bottle over Laura's head and Laura would say, very calmly, "Thank you."

There was plenty of room for Laura on the couch beside Emily, but she wouldn't sit there, simply because Emily got there first. She sat down in the butterfly chair with a sigh. It defied her, as usual, and her narrow skirt made the problem worse. She shifted unhappily and Emily, trying to be helpful, suggested, "Why don't you put your p.j.'s on, Laura? Much more comfortable. Besides, nobody studies in their clothes."

Laura couldn't think of an excuse to keep her clothes on and she got up to change, wondering if Emily just wanted to watch her undress. She performed the operation with determined casualness. Her set teeth wouldn't show, but her manner would. Emily watched her on the sly, wondering why Laura was so embarrassed and self-conscious about herself.

"Hey, Laur, what a pretty bra!" she exclaimed spontaneously as Laura pulled it out from under her pajama shirt. "Let's see it," said Emily reaching out a hand.

Laura gave it a jerky toss.

"Gee, nylon," said Emmy. "They make 'em up just like this only padded, you know," she added. "They're terrific. Ever try 'em?"

"Falsies, you mean?" said Laura. The word struck her as mildly obscene.

"Yeah."

"No, I never did."

"You should," said Emmy realistically. "They're terrific, really. Nobody knows the difference. Unless you're dancing awful close," she amended.

"I guess my busts are kind of small," said Laura.

Emily smiled at her, wondering at the pathetic modesty that made it impossible for Laura to call the parts of her body by their right names.

Laura's small breasts bothered her. She would fold her arms over them as much to conceal their presence as to conceal their size. She wished that they were more glamorous, more obviously there. In their present shape they seemed only an afterthought.

She sat down with her book again when she was safely into her pajamas and Emily sat and toyed with things to say; she had made a start and she wanted to keep the communication line open. At nine o'clock she snapped her book shut and said, "How 'bout some coffee, Laur?"

"No thanks," said Laura, looking up from her book.

"Oh, come on. It won't keep you awake. We've got a big jar of Sanka." She pulled open Beth's bottom dresser drawer and took out the jar, and Laura noted with displeasure her familiarity with Beth's things. "Come on," she said again. "I hate to go down alone."

Laura gave in. She followed Emily down the back stairs to the kitchen.

"We have a coffee break almost every night," said Emily tentatively. She lighted a cigarette and cast about for something new to say. Her perplexity made her pretty face quite appealing.

"Say, Laur," she said cheerfully, "have you got a date this Saturday?" Emily was ready to be friends with Laura; she was willing to be friends with almost anybody. The best turn she could do Laura, as she saw it, was to fix her up with an acceptable male. Emmy knew dozens of them.

"No," said Laura doubtfully. "But in pledge meeting they said something about getting me a date." She thought with fleeting guiltiness of Charlie Ayers, and knew she would never call him; she hadn't the guts and she hadn't the desire.

"Oh. Well, they haven't done it yet, have they?"

"Well, no, but—"

"Listen, Laura, there's a terrific guy I'm thinking of—a fraternity brother of Bud's. I could fix you up with him. Jim's a junior, real tall." And she went on to describe an irresistible young man. They are always irresistible until you're face to face with them. Laura let Emmy talk her into it. She didn't know any men and it seemed a good idea to let Emmy take care of the problem.

"Bud and I will be along the first time out," said Emily, making plans. "It's much easier to have somebody else along for moral support." She laughed and Laura smiled with her. What she said was true enough. It might not be so bad.

"That sounds terrific," she said, borrowing Emmy's favorite adjective to amplify her gratitude. "If it wouldn't be too much trouble for you."

"Oh, Lord no," said Emily. She set one cup into another thoughtfully and went on, "Gee, I wish I could talk Beth into going out."

Laura was suddenly alert. She turned and looked at Emily. "Doesn't she go out?"

"Nope. Crazy girl."

"Not at all?" Laura thought it was a requisite for sorority girls.

"No." Emily stared quizzically at her sudden show of interest.

"I just thought—" Laura looked away in confusion. "I mean, she's so popular and everything. I just naturally thought—well—" If a girl didn't date was there anything wrong with her?

"Oh, she used to," said Emmy, taking the steaming water from the burner and pouring it over the little mountains of dry coffee in the cups she had set out. "She used to go out a lot the first couple of years she was down here. But nothing ever happened, you know? Every time she got interested— Sugar?"

Laura was so absorbed that it took her a minute to collect her wits and answer, "Yes, please."

Emmy dropped it in and handed Laura her cup. "There's no cream. There's Pream, though. Want some?"

Laura wanted to shake Beth's story out of her. "No, thanks," she said briefly. "This is fine." She was hungry for any crumb of information about Beth without stopping to wonder where her appetite came from. She was concerned only with satisfying it at this point.

Emily dipped into the Pream can with a spoon and sprinkled the white powder into her coffee. "You get used to it," she said. "I didn't used to like it, either."

"Well, what happened?" said Laura in a voice that was urgent yet soft, as if the volume might excuse the words. She didn't want to look interested.

"Oh . . . well," Emmy stirred her concoction. "Nothing happened, really. In fact, that was the whole trouble. Nothing *did* happen." She looked cautiously at Laura, as if trying to determine just how much she could be confided in. Laura's face was a picture of sympathetic concern. "She'd find somebody she liked," Emmy went on, "and they'd go together for a couple of months, and just when it seemed as if everything was going to be terrific, it was all over. I mean, Beth just called it off. She always did that," she said musingly, "just when we all thought she was really falling in love. All of a sudden she'd call it quits."

"Why?" said Laura.

Emily shrugged. "If you ask me, I think she just got scared. I think she's afraid to fall in love, or something. It's the only thing I can think of. Otherwise it just doesn't make sense."

"Were they nice boys?" Laura asked.

"Terrific boys! Some of them, anyway."

"Well, didn't she tell *them* why she dropped them? I mean, she must have told them something." Laura was groping for the key to Beth's character, for something to explain her with.

"Nope," said Emily. "Just told 'em good-by and that was it. Believe me, I know. I've had 'em call me by the dozens to cry on my shoulder. But she wouldn't say much to me, either. She just said she got tired of them or it wouldn't have worked out and it was best to end it now than later, or something."

"And now she doesn't go out any more?"

"Isn't that something?" Emily clucked in disapproval. "You'd think she was disillusioned at the tender age of twenty-one. She puts on like she doesn't care, but I know she does. But still, she did it to herself. After a while when the boys called up for dates she just turned 'em down automatically. As if she knew she wasn't going to have any fun, no matter who she went with. As if it just wasn't worth the trouble."

Emily had lost Laura's attention, but she didn't know it. Laura was thinking to herself, She's got a right not to care. Why should she care about boys? She doesn't have to. Emmy doesn't know everything.

"Of course," Emmy went on, "she's told me a thousand times she doesn't want any man who's afraid of her, and if they're all afraid of her, to hell with them. I'm quoting," she added, smiling. "She likes to swear."

"I noticed," said Laura a trifle primly.

"I don't know where she got that idea," Emmy said. "She says she won't play little games with them just for the sake of a few dates. Well, you know men. What's a romance without little games? I mean, let's face it, there isn't a man living who doesn't want to play games." She eyed Laura over her coffee cup and made her feel illogically guilty.

"Maybe she's afraid of men," said Laura. The words popped from her startled mouth like corks from a bottle. For a sickening minute she thought Emily was going to ask her questions or stare at her curiously, but Emily only laughed.

"Lord, she's not afraid of anything," she said. "It's more the other way around. They're afraid of her. She just needs a good man who doesn't scare easy to get her back on the right track. Maybe we can find somebody for her," and she smiled pleasantly at Laura.

Upstairs again, Laura settled into her malevolent butterfly chair and wondered why Emmy was so short-sighted. It struck her as rather fine and noble that Beth didn't go out with men. It never occurred to her that Beth really might like men; without knowing why, without even thinking very seriously about it, she knew she didn't want her to like them.

Laura was a naive girl, but not a stupid one. She was fuzzily aware of certain extraordinary emotions that were generally frowned upon and so she frowned upon them too, with no very good notion of what they were or how they happened, and not the remotest thought that they could happen to her. She knew that there were some men who loved men and some women who loved women, and she thought it was a shame that they couldn't be like other people. She thought she would simply feel sorry for them and avoid them. That would be easy, for the men were great sissies and the women wore pants. Her own high school crushes had been on girls, but they were all short and uncertain and secret feelings and she would have been profoundly shocked to hear them called homosexual.

It would never have entered her head to doubt that Beth was solidly normal, because Laura thought that she herself was perfectly normal and she wasn't attracted to men. She thought simply that men were unnecessary to her. That wasn't unusual; lots of women live without men.

What Laura would never know and Beth would never tell her, was the real reason she had given up seeing men. Beth had, over and above most people, a strongly affectionate nature, a strong curiosity, and a strong experimental bent. She would give anything a first try, and morality didn't bother her. Her own was mainly a comfortable hedonism. What she wanted she went after. At the time she met Laura, she wanted to be loved more than anything else.

Beth had always wanted to be loved. She wanted to feel, not to dream; to know, not to wonder. She started as a little girl, trying to win her aunt and uncle in her search for love. Loving them was like trying to love a foam-rubber pillow: they allowed themselves to be squeezed but they popped right back into shape when they were released.

Unknowingly, her aunt and uncle had started Beth on a long, anxious search for love. When she couldn't find it with them she turned to others, and when she grew up she turned to men. It was the natural thing to do; it was inevitable. For Beth grew up to be a very pretty girl, and when she began looking for a man to satisfy her she found more than one always willing to try.

But none of them made it. First there was George, when she was still in high school. She was just fifteen and George was a Princeton man in his twenties. Beth liked them "older," and the older ones liked her. George fell very much in love with her. He was fun, he had been places, he could take her out and show her a good time . . . and he adored her. Her word was law.

Beth administered the law for two years. The time began to drag interminably toward the end of the second year. George smothered her with love, and she began to doubt and to despise herself for not returning his passion. Here was real love, what she had always craved to make her life complete and meaningful, and what did it give her? A headache. George bored her.

It was in this mood that she gave herself to George. She was seventeen. George, on his knees, had implored her not to go to college; to stay at home and marry him and make him the Happiest Man In The World. She said, "No, George, I can't."

And he said, "Why?"

"Because I don't love you." Her heart rose in her throat, in fear and pity—fear for herself and pity for George.

George wept. He wept very eloquently. "I'll kill myself," he murmured in a misery so genuine that she began to fear for him, too.

"Oh, no, you mustn't! You can't!" she said. "Here, George. Come here, George." She called him like a faithful spaniel, and he came, and let himself be petted. And very shortly he felt a sort of dismal passion rising in him with his self-pity; he began to sweat.

"Beth." He said her name fiercely. "Look at me. Look what you've done to me."

Beth gasped and then covered the lower part of her face with her hands so he couldn't hear her laugh.

"Oh, George," she whispered in a voice shaky with suppressed amusement. George took it very well; he thought her trembling voice was paying him tribute.

And suddenly Beth thought to herself very clearly, Oh, hell. Oh, the hell with it. She was quite calm and she said to George, "Come here." Somewhere in the back of her mind was the hope that this would solve her problem, answer her questions, set things right. She might not love George, but at least she would discover the end of love. Next time she met a desirable man, she would know everything there was to know. She would be prepared and it would all be beautiful as nothing with George had been beautiful.

Beth unbuttoned her skirt and let it slip to the floor.

Hesitantly, with a flushed face and a nervous cough, George approached her. And in less than a minute they were on the couch together and Beth was learning about love.

After that there followed a long procession of boys, mostly college men. The novelty wore off early for Beth, but not the hope and promise; she was an incurable optimist. It took her three years of indefatigable effort to convince herself that it wasn't the men who were at fault —at least not all of them. The laws of chance were against it. But it was one thing to realize that some of the men were good lovers and another thing entirely to admit that not even the best of them could rouse her. What was wrong? She was healthy and eager and willing; she wanted it, she had always wanted some kind of love. Was it George's fault for making her laugh at it? Or her aunt's and uncle's for making her weep? It took her a long time to see that it wasn't the fault of any one of them, but rather of all of them, and of herself. That was the bitterest pill. And after she confessed to herself that something prevented her from finding the love she so wanted she became rather cynical about it. The bitterness never showed, but it was there. She was just a little contemptuous of men because none of them had been able to satisfy her; it was much more comfortable than being contemptuous of herself for a fault she couldn't understand.

Laura, sitting alone in the room with Emily on a lonely Monday night, could not have known any of this. Even Emily, who had been Beth's closest friend throughout her college years, knew nothing of it.

At ten-fifteen Beth walked in and the atmosphere in the room lightened up noticeably. Laura gave her a glad smile.

"Hello, children," Beth said, smiling at them both.

"Long meeting?" said Emily, stretching.

"No, short meeting. Long coffee break." She dropped her notebook on the desk and slipped out of her coat. "Laur, for God's sake, aren't you uncomfortable?" she said suddenly, laughing. "Makes me want to wiggle just to look at you. Here, swing your leg over this thing." And when Laura hesitated she took her leg and lifted it herself over one wing of the butterfly.

"It comes up between your legs," she said. "Now put your head back."

Laura moved her head back gingerly as if she expected it to fall off her shoulders at any moment. Beth pushed it back against the high wing of the chair, laughing at her.

"Now, isn't that better?" she said, mussing Laura's hair.

"Yes, thanks. Much better." And Laura had to smile back at her. The real world, with its real bumps and backslides and perplexities, was never farther away.

THREE

ON SATURDAY NIGHT Laura went out with the two fraternity boys and Emily. They walked to Maxie's, one of the oldest campus joints, and drank beer and listened to the Dixie Six. Bud put on almost as much of a show as the musicians; Bud was Emmy's flame—Bud was "it." He would drop his head in his hands and groan at the bad notes and at the good ones exclaim, "Christ! Listen, Emmy!"

Bud was slender and tall, with thinning brown curls and round green eyes. He had remarkably sensual lips with straight white teeth behind them, and an impish smile. He was a well-known campus musician, one of the best; his reputation with a horn and with women far outweighed his reputation among his professors in music school.

He was a sort of perpetual student; the type that comes back year after year and never quite graduates. He loved music and he loved girls, and he seemed to exist quite satisfactorily on beer and slide oil and kisses. He was a campus character; one of the ones everybody knows, or hears about and wants to know.

Emily was the only girl who had ever come near to hooking him. It wasn't the physical attraction; Bud liked them all pretty; he wouldn't have taken her out the first time unless she had fulfilled that qualification. It wasn't her twinkling charm or her compliancy, either; it was all of these plus her willingness and ability to learn something about music—his kind of music. She was learning how to play the piano, spending long hours at it, so she could talk to Bud in his own language. All these attractions weren't enough to keep him from surveying the field and finding a little competition for her, but as it happened that was the best possible way to intrigue Emmy, who liked to "work for a man." He was fast becoming her major subject, and Laura and Beth had to sit through several monologues on his merits as man and musician.

Laura examined him curiously. The music didn't move her, but everybody else was so excited that she pretended to be. She didn't understand the mass fervor but she was afraid to say so, and she sat and watched the band like the others.

Fortunately it was not very hard to be friendly at beer parties, and the more beer you drank the easier it was. Not that Laura could drink very much. But Jim, Bud's friend, did famously. With every passing quart he got friendlier. Toward the end of the evening anything in skirts was irresistible, and the handiest skirt was Laura's. He made an effort to get better acquainted, draping an arm over her and squeezing her into the corner of the booth with the warm weight of his body. He put a hand on her thigh and began to press it, and Laura looked to Emily in sudden alarm. She hated to let a man touch her and she hated even worse to let him do it in public. But Emily was too preoccupied with Bud to notice that her room-mate wanted help.

"Jim—" Laura said helplessly, and wondered wildly what to say next. Maybe all sorority girls did this. Maybe this was part of the price of membership.

When Laura hesitated in confusion, Jim thought she was searching for a way to encourage him, and he began, as he thought, to make it easy for her. He murmured, "What, baby?" in her ear, and "Tell me, come on," with a nauseating intimacy, and began to plant wet kisses on her neck and cheek, his hand closing harder on her thigh, until it started to hurt.

Laura trembled in revolt and he breathed, "Oh, baby!" and pulled her chin around and kissed her lips. The hot blush burned her face and she thanked God for the bath of pink neon that disguised it.

"I was all wrong about you, Laura," he whispered, and his lips brushed hers as they moved.

Laura wanted to claw at him, to burst from that terrible basement into the cold air and run and run and run until it was all miles behind her.

He kissed her again; a man's lips were claiming her own, and it was all so new, so alarming, that it took her breath from her.

"Jim—" she said.

He kissed her again, harder.

"Oh, Jim, please!" and she turned her head away sharply

against the wall of the booth. It was unbearable. No punishment could be worse than this. She waited, shaking, for him to reprimand her.

Instead he stroked her leg and leaned over her and said softly, "I understand, baby. Believe me. We'll have time later."

Laura thought she might be sick. It was no consolation to her to suddenly discover that she might be attractive to a man. She heard Emily's voice across the table with such grateful relief that she almost reached out to clutch at her.

"Well, look here!" said Emmy. "Look who's hitting it off!" She smiled a pleased smile. Emmy was a born matchmaker.

Jim straightened up a little and grinned at her. "Why sure," he said. "Just took us a little while to find each other. Kinda dark down here." He was delighted to have discovered an unexpected warm spell at the end of a chilly evening.

They laughed, and Emily gave Laura an approving smile that made Laura weak. It was apparently not only right but expected that she should let Jim maul her. Beth! she thought with sudden desperate force. Oh, Beth, if only you were here! The thought came unbidden out of the blue.

The two couples walked home together to the Alpha Beta house, Jim with a tight grip around Laura. She could feel his hip bone grind smooth and hard around its socket where their bodies were pressed together. She hid her cold helpless hands in her pockets and put her head down against Jim's jacket. The grating of the wool on her tender skin was a comfort to her; it was utterly disassociated from human flesh and just irritating enough to assuage her conscience.

She murmured "Yes" and "No" to Jim when she had to and when she tried to keep him from kissing her, he took it affably as part of the game. And all the while Laura thought of Beth, so strong, so lovely, so gentle. She tried to peer through the defiant dark for the lights of Alpha Beta. But when they got there, she wasn't allowed to run upstairs to Beth.

Jim hustled her out on the gloomy patio and emprisoned her on the love seat. He thought she owed him a fair measure of affection to recompense him for the evening's entertainment. Laura's aversion to him mounted higher with every kiss until it reached a screaming pitch inside her.

"Gee, Laura, I thought you were gonna be cold as hell," he said. "You're not, are you?" He chuckled at her.

Laura looked at him wide-eyed, held so hard that she felt she could count his ribs with her own. She hated him. She wanted to spit at him, hurt him, run. But she was afraid.

"Oh, yes," he said. "You and I are gonna get along just fine, Laura. Just fine." And he kissed her. "Just fine. Hey, open your mouth, honey. Hey, come on, Laura."

Laura turned away from him and whispered, "Jim, this is our first date. I mean—please, Jim."

"I know, baby. You're just a kid, you want to do everything right." He tickled her neck. "Well, believe me, Laura, this is right."

Laura's nails bit cruelly into the heels of her hands in a frenzy of revolt. Oh, God, stop! she thought.

"Hey, Laur, how 'bout next week?" He waited. "You busy next week?"

She waited too long; she didn't know how to make up excuses. She turned a helpless face to him.

"Good," he said. "Let's make it Friday."

"Oh, but I—"

"I'll give you a buzz."

The merciful closing chime sounded, and she sat up straight in a spasm of relief. Jim pulled at her arm. "Hey, Laura, they don't beat you if you kiss a boy, you know," he said, laughing and pulling at her.

"Jim, it's closing time," she said sharply.

"You're just nervous, baby," he said with a grin. He got to his feet slowly. "Okay, I don't want to make you a nervous wreck." He pulled his jacket on. Laura wanted to yank it on and force him out the door with all the histrionic haste of an old movie. He got one more long wet kiss from her and then she saw him out the door with an audible sigh of relief.

Laura walked up the stairs feeling weak and miserable. Jim was a handsome boy. Emmy said he was popular, and she had another date with him. She ought to be happy. But for the first time a tiny doubt slipped into her thoughts. What do I want? she asked herself. But she was afraid to answer.

Emily caught up with her on the stairs and said, "Gee Laur, Jim really likes you! I'm so glad. I thought for a while you two weren't going to hit it off. When are you going to see him again?"

"Friday." She wondered if Emily would notice her lack of enthusiasm. . . .

Beth was still up. Laura felt a surge of affection for her.

"Hey, it's past your bedtime," said Emmy.

Beth looked up with a smile. "I wanted to hear about the date," she said to Laura, and Laura had a sudden wild desire to throw herself into Beth's arms and cry; to tell her, with all the violence at her command, what she thought of Jim. But she didn't dare. She looked at Beth for a minute like a lost waif.

Beth smiled at her as if she understood. "How was it?" she said.

"Oh—very nice," Laura said. Emily was watching her.

"Laura made quite a hit with Jim," she told Beth, stripping off her clothes. Laura let her talk, wishing all the while that she would go away. She wanted to be alone with Beth; to talk, to be comforted.

Emmy kept them up for a while. Laura refused to go to bed until Emmy did, and finally she won the game. Emmy stood up and yawned.

"Guess I'll hit the sack, you guys," she said. "I'm beat to the bricks, as my friend Bud would say. See you in the morning."

"Night, Em," said Beth. She lighted a cigarette and settled back to gaze at Laura and when Laura could think of nothing to say, she walked over to the couch and sat down beside her.

"What's the matter, honey?" she said.

"Oh, nothing!" The overemphasis rang false, and her head ached and Beth was so close to her that she was dizzy.

Beth put an arm around her. "Tell me the truth, Laur," she said. And when Laura remained silent, she added gently, "It's not a disaster if you didn't like the boy, you know."

Laura looked down at her lap, still mute, afraid her tears would start with her voice.

"What did he do, honey?"

"He—he— I don't want to talk about it. It wasn't anything awful. Emmy seemed to think it was all right. Only, I—" her voice quavered—"I didn't like it." And suddenly she put her head down on Beth's shoulder and wrapped her arms around her and let the tears come out. The pressure began to lessen a little.

Beth held her and rocked her in her arms. "You didn't like it, baby?" she said softly.

"I hated it! I couldn't help it."

Beth smiled down Laura's back.

"Oh, Beth, I wish so much you had been with me instead of—of Emily." She had been about to say, "Instead of Jim." What a curious idea that was—to have a date with Beth!

Beth held her closer.

"I don't ever want to see that boy again!" she said into Beth's shoulder.

Beth broke the date for her.

FOUR

THE DAYS began to fly in Laura's life so fast that she lost them before she could reckon them. They got progressively brighter; she wanted to memorize each one but there was no time.

A letter came from her father; he was a better correspondent than her mother, but all his notes reminded her of the fresh wounds of their divorce. Laura was ashamed, even afraid to mention it to anyone. Her father wanted to know if she had called Charlie Ayers and Laura revolted vigorously at the thought. She tried to picture herself getting him on the phone and saying stolidly, "Hello, this is Laura Landon." Silence. He would get the point, of course. "Well—uh, gee, yeah, Laura, nice to hear from you. We'll have to get together some time. Tell your dad hello for me." Thanks, but no thanks.

Laura wrote her father that she couldn't get hold of Charlie. She gave the impression that she had given him up in favor of a clamorous press of beaux. Her father wanted her to be popular.

Life with Beth, she soon discovered, was busy and unexpected and at the same time relaxed as if nothing quite mattered enough to worry about. Beth was always occupied but somehow never in a rush. She had a phone installed in the room to accommodate her burden of calls.

"I just don't see how you do it," said Laura one night when the visitor count was high.

Beth stretched and came down from her stretch laughing. "It's easy," she said. "Lots of spare time. No social life. My God, if I had to mess with men I wouldn't have time for anything. I know when I'm well off." She laughed again suddenly, her eyes on Emily. "Look at Emmy," she said. "You don't believe a word I'm saying, do you?"

"Not that 'well off' stuff," said Emmy. "Neither do you."

"Sure I do. Now and then. My God, I have to. I'd go nuts if I didn't." She winked at Laura.

"Don't listen to her, Laura," said Emily in a motherly voice. "She's depraved."

34

Beth shrugged and got up with a grin. "You see?" she told Laura. "Nobody understands me, not even my best friend." She threw a pillow at Emily, who promptly threw it back. Beth dropped it elaborately on the floor.

"You're slowing up in your old age," Emily said.

"Oh, go play your piano!" Beth instantly regretted the remark. She knew why Emily spent most of her free time —and there was very little of it now, since she saw Bud every night—practicing on the old piano in the living room. There was an almost pathetic childish ingenuousness to her plan to capture Bud that made Beth feel sad and helpless. Aside from that, she missed seeing as much of Emily as she used to. Her peculiar schedule usually kept her out with Bud or down in the living room until bedtime. Emily was fun to talk to and gossip with.

Laura carefully put the pillow back where it belonged and then said good night. Pledge rules forced her to go to bed at eleven, and left the other two to talk as they pleased. The curfew irritated Laura. She was afraid that as soon as she left the room her roommates talked about her. She always felt that it was too early for bed, that she was wide awake, that there was more studying to do. It didn't occur to her for a long time that she was jealous of Emily.

Laura was right, in a way. Her roommates did speculate about her. They marveled at her two baths a day. They watched her scrub her face until it was almost raw and red and they noted how she always volunteered for the most dreary and uninteresting tasks in the whole house.

"Darn the girl," Emily said after Laura's polite goodnight, "I wish she'd relax. You know, sometimes when you burp nobody hears you. If you say 'excuse me' everybody looks up and knows you burped."

Beth threw her head back in a strong laugh.

"Well, that's the way she makes me feel," said Emily, grinning ruefully. She thought of Laura's eagerness to please, her conscientiousness, as a sort of magnified normalcy that made Emmy uncomfortable. "I like the girl, I really do," she said. "I can't complain about anything she does, but—I guess that's just it. I can't complain. I wish I could. It'd make her seem real, somehow."

"I don't think she understands herself very well yet," Beth said. "That's why she's so careful of everything she says and does. She wants to be sure it's right."

"Here we go again," said Emily cheerfully. "The old

psychology corner." That meant gossip about a particular female. "What's her family like?"

"I don't know. She won't talk about them at all. I'm afraid I scare hell out of her when I ask about them."

"Well, that's funny," Emmy said. "Wonder why?"

On a Wednesday in late November, just before dinnertime, Laura was called to the house phone. She picked up the receiver without thinking; it was probably someone from her activity committee at the Union, or maybe a man. She had continued going out; it was expected of her. But not with boys like Jim.

"Hello?" she said.

"Hello. Is this Laura Landon?" It was a good voice, strong and low and pleasant.

"Yes." Laura checked the files of her memory against the voice. It wasn't listed.

"This is Charlie Ayers. My father and your father are old friends."

Laura was silent, surprised.

"I just heard from Dad that you were down here. Thought I'd give you a ring."

"Oh. Oh yes, Charlie." She was flustered and awkward on the phone, especially with men.

Charlie sensed it and took over for her. "Well, look," he said, "maybe we could get together for a beer or something tonight."

She started to protest. It was a reflex action.

"Oh, come on, you can study any time," he said pleasantly. "I won't keep you long." Laura was struck again by his smooth voice. She paused a moment and he took it for acceptance. "I'll pick you up around eight," he said. "Okay?"

"Well, I—okay."

"See you at eight," he said.

She hung up wondering if the rest of him was as impressive as his voice.

Beth was interested. "Charlie Ayers," she said reflectively. "Isn't he an ADO?"

Laura nodded.

"Seems to me I've met him somewhere. Where'd you find him, Laur?"

"Oh, he—he just called. I met him on campus." She was amazed at her own fib, only half aware of her motives.

They were many and involved and they boiled down to impressing Beth with her own importance.

At a few minutes past eight her buzz ripped down the quiet halls. She jumped up nervously, pulled her coat on, and opened the door.

"Laura," said Beth, watching her with a smile. "You'll need your scarf. It's cold."

"Oh, yes. Thanks." She pulled it from the shelf and settled it around her shoulders, and started for the door again.

"Got your gloves?" Beth asked.

Embarrassed, Laura turned back to her dresser and pulled them out.

"How 'bout your purse, honey?" Beth chuckled at her.

"Oh!" said Laura impatiently, grabbing it and starting out again.

"Laura," said Beth in a slow teasing voice. "Aren't you going to kiss me good-by?"

Laura whirled and stared wide-eyed at her. Beth grinned. "Go on, honey," she said. "Have fun."

Laura backed out of the room and then turned and almost ran down the hall, her heart pounding, thrumming a thunderstorm inside her. Emily came out of the bathroom one door down and said, "Have a good time, Laur." Laura watched her retreat down the hall toward Beth with a sudden pang of jealousy so strong that she had to admit it to herself for the first time. Her buzz sounded again, and she had to go downstairs and meet Charlie.

She gazed anxiously around the front hall as she came down, and finally she saw a young man with dark hair glancing through a magazine, standing with his back to her. The lower she came the higher he seemed to stand from the floor. He wasn't aware of her until her heels clicked on the marble floor of the hall. Then he turned around, tossed the magazine down, and smiled at her.

"You must be Laura," he said, and walked across the room to take her hand. "I'm Charlie Ayers."

"Hi," she said, intimidated by his height and afraid her nervousness would betray itself. His face went very well with his voice.

Charlie took her arm and said, "Let's go to Pratt's."

He held the door for her and led her down the front walk to his car—an eight-year-old Ford with a dubious repaint job that left it generally green in tone. "It's not beautiful, but it runs," he said, laughing as he let her in. He was so sure, so calm and steady, that Laura began to relax a little. She tried to think of him, not of Beth.

Pratt's had a fair number of customers for a Wednesday night when Charlie and Laura walked in. They found a booth and Charlie helped her out of her coat.

He leaned over the table while she sat down. "Beer?" he said.

"Just a Coke, thanks."

He went to get it—no such thing as service in a student bistro—and left her to think. She made a powerful effort to avoid Beth and concentrate on Charlie. He was handsome and friendly and he didn't seem disappointed to find her ordinary-looking. She thought boys who looked like Charlie wanted only beautiful girls. She pictured him with a beautiful girl. She made a cigarette ad of them, a little TV commercial in which Charlie, in a tuxedo, leaned amorously over a white-clothed table to light the beautiful girl's cigarette, and she inhaled the intoxicating vapors till her strapless gown groaned with the burden of her breasts, and then blew the smoke out at the audience. And then she turned back to Charlie and smiled enchantingly into his wonderful face. They really made an eye-catching couple. When Laura recognized the girl in the picture it shocked her heart into action again. It was Beth.

Charlie set a Coke and a beer and glasses down on the table, and sat down facing her, interrupting her disturbing reverie. She couldn't think of anything to say.

"Well, I guess our fathers have been friends for a long time," he said.

"Yes, they certainly have."

Laura let him talk, but she didn't encourage him. She didn't like to talk about her father. It always made her feel sad and a little frightened, and after a while it tired her out.

"That's a fine house you're in," he said. "Let's see, I should know some of your sorority sisters. Baker?"

"Mary Lou. She's the president."

"Yeah, I remember her. Sort of pretty. Nice gal. Gloria Mark?"

Laura nodded.

"Gee, I knew a lovely dish over there a couple of years ago . . . Beth Cullison. Never see her around any more."

"Do you know Beth?" said Laura, uncertain and faintly alarmed.

"Oh, everybody knows Beth. I've met her a couple of times. I don't think she remembers me, though. This was a few years ago when she was dating a fraternity brother of mine. Pinned to him, in fact."

"Who?" she asked. She had to know.

"Oh, you wouldn't know him. Graduated last year."

"What was he like?"

Charlie smiled quizzically at her eagerness, without answering her. She began to feel the need to explain herself.

"Beth's my roommate," she said.

"Oh." He nodded, smiling. "Well, he was a nice guy. Quite an intelligent boy. They used to have long philosophical discussions. I guess Beth went for that in a big way."

Laura didn't like him, whoever he was. She didn't like to think that Beth had confided in him, kissed him, even. The thought produced a rash of gooseflesh.

Charlie ran his hand over the back of his head, the cigarette jutting out and away from his crisp brown hair, and he watched Laura as he did it. "As I say, I don't really know the girl. Just met her briefly. But I remember her . . ."

Laura didn't answer, and Charlie casually changed the subject. "When's your father coming down to pay you a visit?" he said.

"Oh, I don't know. I don't think he will. He's too busy," she answered, but she was thinking about Beth. What did the boy look like? Was he fun, had he been in love with her? Did she like him? Did she let him . . .

"Too busy?" said Charlie. "Must be traveling, hm?"

"No," she answered absently, "he and mother are—I mean—they—" She was suddenly staring at Charlie in confusion. It was too late.

"They what?" he said.

She looked around helplessly as if some way of escape might suddenly appear, and all of a sudden she felt very weak and lost. Her family was falling apart, and she was falling in love with Beth. The world was inside out, all wrong. She didn't understand it, she hardly even realized what was happening to her. She couldn't stop and she didn't know where she was going. Charlie's eyes burned her face.

Laura put her head in her hands and a tight silent sob shook her. He came around the table and sat beside her, putting an arm around her and trying to comfort her. "You know, we're really old friends, Laura. By proxy, anyway. I'm a great listener. Want to tell me about it?"

She couldn't control her tears. At last she said simply, "They've gotten a divorce. It's all over now. It shouldn't affect me like this. Please don't tell anybody," and she looked up at Charlie anxiously.

"Of course not," he said. "But just remember I've got a dandy shoulder for crying on, any time you're in the mood." And he gave her a warming smile. Laura returned it gratefully.

"Come on, let's go," he said.

At the Alpha Beta front door Charlie said, "I'm not going in with you, Laura." She looked up in surprise, and he chuckled. "You might feel obliged to kiss me good night. Gets pretty hot and heavy in the front hall at closing time —as I recall." He was not in the least tempted to kiss her.

It seemed to Laura a very special favor, one that respected her acute sensitivity, and she didn't know how to thank him. "Charlie—" she began. "It was very nice of you to take me out and listen to my troubles."

"Wasn't nice of me at all. I enjoyed it," he said with a smile. In the little silence that followed it struck him that there was only one way to prove that statement and that was to ask her out again. It occurred to Laura too, only to humiliate her. But Charlie saw her as a nice kid in an emotional jam, and because she seemed to need someone to lean on, because of their families, because she looked forlorn, he thought one more evening wouldn't hurt him. "When can I see you again?"

Laura was astonished. "Why, I don't know—" she said.

"Well, how about a week from Saturday?" he said, figuring only that he hadn't any other plans.

"Oh, that would be fine." She looked at him curiously.

"Swell. I'll call you," he said. And he went off down the front walk.

She went upstairs to the room, wondering why Charlie Ayers had asked her out for the night of the Varieties Show, one of the biggest campus events. Charlie didn't know he had until two days later when he checked the university calendar, and then he cursed himself. But he didn't break the date.

Laura came in the room to find Beth on the phone. She looked up from her conversation and smiled at Laura and after a moment she hung up. She spun around in her chair and said, "Well, is he as good as he looks?"

"Oh," Laura blushed. "He's awfully nice."

"Going to see him again?"

"Yes. For the night of the Varieties."

"Well!" Beth smiled at her. "He must be impressed." Laura didn't answer. "Finally remembered where I met that guy," she went on.

An awful suspense grabbed at Laura's stomach. "Who?" she said.

Beth frowned a little. "Your friend. Ayers. Charlie."

"Oh. Have you met him?"

Beth studied her and Laura could feel her amusement without understanding it. "Um-hm," Beth said. "Real handsome kid, isn't he?"

"Yes," Laura said briefly. She didn't like the way Beth and Charlie remembered each other at all.

"Well, I think I've got it now—I must have met him at a party somewhere."

"A fraternity party?" She was chagrined by her own jealousy.

"I guess so." Beth smiled. "Charlie been telling tales?"

"Of course not!"

Beth began to laugh softly. "Laura, you must be interested."

Laura's face turned red. "In what?"

"In Charlie, of course. What else?" Laura couldn't look at her smile. "I don't blame you," Beth went on, needling her subtly. "He's nice, as I remember. I thought it was a damn waste to give a brain to a guy with a face like that."

Laura wouldn't answer her. She wouldn't even look at her. Beth enjoyed the boycott.

"He's too handsome for me," she said. Laura rummaged defiantly in her closet, her back to Beth. "I like 'em ugly," Beth said.

"Oh, you're just joking," Laura said pettishly to a wall of wool skirts.

"No, I'm not. I like ugly faces. I like interesting faces better than pretty faces . . . You have an interesting face."

Laura turned around then and met Beth's provocative eyes for an instant and then looked at the floor. "I do?" she said.

The door opened noisily and Emily burst in, laughing. "Hi, roomies!" she said.

"Jesus, Emmy!" Beth got up with a grin and walked over to her. "Let me see your face." It was lipsticked from ear to ear and down her neck to the collar of her blouse. Beth laughed at her. "Laura, our roommate is bombed," she said.

Emily studied herself in the mirror. "And it's indelible," she wailed.

"Is she drunk?" Laura whispered to Beth.

"Sure," said Beth. "She's stoned." She took Emmy's chin in her hand and surveyed her face. Emmy submitted docilely to the examination, with her eyes shut. "Open your eyes, Em, I'm not going to kiss you," said Beth. "Bud went home, remember?"

And Emily got the giggles again. She took a piece of Kleenex and began to rub at the lipstick, which resisted her efforts and sat firm on her face. After a minute she gave up and stared at herself in dismay. Beth pulled open a dresser drawer and handed her a jar of cold cream.

"Not that you deserve it," she said. Emmy clung to her and laughed. "Come on," Beth said in a businesslike voice. She smeared cream over Emmy's face, rubbing it in carefully. "Every time she goes out with Bud, this is what happens," Beth told Laura. "She says it's good for his morale."

"Oh, Beth, I do not!" Emily said. "I said it was good for his music."

"God, I'll say it is. When you finish with him, Em, he can play in the key of Q."

Laura didn't like to see girls drunk. She sat on the studio couch and said hesitantly, "Well, it must be sort of exotic to date a musician."

"Exotic-exschmotic," said Emily. "He comes with the same basic equipment as any other man." Beth laughed, but Laura saw nothing to laugh at. "Only he's the deluxe model," Emmy added. She pulled her clothes off vigorously.

"Here, here!" exclaimed Beth. "You have to wear that again. God, Emmy, you act like you wear 'em once and throw 'em away!" And she rescued Emily's skirt and blouse from the floor. She pulled a towel from the rack on the closet door and draped it over Emily's shoulders, stuck her toothbrush in her hand, and propelled her firmly toward the door.

"Shape up or ship out, gal," she said. "You're just too damn sexy."

Emily pulled herself up regally in her underwear and said, "I'm beautiful, I'm beloved, and I have a secret."

"Well, hot damn!" said Beth, and she laughed.

Emily minced into the hall and turned back to announce, "And you're all jealous." And she left to wash up.

"How 'bout that!" said Beth in mock awe.

Laura looked uneasily around the room. She thought Emily had acted disgracefully and it embarrassed her to even think of it. Beth was silent for a moment and then stared at Laura thoughtfully. "Laur, honey," she said, "you free tomorrow night?" When Laura said yes, Beth gave her a friendly smack on the rear. "Be my date," she said. "For the movies."

From then on, they went to the movies regularly and Laura saw the old Garbo films, French imports and Swedish nature films, only to be with Beth. She often turned down parties to be able to go, a practice Beth would have stopped had she known of it. But Laura kept it carefully from her. She liked everything about the movie trips too well: sitting next to Beth in the dark theater, hearing her breathe and shift and laugh or whisper to her. The first time they'd gone to the movies together, Beth had reached over and helped her out of her coat. When Laura tried to do the same for her, Beth stopped her. "I've got it, thanks," she said. And after that they followed the same ritual, without ever referring to it.

Then the night came when *Cyrano de Bergerac* was playing at the local theater. Laura and Beth had hardly been seated before Laura, saturated with the sentiment, found the tears starting down her cheeks. She could never keep them back from an affecting story. Beth saw the quiet little tears and smiled at them. It was then she reached into Laura's lap and found her hand and took it in her own and pressed it. The shock stopped the tears as the warmth of Beth's hand began to spread all through Laura, strange, sweet and inebriating. It was ten minutes before Laura dared to look at Beth. She was gazing serenely at the screen.

They never mentioned it but after that their hands always found each other in the dark of the theater.

FIVE

IT WAS Saturday, the day of the Varieties Show, the day Laura was to see Charlie for the second time. It was also the day that Beth's Uncle John chose to pay his niece a visit. He had made a habit every year of getting down to see Beth for at least one weekend. He liked the Varieties and he liked the football game and he liked to have dinner at the sorority house with Beth. The girls made a fuss over him, and he would sit beaming at the head table, flattering the house mother and flirting with her charges.

Laura was anxious to meet him, to see if he looked and acted anything like Beth. Emily told her he was a very impressive individual; he had been a colonel in the last war and he had a false leg.

Uncle John arrived just before dinnertime and Laura watched with mixed emotions as he folded Beth in a hug. He was a big man with a red, jovial face and he shook Laura's hand heartily and said, "Well, well, you're Beth's new roommate! How d'you do?"

"Fine, thank you," she murmured, overcome with shyness, but Uncle John didn't notice. He was following Beth into the living room and greeting the girls he remembered from the year before.

Laura turned to Emily and said accusingly, "He doesn't look anything like Beth," as if it were Emily's fault.

"Oh, heavens no," said Emily. "He's not her blood relation. His wife is. She and Beth's mother were sisters."

"Oh," said Laura, and had trouble concealing the disappointment she felt. "Does she look like Beth?"

"Nope. Beth looks like her father. He died a long time ago. She has a picture of him around somewhere. It's funny. You'd think she actually knew him if you ever heard her talk about him. She was two, I think, when he died."

After dinner they went into the living room and sat on the floor in the circle of girls talking to Beth's uncle. He

44

was enthroned on the couch with a pretty girl on either side of him, talking merrily in all directions at once. Beth sat in a chair across from him, watching him with a little smile. Every now and then he said, "Isn't that so, Elizabeth?" and she would nod in agreement.

Uncle John was a large man in many ways, fat, generous and well-heeled. He hadn't any idea of what sort of a girl his niece was underneath her pleasant exterior. All her life she had been a bright little girl and pretty, so he simply ignored her spells of melancholy and her love of books. He gave her plenty of spending money, kept her in nice clothes and nice schools, and saw her at dinner and on weekends. He didn't interfere with her private life and feelings; they simply didn't matter to him that much. She was charmingly grateful for his care so he was fond of her and had arranged for her to have an independent income on her twenty-first birthday.

Laura cringed when he began to tease Beth. "We're going to have to lock up her books until she gets herself a man," he said, and roared amiably at his niece.

Beth grinned at him. "He's scared to death I'll wind up an old maid," she told Laura, "and he'll never get me off his hands."

"Now, now, honey, you know that's not true," he chuckled.

Laura sat there almost hating Uncle John and his calm assumption that Beth wanted to get married. Couldn't he see how fine and pure she was? Her face a blank and her thoughts miles away, Laura didn't hear her buzz and it wasn't until one of the girls nudged her and whispered something that she remembered she was supposed to meet Charlie that evening.

He looked even more attractive than she remembered and he said, "Well, Miss Landon, you look very pretty this evening."

Laura tried to feel a spark of feminine interest in him, but she couldn't. She liked him, that was all. He took her arm and led her out to the car. In it was a young man sitting alone. Charlie pointed to him and said, "This is my roommate, Mitch Grogan, Laura. We have an apartment—"

"So called—" said Mitch.

"—over on Daniel. Couple of blocks from campus."

"Compensations of old age," said Mitch. "You don't

have to live in university-approved housing. As a matter of fact, I don't suppose we could get anybody to approve of our housing, Charlie."

"What's the matter with it?" said Laura.

The two boys laughed. "Everything," said Charlie. "You name it, if it's bad we got it—bad pipes, bad wiring, bad landlady, bad everything. But we can give a hell of a beer party in the front room."

"And we keep our own hours," Mitch added.

"How old do you have to be to get an apartment?" said Laura conversationally. They were driving toward the auditorium where the Varieties Show was scheduled to get underway.

"Real old," said Charlie. "God, twenty-two, at least. Would you believe it, Laura, Mitch is damn near twenty-five."

"Really?" said Laura, turning to look at Mitch in the front seat beside her.

Charlie laughed at her seriousness. "He's going to die a bachelor," he told her confidentially. "I just let him tag along with me for kicks. Otherwise he forgets what women look like."

Laura looked at Mitch again and he didn't seem in the least disturbed over Charlie's prediction.

"See?" said Charlie with a grin. "God, they could put him right in the middle of a harem and he'd ignore every damn female until he got his homework done."

Trouble finding a parking space stopped all conversation until they were inside the auditorium. From then on, Laura made no effort to try to listen to Charlie and Mitch over the wild shouts of laughter. She searched the huge audience for Beth and Uncle John, but couldn't see them. When the Varieties were over Laura tried to scan every face she could see of the huge crowd streaming out of the auditorium, but Beth was nowhere in sight. Depressed and silent, Laura walked with Charlie and Mitch to Maxie's.

Maxie's was already jammed when they got there and the Dixie Six was in action, as usual.

"My God, when did Bud Nielsen start playing with them?" said Charlie.

"Where?" said Mitch. "Oh, yeah!"

Laura looked up, and there was Bud with his long gold horn glinting through the smoke, standing in the fore of

the little bandstand that stood in the rear of the room.
"Do you know him?" she asked Charlie.
"Yeah, I know him. Fraternity brother. Good musician."
"My roommate dates him," said Laura.
"Beth dates this character?" Charlie looked at her in surprise.
"Oh, no! My other roommate—Emily."
"Oh," he chuckled. "I didn't think Cullison would go for this guy," and he nodded at Bud.

Cullison, Laura thought in irritation. Her name is Beth. Elizabeth.

"God, it's crowded. Do you see a place?" Charlie said, squinting through the smoky pink gloom.

Laura became suddenly aware of someone saying her name and she turned around a couple of times, straining through the half-light at the myriad faces.

"Laura!" It was Beth. Laura saw her laughing and struggling through the crowd and her first wild impulse was to blindfold Charlie. But it was too late for that. She looked up at him and he was staring at Beth with a smile on his face. Laura was too upset to see that Mitch was smiling too.

Beth was worth staring at. Her cheeks were flushed and her eyes were very bright, as if she had a romantic fever of some sort. Actually, she simply had too much beer in her, and it was making her laugh. The boys in the crowd were squeezing and pushing her and Laura was suddenly furious to see that she was enjoying it.

Beth reached a hand toward Laura and Charlie took it quickly and pulled her past the last few people that separated them. He pulled hard and she fell against him, laughing and off balance. He caught her around the waist to steady her and when she was quite steady he held her still as if he were afraid she might lose her balance again, or as if he hoped she would.

Mitch and Laura watched this artful maneuver together, Mitch with a mild twinge of envy and Laura with raging jealousy. She almost swore at Charlie in her anger. Furious tears gathered in her eyes and her whole body was rigid with emotion. She hated Charlie for holding Beth, she hated Beth for letting herself be held, she hated the two of them just for being near each other. She was afraid to see them together; they had spoken too well of each other.

"My God, I thought I'd never make contact," Beth was saying. "We're over there." She gestured vaguely behind her, still leaning on Charlie. "Emmy talked us into it. Uncle John is getting a lecture on jazz. Bud's playing. Did you see him?"

"We saw him," said Charlie.

Beth looked up into his face for the first time. "Hi," she said. "You must be Charlie." She leaned closer and studied him. "Yes, you are. I'd remember that face anywhere. I'm Beth Cullison."

"Yes, I know." He laughed, holding her a little tighter.

Laura could hardly contain herself. "And this is Mitch Grogan," she said in a sharp, impatient voice.

"Hi, Mitch." Beth leaned away from Charlie to take his hand. Then she said, "Come on back and sit with us. We've got loads of room." She looked up at Charlie again.

"Sure," he said, releasing her slowly. "Think you can make it?" He grinned.

Beth took a few steps away from him and then turned back and said with an air of injured dignity, "Certainly."

Mitch and Charlie laughed at her, and then Charlie took Laura's arm—he failed to notice how stiff and unwilling it was—and followed Beth back to the booth. Beth introduced the boys. Emily smiled beautifully at them.

"Well, now," boomed Uncle John over the racket, "you children can sit together over here and I'll sit next to Emmy. She's a trombone widow tonight." And he laughed at himself, getting up and moving over to Emily's side.

Beth slid into the seat he had left and Laura nearly followed her in an effort to keep Charlie away.

"Whoa, my dear," said Uncle John, catching her sleeve. "Let the gentleman in the middle." She was furiously embarrassed.

Charlie sat between Beth and Laura, and Mitch settled next to Uncle John where he could gaze undisturbed across the table at Beth. He wasn't the only interested party. Laura kept an anxious eye on her, and every time Charlie leaned over Beth to smile or say something Laura crawled with irritation. The loud music prevented her from hearing what they said to one another.

As for Beth, sitting next to Charlie and crowded tight against the wall, she was surprised by the size of him. His eyes were dark and his grin was wonderful and she began to feel inside her an almost forgotten excitement. It was too strong to fight and too sweet to ignore. She didn't do anything about it; she just let it happen, and when after a while she felt his hand on her knee she let it stay there and smiled imperturbably across the booth at Uncle John.

But she was not as calm as she looked. The pressure of the warm firm hand on her leg exhilarated her and confused her at the same time. It had always taken Beth a while to react to a man; there were some she had never reacted to at all, in spite of the fact that she had allowed them to touch more than a knee. But from the moment Charlie's arm had circled her waist she had felt an almost electric delight in him, in his touch and his presence. She almost resented it; she had tried so hard to give her affection to men she thought were worthy of it. But Charlie had done absolutely nothing to deserve it except touch her once or twice and talk to her a little. And that light touch, that low voice combined to thrill her strangely and bother her until she began to wonder if there was something wrong with her . . . or for the first time, something right.

Charlie's hand tightened on her leg and moved up a little while he talked to her. And then it moved up a little more, as if he were asking questions with it that had nothing to do with the words he spoke. Beth sat quietly letting him do as he pleased, too bewildered, too secretly pleased to stop him. She found that his touch made her shy; and the farther his hand traveled the harder it was for her to meet his eyes. But when she did she saw a promise in them.

Laura could see nothing but she suspected everything and she sat beside them, angry and tormented. Her sharp nails crept up her arms and threatened to come down them cuttingly. She was so tense toward the end of the evening that she almost gave a little shriek when Uncle John finally said, "Well, we'd better be on our horses, children." She wanted to get up and bolt.

They went their separate ways home and Laura was greatly relieved to get some distance between Beth and Charlie. She was silent in the car, still nettled, trying to think of a way to make Beth sorry for being nice to Charlie, to make her apologize for Laura didn't know what. Her jealousy rode herd on her, goaded her unmercifully.

Mitch asked her a couple of questions about Beth and

she hardly heard them or knew how she answered. Mitch was no threat, he didn't count; he hadn't sat too close to Beth and claimed all her attention and smiled at her and made her laugh.

There seemed to be only one solution, only one way to make Beth feel guilty, to make her stay away from Charlie, and that was for Laura to pretend that she really liked him. Laura made her mind up and set her chin in determination.

They reached the house and Charlie took her up the walk. Mitch leaned out of the car and called, "Hey, tell your roomie hello for me," and Laura ignored him. Charlie just laughed at him; Mitch admired all sorts of girls but he rarely had the guts to ask them out.

At the door Laura turned and faced Charlie, and began to talk before he said a word. "Charlie, we're having a Christmas party—a dance—two weeks from today. An afternoon dance. Would you—would you be able to come?"

Charlie was trapped. There were always excuses for evening parties but what the hell was there to do in the afternoon that was more important than a dance? And he had only seconds to think of something. He saw the little tremor in Laura's lips, her timidity and distress. There was a letter at home on his desk from his father that read, "Glad you met the Landon girl. Just heard about her family—too bad. Give her a good time if you can. Probably needs some cheering up." Still he hesitated. And then suddenly Laura came so near to tears that he said swiftly, "Why—I'd like to, Laura. Thanks."

His reticence stung and humiliated her, but at least he had said yes, and it was worth it to keep him and Beth apart. He smiled at her to make it up a little and gave her arm a friendly press. "I'll call you," he said. And Laura had to dash into the house without answering him before she lost the last of her composure.

SIX

Laura went heavily up the stairs and into the room. Beth was in her pajamas. She looked up at Laura with a smile as innocent as if she had spent the whole evening playing checkers with a maiden aunt. Laura stood staring at her, her face drawn and pale, and Beth's smile changed to a frown of concern.

"Hi, honey," she said. "You look pretty glum."

"I'm tired," said Laura briefly, and turned away to hang her coat up. She was too proud, too hurt to tell Beth what the trouble was—and she was too afraid.

Beth watched her for a moment in silence, and then she said, "What's the matter, Laur?"

"Nothing!" Laura snapped. She got ready for bed in resolute silence; Beth couldn't get a word out of her.

When Laura came back from the bathroom she found the studio couch opened out and made up like a bed. Beth was stretched out across it with her eyes closed and one arm lying across her forehead. Laura felt a sudden creeping shyness with her.

"Laura," Beth murmured sleepily.

Laura turned her gaze abruptly away. "Yes?" she said.

"It's awfully cold in the dorm."

Laura glanced back at her, her hand poised halfway to the towel rack. "It is?" she said.

"Um-hm . . . Want to sleep in here?"

Laura hung up the towel nervously. "But you're sleeping in here," she said softly.

"There's room for two."

"Oh, I—I think I'll be okay in the dorm." She felt suddenly a little panicky; she didn't know why.

Beth rolled over on her stomach and opened her eyes. She was smiling a little. " 'Fraid of me, Laur?" she said.

"No," said Laura, trying to make it sound very casual.

Beth bounced up and down invitingly, laughing a little. "Come on, then. It's nice and warm in here."

Laura didn't know what to say. She opened her mouth and shut it again and then she turned around and looked

51

at Beth, as if that might give her something to answer
with. "Well—" she hesitated.

"I knew you would." Beth grinned at her.

Laura tried to remember that she was mad at Beth. "I
don't think I will," she said severely.

Beth turned over on her back again and laughed. "Open
the window a little, honey," she said.

Laura opened it slowly and the fresh cold air came in.
Then she went to the dresser and reached for the lamp
cord.

"Laura," Beth said in a drowsy voice.

Laura turned around, startled.

"Come here, Laur."

Laura stood still and gazed at her, wondering if she heard
right.

"Come here, honey," Beth said. "No, leave the light on.
Come sit here where I can see you."

Laura walked slowly to the bed with a strange alarm
growing inside her and sat gingerly on the edge. She was
trembling a little. Beth reached for her arm and said,
"Move over, Laur. Let me see you." Laura moved closer
unwillingly and trembled again.

"Are you cold, honey?"

"No." Her voice sounded too small for the rest of her.

"What's the matter, Laur? Did I hurt your feelings or
something?"

"No." Laura clamped her hands together and stared at
her knees.

"Tonight, I mean. I was acting kind of silly with Charlie,
wasn't I?" Laura refused to answer. "I was a little tight,
I guess. I didn't mean anything by it." She hardly knew
why she said this, why she felt the need to say it to Laura.
It was almost as if she were reassuring herself that it didn't
mean anything, when in reality she wasn't sure at all. "You
know that, don't you, Laur? Don't you?" She wished she
knew it herself.

"I—I hardly noticed it," Laura said, clinging to her
pride. Her arm felt like fire at the place where Beth's
hand rested.

"Yes, you did. You're upset, I can tell. Laura, baby, it
didn't mean a damn thing, believe me. Who's Charlie?
gentle; it almost persuaded Beth herself. She sat up and
My God, I hardly know him." Her voice was lovely and
put her arm around Laura. "Honey . . ." she said. "Am I

forgiven? Hey, Laur?" It was a teasing whisper. She lifted
Laura's chin and Laura wanted to press her hands to her
pulsing temples.

"Yes," she whispered, ashamed of her weakness.

Beth squeezed her and smiled. "Okay, you can turn
out the light now," she said, and released her.

Laura got up and her knees were precariously weak. She
hadn't time or strength to analyze the sudden violence
within her. She pulled the lamp cord and let the darkness
in. And then she stood perfectly still for a moment, knowing she was going to get into bed with Beth. She moved
very cautiously across the room and found the bed; and
then she crept in and pulled the covers up to her chin and
lay on her back, afraid to move or make a sound, afraid
even of her own breathing.

They lay in absolute silence for a minute. Suddenly
Beth rolled over and tickled her hard in the ribs. Laura
gave a little scream.

"Well, thank God," said Beth, laughing. "I was afraid
you were dead. Don't you wiggle when you get in bed,
Laur?"

"Yes—" She caught her breath. "No—" She didn't
trust her voice, her thoughts, her body. She felt a great
rush of warmth through all her limbs, electrifying, wild,
radiating from the powerful thrust of her heart. "Oh,
Beth . . . Beth . . ." she said, helplessly, drowned in it.
Her voice shook and she realized that she was holding
Beth's hands, that she had caught them to stop the tickling and held them still, held them hard against her ribs.
Beth felt her quiver. "Laur, you are cold." She knew she
wasn't. She wanted to make her talk. Charlie had left her
in a state of strange elation that made her restless.

"No, no, I'm not cold—"

"Yes you are. Here, roll over. I'll keep you warm."

Laura turned on her side and Beth followed her, fitting
her body to Laura's and pulling her close in her arms.
"You'll warm up, honey," she said. "Just relax. Shall I
close the window?"

"No," said Laura. Don't move, don't leave me, she
pleaded silently. She wanted to stay like this in the velvet
dark with Beth always beside her, touching her, her arms
around Laura, her warm breath in her hair. Beth was torment so lovely, so amazing, so sweet, that Laura wanted
to cry. She lay very still, afraid that if she moved Beth

would move too, and she would lose her. She felt her own
arm resting on Beth's, and Beth's clasped loosely about
her midriff, and all down her back the thrilling front of
Beth . . . their heads so near, her breath so light on Laura's
ear. The wonderful softness of her breasts, the strong
length of her thighs against Laura's. With the care of love
aborning, Laura pressed back toward her, trying to feel her
even closer as if that might make them inseparable.

Beth was immersed in a reverie of Charlie. "Hm?" she
said when Laura moved, rousing a little. "You all right,
Laur?"

"Yes," Laura whispered. Her whole body seemed to have
stopped functioning in an access of caution.

"Go to sleep, honey," Beth murmured, and pulled her
tighter to reinforce her words.

Laura lay wide awake in her arms for a long time, so
perfectly happy that nothing seemed real; full of a strangely
wedded exhilaration and drowsy bliss.

Beth fell asleep wrapped in her reverie. After a while
Laura raised up a little to let her move. She rolled over on
her back, groaning softly, and then lay still. In a moment
when she was quiet again, Laura turned to gaze at her, her
head lifted and resting on her hand. She studied the curve
of her lips and she wondered if Beth would know if she
kissed her, and she leaned toward her and then became
afraid again and stopped herself.

"Beth," she whispered in a voice not meant to be heard.
"Dear Beth . . . is this wrong? I'm so happy . . ." Maybe
she was wrong, but nothing, no one, was ever more right
than Beth. Laura looked at her face until she felt almost
dizzy with her; with the wild and foreign turmoil she
created in her heart.

"Oh, Beth, Beth," she whispered. "I think I—I think I
love you, Beth. I think I must love you." She pulled herself closer and brought her lips very near to Beth's. Her
heart felt twice its size in her breast and her breath wanted
to rush in and out in great gasps. She felt a sudden sweat
all over and she stared fascinated and shivering at Beth.

"We're so close, Beth . . . I could kiss you. I could kiss
you, Beth, we're that close . . ." She looked from Beth's
lips to her eyes, and still Beth slept peacefully, and Laura's
fever mounted until nothing mattered except Beth and
the intoxicating nearness of her. Laura made the first
concession to her passion. She leaned steadily closer to

Beth until their lips touched, and then she couldn't move away for a long time. She had reached, not a goal, but a first step. The kiss would never calm her—it taught her to crave.

She pulled away, shaking, and drew her hand across her mouth and she wanted violently to kiss Beth awake, to rouse her from slumber to sudden hot passion. Laura sat up in bed and struggled against her implacable desire with tears and tremors.

"Laur?" murmured Beth, and her hand found Laura's startled back.

"I'm all right," said Laura in a quick scared whisper. "I'm all right, Beth," and she lay down and faced away from Beth and drew the covers high.

She slept very little that night, and her whole being was consumed with wonder and hope and powerful misgivings. She had completely forgotten Charlie.

Beth slept, but restlessly. There was the mystery of Charlie to trouble her dreams, and there was the surprise of unexpectedly rousing Laura. She had begun to think that she would never reach Laura, never really be close to her; it seemed that all she ever did was tease, and all Laura did was answer her politely. But when she reached over in bed to tickle her she realized with a shock that she had struck a profoundly responsive chord in Laura. She felt Laura's cold hands grip hers and heard her breathe, "Oh, Beth . . . Beth . . ." and felt her cool, remote courtesy melt away. Beth was surprised and delighted. Unwilling to hurry her and just as unwilling to let her go, Beth simply held her in her arms and enjoyed the feel of her and marveled at the force of her heart. She knew it was more than fright that provoked Laura's heart so, and somehow Laura's reaction complemented the strange mood Charlie had brought upon her.

Beth took Laura in her arms that night, not because she had forgotten Charlie or because the effect he had on her was lessened; but simply because Laura was right there with her in the same place at the same time, because Laura was sweet and warm and accessible and Beth felt a tender fondness for her. And perhaps most of all because Charlie had aroused to painful new life her old craving for love.

It meant a lot to Beth to be loved. It would have meant

even more if she could have loved someone herself. But she had never been able to give her love successfully and so she was ready to take someone else's. She needed it; if she couldn't give it she would take it, that was all. And Beth was not afraid to take, to try new ways, to look in new places. She had not been afraid of George, nor of the boys that followed him. And she wasn't afraid when she felt Laura's unmistakably erotic response to her teasing; startled, intrigued, but not afraid. It did not frighten Beth that Laura was a member of her own sex; it made her only the more curious.

There was, in fact, only one thing that scared Beth a little that night, and that was her reaction to Charlie.

SEVEN

T HE NOISE in the halls woke Beth the next morning. She moaned and stretched and turned to find Laura watching her, and she smiled sleepily at her.

"Morning, honey," she said, and yawned. "What time is it?"

"I don't know. Almost nine." Don't get up! Laura thought anxiously. It all went so fast.

"Ummm . . . got to get up." She raised her arm over her head and squinted at her watch.

"It's early," said Laura hopefully, still watching her.

"I know, but Uncle John rolls out at nine on Sundays. Always has." Her arm fell across her stomach. "He'll be by to pick me up in a few minutes for breakfast." She looked at Laura. "Sleep well, Laur?"

"Yes," said Laura, and she thought she had never seen anything quite so beautiful as Beth with her sleepy head on the pillow and her pale face set in the aureole of her dark hair.

Beth reached up languidly and pushed Laura's hair behind her ear, and that ear tingled to the ends of Laura's fingers. "My God, are you ticklish," Beth chuckled. "I thought you were going to snap at me last night."

Laura smiled sheepishly. "I didn't mean to. I was just—you caught me by surprise."

"I guess!" said Beth, and she lay still and looked at Laura for a long moment. She liked to be looked at the way Laura was looking at her. She was being admired and she enjoyed it. But still, Uncle John got up at nine.

She sat up and Laura's eyes never left her, as if they were trying to pull her back down on the pillow. Beth felt them and they were subtly exciting. She wanted suddenly to arouse Laura and she turned back and looked at her. Laura was propped up on her elbows. Beth put a hand on either side of her and leaned over her playfully. Laura's breath caught and her eyes widened in excruciating suspense.

57

"Did you finally get warm last night, Laur?"

"Yes. Finally." She smiled and Beth took her shoulders with a grin and pushed them into the pillow so that Laura lay flat beneath her.

"No 'thank you'?" she teased. "No 'yes, thank you'?"

"Oh!" said Laura, putting her hand over her mouth. "Oh, I'm sorry—" The weight of Beth on her made her feel a little crazy.

Beth laughed. "Don't be silly! It's a good sign. I've always thought you wouldn't stop being polite to me until you started to like me, Laura."

"Really?" Laura was astonished. Her beautiful manners came to nothing, then. "Oh, Beth, I—I do like you. I've liked you right along, right from the start. I—really." How could she possibly say it? Her earnest frown, her eyes, would have to speak for her.

"No, you haven't," Beth said, and she poked Laura in the ribs.

Laura gasped and twisted her body. "Oh, yes—yes, I have, Beth." She felt compelled to keep talking, to prove it. "Why, I liked you even before I met you."

"You did not," Beth teased.

"Yes, I did. Really, Beth."

"You didn't even know me. How could you like me?" She smiled.

"Well, I—well, I don't know." Her eyes fell then. It was the truth. She didn't. She knew only that from the moment she first saw Beth, nobody else interested her. And from the moment she spoke to her, no one else mattered.

"You must have some reason. Come on, Laur, tell me." Beth leaned over closer, smiling.

Laura had a brief fear of suffocating with her want, of betraying it through every hard breath, every drop of perspiration. "No, no . . . she protested weakly.

"No reason at all?" Her voice was almost a whisper.

"I just thought you looked like—such a nice person. That's all. You looked friendly. I thought you must be a nice person to know," she whispered lamely.

"Am I? Am I nice to know, honey?"

"Yes." She couldn't look at Beth now.

"I don't believe you."

"Oh, you must!" Her eyes flew back to Beth's. "You're

more than nice, Beth, you're—" And she stopped herself, swallowing compulsively, and looking away in something very near panic.

"I'm what? Tell me, Laur. Come on, honey, tell me," she coaxed. "What am I? Hm? Laura?"

"Beth—" Laura pushed her away in a sudden hot desperation. "I don't know!" She sat up panting and swung her legs over the edge of the bed.

Beth watched her with a smile. "Now you're mad at me, Laur. You're mad at me, aren't you?"

"No!"

"Yes, you are."

"Don't say I am when I'm not!"

Beth laughed gently at her and crawled over to her. She put her arms around her from behind with her legs coming around alongside Laura's and gave her a bear hug. Laura stiffened in the embrace, fighting her potent urge to return it and shivering again.

"Okay, Laura. You're not mad at me. You love me," Beth teased. She looked around Laura's head, trying to see her face.

Laura turned it furiously away, pushing at Beth's arms. "Don't make fun of me! Let me go!"

"I'm not making fun of you, honey."

"Let me go!"

"Say you're not mad."

"I've already said it."

"Say it again."

"I'm not mad," said Laura between clenched teeth.

"Okay, honey." Beth was laughing again. "Let's kiss and make up."

"Oh, Beth!" She was torn apart. "Beth, what a thing to say!"

"What's wrong with it? It's a nice thing to say."

"Let me go! Will you let go of me!" And she gave a hard push against Beth, who suddenly freed her and left her pushing against nothing. Laura got up seething with temper and an infuriating desire to turn back and throw herself into Beth's arms again and beg for kisses. But she dared not even look at her.

Beth sat on the edge of the bed and watched her pull her towel from the closet rack with jerky impatient movements. Laura couldn't bear being watched.

"I thought you had to get up and have breakfast with your uncle," she said testily. Her emotion unnerved her; she couldn't leash it and she hated to have it show. Beth sat still on the bed, smiling at Laura's irritation with gentle amusement.

She got up and came toward her. "Laura," she said in a soft conciliatory tone. Laura moved swiftly toward the door but Beth reached her before she escaped, catching her upper arms. She turned her around. "Hey, Laur?" she said. It was soothing and contrite. "Let me tease you, honey. Don't get so angry. I'm not trying to be mean . . . Do you believe me, Laur?"

"I don't know," said Laura as coldly as she could, and she trembled again.

Beth felt it with amazement. "Laur," she said. "Look at me, honey."

"No." And she stared in unhappy defiance at her towel.

"Laura, honey, listen. I liked you too, Laur. Before I met you, I liked you too."

Laura looked up slowly, disbelieving, yearning to believe, trying to hold her anger between them for defense. But it slipped away from her, out of her, and she was looking up at Beth like a little girl; like Laura six years old begging for a candy heart.

"You did?" she faltered, searching Beth's face.

"Yes. Yes I did." Beth was strangely excited again at the intensity in Laura's face and for a precious second Laura saw it. She found herself suddenly on the point of declaring her love, of clasping Beth in her arms. The tension spiraled up like a rocket and she gasped, "Beth!" and so startled Beth that she caught her breath like Laura and nearly crushed her arms with the sudden tight grip of her hands.

"Oh—oh, Laura," she said, shaking her head and trying to collect her senses. They were going too fast, they had to slow down. Her hands dropped and she turned to her dresser and picked up her comb, feeling the trembling in herself now. "We'd better get dressed," she said.

Laura stood paralyzed, watching every motion Beth made, the confession so tight in her throat that the pressure made her giddy. "Beth, I—I—"

Beth turned away from her into the closet. "Go wash up, honey," she said.

"Beth, please. Please, I—"

Beth straightened up suddenly and took Laura's face in her hands and bent over her and kissed her. And then she shut her eyes tight in pure surprise at herself and her hands held hard to Laura's shoulders for a moment. Finally she said, "Now go. Go on . . . For God's sake, Laur—scram!"

Uncle John stayed at the house for Sunday dinner. It was the traditional climax to his traditional weekend. He sat at the housemother's table and Beth sat beside him. Laura was at a table in the back of the room. With a little prudent rubbernecking she could just see Beth, but it was risky to keep looking. And still she had to look, almost to reassure herself that Beth was real.

They teased her about Charlie at the table. Emmy had pried the information from her that she was going to the Christmas dance with him, and when Emmy knew something the rest of the house knew about it soon after. Mary Lou Baker startled Laura at the table by saying, "Laura, it must be love!" Laura was straining to see Beth over the tops of rows of heads and her concentration gave her face a dreamy quality. She looked at Mary Lou with a startled expression until somebody said, "We hear you've got a date for the Christmas Dance!"

"Oh," Laura breathed in relief. From then on she was glad to play along with them. She needed a man just then as insurance against a dozen ills. Charlie stood for Laura-likes-men, men-like-Laura, everything-is-right-with-Laura-so-look-no-further.

When the girls across the table from her moved their heads apart, and the girls at the next table were nodding just so, she could see just enough to know that Beth wasn't looking at her. She was talking to someone, or laughing, or busy with her food, and Laura felt isolated and forsaken, envious of everyone at Beth's table. But between courses, when Uncle John was busy singing a song with the others, she glanced once more toward Beth's table and their eyes met and Beth gave her an almost imperceptible smile before she looked away.

Laura caught it and held tight to it, to the secret recognition in it, and she felt a sudden shock deep in her abdomen—so strong, so strange, so sweet that it invaded all of her before she understood it or could resist. She refused her dessert; she sat tortured in her place, yearning for the interminable meal to be over, for Uncle John to go home and leave Beth to her. She would have given anything to be rid of Emily.

She dared not look back at Beth. The curious feeling flared at the mere thought of her. The sight of her now would make the agitation unbearable. Laura began to fear her own words, her trembling hands, the telltale sweat on her face. It was with a long sigh of thanksgiving that she arose from the table and left the dining room, and went up to the room to wait for Beth.

She tried to calm herself, to tame the whirlwind in her stomach. She reached the room and opened the closet door to get her toothbrush and suddenly the funny feeling burst again inside her and she buried her face in the clothes and thought wildly, Beth, help me! Hold me, help me, Beth darling Beth I need you. Oh, I need—

The room door smacked against the closet door and Emmy said, "Who dat? Laur?"

A pang of caution sharply neutralized the feeling. Laura was on guard. She straightened mechanically and collected her toothpaste and said, "Yes."

Emily yawned. "We're going over to the Modern Design show in the art building," she said.

"You and Bud?" said Laura politely, as if it mattered. It cost her a terrible effort to appear calm.

"Yes, and Beth and Uncle John."

And suddenly it did matter.

"Should be a good show. Isn't Beth's uncle funny? Honestly, we nearly died laughing at him at dinner."

"Yes, he is funny. I thought he was going home early this afternoon."

"Well, he was, but we talked him into coming along to this show. Besides, he's the only date Beth ever has, and she needs to get out once in a while."

They heard Beth coming down the hall. She was talking to Mary Lou and she came into the room looking back over her shoulder and laughing at something. The strange feeling welled irresistibly in Laura at the sight of her back.

"We were just talking about you, roomie," said Emily, foraging through a muddled drawer for her gloves. Laura half envied her ability to be casual with Beth, and at the same time scorned her for not understanding Beth better.

Beth turned around and faced her roommates, and Laura couldn't stop looking at her. "Oh, you were?" she said. "Good things, of course." She smiled at them.

"We think you ought to go out more often," said Emily matter-of-factly, pulling out one glove triumphantly and tossing it on top of her dresser.

"You do, hm? With whom?" Beth gave Laura a quizzical smile.

Laura gave Emmy a brief venomous glance for having said, "We."

"Oh, anybody," said Emmy, burrowing in her drawer again for the other glove.

"Sure," said Beth. "Like, maybe, Santa Claus?"

Emily laughed. "Oh, Beth, you're hopeless. We'll have to make it our special project to marry you off this year, won't we, Laur?"

Laura glared at her, but Beth said, "And ruin a fine record? No thanks, Em. I'm stuck with Uncle John." She walked over to the closet and reached past Laura for her coat. "Hurry up, can't keep them waiting," she said to Emily.

"I'm coming. Can't find that other glove, darn it. I know it's here somewhere. I put it in here with the other one just two days ago. Can't just have walked away. Now where is it?"

While she talked Beth pulled her coat slowly off the hanger in the closet, all the while looking down at Laura, who stared hard at the floor until the wild feeling beat inside and lifted her eyes almost without her willing it. Beth took her hand suddenly and pressed it and Emily rambled on about her glove. Neither Beth nor Laura heard her for an instant. And then, when the instant grew a second too long, Beth drew her coat between them and turned and slipped into it.

"What are you going to do this afternoon, Laur?" she said.

"Found it!" said Emmy, and gave them a disgusted smile. "Underwear drawer."

"Nothing," said Laura. "Study, I guess."

"Why don't you come along with us?"

"Oh, no thanks, I couldn't. I—I have too much to do." She couldn't bear the thought of being so near to Beth all that time and unable to touch her.

Beth smiled at her. "I understand you're going to see Charlie again," she said. "You didn't tell me."

Laura turned hot with confusion. "Oh—oh, didn't I? Yes, for the dance."

"Hey, he's cute, Laur," said Emmy, grabbing her coat, and hurrying out the door.

Laura and Beth looked intently at each other, Laura with an uneasy smile on her face, and then Beth followed Emmy out.

Left by herself, the rest of the afternoon was a lonely one for Laura. Somewhere in the back of her mind was the sickening doubt that it was monumentally wrong to love another girl. And yet she did, and how much!

She thought of the kiss she stole in the night and her breath left her, first with delight and then with shame. And then she crept back to the thought and it was once again pure pleasure. She put her hand against her lips as if to preserve the kiss. Or prevent it? And then she thought of the way Beth had kissed her in the morning, so suddenly, so quickly, and she thought she couldn't have done anything so very wicked after all.

All afternoon, through her thoughts, the lines of print in her textbook, the wandering reveries in her head, slipped the word "homosexual." At first she seemed to glimpse it from very far away and it made her feel sick and frightened, but as the day waned it came closer. And finally she made herself look hard at it until she threw herself out on the couch and sobbed in an agony of self-accusation. She cried until exhaustion stopped her.

She sat up finally and looked at her mental picture of the Landons. They were normal. And then she looked down at herself, and nothing seemed wrong. She had breasts and full hips like other girls. She wore lipstick and curled her hair. Her brow, the crook in her arms, the fit of her legs—everything was feminine. She held her fists to her cheeks and stared out the window at the gathering night and begged God for an answer.

She thought that homosexual women were great strong creatures in slacks with brush cuts and deep voices; unhappy things, standouts in a crowd. She looked back at herself, hugging her bosom as if to comfort herself, and she thought, "I don't want to be a boy. I don't want to be like them. I'm a girl. I am a girl. That's what I want to be. But if I'm a girl why do I love a girl? What's wrong with me? There must be something wrong with me."

But then she thought irresistibly of Beth, and her clean wholesome beauty and her gentleness, and she thought that nothing Beth could do would be wrong. And Beth had kissed her. . . .

The interminable afternoon dragged on. Laura didn't go downstairs for supper but sat in the room ticking off the hours, thinking that Uncle John must surely by now have left and that Beth would be home soon. She was studying quietly on the couch at ten o'clock when her two room-mates finally came in.

"Hey, you cleaned the room! That's terrific! Thanks, Laur," said Emmy.

Laura smiled. "That's okay," she said. She looked back to her book, but a hundred veiled side glances brought Beth to her eyes; Beth slipping out of her clothes, revealing her fine legs, slim-ankled and hard-calved. Laura wanted to know if she ever took dancing lessons. Her thighs were slender too, and firm, not wide and soft like so many girls'. For the first time Laura took a long heady look at Beth in the flesh and then Beth climbed laughing into her pajamas, teasing Emmy for running after "that no-good trombone."

Emily groaned and said she had millions of things to do and she would do them all tomorrow and thank God the evening was over and "Good night, you two, I can't fight it any longer." She went off to bed. It was a stroke of luck Laura hadn't counted on. She was worn out herself, but she didn't know it. She wouldn't have believed it.

Beth drew a book from the shelf and came and sat be-side Laura on the couch.

"Don't know how long I'll last," she said. She felt Laura's warm glance on her and enjoyed pretending she didn't.

The torments of Laura's afternoon began to fade. Beth reached out and squeezed her knee, and Laura jumped.

"You are ticklish," she said with a smile, and then she turned to her book.

Laura looked at her book, waiting for a word, a gesture to invite her; but none came. Beth studied seriously and in a short time she was lost in another world. Laura, seeing her absorption, stared boldly at her, loving her nearness with its wealth of adorable details: the light hair on her arms, the fine skin, the violet eyes so unaware of the pale blue ones that searched them. Her hands were marvelous and long and firm, with trim hard nails on them;

her breathing so gentle, so peaceful, so welcoming. Laura wanted to put her head down on Beth's breast. And as she looked at it, moving rhythmically up and back, swelling with swift grace under the striped pajamas, she wanted more than to rest on it. Her hand tightened, disciplining itself against desire.

She shifted self-consciously on the couch and found her place in the book again and stared at it, unseeing, stamping with her will on the strange madness in her that begged for liberty. When Beth was near her, her careful senses loosened, yearned, burst suddenly from the bonds of caution. Her mail-fisted moral code unclenched, and right and wrong rushed out and ran whooping into limbo.

After half an hour, Beth threw her book down and yawned. "Can't keep my eyes open," she said.

Laura looked at her with nothing for her but a smile—such a beggar of a smile! Beth gave it a bag of gold.

"Laur, honey, will you scratch my back?" she said.

Laura's smile grew. "All right," she said.

"Wonderful. I love to have my back scratched." She rolled over on her stomach, giving Laura room to sit beside her, and she sighed with pleasure as Laura's hands began to trace the curves of her back. "Oh, that's marvelous," she murmured. "Mmmm . . ." She shivered a little, and Laura trembled with her. "Under my pajamas, Laur. Feels better . . ."

Warily Laura lifted her pajama shirt and her cool fingers groped for the ripe smooth warmth beneath them.

"Oh, yes . . ." Beth said.

Laura could see her smile, her eyes shut the better to feel.

"Oh, I love this. Emmy won't ever do it for me. Mmmm . . . you're wonderful."

Laura's hands shook and she lifted them for a moment.

"Don't stop, Laur."

And her fingers descended to their enthralling task again, traveling like ten light feathers over the flawless hollows, the fields of grateful flesh, the sweet shoulders. Laura was lost to reason. She parted the hair that hid Beth's neck and drew her fingers lightly over the white nape. The hair was cool and delectably soft, and at the roots warm and thick. Laura leaned toward it, hardly realizing that she was moving. It smelled clean and faintly perfumed. She looked at Beth's profile, outlined against the burgeoning pillow, the eyes shut, the lips relaxed, the brow fair and faultless.

With a swift thrill of necessity she bent down and kissed the white neck for a long moment. A sudden acute fear pulled her up. She clasped her hand across her mouth and stared in terror at Beth, wondering how she could have let herself do it. Beth lay perfectly still with a faint smile on her lips.

"Beth?" said Laura. "Beth?" The whisper quailed. "Oh, Beth!" Laura clutched her shoulders. "Say something! Forgive me! Say something! Are you mad at me?"

Beth whispered softly, "No."

A wash of heat flooded Laura's face. She bent over Beth again, perfectly helpless to stop herself, and began to kiss her like a wild, hungry child, starved for each kiss, pausing only to murmur, "Beth, Beth, Beth . . ."

Beth rolled over on her back then and looked up at Laura, reaching for her, breathing hard through her parted lips and smiling a little, and her excitement burned the last rags of Laura's reserve. Her lips found Beth's and found them welcoming, and one after another after another shock of intense pleasure hit her.

Her frantic heart shot blood through her veins, the sweat burst urgently from her body and she felt answering movements from Beth's body. All of a breathless sudden it culminated in a sweeping release exploding and reverberating stormily through her.

She heard her faraway voice groan in ecstasy and she held Beth so tightly that it seemed they must somehow melt together. She couldn't stop, she couldn't let go, she couldn't think or speak. And when finally the furious desire abated a little it was only to gather strength for a fresh explosion.

At last Beth pulled herself up on one elbow and leaned over Laura. Her eyes were hot and her hair was wild, yet for all that she looked strangely ethereal.

"Oh, baby," she said in a husky voice. "We'll sleep in here. We'll sleep here tonight. I couldn't leave you tonight." She looked hard at her. "Oh, Laur . . ." she said and her voice trailed away and her lips came down on Laura's again and again and again. Laura answered her with wordless passion.

Suddenly Beth pulled away from her and stood up with a

quick movement as if that were the only way it could be accomplished.

"Beth!" said Laura like a hurt child, as if she were about to lose her.

"Got to fix the bed. Somebody might come in. My God, they can't find us like this. Open the couch, honey. I'll get the blankets." She leaned over to kiss her once more and then she went out of the room.

In a few minutes she was back with the bedclothes. Laura couldn't look at her without touching her. She went over and put her head down on Beth's shoulder, and Beth let her burdens drop around her to free her arms for Laura. After a while they got the bed made up and the light turned out and themselves tucked in. There was still a little noise in the halls.

"What if somebody comes in?" whispered Laura.

"Nobody will. Besides, if somebody does, it won't matter. They won't know. The dorm is cold as hell tonight. A lot of kids are sleeping in their rooms. Don't worry, don't worry," she whispered and drew her closer in her arms.

"Oh, Beth," said Laura, and her voice was light as a breath and as warm. "I love you. I love you so much."

Beth bent down and kissed her. "Hush," she said. "Sleep."

EIGHT

LAURA thought nothing could ever awaken her. The days that followed were dreams. She wrapped herself in her secret; she wore it in her eyes, on her lips, in her stomach where it welled up hotly to ignite the star in her heart. Her moments with Beth were brief but beautiful, precarious and precious.

It took Beth some time to recover from her astonishment. In one swift strange night with Laura she had found that powerful delight that was supposed to be the crown and glory of romantic love. It had been effortless, inevitable, more wonderful than she had dared to hope. But it had been ironic, too, that it had come like this unbidden, so easily, with a girl. Beth thought of the many men she had looked to for it; the countless times she had searched, tried for it, even worked for it, with nothing for her pains but fatigue and eventually boredom. How had a simple girl like Laura been able to spring her emotions free of their trap? It was a little uncanny. Beth eyed her with a new respect, but she couldn't help wondering . . . if it had been Charlie she had slept with instead of Laura, would it have happened anyway? Would it have been as good, or better? Maybe Beth was just ready for it when Laura happened to come along. Or maybe she needed a woman to teach her how a woman can feel. Beth couldn't find the answer, and the more she looked for it the more perplexed she became.

Laura and Beth found all sorts of odd little gratifications. At house meetings Laura liked to sit behind Beth and scratch her back. It went unnoticed, since half the others were doing it too. At the Union they met each other for coffee in the afternoon and they walked home together for dinner. During the long quiet evenings they studied; beside each other on the couch when they could, across the room from each other when Emily got to the couch first.

Emily was now a thorn in the side, now the spice of danger. Her presence inhibited them and at the same time made the least glance, the least casual touch almost unbearably sweet. If Emily sat down at the desk to write, their eyes met over her back and their lips smiled behind her. If she sat in the chair and left them the couch they found means to let their bodies touch somewhere, gently, with seeming carelessness. When she left the room they had a sublime moment to kiss and caress and tease.

Still, Emily wasn't the only threat. Beth was pursued regularly by phone calls and visitors to the room. Someone might walk in at any time. Her minutes with Laura had to be brief. And yet she made time or found it somehow. Then she would hold Laura in her arms, whisper to her, tell her how often she thought of her, kiss her, comfort her, make love to her. And Laura would pour her passion over Beth like honey—rich and sweet and natural, and yet somehow ensnaring. It was delightful, a balm and a succor to Beth, but it wasn't all-engrossing, all-satisfying, as it was for Laura.

Beth knew this, and she knew she had to be honest with Laura before she broke her heart. Once or twice she tried to explain her feelings, but her uncertainty stopped her. She was afraid of hurting Laura, even though she knew that a small hurt now was far better than a great hurt later. But just then any hurt at all seemed too much. It wasn't fair to hurt her so soon. Beth stuffed her logic into this ill-fitting mold, not just to spare Laura, but partly to preserve her own pleasure. It was selfish, and she knew that, but for a while her need was as great as Laura's—different, but just as strong.

It would have been nearly as hard for her to renounce the thing as for Laura, so she let things drift for a while and luck and happiness drifted along with them. They had each other and no one suspected anything.

Into the golden days sailed Charlie, like an unwelcome thunderhead. Laura had almost forgotten about him and the dance she had asked him to. She was ready to plead any strange malady to get out of it but Beth insisted that she go.

"You made that date almost two weeks ago, honey," she said. "You can't just suddenly break it. You can't just quit going out. It'd look pretty damn queer if you did. Besides, you need a little male company now and then."

Laura disagreed by simply not answering. But she didn't say no when Charlie called.

"Does your roommate have a date?" Charlie had asked. Laura bit her underlip. "Oh, yes, she's got a date," she said brightly.

Charlie seemed to see through her ruse almost instinctively. "I don't mean the other one—Bud's girl—I mean Beth. She got a date?"

"Oh. Beth. No, I don't think so."

"Don't you know?" He laughed a little.

"No, she doesn't." Her voice was sharp, but Charlie ignored it.

"Well, my roommate wants a date," he said. "Mitch— you remember?" The whole thing struck him as something of a joke. Even Mitch wasn't serious about it. Two such disparate characters as he and Beth would never last, but they might brighten up the Christmas Dance a little. Besides it would be fun to have Beth around, and Charlie couldn't very well take her himself.

"Mitch?" said Laura.

"Yeah. Beth there?"

"Not till dinner."

"Okay, he'll call her after dinner. Talk to her, will you, Laura?"

"Okay, Charlie. I'll tell her."

She did, of course; she had to. But she didn't like it. The whole thing seemed ominous to her.

"He's a very nice boy, I guess," she said glumly. "I don't think you'd like him, though. He didn't say a word at Maxie's that night."

"Oh, I thought he was adorable," said Beth, and she reached out laughing and took Laura's hands. "Laur, you're jealous!" she said.

"No I'm not! Really, Beth, I'm—you mustn't— Oh, I guess I am. Just a little."

Beth mussed her hair and said, "I'd be crushed if you weren't. Just a little." She lighted a cigarette and said thoughtfully to the smoke, "Well, it might be fun to get back into circulation. Just for once."

"All right." Laura looked at her hands. "He's going to call you tonight after dinner." She got up stiffly and started for the door.

"Laur—where're you going?"

Laura didn't know. She just wanted to express her disapproval.

"Oh, Laura, honey," Beth said, laughing. She came up

and stopped her and put her arms around Laura's waist. "You mustn't be so jealous. You've been going out all fall. How do you suppose that makes me feel?"

Laura hung her head.

"God, Laur, we'll double date. How could I possibly two-time you?"

Laura apologized. "I won't be jealous," she said. "I swear I won't." And she underscored her intention with a kiss.

Charlie and Mitch arrived together for the dance and waited in the living room for Beth and Laura. Charlie was imposing in a tuxedo, and he looked faintly amused and detached from the proceedings. Like Emmy's Bud, he was something of a ladies' man, but unlike Bud, he didn't court crushes from every girl he knew.

The attitude became him, but he was hardly aware of it. It wasn't that he was immune to girls—far from it. It was simply that he was much more susceptible to women. Simpering college girls amused him. They were silly and scatterbrained, many of them, and once in a while he thought they were fun. But a beautiful woman, assured, alluring and feminine, was a wonder he could never wholly resist. He had begun to see the first signs of this mature loveliness in Beth, just as she had begun to find maturity in herself.

Charlie and Mitch stood off in a corner and surveyed the girls of Alpha Beta, and the girls milled about and re-turned the survey. Charlie was fun to look at because he was good to look at. His hair was wonderful stuff—a rich dark brown born of an early blond that left gold traces at his temples.

"A pretty nice-looking bunch," said Mitch. He was en-joying his favorite spectator sport.

"Yeah. I've been away from this house too long."

They grinned at each other.

"Who's that one over there? By the fireplace?"

Charlie followed his gaze. "Oh, in the red? Boy, you're coming back to life." He laughed and slapped Mitch on the back. "That's Mary Lou Baker, the house president. Nice gal."

"You know her?"

"Used to. Haven't seen her for a while. Let's go over."

Mitch hung back. He liked looking better than doing.

But Charlie was striding across the living room and rather than be left stranded Mitch tagged after him. Charlie in action made a beautiful study in savoir faire. Mitch admired it, with secret envy.

Mary Lou looked up and smiled at Charlie as he came up. "Well, Charlie Ayers!" she said. "How are you? Gee, I haven't seen you for ages."

"Mary Lou, I'd forgotten how pretty you are."

She laughed a little, pleased and embarrassed.

Mitch stood and looked at her in the same way he had stood and looked at Beth, with a sort of goodhearted and passive admiration that rarely asked for more than a look.

"I hear you've been seeing Laura Landon," Mary Lou said to Charlie.

"Um-hm." He smiled.

"Isn't she a sweet girl? She's one of our best pledges. We're really fond of her."

"Yes, she is a nice girl," he said politely.

"Here she comes," said Mary Lou.

Beth and Laura came in together in very different moods. Beth was luxuriously pretty. For once she had taken time for every detail of herself, to Laura's alarm.

"After all, I only go out once a year," she explained. "Might as well do it up right."

"Well, if Mitch doesn't think you look terrific, he's blind," said Emmy. "Isn't that so, Laura?"

"Yes."

Laura tried to keep Charlie occupied with her so that he wouldn't have time for Beth. She talked or trapped him into talking as steadily as she could. But the four of them sat together and the conversation jumped about frequently.

Laura couldn't help it if Charlie offered Beth a cigarette and lighted it for her, but Beth could help it if she took his hand to steady the light and watched him while she inhaled. Whenever she spoke or smiled or glanced at Charlie she aggravated Laura's irritation.

They went into the dining room to dance after a while, and Laura had Charlie to herself. Not that she wanted him, but for once she was happy to put up with him, just to keep him away from Beth. The dining room was romantically festive with green lights, and all the furniture had been cleared out to make a dance floor. At the rear of the room was a long elaborately decorated table loaded with

punch and cookies. Now and then, at intermissions, Beth
and Mitch met Laura and Charlie around the punch
bowl. Inevitably, Charlie finally suggested that they trade
partners. Laura hardly had time to think about it before
Beth was swept masterfully onto the dance floor and she
found herself moving off with Mitch.

Charlie was perfectly assured with women and he liked
to be around them. It was almost second nature. They
never gave him much trouble. He was easy and firm with
Beth and she followed him docilely, faintly annoyed with
him for attracting her and amused with his confidence.

"That's a very pretty dress," he said, looking down significantly.

"Thanks." She smiled at him.

"Good color for you."

"I think so, too."

He raised an eyebrow at her. "Do you always wear
purple?"

"Um-hm," she said, pursing her lips sagely and nodding.

He laughed. "Always?"

"Of course. Even my pajamas are purple."

He grinned and gave her a squeeze that brought back
to her the strange sensations in the booth at Maxie's.

"Don't you believe me, Charlie?"

"No," he said calmly. "A girl like you doesn't wear
pajamas."

Beth had to smile at him but at the same time she
wanted to shatter his beautiful composure. He seemed to
know instinctively how to tease her and she couldn't catch
him off guard. He thought he had her perfectly under
control. She had to wait till the dance was nearly over for
a chance to trip him up.

He bent down close to her and pulled her tighter in his
arms and said softly, "Beth, my dear, you're beautiful."

It was just her cup of tea. "Thanks, Charlie, so are you,"
she said.

For the space of a few shocked seconds he was silent.
Beth waited for a tantrum, but she guessed wrong. He put
his head down against hers as the music ended and laughed
at her. And at himself.

"It's my criminal charm," he said, and squeezed her
again, and Beth looked up at him in surprise. And again she
smiled at him against her will. . . .

The four of them went out to dinner together at the

Hotel Champlain. Laura became more and more quiet as her jealousy grew. Only Beth could see behind her deliberate courtesy to her hurt feelings.

The two girls went to the ladies' room and Beth tried to talk some sense into the younger girl.

"Are you all right, Laur?" she asked.

"Yes, of course." Laura looked down into the cascade of blue tulle flowing from her waist.

"Honey, tell me the truth. You look so unhappy."

Laura bit her lip, and then she said, "Beth, I told you I wouldn't be jealous, and I won't."

"Oh, Laura—" Beth couldn't help smiling. "You're such a foolish little girl. Do you know that?"

"Yes." It meant no.

"Who's Charlie Ayers anyway? Just a guy." Charlie was causing the trouble, of course. Not Mitch. "No more foolishness. Okay?" Beth talked to Laura as if she were a little child.

Laura nodded at her. The image of Charlie interfered with her every good intention, spoiled her every smile.

"Laura . . ." Beth's voice was very soft. "We'll be together tonight. We'll be together."

Laura looked full at her suddenly and momentarily forgot her rival till Beth gave her a little shake. "Come on, we've got to get back. They'll think we fell in."

And Laura followed her willingly then, as if a great weight had been lifted from her.

The evening went quickly after that, and everybody drank too much, except for Mitch, who was talking himself into a crush on Beth.

Beth had to stop Laura from a fifth Martini. "God, Charlie, what are you trying to do? Pickle her? She's not used to it," she said.

Charlie grinned and shrugged. "Give the lady what she wants," he said. His interest in Beth grew franker as his inhibitions grew fewer, but it didn't seem to matter. He couldn't stop himself. He began to get quiet and deliberate. When he got drunk he slowed down perceptibly, but there was nothing unmanageable or mean in him. He was quite pleasantly absorbed in pondering the enigma of Beth Cullison.

Now and then he would lean forward lightly on the table and study her as if she were a map. Beth gazed straight back at him in an effort to make him look away, but it was rather more like indicating the way to him; he wasn't in the least abashed. Beth was somehow half afraid that he would read in her eyes something of her concern for Laura; that he would see on her lips the illegal kisses, the extraordinary passion that the girl had inspired in her.

Charlie tried to ignore Beth out of regard for Mitch and Laura, but the other two simply didn't interest him. He asked Beth to dance with him again before the evening was over. The floor was small and packed. He guided her away from Mitch and Laura so they couldn't see, and he spent the dance pretty much in one place, holding her hard against him and talking to her. She had to look up at him to catch the words, and she tried to protest.

"Charlie, we have to get back," she said. And, "You're holding me too tight."

But he only shook his head and kept her there. He had never been so attracted to a girl. It just couldn't have happened any other way. He pulled her out of the crowd and into the shadow of the heavy drapes by the bandstand and gave her just time to say, "No—" before he kissed her.

When he released her she said, "Charlie, please, for God's sake—"

"I know," he said and gave her his handkerchief. "Don't talk about it. I know."

"No, you don't," she said, wiping off the smeared lipstick. "You couldn't. Let's get back." But she didn't want to.

It was a while before she could look at Laura again; the whole evening was different, irrevocably changed. It wasn't Laura she wanted that night, but it was Laura she would have.

NINE

Mitch was mad. It happened very rarely, but Charlie had muscled in on his date. He walked stiffly into their apartment. Charlie sighed and followed him in.

"Okay, Mitch, I'm sorry. So we both like the girl. We both want the girl. Okay, so we both call her."

"But that's just the point. You act as if you own every woman you look at, damn it. You—"

"I act like it but I don't."

"You make them think—"

"Oh, Mitch, for God's sake, that's a lot of crap. That's a lot of damn crap. You go around with your nose out of joint because you think I'm better equipped to seduce women than you are."

"Well, let's face it."

"Oh, let's face it, hell. Do you think a girl like Beth would fall for a face? For a lot of crap? Well, do you?"

"Any girl could be fooled."

"Well, would you like to know how well I fooled your precious date? I danced with her, remember? Do you know what I said to her?"

"No."

"I told her she was beautiful. Yeah, just like that. And what do you think she said to me?"

"I don't know," said Mitch with polite sarcasm.

"She said, 'Thanks, Charlie, so are you.' Now, what do you think she meant by that?"

Mitch glowered at him, and said nothing.

"She meant, 'You're an ass, Ayers. You're a damn ass and you're not fooling me.' Okay, I'm an ass. My God, I know what I am. It's just that women like that crap—most women. Now, do you think a girl like Beth thinks I'm Prince Charming, or something? Hell no, she thinks I'm an ass. Quit harping on the thing."

"Harping? Who's harping? You're doing all the talking."

77

"Oh, for God's sake," Charlie muttered. "All right, the hell with it. Do you want to know what your trouble is, Grogan? Do you want to know what your son-of-a-bitching trouble is? Well, I'll tell you. You don't want Beth Culli-son; you just want a girl." Charlie sighed. "Let's just forget it. We'll talk about it later." Mitch sat motionless. "Women," Charlie growled. He went to the washbowl and brushed his teeth viciously and then he got into bed. "Come on, Mitch, you can't sit there all night."

Mitch stood up slowly and got out of his clothes and into his pajamas without a word. Charlie rolled over and shut his eyes and tried to figure out a way to see Beth, Mitch or no Mitch. He tossed around for a long while before he got to sleep.

Beth was a long time getting to sleep herself that night, too. Emily wouldn't go to bed until the birds were nearly ready to get up. Beth was too tired to want anything but sleep; too full of Charlie, too upset for Laura. But still, she was committed.

When Emily finally went off and Beth and Laura were alone, Laura could see that Beth was in a faraway and pensive mood. For a while she said nothing. Laura sat down on the couch and looked up at Beth as she might have gazed at a distant cloud, so lovely, too hard to know, so impossible to clasp and keep. The first drops of melancholy began to spatter in Laura when Beth turned out the light and came over to the bed and pulled Laura down in it beside her. She held her close and they lay still for a little while, warming each other, occupied with their thoughts.

"Beth," Laura whispered finally, "are you unhappy about something?"

"No, honey." Her voice was very soft. "Should I be?"

"I don't know. You sort of—acted as if you were."

"No, baby, I'm not unhappy." She frowned in the dark.

"Sometimes—sometimes I think I don't know you at all, Beth."

Beth said nothing. It was true.

"I know about the little things, but—I don't know anything about what makes you the way you are. I'm afraid I never will."

Beth squeezed her gently. "Maybe I'm not worth it. Maybe it doesn't matter."

"Yes, it does." She sounded urgent. "We won't always be together like this, Beth."

"Nothing lasts forever."

And Laura fell silent, as silent as her tears. Beth held her, unknowing; wondering sleepily at Charlie's invulnerable composure. She was startled out of near sleep when Laura said, some while later, "What do you really think of Charlie?"

"Mmmm . . . he's conceited."

"Is that all?"

"No. I don't know. He's a nice guy, I guess. I don't know . . ."

Laura felt her uncertainty as a worse threat than her positive admiration would have been. Under the spell of possible threats she snuggled closer to Beth, feeling, like a pain, the fragile sweetness of every moment with her. She thought briefly of Charlie, and she swore to herself, He won't have her! I'll fight for her!

"All right, baby?" Beth murmured.

"No!" Laura whispered. "No, Beth, I love you. Darling, I love you." Her sudden intensity brought Beth back to life. Laura had her way. She vented her passion with bouquets of kisses and her arms full of all the magnificent softness of Beth's body. Beth gasped in a thrill of surprise and then it was just Beth and Laura again, so immersed in each other that no wayward uninvited thoughts could threaten them.

It was the last time they were together before Christmas; the last time for several weeks.

Christmas. Laura went home to Lake Forest, Charlie went home to New York, and Beth went off to Florida to be with her Aunt Elsa and Uncle John.

There was little for Laura to do but visit one parent and then the other, and do school assignments. The holidays were a dreary parenthesis in her romance. She wanted to write to Beth every day but Beth forbade it.

"It would look too obvious," she said. "Just send a couple of notes, honey."

Her notes were rather more like chapters from a book, but at least there were only three of them. Beth's answers were short but affectionate in a noncommittal sort of way; Laura knew them by heart.

She spoke to her parents so many times of Beth that her

mother exclaimed, "Aren't you lucky to have such a nice girl for a roommate!" And she was thankful that her daughter was under the guidance of someone so "sensible" about boys. Laura had told her that Beth spent most of her energies on study and the Student Union.

Mr. Landon muttered, "She sounds like a damn puritan. A girl like that ends up an old maid nine times out of ten. I wouldn't take everything she says as the Gospel, Laura."

And Laura laughed to herself to think that her lovely, warm, passionate Beth could be so easily camouflaged without benefit of a single fib.

Beth, on the beach, sunned herself and studied and thought of Laura. She thought of other things, in her solitude, and all the other things, strangely enough, were Charlie. Her mind was vague, her thoughts indefinite; there was just a cloudy image of Charlie in her head. It could be dissipated like a cloud, but like a cloud it always re-formed and hung about to threaten a storm.

It came to her at odd moments, bothersome and wonderful and completely exasperating. Once, in a restaurant booth, Uncle John leaned past her to reach for the salt shaker, putting his hand on her knee as he did so. It couldn't have been a more innocuous gesture on his part and he was somewhat startled to hear his niece gasp audibly at his touch. The warmth and pressure of his hand in just that spot on her leg brought Charlie back to her with a shock; Charlie in the smoky booth in Maxie's basement, pressing against her, laughing, telling her nonsense, and feeling her leg with an experienced hand. She felt a sudden irritation at the thought of him, as she had so many times before; and as usual, she didn't quite understand it. Before the first week of vacation was up she was impatient to get back to school again.

Charlie, in New York, occupied himself with parties and people, but his head was full of Beth. In the past, whenever he found himself thinking too much about one particular girl, he'd deliberately ignore her and take out dozens of others, another one each night, and soon enough he'd be free of his infatuation. So it was with understandable confusion that he discovered that Beth could not be driven from his thoughts in this fashion. It annoyed him, but after four or five days he accepted the situation and quite simply gave up and thought only of Beth.

He knew her special kind of beauty appealed strongly to him, and she pleased him with her teasing, her talk, even her tantalizing independence. But he had found these qualities in other girls and never been so hopelessly fascinated with them. No, there was a unique delight in being with Beth, a curious essence in her that he couldn't put his finger on, couldn't explain. It was as if she were holding something of herself back, as if there were some secret unsounded depth in her that no one had ever touched. Charlie made up his mind then and there to touch her; to reach for her and find her as she really was, and hold and keep her.

The days dragged for all three of them. Laura crossed them off on a little pocket calendar she carried in her wallet on the other side of a picture of Beth. The picture was a reproduction of her yearbook portrait and although Laura knew every plane and shadow of it, she took it out frequently to study it.

TEN

Laura came back to school in a sweat of excitement. But when she burst into the room the one who turned to greet her was Emily.

"Where's Beth?" Laura demanded. She forgot to say hello to Emmy.

"Hi, Laur. Nice vacation?"

"Oh—yes, thanks. Where's Beth?"

"We just got a wire from her. She's not coming in till tomorrow. Bad flying weather, or something."

"Oh." It was a shocking disappointment.

Emily stared at her curiously. "She'll be back tomorrow, Laur," she said in a comforting voice that Laura was alarmed to have inspired.

"Oh. Oh, I know." Laura laughed nervously to cover her chagrin. "I—I just had something to tell her." She tried to make it sound casual. She had to have something innocent to be disappointed about.

"Oh, what!" said Emily, who loved secrets.

"Oh, nothing," said Laura. She turned away in confusion, suddenly afraid.

"Is it a secret?" said Emily. She was kneeling on the couch and smiling at Laura like a little girl with three guesses to spend. There was nothing malicious in her curiosity.

"Well, I—I don't know." Laura felt rather desperate.

"Can I guess?"

"Oh, Emmy!" she said in a sharp, angry voice. She stopped and caught her breath, and then turned to see how much damage she had done. Emily was looking at her, stung and astonished. Of all people, Laura was the last she would have expected a temper from.

"I'm sorry, Emmy," said Laura, and she was—sorry and scared. "I didn't mean to—say anything. I'm awfully sorry."

"Well . . . that's all right, Laura." Emily frowned curiously at her.

Laura undressed in a state of smoldering resentment, angry with Emily, furious with herself, and irritated with Beth for being a day late. Never mind what the flying conditions were; she should have been there.

Beth came the next morning. It was so good to look at her, to see the color of her and feel the substance, that Laura temporarily forgot her troubles and forgave her. Beth gave her a warm hug and said, "Miss me?" and laughed at Laura's bright eyes before she could answer. Laura was admiring her tan; she had turned a lovely gold-brown from the Florida sun and in her dark face her violet eyes looked almost luminous.

It took Emily only until that evening to wreak havoc. She didn't mean to; she never meant to. She thought there must be some sort of joke between Beth and Laura and she wanted to tease.

The three of them were settled quietly about the room when Emmy snapped her book shut and said, "Hey, Beth, what's this big secret between you and Laura?" She smiled at her.

Beth looked up suddenly with a long silent gasp of alarm. Emily didn't see Laura start in her chair. She was looking at Beth. Beth turned to Laura for an explanation but Laura was too frightened to say a word.

"What secret?" said Beth.

"Laura said you had a secret."

"She did?" Beth looked back at Laura with troubled eyes.

"Emily, I did not!" said Laura angrily, finding her tongue suddenly in this crisis. For the second time she had lost her temper at Emily. "I didn't say anything of the kind!" She had to shout at Emmy; she was afraid to look at Beth.

"Well, gee, Laur, don't get mad," said Emmy. "I'm not trying to start anything. What the heck is this, anyway?" She looked at Beth. "She said she had something to tell you, that's all. She was so let down when you weren't here last night that I asked her what was the matter and she wouldn't tell me. She just said she had something to tell you. Gee, I didn't mean to start anything. I thought it was a joke."

Beth pulled herself together fast. She had to in the face of Emily's sudden suspicion. "You didn't start anything,

Emmy," she said calmly. "You don't mind if I tell her, do you, Laur?"

Laura, who would have followed her naked into hell, shook her head in bewilderment.

"It was just a family thing, Em. Laura wanted to transfer out of journalism school. It all depended on what her father said. Sort of a difficult situation. Her parents didn't agree. I guess Mr. Landon finally decided against it. Right, Laur?"

"Yes." She stared in grateful surprise at Beth, with a sort of perverse pleasure in seeing her father rescue his daughter's Lesbian love affair. It was as good a thing as ever he did for her.

"One of those family things," Beth said. "Not so much a secret, Emmy, as just—sort of—awkward."

Emily was suddenly contrite. She never disbelieved Beth; she never had reason to. "Oh, Laur, I'm sorry!" she said. She looked anxiously at her, wanting to restore a sunny atmosphere.

Laura promptly absolved her, glad to have it over, to have got out of it so well. Emily took the thing at nearly face value, thanks to Beth. Laura was shaken hard and fast into the realization of the pressing need for tact and caution and highly refined hypocrisy.

Mitch called Beth, and ran headlong into the bruising fact that Beth didn't want to go out with him again. She gave him a charming runaround; he couldn't even get mad at her. But she said no, and it rankled in Mitch.

Charlie got out of the way and let him call first. It was the only way to keep peace. Besides, they were friends, they had an agreement, they even had a lease to bind them. But he intended to call and he said so, and there wasn't much Mitch could do about it, being Mitch. He didn't think he was in love with Beth any more, but he thought he might have been if he had had the chance.

Charlie came in and found him sitting by the phone. Mitch waved at it. "She's busy all week," he said with a sort of comic sarcasm. "Try for Friday night. She hesitated a little over that one."

"Mitch—" Charlie felt awkward.

"Go on, go on. We had an agreement."

He called. Beth was rarely called on a house phone.

Anyone with anything to say to her knew her private number.

"Hello?" she said.

"Hello, Beth, this is Charlie." He didn't believe in guessing games.

"Well, Charlie!" she exclaimed, strangely startled.

"I have a problem. I thought maybe you could help me out."

It was somehow possible to tell that he was smiling.

"Well, I don't know." She grinned back at him. "What is it?"

"Classics. An elective. Don't know how I got hooked. Anyway, I'm in trouble. I mean, I may very well flunk out."

Beth laughed at him. "Oh, that's a shame!" she said.

He ignored her. "Laura says you know something about the classics."

"Oh, she does?"

"Thought you might be willing to brief me. I wouldn't take much of your time. You're up at the Union every day, aren't you?"

"Yes—"

"I know you're busy—"

"Oh, I am—"

"But you must have a few free minutes."

"Well, sometimes, but—"

"Any time would do."

She realized that every answer she gave him was affirmative. "Charlie, I just don't know. I never know what to expect up there. My time isn't my own."

"Aren't you the president of the Student Union?"

"Yes, but—" Another affirmative.

"Well, hell, honey, make time. Just half an hour would do it. How about the Pine Lounge this afternoon? Say about three-thirty?"

"Charlie, I can't." She thought of Laura. "I just can't."

"Sure you can, Beth. Oh look, honey—I know you don't owe me anything, that's not the point. I just thought maybe you'd be willing to help me out. My God, I can't even tell you anything about Socrates! That's how bad it is."

Beth laughed.

"Please," he said, and she could tell again that he was smiling. "I'd really appreciate it, Beth."

She would tell Laura as soon as she got back to the room. There would be no cause for jealousy or suspicion. What's more practical and less romantic than a history lesson?

"Beth?"

She just liked to be with him. He was fun, he was different, he wasn't afraid of her. It wouldn't amount to anything.

"Hey, Beth—you there?"

"Yes. I—"

"Good," he said in a matter-of-fact voice. "Thanks a lot, honey. See you at three-thirty. Okay?"

No breath of ulterior motives. "Okay, Charlie."

Back in the room she told Laura, "It's for a Classics final. I guess he's having trouble with it."

"He likes you, Beth." Laura knew it right away.

"Not *that* way." She laughed. "Men like Charlie don't like girls like Beth. I'm supposed to be a real bookworm, you know. I guess I'm just a change of pace for him."

"Well, girls like Laura don't like girls like Beth, either. Until they fall in love with them."

"Oh, baby!" Beth laughed and pulled the troubled face up and kissed it. "I swear I'll tell you every word he says. And all you'll hear is a half-hour monologue on Greek philosophers."

With Laura watching her carefully, Beth only ran a comb through her hair before she left for the Pine Lounge. She had wanted to put on some cologne, change her sweater, freshen her lipstick—but she knew that would cause too great an eruption. She left the room with a great show of casualness and arrived at the Lounge a little early. She sat at a table with a notebook before her, daydreaming. She looked up and let her gaze wander out the window, where it rested motionless on nothing and criticized Charlie's face. She sat like that for almost ten minutes until suddenly a strong hand gripped her neck and she put her head back with a jerk, electrified. She laughed in spite of herself, hunching her shoulders and squirming to be free. Charlie held her firm, grinning down at her.

She said, "Charlie, don't!" still laughing, and then she realized that he wouldn't let her go until she stopped struggling. She froze.

He released her, tossing his books on the table in front of her.

"Sorry I'm late."

"Are you?" She was surprised.

"Um-hm." He took his coat off, pulled up a chair, and sat down.

"Charlie, you've been drinking beer," she said, pulling away from him as if his breath might intoxicate her, and grinning.

"Brethren," he said piously, "I repent."

Beth laughed at him. "Okay," she said. "What is it you want to know? As if you were in any condition to learn."

"I'm forced to agree," he said. "Let's adjourn. There's a jam session at Maxie's this afternoon."

"I thought you were flunking out of Classics."

"Oh, I am."

"Well, maybe you'd better do something about it."

"That's your job, honey." He pulled out a mimeographed list of names and places and questions and handed it to her. "Explain this damn thing to me, will you?" he said.

"All of it?"

"Well—the Peloponnesian War. I can't get the damn thing straight."

Beth gave him a skeptical smile and then she took the list from him. "Okay," she said. She bent over the paper and began to talk.

Charlie studied her hair and the line of her cheek, his head resting in his hand.

"You see, Sparta was up here," she said, and he didn't answer. "Do you see?" She looked up and saw him gazing at her.

"Mm," he said thoughtfully and let his hand come down. He leaned forward on his arms and looked down at the paper. "See what?"

"Charlie, are you listening to me?"

"You won't believe this, but I am. I don't know as I'm remembering any of it, though. Let's go over to Maxie's, honey."

"And let you flunk out of Classics?"

"And let me flunk out of Classics."

"I couldn't, Charlie, even if I wanted to. Sorry."

"Do you want to?"

She smiled a little, wondering why he had put it that way. "I can't," she said.

"That's not what I asked you, honey."

"I have work to do."

"So do I. So does everybody. Don't you ever play, Beth?"

"Charlie, I can't go."

"Half an hour?"

She laughed helplessly. "Ohhh," she groaned, flattered, and gave him a deploring look. "No!"

"Half an hour it is," he said. "Where's your coat?"

"Charlie—" she protested, but the situation struck her, and her laughter took the starch out of her protest. She did want to go. She obviously wanted to go. But she thought suddenly of Laura and her own good intentions, and turned cold.

"Where's your coat, honey?"

"Upstairs." Laura was tormenting her. "Charlie, I—"

"Come on, we'll go get it."

"I can't go, Charlie." She tried to make it sound serious and final.

Charlie stood up and pulled his jacket on and grabbed his notebook. He hustled Beth out of the lounge and down the linoleumed corridor to the elevator.

Beth leaned against the wall of the elevator while he pushed the button and it started up. "I wish you'd believe me, Charlie. I can't go."

He leaned on the wall beside her, one arm over her head, and looked down at her. "I wish you'd tell me why. You keep saying you can't go. Why can't you go?"

"All right, I'll give you a good reason. Mitch. What about Mitch?"

"What about him?"

"He called me this week, you know. Or didn't you know?"

"I know."

"And I turned him down."

"Um-hm." He didn't seem in the least perturbed.

"Charlie, he's your best friend! I agreed to see you only to help you out of a jam. Not to go out and drink beer with you."

"Am I supposed to apologize for asking you out for a beer?"

The elevator doors pulled open and they walked out slowly.

"How would Mitch feel?"

"He expects it."

"He expects it? Well, damn it, Charlie, what are you up to? What is this? You didn't want any help on that final." She sighed, but she was pleased. "Are you afraid to be honest?"

"You make it impossible, Beth. I suppose it's beside the point that I meant to be. I didn't organize the jam session." He followed her into her office and she turned and faced him while he talked. "Mitch was honest with you, and what happens? You force a man to use his ingenuity, Beth." It was the rare kind of compliment she couldn't resist. "Mitch says, 'Beth, I'd like to see you again, will you go out with me this weekend?' and gets a flat 'No.' So what am I supposed to do? Throw myself against the same brick wall?" He smiled at her and she had to laugh. "You can't say I'm not being honest now," he said.

"Still, Charlie," she said in a gentler voice, "it must be hard on Mitch." She was arguing for Laura, not for Mitch.

"Look, Beth, we had this out together. We both wanted to see you, we had a big argument over it, we finally decided to leave it up to you. It was the only way. Mitch called first. Then I called. He knows I called. My God, I'm not keeping any secrets."

Beth said firmly to herself, I can't go out. But she didn't say it to Charlie and when she looked up at him her resolution began to falter.

"Now, where's your coat?" he said, lifting a gray one from the rack. "This it?"

"No. Won't you please give up and go away?"

"This one?"

Oh, Laura—I can't help it, I want to go . . .

"Hey, Beth?" A girl put her head in the door. "Oops, sorry!" she said, catching sight of Charlie. "You leaving?"

"Well, I—what is it, Doris?"

"Nothing vital. Entertainment committee. You can see 'em tomorrow." She grinned at Charlie and left.

"Well, that's settled," said Charlie. "Which coat?"

"The tan one."

"That's more like it." He smiled and held it for her and she slipped into it with the feeling that she was slipping into a trap. She expected to pay for it somehow, but at the moment payment seemed far off.

They walked briskly over to Maxie's and Charlie talked

with her all the way, holding her arm, stopping her at curbs, leading her around puddles. Now she liked it and now it annoyed her but the curious excitement of being with Charlie overwhelmed her other feelings.

"Your friend Emily is over there," he said.

"She is?" Beth was vaguely upset. She would rather have had her escapade unobserved, but better Emmy than Laura.

"Yeah. Bud's playing. He's got her hypnotized."

"It's a way he has." And as a matter of fact it was true that he had held Emmy's affections longer than any other boy she knew.

"I'd like to know when that guy studies," Charlie went on. "Jesus, I only study the bare minimum myself. He studies about half as much as I do. Every time I go over to Maxie's he's down there playing. Damn near lives there, I guess."

Bud managed to stay in music school by conducting all his practice sessions down in Maxie's basement. Everybody loved it except his professors. He saw them only on the rare occasions when he went to class.

At the door to Maxie's Beth tried to hesitate once more, in deference to her conscience, but it was too late. Charlie pushed the door open with one hand and pushed Beth inside with the other.

"Get in there, girl, and behave yourself," he said.

She turned to glare at him and ended up laughing and doing as he told her. "One beer," she said weakly. "One."

The music floated up from downstairs. Maxie had moved the band permanently to the basement in the interest of maintaining the public peace. They went down the narrow flight of stairs to a huge dimly lit room full of long tables and smoke and music. The tables were full of people and the people were full of beer, as a general rule.

Bud was regaling the crowd with a trombone solo when Beth and Charlie found seats in a booth, and Emily was sitting on the floor of the bandstand at his feet, leaning against the piano.

"See?" said Charlie with a grin. He helped her out of her coat. "Be right back," he said, and went off to get beer.

Beth took out a cigarette and settled back to watch Bud perform. He stood with his head cocked toward the trumpet, building a duet for the clarinet to coast on. There

was a cigarette jutting from his left hand and his shirt
sleeves were rolled halfway up his long forearms. His legs
were set wide apart and his right foot beat steadily on the
stand beneath it. He belonged wholly at that moment to
the melody and rhythm he was making, and Emily belonged wholly to him.

Beth studied them with the strange little prick of fore-
boding that Bud always inspired in her. It wasn't that she
didn't like him; he was, as everybody said, a great guy.
But he was no great guy to fall in love with. His eyes were
always busy with other women and his head was full of
music. He was crazy about Emmy, but he didn't love her.
Beth didn't think he ever would. It wasn't Emmy's personal failure; he was just made that way. Some men are.

Charlie set a quart of beer under her nose and pushed
her over into the booth. She looked up at him and smiled.
He kept shoving until he had her pinned against the wall.

"Are you going to let me get away with this?" he said.

"Hell, no. I'm a lady," said Beth.

"Beth honey, you swear too much."

"I know," she said, "it's a defense mechanism."

He slid away from her and poured her beer. Beth felt
the release of pressure from his body with regret. She
watched him while he poured, wondering what it was
that made her follow him, smile against her will at him,
feel content just to look at him.

"Drink up," he said, and gave her her glass. "Cheers."

The music stopped and Charlie looked up and waved at
Bud. Bud put his horn down on the piano for a moment
and nudged Emmy. They both smiled and nodded and
waved. Charlie beckoned to them to come over but the
music started again and Bud picked up his trombone.

Charlie put his arm around Beth and she was astonished
at the force of her pleasure. She turned to smile at him
and it came to her as a shock that their faces were so close.
Charlie pulled her closer and checked her sudden impulse
to retreat with his own obstinate strength.

"Beth," he said, "do you know you bothered the hell out
of me all through Christmas vacation?" She smiled away
from him. "I thought about you all the time. And that's
the God's truth, if I never told it before. I couldn't get
you out of my head. Oh, I know what you're thinking."
He looked at his beer and gave her a chance to watch him
again. "You think I've said the same thing to a dozen dif-

ferent girls. Well, I guess I have, at that. I even thought
I meant it once or twice." He laughed a little at himself.
"Do I sound like a damn fool?"

"Yes," she said, but she smiled gently.

He leaned toward her. "I wish I knew you better, Beth.
I think there must be a lot to know about you." He
reached over and stroked her cheek with his index finger,
and she pulled away, still smiling.

"Why?"

"Because there's so little you tell. You won't talk about
yourself, honey. And yet you're talented, intelligent . . ."
He paused. "You're beautiful, Beth. I say this at considerable risk to my ego."

She laughed and looked at him.

"You are, you know." He reached into her soft hair and
caressed her neck with his hand. "Will I have to resort to
tricks to get you out next time? Or can I just say, 'Beth,
this is Charlie. I want to see you.'?"

"Try it," she said.

"I will. Do you remember meeting me, Beth? At a
party a couple of years ago? You were there with Don.
Remember?"

"Yes." She smiled, warm and aroused.

"Do you know what I thought of you?"

"No," she said and shook her head, wondering at her
wealth of monosyllables.

"I thought you were a beautiful girl who didn't know
she was beautiful. I thought you were antisocial, too. I
figured you for a born spinster. My God, I was blind! I
remember wondering if some guy would have the sense
to see how pretty you were and didn't give a damn that
you were such a square. Or maybe liked you square. I guess
Don did."

"We got along, for a while."

"God, isn't it funny how things work out? I had the
eyes to see you with and not the sense to do anything
about it. I guess I thought you were strange. I mean, it
didn't seem right that you should be so wrapped up in
books. Not you."

"Oh, I've always liked books." She couldn't get a respectable sentence out.

"Better than anything else?"

"Not quite."

"I used to think so."

"They were an escape. They—filled an empty place. I guess you don't know about empty places, Charlie."

"I'm spoiled. I don't say that makes a better man of me. Will you tell me about the empty places, honey?"

It hit close to home.

"Can you talk to me, Beth?" he said gently. She looked down again, and he waited silently, watching her. "Hard, isn't it?" he said. "I remember when I was little I always used to say, 'Can I go outside?' and my mother would say, 'You can but you may not.' It's the other way around for you, I guess. You may, but you can't."

She looked up at him slowly and nodded. "I could, if it didn't matter," she said, and then, as if she had confessed too much, she turned away sharply and looked down into the cool gold in her beer glass.

"Afraid of me, Beth?"

She smiled a little at the heavily initialed table top, remembering the way she had asked Laura that same question, and then she looked up, straight ahead of her. "No," she said.

"Then look at me and say so."

She looked at him but it was very difficult to say it. It was difficult to say anything. She found herself just looking at him, wordless and wondering and excited. His arm tightened around her.

"No, Charlie," she whispered.

"I think you are."

"All right, I am." She swayed away from him but he followed her to the wall of the booth and held her fast. The force of the physical attraction between them overcame their sanity. They wanted each other with a violent desire; wanted to fit their bodies together to forge two physical promises. And still Beth fought him.

"Beth," he murmured.

She turned her head and his lips trailed over her cheek until his tongue found the corner of her lips. And then she turned back to him with the music and the noise and the excitement giving them privacy, and let her lips part a little and give themselves to him. All resistance washed out of her. She put her arms around him and held tight to him and when he stopped in surprise to gaze at her, she pulled his head down again and found his mouth, begged for it with her own, curiously thrilled with the light scratch of his beard, pressing her breasts against his broad flat chest as if she had suddenly found an excuse for their being.

"Beth!" he whispered in astonishment, putting his head down on her shoulder and holding her hard, feeling her tremble. Her response was so unexpected, so strong, that it caught him completely unaware.

"Jesus!" he said, and kissed her neck. "Let's get out of here." And sat up and started to pull her after him.

"Oh, no! No, Charlie, I—" She was frightened then, unwilling and unable to trust herself. They were safe in Maxie's basement; they couldn't do anything wrong. But Charlie had a car and he had an apartment, and Beth wanted him so much that she couldn't have put up a struggle. With another man it wouldn't have mattered; she had given up struggling long ago. It just didn't matter that much to her one way or the other. It was a sort of lost cause. But with Charlie it mattered enormously; with Charlie it had to be right. And the fear that it wouldn't be scared her almost as much as the growing feeling that it would.

"Charlie?" said a girl's voice. He looked around slowly with a frown. It was Mary Lou. "Hi!" she said. There was a boy behind her. "Freddie said there was a jam session down here. Well, Beth! What are you doing here?"

Beth mustered a smile. "Well—Charlie said there was a jam session down here."

"Uh—say, why don't you two sit down?" Charlie said to them. "We were just leaving. You can have the booth."

"Oh, there's room for four," said Mary Lou, sliding in on the opposite side. "Stay a little longer. This is the last set."

Charlie tried to object but she said, "Oh, look—isn't that Bud playing trombone? And look at Emmy." She turned to Beth with a disapproving frown. "Do you think she ought to sit up there like that? In public, I mean? It really doesn't look too good."

"I think it looks damn noble and romantic," said Charlie with a sort of irritated amusement. "Mary Lou, you worry too much."

"Look again!" said Freddie gleefully. "Maybe she's got something to worry about."

Mary Lou turned around in time to see Bud, flushed with beer and pleased with himself, give Emily a pro-

longed and melodramatic kiss. The audience offered some
spirited approval.

"Oh!" said Mary Lou indignantly and the men laughed
at her.

"That's nothing to worry about," said Charlie. "That's
normal. Hell, be thankful she doesn't feel that way about
girls."

Oh, Laura! Beth shut her eyes and put her head down
to ease the pain in her clenched heart. And then she felt
the pressure of Charlie's arm around her and she began
to quiver again.

"She's got to stop that," said Mary Lou firmly, frowning at Emily. "It's just not fair. Not to any of us, especially her. Beth, can't you stop her?" she said earnestly.
"I wish you'd talk some sense into her. I've heard all I
want to hear about it. It's a campus joke. If she'd act like
that right in Maxie's, I hate to think what she'd—"

The men leaned forward to hear what she said.

"Just talk to her, Beth," she finished loftily. "As a favor
to me." Mary Lou had solid confidence in Beth. Beth was
very sensible.

"I will," Beth said, and it was all she had strength to
say.

Charlie got out of the booth and stood up, pulling
Beth after him.

"We're leaving," he said firmly.

"Oh, why?" said Mary Lou. "Dinner isn't for another
half-hour, Beth."

"It'll take me half an hour to get her back to the house,"
said Charlie with a grin, and they laughed at him.

"Okay," Mary Lou sighed. "See you later."

Beth felt a mounting sense of alarm outdistanced only
by her rocketing desire. She tried feebly to protest again,
but Charlie was too much for her; his utter refusal to let
her intimidate him, his gentleness, his strength, his passion and her own overpowered her. She let him take
charge of her.

Charlie put an arm around her and led her the three
blocks to his apartment. She knew where they were going though she had never been there. They said very little
to each other but when they stopped at street corners or
turned and looked at each other their hearts started up
again. Just inside the apartment door she stopped and

turned back, the so-familiar doubts back in her heart.

"Mary Lou?" she said.

"I took you out to dinner. She won't ask questions."

"Mitch?"

"Field trip. Won't get back till tomorrow."

Laura? she thought, and the pain came back, but only for a moment. Charlie swept it away. He put his arms around her and embraced her so tightly that she couldn't breathe. And then he relaxed a little and pressed her to him, running his hands down her back. Her shoulders, her breasts, her hips felt the response of his smooth strength, his desire.

He picked her up and carried her to the bed. "Beth, you're lovely," he said. "So lovely."

A sudden awful fear clutched at her. What if it was wrong? What if it was as dull and empty and depressing as all the others? What if her instincts had misled her? "Wait, Charlie!" she said in a voice pitched high with alarm.

He heard the strain in her words and stopped to pull her close and comfort her. She clung to him on the verge of tears.

"Beth," he murmured. "Beth? Is this the first time?"

She held her breath in an agony of misgiving. What would he think of her if she told him the truth?

"Is it?" he prodded gently, thinking that was probably the cause of her fears. He was surprised to hear her whisper into his sweater, "No."

For a few moments they sat on the bed, neither moving nor speaking. Charlie was completely at a loss for words. Finally Beth lifted a pale face to him, and whispered, as if each word were costing her pain, "It was never any good. It was just a farce, a dirty little game. It was never right. At first I used to think it would be beautiful, if I just kept trying—if I didn't lose hope, if I found the right guy, if there was nothing wrong with me. If, if, if . . . But it never was." She stopped to conquer her trembling voice. "And finally, after a while, I just didn't care any more. I didn't care what they did to me. I guess I was lucky. Most of them were nice guys." A sob betrayed her, and Charlie held her a little tighter.

"And then I got sick of it," she said. "I got just old-fashioned sick of the whole business. I quit; I sort of swore off, I guess you could say. I figured it just wasn't for me. I didn't know why."

Charlie was silent and she began to get frightened again. "I—I don't know why I did it, Charlie. I'm ashamed—so ashamed. I—" She couldn't go on.

"You don't have to tell me all this, Beth," he said at last. He was shaken, surprised. And at the same time her confession made him feel fiercely protective.

"I had to tell you the truth," she said through her tears. "I couldn't lie to you."

"Why?" He looked down at her.

"Because this time I—I want it to be right. I want so terribly for it to be right and I was afraid it couldn't be if I —if I weren't honest with you."

He kissed the tears on her cheeks. "Is that why you're here now, Beth? To see if it's going to be right at long last?"

She hung her head. "I'm here because you told me to come with you," she said. "Because I couldn't help myself. Because for once I want it really and truly, for once I care about it. I care terribly." She looked up at him with tormented eyes. "Charlie," she begged. "Forgive me. Please forgive me."

"Forgive you?" he said softly. "What for? For being lost and mixed up and unhappy? For trying to set things right when you didn't know how? Hell, there's nothing to forgive you for. I'm only thankful they didn't turn you into a hopeless cynic."

She felt herself beginning to smile very faintly at him and in a sudden burst of gratitude she took his head in her hands and began to kiss him. The pain of her confession began to fade. Wherever he touched her she felt good. And when he had all that loveliness in his hands he pushed her down on the bed in a spasm of delight and kissed her all over, feeling her tremble with an almost unbearable pleasure.

Beth shut her eyes and said, "Oh, my God, Charlie, Charlie, Charlie . . ." And knew she had found what she had been looking for for so long.

And they fulfilled their promise in the dark and all the world spun away and left them alone in heaven.

ELEVEN

Laura looked for Beth all afternoon. She looked for her at dinner. And when she went up to her room she felt lethargic and sad. Emily came up at seven and found her sitting in the butterfly chair, staring at a book.

Emily saw that Laura was worried, and she thought she knew why. Laura had a crush on Charlie and so Emmy hesitated to say anything. She just waited until Laura couldn't stand it any longer and said, "Laura, do you know where Beth is?"

"Well, I—she was out with Charlie this afternoon." Laura looked so unhappy that Emmy pulled the desk chair over to the butterfly and sat down.

"It didn't mean a thing, Laur, really. She'll tell you that herself when she gets in."

"Is she still with him? You mean she's been with him all this time?"

"Well, she—they dropped down to Maxie's to hear the music this afternoon." Emmy watched sympathetically as Laura's face fell. "Charlie was there earlier, Laur. Before he met Beth. He loves jazz, you know. I guess he just decided to bring Beth along. They really were good this afternoon." Laura's face was pale and hard. She said nothing. "Beth likes jazz too, you know," Emmy added, afraid of the silence.

"Yes, I know!"

"Laur, you mustn't take it so hard." Emmy reached out and put a hand on Laura's shoulder, but Laura shook it off and her nails pressed cruelly into her brow and scalp, trying to cut out the hurt they could never touch.

Emmy sat beside her in silence, miserable because she couldn't help. "Laur," she said. Her voice was all she could offer. Laura couldn't very well stop her ears. "Laur, please don't cry. She'll be home in a little while. She'll explain it to you, I know she will. Laur . . . there there, Laur, honey. Please don't—"

Laura stood up, suddenly furious, and turned on Emily.

"Don't call me honey! Don't call me that! I hate that word. Emmy, do you hear me?"

"Yes, I hear," said Emily in a whisper.

Laura sank back to the chair, frightened with her temper, her hurt, her jealousy. "Emmy," she said. "I'm sorry. You mustn't pay any attention to me."

"I didn't know you liked him that much, Laur."

"Oh, I don't. I mean, not really. Oh, I don't know what I mean; I can't explain. Please, Emmy . . ."

They sat in silence for a minute and then Emmy said, "Maybe you'd like to be alone for a little while."

Laura didn't answer. She was thankful, but too eager to be rid of Emily for graceful gratitude. When Emmy left she sat perfectly still with her lips tight and her eyes full, and had a talk with herself. She began to see that for all her tolerant teasing and tenderness, Beth simply didn't like her jealousy. And she knew Beth would expect a vindictive temper and tears and recriminations when she got home. Laura faced facts; her good sense was born of desperation. She couldn't swear off her jealousy, but she could tuck it under her love and hope it would smother. If it persisted, at least it wouldn't show. After all, maybe Charlie wouldn't last. Maybe it didn't mean anything.

The door opened suddenly and startled a gasp from Laura. She looked up quickly, but it was Mary Lou. The letdown knocked her temper off again.

"Where's Beth?"

"Not home yet," Laura said testily.

"Not home yet?" Mary Lou repeated in surprise.

"Try again at closing hours," said Laura. She stood up and turned her back on Mary Lou, gazing at the desk top as if she had important business with it.

Mary Lou stared at her back for a minute. The voice didn't sound like Laura's. "Will you tell her I dropped in? I'd like to talk to her when she gets back."

"Certainly."

"Thanks." Mary Lou waited just a second longer for Laura to say "You're welcome." Laura never passed up a chance to be polite. But this time she remained silent and finally Mary Lou turned and left, surprised.

Emily came back to study, and Laura waited with her heart beating high for the closing hour chime and Beth's return.

At closing hour Charlie and Beth said good night in his car. They couldn't let go of each other with any finality. Beth murmured several times, "I have to go in," and neither of them moved, except closer together.

Charlie kissed her, a long, deep kiss. In the pale radiance of the dashboard they gazed at each other.

"Oh, Beth, darling," he said. "I could look at you like this forever." It was unoriginally and beautifully true. "I never met a girl I wanted so much . . . so much . . ." He frowned at the mystery of it. "I can't let you go, Beth. I can't let you go."

"Charlie . . ." She traced the line of his brows with a finger and closed her eyes and felt his lips, and his warm breath flowed over her hand. He bent his head to kiss her hand and she pulled him closer and licked his ear, until he began to groan with the pleasure of it.

"Oh, Beth, where the hell did you come from? Why didn't I know you when I saw you? I've been looking for you for so long, darling."

"This is crazy, Charlie. It's just crazy," she whispered. "It happened so fast."

He stroked her hair. "Are you sorry, Beth?"

Her eyes fell. "I—don't know. I don't know, Charlie." She looked up to him and the sight of him scattered her doubts. "No, I'm not sorry." But when she looked away again she was. "Yes, I am. Oh damn, I don't know."

He pulled her tighter. "Beth—"

"Charlie, what time is it?" she asked suddenly. Laura was waiting. She went cold at the thought.

"Twenty-eight after."

"I have to go in." *Oh, Laura, forgive me!*

"Beth darling, listen to me—wait—"

"I have to go in."

"I want to see you tomorrow," he said. "What time, honey?"

"I don't know. Call me." She opened the car door, looking back at Charlie as she did so. He was frowning at her.

"Call you, hell. What's the matter with you? Tell me now."

She got out of the car and slammed the door, hurrying up on the walk in the direction of the house. Laura was suddenly looming in her thoughts and her conscience began to torture her. Charlie reached her side and took her arm and swung her about to a stop.

"Charlie, it's late—"

"I know it's late, Beth. What the hell's come over you all of a sudden? Wasn't it—wasn't everything all right?" His voice became soft, pleading.

"Yes—oh, yes, everything was—wonderful. Only—"

"Only what?"

"Nothing. I just don't want to be late. Please, Charlie." She tried to shake his arm off but he held her fast. Her concern for Laura chafed and grew with each second that he held her there, and at the same time she wanted to spend the whole night with him. She was helpless, rent between two loves, tormented.

At last he turned and started walking with her toward the house. "When will I see you, Beth?" He sounded a little grim.

"Just call me, Charlie, please. I don't know."

"What's the matter? What in God's name is the matter? Two minutes ago you were—you were happy. Now all of a sudden you panic because you're going to be a minute late. Am I supposed to swallow that?"

"You'll have to," she said. Her affection for Laura was crushing her with reproval.

Charlie spun her around again at the front door and embraced her.

"Beth, talk to me," he said urgently.

She shook her head and tried to pull free.

"Is it me?" he said.

"Oh, no! Oh, Charlie, darling—" She reached for him and he kissed her and let her go slowly. She shook her head at him wordlessly, wondering why she couldn't hide her troubles. They were so strong, so near the surface, that they threatened to spill over.

"I'll call you," he said finally, when the housemother called to Beth to come in. They stared at each other for just a second more, and then Beth left him.

She ran up the stairs, pausing for an instant on the landing to wipe off her smeared lipstick, and then she went down the hall to the room. Her roommates were studying quietly together. She glanced swiftly from one to the other.

"Well!" said Emmy with a big smile. "Welcome home."

Then she thought of Laura and fell suddenly silent.

Laura said nothing, and seeing her, so slender and wan in the big chair, Beth ached to be alone with her, to explain things. She began uneasily to undress.

"Have a nice time?" said Laura.

"Yes," she said cautiously.

"Where did you go?"

Beth was afraid to set off the volcano with every word. She went carefully. "Maxie's," she said. "And then it got too late to come home for dinner, so—we went out."

"Well, I'm glad you're home safe," said Emmy. She left Beth and Laura alone; she understood that Beth would want to talk to the younger girl, and she made a discreet disappearance.

Beth hung up her clothes, feeling as if she might explode with the tension. Charlie was so close, so warm in her head and the pit of her stomach, and yet there was Laura right beside her, real, and hurt. She couldn't let her go to bed before she had explained, or tried to explain, at least some of what happened. It hurt her sharply to know that she had to lie.

Laura sat hunched on the desk chair, her eyes fastened on the floor. Beth felt an unbearable pity for her and an almost exacerbating scorn for herself. She stood gazing at Laura for a minute, unable to talk, to find the right words. Finally she went over to her and knelt on the floor beside her. She took her hands and looked earnestly up at her.

"Laura," she said. "Laura, look at me." There was a film of anxiety over every word; a profound tenderness in her voice that touched Laura. She looked up and Beth reached for her to kiss her, but she resisted.

"Mary Lou wants to see you," Laura said unexpectedly.

"Oh, honey, not now. Not now."

"You'd better go, Beth. She might come looking for you."

"Laura, I don't want to leave you. I want to talk to you. I—"

"You'd better go."

Beth was surprised at her firmness. She squeezed Laura's hands and then lifted them up impulsively and kissed them. "I'll be right back."

She hurried to Mary Lou's room and found her still up. It would never have occurred to Mary Lou to question anything Beth did. Emmy's most casual behavior was subject to suspicion, but Beth's most suspicious behavior was just casual. To Mary Lou, anyway. She trusted her.

"Oh, hi!" she said. "I was just going down to your room. Guess what?"

Beth was in no mood for games. She tried to smile a little. "What?"

"Mitch Grogan called me."

It stirred a little interest. "Oh, that's great. Going to see him?"

"Yes, this weekend. Say, Beth? Is Laura all right?"

That rang the alarm bell. "Yes. Why?"

"She just seemed upset. About your date, I guess."

"Oh, no—"

"I guess she still likes Charlie."

"Oh!" She rubbed a distraught hand through her hair. It was an out; not the best, but the only one. "Yes, I— God, I feel terrible about it. I—"

"I understand," said Mary Lou. "Actually," she added confidentially, and confidence with her was a luxury, just as friends were a luxury, "I'm sort of glad it happened. You need somebody, Beth. I've thought that for a long time. It's a shame about Laura, but she'll find somebody."

Beth had to get back; her nervousness was likely to betray her. "I'm going to talk to her about it," she said. "I think it'll be all right." She turned and almost ran back to the room.

Laura was waiting for her on the couch. Beth went over to her, sat down and searched her face, and then took her in her arms and held her for a long time. Laura submitted docilely, letting Beth cradle and comfort her. As for Beth, every part of Laura that she could see and feel tore her heart; the quiet acceptance was harder for her than an out-and-out tantrum would have been. She touched Laura's face with her hand and felt her wet cheeks and said in a broken voice, "Oh, Laur, honey." It was all she could say for a minute.

"Beth, Beth, that's all right. Please—"

Beth got hold of herself. The immediate hurt in her arms loomed larger just then than the remembered pleasure of the evening. She hated herself for being false to this sweet trusting girl who loved her so completely. She was suddenly appalled with her own cruelty, her own bad faith. She should have told Laura long ago how she really felt and now it was too late. She must pay now; make it up to Laura, somehow heal the hurt.

"Laura," she said. "Laura, honey, get mad at me, or something. I can't stand it like this. I wouldn't hurt you for the world."

Laura made herself keep calm by an immense effort of will. "Beth, don't try to explain. I'd rather not hear . . . I love you, Beth." She looked up at her and Beth bent down to kiss her, and Laura knew she had said the right things. No desperate anger would have brought Beth so close and made her so contrite.

The gentler Laura was, the more Beth's conscience hurt her, the more viciously her deception bit into it. "Oh, Laura, Laura, I don't know what to say. Forgive me, forgive me. I'd do anything to make it up to you."

"There's nothing to make up, Beth. Is there? I mean, you just went out with a boy, that's all. Well, I've been going out with boys too, all year. I'm as guilty as you are."

It was almost more than Beth could take. She had a brief horrible vision of Laura learning the whole truth and she stiffened against it, suddenly furious with Charlie for attracting her as he did. In an access of remorse she said, "Laura—Laura, I won't go out with him again, if you don't want me to." It was so easy to say, so magically comforting.

Laura was too powerfully tempted to refuse. She answered, looking up at Beth with a hopefully happy face that contradicted her cautious words, "Beth, I wouldn't ask you to do that. You know I wouldn't."

"You want me to. I can tell by your face." She took the slim face in her hands and it seemed so anxious and so trusting that she said, "All right. All right, Laur." She embraced her and looked into a dark corner of the wall and thought, Oh God, give me strength. I can't hurt her any more, I just can't. It took a woman, it took Laura, to teach me how to feel. I owe her my love. I owe it to her. She shut her eyes tight against Charlie and found him strong and clear in her mind.

And then Laura said, "Beth, darling!" and hugged her passionately and Beth thought, This is enough. This has got to be enough.

"Laura," she said softly. They fell back on the couch together and Beth let her have her way, tired though she was. A long while later she fell asleep, exhausted and unhappy, plagued by febrile dreams of first Charlie and then Laura and then Charlie again, wondering what Charlie would think when she refused to see him, wondering if she had the guts to stick by Laura. She hardly dared to think of Charlie, for she no sooner reviled him roundly in her head than her body gave him an unconditional pardon.

Laura lay still beside her, worried at her fitful turns but clinging obstinately to Beth's promise. She had a frightening premonition that Beth would resent her bondage, but at least she couldn't break it: she had forged her own chains. Besides, it was so thrilling to feel Beth bound to her, to feel Beth her captive, that Laura couldn't see the dangers clearly. She was too sensitive not to be fuzzily aware that there were dangers, but she couldn't really believe in them just then. Beth was hers.

TWELVE

Emmy could hardly wait to hear about Charlie. She had to run after Beth in a midmorning rush between classes and caught her speeding over the campus toward Lincoln Hall.

"Have coffee with me," she begged.

Beth was afraid; she knew too well what to expect from Emmy. "I have a class, Em."

"Well, cut it! Oh, come on."

Beth slowed down. "Well—" she said. She had to face it sooner or later. Emily would be wondering why she didn't see Charlie again. She'd have to make it sound plausible.

Beth let herself be led to the nearest coffee spot. Emmy could hardly wait to ask questions.

"How was it?" she said.

Beth stirred her coffee carefully, watching the brown and white unite in her cup and come tan. "He's a very nice boy," she said.

Emily waited. "Well, is that all?" she said finally.

"No." She pulled the spoon out and looked at it. It was a tricky business trying to fool Emily. Emily knew her too well. "We had a very nice time."

"What's all this 'nice'? That doesn't mean anything." She leaned back and folded her arms. "What happened, Beth?"

Beth wondered if she could possibly conceal it from her, and the weight of another lie pulled her spirits still lower. "He just doesn't have it, that's all. I know, I know, when you saw us at Maxie's I looked all excited . . . and I guess I was. But it wore off. He's—" She shrugged. "He's just another guy, Emmy."

"You're disappointed, maybe, but not with Charlie. Gee, Beth, I know you better than that. You're not in love with his face. At least that's not all you're in love with."

"Who's in love? With anything? Or anybody? I didn't say I was in love."

"You didn't need to."

106

"Oh, Emmy—" she exclaimed. *My God, does it show?*
Emily took her confusion for confirmation.

"When are you going to see him again?"

Beth emptied the smoke from her lungs and said, "I
don't know." If she had said "never" she would have
provoked a storm from Emily.

"Is he going to call?" Emily felt her way carefully,
surprised by Beth's evasiveness.

"Yes."

"When?"

"I don't know, Emmy. Today, I guess."

"You don't know? Didn't he say?"

"No."

"He's disappointed too, is that it?"

"I guess so. I don't know."

"If he's disappointed, why is he going to call?"

"Emmy, I—" She had to protect Laura. She looked down
again, defeated. "I don't know."

Emmy frowned, reaching for Beth's confidence with her
sympathy, her affection; wondering why Beth suddenly
distrusted her. "What happened last night, Beth?" she
said again. "Or don't you know that either?"

Beth wanted to scream at her. She made one last try to
evade her. In a short dry voice she said, "We had dinner,
we danced, we talked. We made love, we came home." She
sighed, hurting because the relief of truth was denied her
and because now it was Emily she had to lie to. But
Laura must be spared; Laura, whose whole love she had
taken for her some-time pleasure; Laura, whose trust she
had wholly betrayed; Laura, to whom she owed the climax
of love, and perhaps even her physical pleasure with
Charlie.

"Beth," said Emily gently. "Why won't you talk to me?
Is there something the matter?" Beth looked up at her
slowly and Emmy took her hands and squeezed them.
"Beth, you're my best friend," she said. "Don't you think
I want to help, if I can? Gee, Beth, I tell you everything.
I haven't a secret in the world from you. You know you
can trust me." Beth couldn't answer. "Did he hurt you?"

She shook her head.

"Did he threaten you or—or was he disgusting, or—"

"No, no, Emmy. He—" She stopped, helpless. After a
moment she said, "No, he was very nice. He didn't do
anything."

Emily released her hands and sat studying her in silence. Beth sipped her coffee and smoked and sweated in quiet misery. Finally Emily said pointedly, "It's Laura."

Beth looked up at her with such a startled face that Emmy said, "I thought so. I should have suspected this all along."

"Oh, Emmy—no!" said Beth. She was almost sick with apprehension.

"Don't tell me, Beth. I've got eyes. You won't go out with Charlie because of Laura."

"Emmy, I swear to God, it's not true, it's not—"

"Don't try to deny it, Beth. It's the only possible answer. Nothing else makes sense."

"Oh, Emmy, my God." She put her head in her hands, shaken to the core. "How did you know? How did you ever—"

"Simple," said Emmy. "You have the softest heart in the world. Too darn soft for your own good. You won't go out with Charlie because Laura's still got a crush on him." She smiled triumphantly. "I knew it. I'm right, aren't I?"

Beth couldn't answer. She wanted to laugh hysterically with relief, she wanted to get up and run.

Emmy sighed and spun her cup slowly around by its handle. "I know because Laura felt so terrible last night before you got home. She even cried a little. And finally she just plain got mad at me. She said she just couldn't explain it, but I knew it was you and Charlie."

Beth wondered if Emmy would see the tremor in her hands. "I talked to her last night," she said. "I think she's all right now."

"Now that you've told her you won't go out with Charlie, you mean."

"Oh, Emmy . . ."

"Beth, I know you wouldn't lie to me. You'd tell me if this wasn't true. Now listen to me. Laura's a sweet girl and I know you're fond of her, but this is ridiculous. You can't sacrifice a terrific guy—maybe your whole future—to one girl. You'll probably never see her again after next June. Beth, you're crazy about Charlie. Admit it . . ." Beth put her head down on her arms and prayed for her sanity. "Beth, you're hurting yourself forever, trying not to hurt Laura for a little while." For the wrong reasons, Emmy hit the right truth, but Beth was blind with her own distress.

"Oh, Emmy, you've got it all backwards, you—" She

broke off. "Let's not talk about it. Let's please not talk about it."

"But I don't understand."

"Please, Emmy." She restrained an impulse to grasp her shoulders and shake her into silence. She stood up abruptly, suddenly at the end of her endurance, and said, "I'm going up to the Union. I'll see you later, Emmy."

Emmy looked up, surprised and a little hurt. "I'll come with you, Beth," she offered.

"No, no. You—you stay here and finish your coffee."

Emily watched Beth stumble out of the lounge and made up her mind that she would interfere. Laura's crush would just have to give way to Beth's love. There were no two ways about it.

THIRTEEN

Mɪᴛᴄʜ was curious. He pestered Charlie for the facts, and Charlie's evasions gave him the satisfaction of supposing the evening with Beth was a failure.

"How far did you get?" he asked.

Charlie sighed and looked up from his book. His temper was bad but he tried to hold it back. "I got nowhere, boy. I wasn't trying to get anywhere."

"Going to see her again?"

"Of course."

"When?"

"I don't know," he said with martyred patience. And then to illustrate his irritation he added, "God damn it! Now will you shut up?"

Mitch complied, grinning comfortably. To see Charlie make a mistake with a woman was to see Romeo take a pratfall under the balcony.

"What are you grinning at?" said Charlie.

Mitch chuckled. "I didn't know I was."

"You were."

"Oh, I'm just glad to know you're fallible."

Charlie plunged back into his book. He had been trying to reach Beth all day with no success. She wasn't at home or she couldn't be disturbed. They couldn't say where she was or when she'd be back. Sorry. Call again. And he did, again and again, with always the same results and the same obvious reason for them: she didn't want to talk to him.

It was incomprehensible. For a long while he imagined that he had done something wrong. But the harder he pursued the idea the less substance it had and finally he gave it up. Something else was bothering her. Maybe they had gone too fast. Maybe they both had wanted too much too soon. He hadn't pushed it, he hadn't insisted on anything. She'd wanted it as much as he did; it had happened naturally. He couldn't accuse himself of anything there. The whole evening had seemed so right, so fair and lovely, and he wanted her again so much that it was impossible for him to admit that she didn't want him just as much. He didn't think she was a girl with a conventional conscience, but he was willing to admit that he might have been wrong there; she had certainly suffered enough over her past transgressions. What else could it be? He didn't think she was seeing anyone else; she came with him voluntarily and never made an objection to him. The more he thought of it the more puzzled he was.

Charlie didn't know he had an ally. Emily kept her peace as long as she could, but by the middle of exam week she couldn't hold out any longer. She knew Charlie had been trying to see Beth on campus, at the Union, everywhere; that he had been calling every day and getting nowhere; that he was upset and getting mad. She got half of this from Bud, who saw Charlie almost every day, and the rest from watching and listening to Beth, and pretty soon her Samaritan instincts got the better of her. She called Charlie. Mitch took a message for her.

When Charlie got home he found the note under the corner of the phone. "Call Emily at 7-4006. She says you'll understand. What's the mystery?"

Charlie chucked his books on the sofa and picked up the phone, pulling off his jacket while it rang.

"Good afternoon, Alpha Beta," said a bright young voice.

"Hello, is Emily there?"

"Just a moment please."

Charlie lighted a cigarette and waited, fidgeting.

Minutes later, Emmy said, "Hello?"

"Emmy?" he said eagerly.

"Oh, Charlie! I'm so glad you called. Listen, I'm going to be perfectly frank with you. I know you've been trying to reach Beth." She hesitated.

"Yeah?" he said, urging her with his voice.

"Well, she wants to see you, Charlie. I know it. She won't talk to you on account of Laura."

"Laura? What the hell does Laura have to do with it?"

"Beth's got it into her head that Laura's still got a crush on you."

Charlie was floored. "Emmy—my God—she never did! Our fathers were old buddies in college. I never would have met the girl if it hadn't been for that. She doesn't have a crush on me. She never did. What the hell!"

Emily was suddenly concerned. The words she phrased in such good faith seemed always to change character the moment they left her mouth. Not until she heard herself speak them did she understand them as other people did. She paused, trying to grasp the implications of the conversation. "Well," she said, uncertainly, "Beth doesn't know that, apparently. Anyway, Charlie, that's not the point. The point is she wants to see you. She's told me so. She's miserable, and if you could just *talk* to her—"

"How? My God, I've been trying—"

"I know, but she won't talk to you if she knows it's you. Call her on her private phone. We have one in the room. She doesn't know you have the number, so she'll answer it. Once she hears your voice, Charlie, it'll make all the difference, I know it."

"When can I call?"

"Call her tonight about seven. She'll be alone in the room then. Laura's got a final at Greg Hall and I'll just fade away."

"Emmy, you're a good girl."

"Oh, she'd do it for me. I just hate to see you two in a mess because of a silly misunderstanding. You just need a go-between." She laughed.

"What's her number?"

She told him.

"Thanks, Emmy," he said. "I really appreciate this."

They hung up, each wondering what sort of a game Laura was playing. Charlie figured it for some kind of petty jealousy, but Emily came closer. She began to review Laura's behavior systematically: the way she followed and imitated Beth; her disappointment when Beth wasn't at home; her temper when Beth wasn't there to greet her after Christmas vacation; her anger when Beth and Charlie went out.

Emily admitted that it might be some sort of obsessive friendship, but even that idea made her uncomfortable. She was unwilling to accept it but unable to dismiss it. But she said nothing to either of her roommates.

At seven, as arranged, Charlie called Beth on her room phone. He listened nervously to the ring. It rang four times before Beth picked up the receiver.

"Hello?"

"Beth—darling, this is Charlie. Don't hang up."

"Charlie?" She began to tremble.

"Don't ask me anything, Beth, just listen. I have to see you. Tonight. We have to talk. We owe each other that much. Can you be ready in fifteen minutes?" His voice was urgent and soft; it brought him too close to her.

"Charlie—" she whispered, sinking into the desk chair, and tears started down her cheeks.

"I'll be by for you in fifteen minutes," he said. "Beth?"

"Yes?"

"Fifteen minutes, darling." He hung up before she could say anything.

Beth put her head in her hands and gave one short dreadful sob, and then she ran to wash her face and get dressed. She was ready when her buzz sounded a few minutes later and made her heart jump. She sped downstairs as if speed would obliterate her thoughts.

Charlie was waiting at the foot of the stairs. She stopped when she saw him and moved toward him slowly, stopping in front of him in the hall. She hadn't even time to hate her weakness; she resolutely ignored the idea of Laura. She couldn't help herself. They stared at each other for a minute and then he put his arm around her tight and led her outside without a word and down the walk to his car.

He started the motor, and she watched him with her heart pulsing wildly and her hot hands knotted together. After a moment he turned and regarded her and, still without a word, took her in his arms. With a gasp she reached for him and they kissed for a very long time. And then again. He turned the motor off, and for almost an hour they sat there with no words, only their lips and their trembling bodies to speak for them. Finally she put her head down on his shoulder and cried soundlessly. Only her involuntary tremors betrayed her. When she was calm again he said gently, "Want to talk to me, darling?"

She shook her head. He tilted her face up and brushed away the leftover tears and smiled at her. "All right," he said. "I won't torture you with questions. You'll find a way to tell me. Only tell me this, honey. Did I do something wrong?"

"No." She smiled faintly at him and looking at him wanted him again and lifted her lips to be kissed. He took them almost violently and then, holding her, he said, "Is there someone else?"

She couldn't answer. She struggled with herself and couldn't answer.

"I'm sorry, I'm sorry," he said. "I said no questions, didn't I?" He released her, frowning and rubbing his brow. "Let's get a beer." He looked at her but she didn't answer. "I can only take so much of this, Beth. Beer, honey?"

"Okay," she said.

They went over to Pratts' and talked very little because there was only one thing to talk about and it couldn't be said. So they studied each other's faces in the candlelight and locked their hands together and got a little drunk, more on each other than on the beer. And Beth fought off the haunting image of Laura's face from time to time when it got too strong and began to accuse her.

Charlie had to say something finally. "Emmy called me," he said. "She gave me your number."

"Oh." She smiled at him.

"She said something that—made me think you might have a wrong impression, honey."

"Of what?"

He knocked a column of ash from his cigarette and said musingly, "Twenty-eight years ago, my father went to school here with a guy named Merrill Landon. They've been friends ever since. When I found out Landon's daughter was here in school last fall I called her up and we went out a couple of times." He paused to study her. "Do you see what I'm getting at?"

There was a line of worry between Beth's eyes. "What did Emmy tell you, Charlie?"

"She said she thought you wouldn't see me because of Laura—because you thought Laura had a crush on me. Darling, Laura never *did* have a crush on me. We're just friends. Or rather, the children of friends . . . Was that the trouble?"

Beth stared helplessly at him, her fingers pressed against her cheeks. He watched her for a moment, feeling that he was losing her again. "Beth, you can't let Laura come between us. She means nothing to me, except as a family friend. There's no reason—"

"It's not Laura's fault. Don't blame anything on Laura. She has nothing to do with it."

Charlie wanted to squeeze the truth out of her, but her worried face warned him it wouldn't work. She was as stubborn as Emmy had said she was. "All right, darling,

I won't push you any farther," he said. "On one condition. On *one condition*, Beth. Look at me." He pulled her toward him. "That you see me again." Her eyes dropped. "Beth!" His voice ordered her attention.

"All right," she whispered unhappily. She couldn't resist him when she was with him, just as she couldn't hurt Laura when they were together. "All right, Charlie."

"Tomorrow?"

"I don't know."

"Look, Beth," he said, suddenly getting disciplinary with her. "I know you've got trouble, honey, I know you're up against something. I'm not trying to force you or push you around or frighten you. Maybe you've got obligations somewhere else, maybe you can't help what you're doing. Okay. But damn it, Beth, you've got obligations to me, too, whether you want 'em or not. You can't play with people, honey. You can't do—" He groped a little. "You can't behave the way you did with me—say the things you did—and suddenly drop me like a hot potato. Nobody can take that, Beth. Not me, not anybody."

"I wasn't playing, Charlie. I was serious. Only—please, please, don't ask me what the trouble is. I can work it out. Just give me time." She raised her eyes again, imploring him.

He sighed and said a little crisply, "All right. I'll give you time, Beth, if that's what you want. But I won't sit around making phone calls that don't get answered and playing tricks on you just so I can see you. I'm going to see you. And you're going to make a date right here and now and stick to it. Do you hear me?"

She nodded.

"Do you have an exam tomorrow?"

"No."

"Okay, I'm out at four. I'll pick you up at five. We'll go out, have dinner, see a show or something." He paused. "Okay, love?"

She nodded.

He looked at the wall clock and said, "Okay, let's go. Almost closing hours."

Beth got up with a start. Laura would be home already. Her final couldn't have lasted longer than ten o'clock. It was ten-twenty.

At the house, Charlie stopped the car and turned to gaze at her for a minute, and then he got out without kissing her. Beth was chagrined, almost angry. He opened her door and let her out.

"Come on, honey," he said in a businesslike voice. "It's cold."

She got out, watching him hopefully. He took her arm, slammed the door, and started for the house.

"Charlie!" she said, pulling back, and the tone of her voice reproved him.

He stopped and looked at her, and she threw her arms around him and kissed him until he held her and answered her.

"Charlie darling," she said. It was as grateful as it was inadequate. At the door she clung to him, almost afraid to let him go, afraid to face Laura. But the housemother shooed him out with the others, and she had to watch him leave.

She went slowly up to her room and pushed the door open with a sort of dread, and walked in. Emily looked up from the desk.

"Oh, Beth!" she said. "How was it? Was it all right?"

Beth nodded. "Yes, Em. Thanks. Where's Laura?"

"In bed."

"In bed?" Beth could hardly believe it.

"Yes. She got home from the final and—" She shrugged. "She said she was tired."

"Didn't she ask where I was?"

"Well, she asked if you'd gone out and I said yes. She knew right away with who. I just told her you went out for a beer with him. I mean—I *had* to tell her. She would have found out anyway."

Beth turned and took her coat off. Emily watched her with a host of questions on her tongue.

"How's Charlie?" she said.

"Fine. We sort of—made it up. I'm going to see him tomorrow."

"Will you tell Laur?"

"Yes, I'll tell her." She shuddered at the thought.

"Will she understand?" Emmy was half expecting an admission—of what, she didn't know.

"Yes, she'll understand." The hell she will, she thought.

"Beth?" said Emmy, hesitating.

"Hm?"

"You aren't mad at me for calling him, are you?"

"No, Em, I'm not mad."

"You're acting sort of funny."

"I'm tired, Emmy."

Emmy went over to her. "Beth, are you in love? Really?"

"I don't know."

"Yes you do. Are you?"

Beth sighed and her strength seemed to leave her with her breath. "Yes," she said, and suddenly it felt good. "Yes, yes, Emmy . . ."

Emily hugged her. "Oh, Beth, I'm so glad!"

"Emmy, you make me feel—" She tumbled her hair with nervous fingers. "Everything's such a mess right now."

"But it'll all turn out, Beth. Things are never as bad as they seem. Most of the things you worry about never happen, you know . . . Have you told him?"

"No. I—I'm a little afraid to, I guess."

"Oh, well, you'll get over that. Beth, I'm so happy for you!"

Beth had to answer her smile and fight it at the same time. Emily's warmth brought the truth to the surface in her; she wanted awfully to confess. But the thought of Laura, so alone, so lovingly given, so badly used, stopped her again.

"Guess what," said Emmy wth her eyes bright and her yellow hair alive in the lamplight.

"What?"

"Oh, you won't even think it's the truth," she said, looking at her bare toes in the pile of the rag rug.

Beth smiled indulgently at her. It was a brief hiatus of relief from her own troubles. "Yes I will, Emmy. If you say so. What?"

"It's Bud. I really love him. I'd do anything for him."

Beth couldn't help laughing a little. "You've been in love with him all year, Em."

"Not like this. This is it, Beth." She gripped Beth's arms in dead earnest.

Mary Lou's request floated hazily back to Beth. She had completely forgotten to talk to Emmy in the press of her own difficulties.

"Emmy, you haven't done anything—"

"Oh, no, Beth!"

If it were real, as Emmy said, then it was wrong. Bud was too undependable, too uninhibited. "Emmy—don't get carried away. Use your head. Oh, Em—"

Emmy hung her head as if she might begin to cry. "Beth, you don't believe me," she whispered.

"Yes, I do, I do, Emmy. Only, be sensible, honey. I mean in public and everything. I mean—"

"Do you really?" She brightened. "Because I do love him."

"Yes, Emmy. I know." She was too tired to argue.

"And he loves me. He told me so."

"Oh, Emmy, I'm so glad." What else could she say? She fell into bed later too tired to think.

FOURTEEN

THE NEXT DAY, Beth and Laura hedged with each other for a while before either of them would say anything. Finally Laura said in a tight voice, "You saw him last night, Beth. Why won't you just tell me? Why do I have to tell you?"

"Well—because I'm a little ashamed, I guess. Because I'm sorry, Laur. I didn't want to hurt you."

"You didn't have to. Why didn't you just tell me you were going to see him again?" She couldn't keep the bite out of her words.

"Because I didn't know it myself, honey."

"You didn't?" Laura gazed past her coolly and out the window.

"Oh, Laur, honey—" Beth tried to think of something better to say, but there was nothing. "No, I didn't."

"Beth, I didn't ask you not to see him again. You said you wouldn't see him again. You said it, not me. It was your idea. If I had asked you not to and you'd agreed—that would be different. But I didn't ask for anything. You went back on your word, Beth, after you gave it voluntarily." She was shaking with the force of her feeling, and she worked to keep her voice steady.

"Laura, honey, I— He called. He got my number. I didn't know. And when I talked to him, it—I owed him an explanation, Laur. I couldn't just drop him. Everyone thinks I dropped him because you still have a crush on him, don't you see? But he knows you don't, Laur."

"He knows?" Of course he knew. He took her out as a favor to her father. But did Beth know about her family, then? Had he told her of the divorce.

"Yes. He said your fathers were friends. He said you didn't have a crush on him at all. I had to see him—explain it—say something. I had to, don't you see?"

"I see," she said. "How did he figure all this out? If he knew I didn't have a crush on him, why did he think you wouldn't see him for my sake?"

"Well, I don't know. I—"

"Why didn't he figure out that there might have been another boy in your life? Or family troubles? Or something he did wrong? Why didn't he figure out any of those things, Beth? How come the first thing he thought of was me?"

"Laura, I—he didn't, exactly."

"Well, exactly what *did* happen, Beth?" She felt furious tears start up.

"He talked to Emmy, Laur. Emmy thought I wouldn't see him because of you. It was her idea."

"What right does Emmy have to go blabbing to him? What right does Emmy have to think *anything* about us?" She caught her breath, looking for words to cut with. "Why can't Emmy mind her own business and leave us alone?"

"Laur, please don't get excited, honey."

"Answer my question!"

Beth sighed and looked at her hands. "Emmy wanted to help. She knew I was unhappy. She knows me pretty well."

"Well, I guess I don't want to help and I don't know you at all and I made you unhappy. Is that it?"

"Laura—"

"Well, *is* it, Beth?" Suddenly an awful fear overswept her anger. "Oh, Beth—can't we be happy?" she pleaded. "We were so happy before. What happened? Why does Charlie matter?" The tears spilled over. "Do we have to quarrel and make each other miserable like this?"

"Oh, baby. No, no, we'll work it out. Somehow." She reached for her and Laura cried in her arms.

"Beth, we have such a beautiful thing together. We just can't let anything happen to it. We can't let anyone hurt it or come between us."

Beth wondered where the words were that would win her pardon. There didn't seem to be any.

"Beth," Laura whispered. "You won't see him again, will you?"

Beth was silent, not because she was torn again between the two, but because she hadn't the guts to say "Yes, I will see him."

"Beth?" Laura's voice was small and lost, like a child's in an empty room.

Beth pressed her close. "I don't know," she whispered. Laura took it in silence and in a moment Beth added, "I

might have to, Laur. I might have to—to ward off suspicion."

"Beth, please." It was almost inaudible.

"Laura, baby, I can't promise. I think I *have* to see
him."

"Why?" Her voice came out again, demanding.

"I've told you why. What will he think about you—and
me—if I don't?"

Laura sat up and pulled away from her. "I don't care
what he thinks. I don't care, I'm not ashamed. Are we
doing something dirty or wicked to be ashamed of? Are
we, Beth?"

"No." She shut her eyes and said slowly, "But other
people don't understand that, Laur. We have to keep it
secret—absolutely secret. People will say we're queer—"

"But we're *not!* I know what queer is. I've seen people—"

"Laura, we're just as queer as the ones who *look* queer,"
Beth said sharply, looking at her. "We're doing the same
damn thing. Now, let's not kid ourselves. Let's be honest
with each other, at least." Her own deception shut her up.

Laura sat and stared at her with a horrified face.
"Beth—" she quavered, shaking her head. "No . . . no . . ."

Beth grasped her hands. "I'm sorry. Oh, I'm sorry, that
was a terrible way to say it. I'm just so damn upset. I—"

"Are we really—" She couldn't say the word. "Are we,
Beth?"

"Yes."

Laura was mute for a minute, and then she said, "All
right. Then we are." She set her chin. "That still doesn't
make it dirty or wicked."

"No." Beth smiled ruefully at her and kissed her hands.
"It just makes it illegal."

Laura pulled her hands away and for a long while said
nothing. Finally she said, "Are you going to see him,
then?"

"Yes."

"How did he know your phone number?"

"Emmy."

Laura stood up suddenly and turned an outraged back
to Beth.

"Laura, Emmy's a friend. A very close friend of mine."

"Not of mine."

"Try to understand, Laura. She only wanted to help."

"Can't you make her understand you don't need help?"

"That would hurt her terribly. I can't hurt her, Laur."

"You can't hurt her, but you can hurt me?"

"Oh, Laura." Beth put her head in her hands. "I don't want to hurt either of you," she said from between her palms. "I don't want to hurt anybody."

"Well, choose between us, then. Because apparently one of us has to be hurt."

"Laura, will you stop?" Beth cried, looking at her. "My God, who's hurting who? What are you trying to make me do? What do you want me to say?"

Laura went to her and sank to her knees beside her. She put her head in Beth's lap, clutching at her, and said hoarsely, "I want you to love me, Beth, that's all. I want you to love me. Say that's selfish, say it's anything you want to call it, I can't help it. I love you more than life or death and I can't stand to think of losing you. I can't stand it, Beth, do you hear me? Oh, Beth, Beth, my darling, say you love me. Say that, and I don't care what happens. I don't care what else you say or what you do or even what we are. I don't care, if you'll only just tell me you love me . . . Beth? You do love me, don't you?"

"Yes, Laura."

"Say it."

"I love you, Laur."

Laura shut her eyes and didn't see the suffering in Beth's. There was nothing more they could say to each other then. And there was nothing more they could do. Emily would be back from lunch at any moment and both of them realized how dangerous it would be to continue as they were. They silently started tidying up the room.

Emily found her roommates in a state of apparent calm. Laura was collecting a pile of books and getting ready to leave.

"Where're you going, Laur?" said Emily conversationally.

"Over to the library." Laura wouldn't look at her. She was furious with Emily.

"I'll be down in Mary Lou's room, Emmy. We have that Comparative Lit. final tomorrow," Beth said, starting out of the room. "If anyone calls, I'll be down there." She looked cautiously at Laura, but Laura seemed unperturbed.

"Okay," said Emily. "Hey, when are you going out?" She knew instantly, from the look on Beth's face, that

Beth hadn't told Laura about her date. Emmy bit her tongue too late.

"I—don't know," Beth said, and she and Laura looked at each other. "He said he'd call. About five, I think."

Laura stod perfectly still with a book in her hands and stared at Beth. Emmy made the diplomatic move; the coming storm raised enough charge to frighten her out of the room.

"Guess I'll go see Bobbie," she said hastily, and backed out. She pulled the door shut behind her and walked down the hall in bewilderment. She didn't go to see Bobbie, she went to the living room and sat down in an alcoved corner and began, in spite of herself, to analyze the situation. She could put two and two together, but she could not believe in four until she saw it with her own eyes. It was the most difficult logic she ever faced: it was simple, irrefutable, and incredible—a lover's quarrel. Emmy gave an involuntary shudder.

Laura didn't say anything for a few moments after Emmy left. She sat down at the desk and stared out the window, speechless. Beth came up behind her, afraid to touch her, and stood behind her chair for a moment. Finally she said, "I meant to tell you, Laur. I just couldn't, after we got to talking. I can't bear to hurt you. Everything I say, everything I do, hurts you. It was cowardly, I know; I'll admit it. God knows I can't bear pain. And when I hurt you, I suffer too. I suffer terribly."

No sound, no gesture, came from Laura. Beth went around and sat on the desk and looked at her. "Laura, honey, you said—you said it didn't matter. You said nothing mattered as long as we had each other. You said you didn't care, as long as I loved you."

"Do you love me, Beth?"

"You know I do."

"No, I don't."

"I do, Laura."

"Then why didn't you tell me? Why do you lie to me, Beth?"

"Oh, darling—I'm afraid the truth hurts, sometimes. I didn't really lie to you, Laur, I just—tried to shield you."

"You should have told me, Beth. You never tell me anything. I have to guess, and if I ask the right questions, maybe I get the right answers. Otherwise I never learn anything. Not telling the truth is as wrong as telling lies, Beth. You knew all the time this morning you were going out with him this afternoon. It's yourself you're trying to shield."

Beth sighed. "I'm going out with him this evening, Laur. Because there's no way to explain to him why I won't go out."

"All right, Beth. Why didn't you just tell me that? I'd rather be hurt honestly than dishonestly."

"Oh, Laura, don't you understand—"

"I understand that I'm being treated like an irresponsible child," Laura exclaimed. "I'm being shielded from nothing, Beth. It's yourself you're trying to protect."

"Can't you believe I'd do something—anything—for you? Laura, if I've lied, and I have, it's been for your sake. Can't you understand that? My God, I've had to lie to Charlie for you and to Emmy, and—" And even to myself, she finished silently.

"And me."

"No, Laur."

Laura nodded at her. "Yes, Beth. Yes. Beth, I've been honest with you—absolutely honest—but you've got to be the same with me. I know I'm young. I know I'm inexperienced and childish sometimes. But you can't help me to grow up by treating me like a child; by shooing me out while you share your secrets with somebody else."

"Laura, I'm not sharing them with anyone else," she said, and her voice was tired.

"You haven't any right to deceive me, Beth," said Laura unhappily.

Beth's sorrows suddenly swelled and split inside and poisoned her. "God damn it, Laura!" she exploded. "Damn it, damn it, damn it! I've done nothing that I didn't do for your sake, nothing!" She stood up and strode to the other side of the room, and whirled to face Laura. "Will you never understand that? I've made mistakes, I know. I've hurt you, I know that, too. But do you have to harp on it? Do you have to cavil and pester and torment me, day after day—"

"Beth!"

"Like a damn silly little child—"

"Beth—"

"You make it impossible for me to handle this any other

way, Laura. I thought we could handle the thing like adults, but apparently we aren't quite capable of that."

"But Beth, didn't you understand what I meant—what I—"

"Yes, I understand. I understand that you're at least aware that I'm not the only one who's made mistakes. I suppose I'm to be grateful for it." The ache inside her was so awful that she went to extremes for the littlest relief; she hardly knew what she said, or cared. "What do you want me to do, Laura? Never speak to Emmy again? Never speak to Charlie? Lock myself in a damn garret with you somewhere and rot? Is that what you want?"

Laura looked at her, shaking her head, frightened.

"Well, there's a world around us, Laura," Beth went on as if Laura had said no, "and we're damn near grown up, however young we may act, and we've damn well got to go out and live in it. And crying over each other and clinging to each other and denying the rest of the world exists is sure as hell not the way to do it. That's a child's way, Laura. And if you haven't grown up enough by now to see it, then—then, damn it, I don't know. I can't help, I can only mess it up for you. If you're still a child, then go home. Go on back home to your mother and father where you'll be happy. Let *them* worry about you, let *them* take care of you. *I* can't; everything I do is wrong. Well, go back to your happy home and let your parents figure it out."

Laura put her head down on her arms, resting on the back of the desk chair, and never said a word. Beth wanted to see her temper, not her surrender. She wanted a fight and she persecuted Laura still further. She walked to Laura's chair and said, "The world is half men, Laura. The world is one-half men. Does that make sense? Well, does it?"

"Yes."

"And I like men, Laura. Now, that's honest. And I like Charlie. That's honest, too. Does it hurt enough for you? Honesty? Does it?"

"Yes."

"I like Charlie and I'm going to see Charlie, when I feel like it. Is that honest enough for you?"

"Yes."

Beth went to the closet and got her coat. "You can't

love a girl all your life, Laura. You can't be in love with
a girl all your life. Sooner or later you have to grow up."
She pulled the coat on and suddenly she couldn't look at
Laura for knowing how horribly she had hurt her. It began to overwhelm Beth and she had to get out before it
strangled her.

"Tell Mary Lou I had to go out, will you?" she said
brusquely.

Laura lifted her head. "Where are you going?" she said.
Her delicate face was discolored by the eruption of pain
and on her underarms, where Beth couldn't see, her nails
raised red welts, trying to call attention from the great
pain with a lesser. "Where are you going, Beth?" she
whispered.

"Out," said Beth.

"When will you be back?"

"Tonight. Closing." She paused at the door and looked
at Laura. And she knew she'd never forget what she saw.
Then she went out.

Downstairs in the hall she phoned Charlie. "This is
Beth," she said. "Where's your final?"

"Math building."

"When will you be out?"

"About four, maybe sooner."

"I'll be at Maxie's."

"Honey, are you all right?"

"Yes. I'm all right."

"You sure?" He felt the tension and was doubtful.

"Yes. Charlie, I have to go."

"Okay, Maxie's." He hung up worried.

Beth went out and walked. She walked over to the campus, and across it to campus town, and down the block to
Maxie's, half wild with pain and doubt and anger.

Girls didn't usually go into Maxie's alone, but Beth
walked in without looking to right or left, stopped at the
bar to get some beer—they didn't serve anything stronger
—and found a dark booth in a back corner. There was
only a small crowd and no one paid her much attention.
She looked too grim for company.

She sat back there alone until almost four o'clock, with
many trips to the bar for more beer. When Charlie found
her she was slumped in the booth with her head back and
her eyes closed. He slid in beside her and shook her gently.

"Beth . . . darling," he said.

She opened her eyes and looked at him as if she had never seen him before. And then she smiled.

"Let's get out of here," he said. He pulled her to her feet and helped her into her coat. She swayed a little, saying nothing and letting him steady her and lead her out into the cold air. He took her to his car and guided her in.

"How long have you been there?" he said.

She put her head back on the seat. "Since two." She smiled a little at the ceiling of the car.

"Did you have any lunch?"

"Um-hm."

"What time?"

"Noon."

He started the car. "You need some black coffee, darling."

"No, Charlie." She turned her head on the seat and reached for the back of his neck. She stroked it with her long fingers and said, "No, Charlie. Come get drunk with me."

He looked at her with a curious smile. "What's the matter, Beth?"

"I won't tell you unless you get drunk with me."

"I don't want to get drunk."

"Yes you do, Charlie. Charlie, please, darling . . . yes, you do."

"What's got into you!"

She smiled. "Beer," she said. "I'm sick of beer. Can't we go somewhere and drink Martinis?"

Charlie laughed. "Oh, you're a funny girl." He caressed her hair with his hand.

"I know. You'll never find another like me, Charlie. Humor me, get drunk with me." She tickled his ears. "Please . . ."

He turned away, smiling a little out the windshield. "If I get you a Martini, will you tell me what the hell's the matter?"

"Um-hm."

"Promise?"

"Yes."

He paused a moment, and then he drove her downtown. There was a hotel two blocks from the railway station with a small bar in it and he took her there with some misgivings and a firm intention to drag her out after one drink.

She behaved very well. She didn't stumble or mumble and she wasn't loud. They sat quietly at a dark table and she teased him and they talked about nothing and pretty soon Beth wanted another drink.

"You said you'd tell me what the trouble was if I bought you one Martini," he said.

"Yes, I know. Well, I find I'll need two." She smiled charmingly at him.

"That's just what you don't need, darling. You're already loaded on beer. How much beer did you have?"

"Not very much."

"You were asleep when I came."

"I was not. I was thinking."

"Anyway, you promised you'd tell me after one Martini."

"Did I? I can't remember. It's a funny thing about me, Charlie. I never keep my promises. Never believe me when I promise you something."

"What's the trouble, Beth?"

"One more drink," she pleaded. He looked at her askance and she gave him a little-girl smile and said, "I'll be good. Honest." She felt a driving, desperate, relentless need to forget.

"I think you need some black coffee and some food."

"After this drink."

He shook his head. "I don't know," he said.

"Charlie . . ." Her voice was tender and soft. "Please."

With a sigh he signaled the waiter. "Two more," he said, and she smiled. He put his arm around her and said, "Now talk to me, Beth. Talk to me."

She cocked her head a little to one side and said with sleepy suggestiveness, "Charlie, let's go to bed. I want to go to bed with you, Charlie."

He smiled quizzically at her. "Later, honey."

"I want you to make love to me." She put her head back against him and looked up at him so that their lips were very near and Laura was very far away. "I want it. I want to be so close to you that I can't get any closer. I want you to hold me so tight that I can never get away . . . so it won't be my fault if I never go back. Can you hold me that tight, darling?"

Charlie felt his heart speed up and he tried to fight the feeling. "I'm worried about you, Beth. I'm worried," he said. He pushed an errant curl behind her ear and kissed her cheek and said, "Tell me why you want to get drunk."

She pulled away from him and lifted her glass and drank half the Martini. "I just want to get drunk. I like to get drunk. I haven't been drunk for years. Anything wrong with that? Besides, I can't think of anybody I'd rather get drunk with than you."

"That's the truth?"

"Um-hm."

"And nothing but the truth?"

"Yes."

"Beth?" His voice implied that he knew better.

She turned and looked him full in the face and said, "Charlie, I wouldn't lie to you," and shook her head to augment her honesty, and then she picked up her glass and finished her drink.

Charlie watched it go apprehensively. "Why not?" he said. "Why wouldn't you lie to me?"

"Why Charlie," she said, laughing a little. "Because you're the most beautiful man in the world. You know that, darling? You're beautiful."

"Yeah, I know." He grinned sardonically at his drink. "You told me once. But you can lie to anybody, Beth. Doesn't matter what they look like."

"Nobody ever told me that," she said. "Think of all the lies I could've told! I've been lying to the wrong people, Charlie. Maybe I should tell them the truth and see how they like it. Maybe they'd start telling lies themselves. It's awful to be the only one. It's lonesome."

He frowned seriously at her.

"One more drink," she said.

"No."

She picked up his glass and drank almost all the drink before he could stop her. "My God, you're a queer one," he said, laughing.

She put her head back and laughed with him. It seemed unbearably funny. "Oh!" she said, trying to catch her breath. "You called it, Charlie. You're so right. You have no idea—" and she laughed again. When she was calmer she leaned against him and turned her luscious eyes to his face and said, "Charlie, darling?"

"What?" he said, smiling at her.

"Can I excite you? Just looking at you, I mean?"

His mouth dropped a little and then his smile widened and he turned and fingered the stem of his glass. "Don't be foolish, honey."

"Charlie, look at me." He looked. "I'll bet I could."

"Not here, Beth. Not now."

"Oh, yes. Here and now."

"I think it's high time we leave," he said, making a move to get up, but she gripped his thigh and he stopped cold. "Beth, my God!" he said in a low voice. "Are you out of your head? Damn it, stop."

She didn't answer and she didn't obey. "Charlie," she said, smiling with her lips parted. "We can't go now. We can't go now, you'll make a spectacle of yourself."

"Beth—" He stared at her, astonished.

"Waiter!" she said, taking advantage of his confusion. The man saw her two raised fingers and nodded. And now when Beth started to pull her hand away, Charlie caught it and pulled it back. She felt his breath come fast and her own excitement began to mount. She leaned against him and said voluptuously, "We're going to have a nice slow drink. It'll calm your nerves."

"Beth, for God's sake," he said. "Oh, Jesus, Beth, you're crazy. You're absolutely crazy."

"I know. I'm crazy. That's my excuse. That's my excuse, Charlie. I need an excuse. I'm a girl in need of an excuse. You'd be surprised how I need—"

"I hear you," he said, smiling a little. "I need one myself right about now."

"What's it like, Charlie?"

"What's what like?" he said cautiously.

"What's it like to feel the way you do right now?"

"God, Beth," he said softly, and she felt a tremor run through him. "Stop talking, darling." He pushed her away.

The waiter brought their drinks.

"Beth, let's go," he whispered. "Let's go, honey."

"No," she said. "You haven't had your nice drink. Drink your Martini, darling, like a good boy."

"I don't want the damn drink. Damn the drinks. Let's go."

"No," she said and smiled at him. "You don't have to drink yours, but I'm going to drink mine." She drank half of it and leaned toward him. "How do you feel now, Charlie?"

"Beth, you damn little witch," he said.

"Tell me," she begged. "I want to know."

"I don't know," he said, "but I'm going to tear this God

damn table apart if we don't get out of here right now."

She patted his arm. "Drink your drink, dear. Maybe the table will go away."

"Beth," he pleaded. He trembled again and pulled her hard against him.

"Charlie, what will the neighbors think? I mean, we have to think of our reputations. I mean, my God, here we are in public, and everything." She felt giddily funny. Everything was funny. Charlie started to take her drink away from her, but she snatched it back and finished it, and some spilled on her blouse. "Charlie, darling, look what I've done. Wipe it off." She smiled at him like a malevolent siren. "Wipe it off, darling," she whispered.

He looked at the drops of liquor melting slowly into her cotton blouse and swallowed hard.

"You're sweating, Charlie," she said.

"Beth, we've got to go—"

"Oh, no!" she said. "Charlie, you can't."

"Can't, be damned. I have to."

"Your drink. You can't leave your drink."

He picked it up and drank it all down and set the glass hard against the table top. "All right, let's go." He got up holding his coat and pulled her after him. He put an arm around her to steady her, and guided her out of the bar.

They walked toward the car.

"Charlie, you're wonderful when you're drunk," she said. "You're wonderful when you're excited. I want to kiss you, darling."

He propelled her sternly toward the car and when they reached it he sighed with relief.

"Can we go back to the apartment?" she whispered when they pulled away from the curb.

"No. Mitch is there. We'll go out to the motel on Forty-five. Out near the air base."

"Anywhere," she said. She put her head down in his lap.

"Charlie, how long will it be? How far do we have to go, darling?"

"Beth, don't ask me questions. I've got all I can do to drive."

He reached down with one hand and tore her blouse open. Beth chuckled at him and heard the buttons chink on the floor. At stoplights he pulled her up and kissed her violently, nearly crushing her. The tires screamed when he rounded a corner and he drove a wild eighteen miles to the motel.

He pulled Beth out of the car and into the room so fast that he had her laughing again, dizzy and wild and hot, like carousel music. He almost tore her clothes off her. He didn't even turn the light on. She fell back on the bed laughing, teasing him, pestering him, refusing to help with her clothes.

"Oh, Beth," he said, and his voice was rough. "Beth, God, I need you. God, I wish I understood you! Oh, darling . . ." His groan thrilled her. She surrendered passionately to him and for a while she forgot her pain. For a while there wasn't any pain, there was only a heady purifying madness. She let her mind empty as her body was fulfilled.

For a long time they lay in each other's arms, half asleep, murmuring to each other, absorbed with each other.

"Feel better, darling?" he said. "Or do you want to go out and get drunk again?" He laughed against her shoulder.

"No. Don't have to . . . This'll last forever. Oh, Charlie, I don't know what I'd do without you. I just don't know."

"I thought I caused all your troubles."

"Oh, let's not talk about troubles. Please . . ."

"Can't you tell me about it, honey?"

"Not now. Later. Please, later."

He lay still for a minute and then he said, with his lips moving softly against her skin, "What am I going to do with you, Beth? You worry me, darling. I don't know how I'm going to leave you. I guess this is the first vacation I haven't looked forward to since I started college. I'm— almost afraid to leave you, Beth. I wish to hell I knew what was the matter."

"Nothing's the matter. Nothing. Not now." She cuddled against him.

He stroked her hair. "I wish I could believe that, honey."

After a while they got up. It was almost nine o'clock. They were slow and sleepy getting into their clothes and often they had to stop and hold each other. Every time they separated, Beth felt the pain a little more. It was coming back, little by ominous little.

"We'll stop on the way back and get something to eat," he said. "You must be starving."

Beth felt herself, as if that might clarify the matter, and said, "I don't know."

They stopped at a drive-in on the outskirts of town and got a couple of hamburgers and some coffee.

"Well," he said, "did you get Laura straightened out?"

"Straightened out?"

"Wasn't she giving you a hard time? Emmy said something—I don't know."

"Oh, she's just temperamental. She's just—I don't know. Let's not talk about Laura."

He was silent for a minute, eating his sandwich, and then he said, "Why didn't she want you to go out with me?"

"Oh—she had a crush on you. That's all." The bread and meat stuck suddenly as her throat went dry with alarm.

"No, she didn't."

"She did, darling. Anyway, how do you know she didn't?"

"Oh, hell, I don't know. I can tell. Can't you tell when someone has a crush on you?"

"Not always."

"Well, I can. And Laura didn't."

"Well, she did, Charlie. I talked to her. We—sort of had it all out."

"Why was this so hard to tell me?"

"It wasn't. It's not hard. I'm telling you."

"The last time I saw you you couldn't. It was so damn difficult you couldn't even think about it."

Beth forced herself to swallow; she was beginning to feel edgy with anxiety. "Oh, well—I hadn't talked to Laura, then. I didn't have a chance. I didn't want to say anything until I talked to her."

He raised an eyebrow at her. "Well? What did you say when you talked to her?"

"Oh, I told her she was behaving like a child. I was kind of nasty, I guess. I said she was acting like a spoiled brat and spoiled brats belong at home with their doting parents."

"My God, you were nasty. Jesus, honey, that was pretty low, wasn't it?"

She frowned at him. "What do you mean? It wasn't so bad. She was acting like a child. I just told her if she couldn't act grown up she'd better go back to her family where she belongs. Where somebody'll take care of her."

"She can't, Beth."

"She can't?"

"Didn't she tell you? I mean, didn't you know?"

"Know what?" Beth put her hamburger down, feeling suddenly sick. The incipient hangover, the passion, the overcooked beef, combined to aggravate her misery.

"They're divorced. Happened just before she came down to school. I guess it was pretty bad. Anyway, Laura was all upset about it." He paused. "You didn't know this?"

Beth shook her head.

"That's why I kept taking her out. She needed a shoulder to cry on. Poor kid. She really needed somebody. She was terribly alone. Still is, I guess. I felt sorry for her. My God, didn't she tell you all this?"

"She didn't tell anybody."

"You'd think she'd've told you. I mean, roommates . . . you know."

Beth held her head. "Oh, Charlie, I feel awful. Oh, I feel awful."

"Honey, are you going to be sick?"

"I guess so," she whispered.

"Yes, you are," he said with a swift critical glance. "Come on, here we go. Can you make it to the ladies' room?"

"I don't know."

He led her as fast as he could to the john. She made it just inside the door, fell to her knees and let the sickness flow out of her. Ten minutes later she came out, very pale.

"Charlie, I want to go home," she said. "I want to go home."

"I know. I'll take you home. You're going to be all right, darling, don't worry." He took her out to the car and drove her back to the house. She said nothing, leaning heavily against him and moaning a little now and then.

At the house he stopped and took her in his arms. "Poor little girl," he said. "Feel any better?"

"A little."

"Darling, that was my last exam today. How long will you be down here?"

"Day after tomorrow. Leave at noon."

"Will I see you?"

"Charlie— Oh, darling, I—"

"Okay," he said. "When will you be back?"

"February sixth."

"I'll be here the fifth. In case you come early."

"Charlie." She sat up a little and looked at him. "Darling, oh, I've been a bitch. Oh, Charlie, I'm a mess. Darling, I—"

"I love you, Beth," he said. And he kissed her.

She clung to him for a minute and then she said, "I love you, Charlie." It was plain and awesome honesty and it felt deliriously good.

He took her face in his hands. "Beth, take good care of yourself. Take good care of yourself, darling."

FIFTEEN

E MILY and Laura had a brief, bitter exchange of words. Laura precipitated it. She simply looked up from her studies and said, with no introduction, "Emmy, why did you call Charlie?" She was immediately sorry she had said it, but she was frantically worried about Beth and desperately unhappy.

Emily was startled. "Well—" she said. "She wanted to see him, Laur. It seemed as if it was the only way. I didn't mean to hurt your feelings about it."

"How did you *know* she wanted to see him?"

"I could just tell, Laur."

"Did it ever occur to you that Beth might not want to go out with him?"

"No, it never did," said Emmy. This wasn't the Laura Landon of last fall: passive, pleasant, unemotional.

"I don't understand why you don't know Beth any better than you do, Emmy. Sometimes I think you don't know her at all," Laura snapped.

"Laura, Beth wanted to go out with him. She didn't have to go, you know, even after I called him."

"Well, of course she had to go out with him, after she talked to him. What could she say?"

"I don't know, Laur. What could she say?"

Laura went suddenly cold. Her eyes dropped and she fumbled with her book. "I don't know," she said in a small voice.

"Why don't you want Beth and Charlie to go out together, Laur?" Emmy's voice was soft. If what she suspected were true, why hadn't Beth been honest with her about it? Beth had never deliberately lied to her before about anything.

"They just—aren't right for each other, that's all."

"How do you know?"

"Because I know Beth!" Laura flared.

"But you don't know Charlie very well."

Laura turned on her. "Emmy, what are you trying to say?"

136

Emmy, confronted with an angry challenge, was silent. Laura rose slowly to her feet. "I'm going to bed," she said icily and walked stiffly to the door.

Emmy sat on the couch uncomfortably. She had no desire to stay in the room, either. It had suddenly become a sinister, unfamiliar place to her. She gathered some books together, scribbled a note to Beth and ran down the hall.

At ten thirty-five, Beth found the note on her dresser: "Laur's in bed. I'm in Bobbie's room. Come get me if you want me. I'll be up late. Love, Em."

Beth crumpled the note and tossed it into the wastebasket, and undressed. She looked at her blouse with the little rips now in place of buttons, and thought of Charlie. But all the cutting words she directed at Laura that afternoon came back to torment her.

She went to the washroom to clean up, and when she got back to the room, Laura was in it. She was standing looking out the window toward the street with her back to Beth. Beth said nothing. She put her things away and stood at her dresser for a minute, silent.

"Beth," said Laura softly. "I was wrong." She had learned her lesson. The only way to bring Beth back was to be gentle and yielding with her. It worked before where even the most righteous temper failed. Beth scolded her for being a child, but Laura knew she liked her best that way. Laura was willing to play the game—any game—if it meant keeping Beth.

"If you need Charlie, I guess you should have him," Laura said. She didn't turn around; she spoke to the windowpanes.

Beth regarded her back. "Laura, I was hateful to you. I was unforgivable."

"Let's not talk about it. I don't want to talk about it. You're forgiven, Beth."

Beth put her arms around her and her head down against Laura's. "Laura," she whispered.

"I understand. At least, I'll try to understand."

"Laura . . . I need you, honey." I can't just drop you, so hard, so suddenly. And besides, you're so sweet . . . so sweet to hold. Not good like Charlie, but . . . I wonder, if I could have you both.

Laura turned around and put her arms around Beth and looked up at her. "Beth," she said humbly. "Will we be together—just once in a while?"

"Yes, honey." Beth kissed her forehead. "Yes, we will." Behind them Emmy pushed the door open. Beth had forgotten to close it all the way and it didn't make a sound. Emmy stood staring.

"Oh, I'm so glad," Laura whispered. "It's all right, then. I'll be all right, if I can have that."

"Of course you can, baby. Oh Laur, I hurt you so."

"You could never hurt me too much, Beth. You can never teach me by hurting me. I just come back for more. I guess I'll never learn. I love you too much. I love you so much."

They kissed each other's lips and Beth liked the velvety softness of Laura's mouth. She could command Laura the way Charlie commanded her. But the authority fulfilled and invigorated Charlie; it only amused Beth and left her empty.

Emmy stood watching them, transfixed and soundless, while Beth rocked Laura gently in her arms and whispered, "We'll work it out, honey. Don't worry." And then Emmy pulled the door to very quietly, and without letting it catch, and left. She walked down the hall shivering nervously, wondering what to do. She stared unseeing at the bulletin board in the hall with her head full of the strange scene she had just witnessed and the details of it so vivid that she could think of nothing else.

After a little while she heard soft voices down the hall. She turned around and saw Beth and Laura coming toward her.

"Beth?" she said, with a humane impulse to warn them of her presence.

Beth looked up. "Oh, Emmy," she said. "I thought you were in Bobbie's room."

Emmy hesitated, feeling strangely uncomfortable, and Laura started up the stairs to bed.

"What, Em?" said Beth. She glanced quickly at Laura. "Go on up, Laur," she whispered. "See you in the morning." She looked back at Emmy and Emmy found she couldn't say it; she couldn't ask.

"How's Charlie?" she said.

Beth relaxed then and gave her a radiant smile. "Wonderful," she said. "I'm in love." And she went upstairs to bed, leaving Emmy confounded. She knew she would have to talk to Beth about Laura, she couldn't keep the things she had seen and heard locked inside of her. But she would wait, she decided, until the next night. Then Beth and she would be alone for the first time in months— Laura would have left for her semester vacation. So Emmy kept her peace for almost twenty-four hours and then discovered, when the time came for her to speak, that she didn't know how to broach the subject.

She looked at Beth with a sort of new timidity and said, dismayed to find her voice raspy, "Beth?"

"Hm?"

"Beth—"

Beth looked at her. "Why, Emmy, whatever is the matter? You look as if you—" She stopped, wondering. "Emmy, what's the matter?"

"Well—well, I— Beth?" She walked over to her, as if it were too difficult to send her words across the room, and took a deep breath. "Is Laura in love with you?" she asked finally.

"Oh," said Beth, and her face went very pale. She put her head down for a moment and said, "Oh, Emmy . . ."

"I know she is. I heard her say it last night. I had to tell you."

"Oh, Em."

"Beth, I won't tell. I won't ever ever tell. I promise." Emmy held her shoulders and watched her anxiously. Beth couldn't talk. "Do you love her, too?"

Beth lifted her head. "Emmy—come sit on the couch. Listen to me."

They sat down together and Beth tried to explain what had happened to her, and she tried to be honest. Emmy listened without saying a word, watching Beth's face intently. Finally Beth looked up at her and said, "You see, Emmy? Why it's been so hard? Now I'm in love with Charlie. Really in love. But I can't hurt Laura any more. I just can't. I can only wait till it wears off. Till she grows out of it and forgets about me, without my having to hurt her."

"Wouldn't it hurt her less just to tell her you don't want to do it any more?"

Beth played nervously with a cigarette. "Yes, I guess it would. But—you see—that's not it, exactly. I'm not in love with her. That's what I ought to tell her. But—"

"You mean you—still want her?" It was as weird and wonderous to Emmy as sorcery would have been.

"Yes," said Beth. She looked at Emmy with a worried frown. "Em, you must think I'm terrible."

"Oh, Beth, I don't think you're terrible at all." She leaned toward her sympathetically. "I couldn't think you were terrible—we're friends, Beth. I just—I just don't get it, that's all. Why do you want a girl when you could have a man? I mean, why does a girl want a girl? Ever? I mean —well—" She laughed a little. "What is there to want?"

"Oh, Emmy, I don't know how to tell you. I was just— we were both lonely. We just happened to be lonely at the same time in the same place, that's all. It was too easy. It was so good to have somebody to—hold, to talk to . . . sort of play with and play at making love."

"But Laura isn't playing. She is in love. I heard her say so."

"Oh, she thinks she is. She's just so young, she doesn't know. These things never last."

"How do you know?"

"Oh, Em, when you go to a girl's boarding school, you just know. It happens all the time. You grow out of it. It doesn't last. It's just part of growing up. Didn't you ever have a crush on a girl?"

Emmy searched her memory. "No," she said doubtfully. "I don't think so. Oh, once when I was about twelve, I guess . . . No, I don't think that was really a crush . . ." She looked at Beth.

"Well, maybe not."

"Anyway, there were always so many boys around and they were so much more fun. Well, I mean—" She hunched her shoulders.

"I know, I know. It never happens to some people. And it does to others. That's all."

"Beth, how do you know it won't last with Laura? I mean, some people never grow out of childish things, if this is a childish thing. How do you know?"

"Oh, because Laur's a sensible girl. She's sentimental, but she's—well, she's just timid. She hasn't known enough men. She's afraid of them. When she gets over that she'll be all right." She had to be all right.

"Well, I guess you ought to know. But some people go through all their lives queer. Oh, I don't mean you, Beth! I guess that's not a very nice word."

"Oh, it's just a word. What's in a word?"

"Besides, you're in love with a man."

"Yes, I am. Oh, I am, Emmy, I am!"

"Well, how can you love two people at once, Beth?"

"I can't. That's the whole trouble. I'm in love only with Charlie. But don't you see, Em—Laura can't be in love with me forever. I mean, a schoolgirl crush just doesn't last that long. I know, I've had them. You get over them. She'll get used to the idea of dating—of having me date, too—and pretty soon she'll begin to forget about it. And nobody gets hurt. Do you see?"

"Yeah. If it works."

"Emmy, you mustn't worry. Now that she understands about Charlie, there won't be any more trouble. That was the whole trouble before."

"Does she understand about him?"

"Oh, yes." Beth crushed the cigarette out in a bean-bottomed ashtray.

"Does she know you love him?"

"She knows I need him, Em." Emmy frowned at her. "Oh, Em, believe me, I know what I'm doing." She spoke heartily, in order to convince herself. "There won't be any more trouble now. We all understand each other. Everything's going to be all right. Really."

"Does Charlie understand about Laura?"

"Oh, no!" said Beth, and the idea shocked her. "He'll never know."

"I hope not," Emmy said. "Well, okay, Beth, I trust you." She had never seen Beth in a situation she couldn't handle.

Beth was right, for a while. She and Charlie were happy, Laura seemed to be happy, and even Mitch seemed to have deserted his books for a gay social life. He'd called Mary Lou and they were seeing a great deal of each other. Even Bud had settled down to a steady routine. He'd given Emmy his fraternity pin, which was in the nature of a minor miracle. Bud had managed to elude every other girl he'd known and leave them unscathed, his pin still firmly attached to his old tennis sweater. But Emmy had won and she was triumphant. She was teased, however.

As Beth put it to Laura, "That's just the first plateau. She's trying for the sixty-four-thousand-dollar ring." Laura laughed and Beth went on. "She'll never make it. Not with that guy. She'd better switch categories pronto."

Mary Lou said hopefully, "Maybe she'll calm down now and stop panting over him in public."

And so the month went by, peaceful on the surface, but boiling dangerously just below the surface.

The first week in March brought sorority initiation. Laura became a full-fledged Alpha Beta with a pin like Beth's. And she and Beth shared a sentimental bond that Charlie couldn't break.

It eased Laura to think about it on dreary weekends when Beth and Emmy were out with Charlie and Bud and she sat at home alone and studied, for she wasn't going out very much any more. She wouldn't have at all, except when Beth insisted on it, and then she accepted a blind date only to keep peace.

"You've got to go out once in a while, Laur. My God, you dated every week last fall. It'd look just too damn strange if you suddenly quit for no reason."

So she sighed and did as Beth told her. The nicest part of the weekend was at closing hours when Beth came in and Emmy went to bed. Emmy usually went off discreetly and it struck Laura as simple good luck. Beth never told her that Emmy knew.

Once, Laura asked, "Emmy doesn't suspect anything, does she? I mean, I was pretty temperamental a couple of times. Do you think she suspected?"

And Beth laughed and mussed up her hair and said, "Laur, honey, you worry about all the wrong things." And Laura, as always, took her cue from Beth. Beth wasn't worried, so there was nothing to worry about. Beth didn't think they were doing anything wrong, so they weren't.

Usually when Beth came in she was in a good humor. She wanted to tease and play and cuddle Laura and she was easily roused. It seemed to Laura then that Beth would always come back to her, however far she wandered; that she alone could satisfy her, make her happy. But now and then Beth came in quiet and uncommunicative, simply too satisfied for more passion. And then Laura wondered.

Sometimes Beth was a little drunk and then Laura sulked at her. Beth would tickle her to make her giggle and then laugh at her pout.

"Beth, you've been drinking," she would say.

"Not against the law, honey. I'm of age."

"That's not the point. I think it's disgusting." And she would turn her back on Beth's amusement.

"Laura, forgive me," Beth would plead and laugh at her.

"You smell of gin."

Beth squeezed her and said, "You don't even know what gin smells like."

"I do too!"

"Okay, I smell of gin. I guess you don't want me around. I guess I'd better just go off and leave you alone."

"No, Beth!" And she turned around and caught her arm as Beth started to rise.

Beth pushed her away. "Oh, but I smell of gin, remember? Laur, I don't know how you put up with me. I swear I don't know."

And then Laura would have to beg her to stay and protest that she didn't care what her breath smelled like. But she did.

SIXTEEN

In the middle of March Bud's fraternity gave a costume dance, an annual affair for which the girls were required to make their own costumes. They were given one square yard of bright colored cotton for that purpose and the one who returned the largest piece of unused cloth won first prize. Some used the whole cloth out of necessity, some out of modesty, and some used as little as they dared.

Emmy used as little as she dared. She achieved a sort of bikini effect much admired by the men and frowned upon by the conservative element in Alpha Beta, headed by Mary Lou. Before she went out Emmy modeled her creation in the upstairs hall.

"Emmy, I think that's a little—bare," said Mary Lou.

"Oh, heck, Mary Lou, there'll be a dozen others just like it."

"Well, I know, but it's awfully revealing."

The girls laughed at her and said, "Oh, they all wear 'em now, Mary Lou."

"I think she looks great."

"Emmy, if you don't win first prize, nobody can."

"Just don't sneeze," said Beth.

The buzzer sounded and Emmy said, "Oh, there's Bud!" and scampered down the stairs.

Laura watched her go a little spitefully. The thought that Emmy had brought Charlie and Beth together again still rankled inside her. Her sense told her it would have happened anyway; her heart told her it was Emmy's fault. She said to Beth, "Emmy has a pretty figure, doesn't she?"

"Oh, Emmy has a beautiful figure."

That was enough to make Laura hate it. She was even jealous of Emmy. Emmy and Beth were such good friends, Emmy was so pretty, Laura so plain. When Beth and Emmy laughed or talked to each other she found it irritating in the extreme. And yet she knew nothing could be less likely than erotic intimacies between them, and during the span of quiet rational daytime hours she calmed herself, combed out her snarled affections and sprayed them with logic so they might last smoothly through the evening.

After Emmy went out Mary Lou came in to talk to Beth.

"Hi, Mrs. Mitchell Grogan," said Beth with a grin. "When are you going out?"

Laura looked up from the couch, and Mary Lou laughed and said, "Oh, Mitch is coming over around eight. Say, Beth—" She grew suddenly serious. "Did you talk to Emmy?"

Beth felt a guilty pang shoot through her. "Why? Is something wrong?"

"Well—no, not really. But I just don't like it when she wears such a revealing costume to a big dance. I didn't know it was going to be that bare or I would have told her myself."

"None of us saw it before tonight, Mary Lou. In fact she finished it only this afternoon."

"Well, I didn't see it till just now or I'd've stopped her. But—what can you do?" She wrinkled her brow and sighed. "Bud came, and she was all ready to go out. Everybody stands around approving and it's the night of the party. I can't order her not to wear the thing. But I wish she'd use her head. I've been worried about her for months."

It made Beth feel rather nervously defensive. "She's been behaving herself," she said. "She doesn't act up in public."

"Oh, Beth, I've seen her so full of beer at parties—"

"That's just a big act, Mary Lou. Most of it."

"Well, not all of it. I've seen her drink the beer."

"She doesn't drink too much—just likes a good time."

"I'll say she likes a good time. Remember that afternoon at Maxie's when she was kissing Bud?"

"Oh, hell. Everybody kisses everybody at Maxie's."

"Yes, but not up on the bandstand. And not like Bud was kissing Emmy."

"Oh, Mary Lou, don't worry about her. You'd be surprised how sensible she can be."

"I certainly would."

Beth laughed and said, "Oh, come on. Don't worry. I'll answer for her."

"Okay, if you'll talk to her again. If you don't, I will."

"I will, Mary Lou." Bud was a party boy, and Beth knew it. He liked to whoop it up and he expected Emmy to keep up with him. He expected, in fact, quite a lot of Emmy, and Emmy wouldn't disappoint him. But she tried to make him play the game her way; he had to stay within certain bounds, and the bounds were simply discretion, meaning privacy. Unfortunately, the bounds became hazy and Bud began to step over them now and again.

Bud and Emmy hadn't gone to the dance directly, it turned out. They went to a party where beer flowed, spirits rose, and time wandered by unmarked. At a quarter of midnight someone shouted, "My God! The dance!"

They scrambled out and into their cars and made it over to the house five minutes before the orchestra packed up to leave. They were welcomed with a cheer and the girls surrendered their left-over costume material to a committee of judges, which, after a thirty-second squabble, gallantly pronounced Emily the winner.

Amidst the uproar following, Bud picked Emmy up by the waist and lifted her over his head. Flashbulbs flowered around them. He let her down again and she was giggling helplessly, clinging to him for support.

"Hey, pick her up again!" someone shouted. "Nielsen! Hey, boy, ya hear me? Pick her up again!"

"No!" said Emily, clutching Bud.

"Hey, we want another picture. Once more. Come on, Emmy!"

"No!"

"Emmy, you're chicken!"

"Hey, come on, Em," Bud said. "It won't hurt you."

"No, I won't do it. I don't want them to take pictures."

Bud dug his fingers into her ribs and she screamed and laughed, wriggling to be free. With a wretched disregard for discretion the top of her costume suddenly split open, and the evening took an unexpected saturnalian turn. Emmy gasped and covered her dazzling front with her arms and whirled to face Bud, who was laughing as he had never laughed before. He took her in his arms and the general hilarity got them both. Everyone shouted at Emmy to turn around again and somebody finally rescued her with a leather jacket, tossed over the heads of the crowd. The others booed the rescuer.

Bud reached out and caught the sailing jacket and Emily cried, "Oh, Bud, don't let me go!" and everybody cheered. When she had the thing safely on she went to the powder room and got her coat and wrapped herself securely in thick gray wool. She was indisputably the queen of the evening, and in spite of her embarrassment she was so roundly and good-naturedly flattered that the accident didn't seem like quite such a calamity.

Several of the girls who convoyed her to and from the powder room were Alpha Betas. They were laughing because the atmosphere of laughter was irresistible, but they knew, and Emmy knew, that there would be trouble.

"Well," said Emmy, "I certainly didn't do it on purpose. Nobody could say that."

"I hate to think what Mary Lou's going to say," said one of the Alpha Betas. "We can't possibly keep it a secret. Everybody'll be talking about it."

Emmy said in alarm, "Do you think they got any pictures of it?"

"Oh, my God! I hope not!"

"I don't think so," said another girl. "You turned around so fast. I don't think anybody had time."

"Well, pictures or no, Em, you're going to have to explain it somehow."

Emmy shrugged. "My costume broke, that's all. Heavens, it was double stitched. I don't know how it could have happened."

"Maybe you were sabotaged."

"What?"

"Maybe somebody cut the threads."

Emmy laughed, but she disallowed the suggestion.

She got home at closing hours, and ran breathless up to the room. Beth was just undressing and Laura was still up. Emmy came in laughing and threw herself down on the couch. Beth shut the door hastily and ran to her.

"Emmy!" she said, and Emmy laughed even harder. Beth had to laugh with her, while Laura remained disdainfully aloof. "Emmy, what happened? Tell me."

Emmy sat up slowly and said theatrically, "Look," and unbuttoned her coat. Laura gasped, and Beth stared wide-eyed at her for a minute and then she began to laugh.

"Oh, Emmy," she exclaimed when she could catch her breath. "My God, it broke!"

Laura watched their laughter, properly disapproving. Finally Beth began to get serious.

"Emmy, what happened?" she said. "Was it bad?"

"Oh—" Emmy slowed down a little. "It was just one of those things." She giggled again. "Bud was tickling me—Oh, guess what? I won first prize!"

Beth had to chuckle at her again. She threw her hands up and slapped her knees. "Emmy, you're impossible!" she said. "Okay, now be serious. What happened?"

"Well, it just ripped, that's all."

"With how many people gaping at you?"

"I don't know. Oh, I grabbed it, of course. I turned right around and Bud held me so nobody could see."

"After everybody saw."

"Well, Beth, I couldn't help it," Emmy protested, laughing again. "Oh, I was horribly embarrassed. But it was so funny!"

The door snapped open and Mary Lou bristled in. She shut the door after her and leaned on it.

"Emmy . . ." she said and paused, her face solemn. "What happened?"

Emmy stood up, still smiling. "Oh, it wasn't so awful, Mary Lou. It was just an accident."

"Well, I want to know just exactly what happened. Everybody's talking about it, Emmy. It'll be all over the campus by tomorrow. Now tell me." Her voice trembled with indignation and she was pale and earnest. She found no humor in the situation at all. It was a social fiasco that reflected directly on the good name of Alpha Beta.

"Well, I won first prize for my costume and everybody was sort of cheering and teasing me while they took pictures, and Bud tickled me and I sort of—jerked away from him, and the bra broke. That's all. I couldn't help it, Mary Lou. I didn't do it on purpose."

"They took pictures?" Mary Lou looked stricken, and Beth watched her with a worried frown. Anybody could have pleaded Emmy's case better than Emmy pleaded it herself.

"Oh, they didn't take pictures of *that*. I mean, I'm sure they didn't. Oh, Mary Lou, don't look so grim! You frighten me." She laughed, but Mary Lou didn't even smile.

"Emmy, we're going to have a talk about this. You and me and Sarah and Bobbie." They were the ranking house officers; Bobbie was one of Emmy's good friends.

"Mary Lou, you act as if you thought I did this on purpose. I'd never do such a thing."

"The house is in for a lot of bad publicity about this, Emmy. We have to agree on something to say. The dean is going to want to see you, and so are the alumnae."

Emmy sobered up suddenly. "Oh, no," she said. "Do you really think so? But it was just an accident."

"Be in my room tomorrow morning at nine," said Mary Lou. "And don't talk to anybody about it before then."

"Okay," said Emmy, and Mary Lou went out, leaving her honestly worried.

"Gee, Beth," Emmy said, turning anxious eyes on her. "What'll they do to me?"

"I don't know, Em. Depends on how it goes over on campus, I guess. Don't worry, Emmy, it wasn't your fault." Beth felt the weight of a new blame on her shoulders. She had failed both Emmy and Mary Lou. She could have warned Emmy to slow down, if she'd only had the eyes to see how fast she was going, if she'd only re-membered Mary Lou's warning. But she had been too engrossed in her strange little triangle. Emmy was outside that triangle, so Emmy's troubles didn't count. Nobody had troubles but Beth Cullison, and now Beth was ashamed of her selfishness.

Beth wanted to go with Emmy to the meeting the next morning, but Mary Lou said no. So it was Mary Lou, Sarah, who was vice president, and Bobbie, who was secretary, who faced Emmy that morning.

Mary Lou, with her customary unbudging justice, and Sarah, who usually agreed with her, thought Emily and Bud should shake hands and call it quits. The dean had called and arranged a conference with Emily. The incident was in the town papers and the campus was having a good laugh. The faculty and the alumnae of Alpha Beta were furious. Emmy began to feel a little desperate.

"Can anyone possibly think I did it on purpose?" she said.

"Look, Emmy," said Mary Lou. "We know you didn't do it on purpose. That isn't the point. The point is that it happened and it happened to you. And you were very drunk and very bare and in mixed company at the time. Nobody's saying you deliberately undressed in public, but if you'd been willing to wear a little more costume in the first place this wouldn't have happened at all. And this came on top of four months of a pretty hot romance that everybody's been talking about. You just haven't been too careful, Emily. You just haven't cared very much about anything but yourself and Bud."

"But I have, Mary Lou."

"You've completely ignored your obligations to the university and the sorority. You've disgraced us all and it could have been prevented."

"I don't see—" Emmy was near tears.

"It could have, Emmy, if you hadn't insisted on being the barest girl at the party. If you hadn't gone out and gotten drunk."

"I wasn't the only one—"

"If you hadn't led Bud to expect that he could treat you—" she cast about for a word— "promiscuously in public and get away with it."

"It wasn't promiscuous. He was just tickling me. I mean —heavens, it was just—" She stopped, sensing that her own words did her a disservice.

"Well, just what kind of behavior do you think that is, Emmy—proper? What do you think a man thinks of when he sees a girl squirming and wriggling in practically no clothes at all?"

"I didn't ask him to tickle me, Mary Lou."

"Yes you did, Emmy. Don't you see? For the past four months you've been letting him tickle you; you just never told him not to. You let him do it and you let him know you like it. What more do you have to do for a man? Spell it for him?"

Emmy hung her head.

"Emily," said Mary Lou and her voice grew kind again. "I'm not trying to hurt you. Believe me, I'm not. I'm trying to do what I can for the sorority. And it, as a whole, is more important right now than the individual, because it's within the power of an individual to do the whole group a harm, to punish everybody for her one mistake. Well, we have to correct that mistake. We can't let everyone point at Alpha Beta and laugh because one Alpha Bete did something wrong. That one Alpha Bete has to correct the error. It's simple logic, and it's only fair."

Emmy rubbed her head. Simple logic was the hardest kind for her. It always struck her as being inarguable and senseless at the same time. She was awed by it.

Mary Lou sighed and ditched her cigarette. "Emmy, it's up to you," she said. "I don't want to impose any silly useless detention on you. I don't even want to campus you. You'll see the dean; you'll talk it over. I know you'll be sensible about it."

"What can I do?" said Emmy.

"Well . . ." Mary Lou looked around at the others and then sighed and looked back at Emily. "Em, I know you're terribly fond of Bud. I guess that's been the cause of the difficulty, really."

Emmy nodded. It seemed as if Mary Lou was beginning to understand her now and wanted to help her; it gave her a false sense of security.

"And I know too, how much affection you have for the sorority, for the university . . ."

Emmy nodded fervently again.

"Well, somehow the two just don't seem compatible. I know it's hard, Emmy . . ."

Emmy didn't get it at all for a minute.

"But—I think we have to take a positive step right now. Undo the wrong, sort of . . ."

"Oh, yes, I do too," said Emily, walking innocently, willingly, into the trap.

"And I think you just have to make a choice."

"A choice?"

"Yes. Because if you keep on like this, Em, the university and the sorority are going to suffer. That's all there is to it."

"Oh, but Mary Lou, I won't keep on. I mean, the party's over." She couldn't believe they would be so harsh. She laughed a little apprehensively as the light began to dawn. "Is it, Emmy?" Mary Lou's bright, steady eyes hurt her.

"Well, of course."

"Emmy, I think it might be a good idea—for all of us, and especially for you—if you didn't see Bud for a while."

Emmy stared at her, speechless and appalled. "But I love him," she whispered finally.

"I think that's exactly the trouble, Emmy. I think you either ought to leave school and marry the guy, or not see him for a while. I think the temptation is just too great." She said it very kindly.

"But my parents would never let me leave school. My father has his heart set on my getting my degree." *And Bud might not marry me.* Brought face to face with the problem she admitted it to herself for the first time.

"Then I think you ought not to see Bud for a while."

Emmy was thunderstruck, trapped. "For a while?" she murmured in a hardly audible voice.

Bobbie put an arm around her and said, "Don't cry."

"For a while," Mary Lou repeated. "It's the only way, Emmy. I think you're headed straight for real trouble, otherwise. And you're pulling all of us after you. Don't you see, Emmy? It's for everybody's good, really. It won't be forever."

Emmy saw; she saw very clearly now. She tried to steady her breath. "What if I do see him?" She couldn't help asking; it was a last feeble gesture of independence. "What if I keep on seeing him?"

"It's your duty *not* to, Em."

"But what would happen if I did?" It had the fascination of calamity for her.

"Well—" Mary Lou looked down at her lap and found it hard to talk, hard to do what she cherished as her duty, to hit just the right tone—firm but compassionate. "Then I think—I think you would be happier outside the sorority."

It took Emmy's breath away from her for a minute. "You mean you'd jerk my pin?" It was preposterous. "You'd *blackball* me?"

"Oh, Emmy," said Mary Lou, and she patted her arm sympathetically. It was hard to do the right thing, but this was indubitably the right thing. "Emmy, don't say it that way. We wouldn't blackball you. I think we should just have a sort of agreement. If everything works out, you'll see Bud again. It just means time to think it over, time to get to know yourself."

"But you don't know Bud." Emmy put her head down in her hands. It might be love, all right, but with Bud she had to keep feeding the flame. She had to be with him every day, reminding him how pretty, how bright and sweet she was, or he would find someone else. It was that simple. *That* was logic.

She looked up. The three girls were watching her, a jury of friendly executioners, waiting for her answer. She knew they were all of the same mind—Mary Lou's mind. Even Bobbie, who gave her a squeeze and said, "Emmy, I think it might be a good idea."

Emily leaned against her and wept for a few minutes. The sorority had her in a corner; there was no help for her. At last she whispered, "All right," and got up and hurried from the room.

SEVENTEEN

Beth was warmly sympathetic in spite of her misgivings about Bud; she was needled by a sense of guilt and the thought of her own adventures with Charlie. She said over and over, "Emmy, I should have warned you, I should have seen it coming. It's my fault, Em."

But Emmy wouldn't have it that way.

"They're such damn hypocrites," Beth fumed. "They know you aren't the only one who's made a few concessions. My God, they do it themselves, a lot of them. It's just that the one who gets caught gets punished. You were just too much in love to be very cautious, I guess. I guess you really are in love, Emmy, aren't you?"

Emmy's tears answered her.

"Damn," Beth muttered. "They really cash in on that prestige of theirs, don't they? They know there's no disgrace quite so humiliating as getting blackballed out of the sorority. The whole campus talks about you for months. Suddenly you haven't any friends. Why? Because you left them all back in the sorority. And you've left the sorority for good. And then what happens? You can't stand it after a while. You're an outcast, a failure. You're nowhere socially. You're ashamed and lonesome. And pretty soon you call it quits and leave school. Maybe you go somewhere else, maybe you don't. But all over the country, on any campus, that sorority blackball will haunt you every time you try to join a club. They'll find out about it, and there you'll be, right back where you started. God, it makes me sick."

Bud exploded when he found out what had happened. He was furious, frustrated, bitter against the powers that be in universities and sororities. He cut his classes for a week and spent all his time, filled to his ears with beer, in Maxie's basement. He played till his lip gave out and he complained to anyone who would listen to him. It was his way of handling a problem. Bud could make sweet music and sweet girls; he could be supremely pleasant with any-body, anywhere; but he couldn't make or follow a plan, and order and progress were hostile to his happiness.

He was artist enough to admire ideals, but he never pursued them. However, they took Emily away from him at just the time when he had decided that she was one of his ideals, and the sudden loss made her more desirable—not less, as Emily had feared.

"I love that girl," he muttered moodily. "The only girl I ever loved. And what do they do? They take her away from me."

Charlie swatted him on the back. "Cheer up, boy," he said. "This won't last forever. You'll be seeing her. Beth says they'll parole her for good behavior." Charlie had heard the story a dozen times.

"Yeah, sure. When? What the hell am I supposed to do in the meantime? I tell ya, Ayers, I'm going nuts. I can't stand it. Who the hell do they think they are? Who the hell—"

"Okay, boy, take it easy."

"Yeah, take it easy. You gotta help me out. What am I gonna do? Help me out, boy."

Charlie gave him a lot of free advice. . . .

Beth complained to Charlie, too. "It's a damn dirty trick," she said. "God, it makes me mad! There's only one aspect of the whole thing that might do any good, and that's that Bud was never meant for Emmy—or any girl, for that matter. He couldn't support a wife or kids. My God, can you imagine Bud Nielsen with *kids* on his hands? He'd give 'em all slide whistles before they could walk and send 'em out to make their own living."

Charlie laughed at her.

"No one's fonder of Emmy than I am," she added, "but she'll do anything for a man she thinks she's in love with. She hasn't the sense she was born with. She'd never get caught if she'd use her head, but she wants to please Bud. Will she say no to Bud? No, she will not. And do they catch her in bed with him? No, they do not. That's too easy. Her damn silly costume breaks and all of a sudden she's a scarlet woman. An accident. God, it's ironic, isn't it?"

Charlie nodded.

"Well, maybe she'll cool off, now. See Bud for what he is."

"What is he, honey? You're pretty damn hard on him."

"Oh, Bud Nielsen is a bum. A born bum. Let's face it."

"A bum? I don't know, Beth. He's a nice guy."

"Sure, he's a nice guy. He's a great guy. Everybody likes him. And he'll never amount to a row of beans."

"Well, I don't know." Bud was a good friend of Charlie's.

"Oh, Charlie, he's been an undergraduate for six years. The guy hasn't even enough ambition to leave school, for God's sake. Emmy's as much in love with that trombone as she is with Bud. He's a big wheel on campus—talented, everybody knows him. I'd never tell her, but I'm kind of glad they'll be separated for a while. I think they'll both come to their senses. I hope they will."

Charlie disagreed. "Hell, if they took you away from me for a while would you come to your senses? Would I?"

"No, but—we're in love."

"Well, so are they."

"They just think they are."

"You just can't resist analyzing everybody you know, can you? No matter how little you really know about them. You figure them all out and slap a label on them and that's the end of them as far as you're concerned. You never consider that you might be wrong, or they might be different. Try analyzing yourself some time. It's no cinch."

Beth was temporarily confused. "Well—I know Emmy pretty well," she said.

"Yeah. And I know Bud. He may be a worthless character, but tearing him away from Emmy isn't going to cool either of them off. That's the best way I can think of to get them both hot. Right now Bud's in love with Emmy and he's damned unhappy. I feel sorry for the guy."

"Oh, so do I. It's not that I don't, it's just that all men are such—most men are such—oh, never mind."

He grinned at her. "What are most women?"

"You'd never understand."

"What's Beth Cullison?" His eyes were curiously bright and narrow and Beth felt suddenly uncomfortable.

"You tell me," she challenged him.

"I can't," he said. "I don't know. I thought you did."

She couldn't look at his eyes and she despised her sudden shyness.

"Maybe we'll find out together," he said with a light smile. . . .

And so the days went slowly by, with everybody bringing news to Emmy about Bud, with everybody discussing the situation over and over again.

Emily chafed and wept and wondered and beseeched her friends for more news. Bud griped and argued with anyone who would listen, and consoled himself with beer and music.

It got pretty bad. He liked to talk to Charlie because Charlie was a fraternity brother and Charlie saw Beth, Emmy's roommate. Charlie was a friend; he listened.

"I tell ya, dad, it's intolerable," Bud protested. "If I could just see her. Just once. The thing is, nobody'd have to know. If I could just talk to her, work it out somehow."

"They won't let you talk to her."

"If I could meet her someplace . . ."

"Hang on, boy. That's not going to kill you. They'll relent one of these days."

"Yeah, sure, I can hang on. But what I mean is, why hang on if you don't have to? Hell, this is a big campus. Nineteen thousand students. Who's going to check on each one? If I saw her some afternoon where nobody'd suspect anything . . ."

"Yeah, but you have to worry about where. Why don't you just forget it and let the thing ride for a few weeks? They'll give in. Emmy's acting like a damn puritan. They'll have to let her out."

Bud was quiet for a minute, and then he looked at Charlie with an intently confidential frown. "Charlie," he said, "listen. Is there any time during the day when your apartment is empty?"

"No," said Charlie firmly.

"Listen, boy—"

"No! It's never empty. We have a resident truant officer."

"Charlie, listen, it'd be so easy. Nobody'd ever know, believe me."

"No."

"Now listen to me, will ya, God damn it? Now listen. Look, Emmy has a two o'clock Tuesdays and Thursdays. She's out at three, walks south on Wright Street—"

"Listen, Bud—"

"Charlie, you've even got a car. My God, this is perfect. You could pick her up, tell her about it in the car on the way over."

"Way over where?"

"To the apartment, boy." Bud flung his hands out earnestly. "Use your head. Jesus. Now listen, when's your roommate in class? What's-his-name?"

"Mitch."

"Mitch. He there on Thursday afternoon?"

"Look Bud, that's beside the—"

"That's great. That makes it just about perfect. He wouldn't have to know a thing. Nobody'd know but you and me and Emmy. The fewer the better. Charlie my boy, listen to me—we'd be there only a couple of hours." He watched Charlie's face anxiously. "All right, an hour." Charlie was silent, sympathetic but dubious. "Charlie, you hear me?"

"Yeah . . . I don't know, Bud."

"Man, what's the matter with you? You so pure you never had a girl in your apartment?"

"No, but I was never under orders *not* to have her, boy. I was never shadowed by the university. If you get caught, we all get canned. The university doesn't sponsor extracurricular love-making, in case you didn't know."

"Look, Charlie, if we get caught, which we won't, nobody gets canned but us. Emmy and me."

"Are you ready to do that to Emmy?"

"It won't happen. Believe me. Besides, if it did we'd go on pro, we wouldn't be expelled."

"Who wants to be on probation?"

"Charlie, we're just wasting time talking about it. It won't happen, man."

"It's my apartment, my car—my *bed*, for God's sake."

"Okay. And I'm your friend. A brother. I could've asked to use the apartment without telling you why. You can make like you're shocked as all hell if we get caught. Oh, hell, this is a lot of crap—we're not going to get caught. Who's gonna catch us? When does Mitch get in?"

"Oh—about five-thirty."

"Any sooner? Ever get in sooner?"

"No." Charlie shook his head.

"Okay, we're out at five. Emmy walks one block to the bus, I go the other way, toward campus."

Charlie shook his head doubtfully. "Bud, I hate to risk it, boy. Not because I'm afraid for my own sake, but—God, it would be the end for Emmy if she got caught."

"Charlie," said Bud, as if he were talking to an unco-operative first-grader, "we won't get caught. Who the hell's gonna catch us? As long as I don't have to call her, as long as you pick her up and everything, what's to go wrong? Oh, Charlie, be a friend. I need help, believe me. How would you like it if they cut you off for months? And don't tell me there's other girls. I know that, I know. I want Emmy. Like you want Beth, I want Emmy . . . Charlie, I'd do it for you. I swear I would, boy."

Charlie drained his beer and stabbed his cigarette into an ashtray. "You really want to see her that bad?" he said.

Bud looked up at the ceiling as if searching it for his self-control. "Yeah. I want to," he said. "That bad."

"Okay. I'll pick her up. Thursday at three."

"Charlie—" Bud grinned at him and gripped his hand.

"Be at the apartment. And by God, be out at five."

"I will. Jesus, Charlie, I can't tell you—"

"Never mind, boy. Save it. Just keep it quiet."

"My God, you're telling me!"

At three o'clock on Thursday afternoon Emily stood on the steps of Bevier Hall on Wright Street, chattering with some classmates. Charlie didn't see her until she came down the walk with a friend, and then he pulled the car toward her and called to her.

"Emmy!" he said. "Hey, Em! How about a ride?"

She looked up, surprised, and broke into a sudden smile.

"Thanks!" she exclaimed, running over. "Can you take Jane too?"

Charlie was alarmed. "Where's she going?"

"Gamma Delt house." The girl thrust a pleasant young face over Emmy's shoulder.

"Okay, hop in," said Charlie.

"It's right on the way. I hope you don't mind," Emmy said, sensing his reserve.

"Not at all." He had little to say until Jane was de-livered and they were a mile off course from the apartment. He turned the car around while Emily watched him with big questioning eyes.

"Where're we going?" she asked.

"We're going to my apartment, Emily," he said.

"Your apartment?"

"Yeah." He looked at her and said with a smile, "Bud's there."

Emily gasped. And then she cried.

"Emily!" he said. "My God, don't tell me you don't want to go!"

"Yes, I do," she said. "I do. You scared me, Charlie. Oh, is he really there?" She put a hand on his arm.

"Yeah, he's there all right."

"Charlie—it's safe, isn't it? I mean, we won't get caught?"

"No, Em, don't worry. Mitch is out for the afternoon. I won't be there. You'll have till five o'clock."

"Ohhh," said Emily with an uncertain smile. "Charlie, thanks."

"Don't thank me, honey. I wasn't very nice about it. I don't want you to get into trouble. But I guess there's not much chance of that. But Emmy—"

"Yes?" Her heart gave a thump.

"Don't tell anyone about it. Not anyone. Not even Beth. Understand?"

"Yes. Not even Beth?"

"Not even Beth. Promise?"

"Yes," she whispered.

Charlie dropped her off. She walked up to the door with her knees shaking a little, opened it, and went in. For a moment her sun-dazzled eyes saw nothing and then she heard Bud jump to his feet. "Emmy!" he said. He pushed the door shut behind her, and held her against it, leaning on her and kissing her almost savagely.

He pulled her against him and said, "Oh, Emmy. Oh, God, God, God, Emmy! Darling . . ." He could not have said more or said it better. He looked at her as if she were all miraculously new to him. He pulled her down and took her like a man who had never had a woman before and thought never to have another. He took her over and over and over and yet again in a fight with time that raised his passion to a frenetic pitch and made a wild, tireless thing of Emily. And then they lay beside each other, whispered to each other of love and loneliness and relentless longing. Bud wrapped her in his arms, still lightheaded with emotion, and said, "Emmy, darling, I love you."

"Oh, Bud," she half sobbed. "They'll never do this to us again."

"Never," he echoed. "Oh, Em—I'd do anything for you. I love you, chicken."

She clung to him hopefully. "Anything, Bud?"

"Anything," he murmured, kissing her. "They'll never take you away from me again."

"Bud—" Her voice was light and supplicating. "Marry me?"

"What?" He stopped kissing her just long enough to raise himself on one elbow and gaze at her. "Marry you?"

She held her breath, not daring to answer nor yet to keep still, and her perishable perfection ensnared him, enflamed him, wrenched his heart like a lovely tune.

"Yes, Em. I guess I would. I never thought of it, but I guess I would. I will if you want it, Emmy. I'd be one hell of a lousy husband, but I love you. Maybe that'll make up for it."

"Oh, Bud," she cried softly. They leaned toward each other until their lips were together again, and far away, as in the gentlest of reveries, the latch clicked and the door opened. They lay, quiet and complete, whole and serene in each other's need, fulfilled and reassured, lovely and beautifully human.

"Emily!" A poison-tipped voice split them asunder; a girl's voice, high and hard with indignation.

"Oh, my God!" cried a boy at almost the same time. "Oh, my God!" he said again, helplessly.

Bud and Emmy sat up suddenly in a fit of alarm, gazing at the silhouettes, straining against the head-on sun streaming at them from the window to see their faces.

"I'm terribly sorry," said the boy. "I didn't know. I mean—God. We'd better go, Mary Lou."

"We'd better go, Emily," said Mary Lou. "You and I."

Bud looked at his watch. "But it's only four-thirty," he said.

Beth found Emmy just before dinner, face down on the couch and sobbing. The shades were all pulled down and the room was dark and sad and overheated. Laura followed Beth into the room and stood soundless and motionless while Beth dropped her books and shut the door.

"Emmy!" Beth said. "What's the matter?" She threw her coat off and sank to the floor on her knees by Emily's head. Emily turned away. "Emmy, honey," she said, and stroked her hair. Laura watched her without expression. "Tell me what's the matter."

Emily tried to repress her tears. She turned to Beth and whispered sporadically, "They found us. Mary Lou and Mitch. We couldn't stand it any longer. We had to see each other. They found us."

Beth was astounded. "You saw Bud?" she said, squinting incredulously.

"Yes," said Emmy in a tiny voice.

"Emmy! Where? How?" Beth felt the impending catastrophe.

"The apartment. I didn't know. Charlie picked me up. I never thought we'd get caught."

"Charlie? Charlie's apartment?"

"Yes. He told Bud he could use it. Nobody was going to be there. It was just a mistake—"

"You met Bud in Charlie's apartment?"

"Yes." Her voice tricked and trapped and deserted her; her breath came hard and then not at all.

"Oh, Em . . ." Beth put her arms around her and comforted her. Laura watched them, cold and remote as a winter sky, silent as the snow. "Tell me about it."

Emmy pulled herself up and sat gazing at the dead face of the window shade behind the desk. "Mitch wasn't supposed to get in till five-thirty. He cut class. He had coffee with Mary Lou. They came back to the apartment to get some books. We would have left in another fifteen minutes. But they caught us. I'll be blackballed, Beth." She looked desperately at her.

The dinner chime sounded and Beth remembered Laura. "Run along and eat, honey," she said.

Laura stood stolidly in place. There were times when she actively resented the childish role Beth forced on her.

"Go on," Beth said. "I'll be along in a minute."

Laura stayed where she was and Beth turned to Emily again. "Can I bring you a tray, Em?"

Emmy shook her head. "I can't eat," she said, leaning limply on Beth's shoulder. "They're going to kick me out, Beth."

"How bad—I mean—what were you doing when they came in?"

"We were in bed. We were in Charlie's bed."

Laura shuddered with a sharp involuntary disgust.

"We were making love. Oh, Beth!" Emmy wept. "I love him so much. Is it such a terrible crime to love somebody?"

"No," said Beth with a sting in her voice, "but it's a terrible thing to get caught. It's good to love, Emmy, but it's hell to get caught. I'd just love to know," she went on, with her voice getting surer and harder, "just what the hell Mary Lou and Mitch were doing going to the apartment this afternoon? Going to do a little intimate homework, maybe? A little research . . . anatomical variety? We'll never know." She rocked Emily in her arms and Laura, seeing their bodies move together, could feel nothing but spite for Emily. . . .

Laura held her tongue until late that night, after Emmy had gone to bed. "What will they do to her?" she asked.

"Kick her out. Jerk her pin. Disgrace her." She spat the words out.

"Well . . ." Laura studied her nails. "I guess she disgraced them."

Beth looked at her narrowly. "She fell in love, Laura. Is that so disgraceful to you?"

"I didn't mean it that way, Beth," Laura said softly. "I only meant she didn't have to be so obvious about it. Everybody knew—"

"Yeah, everybody knew she loved him. That's good enough reason to expel her, isn't it?"

Laura sighed ill-naturedly. "She got what she deserved," she said. "She broke every rule. She defied authority."

"Laura," said Beth with pointed irritation, "what do you think would happen to you if everybody knew you were in love with me? You'd get the same treatment, honey, and don't forget it. You'd get worse."

Laura stared at her, startled and scared.

"What's so wonderful about rules?" Beth snapped. "Is it obeying the rules for two girls to make love to each other? Don't you think we're defying authority ourselves?"

"I—never thought of it that way," Laura faltered.

"No, of course not. Maybe you never thought of it at all."

"Beth, for heaven's sake! Emily was caught in bed with a man with no clothes on when she wasn't supposed to see him at all. She was—she was—making love to him—"

Beth came over to the couch and sat down beside

Laura, leaning forward with her elbows on her knees, a cigarette in one hand. She pulled on her cigarette and brought two jets of smoke through her nose. "We've made love, Laura."

"But that's different, Beth. That's clean. It's beautiful." She grasped Beth's arm and leaned anxiously toward her. Beth studied the tip of her cigarette.

"A man and a woman are beautfiul, too. And we've been caught making love, Laura . . . you and I. Just like Bud and Emmy."

Laura snatched her hand away as if from a flame and sat for a wounded moment, terrified. "Beth, what do you mean?" she said in a strained whisper.

Beth flicked her ashes thoughtlessly toward a tray. "Just that. We aren't any cleaner or any more beautiful than Emily and Bud, just because we're both women. And we were caught, too."

"Beth!" Laura stared at her with horrified eyes. "We were never caught."

"Yes we were, Laur. We were seen in here one night—right here in this room—kissing each other and talking about it."

"Why didn't you tell me? Why didn't they ever say anything?"

" 'They' don't know. We had the good luck to get caught by Emmy."

"Emmy!"

"Yes. Emmy. Emmy found us in here one night. Just before semester vacation. She heard enough to guess the story. She never told a soul except me. She never will." Beth's quiet, angry voice contrasted vividly with Laura's high anxiety.

To Laura, her love had seemed as secret as it was sacred. That someone else should know; that someone else had known for months; that the someone else was Emily, and Emily would never tell, would spare them what had been inflicted on her—all these thoughts struck Laura at once and she felt a sudden twist of guilt in her heart.

"Oh, Beth . . . if I'd only known," she said, and her voice broke.

"Oh, it would only have worried you, Laur. I hoped you could see some good in Emmy. I hoped you'd learn to like her." She looked up at Laura's face. "I guess you were jealous of her."

"Beth . . ." Laura rested her forehead against Beth's shoulder. "Beth, I'm so sorry. I thought she was—oh, I don't know why she didn't just tell them about me. I was so nasty to her. I couldn't have blamed her if she did."

"She's not that way, Laur. Besides, if she told them about you she'd've had to tell them about me." She fingered her cigarette, musing. "But she wouldn't have said anything anyway. She likes you, Laur . . . or at least, she wants to. I don't know why."

"Oh, Beth, I'm so sorry—"

"Don't tell me, Laur, tell Emmy." Beth wasn't cross with her any more. She was too worried about Emily to think about other feelings.

"Don't cry, Laur." She turned and held her then and chided her gently. "I've had all I can stand of crying today."

Laura stopped slowly, in jerks. "Will they really blackball her, Beth?" she whispered.

"They have to. You can break the rules, but you can't get caught."

"Isn't there anything we can do?"

"All we can do is remind them of what they're going to do to Emmy: her family, her education, her friends . . . all the heartbreak, and things never patch up to be quite the same as they were before."

"Never?"

"Oh, those things get all over your home town. There's always somebody around to let them out. And once it's out they never let you forget it."

"Will they kick her out of school, too?"

"They'll probably just put her on social probation. But she won't want to stay in school. My God, when the whole damn campus knows what happened?"

Beth knew what she was talking about. In no time at all there was the secret chapter meeting of the sorority, with one of the national officers in attendance. Representatives of the alumnae were there, too.

Mary Lou was pale and distressed and she let the alumnae carry the burden of the meeting. They were impressive women, businesslike and efficient, real club women. They enjoyed tackling problems; Emmy's was one of the juiciest in years. They spent a good bit of time congratulating the girls present on their presumed virginity and their unblemished reputations; and a good bit demolishing what was left of Emmy's. They did it with masterful tact.

"Emmy is a good girl at heart, but . . ."

"Of course, you all feel terrible about this. I know she had many friends in the house . . ."

But an hour and a half later, Emily was an ex-Alpha Beta. Her career at the university was ruined.

Emmy was spared the meeting. She sat alone in her room while it was going on with a number of open suitcases around her and tried to find the courage to start packing.

Beth had stood up at the meeting and made an eloquent plea for her. And when that failed she got sharp and sarcastic, and still it didn't change the vote. The sisters were sympathetic but restrained from mercy by the stifling good sense of their elders.

Laura sat in wretched silence, helpless. She couldn't speak as well as Beth, she hadn't nearly the influence, and yet she wanted to stand up and say something, but after Beth sat down there was nothing more to be said.

Beth and Laura went up to the room together. Emmy had one bag packed when they came in. She sat on the floor staring listlessly at her belongings, and she looked up at them when they came in. Their faces were painful to see.

"I know," she said. "I've called home. Dad's going to pick me up tomorrow."

Beth went to her and said, "We did everything we could, Em."

"I know. I knew it would happen. It had to happen, that's all. It couldn't be any other way. I was a fool."

"Did you talk to Bud? They said you could call him."

Emmy gave a bitter little smile. "Now that the damage is done, I can call him. If they'd let me talk to him before, maybe it wouldn't have happened."

"Did you talk to him?"

"Yes. I called while you were all downstairs."

"What'd he say?"

"Oh, you know Bud. He feels terrible. He was furious. But he doesn't know what to do; he never could handle a problem." Her smile became reluctantly tender. "He just rants and raves and says he'll quit school too, as if that would do any good, and they can't do this to me, and . . . Oh, I don't know." She looked at Beth sadly.

"Come on, Emmy," Beth said gently. "I'll help you get your things together. You don't have to go right away. You can take a few days to pack and—" She stopped.

"I want to get out of here as fast as I can," Emmy said harshly. "Oh, Beth, he—he cried!" she said with a sudden hard sob. "My dad cried!" And the stress of that sorrow nearly tore her apart.

Beth got Emily packed by three in the morning. Laura had tried to help but soon realized that she was neither needed nor wanted and left for the dormitory. Emily was afraid to face anybody and Beth sat up with her all night and helped her get ready to meet Bud for breakfast so they could say good-by. He promised to go to see her every weekend, he swore he loved her, he denounced the university, the sorority, the world for his mistake.

He said, "Emmy, darling, I did this to you and I'll make it up to you somehow, by God, I will. I don't know how, but—there must be a way. Oh, honey, I hate to see you so unhappy. And I did it, I did it." He was so miserable that Emily had to comfort him, and it seemed to give her strength. She listened to him, knowing that he sincerely meant what he said when he said it, wondering how long it would affect him so.

"Emmy," he said, "I love you. If only there were something I could do."

"There is," she said, nervously determined. "Don't you remember?"

He looked at her in puzzlement.

"Marry me, Bud," she said.

He dropped his glance and stared at the table for a minute and then he took her hands and nearly crushed them in his. "I will, Em," he said. "If that's what you want, I will." He looked up at her.

"Oh, Bud," she said, and began to smile a real smile for the first time since their disaster. "If I could know that —if I could look forward to that—"

He kissed her hands.

"When?" she urged him.

He shook his head. "I don't know." And seeing her face cloud over again he added, "June, maybe. Or Easter. I don't know."

"Oh, Bud, darling," she whispered, and the world steadied a little.

EIGHTEEN

B ETH brooded for days. She didn't want to see Charlie, she didn't want to go out, she didn't want to do anything. Her every bitter thought had a wicked stinger in it: she and Charlie had done the same as Emily and Bud, and got away with it.

Beth felt a wave of irresistible disgust with herself, her little duplicities, her evasions. In a restless temper she got up and paced the room fretfully. Laura watched her anxiously, wanting to talk to her, to help, but afraid to. Beth pulled the window open and stood in the wash of early April air, chill and dark and soft, and thought of the sorrows that a man can heap on a woman. She thought of Charlie's complicity, she thought of Bud's worthless charm and useless contrition, and she hated them briefly, with violent energy.

The phone on the desk rang. Laura picked it up, watching Beth all the while.

"Hello?" she said, and she frowned. Beth shook her head without a word, and then shut her eyes tight as if that might eliminate the sound of Laura's voice.

"No, Charlie, she's not here. I'm sorry—please, Charlie —I don't know, but—" And she listened a moment longer and hung up. She looked at Beth apologetically. "I hung up on him," she said. "I didn't know what else to do. He sounded sort of—frantic. I didn't know what else to do." She watched Beth hopefully, tenderly, afraid to go near her. Beth leaned against her dresser and stared out the window again, silent.

"Beth?" Laura said softly. Beth turned toward her suddenly and pulled her hard and close against her and put her head down against Laura's. Her hot hands probed and pushed back and forth across Laura's shoulders, the small of her back, her hips, catching in her clothes, rumpling them, and finally her arms tightened around the younger girl and she whispered, "Laura. Look at me."

Laura looked up and Beth kissed her full on the lips, a yearning kiss, warm and deep and slow. She didn't stop

167

for a long while, not until Laura was shivering wildly in her embrace, answering Beth's passion with her own.

"Oh, Laur," Beth said into Laura's ear, "what a fool I am. What a simpleton."

"Beth, I love you," said Laura, clinging to her and letting the delicious tremors shake her body, wondering where this revival of desire came from, but not caring. It had happened; Beth wanted her again the way she had in the beginning.

"Laura," Beth said. "Oh, I hate them! God damn them all, I hate them!" Laura didn't have to be told that "they" were men; she knew it and her heart expanded joyously and floated in her chest.

"You can't trust them," Beth muttered. "You can't trust them. God, I don't know why I ever bothered with them. All they know how to do is hurt. They all want the same damn thing." She hugged Laura tighter and Laura's hope bloomed again like a forced flower. "I'm sick and tired of it," Beth went on. "I'm sick and tired of the whole thing. If you get caught they treat you like a slut, they kick you out. If you don't get caught your conscience gives you hell. I've had enough, Laura. It makes me sick the whole damn business—authority—stupid, stuffy, blind authority—men, deans, school, everything. I want to get out of here." They whipped Emmy in public, she thought; I'll whip myself in private. Exile myself. It was the only way to square with her conscience.

"What about Charlie?" Laura's voice was faint and frightened.

"Charlie can go to hell. Charlie's as guilty as Bud. You don't know how guilty Charlie is. You don't know." She put her head down again.

"Beth, would you really leave school?"

"Yes. Yes, I would, damn it. I would!"

"Will you let me come with you?"

Beth pulled away from her a little and started to shake her head.

"Beth!" Laura cried, "I want to go wherever you go. You said we weren't any better than Bud and Emily; you said we were doing the same thing. Well, we haven't any more right to stay here than she does, then."

"Your family?" Beth said.

"Oh, my family . . ." Laura said, making the word curdle with her contempt. "My family doesn't care what happens to me, just so they have something to tell their friends."

"They won't like it, Laur."

"I won't ask them to like it. There's nothing they can do about it, Beth. I'm of age, in this state anyway. Oh, Beth, you can't ask me to stay here without you—you can't!" She clung tightly to her. Laura was aware that Beth couldn't resist her at that moment, and she made the most of it.

Furious with men and intensely sympathetic for a girl, angry with herself, yet in need of reassurance, Beth turned to Laura again with all the unreasoning joy of their early romance. She said weakly, "I don't know . . ."

Laura said quickly, "Beth, darling, I wouldn't be afraid of anything as long as you were with me."

Beth laughed gently at her, flattered, seeing the exaggeration and yet enjoying it too much to deny it. "I can't do everything," she whispered.

"Yes you can," said Laura positively.

Beth looked down at her with a spellbound smile. "Laura," she said, with her lips against Laura's cheek, drifting over her face toward her lips. "I love you." Laura's arms tightened about her and brought her desire hot to the surface. Beth pulled her over to the couch and down beside her.

Suddenly, unexpectedly, completely, Laura had Beth again. Whatever the sorcery that won her, it was potent, and it lasted. A week passed and they made plans in secret to leave the house. Every night, in defiance of chance, they slept together in the room, and strangely enough, nobody noticed. Nobody barged in on them. Nobody suspected anything.

Beth laughed at their luck. "Wouldn't you know," she said. "We might as well be kicked out as leave by ourselves. Might even be more honorable. But as long as we don't give a damn we're perfectly safe. They'd never dream of anything amiss in *this* room. Lightning never strikes twice in the same place."

Laura laughed with her.

Charlie was getting desperate. He called, and almost never spoke to Beth. When he did, she was brusque with him. He saw her at the Union, where she couldn't escape him, and she gave him only a few cursory minutes in public. He tried to pick her up after classes and she ignored him or took refuge in the ladies' room.

He was aching to explain, to talk, to hold her and to restore the love and logic to his world. Every time he saw her he felt a frantic need to touch her, to force her to listen. Nothing was sensible any more. He stopped her in the hall at the Union one day and said, "Beth, this has gone far enough. For God's sake, talk to me."

She eyed him coolly. "I have nothing to say to you, Charlie."

"Well, I've got something to say to you."

She folded her arms patiently. "All right," she said.

"Here?" His voice was hard.

"This is as good as any place."

He studied her for a minute in silence. "Not quite, Beth," he said finally, and walked off and left her alone. It was the first time he had done it, and he caught Beth by surprise. She stared after him for a minute and then went down the hall in the opposite direction. Charlie went off tormented and angry, wild with impatience and doubt, afraid he might never reach her, never touch her again, and the idea made him half mad.

He went home to the empty apartment, poured himself a stiff drink, and threw himself into a chair. He fixed the wall with an angry stare while he finished the drink and poured another. And then he said to himself, Why? What the hell's wrong with the girl? And then he said it out loud, as if he expected an answer from the listening wall: "What the hell *is* wrong with her?"

He stood up, glass in hand, and began to walk slowly up and down the room. "I'll tell you what's wrong with her," he told himself aloud. "She doesn't want to see you." He turned sharply around and demanded sarcastically, "Does that mean there's something *wrong* with her?" He emptied his glass and then glared balefully at the wall, filling the glass again. "Be sensible, be sensible . . ." he admonished himself. "Okay, we'll be sensible," he said. "We'll be logical. We'll start with her family. Anything wrong there? No, she gets along fine with them."

He fortified himself with a swallow. "Now," he said. "Friends. First category: men. God, let's see. Men." He sat down suddenly. "Damn them," he murmured. "God damn them all." When she had told him about the others, he had taken it in stride. He had been full of her, warm and passionate and wildly in love. He had her in his arms, and she had made a brave and painful confession to him. It had stunned him, but he rallied. It was easy to forgive her; she loved him, she needed him, she hated the others as much as he did. But now, thinking of them, with Beth remote and icy, with the same room they had made love in cold and lonely and haunted with Bud and Emily's sorrows as well as his own—he broke down, enraged.

"Oh, God," he snarled through closed teeth, "send every one of those stinking bastards straight to hell." His voice subsided to a whisper. "And as for her—as for her—" He drank a little more, and then dropped his head in his hands. "Make her love me," he said in a broken voice. "Just make her love me."

After a few minutes he straightened up again and refilled his glass. "Men," he said softly. "I know she has no other men. I'd know that right away—Mary Lou would tell Mitch and he'd sure tell me."

He drank. It was becoming rather difficult to pursue the logical approach. He tried to retrace his steps. "Family," he muttered. "Friends. Men. Women." He laughed a little and lifted his glass and then put it down again on the table. He shook his head to clear it. "God, how drunk am I?" he said, looking at the glass and then at the bottle. After a long pause he said it again, aloud but very quietly, "Women?" And then he took a long swallow. He stood up again and walked uncertainly around the room, pulling at his chin, rubbing his head, squinting with concentration. Finally he walked up to the wall and stopped, leaning against it. From months past came a hazy argument with Beth. He remembered gazing at her over the top of a diner table. He was saying, "I can tell when a person has a crush on me. Can't you? Laura doesn't."

"Well, she does," Beth had said.

She had said it several times, insisted on it. Charlie raised his clenched fists over his head, his whole body relying on the wall. "Laura?" he whispered, and the strength seemed to go out of him. He sagged against the wall. "If I weren't so drunk," he told himself sternly. He slid slowly to the floor and fell asleep where he lay.

While Charlie got drunk that afternoon, Beth began, for the first time, to have doubts about leaving school with Laura. When she got back to the sorority house that evening she, quite unconsciously, gave herself away by saying to Laura, "I wonder if we're doing the right thing?"

"Beth!" Laura exclaimed. She grasped Beth's hands and held them tight. "Of course we are. What a thing to say!"

"I guess so, but—I don't know. As time goes by, I begin to wonder."

"Beth, don't you remember what you said? Don't you remember what they did to Emmy? What they'd do to us if we got caught? Beth, you promised me. Oh, darling— we were going to be so happy, all to ourselves with no house rules, no deans, no men to worry about. Beth . . ." She pulled her hands up and pressed them to her lips and Beth watched her with a warm feeling in her chest. Laura looked up. "Beth, you promised. You said whatever happens. I said it, too. It's like an oath. You can't break it. Oh, Beth, my love!" She threw her arms around her.

"Yes," Beth whispered. "Yes. Oh, Laur, I'm just—I don't know. I'm crazy. Don't listen to me, I don't know what I'm saying."

"Then we *will* go?"

"Yes. We'll go."

But if she could calm Laura she couldn't do as well by herself. Laura could believe in Beth and lean on her, depend on her for everything. But Beth had no one to look to and she was suddenly responsible not just for herself but for Laura as well. It was unnerving. She hadn't expected Laura to take to her idea with such enthusiasm; to take so seriously and so finally what began in Beth's mind as a private emotional revolt. The thing seemed somehow foolhardy and stupid. And yet, when she looked into Laura's face and saw the endless warm love in it, all hers, her reservations faded away.

Laura said, "Beth, when will we go? Let's go soon." She knew if they postponed the thing much longer, Beth wouldn't go at all. The main thing was to get Beth out of Champlain before she changed her mind. And Laura had a sure idea that Charlie was behind Beth's doubt.

"Did you see Charlie today?" she asked.

Beth looked surprised. "Yes," she said.

Laura stroked Beth's cheek with her finger. "He always upsets you, Beth," she said.

Beth kissed the finger. "He reminds me of things I'd rather forget. Laura, you're adorable."

Laura smiled gratefully at her. "When shall we go?" she said, capitalizing on Beth's mood.

"Oh . . ."

"Beth, tell me."

"Oh, I don't know. When do you want to go? Your eyes are such a pretty blue. Where'd you get such blue eyes, Laur?"

"Let's go Friday."

"This Friday?"

"Yes." She watched her hopefully, with parted lips. Beth kissed them.

"Isn't that kind of soon?"

"We have to, Beth. It's now or never," she added truthfully.

Beth kissed the corner of Laura's mouth. "Is it?" she murmured.

"Yes. Beth, answer me."

"Kiss me." Beth's eyes were bright, teasing.

Laura obeyed her. "Now, answer me," she demanded.

"Answer you what?"

Laura smiled. "Say yes, Beth. Say yes, darling."

"Yes, what?"

"Just yes. Never mind what. Say it." She kissed her hard.

"Yes," Beth whispered, smiling. "Yes, yes, yes . . ."

That was Monday night. Laura spent the next few days worrying about Charlie. She was afraid of any further contact between Charlie and Beth, though it seemed inevitable, the way Charlie was trying to see her. She wanted to prevent him from talking to Beth before he could do any real damage, before Friday came and Beth was safely on the train. But she didn't know what to do about it, how to go about it. Unexpectedly, Charlie solved her problem before the week was out.

NINETEEN

Beth and Laura told their friends simply that they were going home for the weekend, a normal thing, especially in spring, for most of the girls to do.

By Thursday afternoon Laura was irrepressibly happy. Her only difficulty lay in trying to keep her excitement from showing. It was wonderful to escape from classes and campus and meetings and people, into her room and Beth's arms; wonderful to free her feelings and see how strong and deep and solid they were; best of all to know that after tomorrow Beth would be hers, irrevocably committed.

Beth, as the time grew closer, began to worry in earnest, but Laura's drive and devotion seemed to pull her inexorably toward the train on Friday. She was sure she loved Laura, but not so sure she didn't love Charlie. She wavered, she wondered, she weighed a thousand things in her mind: freedom against her college degree, a tormented conscience against the sweet warmth of Laura, and all the countless little details that trailed in the wake of either decision.

She tried to keep her mental seesawing from Laura; it would only hurt and confuse her. She felt that Laura had to be protected like a child. She had failed to see that every time she treated Laura to a little adult honesty, Laura responded like an adult. She didn't want to see. Laura was her baby.

By Thursday, Beth had an almost oriental fatalism about leaving for New York. There was nothing she could do to stem the tide of Laura's enthusiasm, no way she had any control over the situation any more.

That afternoon, Laura went over to Campus Town after class to get some last-minute supplies. She walked into the university drugstore and got some toothpaste—one for Beth, she was always running out—and some emery boards. She was standing at the counter waiting for her change when she heard Charlie next to her say, "Hello, Laura."

She looked up with a start. "Hi, Charlie," she said. He smiled down at her while she faltered, a little confused. She had the distinct feeling that he had followed her.

"Your change, miss," said the clerk, dangling a bored hand over the counter.

"Oh, thank you." Laura took it and Charlie simultaneously pulled her books out of her arms and held them while she put the money in her wallet. She stuffed the money away and reached quickly for her books, but he held them out of reach.

"Let me take you home, Laura," he said, steering her toward the door. She didn't like the tone of his voice. "My car's just a block away."

Laura protested; she didn't want anything from Charlie Ayers, not even a ride home. "Oh, please don't bother," she said.

"No bother." She understood then that he intended to take her home, no matter what she said. He had made up his mind and she resented his easy authority. It made her apprehensive.

She walked along beside him in nettled silence, dragging and wishing she could give a hard shake to get his hand off her arm. They reached the car and he held the door for her while she hesitated.

"Get in," he said pleasantly, and when still she hung back he smiled and said, "I'm not going to attack you, Laura."

Laura blushed angrily and got into the front seat.

He watched her with a curious smile and then came around and got in and started the car. "I thought maybe you'd answer a couple of questions for me," he said.

"In return for the ride?" she said. He must have been following me, she told herself.

He laughed. "No," he said. "In return for the sympathy. You cried on my shoulder last fall, Laura. Now I'm going to cry on yours—figuratively," he added when she gave him a cold stare. They pulled away from the curb.

"Well," she said, "I don't know if I can answer any questions, Charlie."

"I think you can," he said. "I hope you will." He paused and then looked at her out of the corner of his eye, amused to see that she was staring spitefully at his long legs. She looked up hastily, sensing his gaze. "Of course you're under no obligation," he said.

"Oh, no." She looked down at her hands, knowing it would be about Beth and tempted to fear Charlie again. He was impressive competition; she had almost forgotten the lines of him. But tomorrow, she told herself. Tomorrow! And thinking of Beth and of the things she did and said and the way she looked, Laura felt a flush of strength and certainty. Beth loved her. You can't be in love with two people at once, and Beth loved Laura. She said so and she meant it. Laura was sure. She looked up at Charlie again. He was lighting a cigarette.

"I want to know," he said, taking it out of his mouth and spewing smoke over the dashboard, "why Beth won't see me."

"Well," Laura shrugged. "She's been terribly upset."

"So have I."

"Well, Charlie, I don't know. Emily was her best friend."

"Does her best friend mean more to her than the man she's in love with?"

Laura turned surprised eyes on him and then she laughed, in spite of herself. He gave her a quick inquisitive glance. "What's so funny?" he said.

"She's not in love with you, Charlie. Oh, I'm sorry, I didn't mean to laugh. You just—surprised me." It was glorious to talk to him like this.

"The hell she isn't," he said. "She's mad, she's insulted, yes. Maybe she hates me, I don't know. But I do know she's in love with me."

Laura smiled at his certainty, suddenly enjoying her ride.

"What's so damn funny, Laura?" he said.

"Nothing," she said, but it was too tempting. "Your egoism, Charlie."

"My egoism?" He smiled a little, suddenly cautious, wondering at Laura's change of mood.

"Charlie," she said solicitously, with the thought of Beth in bed the night before, of Beth's kiss in the morning, of Beth's arms around her that afternoon, "Charlie, I didn't mean to be rude, really. I'm sorry. I know you think a lot of Beth."

"I love Beth, Laura."

Laura smiled into her lap again. Charlie watched her and then pulled the car up. He had been taking the long way back to Alpha Beta. They were at the edge of the university's experimental farm on the south campus. Charlie switched the ignition off and turned in his seat to study Laura. She glanced out the window and then questioningly at Charlie.

"I want to know what's so damn funny about my being in love with Beth. Or Beth with me." He looked straight at her.

Laura fought her smile down. "Nothing, Charlie. It isn't funny. It was wrong of me. I'm sorry." He said nothing. "I think we'd better get back to the house," she said.

"We will. When you explain the joke."

She couldn't feel any alarm, somehow. She just felt delightfully secure, smug as only a successful rival can feel in the presence of the loser. She looked out the window again at the adventuring green of mid-April. "There's no joke, Charlie," she said.

"Then what are you laughing at?"

"I'm not. I just—I don't know." She ached to tell him. Half the joy of a victory is the look on the face of defeat.

"Look, Laura," he said, leaning toward her. "I thought we were friends, you and I. Maybe I was wrong." He watched her narrowly.

"No." She shook her head slowly, letting him work for every word from her.

"Well, then will you clear up the mystery for me? What's the matter with Beth? Or me, for that matter?"

"Nothing's the matter with you. Or her."

Charlie lighted another cigarette from the last leg of the old one. "What's the matter, Laura? Why don't you want to tell me?" She frustrated him, made him feel hoodwinked; he had never thought a transparent girl like Laura could be so enigmatic. "What's all this about my being egotistical?" He watched her. No response, except a little maddening smile. He put his arm over the back of the seat and leaned toward her. "Come on, Laura, deflate my ego," he said cannily. "It seems to be the only way I'll learn anything."

Laura laughed again. "I don't want to deflate your ego, Charlie."

"Come on, Laura," he insisted. "Don't I have a right to know?"

"Well," said Laura, savoring each word, "it's just that

Beth isn't in love with you, Charlie. She was never in love with you." She gave him a sympathetic look. "That's all. I'm sorry."

He knew better. "Yes, she is," he said. Laura shook her head with a smile. "How do you know she isn't?" he said.

She looked at her lap and finally Charlie sat forward and knocked some ashes out the window and said some words he had only thought of once before, vaguely, when he was very drunk. "She's in love with you, I suppose," he said with a taste of sarcasm in his voice.

Laura looked up at him and smiled. It was intoxicating. Charlie gazed thoughtfully out the windshield, waiting for her denial, not taking his own words seriously until the silence forced him to review them. And suddenly, with painful lucidity, the light came; the sense and the reasons fell deafeningly into place.

Laura watched him minutely; saw the tiniest line between his eyes grow and deepen; saw the hand with the cigarette start for his lips and drop slowly back to the steering wheel; saw his lips part a little and his eyes widen. And then he turned and stared at her and she looked full into his face and smiled. He stared, and all Beth's little mysteries and refusals and anxieties and half-finished sentences smiled back at him. Laura never said a word; she just smiled serenely at him.

Charlie shut his eyes for a moment, wishing he were stone drunk, and then looked unwillingly at her again, and then at the floor. Laura watched him hungrily, remembering every second, every detail of him, every sound.

Finally he said in a husky voice, "Laura—is it true? Is it possible?" He looked at her. "Beth?"

Laura didn't answer him. Her lips parted a little as if she meant to, but she didn't. Then she succumbed to temptation. "Is what true?" she said softly.

"Is Beth—is she—" It was hard for him to say, and Laura enjoyed his difficulty. She felt like patting his arm and saying the question for him and then answering it lightly as if it were the easiest thing in the world. Charlie breathed deep. "Is Beth—in love with you, Laura?"

Laura looked down for a moment and her smile widened. And then her eyes came up slowly to his face. Charlie took her shoulders and shook her.

"Answer me!" he commanded. "Answer me, Laura! Is she?"

Her shoulders hurt from the grip of his hard hands and she saw the ripple of movement in his cheeks as his jaw clenched. Laura let her head fall back a little and she smiled gently at him and said, very slowly and luxuriously, "Yes."

They gazed at each other for what seemed a very long time—a tortuous time for Charlie and an exultant one for Laura. And then he let her go suddenly and turned back to the wheel and put his arms across it with his head down on his arms. Laura hoped he would cry. For a few minutes they sat in utter silence, with only April noises to disturb them.

Laura put her head back on the seat and gloated over the handsome broad-shouldered boy beside her, thinking how charming he was, how pleasant, how cock-sure. She let herself feel sorry for him, and her pity threatened to exhilarate her uncontrollably. This was her irresistible rival, a desirable man. And Laura, a plain girl, had vanquished him. She smiled again.

At length, Charlie straightened up. "I could never have believed it," he said quietly. "I thought of everything, but some things you just don't believe."

He started the car without looking at her, without saying anything more. They pulled back onto the road and headed for the sorority house. Laura watched him, but his face was set and blank; not the least tremor, not the palest line betrayed the tumult inside him. She said nothing, respecting his unuttered wish for silence.

Five minutes later they pulled up in front of the house. Charlie stopped the car and turned to look at her. She gathered up her books and opened the door, and then she looked back at him; she couldn't help herself.

"Thanks for the ride," she said.

"You're welcome," he answered. His voice was deep and quiet. She admired his control.

She got out and went up the walk to the front door and opened it and went into the house, knowing that he was sitting in the car watching her, never moving. When she was inside she rushed up the stairs to the first landing and pushed the heavy drapes carefully aside to peek out and see him start the car up and move down the street. He was driving in the direction of Maxie's. He's going to get drunk, Laura thought jubilantly, he's going to get drunk because he can't take it!"

Charlie's first thought was go to Maxie's and drink himself insensible. But he dismissed the idea almost as soon as it came to him. This time he needed a clear mind, uncluttered with alcoholic confusion. He turned the car around and drove slowly in the opposite direction. He was thinking, concentrating intensely in an effort to keep his emotions at bay. "A clear mind," he thought over and over. It occurred to him to go to the library. He hadn't any specific idea why. The library was a temple of learning, of wisdom. He would go there and soak it up. He would find a good sensible book and discover what made Beth and Laura want each other. He would understand.

But he no sooner parked his car by the library and started walking toward the big building than he knew how futile it was. He would be unable to read a single line of print. He paused uncertainly on the steps, looking into the great dark hall beyond the doors, and then he turned around. He didn't know what to do.

He sat down finally in the shade of a statue and leaned against the base. Above him drooped a lush woman in rough stone, rich with female curves. Some feet away a sister statue straddled her pedestal with muscular thighs. Charlie glared at the two women of rock, so warmly shaped that he never passed them without wanting to reach out and touch them. He knew them today for their cold, hard, unknowable selves.

For a long time he sat on the library steps between the stone sisters, and after a while it became possible to think. Just a little at first. It was one thing to reconcile himself to Beth's mistakes of the past; mistakes that were over and done with, mistakes that were above all normal. But it was quite another to accept her strange transgression with Laura.

Charlie thought back over the year. He knew he had satisfied Beth, he knew she wanted him. He had not been putting up a front when he told Laura that Beth loved him. Beth *did* love him. That could only mean one thing: that her feelings for Laura were not true love, not the kind of love she had for him.

He began to breathe a little more freely. Beth was an iconoclast, he knew that. She was an experimenter. And her failures, her frigidity with men might have pushed her to make this most extraordinary experiment of all: to look for release with a woman. Coming at it from that angle it wasn't quite so shocking—and it gave him hope. If Laura were an experiment for Beth, she wasn't a permanent thing. She represented a phase Beth had to go through.

Charlie smacked his fist into his palm. He stood up and slapped the nearest stone woman on the rump. He had made up his mind. Beth needed someone to guide her, to talk to her and straighten her out. She needed someone to love, with real love. He would see to it that she got it.

TWENTY

BETH was pensive that evening, but Laura was so gay that she had trouble concentrating on her misgivings. Laura was learning from her how to tease, and she could rouse and delight Beth very skillfully now. She rarely missed an opportunity to do it. Beth sat on the couch with a book in her hands, and Laura came up to her and pulled it out.

"What's that?" she said, glancing at it as she sat beside Beth.

"James."

"What's it for?"

"Class tomorrow."

"Class doesn't matter any more," Laura said. "Nothing matters any more but you and me. You have to study me now, Beth."

Beth laughed and caressed her, but her doubts grew stronger, nevertheless. She might have revolted against the plan, begged Laura to wait till the school year was up, if a letter hadn't come the next day from Emmy.

There had been several; Beth answered them all and they had been brave and hopeful. But this one was forsaken and bitter for the first time. Emmy hadn't seen Bud for two weeks, her parents were needling her, she couldn't find a job. She said:

"Beth, whatever happens, don't ever let yourself get into a mess like this, ever. Everybody knows what happened—it's so hard to face them all.

"I'd always thought men would give you a fair shake if you were honest with them. But now I'm beginning to wonder. I haven't heard from Bud for two weeks—not a word. And I've written every day. I'd call, but I'm afraid I'd embarrass him—make him mad, or something."

Make *Bud* mad! What's Bud done to deserve any consideration?

"Besides, I have some unwelcome news for him. He may have to marry me, whether he wants to or not."

182

Beth crumpled the letter harshly in her hand, too angry and vengeful even for tears.

Laura came into the room, back from her last class. She was breathless and happy and she threw her arms around Beth and said, "Oh, Beth, I can't wait!"

Beth hugged her. She felt good, the weather was good, the idea was good, the time was right. Emmy was right, there was no good in men.

They planned to meet at the station at four-thirty. The train pulled out at five-fifteen; they'd have time for a sandwich, plenty of time to get good seats.

A lot of trunks went home in April full of winter clothes. Theirs had left with a bunch of others, unnoticed. Beth simply left most of the room furnishings. They were hers and she didn't care about them.

"I'm rich, Laura," she said gaily. "I'm twenty-one and I've got my own money now, and no one can take it away from me, not even Uncle John. I'm free." And it was wonderful.

Beth had an afternoon class, and as Laura didn't, they planned to go down to the station separately and meet there.

Beth got out of her last class at three and headed for the Union. Her conscience troubled her; she was leaving a big job in a big mess. She went up to her office and tried to straighten things out.

"Leaving us?" someone called out, eying her little traveling bag.

She was startled for a minute. "No," she said. "I mean —home for the weekend."

"Lucky girl. Wish I could take a weekend off."

She laughed nervously and went to work. It was after four when she stopped. She tidied up her desk with an unsettling sense of finality, pulled her jacket on, took her bag firmly by the handle, and walked out of her office, through the Student Activities room and into the spacious hall, heading for the elevator.

Charlie stood up from a bench by the stair well. "I've been waiting for you," he said.

She stood frozen for a minute, and then she started briskly for the elevator. "I haven't got time, Charlie."

"Well, make time," he said. He caught her arms and took her bag from her. "Going someplace?"

"Yes. Let me go."

"Not this time, Beth. Where're you going?"

"That's none of your business."

"All right," he said. An elevator stopped and the doors opened and people spilled out. "I'm going to talk to you, Beth, whether you like it or not," Charlie said. People looked at them curiously. "I'm going to talk to you right here and now, in front of anybody and everybody—unless you'd care to give me a little privacy."

"Charlie, don't be a fool," she said sharply. "Give me my bag."

"Beth, there's something I've been meaning to tell you for a long time."

People stopped and watched them.

"All right, Charlie," she said in a brittle voice. She went to the door of a conference room, looked in and found it empty. "We can use this," she said. "But make it snappy."

He followed her in, shutting the door behind him. "Beth, where are you going?" he said seriously, indicating the bag.

Beth sighed impatiently. "I'm going home for the weekend. With Laura. On the five-fifteen." She looked significantly at her watch.

Charlie looked at her in alarm, suddenly alerted. "With Laura?" he said.

Beth turned her back on him. "Yes, with Laura. Now, what is it you're so anxious to tell me?"

Charlie knew he might lose her, then; really lose her. The bag looked ominous, sitting quietly on the long polished conference table. He leaned against the wall, watching Beth pace up the other side of the table, wondering if he could flush the truth out of her with a scare. "Why don't you take her to New York?" he said.

Beth stood absolutely still. The click of her heels died abruptly and she was tense as a guy wire, motionless. He hit home—her back told him so. Finally she turned and looked at him.

"What do you mean?" she said, and her voice was very soft.

He straightened up. "If you're in love with her, go live with her." His eyes were relentless.

Beth gazed at him with a stricken frown on her face, and suddenly she hurried toward the door. Charlie stepped in front of it, and she stopped, unwilling to touch him. She turned her back to him again.

"Is that all you have to say to me, Charlie?"

"No," he said. "Do you love her, Beth?"

"What are you trying to prove, Charlie?"

"What are you trying to hide, Beth?"

"Nothing!" she flared.

"Then be honest with me. Do you love her?"

She paused, looking anxiously for an answer. "What makes you think I love her?"

"Answer me, damn it!" he said.

She said, in a haggard, scarcely audible voice, "I don't know . . . I don't know." And then she turned angry eyes on him. "How did you know?"

"I figured it out. Look, Beth—all I want is a chance to talk to you. I'm not going to strong-arm you into anything; I'm not going to beat you over the head. You ought to know that by this time. I didn't expect to find you running away, but—"

"I'm not running away. Damn it, Charlie, I'm running *into* more problems than I'm running away from. I'm not a coward."

"Listen to me, Beth," he said, and his eyes were intense and his voice was soft. "Just listen to me for a minute. And remember, no matter what I say, no matter what you feel, I love you."

That silenced her. For a minute he regarded her quietly and then he said, "Grow up, Beth. I don't know how much there is to this thing between you and Laura, honey, but it's all off balance, I'll tell you that. It's cockeyed because Laura's in love with you and you aren't in love with Laura."

"I am!"

"A minute ago you didn't know." Her eyes fell, and she rubbed them in confusion. "And what's more," he went on in his firm voice, "she doesn't know you're in love with me. She doesn't know you ever were."

"I'm not."

He ignored her. "This is child stuff, Beth, this thing between you and Laura. You're deceiving yourself, denying yourself. You're a woman, honey—a grown woman. An intelligent, beautiful girl with a good life ahead of you. And that life has a man in it and kids and a college degree. Maybe it can't be that way for Laura. But it's got to be that way for you."

"I want something more than that." Her voice was contemptuous.

"Then you'll find it. But not by running away. And certainly not by running away with a girl, and a girl you don't love, at that."

"Charlie, damn it—"

"You can't run away, Beth." His voice, his gestures, were urgent. "My God, you've read the books. What do they all say—every damn one? They say running away won't help, it won't solve the problem. You can't run away from the problem, you have to stand pat and face it. Look, darling," he said, "you aren't in love with Laura. Laura's in love with you, yes, but—my God, don't you see what you're doing? You're using her as an excuse. You're sorry for her, you want to take care of her as if she were a little girl, without thinking what harm that's doing her. You're sorry for Emmy, you're sorry for yourself. You're mad at the whole God-damned world and me in particular because there are rules that you don't like, and when somebody breaks the rules somebody gets hurt.

"Don't you see how young that is? It's kid stuff, honey. That's the kind of thing you did back in grade school when the world was a big mystery and rules didn't seem to make any sense. You couldn't fight them, you couldn't make sense of them, so you either kicked and screamed or you ran away."

"Charlie," she whispered, and he could hear the tears in her voice, "I can't hurt Laura. I can't hurt her. Not now. It's too late."

"Beth . . ." He came up behind her and took her shoulders in his hands, bending his head down close to hers. "Jesus, Beth, don't you see how much greater the harm would be if you let her go along thinking you love her—let her leave school and home and everything she knows for you—and then let her find out some day that you don't really love her? That you never loved her? That you've only been playing with her, using her for your own self-assurance, lying to her all along?"

"Oh, Charlie." Her shoulders trembled. "You make it sound so terrible."

"It is terrible, darling. But it hasn't happened yet." He felt the first twinge of hope. He was right; she was frightened. The premise he had gambled on was true. She loved him, not Laura; it remained only to convince her of this herself.

"It would hurt her so awfully if I—if I—"

"Not like it will a few months from now. Or a year. Then it could hurt so much that she'd never recover. Beth, my love . . ." He put his arms around her. "Running away now won't help Emmy either. It won't undo the wrong. It won't make Laura happy. And think what it's going to do to you. Face it, honey, look ahead. Think, not just of Laura or Emmy or me, but of yourself. What will this do to your life? Beth," he said, turning her around and lifting her chin.

She looked at him through welling tears.

"You don't need to be loved right now, my darling," he said, and she frowned in wonderment. "You are, but that's not the point. You don't need to be loved one half so much as you need to *love*, Beth. And you need to love a man . . . and you do."

They stared at each other for a long time while her tears slowed and stopped and his face came into focus and his strength held her fast and warmed and thrilled her.

"Charlie?" she said.

He kissed her wet cheeks and her lips for a long lovely while, cradling her body against his own, letting her forget a little, find her courage and will again, pressed hard against the clean friendly power of himself. And then he pushed her firmly away.

"Your train leaves in half an hour," he said. "I'll drop you off at the station."

He picked up her bag and led her out of the room. She followed him in confusion, her mind in an alarming uproar, her heart in knots. They left the Union and walked half a block to his car without saying anything. She got in and settled herself, trying at the same time to settle her frantic nerves.

They drove to the station. He stopped at the corner, some distance from the entrance, in case Laura should be there waiting. Beth hesitated, her hand on the door handle. Charlie watched her.

"It's your decision, Beth," he said.

She closed her eyes and clamped her teeth together, and pushed the handle down. The door gave a little, and still she waited, agonized.

"It's five o'clock. Better get going," he said. "Train leaves at five-fifteen."

"Charlie—" She turned her tortured face to him. "Charlie—"

"I'm going over to Walgreen's and get a cup of coffee," he said. "I'll be there until five-thirty."

Slowly she got out of the car, pulling her bag after her. She gave him a long supplicating look and then shut the car door and watched him drive off. He didn't look back. She turned and walked up the steps and along the station to the entrance and went in. Laura saw her instantly.

"Oh, Beth!" she said thankfully. "For a minute I—I— oh, never mind. You're here. Thank God, you're here."

Beth tried to smile at her. "Laura, I—" she began.

"I got your ticket, darling. It got so late, I— What happened, Beth? Why are you so late?"

"I—I got held up at the Union." Could she never tell the truth?

"Oh," Laura laughed. "I nearly had heart failure. It got later and later and— Well, anyway, you're here. We'd better go on up if we want seats. The train's loading." She gave a little tug at Beth's sleeve.

"Laura—wait. Wait. I—" She stopped, unable to talk, hardly able to face Laura.

With a forced, frightened calm, Laura took Beth's bag from her and led her to a wooden bench near the ticket windows. She made her sit down and then she took her hands and said, with inexplicable dread, "What is it, Beth?" Far away inside her it was turning cold.

"Laura—" Beth's cheeks were hot with a needling shame and uncertainty.

"Beth, you've been crying. What's the matter?"

"Oh, Laura . . ." Beth couldn't find her tongue. Her voice was rough with sorrow.

"Don't you want to go, darling?" Laura sounded unbelievably sad and soft and sweet.

"Laura, couldn't we—couldn't we wait till June? I—"

Laura shook her head gravely. "No, we can't wait, Beth. We have to go now, or we'll never go. You know that."

She did know it, but she couldn't come right out and admit it. "No, Laur, we could do it later. Couldn't we?" For the first time she was asking Laura instead of telling her.

Laura shook her head again and murmured, "No, Beth, tell me the truth. We haven't much time. What's the matter?"

"Laura—darling—I just can't do it. I just can't. Oh, Laura—hate me. Hate me!" And she put her head down against the bench and wept, unable to look at Laura, pulling her hand free to cover her face.

Laura held the other one hard. When Beth was quieter she raised her eyes and saw Laura's face, white and heartbreakingly gentle, and there was a curious new strength in it, an almost awesome dignity that Beth, in her distress, lacked completely.

"Laura, stay with me," she said a little wildly. "Stay here. We'll go back to the house. It's only another month or so. Please—"

"No," said Laura. "I have to go." She was cold all over now, but the frost brought clarity as well as suffering. She began to understand. She heard Beth start to implore her and she stopped her.

"Beth, I have only a few minutes. Listen to me. Tell me one thing—only one. Do you love Charlie? Is that what's the matter?" Beth started to shake her head, but Laura said, "Don't try to protect me any more, Beth. I want to know the whole truth. Do you love him?"

Beth was surprised and touched by her self-command, and she gazed at her a moment before answering, "Yes," in a whisper.

"Then I'll go. And you'll stay."

"No—"

"Listen to me!" Beth was startled into silence. Laura's voice dropped. "Beth, I love you. I'm not like other people—like most people. I can never love more or better than I love you—only more wisely maybe, some day, if I'm lucky. It can never be any other way for me. What I mean is—there can never be a man for me, Beth. I'll never love a man like I love you."

Her voice never lost its steady softness, her eyes never lost their deep hurt, her hand never relaxed its tight constriction over Beth's. She talked fast, racing the clock.

"It's different for you, Beth. I guess I've known all along, when you met Charlie and everything. I just wanted you so much, so terribly, so selfishly, that I couldn't admit it. I couldn't believe it. But you need a man, you always did. Emmy was right, she understood. If I'd only listened. I was the one who was wrong, about you and her. But I'm not wrong about myself, not any more. And not about you, either."

"Oh, Laura, my dear—"

"We haven't time for tears now, Beth. I've grown up

emotionally as far as I can. But you can go farther, you can be better than that. And you must, Beth, if you can. I've no right to hold you back." Her heart shrank inside her at her own words.

"Laura, I misjudged you so. I thought you were such a baby, such a—"

"We've both made mistakes, Beth."

"Can you forgive me? I've been so—"

"You taught me what I am, Beth. I know now, I didn't before. I understand what I am, finally. It's not a question of forgiving. I'm grateful. I can face life, my family, everything now, knowing. That's terribly important. I couldn't before. Don't you see?" She couldn't cry; there were no tears potent enough to relieve her grief. Her control was almost involuntary.

"But I—I've deceived you so. I—"

"It was just an accident, the whole thing, Beth." The train whistle blew. Laura drew nearer, her eyes profound and wise and wounded. Only five minutes left. "Don't you see what happened, Beth? We were in the same place at the same time and we both needed affection, darling. If it hadn't been that way, I wouldn't have known, I wouldn't have learned about myself, maybe not for a long time. And then it could have been a brutal, terrifying lesson. You made it beautiful, Beth.

"I guess that's all loving ever is—two people in the same place at the same time who need it. Only sometimes, for one, love has all the answers. For the other, it's just a game, a beautiful game. That's what happened to us, Beth. Neither of us willed it that way, it just happened. For you it was an accident, a sort of lovely surprise, and you took it that way. You took me for the little girl you thought I was. It was that little girl you wanted, not me. I had to be that little girl to keep you. I should have faced it then, but I couldn't. I couldn't even think about it.

"You see, for me it was love. A revelation, a forever sort of thing. Only nothing lasts forever. You told me that once."

The whistle called again. Laura got up from the bench and walked swiftly toward the exit. Beth ran after her.

"Oh, Laura, Laura, please don't go, not like this. Please."

"I have to, Beth."

"You're running away." She followed her outside as Laura hurried toward the stairs up to the train platform.

"No, I'm facing it," Laura said. "I know what I am, and I can be honest with myself now. I'll live my life as honestly as I can, without ruining it. I can't do that here and I can't do it with you. That's over now."

Beth listened to her words, feeling for the first time the maturity in them; knowing Laura was right and admiring her with a sudden force because Laura had the courage to say these things, these truths, and the strength to do what she knew was right. Beth rushed along beside her, holding her arm, knowing that when she released it, she would release Laura forever; she would never see her or touch her again—and yet knowing that it had to be that way. She would come to Charlie chastened with the knowledge Laura had given her; she would come to him wiser, older, and richer in love because of Laura.

"Laura," she said as they made their way down the platform, "I'm the one who's been acting like a baby, who's been childish about the whole thing. I never dreamed you were so—so brave." She couldn't think of a more fitting word. "Laura, I know I'm not making much sense, but I—you do mean so much to me, Laur. So very much. I want you to know. You're not the only one who's learned and who's grateful."

They reached the last car and Laura turned to her. There was the shade of a smile on her face. The pain was awful but the wound was clean. It would heal.

"Beth, I'm not angry. I thought I'd be bitter. I thought I'd hate Charlie if this ever happened. I thought I'd hate you more than anyone else on earth. But I've thought about it a lot, when you were seeing him so much and so happy with him, and I was spending those long nights at home alone. Even now, when you were late getting to the station, I kind of imagined what it would be like. I knew it would hurt, but—somehow I guess I always knew it would happen. It had to; you can't need men and spend the rest of your life with a girl. I knew you weren't—queer—like I am."

The word slapped Beth cruelly in the face. "Laura—" she protested.

"I knew as well as you did that it wouldn't last. Only I couldn't admit it, because I love you."

"Oh, Laura, darling—"

The conductor shouted, "All aboard!"

Laura put her bag on the steps and took Beth's hands

again. "Beth, you're meant for a man. Like Charlie. I'm not. I'm not afraid to go, I'm not sorry. It hurts, and I love you—" Her eyes dropped and she almost faltered. "I love you—" she whispered, And Beth felt the pressure of her hands as the train gave a preliminary jerk.

"Laura!" Beth cried, walking by the train, and Laura looked up again.

"But I wouldn't have the strength to face it if I didn't."

Beth reached for her and pulled her head down and kissed her, there on the train platform in the late afternoon sun with the train inching away from her and all Champlain free to watch.

"Laura, I love you," she said, letting Laura slide from her arms as the train pulled her away. And she meant it, for the first time. She loved her; not as Laura would have wanted her to, but sincerely, honestly, the best love she could offer.

She leaned exhausted against a post and watched the train pull out and her eyes never left Laura's. She stood with quiet tears stinging her cheeks and watched till the train wound its way out of sight.

Then she turned and walked slowly back down the steps and over to the station. She picked up her bag where Laura had left it and walked outside into the sunshine, set it down, and looked at her watch. There was a sudden flutter of new joy in her heart.

She had to hurry; it was almost five-thirty.

I AM
A WOMAN

Chapter One

TELL YOUR FATHER to go to hell. Try it. It's a rotten hard thing to do, even if he deserves it. Merrill Landon did. He was an out-and-out bastard, but like most of the breed, he didn't know it. He said he was a good father: sensible, firm, and just. He said everything he did was for Laura's own good. He took her opposition for a sign that he was right, and the more she opposed him, the righter he swore he was.

But he was a bastard. Laura could have told you that. But she couldn't tell *him*, because he was her father. That was why she ran out on him. Left him high, dry, and sputtering in his plush Chicago apartment with only his job to console him. And never told him where she went. Never told him why.

Never told him of the angry agony of her nights, spent torching for a love gone wrong. Never mentioned his straight-laced bitter version of fatherly affection that hurt her more than his fits of temper. He never kissed her. He never touched her. He only told her, "No, Laura," and "You're wrong, as usual," and "Can't you do it right for once?"

She had taken it all her life, but it was the worst the year after she left school. It was a year of confinement in luxury, of tightly controlled resentment, of soul-searching. And one rainy night when he was out at a press dinner, she packed a small bag and went to Union Station.

195

She bought a ticket to New York City. She could never be free from herself, but she could be free from her father, and at the moment that mattered the most.

So she rode out of the big city, wet and cold with its January gloss, and left behind Merrill Landon, her father. The man in her life. The only man in her life. The only man she ever seriously tried to love.

All she wanted from New York was a job, a place to live, a friend or two. As long as she won them herself, without her father's help, she would be happy. Much happier than when she had been surrounded with comfortable leather chairs, sheathed in sleek fine clothes, smelling like an expensive rose.

In school Laura had studied journalism. She did it to avoid a showdown with Merrill Landon. He had always taken it for granted that she would follow his profession, just as if she were a doting son anxious to imitate a successful father. She accepted his tyranny quietly, but with a corrosive resentment that he was unaware of. There were times when she hated him so actively for making a slave of her that he saw it and said, "Laura, for Chrissake, don't pout at me! Snap out of it. Act your age."

Laura was more afraid of loving Landon than leaving him. She was afraid the yearning in her would flare someday when he gave her one of his rare smiles. When he said, "Klein says you're learning fast. Good girl." And her knees went weak. But he saved her by quickly adding with embarrassed sarcasm, "But you messed up the water tower assignment. Jesus, I can never count on you, can I?"

When things became intolerable she left him at last with no showdown at all. She had considered going in to tell him about it. Walking into the library where he was working, where she was expressly forbidden to go in the evenings, and saying, "Father, I'm leaving you. I'm going to New York. I can't stand it here anymore."

He would have been brilliantly sarcastic. He would have described her to herself in terms so exaggerated that she would see herself as a grotesque mistake of nature, a freak in a fun-house mirror. He was not above such abuse. He had done it to her a few times before. Once, when she was very young and hadn't learned to tiptoe around his temper yet, and once when she quit school.

Not all his threats and tantrums could send her back to school, however. There was a ghost lurking there that Laura could never face, that Landon knew nothing about. He was forced to let her stay at home, but he committed her to journalism at once, and made her work on his paper with one of his assistants.

Even Laura was surprised when she was able to resist him about returning to school. She wouldn't have thought she could stick it out. Especially when he roared at her, "Why? Why! Why! Why! Answer me, you stubborn little bitch!" And smashed an ashtray at her feet.

She did not, *could* not, tell him why. It took all her courage to admit it even to herself. She simply said, "I won't go back, Father."

"Why!"

"I won't."

"Why?" It was menacing this time.

"I won't go back."

In the end he swore at her and hurt her with the same ugly irrelevant argument he always used when she resisted him. "You know why you're alive today, don't you? Because I saved you! I dragged you out of the water and let your mother drown. And your brother. I could only save one, and it was *you* I saved! God, what a mistake. My son. My wife!" And he would turn away, groaning.

"You weren't trying to save *me,* Father," she said once. "You just grabbed the nearest one and swam for shore. You screamed at Mother to save Rod and then you dragged me to shore. It's a miracle you saved even me. You see, I remember it too. I remember it very well."

He turned a pale furious face to her. "You dare to tell me what *you* remember? You silly little white-faced girl? You don't remember anything? Don't tell me what you remember!"

So she chose a night when he was out and left him without a word, at the start of an unfriendly January, and came to New York. Her first thought was to try to get work on one of the giant dailies. With her experience, surely they could find something for her. But then she realized her father was too well known in journalism circles. She hated the thoughts of his finding her. He had struck her more than once, and his anger with her sometimes reached such heights that she trembled in terror, expecting him to brutalize her. But it never went that far.

No, newspapers were out. Magazines were out. It would have to be something completely divorced from the world of journalism. She studied the want-ads for weeks. She tried to land a job as receptionist with a foreign airline, but her French was too poor.

Then, after about two weeks, she found a small ad for a replacement secretary to a prominent radiologist, someone with experience preferred. It appealed to her, without her exactly knowing why. She didn't really suppose she had much of a chance of getting it and it was silly to try. Who wanted a temporary job? Most girls were supposed to want security. But Laura wasn't like most girls. She was like damn few girls, in fact. She was a loner: strange, dream-ridden, mildly neurotic, curiously interesting, like somebody who has a secret.

The next morning she was in the office of Dr. Hollingsworth, talking to his secretary. The secretary, a tremendously tall girl with big bones, a friendly face, and a sort of uncomfortable femininity, liked her right away.

"I'm Jean Bergman," she said. "Come on in and sit down. Dr. Hollingsworth isn't here yet; he gets in at nine."

Laura introduced herself and said she'd like to have the job. She was a hard worker. Jean was disposed to believe her, on a hunch. It was one of those lucky breaks.

"I've talked to some other girls," she said, "but nobody seems to have had any experience. The girls with training want permanent jobs. So I guess I'll just have to find a bright beginner."

Laura smiled at her. She spoke as if it was settled. "The job will last till June first, Laura," Jean went on. "I'll be gone two months. We'll spend the time till then teaching you the routine. Sarah will be coming in in a minute—she's the other secretary. There'll be plenty for the three of us." She paused, eying Laura critically. "Well? Do you think you'd like a crack at it?"

"Yes, I would." Laura felt her heart lighten.

"Okay." Jean smiled. "I'm a trusting soul. You strike me as the efficient type. Of course, I'll have to introduce you to Dr. Hollingsworth. You understand. Now don't let me down, Laura."

"I won't. Thanks, Jean."

"You might make yourself indispensable, you know," Jean said. "I mean, they really need three girls around here. If they like you well enough—well, maybe they'll keep you on in June. It's just a chance; don't count on it."

Laura felt really worthwhile for the first time since she left home. She had never considered turning back, but there had been moments when the barren want-ads discouraged her and the wet biting weather dragged her spirits down. Now, the sun was shining through the rain.

It turned out to be a fine office to work in. Doctors have a crazy sense of humor and they are often tolerant. Dr. Hollingsworth was small and quiet, quite dignified but tender-hearted. He had two young assistants, Dr. Carstens and Dr. Hagstrom. They were both fresh from medical school—pleasant young men. Carstens was married, but with a wildly roving eye. Every female patient fascinated him, even if he saw no more than her lungs. Hagstrom had a permanent girl friend named Rosie with whom he conducted endless conversations on the phone. Both were devoted to Dr. Hollingsworth and considered themselves lucky to be with him.

Laura fell into the routine rapidly. She was much slower than the other girls at translating the mumbo-jumbo on the dictaphone at first. She spent nearly half the time looking up terms in the medical dictionary and the rest beating the typewriter.

The problem of finding a place to live before the hotel bills broke her was urgent. She discovered in a hurry, like most newcomers to New York, that it was a real struggle to find a decent apartment at a decent price. She asked Jean about it.

"I'm stuck," she said. "Where do people *live* in this town?"

"What's the matter with me?" Jean said. "I should have asked you if you had a place. I know a girl who's looking for a roommate. The one she had just got hitched. I'll call her."

Later she told Laura, "I talked to her. She says a couple of gals have already asked her, but to call if you want to.

She hasn't made up her mind yet. She's a doll, you'll like her. Here's her number."

"What's her name?"

"Marcie Proffitt. *Mrs.* Proffitt." She laughed at Laura's consternation. "She's divorced," she said.

Laura called at once.

"I'm at West End and a hundred and first," Marcie said when Laura got her. Her voice was low and appealing. Laura hoped she looked like she sounded. "The penthouse," Marcie said. "It's not locked. You have to walk up the last flight."

"A penthouse?" Laura said, taken aback. "Jean said—"

"It's not as fancy as it sounds," Marcie laughed. "In fact it's falling apart. That's how I can afford it. But it has a wonderful view. Come over tonight. I'll give you some dinner. I may be late, though, so I'll leave a key for you under the doormat."

"Thanks, Marcie, I'd like to." Laura wondered, when she hung up, if Marcie's hospitality was always so impulsive.

It was dark and getting windy when Laura got off the subway at 99th Street. She walked the two blocks up Broadway to 101st, holding her coat collar close around her throat.

The apartment building was a block off Broadway, up a hill at the corner of West End Avenue. It had been a chic address once, some years ago, when West End was an exclusive neighborhood. But it was deteriorating now, quietly, almost inconspicuously, slipping into the hands of ordinary people—families with lots of kids and not much money, students, working girls. And the *haut monde* was quietly slipping out and heading for the other side of town.

Laura entered the vestibule. It looked like the reception hall in a medieval fort. The only light came from a small bare bulb on a desk in one corner. The whole hall was full of heavy shadows.

Laura found the elevator tucked into a corner and pressed the button. She swung slowly around on her heels to look at the hall while she waited. It gave her the shivers.

She climbed into the elevator with misgivings. It looked well used and little cleaned. There was a paper sticker plastered on the wall above the button panel saying that it had passed inspection until June of that year. Laura looked it up and down and wondered if it would last till June. She reached the twelfth and last floor and walked out into a hall. To the right of the elevator she found a pair of swinging doors, and beyond them a steel staircase. She climbed the stairs, her heels ringing, and found herself in a short dark hall with two doors in it: one to the penthouse, one to the roof. Laura went out on the roof for a look.

She walked over the red tiling toward a stone griffin carved on the railing and looked over it to the city. Below her, around her on all sides, sparkled New York. It honked and shouted down there, it murmured and sighed, it blinked and glittered like a gorgeous whore waiting to be conquered. Laura breathed deep and smiled secretly at it. She could live with a dank front hall and patched up elevator for a view like this.

It was ten minutes before she went into the dark corridor again and found the penthouse door. She rang twice and when there was no answer she fumbled in the darkness for the key under the mat and unlocked the door. It opened into an unlit living room. Laura went in, shut the door behind her and stumbled around looking for a light switch. She knocked something off a table and heard it break before she discovered a lamp in a far corner and pulled the cord.

The room was small and furnished with bamboo furniture—a couch, an easy chair, a round cocktail table. There was a console radio against one wall, and books were lying around on the floor and furniture. There were a couple of loaded ashtrays and one lay shattered on the floor—Laura's fault.

Laura found the switch in the kitchen. It was long and narrow, painted a garish yellow. Beyond that was the bedroom, with two beds and two dressers jammed into it, and some shoes and underwear scattered around. It was bright blue, with two big windows opening onto the roof. The bathroom was enormous, almost as big as the bedroom, and the same noisy yellow as the kitchen. All the pipes were exposed and the plumbing looked as if it were full of bugs.

Laura walked back into the living room and sat down stiffly. She began to have serious misgivings. This was no place for a civilized girl to live. Surely in this tremendous city there was an apartment for a girl that didn't have an astronomical rent. And where she could eat in private out of cans.

Suddenly the door burst open and Marcie came in. And Laura forgot her discomfort.

Marcie smiled. "I'm Marcie. Hi."

Laura cursed the shyness that tied knots in her tongue.

"How do you like this crazy little palace?" Marcie said, gesturing grandly around her.

"It's very nice."

Marcie laughed, and Laura was struck with the sweet perfection of her features. Her lips were full and finely balanced; her nose was of medium length and dainty. Hair with true gold hue that no peroxide can imitate framed her face and hung nearly to her shoulders. She had the lucky black lashes and eyebrows that sometimes happen to blondes, and high color in her cheeks. She was, in short, a lovely looking girl. Laura smiled at her.

"It's a hole," said Marcie. "Don't be polite. The rent is one thirty a month."

Laura gasped.

"I know. It sounds awful. But that's only sixty-five apiece. And it includes maid service—so-called. The maid doesn't pick up a damn thing. Did you see the rest of the place?"

Laura nodded.

"Discouraged?"

"A little." Laura followed Marcie awkwardly into the kitchen.

"You'd better know the worst right off," Marcie went on. "Three other girls have called wanting to share this place with me." Laura's incredulous face made her laugh. "It's not that the place is irresistible," she explained. "It's just that apartments are hard to get in this town. Sit down, Laura." Laura obeyed her, finding a chair at the kitchen table while Marcie fussed at the stove. "Have you been here long?"

"Three weeks."

"Where did you come from?"

"Chicago."

"Oh, *that* place. I was there once with Burr. He was my husband."

"Oh," Laura said softly, almost sympathetically, as if Marcie had announced his demise.

"Well, don't put on a long face," Marcie said with a sudden laugh. "He's divorced, not dead. It was final last November." Her face became serious again and she gave Laura a plate of vegetables and hamburger. "He's very nice to know," Marcie mused. "But hell to live with. Laura, do you cook?"

"I can't boil water."

"Well, I can do that much."

Marcie lapsed into silence then, her burst of charming vitality spent. She ate quietly, as if unaware of Laura's presence, gazing at the table cloth and forking her food up mechanically. She had withdrawn suddenly and soundlessly into a private corner where fatigue and secret thoughts absorbed her.

Laura felt more awkward than ever. She was afraid to interrupt Marcie's reverie, but like all shy people she was convinced that if you can just keep the other person talking everything will be all right. It was an urge she couldn't resist. After a few false starts she said, "Have you been in New York long, Marcie?"

Marcie looked at her, mildly surprised to find her still there. "Yes. Since we were married." She spoke absently, turning to her plate.

"When was that?"

"Three years ago." She came suddenly back to the present. "Laura, did you ever love a man and hate him at the same time?"

Laura was nonplussed. This was more than she counted on. "Well—I don't know exactly." She wasn't sure if she had ever loved Merrill Landon. She knew well enough how she hated him.

"I shouldn't throw my problems in your face like that, before you get your dinner down," Marcie smiled. She reached out and gave Laura's arm a pat that made Laura jump a little. "It's just that that damn character proposed

to me again today. I don't know what to do with him. I
thought maybe you could give me some advice. Have you
ever been married?"

"Me? No," said Laura emphatically, as if it were a
slightly lewd suggestion. "Who is 'that character'?"

"Burr. My ex-husband."

"He wants to marry you again?" It seemed unnatural
to Laura. If the marriage were legally over, physically
over, emotionally over, why beat the carcass?

"Yes. The fool." Marcie smiled ruefully. "He's a very
persuasive fool, though."

Marcie was one of those people with the rare gift of intimacy. You knew her a few minutes, an hour, a couple
of days, and you discovered to your surprise that you felt
close to her. It wasn't the personal revelations she couldn't
help making, as much as it was her look, her questions
that asked for Laura's help. Laura felt curiously like an
expert on marital affairs, and it was so ridiculous that
she smiled.

"What's funny?" Marcie asked.

"You make me feel like Miss Lonelyhearts or something," Laura said.

Marcie laughed. "You don't have to give me advice,
Laura, just because I ask for it. I guess you can't anyway
if you're single. But just for the hell of it, what would you
do if a decent honorable sort of ex-husband chased you
like a demon and swore he'd kill you if you went out with
anybody else?"

"I'd send him to a clinic."

Marcie shook her head. "He's healthy. If I didn't know
we'd quarrel twenty-four hours a day, I'd marry him tomorrow." She sighed. "I almost said yes to him today.
What's the matter with me? I'm not a dope. Or am I?"

"You don't look like one," Laura said uncomfortably.

"Poor Laura!" Marcie laughed. "I'm embarrassing you to
tears. You make a good listening post. Come on, finish
your hamburger. It didn't kill me."

When they cleared up the dishes, Marcie turned on the
tap in the sink. A thin hesitant stream of water was called
up after some pitiful groaning from the pipes. Marcie
kicked a pipe under the sink.

"It's enough to drive you wild!" she exclaimed. "Some

nights you have to wait around till the cows come home before there's enough to wash anything in. Oh, here it comes!"

With a scream the pipes vomited steaming water. Marcie looked at Laura and the little smile on her face widened. Suddenly they were laughing hilariously. Laura felt the laughter soothing and tickling her tight muscles, making her relax.

"It hates me," Marcie said to the sink, grasping the faucets and rattling them furiously. The stream came to an abrupt halt. She turned to Laura again. "Do you think you can stand it?" she said.

"I think I can." Laura knew now why she wanted to move in, but she was ready to ignore the reason. She would bury it, forget it. It had no place in her world any more. She would say to herself, and half believe, that she was moving in simply because apartments were hard to find; because she could pay the rent on this one; because she and Marcie were congenial. Period. "What's your job like?" she asked Marcie casually.

"I'm supposed to be a typist-receptionist," Marcie said. "But I could never type very well. Mr. Marquardt doesn't care, though. He just told me to make a good impression on his customers and don't chew gum on the job. I told him that would be a cinch, and he said, 'You're hired.'" She laughed. "He's nuts. But it's a great job. I just sit around most of the day."

With a face like that, I'm not surprised, Laura thought. It gave her a bad feeling. Laura worked hard, she tried hard at anything she did. It was part of her nature. Either you did a thing the whole way or you didn't do it at all. It was part of Merrill Landon's code that had rubbed off on her. It made her a little jealous to hear this lovely girl brushing idly over a comfortable job that asked almost nothing of her. Marcie would not have understood Laura's feelings at all.

"You'll get along fine with Burr," Marcie said, drying her hands on a towel. "He's always reading something. Those are his books in there." She waved a hand toward the living room. "He brings them over in hopes that I'll improve my mind." She made a face and Laura smiled at her.

"Does he come over a lot?" Laura asked.

"Yes, but don't worry. He's harmless. He talks like Hamlet sometimes—gloomy, I mean—but he's nice to dogs and children. He has a parakeet, too. I always think a man who has a parakeet can't be very vicious. Besides, I lived with him for two years, and the worst he ever did to me was spank me one time. We shouted at each other constantly, but we didn't hit each other."

"Sounds restful," Laura said.

Marcie laughed and went into the bedroom. "See if you think you'll have enough room in here," she called to Laura, who followed her slowly. "It's pretty crowded, but the bathroom makes up for it. We could fence it off and make an extra room of it if we wanted to."

Laura sat down on one of the beds. "I like it fine, Marcie," she said. "I'd like to move in. If you think we'd get along." She looked at her lap, confused. She never said these things right. Marcie laughed good-naturedly and flopped on the bed beside Laura, on her stomach. Laura had to twist around to see her. "Oh, I can get along with anybody," she said. "Even you. I'll bet you're terribly hard to get along with."

"I don't think so. I mean—" She never knew when she was being teased until she had put on a solemn face and felt like an ass. "I'm impossible," she said with a smile.

"That settles it!" Marcie exclaimed, sitting up with the pillow crushed against her bosom.

Chapter Two

THEY GOT ALONG unusually well together, as the weeks passed into months. April came, and Jean left on her European tour. Laura and Sarah were alone in the office with the doctors, and Laura worked with a will to make up for what she still had to learn. With each day, each fact acquired and skill polished, the job meant more to her.

At home, there were no scenes or suspicions, such as female roommates have a talent for. Laura was quiet, shyly friendly, thoughtful. Marcie gave her a cram course in cooking, saw an occasional movie with her, and asked her how to spell things. Most of her free time was spent with Burr.

Laura liked Marcie very much. She tried to keep it that way. She was relieved, as time went on, that her friendship didn't get complicated by stronger feelings.

I like Marcie, and that's all, she mused to herself one time. It gave her a certain satisfaction that most women would not have understood.

As for Marcie, she was somewhat amused with Laura; with her modesty, which seemed so old-fashioned; with her shyness; with her books. But she felt a real affection for her. Laura wasn't much for gossip, but she always listened to Marcie's compulsive confessions. She was gentle and sympathetic. Her ideas were different, and Marcie listened to her with respect.

Laura wasn't pretty, but at certain angles, with certain expressions, she was striking and even memorable. Not everyone saw this quality; not everyone took the trouble to study her features. But they made a curious appeal to those who did. Her face was long and slim, and her coloring pale. But her eyes were deep and cornflower blue. If Marcie had studied them she might have seen more worldly wisdom than she dreamed of in her bookish roommate.

Laura had a good grasp on what it meant to be a woman; on what it meant to live deeply, completely, even when it didn't last; on what it meant to be a loser. And everyone must lose at least once before he can understand what it is to win.

Burr had come over the night after Laura moved in. He was of medium height but powerfully built, with a pleasant face. His brown hair was crew cut, his brown eyes sparkled zealously, like those of a man with a mission. His mission, apparently, was Marcie. He seemed to adore her; it was so plain, in fact, that it made you wonder if it was real.

He walked into the kitchen where Laura and Marcie were finishing the dishes, grabbed Marcie without a word to Laura—he didn't even seem to see her—and kissed her passionately. Laura self-consciously wiped a dish, put it on the cupboard shelf, and started to back out of the room.

"Burr! You could have said hello!" Marcie gasped when he released her. "Laura, don't go. This is—" But he kissed her again. This time when he let go she was mad. It was beautiful to see. Laura was exhilarated with the force of it. Marcie, who was always full of laughter, was walloping Burr with a wet dishcloth and calling him, "You bastard!" Her eyes flashed, and she swiped at his face with long meticulously pointed nails. Laura headed for the bedroom, but Marcie turned and caught her.

"Oh, no!" she said, pulling Laura back. "I want you to see what I married. I want you to tell me if I wasn't smart to get a divorce. Look at him."

Burr, his face damp with dishwater, was gently exploring a nail-inflicted wound with one finger.

Laura tried to back out, but Burr saw her then and smiled. "Hello, Laura," he said. "You'll have to forgive my charming wife. She's very emotional."

"I'm not your wife!" Marcie flared.

Laura couldn't help thinking it was all a joke. They both seemed to be enjoying it too much.

Burr ignored Marcie. "You've probably never seen this side of her," he remarked to Laura. "I used to get it once or twice a day, like medicine. Finally drove me to divorce." Marcie threw a towel at him and he smiled pleasantly at Laura. "But don't let it bother you. You'll never have to marry her, so you'll avoid the problem."

There was a stormy pause. "Have some coffee?" Laura said suddenly to Burr.

"I'll fix him a highball," Marcie sighed. "He hates coffee."

"I don't hate it. Why do you exaggerate, honey?"

"Well, you drink that horrible Postum crap, like all the grandfathers."

"It's not crap. It's a hell of a lot better for you than coffee, I can tell you that."

"Then why don't you live on it, darling?"

"If I wanted sarcasm tonight, I would have gone over to Chita's."

"That whore!"

"I—I think I'll turn in," Laura said softly and hurried toward the door.

"Don't be silly!" Marcie looked at her, chagrined. "You haven't said two words to Burr."

"She couldn't say two words, honey. You've been talking too fast. I couldn't either, for that matter." He went over to Laura and led her by the hand to a chair. "Let's talk about you," he said. "Sit down."

Laura felt ridiculous, but she obeyed him.

"Where're you from?" he demanded.

"She's from Chicago." Marcie handed him his drink and perched on the drainboard of the sink.

"Say something from Chicago, Laura." He grinned at her.

She shrugged and laughed, embarrassed.

"What does your old man do?"

Laura was startled to think of him. He had been out of her mind in the bustle of moving in with Marcie. "He's a writer—a newspaperman," she said. She looked so uncomfortable that Burr let it drop.

After a slight quiet he said, "What do you think of my girl?"

"Burr, please!" Marcie exclaimed, but he waved at her to shut up.

"You know you won't be rooming with her for long, don't you?" He smiled at Laura, and it looked like a warning sort of smile. It made Laura faintly queasy, as if she had already done something wrong.

Laura hated to compliment a woman. It was always

hypocritical because she could never tell the truth without blushing. The more she admired a girl, the harder it was to talk about her. She began to blush. "She's a very nice girl," she said hesitantly.

"Say it like you mean it!" Burr said. "She's a wonderful girl. Even if she is a shrew."

"Damn! Stop humiliating us, Burr. You aren't funny."

Burr stared at Laura, until she had to say something. "We get along just fine," she said.

"Sure. The first two days." He laughed a little.

"Burr!" Marcie exploded. "She's a girl, not an ornery bastard male like you."

"Well, I hope you two will be ecstatically happy," he said, and downed his drink.

"I won't be talked about like this!" Marcie said. She dropped down from the drainboard and started out of the room, but Burr caught her around the waist. He was sitting next to Laura, and he buried his face in Marcie's stomach. Marcie tried to grasp his short hair and push him back. Laura felt the old revulsion rising in her. Burr was doing nothing very shocking or immoral. He was just embracing the girl he loved, the girl who had been his wife. Laura knew that intellectually but her spirit retreated from the sight, repulsed.

"You know something, Laura?" Burr turned his head to look at her, still pressed against Marcie. "She acts like a damn virgin with me. She acts like she didn't have any idea what it's all about. Like we'd never been married at all, and I'd never—well, never mind what I did. She won't let me do it anymore."

"Burr, you're really repulsive," Marcie said, shaking her head at him.

"Am I?" He smiled at her.

"You know you are. Laura doesn't want to hear about that. Do you Laura?"

"I think I'd better get to bed," Laura said.

"That's a good girl," Burr said approvingly. "Always knows when to cut out. Laura, we're going to get along fine."

"Don't go, Laura!" Marcie ordered her.

Laura, halfway to the bedroom, stopped.

"Scram!" said Burr. As she shut the door behind her he added, "Sweet dreams, Laura. You're a doll."

Laura shut the door on them as he took Marcie, still resisting, in his arms. She walked uncertainly around the bedroom for a few minutes. It occurred to her that Burr would be grateful for the use of the bedroom, but Marcie would never forgive her for suggesting it. Laura ran a bath—it took fifteen minutes to get enough water to sit in—and sat contemplatively in it, wondering what her roommate was doing in the kitchen. She tried not to think of it. But when a thing revolted her it stuck stubbornly in her head and tormented her deeply.

Laura climbed out of the tub and dried herself, looking in the mirror as she did so. She had never liked the looks of herself very well. It still amazed her to think that this slim white body of hers; this tall, slightly awkward, firm-fleshed body, had been desirable to someone once. She studied herself. She was not remarkable. She was not lush and ripe and sweet-scented. On the contrary, she was firm and flat everywhere, with long limbs and fine bones. Her pale hair hung long over her shoulders and bangs framed her brow.

I am certainly not beautiful, she thought consciously to herself. *And yet I have been loved. I have loved.*

She gazed at herself for a moment more and the ghosts of old kisses sent shivers down her limbs. Then she rubbed herself briskly with the towel and put her pajamas on.

That's over now, she said to herself. *That happened a million years ago. I'm not the same Laura anymore. I can't—I won't love like that again. I'll work, I'll read, I'll travel. Some people aren't made for love. Even when they find it, it's wrong. I'm one of those.*

She picked up a book she had been reading—one of Burr's—and climbed into bed. There was a small lamp between the beds and she switched it on, drawing her knees up for a book rest. The covers formed a tent over her legs.

For a long while she sat and read about the mixups of other people, the people in the book. Then she closed it and put it on the bedside table. She turned the light off, but still she didn't lie down. She simply sat there in the dark, listening . . . listening . . . and heard nothing. She put her head back, resting, thinking about them in the other room, hating her thoughts but unable to shake them. After a while she slept, still sitting half-upright.

Much later, muscle cramps woke her up and forced her to lie down. She noticed that the light under the kitchen door was out. She pulled the covers over her shoulders, wondering what time it was. In a moment, all was silence again.

"Laura?" It was Marcie, whispering.

Laura sat up with a start. "Yes? Marcie, are you all right?"

"I'm all right."

"Is he gone?"

"Yes. For the time being."

"Oh. What time is it?"

"About three."

"You shouldn't stay up so late. You have to go to work in the morning."

There was a little silence.

"Laura?"

"Yes?"

"Were you ever in love?"

Laura felt a terrible wave of emotion come up in her throat. What a damnable time, what a damnable way, to ask such a question! She was defenseless against her feeling in the soft black night, with the soft voice of a lovely girl asking her, "Were you ever in love?" For a while she tried to keep her mouth clamped shut. But Marcie asked her again and she was undone.

"Were you, Laura?"

"Yes," she whispered.

"What was it like?"

"Oh, God, Marcie—it was so long ago—it was so complicated. I don't know what it was like."

"Was it good?"

"It was awful."

Marcie turned over in bed at this, raising herself on her elbows. "Wasn't it good sometimes? Now and then?"

"Now and then—" Laura whispered, "it was paradise. But most of the time it was hell."

"Did—did he love you? As much, I mean?"

Laura pressed her hands to her mouth, not trusting herself for a minute. Then she whispered, "No."

"Oh, I'm sorry." Marcie's voice was warm with sympathy. "Men are such bastards, aren't they?"

"Yes. They are."

After a moment of thought Marcie said, "Burr likes you."

"I'm glad." She couldn't stand to talk any more. "Goodnight, Marcie."

"Goodnight, Laura." Marcie sounded a little disappointed. But she said nothing more and in a minute Laura heard her roll over and fall asleep. Laura did not sleep again that night.

Chapter Three

I<small>F</small> L<small>AURA</small> <small>AND</small> M<small>ARCIE</small> went along together on greased wheels, Marcie and Burr did nothing of the kind. There was never anything real to argue about. But Burr couldn't pick up a book or clear his throat or make a suggestion without causing a disagreement. And he was as quick to snap at his ex-wife. The only times they weren't shouting at each other, they were kissing each other.

"You probably wonder why we keep seeing each other when we fight like this, "Marcie said to her one night.

"Do you love each other?"

"I don't know—Yes."

"Then I guess it doesn't matter if you fight."

"I hope it doesn't drive you nuts."

"No, not at all." Laura wouldn't even look up from her book. Marcie embarrassed her with these confidences. But she couldn't go on reading. She stared at the page and waited for Marcie to continue.

Marcie couldn't keep a secret. Things poured out of her, even intimate things, even things that belonged to her private soul and should have stayed there. Laura squirmed to hear her sometimes.

"We see each other," Marcie went on, "because we can't keep our hands off each other. We fight because we're ashamed of what we want from each other. At least, I am. I guess Burr doesn't have any shame. No, that's not fair. I guess he's the one who's sure he's in love. Sometimes I think I am, because I want to keep seeing him. And other times, I think it's just his big broad shoulders."

"Don't see him for a while," Laura said. "Or try talking less when you do. See what happens. Or do you just want to keep torturing yourself?"

"I guess I do," said Marcie with such a disarming smile that Laura had to smile back.

"Well, it's not my business. I can't pass out any helpful hints," Laura said. *I won't care about your personal
life, I can't,* she thought.

Marcie laughed, walking around the room, peeling
off her clothes. "Laura, you're a funny girl," she said.
"You're not like other girls I know."

"I'm not?" Laura felt an old near-forgotten sick feeling come up in her chest.

"No. Other girls love to talk about things. They love
to gossip. Why, I know some who would get started on
Burr and keep going until they had to be gagged. But
you're different. You just sit there and read and think.
Don't you get worn out doing so much thinking?"

"What makes you think I do so much?"

"Oh, I don't know. Don't you?"

"Everybody thinks."

"Not as much as you do."

"There's nothing wrong with it."

"I don't mean that. I mean—I guess I mean, why don't
you ever go out?"

"I do. I saw that musical last week."

"I don't mean with me. Or other girls. I mean with
boys."

Laura loathed conversations like these. She felt as if
she had spent her whole life justifying herself to somebody—mostly Merrill Landon, but others too. As if everything she did or didn't do had to be inspected and approved. If it wasn't approved it stuck in her craw somewhere and came up now and then to make her sick. "I'm
new in New York," she said. "I don't know anyone yet."

"How about Dr. Carstens? You said he was good-
looking."

"He's married."

"Well, the other one, then?"

"He's practically married."

"Well, how about the big shot?"

"He's a grandfather." She said it sarcastically.

Marcie threw her hands up and laughed. "Laura, I'm
going to have to do something about you."

"Don't do anything about me, please, Marcie." Something in the tone of her voice sobered Marcie up.

"Why not?" she said.

"I—I just don't want to be a bother, that's all."

"A bother!" Marcie came and sat beside her on the bed, wearing only the bottoms of a pair of blue jersey pajamas, cut like slim harem pants. Her breasts were high and full and unbearably sweet. "Laura, I like you. We're living together. We're friends. I guess I've made a bad impression on you with Burr and everything, but I want you to know I really like you. You're no bother." She smiled. "I'll get Burr to fix you up with Jack Mann. We'll go somewhere together. We need to get out. Maybe we'd quit quarreling if we didn't sit around this apartment all the time."

She paused, and Laura tried not to look at her.

"How about it?" Marcie said.

Laura was in a familiar situation. She'd been in it before, she'd be in it again, there was no escaping it. This is a heterosexual society and everybody plays the game one way or another. Or pretends to play it for appearances' sake.

"I'd love to," Laura said.

"Good! What night?"

"Any night." Laura wanted to shove her off the bed, to throw the covers at her; anything to cover up her gleaming bosom. She felt herself go hot and cold by turns and it exasperated her. She wondered how obvious it was. But even in her discomfort she knew it didn't show as much as it felt. She finally climbed past Marcie and out of the bed, making a hasty way to the bathroom.

"I'll call Burr," Marcie called after her.

Laura closed the bathroom door and leaned heavily against it, panting, her arms clasped tight around herself, rocking back and forth, her eyes shut. Spasms went through her and she shook herself angrily. Her hands stole downward in spite of herself and suddenly all her feeling was fixed in one place, clarified, shattering. There was a moment of suppressed violence when she clapped one hand over her mouth, helpless in her own grasp, and her imprisoned mouth murmured, "Marcie, Marcie, Marcie," into her hand. And then came relief, quiet. The trembling ceased, the heaving breath slowed down. She relaxed utterly, with only just enough strength in her legs to hold her up, depending on the door to do the rest. "Damn her," she said in a faint whisper. "Damn her." It was the first time she realized how strong her "friendly" feelings for Marcie really were and she was dismayed.

Laura went quickly to the washbowl and turned on the tap. She ought to be making some noise. People don't disappear into bathrooms for ten minutes in utter silence. At least not in this bathroom where every pipe had its own distinct and recognizable scream. In a few seconds Marcie was calling at her through the door.

"Laura? Can I come in?"

"Of course."

"We're going to make it for Friday. We'll see a show."

"That sounds fine."

"It'll be fun."

I will not look at her, Laura told herself, and buried her face in a washcloth. She scrubbed herself assiduously while Marcie chattered. *Damn her anyway, I won't look at her. She has no claim on me, that was a silly fool thing I did. I'll pretend it didn't happen. It didn't happen, it didn't happen.* She was afraid that if she did look it might happen again. She rinsed her face slowly and careful in water from the groaning tap, and still Marcie stood there talking.

Laura reached for a towel and dried her face. She hung the towel up again and turned to walk out of the bathroom, ready to ignore Marcie. But Marcie had slipped into pajama tops and looked quite demure. Except for her extraordinarily pretty face. Laura stared at her, as she had known she would, as she did more and more lately.

"We'll take in a show in Greenwich Village, because it's easier to get tickets—at least to this one—and besides, Burr knows—what's the matter, Laura?"

"What? Oh, nothing. Nothing."

"You looked kind of funny."

"Did I? I didn't mean to. That sounds fine, the show I mean." She hurried past Marcie into the bedroom.

In bed she cursed herself for an idiot. *I'm just an animal,* she berated herself. *I hardly know Marcie. I won't start feeling this way, I won't!*

Out of the past rose the image of another face, a face serenely lovely, a face whose owner she had loved so desperately that she had finally been forced to leave school because of her.

Why, they look alike! she thought, startled. *Why didn't I see it before? I must be blind. They look alike, they really do.* In the dark she pictured Marcie's face beside the other, matching, comparing, regretting. It tore at her heart to see them together. She wished the morning would never come when she would have to get up, bright and cheerful and ordinary, like every other morning, and look at Marcie's face again. And Marcie's breasts.

Morning came, as mornings will, and it went the same way. It was not intolerable. Laura was secretly on guard against Marcie now. Or rather, on guard against herself. She wasn't going to fall. Marcie loved a man —men, anyway—and Laura wasn't in any hurry to go through hell with her.

A curious change had come over Laura since the days of the terrible, and wonderful, college romance with a girl named Beth. She had been so frightened then, so lost, so completely dependent on Beth. She had no courage, except what Beth gave her; no strength except through Beth; no will but Beth's. She had loved her slavishly; adored her. And when Beth left her for a man, when she told Laura it had never been real love for her at all, Laura was wounded clear through her heart.

All these things were unknown to Merrill Landon; unknown and unsuspected. They would remain forever in the dark corners of Laura's mind, where she heaped her old hurts and fears.

She had thought of killing herself when she left school and went home to face her father. But she was young and her youth worked against such thoughts. Perhaps the very fact that she had loved so deeply and so well prevented her. She had learned to need love too much to think seriously about death.

Beth had left scars on Laura. But she had been a good teacher too, and some of the things she taught her lover were beginning to assert themselves, now that Laura was on her own and time was softening the pain. Laura walked tall. She felt tall. It wasn't the simple physical fact of her height. It was a curious self-respect born of the humiliation of her love. Beth had taught Laura to look within herself, and what she found was a revelation.

Chapter Four

The following evening Laura got home rather early after seeing a show with Sarah. She rode home on the subway with a dirty gray little man, repulsively anxious to be friendly. He kept saying, "I see you're not married. You must be very careful in the big city." And laughed nervously. Laura turned away. "You mustn't ignore me, I'm only trying to help," he whined. He babbled at her about young lambs in a den of wolves until she got off. He got off with her, still talking.

Laura wasn't afraid—just mad. She turned suddenly on the little gray man at the subway entrance and said, "Leave me alone or I'll call the police."

He smiled apologetically and began to mumble. Laura's eyes narrowed and she turned away contemptuously, walking with a sure swift gait that soon discouraged him. Something proud and cold in her unmanned him. At last he stopped following and stood gaping after her. She never looked back.

Laura arrived home, her cheeks warm with the quick walk with the victory over the little man. *God, if I could do that to my father!* she thought wistfully. She walked up the flight of stairs from the twelfth floor to the penthouse and swung open the front door. The living room was lighted and so was the kitchen. The bedroom door was open, the room showing a cool blue beyond the loud yellow kitchen. Laura walked in, swinging her purse, thinking of the ugly little man and proud of the way she had trounced him.

She stopped short with a gasp at the sight of Burr and Marcie naked together in Marcie's bed. "I'm sorry!" she exclaimed, and backed out, closing the door behind her. She collapsed on a kitchen chair and cried in furious disgust for half a minute. Then she stood up and went to the refrigerator, pretending to want a glass of milk just for an excuse to move, to ignore the hot silence in the next room.

For a while no sounds issued from the bedroom. Laura poured the milk busily and carried it into the living room. She was just putting a record on when the bedroom door opened and Marcie slipped out in her bathrobe. Laura had put her milk down. Just the sight of it was enough to make her feel green. She turned to Marcie.

"Hi," she said, too brightly. "Sorry I had to go and break in."

Marcie burst out laughing. "That's okay. Damn him, I *told* him to go home. I knew you'd get home early. I just had a feeling." She went up to Laura, still laughing, and Laura turned petulantly away. Marcie didn't notice. "We took your advice, Laura," she said. "We haven't said a word to each other tonight. Well—I said when he came in—'All right, we're not going to argue. Don't open your mouth. Not one word.' And he didn't. He didn't even say hello!" And her musical laughter tickled Laura insufferably.

Burr came out of the bedroom, looking rather sheepish, rather sleepy, very satisfied. He smiled at Laura, who had to force herself to wear a pleasant face. He was buttoning his shirt, carrying his coat over his arm, and all he said was, "Thanks, Laura." He grinned, thumbing at Marcie. "We're not speaking. I hear it was your idea." He swatted Laura's behind. "Good girl," he said. He kissed Marcie once more, hard, drew on his coat, and backed out the door, still smiling.

Marcie whirled around and around in the middle of the living room, hugging herself and laughing hilariously. "If it could always be like that," she said. "I'd marry him again tomorrow."

Laura brushed past her without a word, into the kitchen, where she poured the milk carefully back into the bottle, closed the refrigerator door, went into the bedroom, and got ready for bed.

Marcie followed her, laughing and talking until Laura got into bed and turned out the light. She wouldn't even look at Marcie's rumpled bed. But it haunted her, and she didn't fall asleep until long after Marcie had stopped whispering.

Jack Mann was small, physically tough, and very intelligent. He was a sort of cocktail-hour cynic, disillusioned enough with things to be cuttingly funny. If you like that kind of wit. Some people don't. The attitude carried over into his everyday life, but he saved his best wit especially for the after work hours, when the first fine careless flush of alcohol gave it impetus. Unfortunately he usually gave himself too much impetus and went staggering home to his bachelor apartment under the arm of a grumbling friend. He was a draftsman in the office where Burr worked as an apprentice architect and he called his work "highly skilled labor." He didn't like it. But he did like the pay.

"Why do you do it, then?" Burr asked him once.

"It's the only thing I know. But I'd much rather dig ditches."

"Well, hell, go dig ditches then. Nobody's stopping you."

Jack could turn his wit on himself as well as on others. "I can't," he told Burr. "I'm so used to sitting on my can all day I'd be lucky to get one lousy ditch dug. And then they'd probably have to bury me in it. End of a beautiful career."

Burr smiled and shook his head. But he liked him; they got along. Jack went out with Burr and Marcie before and after they got married. And after they got divorced. He was the trouble shooter until he got too drunk, which was often.

When he arrived with Burr on Friday night Laura was irked to find that she was taller than he was. She had made up her mind that she wasn't going to enjoy the evening—just live through it. She'd have to spend the time mediating for Marcie and Burr and trying to entertain a man she didn't know or care about. So she was put out to discover that she did like Jack, after all. It ruined her fine gloomy mood.

Marcie introduced them and Jack looked up at her quizzically. "What's the matter, Landon?" he said. "You standing in a hole?"

Laura laughed and took her shoes off. It brought her down an inch. "Better?" she said.

"Better for me. Very bad for your stockings." He grinned. "Have you read Freud?"

"No."

"Well, thank God. I won't have to talk about my night-mares."

"Do you have nightmares?"

"You *have* read Freud!"

"No, I swear. You said—"

"Okay, I confess. I have nightmares. And you remind me of my mother."

"Do you have a mother?" said Burr. "Didn't you just happen?"

"That's what I keep asking my analyst. Do I have to have a mother?"

"Jack, are you seeing an analyst?" Marcie was fasci-nated with the idea. "Imagine being able to tell some-body *everything*. Like a sacred duty. Burr, don't you think I should be analyzed?"

"What will you use for a neurosis?" Jack asked.

"Do I need one?"

"How about Burr?"

"I'm taken," Burr said. "Besides, you talk like a nitwit, honey. You don't go to an analyst like you go to the hair-dresser."

Marcie's eyes flashed. "Thanks for the compliment," she said. "I'm not as dumb as I look."

"Come on, Mother." Jack took Laura's arm and steered her out the door. "I see a storm coming up."

But it was dissipated when Marcie grabbed her coat and hurried after them.

After the play they walked down Fourth Street in the Village, meandering rather aimlessly, looking into shop windows. Laura was lost. She had never been in the Vil-lage before. She had been afraid to come down here; afraid she would see someone, and do something, and suddenly find herself caught in the strange world she had renounced. It seemed so safe, so remote from temptation to choose an uptown apartment. And yet here she was with her nerves in knots, her emotions tangled around a room-mate again.

Laura pondered these things, walking slowly beside Jack in the light from the shop windows. She was unaware of where she walked or who passed by. It startled her when Jack said, "What are you thinking about, Mother?"

"Nothing." A shade of irritation crossed her face.

"Ah," he said. "I interrupted something."

"No." She turned to look at him, uncomfortable. He made her feel as if he was reading her thoughts.

"Don't lie to me. You're daydreaming."

"I am not! I'm just thinking."

He shrugged. "Same thing."

She found him very irritating then. "You don't say," she said, and looked away from him.

"You hate me," he said with a little smile.

"Now and then."

"I messed up your daydream," he said. "I'm rarely this offensive. Only when I'm sober. The rest of the time, I'm charming. Someday I suppose you'll daydream about me."

Laura stared at him and he laughed.

"At least, you'll tell me about your daydreams."

"Never."

"People do. I have a nice face. Ugly, but nice. People think, 'Jesus, that guy has a nice face. I ought to tell him my daydreams.' They do, too." He smiled. "What's the matter, Mother, you look skeptical."

"What makes you think you have a nice face?"

"Don't I?" He looked genuinely alarmed.

"It wouldn't appeal to just anyone."

"Ah, smart girl. You're right, as usual. A boy's best friend is his mother. Only the *discriminating* ones, my girl, think it's a nice face. Only the sensitive, the talented, the intelligent. Now tell me—isn't it a nice face?"

"It's a face," said Laura. "Everybody has one."

He laughed. "You're goofy," he said. "You need help. My analyst is very reasonable. He'll stick you for all you've got, but he's very reasonable."

Burr, who was walking ahead of them with Marcie, turned around to demand, "Somebody tell me where I'm going."

"Turn right at the next corner," said Jack. "You're doing fine, boy. Don't lose your nerve."

"I just want to know where the hell I'm going."

"That's a bad sign. Very bad."

"Cut it out, Jack," said Marcie. "Where are we going?"

"A little bar I know. Very gay. I go there alone when I want to be depressed."

It sounded sinister, not gay, to Laura. "What's it called?" she said.

"The Cellar. Don't worry, it's a legitimate joint." He laughed at her long face.

Marcie laughed too, and Laura's heart jumped at the sweetness of the sound. It made her hate the back of Burr, moving with big masculine easiness ahead of her in a tweed topcoat, his bristling crew cut shining.

A few minutes later Jack led them down a few steps to a pair of doors which he pushed in, letting Laura and Marcie pass.

Laura heard Burr say, behind her, in an undertone, "It is gay," and he laughed. "You bastard." She was mystified. It looked pretty average and ordinary. They headed for a table with four chairs, one of the few available, and Laura looked around.

The Cellar was quite dark, with the only lights placed over the bar and glowing a faint pinky orange. There were candles on the tables, and people crowded together from one end of the room to the other. Everybody seemed reasonably cheerful, but it didn't look any gayer than any other bar she had been in. She looked curiously at Burr, but he was helping Marcie out of her coat.

"No table service," Jack said. "What does everybody want?"

They gave him their orders and Laura tried to catch his eye, hoping for more information about the place. She was curious now. There were checkered table cloths, fish nets on the wall, a lot of people—all rather young—at the tables and bar. The juke box was going and somebody was trying to pick up a few bucks doing pencil portraits, but no one seemed very interested. The customers looked like students. There were girls in cotton pants, young men in sweaters and open-collared shirts.

"They all look like students," she said to Burr.

He grinned. "I never thought of it that way," he said. "I guess they do, all right."

She stared at him. And then she looked around the room again, and suddenly she saw a girl with her arm around another girl at a table not far away. Her heart jumped. A pair of boys at the bar were whispering urgently to each other.

Gay, Laura thought to herself. *Is that what they call it? Gay?* She was acutely uncomfortable now. It was as if she were a child of civilization, reared among the savages, who suddenly found herself among the civilized. She recognized them as her own. And yet she had adopted the habits of another race and she was embarrassed and lost with her own kind.

They looked at her—her own kind—from the bar and from the tables, and didn't recognize her. And Laura looked around at them and thought, *I'm one of you. Help me.* But if anyone had approached her she would have turned away.

Jack came back with the drinks and sat down, passing them around. He drank a shot of whisky and said to Laura, "Well? How do you like tonight's collection?"

"Tonight's collection of what?" Laura said.

"Of nuts." He looked around The Cellar. "Doesn't anyone tell you anything, Mother? Burr, what's the matter with you? She's a tourist. Make with the old travelogue, boy."

Burr laughed. "I thought you didn't get it, Laura." He smiled. "They're all queer."

Laura's face went scarlet, but the candlelight hid it. She felt an awful tide of anger and fear come up in her at that word. She felt trapped, almost frantic, and she vented it on Jack. "Why didn't you tell me?" she said. Her voice trembled with indignation.

"Take it easy, Mother," he said.

"Tonight's collection!" she mimicked bitterly. "You talk about them as if they were a bunch of animals."

"They are," he said quietly. "So are we."

"We're human beings," she said. "We have no right to sit here and laugh at them for something they can't help."

"Can't help, hell," Burr said, leaning over the table toward her. "All those gals need is a real man. That'd put them on the right track in a hurry."

Laura could have belted ·him. She wanted to shout, "How do you know, you big ape?" But she said instead, "You're not irresistible, Burr."

"I don't mean that!" he said, frowning at her. "Christ! I only mean a man who knows the first thing about women could lay any one of these dames—even a butch—and make her like it."

"What's the first thing about women?" Jack asked, smiling, but they ignored him.

"If men revolt her and somebody tried to—to lay her —he'd only make her sick. No matter how much he knew about women," Laura said sharply.

"Any girl who doesn't like men is either a virgin or else some bastard scared the hell out of her. She needs gentling."

"You talk about us as if we were horses!" Laura flared.

"Us?" Burr stared at her.

"Us—us women." Laura's face was burning.

Burr watched her as he talked. "Some girls get a bastard the first time," he said. "It's too bad. They end up in joints like this swapping horror stories with the other ones."

Laura hated the way he talked. She couldn't take it. "What if the bastard is her father?" she said. "And he scares the hell out of her when she's five years old? And twenty years later some ass who thinks he's a great lover comes along and throws her down and humiliates and horrifies her?"

Jack remarked, with amusement, and probably more enlightenment than the others, "Jesus, we have a moralist in our midst." He looked at her as if she were a new species of fish.

"Damn it, Laura, that's the point," Burr said. "He *wouldn't* humiliate her. I don't mean some God-damn truck driver with nothing but a quick lay on his mind. I mean a considerate decent sort of guy—a sort of Good Samaritan—" He grinned and Marcie said, "God!" and rolled her eyes to the ceiling.

"—who really wants to help the girl," Burr finished.

"Why don't you try it?" Jack said.

Marcie's face darkened. "Yes, darling, why don't you prove your little theory? I'm sure we'd all be fascinated."

"Now damn it, don't you go yammering at me. I'm talking to Laura."

"Excuse *me!*" Marcie said.

Laura leaned toward her. "I didn't mean to start anything," she said.

"Nobody ever does," Jack remarked to himself.

"He said he could lay any girl and make her like it," Marcie said.

"I said," Burr said, turning to her and intoning sarcastically, "That any guy with any—"

"We know what you said, boy," Jack interrupted. "Let's keep it purely theoretical. Nobody has to prove anything. Burr loves Marcie and Marcie loves Burr. Jack loves whisky and whisky hates Jack. Laura loves animals. Everybody happy?"

Thinking over what she had said while Jack talked, Laura began to feel sick. She wished she had been perceptive enough to see where she was when they first came into The Cellar. But she took things at face value. They had entered a little bar and they were going to have a nightcap. Okay. What was so sinister about that? Why did it have to turn out to be a damn gay bar? And why did she have to react like an angry virgin when she found out?

They stayed long enough to get pretty high. They were stared at by the regular customers, but Laura was afraid to stare back. When she did, once or twice, she couldn't catch anyone's eye. She was ashamed of herself for trying to, but she couldn't help it.

There was a girl at the bar, standing at one end, in black pants and a white shirt open at the collar. Her hair was short and dark and there once again was that troubling resemblance to Beth. There were some other people with her and they were all talking, but the short-haired girl seemed somehow apart from them. Now and then she would turn and smile at one of them and say a word or two. Then she turned her gaze back to the bar or into her drink, or just stared into the mirror behind the bar without seeing anything.

Laura glanced at her now and then. She had an interesting face. It made Laura want to talk to her. *It must be the drinks,* she thought, and refused another.

"I see by the look in your eye," Jack said, "that you've had enough of this place. It's nearly midnight. Are you going to turn into a pumpkin?"

"God, I hope not," said Laura.

"It's *after* midnight," said Marcie. "Let's go. After all, poor Burr had to get up at six this morning to get to work. He's probably exhausted. Maybe we should leave him here and let him organize a night school for the ladies."

"Wouldn't be any takers in here," Jack observed, looking around. "They aren't ladies, they're lessies."

"Do you have to talk about them as if they were exhibits in a zoo?" Laura exclaimed.

"God, now *we're* quarreling," said Jack, laughing. But they weren't really, for it takes two to make a quarrel and he was feeling powerfully good natured with all that booze in him. "Leave us not forget our dignity," he told Laura. He enunciated with meticulous care, not to let the liquor trip his tongue.

Marcie laughed at him, and pulled Laura aside as they got up. "Let's go," she said, and Laura walked with her to the ladies room. It was a glaring change from the softly lighted Cellar. They were nearly blinded with a big bare bulb which hung by a frayed wire far down into the room and watched all the proceedings with an unblinking eye.

"You go first," Laura said to Marcie. There were few things less appealing to her than a public rest room —especially a one-horse job like this with its staring light, cracked mirror and mounds of used paper towels on the cement floor. She wet her comb slightly in the tap and ran it through her hair. The door opened and the girl with the short dark hair and black pants came in. She lounged indolently against the wall, studying Laura. Laura recognized her from the bar, but ignored her royally. Marcie was talking to her through the john door.

"How do you like Jack?" she said.

"A lot," Laura said, for the benefit of the girl in the black pants. Her voice was warm enough to surprise Marcie.

"I'm glad," she said. "I thought once or twice you were mad at him."

Laura's cheeks went red again. God, how she hated that! And there was nothing she could do about it. She pulled the comb hard through her hair, afraid to look

into the mirror. She knew she would meet the eyes of the
girl in the black pants. "He's very intelligent," she said
to Marcie.

"He's funny," Marcie said, coming out of the john. She
nearly walked into the strange girl and said, "Oh! Excuse me."

"My pleasure," the girl murmured with a grin.

Laura felt suddenly jealous. It was maddening. She
didn't know who she was jealous of. She wanted the other
girl to notice *her*, not Marcie. And she wanted Marcie
to notice her, too. She stood a moment in confusion and
then she said to the girl in the black pants, "Go ahead."
And nodded at the john. She said it to make her look up,
which she did, slowly, and smiled. She looked shockingly
boyish. Laura stared slightly.

"Thanks," said the girl.

She shut the door behind her and Marcie laughed silently, covering her mouth with her hand. But Laura
turned away, excitement tight in her throat. "Let's go,"
she said impatiently, dragging Marcie away from the mirror. She was afraid the strange girl would come out and
talk to them. She was anxious to get out of The Cellar,
out of the Village. She felt a pressing sense of danger.

Marcie turned to her as they went back to the table, and
said, "I'll bet Burr couldn't have gotten anywhere with
that one!" And she laughed. "She'd throw a hammer lock
on him and tell him to pick on somebody his own size."

Laura smiled faintly at her.

"Did you see how she stared at you?" Marcie said.

"Did she stare at me?"

"Yes, but she stared at me too. That's the awful thing
about Lesbians, they have no discrimination."

Laura suddenly wanted to scream at her. It was so
wrong, so false; so agonizing to have your lips sealed when
you wanted to shout the truth.

They left the smoky Cellar and walked a few blocks,
talking. Jack took a weaving course, and Laura had to
steer him with one arm.

"Let's take a taxi," Marcie said.

"It's only two blocks to the subway," Burr reminded her.

"Can't you ever spend a little extra on me?" she exclaimed. "Don't you think I'm good enough to ride in a

taxi? Don't you think I'm worth another buck once in a while? You did when we got married."

"Yeah, and I went broke. Subway's cheap."

"Well, I'm not!"

"Here, here," said Jack. He took a quarter from his pocket and held it up to Marcie's face.

"Heads," she said.

He flipped while Laura thought to herself what child's play it all was. Jack seemed unsophisticated now and Marcie and Burr had lost the beauty and excitement they seemed to generate together, even in the midst of their quarrels, perhaps because of them. *We all look tired and silly,* Laura thought, *and I wish we were anywhere but the middle of Greenwich Village flipping over a taxi ride.*

"Heads!" said Marcie. She poked Burr in the stomach.

"No show next week," he said.

"You don't think I care, do you?"

"Never mind, children, this is my treat," said Jack. He smiled foxily. "I'm no fool with money," he said. "I grow it in my window box. I give it all to Mother, here, and she invests it for me. Don't you, Mother?"

"Don't be an ass," said Laura, but she laughed at him.

"She loves me," Jack explained to Burr and Marcie. Suddenly he left them all to dash into the middle of the street, waving his arms wildly at a pair of headlights that were bearing down on him. They screeched to a halt with an irate taxi driver behind them. Marcie gave a little scream and the driver leaned out and said, "You damn fool!"

"You'd better get that punk home and give him some black coffee, lady," he told Laura as they started uptown. "If you don't mind a little advice."

"He's going to hate himself tomorrow," Marcie said.

"He's damn lucky he's gonna be *around* tomorrow," said the cabbie. They all talked about him as if he were deaf. And in fact, he was, for he had fallen asleep almost as soon as he got into the cab.

"Does he do this all the time?" Laura asked Burr.

"He's a great guy, Laura," Burr said, as if trying to bolster Jack in Laura's eyes. "He just flies off the handle now and then. I guess he's got problems."

At the apartment Laura got out first. Burr said, "I'll

wake him up, Laura," but she protested. "Just let him sleep," she said. "I'd hate to interrupt his dreams."

"I heard that," said a ragged voice from the shadows inside the car. "You're a doll, Mother. Sleep well."

"Goodnight," Laura said, smiling.

Chapter Five

SHE WAS under the covers and almost asleep when Marcie
tiptoed in after bidding Burr goodnight. She moved
around the room for a few minutes, getting ready for
bed. Laura was just barely aware of her. After a little
while she heard her turn the light off and cuddle the
covers around herself. The silence, up above the city late
at night, was deep, lulling, almost country-like. Only an
occasional stray horn filtered up to their level. It sounded
like a far-off echo.

"Laura? Are you asleep?" Marcie whispered.

"Yes."

"Oh." She was quiet for a minute. Then she whispered,
"I have to ask you something."

"Don't marry him. It'll never work."

"No, I don't mean that. I mean—does it make you feel
funny to see those people?"

"What people?"

"Queers?"

"They aren't queer, Marcie. That's a cruel word." Her
eyes were wide open now in the dark.

"What are they, then?"

"Homosexuals." She said it shyly.

"That's too long. Well, *does* it make you feel funny?"

"I don't know what you mean, Marcie."

"Well, I mean like the butch in the ladies' room. Didn't
she make you feel queer—I mean funny—" She laughed.
"—looking at us like she was a man, or something?"

"I guess so."

"She was looking at us when she was at the bar, too."

"She was?" Laura was amazed that Marcie would notice such a thing. "How do you know?"

Marcie laughed again. "I was looking at her," she said.

"You what?"

"Oh, not the way you think. I was just sort of looking
around and she was looking at our table. I think she

wanted to come up and talk to us but she didn't dare with the boys there. She knew we weren't gay."

"Is that what they call it—gay?"

"Yes. You know, it gave me the funniest feeling, her staring at us like that."

Laura turned over in her bed, very wide awake. She said to herself, *I won't ask her about it,* but she couldn't help asking. "What sort of feeling?" she whispered.

"Well, it was like . . . if I tell you you won't think I'm like *them,* will you?"

"Oh, no! Of course not." Laura felt the blood beating in her throat.

"It was like I wanted to know what she'd do to me. If we were alone, I mean. I was sort of curious. I wondered what it would feel like. Not that I'd ever let a girl—I mean—Laura, did you ever kiss a girl?"

"No," Laura said. In the dark she could lie pretty well. Her blushing cheeks didn't show.

"I did, once."

Laura put her hands to her throat and tried to still her breathing. "Did you like it?" she whispered.

"Not much. But I didn't dislike it. I was at that age. She was a friend of mine in Junior High. Maybe she turned out queer. I mean homosexual. She probably thinks *I* turned out queer," and she laughed. "She was always wanting to touch tongues."

Laura shivered. "Did you?"

"A couple of times. It gave me the creeps. With a man it's so lovely." Laura heard her turn in her bed to face her. "Didn't you ever do that when you were little? We used to do it a lot, just because it felt so awful. But Lenore was always wanting to do it with me when we got older. We were sort of best friends for a while."

Laura was sitting up, shivering, on the edge of her bed. She thought, *Dear God, if there is a God, help me now. Don't let me touch her. Please don't let me.*

Suddenly Marcie got up and crossed the small aisle between the beds. She felt Laura and sat beside her. "Stick out your tongue," she commanded, giggling.

"No!"

"Come on. I want to feel twelve years old again. I feel silly. Stick your tongue out." She was teasing and Laura could see the flash of gold hair in the moonlight that struck them from the window by the bed.

"Marcie, don't do this! Don't! You're playing with fire. Please, this is crazy." But her voice dwindled to a whisper as Marcie took her face in her hands, and she was powerless to resist. She let herself be pulled toward Marcie, felt Marcie's soft wet tongue searching for her own. Laura opened her mouth with a slight gasp. Her arms went out to grasp Marcie's slender body as a groan escaped her.

Suddenly the phone rang. Laura gave a little scream of shock. They were both utterly silent and motionless until it rang again. Then Marcie began to laugh. "Oh, wouldn't you know!" she said. "Saved by the bell. Saved from a life of sin." The phone rang again. "I'll get it," Marcie said. She sprang up from the bed. Laura sat frozen where she was, hugging herself, trembling and miserable. "It's probably Burr wanting to apologize for being such a skunk," Marcie said. She threw herself across her bed and lifted the receiver. "Hello? . . . Laura, it's for you." She put her hand over the mouthpiece and said, "It's Jack."

"I don't want to talk to him."

"Don't be silly. Talk to him."

Unwillingly Laura took the phone, sitting on the bed beside Marcie. She was so conscious of Marcie's body stretched out there beside her that she had trouble concentrating on Jack.

He said, "Mother, I've been an ass."

"I know."

"Forgive me."

"You're forgiven," she said. "Now go to bed. Goodnight."

"But I am in bed," he said. He was still pronouncing each word with elaborate care. "My question is this—did you really mean it?"

"Mean what?" said Laura looking at the faint moonlit curve of Marcie's leg.

"I'd swear you said you loved me," he said.

"You were dreaming."

"Do you?"

"No. Jack, please go to bed. Let me go."

"If I went any more to bed than I already am, Mother

—and don't think that was easy to say, because it wasn't
—I don't know where I'd be. Say you love me."

"No. Jack, it's late. I'm tired."

"Tomorrow is Saturday. You can sleep."

"I don't care what tomorrow is, I'm tired right now.
Now good-night."

"Do something for me, Mother."

Marcie turned over, lying across her pillow on her stomach.

"What?" Laura said softly, losing contact with him.

"Promise."

"Okay." She whispered it.

"Kiss Marcie for me."

"*What?*" Laura was shocked into total awareness.

"Good night, Mother," Jack said. And hung up.

Laura replaced the receiver and sat uncertainly on the
bed next to Marcie for a minute. She didn't dare to wonder what Jack meant. She had enough to do just keeping
her hands off Marcie's smooth behind. She felt afraid
of her.

*What would Beth have done if it had been me lying
there?* she wondered, and knew at once. Beth would have
laid down on top of her, her front to Marcie's back. Beth
would have kissed her neck, her ears, her shoulders. Beth
would have—

"Laura," Marcie murmured.

"Yes?" Her throat was dry, making it hard to answer.

"We'd better get to sleep."

It was all over, then. Laura had waited too long. Maybe
Marcie would have repulsed her anyway. Maybe her hesitation had saved her. On the other hand, maybe—Laura
burned to know. But Marcie had lost the playful, childish,
experimental mood, and was already half asleep. There
might never be another chance.

Chapter Six

At work on Monday Laura's phone rang halfway through the morning. "Doctors Hollingsworth, Carstens, and Hagstrom," she said, business-like. What a mouthful! she thought to herself.

Her listener apparently had the same idea. "Jesus, what a tongue-twister," he said. "What happened to Smith?"

"There is no Dr. Smith," she said, taken aback.

"Oh, don't be so damn formal, Mother. It's not like you. I thought I'd better apologize while I'm sober. I was drunk the last time."

"I know. How are you, Jack?" She smiled at the thought of his face.

"Bored. But healthy. I didn't mean to fall asleep in your face Friday night."

"It's okay. Forget it."

"Just for that I'll give you a free ticket to see my analyst. He's a great guy. He needs you."

"He needs me?"

"Have you got fifty bucks a week to spend on your salvation?"

"I haven't got fifty bucks a week to spend on my *groceries*," she said.

"Well, I guess he doesn't need you as much as I thought. But I'd be glad to stake you to your first session. After that it becomes habitual. You crave it. You'll find the money somehow."

Laura was laughing. "Give it to Marcie, not me," she said. "She's the one who loves to talk."

"You do some pretty good talking yourself."

"I do?"

"You got lyrical in defense of oddballs Friday night."

"I did not! Let's not go into that again anyway," she said. "Look, Jack, I'd like to talk to you, but—"

"I know, you're at work. So am I. Don't you **ever get** tired of work?"

"I'm on probation here. If I don't do well they'll fire me in June."

"So your poor virtuous hardworking little life revolves around that office."

"Now you're being an ass again."

"I'm telling you, Laura, you'd make a good soap opera. So would the rest of us. We're all a bunch of nuts in a million nutsy little soap operas. Will Burr marry Marcie? Will Jack take the pledge? Will Laura stick it out till June? Tune in tomorrow. We won't have the answer for you, but we'll sell you soap like all hell. Do you know why people buy soap?"

"To wash themselves."

"No. They like to play with themselves in the bathtub."

Laura had to laugh at him. "You fool," she said. "Jack, I can't talk to you, honestly."

"Okay. I'll call back."

"No, no call tonight."

"But I want to see you tonight."

She was unaware that she might have impressed him on their date, and he took her by surprise. "You do?"

"Well, don't sound so damn shocked. You're a nice girl even if you are ten feet tall. I'll pick you up at seven thirty."

"No, I can't, Jack."

"Okay, eight."

"I'm busy."

"The hell you are."

"I am."

"You lie! I have an instinct about these things. Eight sharp."

All at once Laura became aware of another voice calling her. "Laura?" It was Dr. Hollingsworth. He was standing over her desk and she looked up suddenly like a scared little kid.

"Yes, sir?" she said. She hung up without even saying goodby to Jack.

Jack Mann was not a pushy type. On the contrary, he was rather shy, although it rarely showed. He went to parties and hid behind a stream of wisecracks. He did the same thing on dates. He did it with anyone and everyone. It

was a sort of defense mechanism, a way of hiding his real
self, and he had done it for so many years that by now
it was second nature. Even people who knew him fairly
well, like Burr and Marcie, never saw beneath this facade
of witticism. They thought that *was* Jack: all funny asides
and not much serious straight talk. It was hard to take
him seriously. He didn't want that. He wanted to be
laughed at, to be amusing, and he usually contrived to be.
He was content to let people take him for a wag.

But once in a while he ran across somebody who made
him feel sick of the mask he hid behind. Somebody who
made him yearn to talk, quietly and seriously, about the
things that mattered to him. It happened when he was unlucky enough to fall in love. Or when he met a loner like
himself and felt an unspoken sympathy. It happened with
Laura.

It wasn't easy for him to call her back. It would have
been, if she hadn't appealed to his emotions. There were a
lot of girls he called just for the sake of their mutual
amusement, or just to amuse himself. But if he bantered
lightly with Laura it was more because he couldn't help it
than because he wanted to, more because he had found it
almost impossible to talk straight anymore.

At eight o'clock he showed up at the apartment. He
walked into the living room without knocking and said,
"It's me." When nobody answered he wandered through
to the bedroom and found Laura giving Marcie a home
permanent. "God, what a stink!" he said.

Laura looked up in surprise. "I thought you were kidding," she said. "About the date."

He smiled at her. She was dressed in tight chinos and a
boy's shirt. It was her favorite after work outfit. "You
weren't planning on the Stork Club, I see," he cracked.

"I wasn't planning on anything."

"That's a dangerous attitude, Mother. Always plan
on something. Avoid accidents."

"Jack, you can't have her," Marcie said. "I'll never
get this thing right without her." She waved a plastic curler at him helplessly.

"You're better off without it, doll. Take it from me.
Come on, we'll go as you are."

"Jack, I can't. I had no idea—"

"Come on, I want to talk to you."

"We can talk here."

"No we can't. Marcie's here."

"I won't listen," Marcie said with a smile.

"Besides, I can't talk," he said, and Laura caught a glimpse of the shyness hidden in him. "I'm sober as a post." He shrugged. "Let's go."

"I can't go like this."

"Never mind the pants, they're becoming."

For some deep buried and curious reason she was flattered. She stood there hesitating and Jack took advantage of her. He grabbed her arm and pulled her toward the door.

"Kidnaper!" Marcie wailed.

"My coat—" Laura said.

"You don't need one. It's balmy."

"So are you."

"Thanks." He guided her down the steps.

This was a switch for Laura. She had never been especially attractive to men before, starting at the beginning with her father and going right on up through college. She didn't look warm and soft and yielding. She was remote and involved in herself, aloof from everybody, men included. She didn't like them very much and they sensed it.

Now, here was a well educated intelligent male giving her the rush. She didn't understand it. Jack didn't appeal to her physically any more than any other man; in fact, a little less. He was small, wiry, rather owlish in his horn rims. He looked like an ivy league undergrad. She guessed he was about twenty-five. Laura was twenty. But she supposed that in five or six years she might be as cynical as Jack was. She liked to hear him say things she never dared to say herself.

They went to a little bar a few blocks away where Laura had gone once with Marcie for a beer. It was a quiet spot with a steady clientele.

They walked in and took a booth in the back. "I usually prefer the bar," said Jack, "but I always end up telling my troubles to the bartender. So we'll sit back here."

Laura felt a little strange walking into a bar in a pair of pants, but she was with a man and she hoped that made it all right.

"Just a beer," she said to Jack. A year ago she would have said. "Just a coke." And said it in a way to make him think she disapproved of liquor. But lately she had picked up a taste for beer. Beth liked it and so did Marcie. That was too much for Laura. There must be something to it. So she had gotten into the habit of having one now and then in the evening when she got home from work. It relaxed her. It made her feel that she could think of Merrill Landon without exploding, or of Marcie without crawling out of her skin. She felt like maybe she could stand it, living this way with Marcie, and everything would turn out all right.

The waitress brought their drinks, and Jack poured her beer for her. Then he downed his shot and drank some water. He seemed to be looking for a way to talk to her. "How long have you and Marcie been together?" He said finally.

That's an odd way to put it, Laura thought warily. "Since January," she said.

"Oh, yeah. I guess Burr mentioned it. He likes you." He smiled at her and she relaxed a little.

"Why don't Burr and Marcie get along?" she asked.

Jack shrugged and hailed the waitress. Then he looked at Laura. "They don't want to," he said. "It would spoil the fun."

"They love each other," said Laura.

"Physically, yes, they do."

Laura didn't like his definition. "Marcie says they might get married again."

"Yeah. They're just blind enough to do it, too."

"Marcie's not blind!"

"Sorry. A slip of the tongue." He grinned and drank the fresh drink the waitress had just delivered.

"Well, she's not," Laura said, disconcerted by his manner. "She really loves Burr—at least, she thinks she does."

He put his glass down. "Marcie hasn't learned to love yet," he said.

"You mean she doesn't love Burr?" She asked the question eagerly.

"No," he said quietly, studying her. "She loves physical excitement. She loves a big virile passionate sonofabitch to make a fuss over her."

"You're wrong," she said, disappointed. "She doesn't fight just for the sake of fighting. It's just with Burr. She never fights with me."

Jack laughed a little, privately. "That's because you're a girl, Mother," he said. "I can tell 'cause you got long hair."

Laura began to sweat under his searching eyes. "That's not the point," she said, exasperated. "Marcie has a sweet disposition. She's very quiet. It must be Burr."

"Quiet?" Jack laughed. "The way that girl talks she's about as quiet as Grand Central during rush hour."

"All right, she talks a lot." Laura was getting mad. "That doesn't mean she likes fights. Or men who thrive on them."

"That's just what it does mean. Believe it. It's true."

"You're screwy."

"You're in love."

"What?" She said it in a shocked whisper, staring at him, feeling her cheeks go scarlet. "What does that mean?" she said. Her voice was dry and small and her hands were wet.

Jack drank another shot. Then he put the glass down and leaned toward her over the table, his face serious. "You're gay, Laura."

Laura was speechless for a moment, surprised beyond her capacity to think or feel. Then an awful sick trembling came up in her throat. For a minute she hung between flight and a fight. She was furious, scared and humiliated. It never occurred to her to deny the truth. Jack had hit the bull's eye. She clenched her fists on the table top and violent things came to her lips. But before she could utter them Jack spoke again.

"Oh, don't look so damn mad. You're not the only one." He sighed, crushing his cigarette in a scorched ashtray. "I am too. So don't give me a martyr act." And he nodded again to the waitress.

Laura put her hands over her face suddenly, pressing one hand over her mouth to catch the sobs. She heard the waitress come up and turned her head to the wall.

"Same for me," Jack said.

"How about the lady?"

"Bring her a double whisky."

Laura could feel the woman looking at her curiously.
She wanted to evaporate. She hated the impersonal curiosity of this stranger. After a minute Jack said, "She's
gone."

Laura put her hands down, but she couldn't look at
him. She just said, rather hopelessly, "How did you
know?"

"Takes one to know one," he said with light sarcasm.

"*How?*" Laura demanded. "You're a man."

"So I'm a man. You're a girl. We're both queer."

"How did you know?" she said sharply, looking at
him now.

"You've got a crush on Marcie. That's how."

Laura gasped a little. "Is it so obvious?" she asked,
frightened.

Jack shook his head. "To me, maybe, but only because I was looking for it."

"You were? Why?"

"I'm always looking for it." He was bantering
again. She realized now that he had called her Laura
when he said it: *You're gay, Laura.* He was dead serious
then.

"Do you look for it even in girls?" she said.

"In anybody. You might say it's a hobby with me. I
spot one and I think to myself, 'Another poor bastard
like me.' It boosts my morale. I guess it's a case of misery loves company."

"I'd rather suffer alone," she said, not without pride.

"You'll get over that. When you learn your way around."

Laura was still trembling all over. "Listen to me,
Jack," she said, leaning over the table and brushing
the last tear impatiently from her cheeks. "I never
heard that word—gay—like you use it until our date
Friday. Nobody ever called me 'gay' before. I didn't
even know what it meant. But I'll tell you this: I never
touched Marcie. I've never tried to get away with anything with her. Never. She doesn't know and she never
will." She said this almost fiercely, but Jack only smiled
at her.

"Okay," he said. "Don't preach at me. I believe you.
I believe you haven't been climbing into Marcie's
bed after hours, anyway. But don't let Marcie fool you.

She can be wild sometimes. She gets in crazy moods and she'll do anything. I saw her go up to a bum in Central Park and kiss him once on a dare. A big ugly slob of a guy. It was enough to get her killed, but she loved it."

Laura was revolted. But not surprised. Not after what Marcie had done to her last Friday night.

"She couldn't possibly suspect me," she said stubbornly. "I never do a thing."

"You did plenty in The Cellar Friday night."

"I—I did?" She felt that old sick feeling come over her again.

"You looked at her like you had ideas. You held the door for her. You argued with Burr."

"But all I said was—"

"All you said was you were gay. To anybody who bothered to figure it out. Well, I did, that's all."

Laura's face was hot and she tried to defend herself. "All I did was defend them—homosexuals, I mean. I just said they were human beings, not animals. Is that against the law?"

"Not 'they,' Mother," Jack said softly. " 'We.' You're one of us."

"But Burr and Marcie don't know that," she said, almost pleading with him to agree.

Jack raised a finger to his lips. "Everybody will know it if you don't keep your voice down," he said. "Okay, Burr doesn't know it. As for Marcie, you live with the girl. You should know."

"She couldn't," Laura said, but she felt shaky.

"You aren't sure, are you? Why don't you find out?"

"How?" She looked at him eagerly.

"Ask her." He laughed to see her face fall.

"Damn you!"

"Okay. Don't ask her. Make a pass at her."

"You're mad!" Laura stared at him, shocked. "I'd never do such a thing! She might—why, my God, she might call the police. Or Burr. She'd hate me. I couldn't stand it. Jack, don't tell me to make a fool of myself. Do you want to get me into a tragic mess?"

"I want to keep you *out* of one, Mother. That's why I'm talking this way."

"Well, act like you did, then. You drag me down

here, when I didn't want to come in the first place, and tell me—" She swallowed convulsively. "—tell me I'm *gay*." She spat the word at him. "And then you have the gall to sit there and tell me to make love to Marcie—" She almost choked on the words. "—when you know damn well she'd probably be revolted by it, she'd—"

"Calm down, Mother, have a drink." And he held her glass up to her until she took it from him. It burned her throat but she was too worked up to care.

"Now," said Jack. "I asked you down here to tell you I know you're gay. And so am I. I want to be friends with you, Laura." She glanced up at him, and found that he was embarrassed, for all the liquid courage he was consuming, and it was hard for him to talk. "Damn it," he said. "I'm so used to talking like an idiot, I can't say what I mean anymore. I—I wanted to tell you—to warn you, Laura—I was in the situation you're in now. Once. Long ago. I fell for a roommate of mine, I didn't think he knew anything either. I didn't see how it was possible. I was so damn careful. I never said anything, I never *did* anything. Jesus Christ, I even avoided the guy. I went out of my way to avoid him. But I was nuts about him, Laura. I wanted him so bad it hurt. I'd lie there in the dark and tell myself, 'You can't have him, you can't have him' over and over. I'd say, 'Who the hell do you think you are? If you were the prettiest boy on earth he wouldn't look twice. And, Mann, you aren't the prettiest boy on earth. You're the ugliest.' Whenever we talked late at night, whenever we went anywhere together, whenever we touched I used to burn up inside, I used to die of it. I wanted to kiss him, feel him all over, just hold him. God, it killed me! But I never let on. Never. And one day—this'll give you an idea of what to expect, Mother—one day after all this noble chastity and virtue and self-denial crap I was going through, he came up to me and said, "Jack, I hate to say this, but I'm moving out."

"Why?" Laura asked softly, her forehead wrinkled with sympathy.

"Because I was gay. He didn't say it that way, of course. He didn't say, 'Because you're queer, you poor bastard. I'm sorry for you but I can't take it any more.' I could have stood that. But he just handed me a lot of bull."

Laura felt like crying again. But she only said, "Isn't that something to be grateful for? He tried, anyway."

"Yeah. He tried." He said it so acidly that Laura was afraid to say any more.

"There've been a lot since Joe," he said, after a while. "Just like there'll be a lot for you after Marcie." Laura tried to protest but he waved her down. "I know, I know, you're going to keep hands off. You're going to spend your whole life ignoring sex, ignoring what you are. Denying that you want it, running away from it. I was going to, too. That was twenty-five years ago."

"Twenty-five years ago!" Laura stared at him. "How old are you, Jack?"

"Forty-two. Surprised?" He smiled at her gaping astonishment.

"I thought you were maybe five years older than I am. Twenty-five or so. You *can't* be forty-two."

"That's what I keep telling myself. I can't be. But I sure as hell am."

"I don't believe it."

He grinned. "Good," he said. "I like to fool people."

"Why?" It seemed crazy. "What does a man care how young he looks? I thought that was for women," Laura said.

"Women and gay boys. Do you think some pretty twenty-year-old is going to fall for a fat bald, middle-aged bastard with not even a bankroll to offer? I'm ugly, Mother. That's enough of a handicap. When I start looking old, I'll quit."

"You're not ugly, Jack," she said gently, trying to console him.

But he took it with a sardonic laugh. "Only a Mother could love me," he said.

"Don't talk like this. You make me so sad."

"Ahhh, Christ," he said, and drank. He looked up at Laura, and she could see he wasn't focusing very well now. "I came here to talk about you anyway, not me. What did your father do to you when you were five years old?"

Laura started. "When did I say that? Did I mention my father?" she asked.

"Yes. In The Cellar. Probably as good a place as any."

"I—I didn't mean *my* father," she said.

"Don't fib to me, Laura. Let's be friends."

After a few moments, she said, "I can't talk about it, Jack."

"What did he do?"

"We—we were at a summer resort." It began to spill out of her. Jack had bared his anguish, and she felt suddenly safe with him, and needed. "We were there for a vacation one summer. We went fishing on the lake—Father and Mother and my brother and me." Her voice grew soft as she spoke. "The boat capsized. I was the only one he could save. I was the closest to him. Mother and Rod drowned." She shut her eyes with a little gasp against the old horror, still so sharp in her heart, like a big ugly needle stuck there to remind her she had no right to be alive. "All my life I've felt as if I killed them. He says I did. He hates me because I'm not his son. He hates me because I'm not my own mother, his wife." Jack seemed completely sober for a minute, staring at her with his brows knit. She put her head down and cried quietly. "That's all," she said. "I can't tell you any more."

"You don't need to," he said softly. "Jesus."

She took a deep breath and sat up, feeling as if she had lightened the weight of that leaden secret by sharing it. She was somewhat surprised to find that she was able to share it. She felt very close to Jack, as if they were now truly friends. Each of them had risked a little of himself to the other. And neither, now, was sorry.

With a sigh, she looked at her watch. It was getting late. "I have to get up early," she said, her voice still unsteady. "So do you. I know, Burr's always yelling about the hours. Let's go."

"One more," he said, holding up his glass. "I'm not quite through with you yet."

"I don't get it," Laura said to him. "We don't even know each other. This is the second time we've seen each other. And here we are talking like old friends."

"You're wrong, Laura. We know each other a lot bet-

ter than some people who've been acquainted for years.
Like Burr and Marcie. We know each other instinctively, don't you feel that? I wouldn't have called you
otherwise. You wouldn't have let me drag you out tonight otherwise."

"Don't talk about Marcie as if she didn't have a
brain in her head," Laura said.

Jack smiled. "You *are* in love," he said. "This is
serious. She has a few brains, Mother, she just doesn't
use them."

"She's not stupid," Laura defended her eagerly.

"She's not sacred either."

"I didn't mean that."

"Oh, yes you did. I thought Burr was once."

"Burr?" Laura stared at him. "Did you—were you—"

"Nuts for Burr? Yes. Once. When I first met him."

"What happened?"

"Nothing. Thank God. I got over it. I go for big
virile sons of bitches, just like Marcie. But I take care not
to room with them anymore."

Laura shook her head, a wry little smile on her face.
"Don't you ever fall for the gay ones?"

"I try to make a point of it." He grinned sadly. "Unfortunately I sometimes miss the point. If you know what
I mean."

"I'm not sure."

"It's just as well. I met Burr at work when he was hired
about four years ago. I knew he was straight."

"What's 'straight'?"

"Everything that's not 'gay'—so I pussyfooted around
the issue. I made him like me. I did his homework for
him. I made him laugh. I told him what to tell the boss.
I double-dated with him and Marcie and I was an usher
at the wedding. I was Number One trouble-shooter *after*
the wedding. He thinks I'm indispensible."

"But you—you don't still—"

"No, I don't. Not anymore. But I still like to be with
him. I like to watch them fight." He smiled at her. "You
do too."

She felt embarrassed, as if he were looking through her
clothes to her naked feelings.

"However," he went on, "I'm not under any lovely illusions about him being an intellectual giant. Or Marcie either. And I know damn well he won't give me a tumble if I just stick around long enough." He gave her a piercing look. "Those are your illusions, Mother," he said. "I suggest you drown them."

"What does that mean?"

"You can set Marcie's hair till the moon turns blue and she's not going to crawl into your bed to thank you for it."

"I don't expect her to."

"Sure you do. It's a mark of our breed. We're hopeless optimists. Otherwise we'd all commit suicide. We get a crush on somebody, and if he's straight we figure we'll just love him so much he'll *have* to turn gay. It doesn't work that way. Marcie isn't going to start kissing you just because you want her to."

Laura was incensed. "She already has," she snapped.

Jack's eyebrows went up. "When?" he said.

"The night we got back from The Cellar. She said she felt funny in there with all those girls staring at her. She said she used to touch tongues with a girl when she was in her teens, and she wanted to do it again. And she did. You—you—" She didn't know what to call him. "You had to call me up right in the middle, just when I thought—" She stopped herself. "Oh, this isn't like me," she moaned. "I never talk like this."

"Only to yourself, hm?" He laughed. "I mess up your daydreams and your affair. God! What more can I do? I'm becoming the Man in your Life, Mother." His laughter fizzled slowly, and Laura could tell he was quite drunk from the way he let his head hang for a minute. "You know," he said and wagged a finger at her, articulating cautiously, "I never have trouble thinking when I'm drunk. But my tongue gets sloppy." He laughed a little. "I say what I want to say, that's one good thing. But it sounds sloppy as hell." He finished the drink in front of him. Laura started to get up, but he caught her wrist and said, suddenly very serious again, "You're in trouble, Laura. Marcie's straight. Accept that. It's a fact. If she's playing games with you, she's doing it for private kicks, not to give you a thrill. And her kicks have nothing to do with being gay. They have to do with going out on a limb, with acting nuts once in a while. Maybe she's just pushing *you* out on a limb to see if you'll fall off. And you'll fall all right. Flat on your can." He stopped for a minute to focus his gaze on her. "Marcie's about as queer as Post Toasties, Laura. Take my advice: move out."

"But I can't! I won't!" she exclaimed defensively. "Why should I? I've done nothing wrong!"

"I hadn't either when Joe gave me the glad news."

"I'm not you. I've done nothing I'm ashamed of."

"No, but you will. If you hang around, feeling like you feel. You were saved by a phone call Friday night. What if my timing isn't so good next time?"

"I don't want to move out." She said it stubbornly like a thwarted child.

"All the more reason why you should."

Laura got indignant. "I've got more will power than you give me credit for and I'm not going to be scared out."

"What are you going to do for will power if she gets cold some night and crawls into your bed to keep warm? Or you take a shower together? Or she feels like pulling your nerves out by the roots one by one again, and makes you play let's-touch-tongues just for the hell of it? Just to see if she can get you sent up for sodomy? Be thankful you're female, Mother. At least your passion won't stand up and salute her."

"I've had enough from you tonight!"

"Okay, okay. But I advise you to find a nice butch somewhere and set up housekeeping in the Village. Or at least, cultivate a few lovelies down there so you'll have a place to let off steam when Marcie feels like playing games."

"You're drunk and repulsive."

"I know what I am, Laura. Don't change the subject."

"I'm going home."

"I'm coming with you." He got up unsteadily and followed her toward the door. Outside he stopped her. "Don't hate me, Laura," he said. And she couldn't, looking at him there in the pink glare of neon, short and plain, brilliant and miserable, offering her his curious stinging sympathy.

"I wish I could," she said and shook her head.

He smiled at her. "I'll walk you home," he said.

"You don't need to. Why don't you get a taxi and get yourself home?"

"Are you suggesting I can't walk?"

"No." She laughed.

"You are. Just for that I'm going to walk you home whether you like it or not. To prove I can."

"All right." But she had to lead him most of the way. Jack could talk better than he could navigate when he was high. When they reached the apartment she hailed a cab for him and put him in it. She stood there watching it pull away down West End Avenue, watching it till it was indistinguishable from the sea of red tail lights traveling with it. And she felt an awakening affection for him.

Chapter Seven

Iᴛ ᴡᴀꜱ ʜᴀʀᴅ to get up the next day. Not impossible, just hard. Discouraging. Her head ached, and she was dissatisfied with herself. For the first time she wanted to cut work. But she went and she did her job. It wasn't until the middle of the afternoon that she jumped to hear Sarah ask, "What's the matter, Laura? A little under the weather?"

Laura looked up at her. *Do I look that bad?* she wondered. "I'm a little tired. Why?"

"The reports are piling up," Sarah said, nodding at them.

Laura rubbed her forehead. "I'm sorry, Sarah. I'll catch up. I'll work late."

"Don't be silly!" Sarah laughed good-naturedly. "Catch up tomorrow. There's not that much of a rush."

But the next day she didn't quite catch up; she got farther behind, in fact. Burr and Marcie had kept her up. It was partly the quarrel and partly the torturing silence that followed it. he went to work still more tired than the day before. Dr. Carstens came in to tell her a story about one of his woman patients, and she was frankly irritated. He picked himself up from her desk, where he was sitting, and huffed out, offended. "Okay, don't laugh," he said. "The others thought it was funny."

Laura drove herself almost crazy with her errors that afternoon. When her phone rang she jumped half out of her chair. It was Jack.

"Good afternoon, Mother," he said. "I'm selling used tooth brushes. Interested?"

"No. I'm very busy. Goodby."

"I'll see you at eight."

"No."

"Eight-fifteen."

"No."

"Eight-thirty."

"All right! All right! All right! Goodby!" She slammed the receiver down and Sarah stared at her.

Laura decided to work late, and it was close to eight-thirty when she got up to go. The reports, though fewer, were still not done.

At the elevator the boy said, "Nice evening."

"Is it?" She answered him apathetically, involved in her own world.

"Yes, ma'am. It's really spring tonight." He smiled at her.

He was right. The air was soft and gentle, lavender and clear. It even smelled good, right there in mid-Manhattan, although that was probably an hallucination. Laura smiled a little. She hated to go underground to the subway, but it was late, and she wanted to get home in a hurry. It would really be gorgeous out on the roof tonight.

She walked in to find Jack and Burr playing checkers. Marcie was cross-legged on the floor, in velvet lounging pants and a silk shirt, humming while she covered the top of the round cocktail table with a plastic veneer treated to look like marble.

She smiled up at Laura, who paused to admire her. "Alcohol proof," Marcie said, rattling the table cover. "Mr. Marquardt gave it to me. We're advertising it for a new client, and they passed some around today. It sticks by itself. How do you like it?"

"It looks wonderful," Laura said. So did Marcie, her cheeks pink with enthusiasm.

"You've had it, Mann," Burr said, and Laura heard a checker smacking triumphantly over the board in a devastating series of jumps. "Touché, boy."

"Why don't you take up tiddly winks? I could beat you at tiddly winks." Jack sat with his elbows on his knees and his chin in his hand. He looked up at Laura without raising his head and smiled. She looked at him, absorbed in the idea that he had once been infatuated with the man beside him, and Burr had never known it. Burr thought he was as normal as himself. But of course, they had never roomed together. Suddenly Laura recalled that she had agreed to go out with Jack.

"Jack—" she began, but he cut her off.

"I see I have less allure than your typewriter," he said. He cocked an eye at her. "Well, never mind, I don't have so many friends I can afford to be jealous of their typewriters."

"Thanks, Jack," she said with a little smile. She turned to go into the kitchen, but he jumped up and followed her.

"Where the hell do you think you're going?"

"Straight to the icebox. I'm starved."

"We have a date. I'm taking you out to dinner."

"Why don't we just stay here?" she pleaded.

But all he said was, "No," and she understood that he had made his mind up and had something planned.

She was reluctant to leave Marcie, who looked so pretty. But the prettier Marcie looked, the worse Laura suffered. Maybe it would be better just to talk about her tonight. Talk to Jack about her. It sounded good.

"Okay, but let's get home early. I'm beat, I really am," she said.

"Whatever you say, Mother." He smiled, and she felt suddenly that it was terribly good to have him for a friend.

When they got outside she said, "Let's go over to Hempel's. It's only a block."

"No. We're going to The Cellar."

"Oh, God no! It's miles away. We wouldn't get home till midnight."

"A friend of mine wants to meet you."

"Who?"

"The name wouldn't mean anything. It would just scare you away, probably. She saw you when we were there last week. She likes your face."

"Oh, that's ridiculous. Come on, I'm starving. I've got to eat or I'll faint."

"This is a very interesting girl. She could teach you a lot."

"I know everything I want to know." He laughed, but she went on, "Jack, I'm not going to the Village with you."

But when they reached Broadway he hailed a cab and she let him put her in it, as she knew she would. "I can't.

I won't. I'm tired and hungry," she said. But she got in.
"I'll fall asleep over my typewriter tomorrow," she
moaned.

When they reached the Cellar she felt a lift of excitement in spite of herself. They arrived after the kitchen
had closed, but Jack was a regular customer, and they
were willing to fix him up.

They followed a waitress to a table. Laura walked with a
strange light queasiness in her stomach and sat down with
Jack feeling terribly self-conscious and looked-at, as if
every pair of eyes in the room was inspecting her. Jack
laughed, waving at somebody. "All my friends'll think I've
gone straight," he said. He gave the waitress an order
and she scuttled off. He leaned back in his chair to look
at Laura then. "Sorry you're here?" he asked.

"No. But I wish it was Friday night."

"Relax. We'll leave when you say the word."

She began to feel adventurous and crazy. Jack went up
to get them both a drink. She eyed it with suspicion, but
then she picked it up and drank half of it down, and it
hit her like a bomb, a big soft lovely explosion of warmth
in the pit of her stomach. She blinked at Jack, who only
smiled, knowing the feeling.

"How would you like to be in here some night," he said
slowly, "with Marcie beside you? And sit alone together
at that little table over there? And tell her you love her?"
Laura took another gulp of the drink and almost finished it. "And hear her say the same thing?"

Laura put the glass down with trembling hands. "Oh,
Jack, you bastard," she said, her insides aflame. "Cut it
out."

"You want it so badly," he said, "that it's tearing your
guts out. And it's never going to happen. So open your
eyes. Look around. There are some beautiful women here
tonight. There's one as pretty as Marcie." He squinted
over her shoulder. Laura turned around indignantly to
look, and saw a charming face framed in short brown
curls smiling at a table partner. She looked up at the sudden sight of Laura's own face, pale and compelling.

"Nobody's as pretty as Marcie," Laura told him.

"Somebody was," Jack said, with his peculiar intuition
taking him straight to the point.

"What do you mean?" Laura said defensively, and finished her drink.

"Whenever you know damn well what I mean," he said with a smile, "you ask 'what do I mean.' As if I were nuts. Well, I'm not. Give me your glass." He took it and got up. "Never thought you'd beat me to the bottom, Mother." He peered into it with one eye and then left to get it refilled.

Laura leaned back in her seat and shut her eyes. After all, what did it matter if she were here? She felt wonderful. She had put in a terrific day's work, she had a right to a little fling. Her body glowed through its whole length. Marcie loomed in her mind like a lovely apparition, not quite real.

I'll have her someday, Laura thought. *No matter what he says.*

She looked around her, half consciously searching for someone. But the girl in the black pants wasn't there. The crowd was much the same as before, but thinner. The artist was walking around with his sketch pad, stopping to talk to tablesful of friends. The bar was crowded, more than the tables.

Jack came back, put a fresh glass in front of her, and sat down. "Now. What was her name?" he said.

Laura opened her eyes slowly. "Who?"

"Number one."

She wrinkled her nose in some disgust. "Jack, she wasn't a number. Or an animal. Or part of a collection."

"What was she?"

"She was a wonderful girl."

"Beautiful like Marcie?"

"No. Beautiful—but not like Marcie. They have some features in common. But Beth was taller. She was quite boyish." She felt a little embarrassed suddenly, putting it this way. "Marcie's very feminine."

"What are you?"

Laura stared at him over the rim of her glass. "What am I?" she repeated, confusedly. "Do I have to be anything? I don't know."

"You'll find out fast enough," he said. "Beth probably taught you a lot. The one who brings you out always does."

"Yes, she did," she said dreamily. Beth had loosened her up wonderfully when they were together. She had taken her by the hand and led her to herself. She had also abandoned her there. But Laura couldn't hold anything against her. That had been a sacred love and always would be in her memory, like all loves that are broken off in full passion. If they had been together till it had worn off a little, Laura might have left her without any desperate regrets and loneliness. She might have been able to see Beth as a whole person, not as an ideal. But it hadn't happened that way, and Beth still looked like a goddess to her.

Now, in a new world, with new people, she wasn't sure what she was. With Marcie she felt aggressive and violent. Here, in the Cellar, with so many eyes on her, she felt timid.

Jack grinned at her. "You're a boy," he said. "With Marcie, anyway. My friend won't like that."

Laura put her glass down. "I'm a girl," she said. "Don't look at me that way."

Jack put his head back and laughed. "Correction," he said. "You're a girl. Why don't you move down here where you don't have to be either?"

"Everybody has to be one or the other."

"You're too literal, Laura. Cut off your hair. Wear those pants you look so nice in. Get some desert boots, a car coat and some men's shirts, and you're in business."

"Jack," she said, "You are positively revolting."

"That's the uniform," he said. "Can't join the club without it."

"I don't want to join."

"Yes you do. You feel good in pants. You swagger."

"I do not!" But she was laughing at him. At herself.

"Shhh!" he said softly. "Or they'll cut you off. Here comes dinner."

The presence of the waitress made it impossible to talk. She set a delectable dinner in front of Laura. But somehow, after the first few bites, it lost its appeal. She sat gazing at the plate, wondering where her enormous appetite had gone, pushing a mushroom dreamily from one side to the other. Jack smiled, watching her. He leaned over the table on his elbows and picked up her knife.

"Laura," he said, pointing at her mushroom. Then he pushed another one slowly across the plate from the other side. "Marcie," he said, nodding at it. The two mushrooms made contact south of the fried potatoes, and Laura felt crazy, watching it. It made her smile; she thought it was ridiculous. It made her want to laugh, and it brought a warm, unwanted, urgent feeling up in her legs at the same time. She pushed "Laura" behind the steak.

"Ah," said Jack. "Laura's afraid of Marcie. But Marcie's not afraid of anything. Marcie's a little heller. Here she comes." And he pushed his mushroom after hers. Laura felt her cheeks get hot.

"I'm not going to run away," she said, and took a large swallow from her drink, letting "Laura" stay put.

"Okay, be a hero," said Jack. "Make it easy for her. Look at that little bitch!" and he scooped "Marcie" over "Laura," back and forth, the passage facilitated by the gravy. "She's nuts. She's on a kick. She wants you to make a fool of yourself."

Laura wouldn't watch. She finished her drink for an excuse not to look.

"But look at Laura," Jack went on. "She can't stand it. Where Marcie goes, Laura goes." And he pushed "Marcie" and "Laura" around the plate together.

"Stop it, Jack. Get me another drink."

"Here's where Laura goes crazy."

"Now stop it!"

He crammed the two mushrooms into the potatoes, helter skelter, one over the other. "Laura got what she wanted," he said, after a minute, looking up at her briefly. "But see what happens to her." And with one sudden cruel stroke he sliced "Laura" in half. Laura gave a little start. " 'Marcie' got bored with the game," he explained.

Laura laughed nervously. "Now cut it out and get me a drink," she said.

He got up smiling, without a word, and went to the bar. Laura couldn't look at the plate. She signaled the waitress, who came over with a water pitcher.

"Will you take this out please?"

"Something wrong with it?"

"I can't eat mushrooms."

"Well, why dincha say so!" She took the plate with an angry "Jeez!" muttered under her breath.

Jack came back to find her laughing. "Couldn't take it, hm?" He nodded at the vacant space where the plate was, and then looked at Laura. "Want to leave?"

"No. I don't want to go anywhere, Jack. Let's just sit here a while and talk."

"About Marcie?"

"About Marcie." She laughed again.

"By Jesus, you're a pretty girl," he said quietly. "I didn't realize it till now. You ought to get soused more often."

"I'm not soused, I'm in love."

He gave a snort of disbelief. "Okay not-soused and in-love. You're headed straight blind for misery. You know that."

"My eyes are wide open. She'll never love me."

"Don't tell me. Tell yourself. Believe yourself."

"I do."

He shook his head and laughed a little. "I see it coming and I tell you 'Look out, she's murder' and you say 'You're absolutely right' and then off you go to slit your own throat." He leaned over the table seriously. "Leave her, Laura," he pleaded, and took her by surprise with his earnestness. "It's no good falling for a straight one. Believe me."

"I won't leave her," she said stubbornly. "I know what I'm doing."

He leaned back with a sigh. "Then at least look at somebody else," he said. "Look at Beebo. She's cruising you like mad."

"Who's Beebo? I wouldn't look at anybody with such a ridiculous name. What's cruising?"

"Beebo's a friend of mine. And cruising—well—you'll catch on." He grinned.

Laura turned warily around. At the bar sat the handsome boyish girl she had admired the week before. She was gazing boldly, but without great interest, at Laura. When Laura turned to see her she smiled, very slightly.

Laura turned back to Jack. "Is that Beebo?" she asked. "In the black pants?"

Jack laughed at her. "You mean tan shorts?"

Laura looked again. "Well, she had on black pants last time."

"Did she?" He grinned. "She says you had on a blue dress with a white collar. You did, too. I remember it. She liked it."

Laura stared at him and then got indignant. "What's she doing, remembering my clothes like that? That's silly."

"So are you. You noticed hers."

"I just—oh, damn! She followed us into the john."

"I know. She talked to me before she went after you. I told you, Mother. She likes your face."

"She likes Marcie's. That's why she followed us," she snapped.

He shook his head "no."

"How do you know?" Laura flared, the jealousy working in her.

"I know Beebo," he chuckled.

Laura was getting curious. She finished her drink in three big swallows, which made Jack laugh. "Is she a friend of yours?" she said.

He shrugged. "More or less. I keep running into her at parties. For years we ran into each other before we finally got acquainted. I like her. She's a hellion, but I like her. She's a cynic like me."

"What a pity." Laura feigned unconcern, running a wet finger around the edge of her glass. "She looks like Beth," she said. "A little."

Jack blew smoke through his nostrils from a freshly lighted cigarette. "That means you like her," he said.

Laura refused to honor such nonsense with an answer. She was rather drunk now. She turned again to look at Beebo. Beebo was still gazing at her, and she winked, with that faint private smile still on her face. Laura turned quickly back to Jack. "Is she coming over?" she said, feeling slightly elated.

Jack was grinning past her at Beebo and nodding. At her words he glanced at her. "No," he said. "She's an uppity bitch."

Laura was disappointed.

"Another drink?"

"One more. That's all. What time is it?"

"Eleven-thirty."

"No!" She tried to collect her thoughts, to right her time sense, while Jack fetched the drinks. When he came back she said, "How many drinks have I had?"

"Jesus, Mother, what a thing to ask a man. I can't even keep track of my own."

"I'm lost," she said. "I've lost count."

"Shall we take off, Mother mine?" Jack said, very carefully.

Laura tried to clear her head by shaking it and pressing her eyes shut. "I guess we'd better," she said.

"I guess we *have* to. It's four o'clock. They're closing."

"Four!" Laura came half awake at this.

"Four o'clock," he repeated elaborately.

"Oh, God. Oh, my head."

"Never mind, Mother, you can stay with me tonight. I'll try to keep my hands off you." He laughed to himself.

Laura saw Jack looking up at somebody with a grin and heard him say, "Hi, doll. I want you to meet my mother. Mother, look alive." He squinted at her doubtfully. "If possible," he added.

Laura looked up and saw a startlingly handsome face gazing down at her: black hair, pure blue eyes, a slight smile that widened a little when Laura turned her face up.

"Hello," Beebo said. "Laura." Her smile gave emphasis to the way she said Laura's name.

Laura put her hands to her head dizzily. "You look just like Beth," she murmured.

At which Beebo grinned, turning to Jack. "Three aspirins and some warm tomato juice," she said. "First thing when she gets up. She'll live."

Laura watched her, fascinated, half smiling.

Beebo turned back to her and returned the smile. Then she reached into her pocket and pulled out a dime. She flipped it in the air and then dropped it insolently in front of Laura. "Here's a dime, sweetheart," she said. "Call me sometime." And with a little grin at Jack, she turned and left them.

Laura stuck her chin out indignantly. She was not too drunk to be insulted. "Well, thanks a bunch, your majesty!" she said sarcastically to Beebo's back. She could hear Beebo laughing but she wouldn't turn around. She was already headed for the door.

Laura let Jack drag her to his apartment, three blocks away. He took her up a few stone steps into a long dim hall, and opened the first door on the left. He steered her to his bed and pushed her till she collapsed backwards on it. She fell asleep at once. Jack pulled her shoes off and her skirt, with total unconcern for her feminity, and got her under the covers.

Laura slept like a stone, a deep almost motionless sleep that could have lasted far into the next day. But Jack got her up at seven-thirty. She had three and a half hours sleep, on virtually no dinner and eight or ten stiff drinks. She felt strange new pains all over. Jack was used to such excesses, though he tried to ration himself to one or two a week. He took it pretty well in stride, but Laura felt awful. Her first words when Jack shook her were, "Oh, God! What time is it?"

"Seven-thirty."

She turned over on her stomach and put her head down on the pillow. "Where's Marcie?"

"At home. Where else?"

"What time is it? Oh, I asked you that. My head hurts."

"Take these, Mother," he said, handing her some aspirin and a glass of water.

"I don't think I can swallow."

"That's a chance you'll have to take. Here we go." He popped the pills into her mouth and gave her the water. She gulped them convulsively. "That'll see you through till—" He looked at his watch. "—about noon. After that, take three more and a No-Doz tablet. And hit the sack tonight about six. It's Friday. You can sleep for two days."

"I will, too." She rolled gingerly to a sitting position, and looked at Jack with aching eyes. "You did this to me," she said mournfully.

"Be fair, Mother. I said I'd go whenever you wanted to. I kept asking and you kept saying no."

She stared at him, disbelieving. "Jack, you louse. You should have dragged me out, you knew I—what's that?" There was a dime on the bed table.

Jack grinned at her. "Beebo's calling card," he said.

Laura remembered it in a flash, although the rest of the evening was little more than a blur. She picked it up and threw it angrily across the room. "Give it back to her for me," she said. "All I remember about last night is that awful girl and those awful mushrooms! God!"

Jack went out of the room laughing.

Chapter Eight

THE FIRST THING Laura did when she got to work was to call Marcie.

"Where were you?" Marcie demanded. "I was just going to call you. I was worried sick."

"You were?" She felt a momentary relief from her headache.

"Are you all right?"

"I think so. It got so late. We were talking. I finally spent the night—" It suddenly occurred to her, as if a brick had dropped on her tender head, that she had spent the night in a man's apartment. For the first time in her life. Never mind that it was an innocent stay, or a short one. Or that the man had no designs on her. It was the idea of the thing.

"I spent the night with Jack," she blurted. Marcie was silent, having suspected as much, but not sure what to say. And it was then Laura realized that she had said the best possible thing. Even if it hadn't happened it would have been the best thing to say. Marcie didn't know either of them was gay. She only knew they were man and girl and they had spent a night together. What could sound more normal, more straight? Immoral, maybe, slightly immoral. But straight.

Marcie laughed finally.

"Is it funny?" Laura said.

"I'm sorry," Marcie said through her giggles. "I never dreamed you and Jack would hit it off like this. He must really like you, Laur." She sobered suddenly. "He never took much to the other girls we fixed him up with."

Laura squirmed a little.

"But he talked you up for half an hour before you got home last night. He thinks you're very pretty."

Laura felt grateful to him. He must have done it to enhance her in Marcie's eyes, even if he did disapprove of her infatuation.

264

"Did he say that?" she said, pleased.

"He did. And he's right."

Laura was taken aback. Then she said quickly, "You're both crazy."

"No, you are. We're right. You never looked at yourself, you silly girl. You don't *know* what you look like."

"Do you?" It sounded stupid, but it came out in spite of her.

"Sure. I've looked at you when you weren't noticing."

When could that have been?

"I think you have a fascinating face."

"But not pretty."

"Lovely."

"Marcie, listen to me, I—" She was shaky, mixed up from the hangover and the unexpected flattery. She should have said something terrible, something intimate, if Dr. Hollingsworth hadn't come in early. He nodded at her as he walked through the office. Sarah was still in the wash room putting on her face.

" 'Morning, my dear," said the doctor with a sort of modified bow as he sailed past.

She returned the greeting and Marcie said, "I'll get you in dutch. You'd better hang up. Will you be home tonight?"

"Yes. I'll be home."

"Good girl. See you at six."

Laura hung up bewildered. She felt good and she felt lousy. Her head was throbbing but her heart was high. She wanted to talk to Jack. She didn't care who caught her. She picked up the phone and dialed his office.

"I just talked to Marcie," she said, unable to keep the pleasure out of her voice.

He sensed her excitement. "Did she propose?" he said, wryly amused.

"No, you idiot!" Laura burst out laughing. "She said I was beautiful." Unconsciously she exaggerated.

"Jesus, she has a screw loose," he said.

"She said you were talking about me before I got home. Thanks, Jack."

"Listen, Mother," he said. "Let's get this straight. I want her to think we're nuts for each other. I also think you're a pretty girl, and I said so. But I didn't say it to get Marcie all steamed up."

"Well, I don't care why you did it. She is steamed up."

"You're making a mountain out of a molehill."

"Oh, Jack, be nice to me! I'm in love, for God's sake!"

"Okay, you're in love. I believe you. Worse things have happened. I'll have to work a drastic cure on you."

She laughed at him. "Too late," she said.

"You're not going to get stabbed like I was, Laura."

She recalled the defenseless mushroom with a little shiver of distaste. "Don't be morbid," she said.

"I'm a realist."

"You're blind. She's falling for me. I can tell. She must be, or she wouldn't—" Here Sarah walked in. "Jack, I'll call you back," she said.

"I dare you to. Call me back this afternoon, when you're hung over to your knees, and tell me how much you're in love."

"I'm telling you now!"

"You talk like a fish. Go on, type your damn reports. Send some poor bastard up for TB. Or enlarged heart. At least it'll be a normal disease."

She hung up with a smack. *He's a morbid miserable old man,* she thought. *I'm not that cynical yet.*

"Was that your friend?" Sarah said. "Jack?"

"Yes." She put paper and carbons into her machine.

"He's giving you the rush, hm?"

"I guess so."

"That's one of us, anyway."

Laura looked at her, and caught an expression of frustration on her face that made Laura's problems seem smaller. Sarah was plain. She was unremarkable. But so nice. It was depressing. Laura put a hand on her arm. It would cheer her up if she could cheer someone else. "Maybe Jack could fix you up with a friend of his," she said. "We could make it a foursome."

Sarah shook her head. "They all want to know 'Is she pretty?' Never mind if she's nice or wants a man so badly she could . . . excuse me, Laura, I sound like an old maid already. I haven't given up yet."

Laura studied her on the way down in the elevator. She ached to say the things she thought, but she didn't know Sarah well enough. They were walled up in them-

selves. *Poor plain Sarah,* she thought. *I'm not beautiful
either. But I've been loved. I know love and I can tell
you, you don't have to be a beauty to feel passion. Sometimes it helps if you're not. I wonder if you know that
already.*

"I'll talk to Jack," she said as they walked out.

"That'd be awfully nice, Laura." She laughed diffidently. "At twenty-eight you begin to feel kind of frantic," she said.

Outside she left Sarah and walked toward the subway
station. All the way she noticed the women, as she never
had before. She was at a loss to explain it. Before, she
had always hurried, on her way somewhere, with a
deadline to beat, somebody to meet, things on her mind.
Now—perhaps it was the fatigue that made her slow
—she sauntered, looking at the women.

Looking at their faces: sweet, fine-featured, delicate, some of them; others coarse, sensual, heavily female. They all appealed to her, with their soft skirts,
their clicking heels, their floating hair. It caught
in her throat, this aberration of hers, in a way it
never had until that moment. It suffused her. She surrendered quietly to her feelings, walking slowly, looking without staring but with a warm pleasure that
made her want to smile. She had trouble controlling
her mouth.

God, I love them, she thought to herself, vaguely surprised. *I just love them. I love them all. I know I'm nuts,
but I love them.* She stopped by a jewelry window where
an exquisite girl was admiring a group of rings.
She was all in gray, as fine and soft as twilight. Gray
silk graced her slim legs, gray suede pumps with the
highest heels were on her feet. A gray suit, impeccably
tailored, terribly expensive—gray gloves—a tiny gray
hat. Laura had never liked gray much before, but suddenly it was ideal on this cool dainty little creature,
with her small nose and moist pink lips. She was extremely pretty. She looked up to find Laura gazing at
her, collected herself with pretty confusion, and went
off, pulling a recalcitrant gray poodle after her. Laura
had not even noticed it till it moved. She looked after
the girl for a minute with a foolish smile.

When she finally reached the subway she collapsed

on a seat, exhausted. She wanted to get home and into bed so badly that she could hardly wait.

She was late getting home but even so, Marcie had not arrived. She wanted very much to see her, but there was no help for it. She would have to wait. She fell on her bed, meaning to rest for a minute before she took her bath. But so tired was she that before five minutes had passed she was asleep. She woke up to hear small sounds in the bedroom, and it seemed like perhaps half an hour had passed.

She opened her eyes and found herself all tangled up in her clothes, her shoes still on, her dress wrinkled. There was a light on, the small table lamp between the beds. She pulled herself up and turned around. Marcie was standing in the bathroom door, with a frame of light around her, holding her toothbrush and smiling at Laura. She was all in white lace, in a short gown that barely reached her thighs. Laura smiled at her and blinked, shaking her head slightly.

"Know what time it is?" Marcie said.

"About seven."

"Quarter of twelve." Marcie laughed at her surprise. She walked over to her bed and stood beside her for a moment. She smelled gorgeous—intoxicating, sweet and clean, faintly powdered, warm and damp from her bath. She looked sleepy, soft, very feminine. Laura began to tremble, desperate to touch her, afraid even to look.

"You must have been awfully tired, Laur. You've been asleep for hours."

"I could sleep till Monday and never wake up," Laura murmured. She spoke without looking at Marcie. She couldn't. The scent of her was trouble enough.

"Burr and I went out for dinner. We didn't want to bother you."

"Did you have a nice big fight?" Irresistibly Laura's eyes traveled up Marcie to her face.

Marcie sighed. "We always have a nice big fight."

"You must enjoy them."

Marcie sat down beside her. "Don't talk that way, Laur," she said. "I wish I could get interested in books, like you."

Laura smiled at her, so close, so distant.

"Help me, Laura," she said.

"How?" Laura felt herself on very shaky ground.

"I don't know how," Marcie said impatiently. "If I knew I could help myself. There must be something in life besides fights, Laur."

"Don't call me Laur."

Marcie looked at her in surprise. "Why not?"

"Somebody else used to call me that. It still hurts a little."

"I'm sorry. I remember, you told me about him."

Laura felt confession working itself urgently into her thoughts. She wanted to clasp Marcie to her and say, "Not 'him'. Her. *Her*. It was a girl I loved. As I love you." *No, not as I love you. I can't love you that way, not even you.* To her sudden disgust the face of a handsome arrogant girl named Beebo came up in her mind. She frowned at her, trying not to see.

"What's the matter, Laur? Laura?" Marcie smoothed Laura's hair off her hot forehead. "You must have loved him a lot."

In a sudden convulsion of desire, Laura threw her arms around Marcie, pressing her hard, tight, in her arms. Her need was terrible, and a sort of sob, half ache and half passion, came out of her. Marcie was frightened.

"Laura!" she said, pushing at her. Laura was always so docile; now suddenly she was strange and violent. "Laura, are you all right?" Laura only clung to her the harder, wrestling against herself with all her strength.

For a moment, Marcie tried to calm her, whispering soothingly and rubbing her back a little. But this only aggravated Laura.

"Marcie, don't!" she said sharply. Panic began to well up in her. "Oh, God!" she cried, and stood up abruptly, shaking all over. She covered her face with her hands, trying to force the tears back with them. Marcie watched her, astonished, from the bed.

With a little gasp Laura turned and ran out. Marcie rose to her feet and called after her, but it was too late. She heard the front door slam as she ran toward it. She pulled it open but Laura was in the elevator a floor below her and on her way out. Marcie stared into the black stairwell, feeling shocked and confused.

She slipped back into the apartment and into her bed, but she couldn't sleep. She simply sat there, her eyes wide and staring, oscillating between a fear of something she couldn't name and bewildered sympathy for Laura. For whatever it was that tortured her. She shivered everytime she thought of Laura's near-hysterical embrace, returning to it again and again. It gave her a reckless kick, a hint of shameless fun, like the night she kissed the bum in the park. She didn't know why it recalled that to her mind. But it did. Laura had scared her; yet now she felt like giggling.

Laura ran all the way to the subway station, three blocks off. She fell into a seat gasping, trembling violently. People stared at her but she ignored them, covering her face with her hands and sobbing quietly. She rode down to the Village and got off at Tenth Street. She had managed to control herself by this time, but she felt bewildered and lost, as if she didn't quite know what she was doing there. She stood for a moment on the platform, shivering with the chilly air. It was nearly the end of April, but it was still cold at night. She had run out in nothing but a blouse and skirt, with a light topper over them—the clothes she had fallen asleep in. She was aware of the cold, yet somehow didn't feel it.

Resolutely she began to walk, climbing the stairs and then starting down Seventh Avenue. She walked as if she had a goal, precisely because she had none and it frightened her. It was Friday night, and busy. People were everywhere. Young men turned to stare at her.

Within five minutes she was standing in front of The Cellar, rather surprised at herself for having found it so quickly. There was a strange tingling up and down her back and her eyes began to shine with a feverish luster. She walked down the steps and pulled the door open.

Almost nobody noticed her. It was too crowded, at this peak hour of one of the best nights of the week. She made her way through the crowd to the nearest end of the bar. She had to squeeze into a corner next to the juke box and it was work to get her jacket off. It was sweaty and close after the chill air outside.

Laura stood quietly in her corner, looking at all the faces strung down the bar like beads on a necklace. They were animated, young for the most part, attractive . . . There were a few that were sad, or old, or soured on life —or all three. Across the room the artist, with his sketch pad, was drinking with some friends.

Laura felt alone and apart from them all somehow. There were one or two faces she might have recognized from the night before, people Jack might have introduced her to, but she couldn't be sure. She had been too drunk to be sure of anything last night.

God, was it only last night? she wondered. It seemed like a thousand nights ago. She didn't really want to be noticed now. She only wanted to watch, to be absorbed in these gay faces, in the idioms, the milieu.

"What'll you have?" She realized the bartender was leaning stiff-armed on the bar, looking at her.

"Whisky and water," she said, wondering suddenly how much it would be. She pulled out a dollar and put it on the counter self-consciously. When he brought her the drink she gulped it anxiously. Marcie kept coming into her thoughts; Marcie's face, her shocked voice saying, "Laura—don't!"

The bartender took her dollar and brought some change. It meant she could have another drink. Drinking your dinner. Where had she heard that? One of her father's friends, no doubt. She gazed at the ceiling. She wanted to talk to Jack, but she was ashamed to call him. She thought of her father again, and it gave her a sort of bitter satisfaction to imagine his face if he could see her now, alone and unhappy, disgracing him by drinking by herself, in a bar—a gay bar. Gay —that would strike him dead. She was sure of it. She smiled a little, but it was a mirthless smile.

After a moment, she ordered another drink. She counted her change fuzzily. There might be enough for a third. She slipped it back in her pocket and looked up to find a young man forcing himself into a place beside her.

Damn! she exclaimed to herself. *As if I didn't have enough on my mind.* Her slim arresting face registered subtle contempt and she turned away. It would have frozen another man, but this one only seemed amused.

"Hello, Laura," he said.

At this, she looked at him. Her mind was a blank; she couldn't place him. "Do I know you?" she said.

"No." He grinned. "I'm Dutton. This is for you." He held out a piece of paper and she took it, curious. On it was a devilish reproduction of her own features mocking her from the white page.

"You're the artist," she accused him suddenly.

"Thanks for the compliment."

"I don't want it."

"Keep it."

"I won't pay for it."

"You don't have to." He laughed at her consternation. "It's paid for, doll. Take it home. Frame it. Enjoy it."

Laura stared at him. "Who paid for it?"

"She said not to tell." He laughed. "You're a bitch to caricature. You know? Look me up sometime, I'll do a good one. I like your face." And he turned and wriggled out of the crowd.

Laura was left standing at the bar with the cartoon of herself. She was suddenly humiliated and angry. She felt ridiculous standing there holding the silly thing, not knowing who paid for it. Her glance swept down the bar, looking for a face to accuse, but she recognized no one. No one paid her any attention.

She studied the sketch once more. It was clever, insolent; it made a carnival curiosity of her face. Quietly, deliberately, with a feeling of satisfaction, she tore the sketch in half. And in half again. And threw it down behind the bar where the bartender would grind it into the wet floor. Then she picked up her glass and finished her drink.

"What did you do that for?" said a low voice, so close to her ear that she jumped and a drop of whisky ran down her chin. "It was a damn good likeness."

Laura looked up, gazing straight ahead of her, knowing who it was now and mad. She pulled a dime out of her pocket and smacked it on the bar in front of her.

"I owe you a dime, Beebo. There it is. Thanks for the picture. Next time don't waste your money."

Beebo laughed. "I always get what I pay for, lover," she said. Laura refused to look at her, and after a pause Beebo said, "What's the matter, Laura, 'fraid to look at me?"

Laura had to look then. She turned her head slowly, reluctantly. Her face was cold and composed. Beebo chuckled at her. She was handsome, like a young boy of fourteen, with her smooth skin and deep blue eyes. She was leaning on her elbows on the bar, and she looked sly and amused. "Laura's afraid of me," she said with a quick grin.

"Laura's not afraid of you or anybody else. Laura thinks you're a bitch. That's all."

"That makes two of us."

Under her masklike face Laura found herself troubled by the smile so close to her; the snapping blue eyes.

"Where's your guardian angel tonight?" Beebo said.

"I suppose you mean Jack. I don't know where he is, he doesn't have to tell me where he goes." She turned back to the bar. "He's not my guardian angel. I don't need one. I'm a big girl now."

"Oh, excuse me. I should have noticed."

Laura's cheeks prickled with embarrassment. "You only see what you want to see," she said.

"I see what I want to see right now," Beebo said, and Laura felt her hand on the small of her back. She straightened suddenly.

"Go away," she said sharply. "Leave me alone."

"I can't."

"Then shut up."

Beebo laughed softly. "What's the matter, little girl? Hate the world tonight?" Laura wouldn't answer. "Think that's going to make it any prettier?" Beebo pushed Laura's whisky glass toward her with one finger.

"I'm having a drink for the hell of it," Laura said briefly. "If it bothers you, go away. You weren't invited, anyway."

"Don't tell me you're drinking just because you like the taste."

"I don't mind it."

"You're unlucky in love, then. Or you just found out you're gay and you can't take it. That it?"

Laura pursed her lips angrily. "I'm not in love. I never was."

"You mean love is filth and all that crap? Love is dirty?"

"I didn't say that!" Laura turned on her.

Beebo shrugged. "You're a big girl, lover. You said it yourself. Big girls know all about love. So don't lie to me."

"I didn't ask you to bother me, Beebo. I don't want to talk to you. Now scram!"

"There she stands at the bar, drinking whisky because it tastes good," Beebo drawled, gazing toward the ceiling and letting the smoke from a cigarette drift from her mouth. "Sweet sixteen and never been kissed."

"Twenty," Laura snapped.

"Excuse me, twenty. Your innocence is getting tedious, lover." She smiled.

"Beebo, I don't like you," Laura said. "I don't like the way you dress or the way you talk or the way you wear your hair. I don't like the things you say and the money you throw around. I don't want your dimes and I don't want you. I hope that's plain because I don't know how to make it any plainer." Her voice broke as she talked and toward the end she felt her own crazy tears coming up again. Beebo saw them before they spilled over and they changed her. They touched her. She ignored the hard words Laura spoke for she knew enough to know they meant nothing.

"Tell me, baby," she said gently. "Tell me all about it. Tell me you hate me if it'll help."

For a moment Laura sat there, not trusting her, not wanting to risk a word with her, letting the stray tears roll over her cheeks without even brushing them away. Then she straightened up and swept them off her face with her long slim fingers, turning away from Beebo. "I can't tell you, or anybody."

Beebo shrugged. "All right. Have it your way." She dinched her cigarette and leaned on the bar again, her face close to Laura's. "Try, baby," she said softly. "Try to tell me."

"It's stupid, it's ridiculous. We're complete strangers."

"We aren't strangers." She put an arm around Laura and squeezed her a little. Laura was embarrassed and grateful at the same time. It felt good, so good. Beebo sighed at her silence. "I'm a bitch, you're right about that," she admitted. "But I didn't want to be. It's an attitude. You develop it after a while, like a turtle grows a shell. You need it. Pretty soon you live it, you don't know any other way."

Laura finished her drink without answering. She put it down on the bar and looked for the bartender. She wouldn't care what Beebo said, she wouldn't look at her, she wouldn't answer her. She didn't dare.

"You don't need to tell me about it," Beebo went on. "Because I already know. I've lived through it, too. You fall in love. You're young, inexperienced. What the hell, maybe you're a virgin, even. You fall, up to your ears, and there's nobody to talk to, nobody to lean on. You're all alone with that great big miserable feeling and she's driving you out of your mind. Every time you look at her, every time you're near her. Finally you give in to it—and she's straight." She said the last word with such acid sharpness that Laura jumped. "End of story," Beebo added. "End of soap opera. Beginning of soap opera. That's all the Village is, honey, just one crazy little soap opera after another, like Jack says. All tangled up with each other, one piled on top of the next, ad infinitum. Mary loves Jane loves Joan loves Jean loves Beebo loves Laura." She stopped and grinned at Laura.

"Doesn't mean a thing," she said. "It goes on forever. Where one stops another begins." She looked around The Cellar with Laura following her gaze. "I know most of the girls in here," she said. "I've probably slept with half of them. I've lived with half of the half I've slept with. I've loved half of the half I've lived with. What does it all come to?"

She turned to Laura who was caught with her fascinated face very close to Beebo's. She started to back away but Beebo's arm around her waist tightened and kept her close. "You know something, baby? It doesn't matter. Nothing matters. You don't like me, and that doesn't matter. Someday maybe you'll love me, and that won't matter either. Because it won't last. Not down here. Not anywhere in the world, if you're gay. You'll never find peace, you'll never find Love. With a capital L."

She took a drag on her cigarette and let it flow out of her nostrils. "L for Love," she said, looking into space. "L for Laura." She turned and smiled at her, a little sadly. "L for Lust and L for the L of it. L for Lesbian. L for Let's—let's," she said, and blew smoke softly into Laura's ear. Laura was startled to feel the strength of the feeling inside her.

It's the whiskey, she thought. *It's because I'm tired. It's because I want Marcie so much. No, that doesn't make sense.* She caught the bartender's eye and he fixed her another drink.

Beebo's arm pressed her again. "Let's," she said. "How about it?" She was smiling, not pushy, not demanding, just asking. As if it didn't really matter whether Laura said yes or no.

"Where did you get that ridiculous name?" Laura hedged.

"My family."

"They named you *Beebo?*"

"They named me Betty Jean," she said, smiling. "Which is even worse."

"It's a pretty name."

"It's a lousy name. Even Mother couldn't stand it. And she could stand damn near anything. But they had to call me something. So they called me Beebo."

"That's too bad."

Beebo laughed. "I get along," she said.

The bartender set Laura's glass down and she reached for her change. "What's your last name?" she said to Beebo.

"Brinker. Like the silver skates."

Laura counted her change. She had sixty-five cents. The bartender was telling a joke to some people a few seats down, resting one hand on the bar in front of Laura, waiting for his money. She was a dime short. She counted it again, her cheeks turning hot.

Beebo watched and began to laugh. "Want your dime back?" she said.

"It's your dime," Laura said haughtily.

"You must have left home in a hurry, baby. Poor Laura. Hasn't got a dime for a lousy drink."

Laura wanted to strangle her. The bartender turned
back to her suddenly and she felt her face burning. Beebo
leaned toward him, laughing. "I've got it, Mort," she said.

"No!" Laura said. "If you could just lend me a dime."

Beebo laughed and waved Mort away.

"I don't want to owe you a thing," Laura told her.

"Too bad, doll. You can't help yourself." She laughed
again. Laura tried to give her the change she had left,
but Beebo wouldn't take it. "Sure, I'll take it," she said.
"And you'll be flat busted. How'll you get home?"

Laura went pale then. She couldn't go home. Even if
she had a hundred dollars in her pocket. She couldn't
stand to face Marcie, to explain her crazy behavior, to try
to make herself sound normal and ordinary when her
whole body was begging for strange passion, for forbidden
release.

Beebo watched her face change and then she shook her
head. "It must have been a bad fight," she said.

"You've got it all wrong, Beebo. It wasn't a fight. It
was—I don't know what it was."

"She straight?"

"I don't know." Laura put her forehead down on the
heel of her right hand. "Yes, she's straight," she whispered.

"Well, did you tell her? About yourself?"

"I don't know if I did or not. I didn't say it but I acted
like a fool. I don't know what she thinks."

"Then things could be worse," Beebo said. But if she's
straight, they're probably hopeless."

"That's what Jack said."

"Jack's right."

"He's not in love with her!"

"Makes him even righter. He sees what you can't see.
If he says she's straight, believe him. Get out while you
can."

"I can't." Laura felt an awful twist of tenderness for
Marcie in her throat.

"Okay, baby, go home and get your heart broken. It's
the only way to learn, I guess."

"I can't go home. Not tonight."

"Come home with me."

"No."

"Well . . ." Beebo smiled. "I know a nice bench in

Washington Square. If you're lucky the bums'll leave you alone. And the cops."

"I'll—I'll go to Jack's," she.said, suddenly brightening with the idea. "He won't mind."

"He might," Beebo said, and raised her glass to her lips. "Call him first."

Laura started to leave the bar and then recalled that all her change was sitting on the counter in front of Beebo. She turned back in confusion, her face flushing again. Beebo turned and looked at her. "What's the matter, baby?" And then she laughed. "Need a dime?" She handed her one.

For a moment, in the relative quiet of the phone booth, Laura leaned against a wall and wondered if she might faint. But she didn't. She deposited the dime and dialed Jack's number. The phone rang nine times before he answered, and she was on the verge of panic when she heard him lift the receiver at last and say sleepily, "Hello?"

"Hello, Jack? Jack, this is Laura." She was vastly relieved to find him at home.

"Sorry, we don't want any."

"Jack, I've got to see you."

"My husband contributes to that stuff at the office."

"Jack, please! It's terribly important."

"I love you, Mother, but you call me at the God-damnedest times."

"Can I come over?"

"Jesus, no!" he exclaimed, suddenly coming wide awake.

"Oh, Jack, what'll I do?" She sounded desperate.

"All right now, let's get straightened out here. Let's make an effort." He sounded as if he had drunk a lot and just gotten to sleep, still drunk, when Laura's call woke him up. "Now start at the beginning. And make it quick. What's the problem?"

She felt hurt, slighted. Of all people, Jack was the one she had to count on. "I—I acted like a fool with Marcie. I don't know what she thinks," she half-sobbed. "Jack, help me."

"What did you do?"

"Nothing—everything. I don't know."

"God, Mother. Why did you pick tonight? Of all nights?"

"I didn't pick it, it just happened."

"*What* happened, damn it?"

"I—I sort of embraced her.

There was a silence on the other end for a minute. Laura heard him say away from the receiver, "Okay, it's okay. No, she's a friend of mine. A friend, damn it, a girl." Then his voice became clear and close again. "Mother, I don't know what to say. I'm not sure I understand what happened, and if I did I still wouldn't know what the hell to say. Where are you?"

"At The Cellar. Jack, you've just got to help me. Please."

"Are you alone?"

"Yes. No. I've been talking to Beebo, but—"

"Oh! Well, God, that's it, that's the answer. Go home with Beebo."

"No! I can't, Jack. I want to come to your place."

"Laura, honey—" He was wide awake now, sympathetic, but caught in his own domestic moils. "Laura, I'm— well, I'm entertaining." He laughed a little at his own silliness. "I'm involved. I'm fraternizing. Oh, hell, I'm making love. You can't come over here." His voice went suddenly in the other direction as he said, "No, calm down, she's not coming over."

Then he said, "Laura, I wish I could help, honest to God. I just can't, not now. You've got to believe me." He spoke softly, confidentially, as if he didn't want the other to hear what he said. "I'll tell you what I'll do, I'll call Marcie and get it straightened out. Don't worry, Marcie believes in me. She thinks I'm Jack Armstrong, the all-American boy. The four-square trouble-shooter. I'll fix it up for you."

"Jack, please," she whimpered, like a plaintive child.

"I'll do everything I can. You just picked the wrong night and that's the God's truth, honey. Where's Beebo? Let me talk to Beebo."

Laura went out of the booth to get her, feeling half dazed, and found her way back to the bar. "He wants to talk to you," she said to Beebo, without looking at her.

Beebo frowned at her and then swung herself off her seat and headed for the phone. Laura sat down in her place, disturbed by the warmth Beebo left behind, twirling her glass slowly in her hand. She was crushed that Jack had turned her down.

Perhaps he had a lover, perhaps this night was so important to him that he couldn't give it up, even though she had all his sympathy. These things might be—in fact, were—true. But Laura could hardly discern them through her private pains.

Beebo came back in a minute and leaned over Laura, one hand on the bar, the other on Laura's shoulder. "He says I'm to take you home," she said, "feed you aspirins, dry your tears, and put you to bed. And no monkey business." She smiled as Laura looked slowly up into her face. It was a strong interesting face. With a little softness, a little innocence, it might have been lovely. But it was too hard and cynical, too restless and disillusioned. "Come on, sweetie pie," Beebo said. "I'm a nice kid, I won't eat you."

They walked until they came to a small dark street, and the second door up—dark green—faced right on the sidewalk. Beebo opened it and they walked down a couple of steps into a small square court surrounded by the windowed walls of apartment buildings. On the far side was another door with benches and play areas grouped in between on the court. Beebo unlocked the other door and led Laura up two flights of unlighted stairs to her apartment.

When they went inside a brown dachshund rushed to meet them and tried to climb up their legs. Beebo laughed and talked to him, reaching down to push him away.

Laura stood inside the door, her hands over her eyes, somewhat unsteady on her feet.

"Here, baby, let's get you fixed up," Beebo said. "Okay, Nix, down. Down!" she said sharply to the excited little dog, and shoved him away with her foot. He slunk off to a chair where he studied her reproachfully.

Beebo led Laura through the small living room to an even smaller bedroom and sat her down on the bed. She knelt in front of her and took her shoes off. Then, gently, she leaned against her, forcing her legs slightly apart, and put her arms around Laura's waist. She rubbed her head against Laura's breasts and said, "Don't be afraid, baby." Laura tried weakly to hold her off but she said, "I won't hurt you Laura," and looked up at her. She squeezed her gently, rhythmically, her arms tightening and loosening around Laura's body. She made a little sound in her throat and, lifting her face, kissed Laura's neck. And then she stood up slowly, releasing her.

"Okay," she said. "Fini. No monkey business. Make yourself comfortable, honey. There's the john—old, but serviceable. You sleep here. I'll take the couch. Here! Here, Nix!" She grabbed the little dog, which had bounded onto the bed and was trying to lick Laura's face, and picked him up in her arms like a baby. She grinned at Laura. "I'll take him to bed, he won't bother you," she said. "Call me if there's anything you need." She looked at Laura closely while Laura tried to answer her. The younger girl sat on the bed, pale with fatigue and hunger, feeling completely lost and helpless. "Thanks," she murmured.

Beebo sat down beside her. "You look beat, honey," she said.

"I am."

"Want to tell me about it now?"

Laura shook her head.

"Well . . ." she said. "Good night, Little Bo-peep. Sleep tight." And she kissed her forehead, then turned around and went out of the bedroom, turning out the light on her way.

Laura had gotten off the bed without looking at her, but feeling Beebo's eyes on her. She shut the door slowly, until she heard the catch snap. Then she turned, leaning on the door, and looked at the room. It was small and full of stuff, with yellowed walls. Everything looked clean, although the room was in a state of complete confusion, with clothes draped over chairs and drawers half shut.

All of a sudden, Laura felt stronger. She undressed quickly, taking off everything but her nylon slip, and pulled down the bedclothes. She climbed in gratefully. She didn't even try to forget Marcie or what had happened. It would have been impossible. Mere trying would have made it worse. She relaxed on her back in the dark, her arms outflung, and waited for the awful scene to come up in her mind and torture her.

Her mind wandered. The awful embrace was awful no longer—only wrong and silly and far away. The damage was irreparable. She stared at the ceiling, invisible in the dark, and felt a soft lassitude come over her. She felt as if she were melting into the bed; as if she could not have moved if she tried.

Time flowed by and she waited for sleep. It was some time before she realized she was actually waiting for it. It didn't come. She turned on her side, and still it eluded her. Finally she snapped the light on to squint at her watch. It said five of four. She switched it off again, her eyes dazzled, and wondered what the matter was. And then she heard Beebo turn over in the next room, and she knew.

An old creeping need began to writhe in Laura, coming up suddenly out of the past and twisting itself around her innards. The pressure increased while she lay there trying to ignore it, becoming more insistent. It began to swell and fade with a rhythm of its own; a rhythm she knew too well and feared. Slowly the heat mounted to her face, the sweat come out on her body. She began to turn back and forth in bed, hating herself and trying to stop it, but helpless with it.

Laura was a sensual girl. Her whole being cried out for love and loving. It had been denied her for over a year, and the effects were a severe strain on her that often brought her nerves to the breaking point. She pretended she had learned to live with it, or rather, without it. She even pretended she could live her whole life without it. But in her secret self she knew she couldn't.

Beebo turned over again in the living room and Laura knew she was awake, too. The sudden realization made her gasp, and she could fool herself no longer. She wanted Beebo. She wanted a woman; she wanted a woman so terribly that she had to put her hand tight over her mouth to stop the groan that would have issued from it.

For a few moments more she tossed feverishly on her bed, trying to find solitary release, but it wouldn't come. The thought of Beebo tortured her now, and not the thought of Marcie. Beebo—with her lithe body, her fascinating face, her cynical shell. There was so

much of Beth there. At that thought, Laura found herself
swinging her legs out of bed.

Moonlight glowed in two bright squares on the living room floor. Laura could see the couch, draped in
blankets. She wondered whether Beebo had heard her and
waited breathlessly for some sign. Nix lifted his head but
made no sound, only watching her as she advanced across
the room on her tiptoes, her white slip gleaming as she
passed through the light.

Laura stood and hovered over the couch, uncertain
what to do, her heart pounding hugely against her ribs,
Beebo was on her side, turned toward Laura, apparently
asleep. Nix was snuggled into the ditch between the
back of Beebo and the back of the couch.

Beebo stirred slightly, but she didn't open her eyes.
"Beebo," Laura whispered, dropping to her knees and
supporting herself against the couch with her hands.
"Beebo?" she whispered again, a little louder. And
then, sensing that Beebo had heard her she bent down
and kissed her cheek, her hands reaching for her. Beebo
was suddenly completely roused, coming up on her elbow
and then falling back and pulling Laura with her.

"Laura?" she said huskily. "Are you all right?" And
then she felt Laura's lips on her face again and a shock
of passion gripped her. "Oh, God—Oh, baby," she said,
and her arms went around Laura hard.

"Hold me," Laura begged, clinging to her. "Oh,
Beebo, hold me."

Beebo rolled off the couch onto Laura and the abrupt
weight of her body fired Laura into a frenzy. They
rolled over each other on the floor, pressing each other
tight, almost as if they wanted to fuse their bodies,
and kissed each other wildly.

Laura felt such a wave of passion come up in her that
it almost smothered her. She thought she couldn't stand
it. And then she didn't think at all. She only clung to
Beebo, half tearing her pajamas off her back, groaning
wordlessly, almost sobbing. Her hands explored, caressed,
felt Beebo all over, while her own body responded with
violent spasms—joyous, crazy, deep as her soul. She
could no more have prevented her response than she could
the tyrannic need that drove her to find it. She felt

Beebo's tongue slip into her mouth and Beebo's firm
arms squeezing her and she went half out of her mind
with it. Her hands were in Beebo's hair, tickling her
ears, slipping down her back, over her hips and thighs.
Her body heaved against Beebo's in a lovely mad duet.
She felt like a column of fire, all heat and light, impossibly sensual, impossibly sexual. She was all feeling,
warm and melting, strong and sweet.

It was a long time before either of them came to
their senses. They had fallen half asleep when it was
over, still lying on the floor, where Nix, after some trep-
idation, came to join them. When Laura opened her
eyes the gray dawn had replaced the white moonlight.
She was looking out the window at a mass of telephone
and electric wires. She gazed slowly downward until
she found Beebo's face. Beebo was awake, watching her
—no telling for how long. She smiled slightly, frowning at the same time. But she didn't say anything and
neither did Laura. They only pulled closer together,
until their lips touched. Beebo began to kiss Laura
over and over, little soft teasing kisses that kept out of
the way of passion, out of the way of Laura's own kisses
as they searched for Beebo's lips. Until it was suddenly
imperative that they kiss each other right. Laura
tried feebly to stop it, but she quickly surrendered.
When Beebo relented a little it was Laura who pulled
her back, until Beebo was suddenly crazy for her again.
"No, no, no, no," Laura murmured, but she had asked
for it. A year and a half of abstinence was too much
for her. At that moment she was in bondage to her body.
She gave in in spite of herself, rolling over on Beebo,
her fine hair falling over Beebo's breasts in a pale
glimmering shower, soft and cool and bringing up
the fire in Beebo again.

Once again they rested, half sleeping, turning now
and then to feel each other, reassure themselves that the
other was still there, still responsive. Now and then
Beebo pushed Nix off Laura, or out from between them,
where he was anxious to make himself a nest.

It was Saturday afternoon before they could drag themselves off the floor. It was Laura who pulled herself to

her knees first by the aid of a handy chair, and squinted at the bright daylight. For a few moments she remained there, swaying slightly, trying to think straight and not succeeding. She felt Beebo's hand brush across her stomach and looked down at her. Beebo smiled a little.

An elusive feeling of shame slipped through Laura, disappeared, came back again, faded, came back. It seemed uncertain whether or not to stay. She swallowed experimentally, looking at Beebo. After a minute Beebo said, "Who's Beth?"

"Beth?" Laura was startled.

"Um-hm. She the blonde?"

"No. That's Marcie."

"Well, baby, seems to me like it's Beth you're after, not Marcie."

Laura frowned at her. "I haven't seen Beth for almost a year. She's married now. It's all over."

"For her, maybe."

"I won't discuss it," she said haughtily, getting up and walking away from her, while Beebo lay on the floor admiring her body, her head propped comfortably on her hands. "It happened long ago and I've forgotten it."

"Then how come you called me Beth all night?"

Laura gasped, turning to look at her, and then her face went pink. "I—I'm sorry, Beebo," she said. "I won't do it again."

"Don't count on it."

Laura stamped her foot. "Damn you, Beebo!" she said. "Don't talk to me as if I were an irresponsible child!"

Beebo laughed, rolling over and nearly crushing Nix, who reacted by licking her frantically and wagging his tail. Beebo squashed him in a hug, still laughing. Laura turned on her heel to leave the room, looking back quickly to grab her slip, and went into the bedroom, slamming the door. Within seconds it flew open again and Beebo leaned against the jamb, smiling at her. She sauntered into the room.

"Now, don't tell me you didn't enjoy yourself last night, Little Bo-peep," she said.

Laura ignored her, moving speedily, suddenly embarrassed to be naked. In the heat of passion it was glorious, but in the morning, in the gray light, in the chill and ache of waking up, she hated it. Her own bare flesh seemed out of place. Not so with Beebo, who sprawled on the bed on top of the underwear Laura wanted to put on.

"Did you?" said Beebo. "Enjoy yourself?"

"Get up, Beebo, I want to get dressed."

"After all, it was your idea, baby."

"Don't throw *that* in my face!" she exclaimed angrily, ashamed to remember it.

"Why not? It's true. Besides I'm not throwing it in your face, I'm just saying it."

Laura turned away from her, unbearably conscious of her own slim behind, her dimpled rump, and her long limbs. She yearned to be shrouded in burlap. "Beebo, I —I couldn't help myself last night." She worked to control her voice, to be civilized about it. "I needed— I mean—it had been so long."

"Since Beth?"

Laura fought down a sudden impulse to strangle her. "I was a fool," she said, and her voice trembled. "A fool with my roommate and now with you. It got so I couldn't stand it at home. It got intolerable."

"So you came down here. And I was a nice convenient safety-valve."

"I didn't mean that!" she flared.

"Doesn't matter what you mean, baby. It's a fact. Here you were, desperate. And here was I, ready and willing. You knew I wouldn't turn you down."

Laura's face began to burn. She had a wild idea that her back was blushing with her cheeks.

"What would you have done if I *had* turned you down, Laura?" Beebo spoke softly, insinuatingly, teasing Laura, enjoying herself.

But Laura was too humiliated to tease back. "I don't know," she exclaimed miserably. "I don't know what I *could* have done." And she covered her face with her hands.

"I'll tell you, then. You'd have begged me. You'd have gotten down on your knees and begged me. Sometime you will, too. Wait and see."

Laura whirled toward her, insulted. "That's enough!" she said harshly. She pulled her underthings forcibly from under Beebo, but Beebo caught the shoulder strap of her brassiere and hung on to it with both hands, her heels braced against the floor, laughing like a beautiful savage while Laura yanked furiously at it.

"You're going to get about half," she said. "If you're lucky. I'll get the other half. Half isn't going to hold much of you up, baby."

Laura let go suddenly, and Beebo fell back on the bed, grinning at her.

"Laura hates me," she said. "Laura hates me." She said it slowly, singsong, daring Laura to answer her.

Laura glared at her, defiant and fuming. "You're an animal!" she hissed at her.

"Sure." Beebo chuckled. "Ask Jack. That's his favorite word. We're all animals."

"You're nothing but a dirty animal!"

"What were you last night, Miss Prim? You were panting at me like a sow in rutting season."

Laura's eyes went wide with fury. She grabbed the nearest thing—a hairbrush—and flung it violently at Beebo. Beebo ducked, laughing again at her young victim, and Laura turned and fled into the bathroom. She slammed the door so hard it bounced open and she had to shut it again. With frantic fingers she tried to turn the lock, but Beebo was already pushing on the other side. Laura heaved against it, but Beebo got it open and she fell back against the wall, suddenly frightened.

"Don't touch me!" she spat at her.

Beebo smiled. "Why not? You didn't mind last night. I touched you all over. Did I miss anything?"

Laura shrank from her. "Let me go, Beebo."

"Let you go? I'm not even touching you."

"I want to leave. I want to get out of here." Laura tried to push past her but Beebo caught her, her strong hands pressing painfully into Laura's shoulders, and threw her back against the wall.

"You're not going anywhere, Bo-peep," she said. And began to kiss her. Laura fought her, half sobbing, groaning, furious. Beebo's lips were all over her face, her throat, her breasts, and she took no notice of Laura's blows and her sharp nails. Laura grabbed handfuls of her hair, wanting to tear it out, but Beebo pulled her close, panting against her, her eyes hypnotically close to Laura's. And Laura felt her knees go weak.

"No," she whispered. "Oh, God no. Oh, Beebo." Her hands caressed Beebo's hair, her lips parted beneath Beebo's. All the lonely months of denial burst like fire-crackers between her legs. Once it had started her whole body begged for release. It betrayed her. She clung sweating and heaving to Beebo. They were both surprised at the strength and insistance of their feelings. They had felt the attraction from the first, but they had been unprepared for the crescendo of emotion that followed.

It was a long time before either of them heard the phone ringing. Finally Beebo stood up, looking down at Laura, watching her. Laura turned her face away, pulling her knees up and feeling the tears come. Beebo knelt beside her then, the hardness gone from her face.

"Don't cry, baby," she said, and kissed her gently. "Laura, don't cry. I know you don't want to make love to me, I know you *have* to. Damn that phone! It's not your fault. Laura, baby, you make beautiful love. God grant me a passionate girl like you just once in a while and I'll die happy."

"Please don't touch me. Don't talk to me." She was overwhelmed with shame.

"I have to. I can't help myself any more than you can. I had no idea you'd be like this—Jesus, so hot! You look so cool, so damn far above the rest of us. But you're not, poor baby. Better than some of us, maybe, but not above us."

Laura turned her face to the wall. "Answer the phone," she said.

Beebo left her then and went into the living room. Laura could hear her voice when she answered.

"Hello?" she said. "How are you, doll? Fine. Laura's fine. No, I didn't rape her. She raped me." Laura sat straight up at this, her face flaming. Beebo was laughing. "Tell her what? It's all fixed up? You mean I can send her home to Marcie?" Her voice became heavily sarcastic. "Well, isn't that too sweet for words. Okay,

Jack, I'll tell her. You what? . . . With who? . . . Oh,
Terry! Yeah, I've seen him. You got a live one there,
boy. Hang on to him, he's a doll . . . Okay, don't mention it. It's been a pleasure. Most of it. She's lovely
. . . So long."

When Beebo returned to the bathroom, Laura was
standing at the washbowl, rinsing her face, trying to
compose herself.

"What did he say?" she asked Beebo.

"It was Jack."

"I heard."

Beebo put her arms around Laura from behind, leaning a little against her, front to back, planting kisses
in her hair while she talked. "He says you're forgiven.
He handed Marcie some psychological hocus pocus
about a neurosis. You are neurotic, love. As of now. As
far as Marcie's concerned, you have attacks. She should
have a few herself."

"Don't be so sarcastic, Beebo. If you knew what I've
been through—how scared I was—"

"Okay, no more sarcasm. For a few minutes at least.
God, you're pretty, Laura." Like Jack, like Marcie,
like many others, she realized it slowly. Laura's singu-
lar face fit no pattern. It had to be discovered. Laura
herself had never discovered it. She didn't believe in
it. She grew up convinced she was as plain as her
father seemed to think, and when she looked into the
mirror she didn't see her own reflection. She saw what
she thought she looked like; a mask, a cliche left over
from adolescence. It embarrassed her when people told
her she was pretty.

"Don't flatter me," she said sharply to Beebo. "I hate
it."

Beebo shut her eyes and laughed in Laura's ear.
"You're nuts," she said. "You are *nuts*, Bo-peep."

"I'm sane. And I'm plain. There's a poem for you.
Now let me go."

"There's no rush, baby."

"There is. I want to get home." She twisted away
from Beebo, turning around to face her.

Beebo let her hands trail up the front of Laura. "Home
to Marcie?" she said, and let them drop suddenly.

"Okay. Go home. Go home, now that you can stand it for another couple of days. And when the pressure gets too great, come back down again. Come back to Beebo, your faithful safety valve."

"You said you wouldn't be sarcastic."

Beebo wheeled away, walking into the bedroom. "What do you want me to do, sing songs? Write poems? Dance? Shall I congratulate you? Congratulations, Laura, you've finally found a way to beat the problem. Every time Marcie sexes you up, run down to Beebo's and let it off. Beebo'll fix you up. Lovely arrangement."

She turned to Laura, her eyes narrowed. "Laura gets loved up for free, Beebo gets a treat, and Marcie stays pure. Whatever happens, let's not dirty Marcie up. Let's not muss up that gorgeous blonde hair."

"Don't talk about her!" Laura had followed her into the bedroom.

"Oh, don't get me wrong, Bo-peep. I'm not complaining. You're too good to me, you know. You give me your throw-away kisses. I get your cast-off passion. I'm your Salvation Army, doll, I get all the left-overs. Throw me a bone." She was sitting on the edge of her rump on her dresser, legs crossed at the ankles, arms folded on her chest—a favorite stance with her.

Laura was suddenly ashamed of the way she had used Beebo. Beebo was hurt. And it was Laura's fault.

"Everything's my fault, Beebo," she said. "I'm sorry." There was silence for a minute. Laura was acutely aware that "I'm sorry" was no recompense for what she was doing to Beebo.

Beebo smiled wryly. "Thanks," she said.

"I am, Beebo. Really. I didn't come to you last night just because of Marcie." It was suffocatingly hard to talk. She spoke in fits and starts as her nerve came and left her.

"No?" Beebo remained motionless with a 'tell-me-another' look on her face.

"No. I came—I came because—" She covered her face with her hands, stuck for words and ashamed.

"You came, baby. That's enough," Beebo finished for her, relenting a little. "You came and I'm not sorry. Neither are you, not really. The situation isn't per-

fect." She laughed. "But last night was perfect. It isn't
like that very often, I can tell you."

Laura looked at her again. Then she moved toward
her clothes, afraid to stay naked any longer, afraid the
whole thing would start over again.

Beebo came toward her, pulling the slip from her
hand and dropping it on the floor. "There's no hurry,"
she said.

"I'm going, Beebo. Don't try to stop me."

For a moment Beebo didn't answer. Then she scooped
up some of Laura's clothes on her foot and flung them at
her. "Okay, baby," she said. "But next time, you don't
get off so easily. Clear?"

"There won't be a next time." Laura concentrated
on dressing, on getting her body covered as quickly as
possible. "I'm grateful to you, but I'll never do it again.
It isn't fair, not to you."

Beebo laughed disagreeably. "Don't worry about being
fair to *me*, baby. It didn't bother you last night."

"I couldn't think last night! You know that."

"Yes. I know that. I'm glad. I hope I drive you out of
your mind." Beebo's eyes bored into her and made her
rush and stumble. She was afraid to confront her, and
when she had her clothes on she caught her jacket up
with one hand and headed for the door without looking back.

Nix pranced after her. Before she got the front door
open, Beebo caught her and turned her around. "Goodby,
Beebo," she said stiffly.

Beebo smiled, upsetting Laura with her nude closeness. "You'll be back, Little Bo-peep. You know that,
don't you." It was a statement, not a question.

I'll never come back, she told herself. *I'll never open
this door again.*

And, confident that she meant what she said, she turned
and walked away. Within minutes she was riding uptown
on the subway. In less than half an hour she was climbing
the flight of stairs to the penthouse, her heart pounding.

The door was open. Laura went in, feeling her legs start
to shake. There didn't seem to be anyone around. She
walked through the apartment: no-one. She slipped her

jacket off and went into the kitchen to find something for breakfast. Out on the roof she could hear people laughing, while competing portable radios squeaked from different corners. The population of the apartment building had taken to sunning itself on the roof on fair weekends.

Laura ate some toast and orange juice, sitting quietly, on the kitchen table. *She's out there on the porch. I know she's out there,* she told herself. She was afraid to face her, afraid to go looking for her. She wanted to fall into bed and sleep, but she knew she would never rest until the thing was straightened out.

Laura emptied her orange juice glass and put it down resolutely on the table. She set her chin and slipped off the table, heading for the door. She bumped flat into Jack as he came in.

Laura gave a little scream and jumped backwards. "Oh," she said, shutting her eyes for a minute to let her heart come back to normal. "It's you."

"Say it like you're glad to see me, Mother," he said, smiling wistfully.

"I am," she exclaimed, coming toward him then and taking his hands. "Oh, Jack, I am. I don't know what I would have done—"

"Now you're embarrassing me," he said. "They're out on the roof sunbathing, by the way."

"They?"

"Burr's here."

Laura started for the door, but Jack caught her sleeve. "Are you cracked?" he said. "This isn't the time. Wait till Burr leaves." Laura stopped, unsure. "You don't want to go out there and try to explain it to her now, do you?" Jack said.

"I just want to get it over with."

"It'll keep. Don't be pushy."

Laura rubbed her forehead. "You're right," she said. "I can't talk to her in front of Burr." She laughed a little. "I *am* cracked. People have been telling me that all day."

"You don't have to say much anyway," Jack said. "I did a smooth patch job. She thinks you're a little goofy. But harmless."

Laura smiled at him in relief. But as they gazed at each other the ghost of Beebo came up in her mind and she was suddenly blushing without Jack's having said a word. "I—I think I'd better go in and lie down, if you'll excuse me," she said, anxious to get away from him.

"Didn't get much sleep last night?" he said.

"Not much." She looked at the floor, not quite forgiving him for leaving her in the lurch the night before. "You sent me home with her," she reminded him.

"I didn't send you to bed with her. I gave her orders. I told her no monkey business. She promised to behave." He was still smiling, curious to hear her defend herself.

Laura wondered quickly whether she could get away with a lie, ashamed as she was of the truth. But she knew her hot cheeks would betray her. They always did.

"She did behave, Jack." His eyebrows went up skeptically. "She—what I mean is—it was me."

He looked at her sideways. "You mean you just sort of fell into each other's arms?"

"Well, sort of."

"By mistake? In the dark?"

"I—I—"

"You're fibbing. I know Beebo. Who made who?" He opened the ice box and fished out a beer. "Do I have to say it, or are you going to tell me?"

"Well, damn it, who are you?" she exclaimed. "You have no right to know anything."

"Okay. I'll get it from Beebo. She says you raped her."

"She's a liar! I heard her say that. Damn!"

Jack laughed, opening the beer. He sniffed it. "God, what awful stuff," he remarked. "I only drink it before noon. Cheers." He drank, and held the can toward her. "Want some?"

"At this hour?"

"Your stomach doesn't know what time it is."

"*Your* stomach, maybe."

"Did Beebo jump you, Laura? If she did I'll break her head." He asked it suddenly and quietly, and she saw that he meant help and comfort to her. He had to stick a few pins in her, only to pull them out and offer first aid. It was the way he did things.

"She didn't—no," Laura said, turning away. "Jack, don't make me talk about it."

"You could talk to me before."

"You turned me down last night," she said pettishly.

"I had to. There was someone else last night."

"I . . . oh damn it, Jack, I'm ashamed of myself. It was my fault, I made it so easy. No, that's a lie. I did it on purpose." A wave of tears welled through her and subsided, leaving her with her hands over her face. Jack started to speak but she silenced him with a wave of her hand. "It's been so long, Jack. It's been hell. I've been so lonely. I didn't know a person could be that lonely and live. And then I moved in with Marcie and it was suddenly torture. All these months I've been here. And most of the time I've been dying for her. And last night—I was so tired, so mixed up and I had a couple of drinks—"

"You sounded nuts on the phone."

"I felt nuts. I felt awful. She took me home, and she was very decent. She really was. She wanted to, I know that. But she didn't. She gave me her bed and she went in the living room and slept on the couch. I thought I'd fall right to sleep. But I couldn't. I just tossed and turned, and every time I heard her turn over I was on fire. It got too strong for me. I finally gave in. *I* did it. It was my fault, Jack."

"Poor Laura." He said it sympathetically. "Come here, honey." He put his arms around her and held her, stroking her back. When he did it, she didn't mind. She'd have resented any other man . . . except maybe Merrill Landon. But Merrill Landon never showed affection to anyone.

"I know how it is, believe me," Jack said. "You're starving, and somebody puts a feast in front of you. What happens after that is Instinct. Overwhelming. You eat. Or you die of hunger, right there, with all that food in front of you."

Laura clung to him, letting herself cry softly and gratefully into his shoulder.

"Let me give you just one little word of advice, Mother. Don't starve yourself anymore. Or that hunger is going to kill you."

She looked at him with wet eyes. Her face was strangely different, and Jack could see it. A night of love, a night of luxurious satiation, had changed her. For all her fatigue, her shame at herself, her body was happy and relieved. She couldn't help that. She felt physically good, for the first time in over a year, and she had Beebo to thank for it.

"You're different," Jack said, smiling. "You look good. I don't care how tired you are. It's becoming—love."

"That wasn't love."

"What was it, then?"

"Just purely physical. Animal. Vulgar."

"Love has a body, Laura. Eyes and lips, legs and sex. We humans can't help that."

"Love is bigger and better than that. There hasn't been any of that with Marcie and me, but I love her."

"That's idealistic crap."

Laura gasped, her eyes widening in sudden anger, but he interrupted her sharp retort before she could make it.

"Love is no bigger and better than the people who feel it," he said. "What has your love for Marcie got you? A fat neurosis, a lot of misery, and a night in bed with somebody you hardly know because you couldn't stand it any longer. If that's what makes it bigger and better, the hell with it. Feed it to the crocodiles." And he turned brusquely away.

Laura stared at him, unable to answer him. It struck her harshly that he might be right. "But I love Marcie," she whispered hoarsely.

"Sure. You love her because she looks like Beth, or whatever the hell her name is."

Laura was shocked. "No, no, Jack you don't understand. That has nothing to do with it. I love her." He turned to look at her, cynicism written plain on his face. "I love her because—"

"Because she's under the same roof with you, two feet away when you go to bed at night. Because she's young and pretty. Because you can't have her."

"Because I can't have her!" she exclaimed contemptuously. "That's exactly why I'm so miserable, you idiot! I love her so much—"

"We all do. She's a great girl," he said, so vaguely and quietly, that it calmed her a little.

But when Marcie said, "What are you two talking about?" Laura jumped, visibly startled. "Oh, I didn't mean to scare you," Marcie said. She had made up her mind to treat Laura gently and carefully. Burr came in noisily behind her. "Hi, Laura," he said, and stared at her pale face.

"I didn't hear you coming," Laura said nervously. She wondered what Marcie had told Burr, and suddenly it was too much to stand there and face them. "I'm going to bed," she said suddenly, briefly. "I didn't sleep much last night." It came to her then that she didn't know what she was supposed to have done last night at all. Jack hadn't told her.

Jack, faster than Laura when he was on the spot, said, "Laura spent the night with Beebo Brinker. She's an old friend of mine." He spoke to Burr who apparently didn't know what to think.

Damn Jack! Laura thought. *He didn't have to say her name. That ridiculous name!*

Chapter Nine

M<small>ARCIE</small> tried to be understanding with Laura when they were alone later. She said, "Jack told me all about it, Laura. I understand."

What did he tell you? What do you understand? Why didn't he tell me? She didn't know how to act with Marcie. Her discomfort made her awkward and for the first time she found herself wishing to be without her for a little while. She didn't want Marcie to try to comfort her. She just wanted to let it blow over.

But Marcie was a warm-natured girl, and she was curious. She wanted to sit on Laura's bed and talk about it. She kept saying, "Tell me about it, Laur. Tell me what happened. Don't you know I wouldn't be shocked?"

At this point Laura revolted. "No, I *don't* know!" she said, and was immediately sorry. She raised her hand to her mouth. "Marcie, please. Please drop it."

"I'm sorry, Laur. I can't do anything right tonight." She looked so disheartened that Laura had to smile at her a little.

"You do everything right, Marcie," she said soothingly. "I'm the one who's wrong. No, it's true. I'm not like you. I can't confess to people."

"You tell Jack things."

Laura was suddenly alert, alarmed. "How do you know?" she demanded. "What things?"

"Oh, you're always going off and talking. Like this morning. Why don't you have long talks with me?"

Laura sighed, relieved. "I don't know. Jack is so easy to talk to, Marcie."

"Does that mean I'm not? I try to be." She smiled invitingly.

Laura, who had been lying on her bed, raised herself up on her elbows. "I never say these things like I mean them," she apologized. "I only mean, I—" *I can't talk to you because I'm in love with you, that's what I mean. But that's not what I can say.*

297

She rolled over on her stomach and buried her face in the pillow. Marcie sat motionless for a minute, afraid to say anything and start her off again. Then she leaned over her and touched her shoulders. "You don't have to tell me, Laura, honey," she said. "I guess I shouldn't pester you. Jack says you've been through a lot and that's why you're nervous. I don't want to make you unhappy, Laura. I'm afraid I do sometimes. I don't know why, I just get the feeling now and then, when you look at me, that I make you sad. Do I?"

Laura's nails cut into her smooth white forehead. "Marcie, don't torture me," she said. Her voice was low and strained. It was such an odd thing to say that Marcie withdrew, and climbed into her own bed.

"I'm sorry," she whispered, pulling the covers up and turning out the light. Then she put her hands over her face suddenly and sobbed.

"Oh, Marcie!" Laura was out of bed before she had time to think, sitting next to Marcie and holding her. "Don't cry, Marcie. Oh God, why can't I ever say anything right?" She implored the ceiling for an answer. "I didn't mean to hurt you."

Marcie slowed down and stopped almost as suddenly as she began. "I know," she said. "I know what it is. I used to drive Burr nuts this way, asking questions and talking and talking. And when he wouldn't answer, I just kept asking more and more till I drove him crazy. I don't know why. I guess I *wanted* to drive him crazy. But I don't know why I do it to you." She looked away, embarrassed. Laura's arms tightened involuntarily around her. She had no idea how to answer this unexpected outburst. She was afraid to try to comfort Marcie, for the very act of soothing her brought Laura's own emotions to a boil. The safest course was to get back in bed at once and forget it. Or at least, stop talking. But Marcie was clinging to her and she couldn't roughly shake her off.

"I've learned a lot from living with you, Laur," Marcie said quietly. Laura listened, her nostrils full of the scent of flowers. "This may sound silly to you but—don't take this wrong, Laura—but I admire you, I really do. You have a quality of self control that I could never learn. You keep your thoughts to yourself. If you don't have anything to say, you don't *say* anything. If you don't want to talk, you don't."

She looked up and laughed a little ruefully. "I talk all the time, as if I had to. Just living with you, I'm beginning to see it. I talk all the time and say nothing. You almost never talk, but when you do it's worth listening to."

Laura began to squirm uncomfortably, but Marcie grasped her sleeves and continued. "You know something, Laur? I think I just drove Burr crazy. I talked him to death."

"He still loves you, Marcie." Laura found her hand on Marcie's hair, without quite knowing how she had let it happen. "He wants you back."

"I know. We've hardly quarreled at all this week, Laur. You haven't been around much, you haven't seen us. But we've been getting along unusually well. But the screwy part is, it's not like I thought it would be."

"You mean, you miss the quarrels?"

"I mean I just wish he wouldn't come around so much any more. I want time to change. To think."

"Think about what?"

"About me. No, about anything *but* me. That's all I ever thought about before. You think about other things. You know what's going on. You come home at night and you read all these books that are sitting around. You can't even talk to me about them, because you know how stupid I am."

Laura was astonished. All these critical thoughts had gone through Marcie's head, and Laura hadn't been aware of it. Marcie had been watching her, admiring her, and she hadn't known that either. *I'm plumb blind,* she thought. *And I thought I couldn't know Marcie any better. Because I love her. And she talks like this to me. God!*

"Marcie, you don't need to read books. It's just a bad habit for introverts." Marcie shook her head silently while Laura went on. "Beautiful girls like you don't need to read," she said.

"That's just it," Marcie said. "I'm not going to be just another pretty idiot. I want to know something. I'm sick of knowing absolutely nothing. I want to be different. I want you to help me."

She wants me, Laura thought happily. *She wants me.* It was all she heard.

"When you were gone all night with Jack—" She paused and looked away. "—I started to think. I couldn't sleep, I don't know why. I was thinking about you, Laur. I was wondering why you never talk to me, why we have so little to say to each other. We sit at the breakfast table and read the paper and go off without anything more than 'good morning'. At night we go to bed and sometimes I talk, but it's not a conversation. You listen, I guess you listen."

"I do!"

"And I, say the wrong things. And you go to pieces, like Friday night."

"No."

"Or else you run away. You go sleep with Jack."

"Marcie!"

"I know you were with Jack again last night. He didn't have to lie to me about it."

"But he didn't. I wasn't!"

"Now don't *you* lie to me!"

Laura stared at her, unable to speak.

"Help me, Laura," Marcie said, leaning toward her. "I want to change. I'm sick of myself. I'm sick of Burr."

The strangest craziest feeling started up in Laura; just an echo, faraway in herself. *She wants me to help her, to be with her. She admires me. Dear God, I'm afraid to wonder how much.* A very small smile curved the corners of her mouth.

"I have to start somewhere," Marcie said. "I want to talk to you like an intelligent human being, not an ignoramus."

Laura smiled at her. Almost without her realizing it, her hand had stolen back to Marcie's yellow hair. "Do you, Marcie?" she said. It was a simple question, but it asked a thousand others.

"Yes."

"Why?"

"Oh, I'm fed up with myself. I never realized, till I lived day-in-day-out with you, how much I'd been missing. Give me a book to read, Laur."

"In the morning." Laura smiled at her and got up, edging away from her bed.

"Now."

"It's too late, Marcie. You won't read anything now."

"I want to tell Burr I read a book."

"I'll give you something later," Laura said. It sounded strangely insinuating, the way she said it. She scared herself. She ducked into her bed as into a safe harbor, and hid her body under the blankets.

With a sigh Marcie turned the light out. After a moment's silence she whispered, "Laur? Will you talk to me after this? Really talk to me? Tell me things?"

"I'll try," Laura murmured, frowning in the dark. She lay in bed daydreaming for hours, seeing the first signs in Marcie of an influence she had been unaware of. Where would it lead? What doors would it open? Would it lead them both to bitterness? Or mutual ecstasy?

In the morning Laura was very matter-of-fact. She almost ignored Marcie. She made her work for her attention and it delighted her that Marcie was willing to work for it. Instinctively Laura knew she had to play hard to get, and she liked to play that way for once.

At breakfast, after a few false starts, Marcie blurted, "I'll be late tonight." She put her paper down and faced Laura.

Laura looked up slowly. "Date with Burr?" she said.

"No. Mr. Marquardt is having some out-of-town guests for dinner downtown. He asked some of us to go. I told him I would."

"Have fun," Laura said, and looked back at the front page.

"Ha! Some drunken idiot of a reporter'll probably pester me to death."

"A reporter?" Laura looked up again suddenly.

"Oh, I don't know." Marcie saw Laura's interest and it sparked her own. "A journalist, or something. It's a convention—professional fraternity, I guess."

"What fraternity? What's it called?"

"Ummm." Marcie bit her lip and concentrated. "It's Greek. Let's see. Something the matter?"

"No. Is it Chi Delta—"

"—Sigma. That's it, I remember. How did you know? Now something *is* the matter, Laura!"

Laura had gone very pale. She swallowed convulsively.

"I just remembered, I was supposed to run an errand for Dr. Hollingsworth. I'd better get going." She got up suddenly and went into the bedroom for her jacket.

Marcie stood up and followed her. "You didn't finish your breakfast, Laur," she said, concerned, a line of worry in her forehead.

"I'm not hungry. I'll see you tonight," she said, and turned quickly to almost run out.

Marcie came after her, bewildered. "Laura, you don't make sense," she said. "What's the matter with you?"

But Laura was running down the stairs to the elevator. Marcie turned and went back into the kitchen and drank her coffee standing, gazing perplexed at Laura's plate.

Chapter Ten

MERRILL LANDON. *Merrill Landon. My father. My father is coming to New York. He never misses these damn things, he goes every year. Oh, God, help me.* Laura rode down to work on the subway, her fists clenched in her lap, her face set like a mask to cover the torment inside. *He doesn't know I'm here, that's one good thing. He'll never find me, either. How long will he be here? It must be in the papers. I missed it at breakfast.*

She picked up the *Times* on the corner where she left the subway. She took it up to the office with her, impatient to look at it. Sarah was already there.

"Hi, gorgeous," she said.

Laura looked up, startled. "Hi," she said. "Who's gorgeous?"

"You are. You must be, you've got a man."

Laura stared at her blankly, her mind full of the threat of her father's presence in the city. Finally it came to her. "Oh, you mean Jack," she said.

"Did you talk to him?"

"Oh, yes. Yes." *Now what the hell does she mean? Why would I—Oh! I promised her a date.* Laura felt suddenly sunk. All those reports to do that should have been done before. Lies to tell, at nine in the morning. Merrill Landon somewhere in New York. It was too much. The day stretched away in front of her like an endless obstacle course.

"What'd he say?" Sarah said eagerly.

"He's working on it. Maybe this weekend."

"Gee, that sounds great."

Laura had to look at the paper; she *had* to. It gnawed at her, as she sat at her desk, sneaking through it between reports and unable to find anything. Her father's name ran through her mind like a robot tune from a TV commercial.

It was a rushed day. Sarah didn't take a break on days

when they were behind, but nothing could have stopped Laura. She got up and almost ran to the washroom at eleven, the paper in hand. She felt herself trembling, going over the pages again and again, until she suddenly found it at the bottom of page 12. "Chi Delta Sigma, national journalism fraternity, opens its convention today at the McAlton Hotel. The convention will last until next Saturday, at which time . . ." etc. There was an agenda listed, a few names—the national officers. There it was— Merrill Landon, corresponding secretary. Laura shut her eyes and groaned a little.

The day dragged. She typed until the small round keys seemed to weigh a pound apiece under her fingers, and still the reports piled up.

Laura sat hunched over her machine for a long time after the others had left for the day. She meant to work, but she never did any. She wanted to cry and she couldn't. She wanted to move, to talk to someone, to explode, and she just sat there until the cramps in her back made her groan. She got up stiffly and put her jacket on and stood for a moment, aimless and lost. There was nowhere to go, nothing to do. Marcie wouldn't be home yet.

She rummaged idly in her pockets, pulling out some change and a shopping list. The list was from the week before and she started to drop it in the wastebasket, when she noticed something on the other side. A phone number —Watkins 9-1313. And the initials B. B. Laura crumpled it in her hand, seized with an uncontrollably pleasant shudder. Then she threw it indignantly into the wastebasket, wondering when Beebo had scribbled it out. And then she leaned over slowly and took it out of the wastebasket and shoved it furtively back into her pocket, without looking at it. She sat down abruptly in her chair and put her head down on her arms and wept.

"Father . . ." she whispered. "Why did we have to hate each other? We're all we have . . . Father . . ."

She got up fifteen minutes later, turned out the lights, and stole out, quiet as a thief.

She walked over to the McAlton Hotel. She had no idea what she expected to find or to do. But she went into the big softly carpeted lobby and walked, almost as if she were sleep walking, toward the desk. It was crowded and noisy, with that ineffable air of excitement that big hotels seem to generate.

Laura felt gooseflesh start up all over her. Many of these people must be conventioneers. If Merrill Landon didn't see her one of his Chicago friends might, and the secret would be out. He would run her down if it took the whole New York City police force.

She leaned apprehensively on the marble topped counter of the desk, waiting until a clerk could serve her. He came up after a couple of minutes, looking enormously efficient and busy. "May I help you, Miss?" he demanded.

"Is a Mr. Merrill Landon staying here?" she asked.

"Just a minute, please." He disappeared briefly and Laura looked around the lobby, her hand partially covering her face.

He might see me. I must be out of my mind to come here. But she waited none-the-less.

"He's in 1402," the clerk said loudly in her ear.

Laura jumped.

"Shall I call him?" asked the clerk.

"Yes, please." She had no idea why she was doing this. She felt as if she were two people, one acting, the other watching; one compelled to act, the other shocked by the action.

"Who wants to see him, please?"

"His daughter." She almost whispered it, and he made her repeat it. Then he buzzed off. She watched him, perhaps ten feet from her but impossible to hear, as he lifted the receiver, gave the number, waited. Then his face lighted into a business-type smile, and she saw his lips form the words, "Mr. Landon?" He went on, and she watched him, feeling almost sick with anticipation.

The clerk came back after a brief conversation. "Well, Miss—" he began, eyeing her closely.

"What did he say?" Laura looked at him with her stark blue eyes. Her chin trembled.

"He says he has no daughter, Miss," the clerk drawled. He grinned. "Tough luck. Want to try someone else?"

Laura's mouth dropped open. Her face twitched. She couldn't answer him. She turned and ran, bumping into people, stumbling, until she found a phone booth empty in a row of booths along a far wall and she took refuge there. She buried her face in her hands and wept. "Merrill Landon, go to hell, go to hell," she said fiercely, under her breath. "I hate you. Oh, God, how I hate you!" And she sobbed until somebody rapped on the door of the booth. She wiped her eyes hastily, knowing they were red and swollen, and turned to glare at the impatient rapper. He glared back.

Defiantly she put a dime in the phone and lifted the receiver. She called Jack.

A voice answered almost at once. A strange masculine voice. "Hello?" it said.

"Jack?" Her voice trembled.

"Just a minute." He called, "Jack, it's for you."

A few seconds later Jack answered.

"Jack, it's Laura."

"Are you all right?"

"I have absolutely nothing to say," she said. "I'm only calling because—because I'm in a phone booth and some fool wants to use the phone. He's rapping on the door."

"Mother," he said slowly, "you have a screw loose. Now listen carefully and do what I tell you. Just go along quietly and don't tell them anything. I'll send my analyst over right away."

"My father's in town." Her breath caught while she spoke.

"Oh! No wonder. Did you tell him to go to hell?"

"The desk clerk called his room and said his daughter wanted to see him." She stopped to swallow the fury in her throat.

"And he told *you* to go to hell?"

"He said, 'he had no daughter.'" Her voice trembled with the immensity of it.

Jack, for once, was momentarily speechless. Finally he said, "He is a bastard, Laura. By God, he is. Don't mess with him. Come on over, I'll buy you a drink."

"Thanks, Jack." She broke into tears again.

"Don't cry, Laura. Just think what satisfaction that would give the old s.o.b."

"You're right!" she said sharply, pulling herself up. "I won't. I'll be right over."

Jack was waiting for her on the front stoop, sitting on one of the cement railings and looking up at what few stars were available between the roofs. Without a word he got up, slipped an arm around her, and turned her away from his apartment. They walked over to a small bar she hadn't seen before called Mac's Alley, without speaking to each other.

The bar was in a basement and you walked down a flight of twisting stairs to reach it. There were booths around the walls, tables and a jukebox in the middle, and a long bar ran across the back. Laura walked halfway towards the bar with Jack before she realized that there were no other women in the place. She turned to Jack with anxiety.

"Do they want me in here?" she asked.

He smiled. "They're not going to give you a rush, Mother. I'll stake my life on it."

"I didn't think they liked women in a place like this."

Jack guided her to a barstool. "Oh, they're friendly enough. They know you wouldn't be here if you weren't gay. They figure, you leave them alone and they'll leave you alone."

Laura looked around her uncomfortably. "I can't help thinking I embarrass them."

"Maybe they embarrass you. Would you rather go over to The Cellar?"

"No ... I don't know."

"You don't want to run into Beebo. She's usually out making the rounds about now. That's why I brought you here."

Laura smiled gratefully at him. "Thanks," she said. "I should have seen it myself." But she found herself so shaken by the sudden idea of Beebo loose among scores of desirable girls that she couldn't concentrate for a minute.

Jack ordered them a drink. Then he turned to her, pushing his glasses back into place on his nose. They tended to slide down to the halfway mark. "Well?" he said, and paused. "Let's tear Papa Landon apart."

"I don't want to talk about him," Laura said.

"Then why am I buying you a drink?"

She turned to snap at him and then saw he was kidding her. "Sorry, Jack," she said. Looking at him brought back

her faith in him, and she smiled a little. "I always knew
he was a hard man," she said softly, "but I never dreamed
he'd go as far as this. I always thought, in spite of everything, in spite of all the bitterness and misery we've had
together, that he must love me a little. After all, I'm all
he has left . . . of my mother, my brother . . . his family.
I was five when it happened, and I wish to God I could
remember what he was like before. But I can't. I like to
pretend he was generous and gentle and kind. And I can
remember sitting on his shoulders when we went to a
Fourth of July parade. It was that same summer, before
our vacation. I remember he hoisted me up and bought
me a balloon and held me while the parade went by so I
could see. Afterwards he walked around and talked to his
friends, and he didn't make me get down. I felt like a
queen on a throne. It's been my one good memory of him,
to this day. But Mother was with us. Maybe he did it for
her sake.

"I remember her better than him from those years.
Sometimes I miss her terribly. She was very loving."

"Maybe," said Jack, "your father wouldn't hate you so
now if he hadn't loved you so much before."

"You give him too much credit," she said. "After what
he did to me tonight, I'll never speak to him again. I'd
kill him if I could. But I wouldn't go near him, even for
that. I wouldn't give him the satisfaction of seeing my
face. He has no daughter, has he? All right, God damn
him, I have no father! Two can play at that game."

"Don't hate me for saying it," Jack said, "but I think
you still love him. I think you'll see him again."

She turned on him. "You're crazy!" she said. "You don't
know anything! What makes you think such a thing?"

He shrugged. "Only that it matters so terribly to you."

Laura finished her drink and placed the glass carefully
on the bar, trying to sort out her thoughts. "If I do see
him again," she said, "it'll be when I can tell him I'm a
success. Financially. Socially. Every way. I want to tell
him, 'I have a good job, nice friends. I can get along fine
in this world without you, and I'll never need you again.'
And you know what else I'd like to say to him, Jack?"

"Yeah." He lit a cigarette. " 'Father, I'm queer. And
it's all your fault. Shove that up your rear and live with

it!' Yeah, I know. Shock the hell out of him. I tried that
on—on a close relative once."

"What happened?"

"I don't really know. When his face went blue I took
off. I haven't been home since. I can't go home to find
out, as a matter of fact. I'm—shall we say—not welcome."
He said this with slow sarcasm.

"Jack, I'm sorry," she said gently, and looked at him
sympathetically. It occurred to her now, when she found
his own troubles paralleled her own, that he was very
human and not a slick witty party boy without real
feelings. He was lonely. *Everybody's lonely,* she thought.
*Marcie for a perfect mate. Beebo for a perfect girl.
Jack for an affectionate boy. Me . . . Poor Sarah . . .*

That recalled Sarah to her mind. "Jack, I have a
friend," she said.

"Congratulations."

"—named Sarah."

"Does Beebo know?"

"And she wants a date."

"With a girl?"

"—With a boy. She's straight."

"What a shame."

"Can you help me out?"

"I can help *you,* Mother, but can I help Sarah?"

"You must know somebody. How about that boy who
answered your phone tonight? Could he take her out?"

"If he does I'll break his head for him," he said and
laughed softly, knocking his cigarette ashes into a
scorched aluminum tray in front of him.

"Who is he, Jack?" she asked.

"A friend. No, a lover. For the moment, anyway."

Laura put her hand on his arm. "Don't be so cynical," she said.

"These things never last." He shook his head. "Better to face it at the beginning."

"He must see something worthy in you or he never
would have come to you in the first place." She spoke
awkwardly, but with sympathy.

"He sees dollar bills." Jack smiled.

"Jack! Don't be so hard on yourself. It hurts me." She
didn't like to see him stick the pins in himself. It

was all right when he did it to her, because it was in
fun. She didn't mind, she understood his need. But
when he hurt himself he hurt in dead earnest.

"Besides, you aren't rich," Laura said. "If that's all
he wanted, he'd find somebody else."

"I have a little put away," he said. "I save it up in
between affairs. When somebody irresistible comes
along, I spend it like a fool. Makes a wonderful impression the first couple of weeks. Then I'm flat broke and
all alone again. My chronic condition."

It was a pathetic revelation. Laura was taken aback
by it. "You shouldn't do it, Jack," she said.

"I can't help it. I'll hang on to him with anything.
Anything I've got. Even dollar bills."

"If all he wants is your money he's not *worth* your
money! Or your time, or your friendship."

"Laura, this isn't friendship. This is another subject entirely. Honest to God." Laura blushed. "A man
can't buy a friend. But there's always a little love for
sale."

"Not real love."

He shrugged. "I don't ask for the moon."

Laura finished her drink. "What's his name?" she
said.

"Terry."

"Terry what?"

"Just Terry."

"You don't trust me." She said it quietly, but she
was hurt.

"Terry Fleming." He spoke the name gently and
Laura saw a look on his face that changed him entirely.
She studied him, surprised.

"Jack, I think you're in love." Once said, it
sounded gauche and unfair.

But he only said, "I think so, too."

Laura was lost. What do you do on the spot like this?
"I don't know whether to give you my congratulations
or my sympathy," she said seriously.

Jack laughed. "Both, Mother. That's a beautiful sentiment, whatever it is. Thanks."

He seemed unable to talk about it and Laura finally
returned to Sarah. "Is there somebody in the office you

could get for Sarah?" she asked. She described her to
him. "She's not pretty, but she's just a swell girl."

"I know, there are a million of 'em," he sighed. "I
wish to God I were straight. I'd marry her, poor kid."
Laura stared at him, then smiled. "I guess I can ar-
range something," he said. "Do we have to double with
them?"

"She expects it. I hate to ask."

"Okay, okay. It won't kill me. But dinner only. And
I'll be in a hurry."

"Thanks, Jack."

"I'd better find a tame one for her," he mused and
then laughed a little. "Whatever that means. Jesus, the
poor girl has probably dreamed all her life of a good
thorough raping. But I can't assume the responsibility. Maybe Jensen can go. I'll call you in the morning
on it."

"Thanks. She'd be so happy." Laura finished a second drink. Jack was two up on her. She looked at him
out of the corner of her eye, wanting to tell him about
the change that had come over Marcie but afraid of his
sarcasm. Finally she said, in the characteristic blunt
way that disguised her uncertainty, "Jack, Marcie is
different. Something's happening to her. I—I'm
scared." She could go no further. She looked away from
him.

Jack chuckled. "Well, what's she doing, filching undies from Macy's basement?"

"She doesn't want to see Burr any more."

Jack frowned slightly. "She's finally coming to her
senses? That was a screwy match to begin with. Burr
wants to worship one gal. Marcie wants to raise a little
hell with every other man she sees."

"She wants to be like me. That's what she said. She
wants to read books. Spend more time at home. She
wants me to help her."

"Help her what?"

Laura frowned. "I don't know what. She says she's sick
of herself and she wants to be a better person."

Jack bit his underlip reflectively. "I know what
you're thinking. And you're wrong. She's not turning
gay."

"I didn't say that." Laura turned to him indignantly.

"You don't have to. You're thinking it so hard I can hear the wheels going around in your head." He looked at her. "Once and for all, Laura, she's *not* gay. Maybe she's got room in her somewhere for a little curiosity. Maybe living with you really has made her dissatisfied with herself. If so, so much the better. But she's not mooning for you every night."

"She acted so funny, Jack. Like—like she enjoyed having me near her. Like she wanted me to touch her. I mean, comfort her. You know."

"The more you want her to enjoy it, the more it'll seem like she does."

"I'm not making up stories," Laura said with some heat.

"No, Mother, I know. I believe you. I'm just telling you a fact. I've known Marcie for a couple of years. From the time she and Burr started dating right through their divorce. She's capable of—let's say—wondering. Like the night she wanted to touch tongues." Laura shivered involuntarily. "Once in a while she gets a kick out of a fling in the Village. Maybe she just wants to see how far you'll go. Maybe she's egging you on, Laura. Did you ever think of that? Just to see what the hell you'll do?"

"She wouldn't do that," Laura said positively, somewhat shocked. "Never."

Jack gave a little snort. "Okay, maybe not. But she's not about to fall for you. Not now or ever."

"She meant it when she talked to me last night. She was sincere."

"Sure she meant it. She's on a book kick. She's obviously very impressed with you. It shows when she talks about you. Temporarily, you're somebody to imitate, somebody to admire."

"Temporarily?"

"Don't fall into a trap." He put a hand on her knee.

"It's no trap! She's too innocent to set me a trap."

"Innocent?" He laughed. "Don't count on it. Besides, you're too innocent to avoid one. Right now you have a lot to learn."

Laura glared at him. "I'm not stupid."

"No, you're not. You're very bright, honey. You're just uninformed. If you want to learn, go scout up Beebo and take the Grand Tour of the Village."

"I could no more fall for her than I could fall for—for—"

"For me?" He laughed.

She smiled suddenly and laughed with him. "Oh," she said with a wave of her hand, "You're taken."

"Mother, that's a beautiful one-line definition of my dilemma. My analyst could use you."

"Are you being analyzed?" she asked.

"Aren't we all?"

"Answer me!"

"I did. Let's go. I hate to keep people waiting."

"Who's waiting?"

"My friend, Mr. Fleming."

She slipped off the barstool, pulling her jacket on. "I'd like to meet him."

"If it lasts another couple of weeks, I guess it'd be safe." He took her arm and steered her through the crowd. They stared at her but it didn't disconcert her so much now that she had had a drink or two.

"Where's your adoring roommate tonight?" Jack said as they went up the stairs.

"Having dinner downtown."

"Why don't you go over to The Cellar? Let Beebo tell you some fairy stories. She's got a million of 'em."

"I couldn't take Beebo tonight."

"Suit yourself. I'll walk you to the subway."

"No, don't bother. I know you want to get home. Thanks a lot, Jack. I don't know why you're so good to me."

"My interest is purely academic. Your innocence amazes me."

"You make me feel like a hayseed," she said.

He laughed. "Okay, Hayseed. I'll call you in the morning on what's-her-name."

"Sarah."

"Sarah. See you." And he turned and walked off.

Laura walked toward the subway but she knew she wasn't going home. She knew she would walk right past

it and she did. She walked for four blocks, seething
with a renewed fury at Merrill Landon. Her hot hand
was cramped around the slip of paper with Beebo's
number on it, in the pocket of her jacket. . . .

*I'll pay her back. I'll just give her the money I owe
her, have one drink, and go home.* She looked at her
watch—a little past nine. For a moment she stood at
the head of the stairs looking down at the double doors
that opened into The Cellar, feeling her heart bound
nervously. She never seemed able to walk into this place
confidently. There was always a moment of fear and reluctance. But the need to be with her own kind quickly
overpowered it.

She walked in, heading for the bar, ignoring the
curious stares that greeted her. She stood at the end of the
bar and when the bartender came up he recognized her.

"Hi," he said. "What'll it be?"

"Whisky and water, please," she said. She looked
around the place, up and down the bar, around the
tables, but she didn't see Beebo. She drank half her drink,
and then walked back to the ladies' room, looking into
the rear of The Cellar, but Beebo wasn't there. In extreme irritation she walked back to the bar, wondering
whether to crush her pride and ask the bartender where
Beebo was, or let it go. She finished her drink and decided if she had come this far she might as well go
the whole way.

"Where's Beebo tonight?" she asked the bartender the
next time he got near. "I owe her some money," she explained compulsively. He smiled.

"Oh, she's been and gone already," he said. "She's
probably over at The Colophon. She likes it over there.
No boys." He grinned.

"Thanks," said Laura, slipping off her seat at the
bar and heading for the door. She was embarrassed
enough without asking him where The Colophon was.
She didn't want to advertise her "innocence."

Near the door a slim pretty girl, who had kept an eye
on her at the bar, approached her. The girl wore her
hair in a short soft curly cut. She was blonde and feminine. Laura let herself be approached simply by returning the girl's gaze as she came near her. She stopped
when the girl spoke.

"Excuse me," the girl said. "We noticed you were all alone. My friends and me. Like to have a drink with us?" She nodded toward a table where three other girls were sitting, watching them. One of them, sitting alone on one side of the table, stared coldly at Laura.

Laura was flattered. But the feelings in her were too personal, too rough, to dissipate with strangers. "Thanks," she said. "I'd like to, but I'm looking for somebody. I'm in a hurry."

"Who're you looking for? Maybe we can help you out," said the girl, stopping Laura as she started to move away.

Laura realized the girl was interested in her, and it made her turn back once more. "Oh," she said with a little shrug, "you wouldn't know her."

"Somebody might. We're over here a lot. What's her name?"

Laura was dead certain they'd know Beebo, who came over here all the time. The last thing she wanted was to have everybody run up and tell Beebo that Laura had been looking for her. The bartender would no doubt tell her. That was bad enough.

"What's her name?" the girl prompted, and then smiled. "Don't want to tell?"

Laura blushed and backed away from her. "I just owe her some money. I thought she'd be down here tonight."

"Who?" the girl goaded her, with a pretty smile.

"Beebo Brinker." Laura didn't mean to say it. Yet saying it was better than trying to hide it and getting laughed at. They could always ask the bartender who she was looking for after she left, and she would look even worse. They would take her stammering reluctance for infatuation. She said the name as casually as she could.

"Oh, Beebo!" The girl laughed. "She left half an hour ago. She's over at the Colophon. She said this place was dead tonight. I guess if she'd known you were coming she would have waited—hm?" She smiled.

"I guess," said Laura briefly. She stared at the girl. It occurred to her that she saw a slight resemblance to Beth in her face. Then she turned and walked out.

The slim girl walked back to her table. Her partner said peevishly, "Maybe that'll teach you you're not irresistible."

"Oh, shut up," the slim girl said quietly. "She's Beebo Brinker's girl."

"Beebo's girl, hell. Beebo's got a dozen girls. She can really pick 'em though, I'll say that much. I should get one like that." And she made a face at the slim one by her side.

Chapter Eleven

Laura went home. She arrived before ten, but Marcie wasn't back yet. Laura put a book she had been reading on Marcie's bed and climbed into her own bed. She tried to read herself, but she couldn't. An hour went by, and no Marcie. Nervously, Laura shut her book and dropped it to the floor. She got up and went into the bathroom to brush her teeth, and remembered she had already done it.

Then she went to the phone. She didn't know what was coming over her. She only felt a deep will-defying unhappiness. She pulled out the phone book and looked up the number of the McAlton Hotel. She sat for a moment with the book open in her lap, unable to move. Then she reached slowly for the phone.

Suddenly it rang. Laura screamed, a small quick cry of extreme surprise. Her heart had taken a tremendous leap at the piercing bell sound in that still apartment. She let it ring twice more while she caught her breath. *It must be Marcie,* she thought. *Maybe she's in trouble.* She lifted the receiver. "Hello?"

"Hello, Bo-peep."

Laura's heart gave another bound. She felt the sweat break out. "Beebo?" she said faintly.

"How are you, sweetheart? I hear you were looking for me tonight."

"You didn't waste any time." Her voice was sharp.

"I hate to keep a lady waiting. What's on your mind?"

"I just dropped in for a drink. I was down there in the Village to see Jack and I just wanted to pay you back." She spoke in fits and starts.

"You don't owe me a thing, Bo-peep. Not a thing."

"A drink." Laura hated to owe anybody anything. She was meticulous about her debts, however small the sum.

317

"You're right." Laura could feel her smile. "I nearly forgot. Okay lover, you owe me one drink."

"Beebo, I can't talk now, really."

"You're doing fine. What's the matter, Marcie breathing down your neck?"

"It's not that."

"You don't have to say you love me, you know. Just say you'll meet me tomorrow night. About eight."

"No."

"Don't be late, doll. I'll call Marcie and ask her where the hell you are."

"You wouldn't! You won't! Damn you, Beebo!"

"I would and I will." She laughed. "Eight on the dot."

"I won't be there."

"Want to bet?"

Laura hung up on her. She was trembling. Angrily she slammed the heavy phone back into place, switched out the bedroom light, and got into bed.

The black night settled around her but it brought more restless tossing than repose. The hours slipped by. No Marcie. No sleep. Only an endless bitter reviewing of what her father had done to her; the look on the clerk's face when he gave her the message; the impotent fury and shame that beseiged her. At last she turned the light back on and began to pace the room. The electric clock on Marcie's dresser said two-thirty. Laura wondered whether to call Burr. Or Jack. She was getting afraid for Marcie. But nobody knew how to reach her. There was nothing to do but wait.

It was a few minutes past three when Marcie came in. Laura had left the living room light on for her and she heard her come in laughing and heard a male voice answer her. Not Burr's voice. Somebody else. A deep mature voice. Laura peeked out through the crack in the kitchen door but couldn't see him. Marcie was giggling, as if she were tight, and pushing him away. Laura could see her now and then.

Marcie said, "I'll call my roommate. She'll make you go home."

"I can't go home tonight. I live in Chicago."

"That's where she's from!"

"Who?"

"My roommate."

"To hell with her. Come here, Baby."

"No!" High as she was, she nevertheless sounded a little scared. She had stopped laughing.

Laura threw a coat hastily over her pajamas and went into the living room. A large man, partly bald and handsome in a heavy featured way, had Marcie wrapped in a bear hug and was trying to drag her to the couch.

"All right," said Laura sharply. "Get out."

She startled them both so much that they froze where they were. The man stared at her. He was drunk, and his balance wasn't the best. Laura, pale and silver blond, her long hair falling down her shoulders, her face strange and sensitive and imperious, looked like an apparition to him. Without taking his eyes off her he asked Marcie, "Who the hell is *that?*"

"My roommate." Marcie took advantage of his interest to slip free. Laura took her arm firmly and sent her through the kitchen door. Then she turned back to the man.

"All right, you," she said as if he were a servant. "Out."

The impudence of it amused him and angered him at the same time. "You can't talk to me like that," he said.

She advanced on him briskly, pulling the door open sharply and facing him. "It's my home and I'll speak as I please," she said. She looked as cold and unapproachable as she was hot and angry. He stared at her, not sure how to take her, and then came toward her to put a hand on her shoulder.

"Marcie's no good," he said confidentially. "Let's you and me—"

Laura swept his hand off her shoulder. "Get out of here or I'll call the police," she said..

He got mad. "Jesus, what a chilly little bitch you are!" he growled.

"Get out," Laura said, so cold, so controlled, that she froze him into submission. She shut the door after him, resisting the urge to slam it. *Dear God,* she thought intensely. *If I could do that to my father. Just once.*

"Laura? It was just a party, Laur," Marcie said. "We

went out after dinner. Just for kicks. He got sort of out of hand. Thanks, Laur, I don't know what I'd have done."

"Come on to bed." Laura turned and walked toward her and Marcie preceded her into the bedroom. It occurred to her then that she was behaving with Marcie much as Beth used to behave with her. She was asserting herself, taking the lead. She liked it; with Marcie, anyway. She felt her influence and reveled in it. A feeling of tremendous strength swept through her when the man turned and left, like the other poor demented little fellow who pestered her on the subway. Only he was such a weakling he hardly counted. She had a mental image of herself treating Merrill Landon that way, and it worked a strange exaltation in her. She smiled.

Marcie grinned at her crookedly. "I thought you'd be sore," she said.

"No. No, of course not. Why should I be?"

"I don't know. Maybe because I felt kind of guilty going out with somebody besides Burr. But I had fun. Up to the end, anyway. I wouldn't have minded that if he hadn't slobbered so much." She giggled and Laura ignored what she said. They were standing less than a foot from each other and suddenly Laura reached for her and gave her a little hug. "I'm not mad. I'm just glad you're all right," she said.

Marcie submitted, but she seemed embarrassed, and Laura quickly released her. With the release came a letdown, a loss of strength and confidence. She slipped quietly into bed and spent the hours till dawn wrestling with the bedclothes.

Laura didn't feel much brighter than Marcie in the morning. She got to work on time, but all she wanted to do was sleep. *I've got to catch up. I've got to catch up,* she kept telling herself. *Less than three weeks and Jean'll be back. And I haven't done a really good day's work since she left. Even if they like me, they can't keep me on as a charity case.*

The episode at the McAlton flamed up in her mind and gave her an angry energy through most of the morning. Sarah said nothing to her, but she kept looking at her over her typewriter, apparently afraid to bring up the date subject again. It wasn't till Jack called that Laura even remembered it.

"All set," he said. "Carl Jensen can go. Friday night. Dinner and a show. What's Sarah's number?"

Laura got it from her and made her face light up with expectation. Jack put Carl on the phone, and Laura gave her end to Sarah. It gave her a momentary lift to see somebody else stammering with pleasure and anticipation. But the day she lived through was endless, bleak with undone work, dragging will, impotent anger.

"You're late," Marcie said when Laura walked in. "I wanted you to tell me about that book Burr brought over last week."

"Nothing to tell." Laura felt too low to talk, to joke, even to eat. She picked listlessly at her food. After a while Marcie fell silent, too.

When the dishes were done Marcie said, "I called Burr. Broke our date tonight." She looked expectantly at Laura, as if this were a significant revelation, and she wanted a proper reaction.

But Laura only said, "Oh?" and walked into the bedroom.

Marcie followed her. "What's the matter, Laur?" she said. And when Laura didn't answer, she asked, "Bad day?"

"Um-hm. Bad day." Laura lay down on her bed, face downward, one leg hanging over the edge, her mind wholly occupied with her father: her hatred, her stifled love for him, her fear of him.

"Talk to me, Laura," Marcie said, coming over to sit next to her.

"Not tonight."

"Please. You said you would."

"I can't, Marcie. I can't talk. I'm too tired." She rolled over and looked at her. "Don't look like that," she said. "I'm—I'm worried about my job, that's all. I'll be all right."

"What's wrong with your job?"

"Nothing."

"Oh, Laura! God! Make sense!" Marcie exclaimed.

But when she evoked no response she dropped it with a sigh. "Let's go out on the roof," she said, "and get some fresh air. It's a beautiful night."

"Looks like rain."

"How would you know? You're staring at the ceiling."

"It did, earlier."

"That's what's beautiful about it. Maybe there'll be thunder. I love to stand naked in the rain." She glanced down slowly at Laura.

But Laura turned back on her stomach without a word. A terrible apathy nailed her to the bed. Not even the nearness of Marcie could arouse her. They sat quietly for a few minutes, Laura lost in herself, and Marcie searching for a way to cheer her up. The phone rang.

"I'll get it," Marcie said, and got up. She walked across the room and picked up the receiver when Laura suddenly remembered Beebo. She sat up in a rush.

"No," Marcie was saying, "I can't. I'm sorry. I don't want to argue, not any more. I've had enough, that's all. I won't talk to you, Burr. No, it's not her fault, it's nobody's fault." She looked at Laura stretched out again on her bed. "That has nothing to do with it. No. Goodnight, Burr."

She hung up and stood for a moment motionless, watching Laura, who lay with her face turned away, apparently relaxed. Burr was getting jealous, impatient. He was ready to accuse anybody of anything to get Marcie's favor back. Their phone converstions were little more than arguments which Marcie terminated by hanging up on him. But he wouldn't be put off for long.

Marcie sat down on her own bed with a book, the one she meant to ask Laura about. She stared at the pages without reading, and wondered about her moody roommate.

Laura was watching her wristwatch. It was two minutes fast. She lay still, but she was alert, poised to jump. At two minutes past eight, by her watch, the phone rang again. "It's for me," she told Marcie, who had no-intention of going for it. Laura came across the room and sat on Marcie's bed.

"Hello?" she said into the receiver.

"Hi, lover. Where are you?"

"At home," Laura said sarcastically. "Where else?"

"You want me to come over?"

"I'll be down in a few minutes. I was delayed."

"Okay, but make it fast. I'll call again at eight-thirty. And every ten minutes after that."

Laura hung up without a further word and turned to look at Marcie. "I met him at work," she said, her face flushing. "He's been pestering me. I don't want to see him." She didn't know what she was going to do.

"Oh," said Marcie. *Then why all the fuss?* She looked curiously at Laura's pink face. Laura turned away and began to walk up and down the room, feeling as if there were a bomb sealed in her breast, ticking, about to go off. She knew her nails were cutting her underarms, yet she hardly felt them. It was an expression of terrible tension in her. Suddenly she whipped the closet door open and pulled out her coat.

Marcie, watching her, said quickly, "Where're you going?"

"I'll be back early," Laura said, heading for the door, propelled by the tight violence that was boiling inside her.

"Laura!" Marcie jumped up and followed her. "Damn it, Laur, please tell me, I'm worried about you."

Laura turned abruptly at the door. "I'm just going out for a little while," she said. "I won't be late." She tried to leave, but Marcie grabbed her arms.

"You're not fit to go anywhere, Laura. I never saw you so upset," Marcie said. "Except once. And you—you spent the night with Jack that time. It was my fault. Is this my fault? Am I driving you out again?"

"No, no, nothing's your fault." Laura covered her face with her hand for a minute and when Marcie's arms went around her to comfort her, she wept. "Please don't let me go," she whispered. "I mean—God!—I mean, let me go. Let me go, Marcie." She began to resist.

But the curiosity in Marcie had taken over. "You're trembling all over. Come to bed, Laur. Come on, honey, you're in no shape to go anywhere. Come tell me about it," she coaxed, trying to guide Laura away from the door. But Laura knew what was in store for her if she obeyed. She uncovered her face to gaze for a moment at Marcie, so close to her, so tantalizing. And that terrible storm brewing inside her made her feel as if she might do any wild thing that her body demanded of her. She was afraid.

"Please," Marcie said softly. "I'll give you a rubdown, I'm a great masseuse. My father taught me how." She smiled. "Please, Laur."

"Your father?"

"Yes."

"Do you love him very much?"

"Yes." Marcie frowned at her.

"And he loves you?"

"Of course."

"You're lucky, Marcie."

"That's the way it's supposed to be, Laur. I'm not lucky. I'm just normal. Ordinary, I mean."

Laura stared at her. The emotion in her simmered dangerously near the top. With a sudden swift movement, Laura kissed Marcie's cheek lightly, leaving the wet of her tears on Marcie's face, and then whispered, "So lucky . . . so lucky . . ." Then she turned and ran down the stairs to the elevator.

Marcie sat down on a living room chair and put her head in her hands and tried to think. Laura's strange behaviour made her tickle inside. She felt close to the storm that had barely brushed past her, and yet she remained untouched. There was only the wet on her cheek as a token, and she brushed it off, inexplicably embarrassed.

Laura made the taxi driver take her past the McAlton. She counted to the fourteenth floor, as nearly as she could figure it, and stared at the golden blocks of windows, and wondered which ones opened into 1402. And if Merrill Landon was in his room.

She walked in quickly when she reached The Cellar, with no hesitation, and made for the bar. It was a little past eight-thirty by her watch. She hoped anxiously that Beebo hadn't called Marcie again. She saw her at the far end of the bar talking to two very pretty young girls. They looked like teenagers. Laura was dismayed at the flash of jealousy that went through her. She walked right up to Beebo, without being seen, until she stood next to her. She took a seat beside her, watching Beebo while she talked, until one of the teens nudged her and nodded curiously at Laura. Beebo turned and broke into a smile. "Well, Bo-peep," she said. "Didn't hear you come in. How are you?"

"Am I interrupting something?" Laura looked away.

Beebo laughed. "Not a thing. This is Josie. And this is Bella. Laura." She leaned back on her stool so they could all see each other.

The younger girls made effusive greetings, the better to exhibit luscious smiles, but Laura only said, "Hello," to them briefly. Beebo laughed again, and leaned closer to her.

"Jealous, baby?" she said.

"I owe you one drink," Laura snapped. "What do you want?"

"Whisky and water."

Laura nodded at the bartender.

"Is that all you came for, Bo-peep?"

"Don't talk like that, Beebo, you make me sick." Laura still wouldn't look at her.

"I didn't last time."

"Yes you did. I hope you've bought your friends there one of Dutton's cartoons. It's the quickest way to get rid of them I know."

"Why didn't it work with you?" Beebo laughed softly in Laura's ear. "You came home with me that night, if you recall."

Laura turned angrily away from her. "What happened was in spite of the God damn juvenile cartoon, not because of it. I nearly walked out when he gave it to me."

"But you didn't."

"I should have."

The bartender came up and Laura started to order. She wanted to buy Beebo the drink and have one quick one herself, and then get out. Go home. Forget she had come. But before she could give an order, Beebo said, "Come home with me, Laura."

"No."

"Come on." Beebo spun her slowly around on the barstool with one arm. Laura looked reluctantly at her for the first time since she had been noticed. Beebo smiled down at her, her short black hair and wide brow making her face more boyish even than Laura remembered. She was re-

markably handsome. Laura was deeply ashamed of what
she was feeling, sitting there on the barstool, letting herself be influenced by this girl she tried so hard to despise.

"Why don't you invite Bella?" she said.

"She's busy."

Laura's cheeks went hot with fury, and she shook Beebo's arm off and started to get up, to walk past her, to
get out. But Beebo caught her, laughing deep in her
throat, thoroughly amused. "By Jesus, you *are* jealous!"
she said. "Sorry, baby, I had to know. Come on, let's go."

Laura, who was pulling against her, suddenly found
herself going in the same direction as Beebo, heading for
the door, all her resistance dissipated.

"Beebo, I didn't come here for that! I came to keep you
from calling Marcie. To pay you back that drink."

"I want you to owe me that drink all the rest of your
life, Bo-peep."

Laura gasped. Then she walked hurriedly ahead of
Beebo, trying to get far enough ahead to escape. In the
faces around the tables she spotted the slim little blonde
who had approached her before about Beebo. She was
laughing and the sudden humiliation that filled Laura
sent her running up the steps to the street. But Beebo was
close behind her, and Laura felt her arms come around her
from behind, and Beebo's lips on her neck, and her own
knees going shaky.

"No, no, oh Beebo, please! Not here, not here
please."

"Laura, darling." Beebo kissed her again. "Not here
is right. Come on." She put an arm around her and led
her away as she had before, and suddenly, strangely, Laura
felt like running. She felt like running with all her strength
until they reached Beebo's apartment. For there was no
doubt about it any longer, that was where they were going.

She wanted her arms around Beebo, their hot bare
bodies pressed together as before. Almost without realizing it she began to speed up and then to run. Instantly
Beebo was after her, then beside her, laughing that pagan
laugh of hers. She caught a handful of Laura's streaming
hair, silver in the street light, and pulled her to a stop,
whirling her around. In almost the same gesture she swept
her into a dark doorway and kissed her, still laughing.

"You're wonderful," she said in a rough whisper. "You're nuts. I love you."

"No no no no no," Laura moaned, but she returned Beebo's kisses passionately. It was Beebo who had to quit suddenly.

"Oh, God, Laura, stop. Stop!" she said. "We can't come in the streets. Come on, baby." She dragged her on for another two blocks. Laura walked if she were drunk. She had no liquor in her, but she was not sober. Not at all. She felt punchy. She half ran, half skipped, to keep up with Beebo's stride. For the last two blocks they ran as fast as they could go. Beebo led her into Cordelia Street, and through the green door into the court.

Inside the door, standing in the little court, the urgency left Laura. She stood gasping for breath, leaning against the brick wall by the door. She was where she wanted to be, next to a fascinating woman whom she wanted to make love to. It was a huge physical need, an emotional hypnotism, that drew her to Beebo. After the wild race she had just come through Laura wanted suddenly to slow down. To tease, to tantalize. She felt like somebody entirely different. Not the tightly controlled Laura who lived anxiously with Marcie, with an uncertain job, with the spectre of a hated father. Not the nerve-tortured cautious girl her roommate knew, but a warm excited woman on the verge of the ultimate intimacy. She wanted it, she asked for it, she accepted it. She stood watching Beebo, her eyes enormous with it, her nostrils flared, her lips parted. Beebo came toward her, smiling, but Laura slipped away.

She moved, almost glided, to a circle of benches in the center of the court. Beebo followed her. And again when she reached for her, Laura slipped around the benches. Beebo reached again, and Laura faded out of her grasp. And suddenly Beebo was on fire.

"Come here, come here, baby. Pretty baby. Pretty Laura," she chanted like a spell. But Laura eluded her, moving just a little faster each time, until they were running again, and Laura felt the laughter coming out of her, soft and light at first, but growing wilder, uncontrollable. She fled, inches from Beebo's hands, into the dark hallway, and scrambled up the stairs, losing her footing, and nearly losing her freedom, twice. Beebo was so close behind her near the top that she could hear her breath. With a little shriek of unbearable excitement, she fell against Beebo's door, and felt within a second Beebo's weight come hard against her. The laughter burst out of her again until Beebo got the door open and they almost fell into the living room.

Nix was all over them instantly, but Beebo, dragging Laura by the neck and Nix by his collar, locked him in the bathroom. Then she turned on Laura. Laura, seeing her, suddenly stopped laughing. Beebo looked unearthly. Her black hair was tumbled, her cheeks were crimson, her chest.heaved. But it was her eyes that almost frightened Laura.

Laura let her jacket drop from her shoulders slowly, provocatively, and Beebo approached her. They stood motionless, so close that just the tips of Laura's breasts touched Beebo, and they stood that way, without moving, until Laura shut her eyes, letting her head rock back on her shoulders, and groaned.

"Do it, Beebo," she said. "Do it. I can't stand it, do it to me."

"Beg me. Beg me, baby."

Laura's eyes opened. She didn't know how hard her breath was coming, how strange and wonderful she looked with all her inhibitions burning up in her own flame of desire. "Beebo, Beebo, take me," she groaned.

Still Beebo didn't move. Her breath was hot and pure on Laura's face when she spoke. "When I start, Laura," she said slowly, "I'm never going to stop." She put her hands against the wall over Laura's head and leaned on them, her eyes boring into Laura's, her body closing gently in on Laura's, pressing. "Never," she whispered.

"Do it, Beebo. God! Do it!"

"I'll never stop. Never." Her lips grazed Laura's brow.

Laura shook all over. She couldn't talk, except to repeat Beebo's name over and over and over, as if she were in a trance. Beebo's hands came slowly over her hair, her face, her breasts, her waist, her hips. And then one strong arm went around her and Laura groaned. They sank to the floor, wracked with passion, kissing each other ravenously, tearing at each other's clothes.

They never heard Nix's indignant barking from the bathroom, or the phone when it rang a half hour later. They never felt the chill of the rainy night nor the hard discomfort of the floor where they lay. Or the phone when it rang again. And later, yet again. It was not until late morning and brilliant sunshine invaded the room that they were aware of anything but themselves.

Once again it was Laura who woke up first. She was too bewildered to think straight at first, and the sight of Beebo, turning over slowly and opening her eyes, did nothing to straighten her out. Physically she felt wonderful. For a few moments she luxuriated in her body, letting her mind go blank.

She rubbed her hands gently over herself and discovered a bruise on her thigh. The little ache gave her a sudden hard thrill and she remembered how Beebo made the bruise with her mouth. She had to fight hard against the need to roll over on Beebo and start loving her all over again. She touched the small bruise once more and felt the same shameless pleasure. She stretched, more for Beebo's benefit than her own.

Beebo caught her and pulled her down and rubbed her black hair against Laura's breasts. Laura laughed and struggled with her.

"Beebo, I've got to get up. I have to get to work."

"To hell with work. This is love."

"Don't keep me, Beebo. This job means the world to me. I don't want to be late." She spoke the truth, yet she had no idea of how she was going to get up and get out.

"What time do you think it is, baby?"

"I don't know."

Beebo peered over her head at the dresser clock. "Eleven-thirty," she said.

Laura gasped and tried to get off the floor, the surprise giving her impetus, but Beebo held her. "You're going nowhere, Bo-peep," she said. Her tone, her self-assurance, brought out the fight in Laura.

"I've got to get there. You don't know how far behind we are. I could lose my job. And if my father ever—" She stopped, still squirming to get up. She got as far as her knees but Beebo grasped her wrists and held her there.

"I said, you're not going anywhere, baby," she said, and she wasn't kidding.

"Beebo, be reasonable. Please. You can't know how important it is to me." It was suddenly important in a new way, too; it meant distance between her and Beebo. She was vaguely afraid that Beebo was strong enough to overwhelm her, to dominate her life. She needed something else to keep her perspective, her independence.

"You don't know how important *you* are to *me*," Beebo returned. "What the hell, you're half a day late already. Call 'em and tell 'em you're sick."

"I can't."

"Why not?"

"I can't lie worth a damn, Beebo."

"You can say 'I'm sick' can't you? It's a cinch, I do it all the time. Come on, let me hear you say it."

"I can't. I turn bright red when I lie."

Beebo released her and turned over on her stomach, laughing. "Jesus, Laur, you could turn bright green. Who's going to see you over the phone? Do your damn radiologists have X-ray eyes?"

Laura was on her feet and heading for the phone in Beebo's kitchen. She dialed the office, while Beebo got up and followed her to listen.

"Sarah?" Laura said.

"Laura! Are you all right?"

"Yes. I'm all right. I'll be down as fast as I can get there. I'm terribly sorry. Is Dr. Hollingsworth mad?"

"No. You know him. He's awfully nice about these things. He did ask if you called in, through. He asked twice. Are you sick?"

She looked at Beebo, who grinned at her. "Yes, I'm sick," she said, setting her chin.

"Well, gee, maybe you'd better not come in, then."

"No, I'll be all right." She glared at Beebo who was laughing at her red cheeks. "I'll be in right away." She hung up and brushed past Beebo haughtily without looking at her.

"Laura," said Beebo, coming after her, her arms crossed over her chest. "You're not going to work."

Laura picked up her wrinkled clothes and said, "Do you have an iron?"

"You won't need it."

"I can't go out like this." Laura held up her rumpled dress, trying to shake it out.

"Then you just can't go out." Beebo stretched out on the bed and made a clucking noise at her. "Poor baby," she said.

"Why is it you're such an angel in bed and a bitch out of bed?" Laura snapped.

For answer, Beebo only lay on her back and laughed at her. Laura looked at her lithe body and after a moment she had to turn away to keep from lying down beside her. "I don't even like you, Beebo," she said harshly, hoping it would hurt. "I don't know why I can't keep away from you."

"It's because I'm such an angel in bed, Bo-peep," Beebo said. "That's all you care about. That's all you want from me."

Laura whirled and threw one of her shoes at her. "Bitch!" she exploded. The hurt had backfired. Beebo spoke the truth. And then Laura turned away to hide the surprise she always felt when the passion in her burst to the surface. In silent embarrassment she slipped into her panty girdle, burningly aware of Beebo's amused stare while she pulled it over her hips.

"I wouldn't bother, baby," Beebo said lazily.

"Why not?" Laura wouldn't look at her.

"Number one, I hate the damn things. Number two, you don't need one. Number three, you can't go to work in a girdle. Period. And that's all the clothes you're going to get."

"What?" Laura turned around.

Beebo had gotten off the bed and with two or three sweeping gestures she grabbed Laura's clothes and headed for the bathroom.

"Beebo, what are you doing? What's the matter with you? Give me those things! Beebo!" Laura tugged at her but Beebo, laughing, was too much for her. Nix burst out of the bathroom as Beebo shouldered in. She turned on the shower full force and threw the clothes over Laura's head into the drink. And while Laura was still spluttering at her she threw Laura in, too, gently, dumping her on the clothes. Everything, everybody, was soaked.

"Beebo, you animal! You're impossible!" Laura said furiously. She turned off the water angrily and snatched up her clothes, wringing them out into the tub. She was trembling with anger. She faced Beebo with a crimson face and threw the clothes at her.

"Take the girdle off, Bo-peep," said Beebo with unconcern. She threw the clothes over a wooden drying rack. "It doesn't do a thing for you."

Outraged, Laura tried to scratch her, but Beebo pinned her back against the bathroom door and kissed her. Laura bit her and only made her laugh. With a feeling of excitement so strong it almost made her sick, Laura knew what was coming.

"No!" she exclaimed, suddenly sobbing. "No, I won't! No!" But it was submissive, helpless. Beebo forced her to her knees. Standing spreadlegged beside her, she put her strong hands behind Laura's neck and pressed Laura's face into her belly. "I said I'd never stop, Bo-peep. I said never, remember?"

"Please, Beebo . . ." Frustration and desire were both so strong in Laura now that she was nearly out of her mind. Her weakness had got her again, and Beebo would make the most of it.

It was late afternoon before she called Marcie. She had left under such peculiar circumstances that she was afraid of what Marcie must be thinking. She didn't want to call. Marcie was angry with her, to Laura's surprise.

"You told me you were coming right back," she said.

Laura was bewildered. "I meant to," she said. "I swear, Marcie."

"You lied to me."

"No, I didn't, I just didn't know—I mean—"

"Don't lie to my any more, Laura. It makes me sick. I thought we were finally getting close to each other. I thought we were finally going to be friends." She sounded upset.

"But Marcie, we are."

"I know where you went, Laura."

Laura went white, and Beebo, who was lounging around the kitchen making dinner, turned to watch her with a frown. "What do you mean, Marcie?" Laura said.

"I nearly lost my mind," she said. "I would have called the police and made a fool of myself. But I called Jack first, thank God. Laura, why won't you tell me the truth? Why won't you just admit that I make you nervous? This isn't the first time I've driven you over to Jack's. If you don't tell me what I'm doing wrong how can I ever do anything right?" Her voice broke. "I feel as if I'm making your life intolerable. As if you'd rather move in with Jack and live in sin than put up with me. You might as well, you spend so much time in his bed."

"Marcie! Marcie, I don't!" Laura was thunderstruck.

"I've already talked to him, so don't deny it, Laura."

"Marcie, honey, listen to me. I—" She looked up at Beebo and the look on Beebo's face silenced her. "Marcie, we'll have a long talk tonight. I'll try to explain it to you. We can't talk over the phone."

There was a brief pause on Marcie's end. Then she said, "Are you at Jack's now?"

"I—no—I'm at the office."

"You must have just gotten there. I've been trying to get you all afternoon."

Laura got more bewildered, more tongue-tied, the more she lied. "Marcie, I can't talk now," she said urgently. "Please. I'll come right home. I'll explain."

"All right, Laura. But I'll tell you right now, I'm ready to move out if you want me to. I'm sick and tired of getting on your nerves and not knowing why."

Laura shut her eyes and tried to control her voice.

"Laura? Are you still there?"

"Yes." She cleared her throat. "I'll see you tonight, Marcie." She hung up and turned a pale face to Beebo.

Beebo snorted and opened the refrigerator door. "She still straight?" she asked sarcastically.

Laura was stung. "No," she flung at her. "She's falling in love with me."

"Don't kid yourself, Bo-peep."

"I'm not kidding. And I'm not blind . She's jealous of Jack. She thinks I spent the night with him and it's her fault. She wants me home."

"How sweet," said Beebo and chucked her under the chin. Laura pushed her hand away impatiently.

"My clothes should be dry by now," she said, getting up.

"Call Jack," said Beebo. "Ask him what he told your roommate."

Laura hated to do anything Beebo suggested, just because Beebo suggested it. But Beebo was right. Laura called him at the office. She got him five minutes before closing.

"I found out from Mortin—the bartender at The Cellar," he said. "And if you pull another fast one on me, Mother, by Jesus, I'm going to let you stew in your own juice. I called you a dozen times last night. You must have been out on Cloud Nine. Marcie's mad as hell. She thinks I'm corrupting you."

"I know. I'm sorry," Laura said earnestly. "Jack, what would I do without you?"

"I don't know. But I wish to hell *you* did. Marcie'd like to see me behind bars."

"Jack, isn't that a good sign? I mean she seems almost jealous."

"Oh, Christ," he said, and then he laughed. "You're really goofy for her, aren't you?"

Laura looked up at Beebo. "Yes," she said. "I am."

"Well, watch it. I don't know what to tell you. Nothing seems to register. If I say 'she's not gay' to you once more I'll sound like a broken record. But she's not. I don't want to see you get stabbed, that's all. Better you should blow off steam with Beebo until you get over Marcie."

"I've blown off about as much steam as I can stand," Laura said, and Beebo laughed. "I'm through."

"Don't be so dogmatic, Mother mine. You'll only have to swallow your words and you'll look like an ass doing it."

Laura wouldn't believe him when he told her Marcie was straight. She wouldn't because she didn't want to. She had told him, she had even told Beebo now, that Marcie was falling for her. She didn't dare believe it herself, but if somebody else did, maybe somehow that would help. Her desire, her pride, trapped her. "Thanks

again, Jack," she said. "One of these days I'm going to
do the same for you. I swear."

"One of these days you may have to. And Laura—"

"Yes?"

"Watch out for Burr. You're on his black list."

"What'd I do?"

"He thinks you're turning his pretty little sex-pot
into a neurotic. He's jealous."

Laura smiled, surprised.

"Well?" said Beebo, when she hung up. "Going
home to your little wife?" She grinned.

"Beebo, sometimes you make me sick."

"I know. I'm enough to make you go straight. Go sleep
with Jack tonight, it'll do him a world of good."

"Oh, shut up!"

"At least it'll give him a whopper to tell his analyst."

Laura turned on her heel and left the room. She felt
her clothes, hanging in the bathroom. They were still
damp, but dry enough to iron. She brought them into
the kitchen. "Where's the ironing board?" she said.

"Pretty determined, aren't you?"

"I certainly am."

"I've got dinner ready. You can eat before you go."
There was a faint tone of pleading in her voice, as
if she knew the time had gone when sheer force was
useless. Laura had made her mind up.

"I don't want another thing from you, not even dinner."

"No, not for another day or two," Beebo said and her
voice became rougher as she talked. "You just want to
run down for kicks once or twice a week. I'm pretty
damn convenient, aren't I?" She pulled the board out
from the wall and plugged the iron in, her movements
sharp and angry. Laura felt a little afraid of her. Her
blue eyes snapped and there was no trace of her usual
humor in her face.

"You're the bitch, Laura, not me. You're using me,"
she said. "Go on, iron the damn thing." She waved a
hand at Laura's dress and Laura spread it out on the
board.

"I'm sorry, Beebo," Laura said, taken aback.

"Sure you are."

"All right, Beebo," she said softly. "I won't bother you any more. Ever."

Beebo snorted at her. "You try it and I'll beat you, I swear I will," she said. "I've had enough from you, Laura. I'm not made of stone. Am I nothing to you? Am I supposed to *believe* I'm nothing to you? Do you think I like to stand and listen to you slobber over that simpering little roommate of yours? Can she give you what I can give you? Well damn it, *can* she?"

Laura couldn't face her, much less answer her. She only worked the iron over her dress and glanced at Beebo's shoes.

Beebo's voice softened a little. "Jesus, what a mess," she said, leaning on the refrigerator. "Here I am falling for you. I ought to have my head examined. I ought to know better." She came over to Laura and took the iron out of her hands and Laura had to look at her. "Laura," Beebo said, leaning toward her, "I'm nuts for you. I wasn't kidding." They gazed at each other, Laura surprised and scared and flattered all at once. "I need you, baby," Beebo whispered. "Please stay."

"I can't, Beebo," Laura said.

"You don't really think you're in love with that little blonde, do you?"

"Yes."

Beebo shook her head and shut her eyes for a minute. "Jack says she's straight. Jack is a shrewd boy. Don't you believe him?"

"No."

"You want to get the Miseries, Baby? That's the quickest way."

"You don't know her, Beebo. Even Jack doesn't know her as I do. She's changing. She seems interested in me. She's sort of approachable. She doesn't even want to see her ex-husband anymore. She wants to stay home at night with me. She breaks dates with him to do it."

"All right." Beebo turned away. "Suppose she's gay. Suppose she is. What then?" She turned to look sharply at Laura.

Laura was stumped. She had never looked beyond the present into that possibility. What would it be like,

just the two of them, both gay, living together, in love?
"Well, then everything will be wonderful," she said.

Beebo gave a short unpleasant laugh. "Yeah," she said.
"Wonderful. You walk hand in hand into the sunset."

"I didn't mean to hurt you, Beebo. I never made a secret of my feelings for Marcie."

"I never made a secret of mine for you, baby."

"We'd never do anything but fight, Beebo."

"Fight and make love. I could live forever on such
a diet." She smiled a little.

"It would drive me crazy. I couldn't take it."

"Do you think there won't be fights with your little
Marcie if she turns out gay?"

"I suppose there will."

"You know damn well there will. And if she's
straight, what happens? She reads you the Riot Act.
Calls the cops. Sics her husband on you."

"She wouldn't do any of those things, Beebo. She's a
sweet girl. She wouldn't get wild like you."

"Not according to Jack. You've known her four
months. Jack's known her for years." Beebo lighted a
cigarette and blew the smoke through her nose. "Want
to know something, Bo-peep? Want to know what it's
like? I've had it happen to me—more than once. If
you're gay, it just happens now and then, that's all. You
get the bug for some lovely kid and you can't keep it
to yourself. You get closer and closer. And if she plays
along it's worse and worse. And finally you give in
and you grab for her. And she turns to ice in your arms."

She looked at Laura and there was a deep regret in her
eyes. "And she gets up with the God damnedest sort of
dignity and walks across the room and says 'I'm sorry.
I'm so sorry for you. Now go away. Don't talk, don't try
to explain, I don't want to hear. It makes me sick. Just
go away, and I won't tell our friends. You don't need to
worry. Just so I never see you again.' It makes you heart-
sick, baby. You get so sick inside. You give yourself
the heaves. All you want in God's world is to get the
hell out of your own skin and be normal. Fade into the
crowd like a normal nobody." She crushed her cigarette
out, grinding it into the ashtray with her thumb till
the paper burst and the brown tobacco spilled out.

Laura felt closer to her. All the insults of the day faded in her mind. She walked over to her, her pressed dress over one shoulder. "Beebo," she said softly.

But Beebo wasn't ready to let herself be touched. "Just remember one thing," she said. "Too many Marcies in your life, and you commit suicide. That's what it is to be gay, Laura. Gay." Laura stepped back a little shocked. "Sometimes all it takes is one," Beebo said.

"No," Laura whispered. "Oh, no."

"Okay, baby, go find out for yourself. I can't stop you, Jack can't stop you." Beebo's eyes were brilliant with bitterness, with the hard knowledge of her own experience. "Go play with your little blonde. You'll find out soon enough she has claws. And teeth. And when you get to playing the wrong games with her, she'll use them."

"Never!" Laura said. "Even if she's straight she won't hurt me. She's not that kind."

"She doesn't *have* to hurt you, idiot. Can't I get that through your head? All she has to do is say 'no thanks'. Kindly. Sympathetically. Hell! If you want her bad enough, you'll die of it. I know, Laura, I know!" And she took Laura's shoulders and shook her head until Laura felt like sobbing. Beebo released her suddenly and they stood in silence, unable to talk, heavy with feeling, trembling.

Finally Beebo said quietly, "Go on, baby. Go home and get it over with. You've been warned." All the fight seemed gone out of her.

When Laura left, Beebo came to the door with Nix at her heels. She was unsmiling. "Come back, baby," she said. "To stay. Or don't come back at all." And when Laura turned away without answering she called after her, "I mean it!"

Chapter Twelve

Laura entered the penthouse and walked slowly back to the bedroom. It was hard to imagine Marcie's mood. Marcie looked up from her bed, her hair in pincurls. She was a relief to Laura's eyes after the stormy, ranting handsomeness of Beebo. Marcie looked beautiful, even with tin clips in her hair. But she looked cool, too; ready for a fight.

Laura slipped her jacket off without a word, thinking of the loud quarrels she and Beth used to have. And how they resolved them with love. A little curl of excitement twisted around her innards.

"Well?" Marcie said sharply. "Did he throw you down in the street?"

Laura was startled, offended. Marcie had no right to say such a thing. "What do you mean?" she said.

"Your dress," Marcie said, nodding at it.

Laura looked down at it. Beebo had dragged it over the bathroom floor and the dirt, together with a hasty pressing job, made her look like she'd been through a scuffle. "Marcie," she said, trying to control her voice, and not sure when she started talking what she was going to say, "Marcie, I didn't sleep with Jack."

Marcie turned her eyes down to the book she was holding, and her expression said, Tell me another one. "With who, then?" she said.

Laura pressed her lips together and sat down on Marcie's bed. *I won't yell at her,* she told herself. *I can't take the chance. I'd say the truth, I'd blurt it out by mistake.* "Marcie, I just ended up down in the Village."

"Did you wander around all night?"

"No. No." She looked down at the floor. "Well, I—"

"You what?" Marcie looked at her.

"Marcie, I *didn't* spend the night with Jack." Her voice begged for understanding.

"Jack has friends."

Even in her mounting irritation Laura sensed jealousy

and it thrilled her. "Yes, Jack has friends. And they aren't all men."

"Don't tell me you spent the night with a girl. Ha! That's even better. You just hang around with anybody who's handy, don't you."

"You aren't very choosy yourself, Marcie."

"Only with Burr!" Marcie flashed angrily. "I only sleep with Burr. And I was *married* to him. Besides, I haven't let him touch me for weeks. You've never been married, not to Jack or anybody else."

"And I've never slept with Jack or anybody else."

"I don't believe you!"

Laura stood up and looked down at her. "You don't have to, Marcie," she said. "What the hell do you care who I sleep with? Or why? Are you guardian of my morals? Yours aren't perfect, you know. I haven't slept with Jack, for your information. Not once. But if I had, what would it matter? You thought it was all a good joke at first."

Marcie's face began to color. She put her book down and looked diffidently at Laura, who was standing by her dresser taking off her clothes. Marcie ran her fingers over her lips, as if warning herself to shut up and Laura thought to herself, *Just like me. Just like me when Beth used to taunt me. I wanted her so. And I was so afraid.*

"I didn't know it would get so serious, at first. With Jack," Marcie said, her attitude softening. "I feel like it's my fault, what you're doing, and I—I feel real bad about it. I'm scared. Maybe you'll get into trouble, maybe you'll blame me then. You get so *odd* sometimes. I guess I'm just being selfish, Laur. But—" She gave an audible sigh that made Laura turn to glance at her. "Laur, will you tell me—will you *please* tell me—why you keep running out of here at all hours of the night? What am I doing wrong? If you don't tell me, I'm going to move out of here tomorrow, I swear. I can't stand it!"

Laura had to tell her something. She had to lie and she couldn't lie and as she walked toward Marcie's bed, she felt something like panic at the thought of losing her. But when she sat down beside her something popped into her head and saved her. She didn't have to stammer and blush, and she didn't have to confess her homosexuality. She told Marcie about her father.

She was almost ashamed to recount what had happened. It was humiliating, and it looked like a bald bid for sympathy. And yet she wanted terribly to touch Marcie's heart, to win her compassion. "He told the clerk he had no daughter." She finished. Her shame made her drop her gaze and cover her face with her hands. But Marcie, suddenly moved, put her arms around Laura and cried.

"Forgive me, Laura," she whispered. "I've been a stupid idiot about this. I don't know what got into me. Honey, forgive me, I should never have tortured you about it. Whatever your father did to you, he must be a beast. He doesn't deserve to live."

But that was going too far, even for Laura. There had been violent moments of shame and rejection, when she wanted to kill him. But there were others when she wanted only to be allowed to love him. "Don't say that, Marcie."

Marcie looked up at her, her face so close that she gave Laura a start. "Don't tell me you still feel anything for him?" she said. "After what he did to you?"

"I don't know what I feel. I hate him sometimes, Marcie, I hate him so much sometimes that I'm terrified of myself. I think 'If he were with me right now—if he suddenly appeared—I'd kill him. I'd *kill* him!' " And she said it with such force that Marcie shuddered. "And then, other times, all I want to do is cry. Just cry till there aren't any tears left. Get down on my knees and beg him to love me."

"It seems so crazy, Laur. My Dad is so nice and ordinary. I couldn't take it if he ever hurt me like yours. God, you must feel so alone. Laura, let me be close to you. Let me be friends with you. You haven't up to now, you know."

Laura began to feel dizzy. *This is too much, this is too easy,* she thought, and pangs of conscience came up in her. *All I have to do is pull her close, caress her, kiss her, all I have to do—oh, my God! But I can't! It'd be like corrupting her, like leading her astray. Damn! Why have I got a conscience? Beth didn't have one. Neither does Beebo. Why me? Why can't I just take her?* But she was too afraid.

"Laura, talk to me. You're off in another world again."

Laura looked down at her, balanced between desire and fear, between desire and conscience, between desire and ... desire, desire ...

"Marcie," she whispered. "Remember the night you wanted to touch tongues?"

Marcie laughed a little, embarrassed. "Yes," she said. "I told Burr about it. He says I'm cracked."

Laura was shocked. "You told Burr?" she said, hurt by the betrayal.

"Well, don't look so horrified." Marcie giggled. "Don't tell me you didn't tell Jack?"

And Laura, by her sudden confusion, admitted that she had. With the admission, and the shock, came a clear head. She stood up. Marcie watched her. "I'm going to bed," Laura said. "I'm too beat to talk. I'm just worn out."

Marcie let her go without a word. Her eyes followed Laura around the room. Laura ignored her studiously. She was asleep within minutes after she lay down, too tired even to worry.

Laura knew she would have to lie to Sarah in the morning about where she spent the day before. She made up her mind to do it fast and simply. She organized a little story about a sick headache and she delivered it quickly, even before Sarah had a chance to ask. Sarah took it at face value.

At the end of the day, she called Marcie and told her she'd be late. "I've got to stay here and catch up," she explained. "I've done nothing but get behind the whole time Jean's been away. I just can't seem to get the work done. I'm not going to lose this job."

"You're wearing yourself out, Laur. I think you're crazy. You can get a much softer job and earn a lot more money. In fact I talked to Mr. Marquardt about you."

"You *what?*"

"Yes." She laughed. "Today. I thought it would be fun if we could be in the same office. Besides, I never saw anybody work like you do. It's insane, when all you have to do is sit around."

"Marcie, I don't *want* to sit around! I don't need help! I can do this myself. I know you did it out of friendship but damn it, I *want* to work. I don't want to sit around on my behind all day, counting the minutes till the next coffee break."

Marcie was taken aback by the forcefulness of it. "Laura, I didn't mean—" she began, and her voice was hurt.

"I know, I know. I'm grateful, Marcie, forgive me. But I have something to prove, staying here. It's only hard at first, when you're learning. It'll get easier. And in another two weeks there'll be three of us at the office."

She knew she had hurt Marcie's feelings and when she hung up she wondered if it was worth it. *Why don't I quit? Why don't I take a soft job, like Marcie?* But she knew what scorn her father would pour on a job like that. It was only the tough ones, the ones that took it out of you, that demanded your best, that he had any respect for.

Laura stayed on until nearly eight by herself. The building was crypt-quiet and she was deep in the last round of reports she intended to do, when the door opened and a voice said, "Laura!"

Laura gave a gasp of shock, throwing her hands over her face. She was so startled that she found herself trembling all over. For a moment she was unable to move.

"Laura?" he said again.

Laura turned slowly around in her swivel chair, taking her hands away from her face. She looked up, her face cold and white and resentful. It was Burr. She didn't say a word. She only stared at him in surprise. She felt overflowing with hatred for him, as if Merrill Landon were standing there.

Burr was somewhat taken aback. "Marcie said you were down here," he said, a little awkwardly. "I wanted to talk to you." He shrugged, and pulled Sarah's chair out from her desk, sitting down about five feet from Laura. She said nothing.

"Laura," he said, embarrassed. "We started out to be pretty good friends, you and I." He turned his hat around and around in his hands, studying it while he talked. "Then—I don't know why—we seemed to—well, we just didn't have anything to say to each other. I guess maybe because we always talked about books. And Marcie. You don't seem to be reading any books any more. And Marcie —well . . ." He seemed at a loss for words here. He twirled his hat assiduously, as if that might give him some answers. But it was no help. "Of course, I haven't been around much lately, either," he said.

Laura was suddenly a little scared. But she was determined not to be any more helpful than his hat. She only glared at him. She still hadn't said a word to him. *After all*, she thought, *I haven't done anything. He still hasn't said what he wants.*

"Well, frankly Laura, Marcie's changed. I don't know what the hell's come over her. I thought maybe you could help me out." He eyed her closely. "I guess it sounds pretty silly. But I love her, and all of a sudden I can't even see her any more. I can't get near her. She's just not interested." When Laura still said nothing he went on, "I mean, I know it's not your problem, but I thought, being her roommate, you know, you might help me out." He looked up at her, smiling a little, but his smile faded when he saw the look on her face.

Laura was thinking, *Why the hell should I help you?* But she said, "Why don't you stop fighting with her, Burr? Maybe that would help." Her voice was faintly sarcastic.

"When we fought," he said, "at least we could always make up. That was fun. We both enjoyed it. Then all of a sudden, a couple of weeks ago, Marcie wouldn't fight any more. I don't know what the hell got into her. She just got quiet and thoughtful. She wouldn't fight and she wouldn't make love. I'm beginning to think she needed to fight before she could make love. Maybe that's the only thing that excited her." He looked quizzically at Laura.

"How would I know? Maybe *you* needed it," Laura said, and shrugged.

By her reticence she had made Burr uncomfortable. "Well, I know it isn't exactly the sort of thing to bother you with," he said, making a visible effort to control his temper. "But damn it, Laura, I love her. She's my wife. I still think of her that way, I can't help it. I was a fool ever to let her have that divorce."

"Do you think getting married again would change any of that?" Laura said. "Don't you think it would just be the same old fights all over again?"

"I don't know." He shook his head. "Maybe. But I'd rather live with Marcie and fight than live without her and be this miserable."

"Does fighting make you happy?"

"I don't mind it. Not enough to make me give her up again."

"You talk like a kid, Burr," she said, wondering what authority gave her the right to pronounce judgments. And then she reasoned that Burr himself gave her the right. He asked for it. Okay, he'd get it. "If you want to win Marcie back, find out what's the trouble and change it. If you want my opinion—and I guess that's why you're here—I don't think you should go back together. I think Jack's right; you were never meant for each other. It's purely physical."

These were hard words, but even so Laura wasn't prepared for the effect they produced. Burr went pale and his mouth dropped open. Suddenly he stood up. "Jack said that?" he said incredulously. "*Jack?*"

And Laura went a little sick. She had violated a confidence, without even meaning to. The one person she couldn't bear to hurt, to alienate right now, was Jack. "Maybe I'm mistaken," she said quickly. But who else could it be? "It was me, Burr, I don't know why I said that. It wasn't Jack."

"Oh, it was *you!*" He had been surprised into a fury. He had been nursing his grievance, trying to talk calmly to Laura. Now his feelings got out of control. "Well, I'll tell you something, Laura. I don't believe you. It was Jack or you wouldn't have said so. You're a lousy liar. Now suppose you explain something to me." He leaned with his fists on her desk.

Laura leaned away from him, frightened now. "Calm down, Burr," she said, but he ignored her.

"You and Jack can both go to hell!" he said. "You've been psychoanalyzing the situation over a couple of beers in your spare time. A couple of cocktail hour psychologists. Oh, don't think I can't see it. Well, I don't give a damn for what you think. I love Marcie!" He was shouting. "I love her! And I'd like to know why the hell she doesn't love *me* any more. *Why,* Laura? *You* tell me. Why would she rather stay home with you at night than go out with me? Why does she talk about Laura, Laura, Laura all the time? Laura reads this, Laura does that, Laura says! God, I'm sick of it!" His ugly suspicions exploded in her face.

"She doesn't, Burr, you're mistaken."

"Mistaken!" he roared, his face turning scarlet. "Mistaken! Oh, you're a bitch, Laura! Mistaken! And she won't make love to me any more. She won't see me. You're the only one she gives a damn about. She can't get enough of you at home, she's got to get you a job in her own office. Yes, she told me about it," he interrupted himself, when Laura gave a little gasp.

"Burr, you fool, you're making things up," Laura said. She looked cold and controlled, but there was a terror inside her that he couldn't see. She rose in her seat and faced him, their faces not a foot apart. "Now get out of here." It had worked before with other men. It had to work now with Burr. She would give him no satisfaction.

"Don't tell me you're not up to some God-damn funny business," he growled.

"I'm not up to any God-damn funny business," she replied quietly.

"Then what's all this crap about touching tongues? In the dark? In bed? Why does Marcie follow you around like you were Svengali?"

"She doesn't."

"Don't tell me she doesn't!" he shouted in a fury, bringing his fist down with a huge thump on her desk. "I know she does. I know!"

"Burr, you're insane with jealousy."

"What's going on between you two?"

"Nothing. Absolutely nothing. I'm a bad liar, you said it yourself. If I had ever touched Marcie I couldn't lie about it." She glared at him, her face a mask, almost white; her eyes brilliant and her body tense.

"You want her. Admit it." He was quiet now, but it was the quiet of hatred.

"I won't admit anything. Who the hell are you? I don't owe you any explanations."

"She's my wife."

"So she's your wife. She's *my* roommate. She prefers to live with me." Laura was dangerously near throwing her advantage in his face.

"You *are* queer! By God, I knew it!"

"How dare you!" And the hot blood came to Laura's face. "Get out of here! You bastard!"

"All right, deny it, then!"

"I'm not accountable to you, Burr. I won't admit or deny anything. I don't have to. I'll call the police if you don't get out of here. I'll sue you for libel if you make that accusation in public. I never laid a hand on Marcie."

"That's not what Marcie said."

For a shocked second Laura was unable to move or respond. Then she gasped and staggered a little. There was a terrible silence, heavy with the awful meaning of his words.

Laura sat down shaking. She began to cry.

Burr watched her in silent fury for a moment. Then he said, "I thought that'd get you, you bitch." His voice was low and dry. "I came here to talk to you like a human being, to give you a chance. But you act like a God-damn queen. You act like I was in the wrong, not you! Like I was an animal. Well, you're no better. You're a pervert, Laura. And I'm going to get Marcie away from you if I have to call out the cops to do it. You're not going to touch her again." He turned sharply and started out.

"Burr! Burr! My God, wait! What did she say? What did she tell you?"

"Can't you guess?"

"She made it up, Burr, believe me. Please believe me." She was begging him now. "You know how she is."

"Yeah, I know how she is. She didn't make this up."

"She did! She's lying."

"She's telling the truth. You're perverting her. It's obvious, even I can see it. Perverting her! My Marcie!" He almost wept when he said it, and Laura instinctively put a hand to her throat as if to protect herself.

"Burr," she said and her voice was deeply intense and quite, "I swear to you by God and Heaven and everything I hold sacred, I never—"

"You hold nothing sacred! You're a walking profanity! You're a mockery of womanhood. You're queer. *Queer!* And you're infecting Marcie. I'm going to get her away from you. Now, Tonight!" And he turned on his heel and walked out.

Laura called after him until he walked into the last operating elevator and disappeared. She sobbed wildly for a minute, collapsed in her chair. Then, as if electrified, she picked up the phone and dialed the penthouse, as fast as her trembling fingers would let her. She almost died of impatience before Marcie answered. "Hello?" Marcie said.

"Marcie! Marcie, what have you done to me? Answer me!"

"Laur?" Marcie's voice sounded small and frightened. "What's the matter, honey?"

"Burr just left me. I thought he was going to kill me. Marcie, what did you tell him?"

"Oh, Laura." Marcie's voice was only the faintest whisper. "I had no idea he'd—I didn't think he'd bother you. I didn't think he'd even mention it."

"What did you tell him, Marcie?" Laura's voice sounded almost hysterical.

"I—we quarreled." Marcie was crying quietly while she talked. "We quarreled, for the first time in weeks. It was terrible. As if to make up for all those weeks when we didn't fight at all. He accused me of—forgive me, Laura, I'm ashamed to say these words—of falling in love with you."

Laura groaned despairingly.

"Laur, I'm so sorry. I guess I talked about you all the time. I get interested in somebody, or something and I just don't talk about anything else for a while. I talked about you because I admire you so much. I—well, you know. He got the wrong idea, that's all. But I didn't realize it, I swear I didn't, Laur. I would have stopped him if I had. And then we had this quarrel tonight and I said some things I shouldn't have."

"What things? *What things,* Marcie?"

Marcie sobbed. "He accused me of trying to tempt you, of egging you on. Oh, Laura, this is too horrible, I can't go on."

"Tell me!"

"And I got so furious. It was so unfair. You know we haven't done anything! He was just determined to believe it. He can't believe I just don't want to see him any more, that's too hard on his damned pride. So he was just waiting for somebody to blame, and there you were. And I was so damn mad at him. It was hopeless, there was no talking to him. He was losing me because somebody else was winning me, that's the only way he could see it. So I finally just shouted at him, 'All right, have it your way, you big fool. Believe what you want to believe, I can't stop you!" She was interrupted by her own sobs.

"Marcie," Laura said, making a huge effort to control herself, "Did you tell him that I . . ." She could hardly get the words out. ". . . made love to you?"

"No! No, Laura!" Marcie cried.

"Did you tell him anything specific?"

"Absolutely not, I swear!"

Laura gave a sigh of relief. She began to cry again herself. After a moment she said softly, "Marcie, he's on his way to the penthouse. He says he's not going to let you spend another night in the same apartment with me. I'm infecting you."

"Oh, Laura, honey. God!"

"So you'd better lock the door."

"We don't have a key!"

"Get one from the janitor."

"I'm afraid of him. He's down in the basement. It's so dark down there and he always tries to make a pass at me."

"I shouldn't think that would bother you." Laura couldn't help the dig; it made her feel better.

"Laura, he's nuts. He's a meatball."

"Well, damn it, do *something!*" Laura cried, exasperated. Then she forced herself to speak quietly. "All right, call the police," she said. "Say your former husband is threatening you. Say you're afraid of him, you think he wants to kill you. Say anything! Tell them he's on his way over right now and you want protection."

"Laura, I've never done such a thing in my life! Poor Burr! I've known him since I was a kid, I worshipped him."

"You stopped worshipping him in a hurry when you had to live with him. Listen to me, there's not much time. If you don't want him to do something violent you'd better get some protection. I can't fight him off for you. Unless you want to go with him tonight."

"Go with him! That bastard! After what he did tonight? He can go to hell. Without me."

"That's where he'd like to see *me,*" Laura said. "I'd bet-

ter not show up. I'll stay down here for another hour or
so. I'll call you before I come home, to be sure the coast
is clear."

"Laura? I hate to call the police, Laur. It makes me
sick." She sounded miserable.

"Marcie for God's sake, you're a taxpayer. You're en-
titled to protection. Burr was in a fit when he left here."

Marcie began to weep again. "Laura, I'm so sorry. I'm
so sorry," she said softly over the phone.

Laura's heart softened too. "Oh Marcie," she moaned.
"I guess it really isn't anybody's fault. Burr's still in love
with you. None of us realized how much. He had to be
jealous of somebody, and he knew you weren't dating anybody else. We've all been pretty stupid about the whole
thing. I just hope to God it blows over." All of a sudden
she felt powerfully tired.

"It's all my fault," Marcie said. "Everything's my
fault. I'll make it up to you, Laura, I promise."

"Never mind, honey. Just keep out of trouble tonight.
I'll be home about ten. I'll call you first."

"Okay." Marcie was still crying when she hung up.

For a long time Laura sat at her desk, staring into space.
The windows were black, gold-spangled with the city
night, and everything was still.

She got up, feeling weak and tired, and yet not desperate or frightened any more. Burr had no proof of anything. Marcie would deny everything. And if things went
as it seemed they must, Burr would act like a crazy man
and convince the police he was bent on violence. Marcie
would be genuinely frightened and it would show. There
ought not to be any difficulty about it. She got her things
together and turned out the office light.

The hall to the elevator was bare and echoing as she
walked down it. The elevator boy was silent, as if he too
had been touched by the vast quiet of the night.

Laura walked out on the street. People hustled by,
lights shone, cars honked. But it all seemed far away, not
very real. Her senses registered only half of what they perceived.

*Where shall I go? I'd better not try to go home for a
while. Not till Burr leaves. Another hour, at least.*

She looked at her watch: eight-thirty. She walked slowly, gazing ahead of her like a sleepwalker. *I'll go somewhere where I can sit down and read,* she thought. She bought a magazine from a corner stand and sauntered on another couple of blocks until she saw the McAlton on the next corner.

She almost exclaimed aloud, as if the hotel had been sneaking up on her while she marked time on the sidewalk. She stopped in her tracks to stare at it and then looked self-consciously into a shop window. After a few minutes she moved on to the hotel.

If I just sit in a corner, as if I'm waiting for somebody, they can't do anything. I'll just read this thing till nine-thirty or so.

A tiny unworded excitement knotted itself around her heart and stuck there, prepared to stay for as long as Laura stayed in the lobby. She didn't go over to the desk. She just sat down in an alcove on a leather covered sofa next to a fat middle-aged woman. She read until nine-thirty.

Then she got up and walked halfway across the lobby to the phone booths, entered one, and dialed the penthouse. Marcie answered.

"Is everything all right, Marcie? It's Laura."

"Yes." She sounded tired, reticent.

"What happened?"

"Nothing. The policeman got here right after Burr did. Burr was yelling like a crazy man. The policeman took him out and told him to stop bothering me or they'd take him down and book him. He was furious. He cried. But he went. Damn it, he deserved it, after what he did to you."

"Are you alone now?"

"Yes."

Laura suddenly felt enormously relieved. "Thank God," she said.

"Will you be right home?"

"Yes. Right away." She hung up and left the booth, putting some change in her purse. She felt much better. Burr was mad as hell, that was certain. But for the moment he would have to watch himself; he would have to be careful. Marcie was disgusted with him. Obviously force was the wrong way to get her back. And suddenly Laura saw her father.

Merrill Landon was about twenty feet from her, his face turned profile to her, talking to some men.

Laura gave a low cry, almost inaudible, and her heart stopped. The knot around it gave a tremendous squeeze, like a big angry fist, and stopped it altogether for a moment. It started again with a tremendous thump. She darted toward the little alcove, her face averted, but found all the seats taken. She stood facing away from him for a minute, her heart kicking wildly, wondering frantically what to do.

I've got to be calm, I've got to be calm, she said under her breath, but each time she said it it seemed more hysterical. She gulped convulsively and barely heard someone say in her ear, "Excuse me, dear. Are you all right?"

"Yes. Yes, thanks," she said, her voice staccato, afraid to identify her questioner.

She shut her eyes tight for a minute. *If I just walk out quickly, he'll never see me. The lobby is full, there are dozens of people in here. He's not looking for me, he's talking to some men, he won't see me. I'll just walk out.*

She took a very careful glance behind her. He was facing her now, but not seeing her, gesturing, talking, engrossed in his words. He would never see her. For a second she permitted herself the luxury of looking hard at him; his big maleness, his strong face that could never be called handsome and yet compelled interest. That face that almost never smiled at Laura since she was five years old. That face she was condemned to love.

Laura turned away then and began to walk toward the door, keeping her face averted, hurrying, her heart pounding as if she were running up a steep hill. Near the door she slowed down a little. *I'll never see him again,* she told herself fiercely. *Just one more glance. It will have to last me my life.* She turned around slowly, carefully, just five feet from the door and safety.

He was looking at her. Looking straight at her, as if he had been following her through the crowd with his eyes, not quite sure but wondering. For a split second Laura didn't believe it; thought he didn't really see her and was just looking that way. But then he cried, "Laura!" in his

big rough voice, and her eyes went huge with fear and she
gasped and turned and ran as if the devil were after her.
She ran headlong, panicky, her heart huge and desperate,
struggling to get out of her throat. She ran with all her
strength and with an unreasoning terror whipping her
heels, all the way to the subway. She never once looked
back. People turned to stare, they jumped out of the way
and she collided with a dozen of them. She almost fell
down the subway steps and ran and dodged and shoved
her way into the ladies rest room.

There, she fell on the floor, whimpering, crying despairingly, unable to lift herself off the filth of the black floor
and completely unaware of anything but the hysterical fear
that gripped her. After a while she felt hands on her
shoulders and she gave a wild scream and sat up. A terrified Negress was bending over her, saying, "There now,
there now." Her eyes were all whites.

Laura panted, speechless, gasping for breath. She
leaned exhausted against the door of a booth until her
wind came back to her and then she tried to get up. The
Negro woman helped her, handling her like heirloom
china, watching her every second for fear she would take
off on another fit.

Laura half staggered to the wash basin and turned the
water on. She looked at her haggard face in the mirror
and an attack of real crying, soothing relief with real tears,
overwhelmed her. "Father, Father, Father," she cried
softly, her face in her hands.

"Can I help you, Miss?" the colored woman asked.
She was scared by Laura's behavior, but fascinated.

Laura shook her head.

After a moment's pause the woman said, "You came
in here like a bat out of hell. You was out of your mind,
honey, that's for sure. Was some sonofabitch chasin' you?"

Laura put her hands down to look at the woman in the
cracked mirror over the basin. She nodded.

"Well, I never seen a girl so scared in my life. Never."
She shook her head positively. "You better get yourself
some help, honey. Is he still out there?"

At this Laura went so white that she frightened the
woman again, who said, "There now, there now. Didn't
mean to start nothin'. Don't go off like that again."

Laura turned around to look at her. And in her awful unhappiness she went to her and put her arms around her, to the bottomless astonishment of the woman, and wept on her shoulder. "I never had a mother," Laura sobbed. "I never had a mother." And her heart was broken.

The woman held her like a child and said, "There now, there now. Everybody's got a mother, even you."

"Nobody knows me. I don't even know myself. I don't know what I'm doing here," she said brokenly. "I'm a stranger in this world."

"Well, now," said the woman, "Everybody's a stranger when you look at it that way. But everybody got a chance to find a little love. That's the most important thing. When you got a little love, the rest don't seem so strange or sad no more. There now, honey, there now."

Laura suddenly shied away from her. "Don't call me honey!" she said, her face twisted with misery.

The Negro woman let her go, shaking her head. "You pretty sick, girl," she said. "You need a doctor, and that's the truth."

Laura turned and walked out of the rest room on shaking legs. Outside she looked warily up and down the waiting platform. Only a handful of people were there. A train had gone through just after she entered the rest room and had taken most of the crowd with it. She waited in silence for the next train.

The woman came out of the rest room after Laura. She stood some distance from her, staring at her with a mixture of distrust and pity, until the train arrived and the crowd separated them.

Laura came home too exhausted to talk about it, to be embarrassed with Marcie about the fight with Burr. She was so full of her experience, so absorbed in her father, that nobody else seemed real. She almost fell into her bed, with hardly a word to Marcie, and lay there wrapped up in herself, crying quietly for a long time.

Things were no better in the morning. Somehow the enormity of Burr's accusation hung between them like a curtain. They could look at each other only furtively; they couldn't speak. They were embarrassed, a little afraid of each other, and it made them overly polite. All they said was, "Excuse me," "pass the cream, please," "I'm sorry." Laura had the additional burden of her terrible flight from her father to keep her both silent and preoccupied.

She was unable to figure it out. She knew she didn't want to talk to him, to show him any forgiveness at all, to satisfy his curiosity about her—if he had any. She only wanted a glimpse of him; she wanted to reassure herself that he was still in New York, even though she knew he was. And she knew he might see her if she hung around his hotel. And she was ashamed that he should see her and know how important he was to her, even after his cruel denial of her. All these things were plain to Laura and yet when she looked back on the night before it seemed incredible. Especially her own terror.

They parted for work without more than a perfunctory goodby. Laura knew it was going to be a rough day. She had had almost no sleep. And for the first time since she took the job she didn't even give a damn what happened. She was too engrossed in herself and the urgent unnameable feelings that plagued her. Not even the head start she had given herself the night before encouraged her. It only reminded her of Burr and the ugly quarrel they had had. The thought of her father, which usually spurred her on, even on the darkest days, now filled her with a shaky apprehension and so engaged her mind that it was hard for her to think about anything else.

Bombshells fell around her all day. Marcie called in tears at ten to say she couldn't stand it any longer and wouldn't Laura forgive her. And Laura was forced to take time out, while Dr. Hagstrom was in the room, to reassure her. Marcie wouldn't be put off; there was no help for it.

Sarah reminded her that they were all going out for dinner that night. They had arranged to meet Jack and Carl Jensen at a small bar a couple of blocks away for cocktails and to go on from there. It wasn't until Sarah mentioned it that Laura even remembered it, and then she was dismayed.

Just before lunch, Jack called.

"Laura," he said firmly, "what the hell are you trying to do to me?"

"Nothing. What's the matter; Jack, can't you make it tonight?"

"Tonight be damned. I'm liable .to get skinned alive. Right *now.*"

"Did something go wrong with Terry?" Laura was startled into attention.

He paused a minute before answering, taken aback to hear his lover mentioned right out on the phone. "No," he said. "I spoil him rotten, but that's nothing new. Guess again."

"Well, Jack, I don't have time for guessing games, we're—"

"I know, you're behind. Burr told me you stayed late last night to catch up."

"Burr told you? Oh!" Suddenly she remembered. "What's the matter with me?"

"You tell me. I'd like to know. Burr was real sweet. He told me I was a lousy bastard and no friend of his, and I could take my psychoanalysis and cram it. Oh, he told me some very interesting things. He told me you're queer and you're perverting Marcie, and you two are lovers, and Marcie sicked the cops on him last night, and God knows what else. Would you care to explain to me what the hell is going on? Just so I won't put my foot in my mouth? You know how it is." There was the forgiveness in his bitter humor and it made her miserable.

"Jack, I'm so terribly sorry," she said. "I blurted out something about the way you felt about Burr and Marcie. I was trying to calm him down. I should have known better. He was out of his mind."

"Since when are you and Marcie lovers?"

"We're not! I would have told you, you *know* that." She glanced surreptitiously across the office at Sarah, but Sarah had her eyes on her work. "Burr got it into his head we were because Marcie talked about me so much. Because she stayed home and wouldn't go out with him. When he accused her, it made her so mad she just told him, 'Okay, believe it.' And he did. I thought he was going to kill me last night."

At this Sarah did look up, but Laura didn't notice.

"Well, that's a hell of a story," Jack said.

"It's the truth, Jack! I swear."

"Never mind the truth. You've got me in a lovely mess. Burr thinks I promoted the whole affair."

"My God! Jack, what'll we do?"

"What *can* we do? Have you done anything with Marcie you wouldn't want to write home about?"

"Nothing! I wish to God now I had. As long as he's going to believe it anyway."

"Oh, no! Christ! Whatever you do, Laura, don't touch Marcie. Not till Burr straightens out. Never, if you have any sense."

Laura wouldn't answer him. She felt closer to winning Marcie, in spite of their awkwardness with each other this morning, than she ever had. She wouldn't make any promises to Jack.

"You hear me, Mother?"

"Yes."

He apparently took that for a promise. "And one more thing."

"I can't take any more right now."

"This won't hurt. What have you done to Beebo?"

"*Done* to her? Nothing. Ask her what she's done to me," she said, and her voice was hard. Sarah watched her with considerable interest now.

"Keep your voice down, Mother," Jack said. "Beebo's goofy for you. And when she gets a girl on her mind, that girl had better watch out. She's a stubborn bitch."

"So am I," Laura snapped.

"She's in love with you, Laura. Don't cross her."

"I'd walk all over her if I could. She treats me like a slave."

"Christ, keep your voice down," Jack said, and Laura was surprised at her own lack of caution. Usually she was meticulously careful. Today, nothing seemed to matter. "She's in love with you," Jack said. "That explains a lot of things."

"It doesn't excuse them. Besides, she isn't. How do you know she is?"

"She said so."

"When?"

"Last night."

Laura couldn't help being flattered. The pleasure in her was warm and sudden and overwhelmed her bad conscience briefly. "I'm not going to see her again." she told Jack. This time she almost whispered, which intrigued Sarah still more.

Jack laughed. "Have it your way," he said. "Only don't drag me into your messes any more, Mother. I've got enough of my own."

"Is everything all right between—I mean—" She looked over at Sarah for the first time and surprised Sarah staring at her. Sarah went quickly back to work and Laura felt suddenly nervous. "Jack, I'd better hang up. We'll talk tonight."

"Okay. See you at five-thirty."

Laura spent the rest of the day reassuring herself, *I'll never go back to that hotel. He'll be gone tomorrow. Or Sunday at the latest.* The thought gave her considerable relief.

Chapter Thirteen

Carl Jensen was a clean cut young man, very fair with freckled skin. He engaged Sarah in conversation right away; it was a part of what he considered good technique to get a girl talking, and he wasted no time.

Jack and Laura had dinner with them, but Jack was obviously chafing to get away. They hadn't even finished their after-dinner coffee before he was whispering in Laura's ear, "Let's get the hell out of here." Laura, who was almost wordless through dinner, agreed.

Jack did the dirty work. He told them a joke, he made them laugh, and then he said he had a meeting the next day up in Albany. Very unexpected. Would they mind, etc.

They were a little startled, Jensen especially, for he had expected Jack and Laura to stick with him and lend moral support through the evening—but they replied, almost together, "No, go ahead. We don't mind."

As soon as they were in the street Jack sighed, "God. I couldn't have stood another minute of it. Straight people are so depressing."

Laura smiled at him and noticed for the first time that evening how tired and worried he looked. She was so wound up in Laura Landon that nobody's troubles counted for her but her own. But now she saw Jack's anxiety and she was afraid she had caused it. She started to apologize. "Jack, I want you to know . . ." she began.

"Skip it."

"Please."

"I said skip it." And his voice was harsh enough to hurt her.

They walked along in silence for a minute and finally Laura said, "Jack, I have to talk. I feel awful about it. I saw my father last night. He saw me, too. I don't know what came over me. I've never been so terrified in my life, as if he were the devil and I had to get

away from him. I ran all the way to the subway. I think
I was hysterical."

He looked at her and then he sighed. "Everybody's hysterical. Even me."

"There was an old colored lady there. In the rest room.
She said something I didn't understand then, but I've
been thinking about it. She said everybody is a stranger in this world until he finds a little love. That's
the most important thing."

"Wise lady," Jack said.

They walked without talking for half a block. "How's
Terry?" Laura asked.

"He needs a spanking. I act like a lovesick cow with
him. I can't help it. I know I'm doing it, and I can't
help it. He laughs at me." Jack looked at the pavement as he walked, his hands shoved into his pockets.
"Mother," he said slowly. "Do you want to get back in
my good graces?"

"I do," she said gently. "Yes. I do."

"Well," he said, and stopped walking. She stopped
beside him and saw that he was embarrassed. "This is
a rotten thing to do. But I'd do it for you, bear that
firmly in mind." He poked her chest between her
breasts, as if he were making a point with a fellow
business man. It was intended to lighten the atmosphere a little, but the atmosphere was too heavy already.

"I'll help you, Jack, you know I will. Any way I can.
You've been so wonderful to me. I don't know what I
would have done."

"Okay, okay." He stopped her abruptly and then
seemed unable to speak himself for a minute. Finally
he said, quickly, "I'm losing him, Laura."

"Oh, Jack!" She was suddenly full of sympathy, but he
cut her off again.

"What the hell," he said cynically. "I expected it. I
predicted it. And I know why."

"Why?"

"Mother, you have a short memory." He smiled wryly.
"My little friend likes nice things. Nice things cost
money. And besides," he looked at his shoes, scraping
one toe along a crack in the pavement, "I can't handle
him. I should shove his teeth down his throat. I should

make him behave. And I can't. I feel more like falling on my knees and worshipping him. He has no respect for me." He spoke so softly that Laura had to strain to hear him.

She put her hands on his arms. "Jack, he's not worth your time," she said. "Anybody who would take advantage—"

"No, no, no, it's normal. In this abnormal world we live in, you and I. If I were young and beautiful, he'd settle for that. But I'm not. I'm middle-aged and ugly. And a sap. So it takes something else . . . money. I wish I had the knack of being a millionaire."

"Damn it, Jack, you need somebody who can appreciate you." He laughed bitterly, but she went on. "You make me hate Terry already without ever having seen him."

"No, Laura," he said seriously. "Don't hate him. He's very young. He'll learn. It's my fault. I can't give him what he needs."

"Dollar bills?"

Jack sighed. "That's my last chance. I know it takes something else, but I haven't got it. And now I haven't got the dollar bills, either."

"If I were a boy I'd fall madly in love with you," Laura said.

This was such a startling remark that Jack had to drop his cynicism and take it in the spirit in which it was given. "Thanks, Mother," he said softly. He looked at her, his ugly intelligent face prey to a number of strong emotions that he made no attempt to hide. It was a measure of his regard for Laura that he could let her see him stripped of wit and laughter like this. "How much do you have in the bank, Laura?"

Laura stared a little at him. But then she said quickly, "All I have is yours, Jack. It's not much, but if it'll help . . ."

He smiled a little and then he leaned over and kissed her cheek. "You're a doll," he said. "We both know this is a losing investment. But it'll give me a few more days with him. After that . . ." He shrugged. "Well, I always seem to live through these things. I don't know why."

They stood uncertainly on the corner for a minute and suddenly he asked, "Where are you going now?"

"Home."

"To Marcie?"

"Yes. I hope Burr hasn't tried to bother her."

"He's pretty sick about the whole thing. I think he'll drink it off for a day or two. You should, too. The whole thing looks screwy to me." He looked at her. "Come have a nightcap with me."

"Where?"

"The Cellar. Where else?"

"I'm afraid I'll run into Beebo."

He shrugged. "I've gotten to know her better." He gazed away from her thoughtfully.

"You have?"

"She calls me all the time. 'Where does Laura work, what does Laura like, tell me all about her.'"

"She asked you that?" Laura was slightly incredulous, but once again, she liked it. She was sorry she liked it, but she did.

"Yeah. I'm beginning to think I like her."

"You liked her before."

"I know." He laughed. "I'm not making sense. I guess I mean I feel sympathetic toward her. We're both unlucky in love. At the moment." He looked hard at her then and said, "Please come with me, Laura. I don't want to go home."

"Why not?"

Again he laughed, not so pleasantly this time. "I'm afraid of what I'll find."

"Like what?"

"Like somebody else in my bed with Terry."

After a moment of shocked silence, Laura put her arm in his. "Okay," she said. "Let's go somewhere and flatter the hell out of each other."

He chuckled at her. "Mother, damn it, sometimes I suspect you of having a sense of humor."

They went down to The Cellar, in spite of Laura's misgivings. Jack seemed so unhappy that she wanted to indulge him. It was crowded as always on Friday nights, but Beebo wasn't in sight.

"She'll be in," Jack observed. "She's late on Fridays."

They stood at the bar until a couple of stools were vacated and then sat down.

"What does she do?" Laura asked rather shyly.

"Who? Beebo?"

"She must get money somewhere. She has to pay the rent like everybody else."

"She runs an elevator. In the Grubb Building. They think she's a boy."

"My God—an *elevator*." It seemed wrong, even ludicrous. Beebo had too much between her ears to fritter her youth away running an elevator. "What does she do *that* for?"

"She doesn't have to wear a skirt."

Laura was stunned. It was pathetic, even shameful. For the first time she saw Beebo not as an overwhelming, handsome, self-assured individual, but as a very human being with a little more pride and fear and weakness than she ever permitted to show.

Laura didn't know how long they had been there when Beebo walked in. She only knew she had had plenty to drink and it was time to go home. Beebo walked up to her, and Laura saw her face first in the mirror. She turned around with a start and stared at her. Beebo was wearing a dress.

A dress. And high heeled shoes. She was over six feet in the high heels. Strangely enough she wasn't awkward in them, either. She wasn't comfortable, but she could walk a straight line and keep her balance.

"Hello, Bo-peep," she said quietly in Laura's ear.

Laura felt a grateful response flow down to her toes from the ear. "Hello," she said to the mirror image and then turned to face her. "Hello, Betty Jean." She looked at her skirt.

Beebo gave her a wry smile. "You remembered?" she said. "Do you remember the good things, too?"

"Yes," said Laura, smiling back. And surprised herself. For a moment she felt curiously receptive. She had no idea why.

Beebo gazed at her and then she put a hand on Jack's shoulder. "Hello, fellow sufferer," she said.

"Hi, doll." He turned around. "We're drowning our sorrows." He gestured at Laura with his glass.

"So I see. Mind if I drown a few with you?"

"We'd be delighted."

Beebo nodded at the bartender, who nodded back and fixed her a whisky and water. Beebo was on good terms with the bartenders in all the gay bars. They knew what she drank and they served her without being told. Beebo leaned on the counter between Jack and Laura.

"Where've you been, doll?" Jack asked, waving a hand at her dress. "Masquerade ball?"

"Party," she said laconically, hoisting her newly arrived glass.

"Gay?"

"Straight."

"How dull. What's the matter with you, Beebo? You're no fun anymore. You wear skirts and go to straight parties. Jesus."

Beebo grinned at him. "I have one dress, lover. I get it out once a year and wear it. In honor of my father. He likes dames."

"Yeah, but he's not around to appreciate it."

"Well, you are, Jackson. Give me a kiss." And she took his chin in her hand and extracted one from his reluctant mouth.

"God!" he said, and made a face. Beebo laughed. And Laura sat and watched them and wondered what they were all doing there and why they laughed at themselves when they were all aching inside from unspeakable hurts. She felt vaguely jealous to think of Beebo at a party with people she didn't know and had never seen. Beebo surrounded by women. Laura looked at her until Beebo returned the stare without talking, only looking at Laura until Laura had to lower her eyes. "What's eating you, Bo-peep?" Beebo said, running a finger around the edge of her glass.

"Are pants really that important?" Laura said. She said it sarcastically because she was afraid of her tears.

Beebo laughed a little. "I don't know. How important is *that* important?"

"Why don't you get a decent job?"

"Oh," said Beebo as she understood. She finished a second drink. "I've got one, baby. I'm a lift jockey. Very elevating work."

"Not funny," Laura said. "You work all day at a lousy job like that, and then you drink all night."

"Does that bother you?"

"Yes. Not very much, of course. You're not worth it. But it seems awful. All for a pair of pants."

Beebo laughed. "Reform me, baby."

"I don't have time."

"What do you have time for?"

"Work."

"And Marcie?"

"And Marcie." Laura didn't know why she said it. She knew how badly it would hurt. But she was high, the go-to-hell feeling was still with her from the morning. It was either hurt or be hurt; sarcasm or tears. She looked up slowly at Beebo. At her blue eyes and her lips turned down, with an unaccustomed trace of lipstick on them. Laura wanted to hurt her. She couldn't stop herself. She turned on her stool to face her. "You're ridiculous," she said. "You're a little girl trying to be a little boy. And you run an elevator for the privilege. Grow up, Beebo. You'll never be a little boy. Or a big boy. You just haven't got what it takes. Not all the elevators in the world can make a boy of you. You can wear pants till you're blue in the face and it won't change what's underneath."

Beebo just stared at her, her face suddenly pale and frowning, in silence. Then she turned, leaving her cigarette still lighted in a tray on the bar, and left them without saying a word to either.

Laura and Jack sat in silence for a while after she had gone, watching her cigarette burn itself out. Finally Jack said, "If Terry had done that to me, Laura, I'd have strangled him."

Laura put her head down on the bar and cried.

The weekend was a stalemate for Laura and Marcie. Laura was so deeply involved in her conflicts that it was impossible to talk about them. In two weeks Jean would be back. In a day her father would be gone. Burr would start hounding Marcie, and Laura still didn't know why Marcie had let him think they were lovers. And Beebo . . . Beebo . . . that hurt the worst, somehow. It was so needless, so brutal. The kind of thing Merrill Landon had done to her when he was in a temper. Just to blow off steam, to dissipate the mood. Only he went even farther. He would shout and call her names, slap her, call down the wrath of his dead wife and son on her head.

Marcie couldn't get through to Laura, hard as she tried. She, too, began to get moody. She launched into long self-reproaching speeches which tortured Laura until she begged her to stop.

On Monday Laura went to the bank before she went to the office and withdrew one hundred and ninety-two dollars. She was going to leave herself twenty, just in case, but she left herself five instead. She had a little at home. She could get along until the end of the week. The rent wasn't due and there was food in the house.

Jack came by at five and picked it up. "Come out for dinner with me," he said. "I seem to have come into a little money."

"No, thanks."

"My treat," he said, directing his sarcasm at himself and waggling her dollars at her.

Laura smiled faintly. "Take it," she said. "I can't talk to anybody tonight."

"How's Marcie?"

"Brooding. I get on her nerves, I guess."

"That's only fair. She's made a mess of yours. How's Burr?"

"He called her. They talked for a few minutes. He asked her to see him."

"Will she?"

"No."

"Not yet, hm?"

"Never," Laura said sharply. "She's fed up with him."

"Well, if not Burr, somebody else." Laura covered her face with her hands suddenly and Jack looked at her sympathetically. "Just won't believe me, will you, Mother? You love Marcie so sooner or later Marcie will have to give in and love you."

"No!" she said, looking up. "I know it's not that simple. It's just that I'm convinced I have a chance. I live with her, I know her, and she was willing to have Burr believe we were lovers."

"She was willing to get him the hell out of her hair after a bad quarrel," he said. "That's all. She just let him believe it to get rid of him."

"Please Jack," she said with forced patience. "How's Terry?" *If he's going to torment me, I'll give him the same treatment,* she thought.

Jack lifted his eyebrows slightly and shrugged. "Healthy," he said. "And hungry. Jesus, how that kid eats. And he likes smoked oysters."

Laura had to smile, though she didn't feel like it. "Get him a bale of smoked oysters," she said, "and leave me alone for a while. Please."

Jack gave her shoulder a squeeze. "Okay." He started out and then turned to ask, "How did Sarah like Jensen?"

"She said she liked him. She has a crush on Dr. Hagstrom, but she liked Carl anyway."

"He's smitten. Says he's going to call her again."

"Good." They smiled a little at each other. "Somebody's doing it right," Laura said wistfully.

Jack laughed. "Never mind," he said. "Someday we'll die and go to heaven. All the angels are queer, you know." And he left.

Laura followed soon after. She knew just where she was going—the McAlton Hotel. She would walk right in and ask for Merrill Landon and the clerk would say he had left, the convention was over, and Laura could quit suffering over him. He would be hundreds of miles away and she could start to forget him.

She walked over to the hotel in a matter of minutes and went into the lobby with a confidence she had not felt during the week her father had been there. She was about to kill her ghost. She looked forward to great relief.

At the desk she waited for a moment or two until a clerk could take care of her. She recognized him from one of her previous visits but fortunately he didn't seem to remember her. "Yes?" he said.

"Is the Chi Delta Sigma convention over?" she asked.

"Yes, ma'am it is."

"Oh. Then I guess Merrill Landon isn't staying here any more."

"Oh, yes he is."

Laura was startled. "He said a young lady might be asking for him," the clerk said. "He left a message." He looked at her dubiously, unnerved by the strange expression on her face. "Would you be his daughter, by any chance?"

Laura shook her head numbly. The clerk brought her an envelope and Laura opened it and read, in her father's hand: "Laura, I will be here till the end of the month. Come up to my room any evening after eight." It was not even signed. *Nice and sentimental,* she thought. *Just like him.*

"Thank you," she told the clerk.

"Will there be any answer?" he asked.

"Yes," Laura said. She took the pad of paper he pushed toward her and wrote on it, "Go to hell." Then she folded it, put it in the envelope, sealed it, and wrote "Merrill Landon" on the front.

She shook all the way home. He was still there, still haunting her, waiting to pounce on her and punish her. When Marcie asked her what was the matter, Laura couldn't tell her. It was Laura's problem, it was intimate and awful, and she had no wish to share it. She hardly noticed how little she had looked at Marcie the past few days, how little she had responded to her. And yet in the back of her mind the question rankled: Why did Marcie let Burr believe that lie? Even for a short while? Why hadn't she fought it harder?

But the fact of her father's physical presence in New York obliterated other considerations. He was waiting for her around every corner, in every doorway. She was even afraid to answer the phone, and afraid to return to his hotel for fear he would have the police there waiting for her. She didn't know on what grounds he could arrest her, but she believed her father could do anything violent and forceful. Her work suffered still more at the office. And she hadn't the interest to stay late and make it up.

Sarah talked to her one afternoon at the end of the week. "Guess what?" she said, to start out in a friendly vein.

"What?"

"Carl Jensen called me again. We're going out tomorrow night."

"How nice, Sarah. I'm glad for you." But she spoke without enthusiasm.

"Are you?" Sarah's voice was pointed enough to catch Laura's attention and warn her that something was wrong. She looked up. "Yes, of course I am, Sarah. I'm sorry, I'm not myself lately. I—"

"You've been in a fog all week. Another one of those headaches?"

"No. I mean yes. I don't know. I just don't feel alive." She laughed listlessly.

Sarah sat down beside her. "Laura," she said firmly, "you could do real well in this job. If you wanted to. Everybody here likes you. Everybody's pulling for you. You're a good typist and you're a smart girl. Jeanie liked you a lot, and she'll be back here in another week. There'll be three of us, and things could go a lot better . . . but Laura . . ."

"But I haven't worked out too well," Laura said for her. "Is that it?"

"You haven't worked at all sometimes. Other times you work your tail off. That's the trouble, Laura, you're so erratic," Sarah said. "You stay late and knock yourself out one night, and then a week goes by and you can't do a damn thing. You drag along all day, you just don't seem to care.

"I hate to pull a philosophical on you, but gee, Laura, we're dealing with sick people. Sometimes these X-ray reports spell life and death for somebody. We can't dawdle over them. Doctors are waiting all over the city for these things. Dr. Hollingsworth is swamped. We can't let him down."

"I know." Laura felt the way she had in third grade when she feigned sick to get out of playing a role in the annual spring pageant. The teacher had talked to her in much the same tone of voice, and used much the same arguments. "Everybody's pulling for you, we all like you, don't let us down, Laura, don't let us down." But the thought of going out on that stage had appalled her. The whole audience melted down to one man—Merrill Landon. She had done it, finally, to prove she could. But his amused criticisms afterward had nearly killed her.

"I haven't been feeling well," she murmured to Sarah.

"Well, you'd better start feeling better, honey. Because Dr. Hollingsworth and I had a little talk today. He asked me what was wrong with you. He thought maybe if you and I talked it over you might tell me what was the matter." She spoke carefully, in a discreet voice.

But Laura stood up, offended and frightened. "Nothing's the matter," she snapped. "If he doesn't like my work let him come to me and tell me about it himself."

Sarah stood up, herself slightly offended at this display of ingratitude. "He came to me because he wanted to spare you any embarrassment, Laura. I should think that would be obvious."

Laura relented a little. "I'm sorry, Sarah. I can't explain it. I just can't, it's impossible. If he wants to let me go, I have no choice. I'll leave." But she was not as resigned to it, as stoical, as she sounded.

"Can't you *try* to do a little better, Laura?" Sarah said kindly. "If I could tell him we had a little talk and you promised to try to do better. Or you'd been sick, or had a problem at home, or something. *Anything.*"

Laura gave an unpleasant little laugh. Then her face dropped and she said, "I have no excuses, Sarah. I'm not a good enough liar to cook one up. I just—" And here she burst unexpectedly into tears and Sarah had to try to comfort her.

"Look, honey," she said, after Laura had recovered a little. "Do you want the job? Do you?"

"Yes," Laura said. "I want it."

"Will you try to be more consistent, then? And I'll tell Dr. Hollingsworth you've been having trouble at home you don't want to talk about."

"That's such an obvious fib, Sarah."

"No, it's no fib. I heard you talk to Jack on the phone last week," Sarah said. "I know there's something going on."

Laura went shaky and pale, and the blue shadows that had been growing in the past weeks under her eyes deepened. "What do you know?" she demanded.

Sarah became alarmed at her appearance. "Well, nothing really, only you sounded so upset, I thought maybe—"

"What did I say?"

"Oh, I don't remember." She tried to push it off casually, but she had thoroughly scared Laura, who recalled with biting clarity now Jack's voice saying, *For God's sake, Mother, keep your voice down.* "What did I say, Sarah?"

"Nothing so very bad, Laura." Sarah stared at her. "I just got the impression you had a quarrel."

"You had no right to listen!" Laura exclaimed harshly.

"You had no right to make personal calls during working hours, for that matter," Sarah said defensively.

Laura picked up her purse and ran out of the office without another word. She went into a phone booth and called Jack. "Can I come over?" she said.

"No. I'm in a mess."

"Please, Jack."

"Mother, for Christ's sake! Be empathic for once, will you?"

"All right, I'll call Beebo."

"No don't. She's p.o.'d at you. She may never speak to you again after what you said to her."

Laura felt frantic. "Well, what am I supposed to do?" she said, half crying into the receiver. "I've practically lost my job."

"Go home to Marcie, Mother. Do *something.* I can't help you out tonight. I'm sorry, honey." And he was.

"Oh, Jack, say something to me. Say something kind. Anything."

After a pause he said, "I love you, Mother. Only I'm not *in* love with you. I wish to hell I was, it couldn't be worse than Terry. Now be a doll and let me go. I'll call you tomorrow."

She felt the urgency to get away in his voice and let him go. For a moment she sat in the booth and dried her tears. She felt sick about Beebo but she was afraid to call her.

It was another torturous weekend for Marcie, who was beginning to feel as if she had ruined Laura's life. It was Sunday night before they actually made any sort of communication with each other.

Burr had been calling Marcie every night, trying to talk her into leaving the apartment. Their talks were short but the animosity had faded from them. Laura listened to them listlessly; she could not avoid hearing them in the

small apartment. Marcie said things like, "Yes, she's here."
"No, you *know* I don't want to see you." "No, we aren't,
and don't bring that up again." "I know I did. I know
what I did, Burr, don't throw it in my face." She refused
to see him.

Laura winced at all this, and finally she took to going
out on the roof when he called. The windows were wide
open, the weather being soft and pleasant now, and
Marcie's voice carried even out there. But it wasn't so
pervading, so persistent. On Sunday night, Laura went out
and looked at the city while Marcie talked. The time
passed almost without Laura's being aware of it. She gazed
across New York in the direction of the McAlton, wondering if her father was sitting in his room waiting for
her. And then she looked down toward the Village and
her heart gave a sick squeeze at the thought of Beebo.
Beebo, who told her how terribly a love affair could hurt.
Beebo, who told her to beware and then got caught in her
own trap. Laura wondered if Beebo really loved her. If
she could ever forgive her. Laura had attacked the very
basis of her being: her body, her pride, her deepest needs.
In that one quick wicked speech, Laura had ridiculed
her. She felt the tears come. And she could hear Jack saying, "If Terry said that to me, I'd strangle him." It was
shameful.

She grew very depressed, thinking of the necessity of
going back to work in the office the next morning, with
Sarah trying to put on cheerfulness and Dr. Hollingsworth—so kindly, so tolerant—watching for signs of stead-
iness and application in her. And herself, so heavily aware
of their good will toward her, their frustration, and her
own overwhelming complexities that sapped her strength
and effort.

She was startled when Marcie said at her elbow, "Burr
wants to see me." When Laura didn't answer, Marcie said,
"He feels God-awful about the whole thing. He wants to
apologize to me." Another silence. "I want to apologize
to *you*, Laura. But you won't let me."

Laura shut her eyes in pain for a moment, as if to avoid
the sight of Marcie's face. And then she opened them and
without looking at her, said, "We've been all through this
before, Marcie. I don't want your apologies. You have
nothing to apologize for."

"I do."

"You don't!"

Marcie gave a long sigh of exasperation. "All right, then why won't you speak to me?"

"I *will*, Marcie. When I can."

"When will that be?"

"I don't know."

"Why not now?"

"I guess I'm sick. Maybe Jack was right, I need to see his analyst." She tried to smile a little.

"Because of your father? What he did to you?"

Laura looked down at her arms, folded on the cement railing. "I guess so," she almost whispered.

"Laura, say something to me. This is unbearable." Marcie was pleading with her, as Laura had pleaded herself with Jack on the phone. She turned and looked at Marcie, standing close beside her, two delicate lines between her eyes betraying the tension inside her. For a moment Laura just looked at her. It had been over a week since she looked at Marcie that way. In the soft spring night, in the golden light fading up from the streets below, with the myriad muffled noises that are the music of a great city around them, they gazed at each other. And Marcie was very beautiful with her hair lifted gently in the breeze and her eyes big with anxiety. She was wrapped in a blue silk negligee and the lines of her slim young body showed through it.

Finally, prompted by the necessity to speak, Laura said, "It's so hard to talk, Marcie. Words are so inadequate sometimes."

"Any words will do, Laura. Except 'Excuse me.' That's all you've said to me for days on end."

They smiled a little at each other, and Laura took her hands. She pulled just a little on them, and Marcie responded softly, coming toward her. "Laura, tell me I'm forgiven. Don't say there's nothing to forgive me for. I just want to hear you say it."

"No."

"Please." Her voice broke.

"No, no, no," Laura said, gazing curiously at Marcie. Did she really feel so guilty? She hadn't done anything that bad. Laura had a strange feeling of finality, of the end of things, of everything ending at once so that nothing really mattered any more. As if Marcie would turn and walk out of her life, and her job would end, and Beebo would never see her, and Jack and Terry would break up. It made her pensive and sad. She wondered at all the new feelings in her: the inability to care about her job, her meanness with Beebo, her unreasoning fear of Merrill Landon in the hotel lobby. Nothing seemed very real, up there on the roof. It didn't seem to make much difference what she did. She gave another little pull and Marcie came still closer, touching her up and down the length of her body.

Laura touched her hair. "You look so much like a friend of mine," she said. Marcie reminded her of Beth again at this moment; the Beth she had lost so long ago, a million years ago, it seemed.

"I do? You never told me that."

"I forgot."

"What's she like?"

"Oh, she was tall, short dark hair, purple eyes. Rather boyish."

"You talk about her as if she were dead."

"She is. As far as I'm concerned."

Marcie frowned at her. "She doesn't sound at all like me."

"No, I guess she doesn't," Laura said. "There's something about your face; I don't know how to define it. I thought I saw a resemblance." She had seen it in Beebo, too. And even in the curly-headed little blonde who had approached her in The Cellar the night she was looking for Beebo. They couldn't all look like Beth. It was very strange.

"Were you good friends?" Marcie asked.

Laura smiled a little and put her arms around Marcie. In the still night she answered simply, "We were lovers." It was very quiet, dreamlike, as if she spoke in a trance.

Marcie stared at her, motionless, as if to determine whether she were joking. She stood in Laura's arms, unable to move one way or the other; uncertain and a little scared.

Laura saw her consternation, but it didn't worry her. She spoke again, still feeling as if it weren't real, any more than the glittering city below was real, or her father's

wrath, or Jack, or Beebo, or the doctors and Sarah . . .
"That was the 'great love' I told you about, in college,"
she said. "It was Beth."

After a long pause, Marcie said in a whisper,
"What happened?"

"She got married," Laura said.

Marcie was dumbfounded. "I'm sorry," she said awkwardly and then retreated into herself, embarrassed. She
had no idea what to say, what to do.

Laura could see that, but at first she didn't try to in-
terpret it. It didn't frighten her yet. "That's why I
was so shocked when Burr said you told him we were
lovers," Laura said. "I wish we were, Marcie. But I
never touched you." Marcie was studying her now, her
eyes brimming. "When he accused me of it and believed it and said you told him so, I was so hurt I
didn't know what to do or say. I thought of a million
crazy explanations. The only one that seemed to make
sense was that you felt the way I do." She looked hard at
Marcie. Their faces were very close together, and Laura
was holding her tightly, her arms locked around Marcie's small waist. "Do you, Marcie?" Laura whispered. "Do you?"

They stayed that way for awhile, not moving, looking at each other. Laura felt her breath speed up and she
felt a powerful longing to kiss Marcie. It grew stronger
by the second. She began to press Marcie against her
rhythmically and suddenly all the months of repression
exploded inside her and came out kisses on her lips.
She began to kiss Marcie intensely—her face, her neck
and arms, her ears, her throat. "Marcie," she said
hoarsely, suddenly holding her tight with the strength
of desire. "I've wanted you for so long. I thought I'd die
of it. Living with you, so close to you, seeing you all
the time . . . undressing, bathing . . . It drove me crazy.
Marcie, you're so beautiful, so sweet. Oh, God, it feels
so good to say it. You're impossible. I want you so terribly, so terribly. You want me too, don't you? I know it,
I always knew it. Oh, Marcie, let me, let me. Don't
stop me! Please!" A note of anguish crept into her voice
when Marcie began to resist her. "Please, Marcie!" she
implored her.

But Marcie put her arms up and pushed hard against Laura. "Let me go!" she said. "Let me go!" And she began to cry. Laura, shocked, released her so suddenly that Marcie staggered backwards a little. She gave a cry, recovered her balance, and stared at Laura with her eyes wide for a moment. Then she turned and ran inside.

Laura stood where she was for a long time, afraid to think or feel. She had no idea how much time had passed before she dared to go inside. Had she frightened Marcie? Revolted her? Would Marcie greet her with love or hatred? As a witch or a lover? She was in a state of nervous agony when she finally gathered the strength to walk around to the penthouse door.

She opened it and walked slowly through the living room and kitchen. She pushed the bedroom door open slowly. Marcie was sitting on her bed, her back toward Laura. She had apparently sat like that without moving for some time. She turned very slowly when she heard Laura come in, and looked up at her. Laura felt her heart turn over. Marcie was so lovely, so miserable. It showed plainly in her face. Laura went to her and dropped to her knees in front of her and put her head in Marcie's lap. And when she felt Marcie's hand stroking her head, she wept.

"Forgive me," she begged. "It's your turn now, Marcie. I frightened you. I didn't mean to, I didn't!" And she caught Marcie's hand and kissed it.

"Laura," Marcie said quietly. "I've been trying to talk to you for weeks and you wouldn't let me. Now it's eating me up. I'm going to tell you something. And you're going to listen." Her voice trembled so that Laura looked up at her.

"Laura, I'm so ashamed, so ashamed."

"Tell me, Marcie. Tell me. I'm listening now." She searched her face anxiously.

Marcie swallowed her tears and with a tremendous effort, said, "I did an awful thing, Laur. I've known for a while about you." She looked away, struggling with herself; her shame, her pity, her shaking voice.

"You—you knew?" Laura whispered, going white.

"Yes. I couldn't help knowing. You couldn't hide it, Laura. You couldn't come near me without it showing

—in your eyes, your face. The way you touched me, the things you said, all the crazy moods you had. You seemed afraid of me. You let things slip. You even kissed me once. I've been around enough to know. I knew about you." She wiped the tears from her cheeks embarrassedly and went on, unable to look at Laura, "I should have told you. Or else I should have let it drop. But I guess it interested me. It seemed like a game. I got sort of intrigued, you might say. I even told Burr what I suspected . . . months ago . . ." She stifled a sob.

Laura's face was colorless, tortured. Her hands were over her mouth.

"It kills me to say these things," Marcie whispered. "But I did everything to earn your contempt. I can't lie to you any more, Laura. I even *bet* Burr I could make you make a pass at me."

"No," Laura gasped. "Oh, no—"

"He thought it was all a joke. He wouldn't even listen to me. Until I got fed up with him and started hanging around here so much. Then he got it into his head that we were having a hot and heavy affair. I couldn't talk him out of it. I'd gone too far for that."

Laura turned away from her and rested her head against her own bed, too stunned, too wounded, to answer or understand half of it.

"Laura." Marcie bent toward her. "I don't know what crazy imp gets hold of me sometimes. I swear I don't. I never even wondered what I'd do if it ever came to this, if you ever tried to make love to me. I guess I thought it would be a game, like everything else. I guess I thought it would be a lot of kicks. Or just a stupid silly thing that wouldn't really matter. To either of us. I guess I didn't think at all.

"And just now—on the roof—when you told me how you felt, and how you wanted me—Laura, I had no idea you could love like that. I didn't know it could be beautiful, or touching, or tragic. I thought it was mostly play-acting. I thought the only real love was between men and women. But you made it beautiful, Laura. I don't know what else to call it. I'm ashamed. Clear through my soul. I played you for a fool, and all the while you were an angel."

Laura began to sob.

"I'd do anything for you, Laur," Marcie whispered. "Anything to make it up. If I could love you the way you want me to, I'd do that. I'll even try, if you want it."

Laura slumped to the floor, her arms over her head, and sobbed helplessly.

Marcie knelt beside her, profoundly afraid and ashamed. "Laura," she said, "Do whatever you want with me. I've hurt you so terribly. Hurt me back if it'll help. Do something. Do anything. I can't stand to see you like this. Oh, Laura, Laura. Please don't cry like that. Please."

Chapter Fourteen

In the morning—the bleak morning that came in spite of everything and had to be faced—she could hardly look at Marcie. And Marcie, brimming with shame and pity, avoided her, breaking softly into tears from time to time.

At breakfast Marcie said, "Laur, if you think you can bear to live with me I don't want you to move out. Nothing was your fault, nothing."

"I couldn't stand it, Marcie," Laura said hoarsely without looking at her. "Neither could you." She got up abruptly and left the table without having eaten a thing.

Marcie got up and followed her. "I wish we could still be friends, Laur."

"We never were."

"Oh, but we were. I like you so much, Laura."

"Marcie, this is unbearable. Don't talk to me. Please don't."

"But I can't just leave things like this, it's too awful."

"I can't help it."

"Laura, I'll never get over this. I'll never forgive myself. I hurt you so."

"Marcie, stop it!" She almost screamed at her. "I was a fool, a blind fool. I wouldn't listen." She was thinking of all the warnings from Jack and Beebo that she willfully ignored. But she caught herself and spared Jack another betrayal. That, at least, was something Marcie didn't know and never would. "Never mind," she finished. "Just drop it." She turned away and busied herself, but Marcie wouldn't let her go.

"You will come back tonight, won't you, Laura? You'll stay here until you find another place? I'll be sick if you don't. This is your apartment as much as it is mine. I'll move out if you'd rather. You know

that, don't you, Laur?" She was so anxious, so eager for
conciliation, so disgusted with what she had done,
that Laura felt a momentary relenting and looked shyly
at her. "Please come back tonight," Marcie whispered.
"I'll worry myself sick if you don't. Please. Promise?"

Laura shut her eyes for a moment and tried to control
her voice. She hadn't the courage to argue. She just said,
"Yes," and grabbed her purse and rushed out.

Laura knew, even before she reached the subway, that
she wasn't going to work that day. She knew it would be
impossible for her to read, to type, to look up words, to
answer the doctors, to joke with Sarah. It would be a
nightmare of hypocrisy, utterly beyond her strength.

She felt shattered, ready to scream if anyone touched
her, like someone with an open wound. But she held
herself tightly in check. She rode aimlessly on the subway for an hour or two. She stood in bookshops with a volume in her hands and stared at the pages until the
clerks, in turn, stared at her. She sat on benches in Central Park. She stopped now and then to get a cup of coffee, and late in the day, a sandwich. It enabled her to
keep walking. She walked, looking at nothing but the
pavement ahead of her, for a couple of hours. She paid
no attention to where she was going or why. She walked
to exhaust herself, to reach that country of fatigue where
even the mind cannot operate and the emotions are
dead.

Abruptly she found herself standing outside the Mc-
Alton in the last hour of daylight. She was not strong
enough to feel surprise. On the contrary, it was as if
she had been working toward it, all through that empty
endless day, knowing she would end up here. And knowing, she had not needed to think of it, to make a decision. It was unavoidable.

She stood outside the main door to the lobby, looking at the people hurrying past and hoping somebody
would come up to her, talk to her, even make advances to
her. Anything to postpone what she knew was coming.
She looked at the door and away again, and then back to
it, as if it were a great sinister magnet. Sooner or later
she knew she would walk through it.

She stood leaning against the gray stone of the Mc-Alton, her fine face pale and vacant, her body apparently relaxed. She looked like a tired young career girl, waiting at the appointed place for a date. She knew it and took advantage of it. The hotel doorman strolled over to her and said, "Lovely evening, isn't it?" And later, "Looks like he's a bit late, Miss." With a little smile.

Laura returned the smile faintly. She tried to engage him in conversation, but he was called away frequently, and finally, with the evening crowd converging on him, got too busy to talk to her at all. The night was violet now, turning fast to black. It was eight o'clock.

Laura turned to the door and walked through it almost automatically. Once inside she was suddenly profoundly afraid. Flashes of fear went through her; long sweeps of tremors and gooseflesh. She didn't bother with the desk this time. She knew what floor he was on. She got the elevator and said, "Fourteenth floor, please." She wondered if her voice sounded as shaky as it felt in her throat. She thought of simply getting off the elevator on the fourteenth floor and taking another elevator right back down. And when she was let off, she stood there in the deep carpeted hall with her heart crying "No-no, no-no, no-no," at every beat.

"He's my father," she told herself. "He won't kill me, after all. He might beat me, but he's done that before and I've lived through it. I'll be twenty-one in three weeks, so he can't say I'm a minor. All he can do is make a speech about my ungratefulness. He's a human being, not the devil." She said the last aloud, in a whisper, and her own voice startled her.

Cautiously, Laura investigated room numbers, half expecting him to burst from his room and discover her unprepared. After a few false starts she found 1402 and standing there, looking at that door, she felt an enormous need to cry. She shut her eyes hard and said softly, "I won't, I won't." Then she opened them, and, with her heart in her mouth, she rapped on the door.

The noise sounded huge. For a moment she wanted to run. But she didn't. *He mustn't see me looking panicky,* she thought. She listened. There was no sound au-

dible. *Maybe he's not in. Oh, dear God, maybe he left.*
She didn't know whether to exult or despair. *If I don't
face him now, I'll never be able to face myself,* she
thought. *I'll never stand alone. I've got to tell him everything.* She felt desperate at the thought of having to go
and search him out, to win her freedom from him. The
hope that she had missed him, that he had already left
for Chicago, was too sweet to banish.

She was ready to flee when the door swung open, without any preliminary sounds to warn her. She blanched
uncontrollably and found herself looking at her father's
feet. Very slowly, she looked up the rest of him to his
face. There was a slight frown on his heavy features.
But he wasn't at all surprised. He let her stand there until
she was miserably uncomfortable, and then—only then
—he spoke.

"Come in," he said. Not "Hello, Laura." He spoke as
if she might have been the maid come to clean his
room. He stepped aside slightly to permit her to walk
past him. She clutched herself in her arms, fearful of
touching him as she brushed past, and walked quickly
across the room to a half open window on the opposite
side. She looked resolutely out at the city, afraid to let
him see her face.

*The minute I look at him, I'll cry. I'll do some damn
silly weak thing, and he'll lord it over me, and I'll wind
up promising to go home to Chicago with him. I
can't look at him. Not yet.*

She listened to him moving around the room behind
her and felt his eyes on her. But he said nothing. After
a few moments, Laura could stand it no longer. She knew
he was laughing at her. Not with his voice or his
lips, but silently, inside. She turned and looked for
him. He was standing across the room, his enormous
back planted against the wall, his arms folded over his
chest, studying her. She flinched a little, seeing his
face.

"I never knew before," he said slowly, savoring it,
"how fast you could run." He gave her a slight sardonic
smile.

Laura felt her insides turn to water. Her face was
white and set as plaster. She forced herself to return his
gaze.

"I never knew you could swear, either," he said. "Especially at me. As a matter of fact, I doubt whether you can, now that we're face to face."

It was a dare. Laura, stung, felt a flush of resistance come up in her. "If I do," she said, "you'll beat me. That's your answer to everything."

"It always worked before," he said, mocking her.

"It worked so well that it drove me out of your house forever. It made me hate you, Father."

"You don't need to spell it for me, Laura. I get the idea."

She hated his sarcasm! Her hatred flowed in her now and revived her spirit. "Is that what you wanted? To make me hate you?" she asked. "Because you've done a fine job. A masterful job."

"Thanks. I'm glad we agree on one thing anyway." He stood immovable, still smiling slightly.

He wants to drive me frantic. He wants me to end up on my knees, incoherent. Kissing his feet. God damn him! He doesn't care what he says as long as it'll drive me wild.

"I must say, you took a prosaic way out, Laura. Running away is no way to solve a problem. Running away to New York is the classic cliché. There are a lot of you here in New York, you know. Silly little girls who left one set of problems at home for another set in the big city."

Laura turned her back on him. *I won't even answer him. If I could just hurt him somehow. Hurt him like he hurts me. What would hurt him the worst? Mother. My Mother.*

"Did you slap my mother around the way you do me?" she asked him abruptly.

At this his smile faded and his face grew very hard. "Your mother never deserved it," he said.

"Neither did I," she retorted. "As far as I can see."

"You are notoriously shortsighted, my darling daughter."

"And you, Father, are blind." Her face flushed.

Again he smiled, but his smile frightened her. "What have you been doing, Laura, that gives you such intestinal fortitude in the face of such obvious physical risk?"

She wanted to scream at him, "I hate you! I hate your

God-damn sophisticated sarcasm!" But she only said tersely, "I have a job. I have some nice friends. I have money in the bank. I have a life of my own without you. I have a little confidence I never had before." They were all lies, that started out so beautifully true. Almost all lies, anyway. But she had flung them in his face, and now he was not sure. He studied her. "Those are the problems I came to face in New York, Father. Nothing could ever persuade me to trade them for the ones at home." *If I didn't hate him so much I couldn't do it. He started out wrong, trying to drive me in a corner. He gave me a chance without realizing it.*

He moved away from the wall then, his face registering contemptuous amusement. He lighted a cigarette, and, to her astonishment, offered her one. She shook her head. "Well," he observed. "You apparently haven't taken up all the vices yet." He turned away from her and walked about the room, firing questions at her. "What kind of job do you have?"

"Medical secretary."

"Where?"

"With Dr. Edgar Hollingsworth."

"Who's he?"

"The top radiologist in the city."

"Where's his office?"

"Fifth and fifty-third."

"Who are the friends?"

This abrupt switch threw her for a moment. "The friends?"

"You said you had some."

"Oh," she said quickly. "Do you want their names?" The little sarcasms she mustered added to her bravery.

He curled his mouth disgustedly. "Anything that will help," he said. "Names mean nothing. Who are they?"

"Well," she said, "some are men and some are women." For a triumphant moment she felt like laughing in his face. But his face had grown dark, and a flash of fear prevented her. "My roommate," she went on, more timidly. "For one. She's a very nice girl. I've met a lot of wonful people through her. The doctors have been wonderful to me."

"Everybody's 'wonderful'," he mimicked.

"I was surprised to find that people can be nice, Father."

"God! If a man accused me of being 'nice' I'd spit in his face."

"And decent and human!" she said hotly.

His face grew dangerous now and his body tense. "Are you implying that I'm not human?"

Her fear grew suddenly quite strong and for a moment she wavered. Then she said softly, "If you're going to beat me, Father, do it now and let's get it over with."

He laughed; an awful laugh she remembered very well. It was usually the prelude to violence. "Well, isn't that noble," he said. "Why don't you pull down your pants and bend over? Make it easy for me?"

"You've beaten me all my life, whenever I displeased you. And I seem to displease you just by existing. I've never seen you beat anyone your own size, Father, but you're awfully damn good at beating me."

"My, aren't we grown up!" he said. "We not only talk back to our Father now, we swear at him. That's real sophistication."

"You don't know how much I hate you, Father! You can't know! I've begun to think that's what you want. You've worked hard enough all my life to make me hate you."

His face changed again, became grave and heavy. Her eyes watched him intently, like eyes that have witnessed floods scan the skies for sun. He turned away from her, dragging on his cigarette, knocking ashes into a heavy glass tray on the dresser. "Why do you hate me, Laura?" he asked dispassionately. "Because I discipline you now and then? Isn't that a father's prerogative?"

"Not when it ruins his child's life."

"Is your life ruined?" he said sharply. "You have a 'wonderful' job, 'wonderful' friends. Wonderful money in the bank, wonderful everything. Hell, I seem to have done you a favor."

"A favor! You call it a favor!" She stared at him, his hardness still astonishing her after all these years. And then she felt her resistance begin to wilt. Sooner or later all her arguments were doomed. She never won with him. The sheer physical fact of him, massive and dominant, exhausted her after a while. "I—I never wanted to hate you, Father. You were all I had. I wanted to love you. But you wouldn't let me," she almost whispered. *I mustn't go on like this. I'll cry,* she thought desperately. "I hate you because you hate me!" she flung at him.

He looked at her for some time before he answered quietly, "What makes you think I hate you, Laura?"

She was so taken aback by this that she could only stammer at him. "I don't know, but you know you do."

"Oh, come now. I haven't been *that* harsh with you."

It's a trap! A trap! He wants to soften me up. He wants to see me whimpering. Oh, God, if only I could stop him, freeze him up, like other men. "You've been brutal," she said harshly and the sobs were crowding close in her throat. "You've treated me like a slave. Worse! you've beaten me sometimes for nothing. Just for the exercise."

"I never once beat you without a reason," he said.

"You lie!" And her voice was a furious hiss.

He glared at her. "I'm not in the habit of lying to you, Laura. Your life has been more than beatings. I sent you to the best schools. I let you go to the college of your choice. I let you join a sorority and paid all your bills. And when you came home and quit like a damn coward—without so much as an explanation, I didn't force you to go back. I found you a good job with excellent training and a big future. I've given you a good comfortable home, a lot of clothes, travel." His voice was low, controlled, but it was the calm before the storm and he was tense.

"I would have traded them all for love." Her voice broke and she turned suddenly away, afraid to shame herself with tears in front of him.

"Let's not get maudlin," he said sardonically, and once again smothered the spark of tenderness that had waited so many years in Laura for expression.

"All right," she said sharply. "Let's not be maudlin. I have a good job here and I'm not going to leave New York. That's what I came to tell you. Now maybe I'll better go." She turned and walked resolutely toward the door, but she should have known it wouldn't be that easy. He merely placed himself between the door and Laura and she stopped, afraid to go near him. He smiled slightly at this evidence of his power over her.

"Before you leave," he said, "suppose you explain the filial affection that made you write me to go to hell, in your little billet-doux last week?"

"Why did you say you had no daughter?" she flared.

"To teach you a lesson."

"Are there any lessons left for you to teach me?" she said.

"Quite a few, my dear. You don't know it all yet, even if you are almost twenty-one."

"It almost killed me, Father," she said, the anguish showing. "You don't know how terribly I—" But she stopped herself, ashamed. He didn't know, and she didn't want him to know. She was the one who cared about their relationship, who wanted love and trust and gentleness between them. Not her father. He didn't give a damn, as long as she minded him. "You said you had no daughter," she repeated bitterly.

"You wanted it that way, Laura."

She turned to stare at him, incredulous. "I?" She said. "I wanted it that way?"

"You denied my existence before I ever denied yours," he said. "You ran away from me."

"You forced me to."

"I did no such thing."

"You made life intolerable for me."

"I didn't mean to." It was an extraordinary admission, completely unexpected, and she looked at him speechless for a moment.

"Then why didn't you show me some kindness?" she said. "Just a very little would have gone a long way, Father."

He crushed out his cigarette in the heavy ashtray with an expression of contempt on his face. "You women are all alike, I swear to God." he said. "Give you a little and you demand a lot."

"What's wrong with a lot?" she said, trembling. "You're my father."

"Yes, exactly!" he said, so roughly that she ducked. "I'm your father!"

"Did you treat my mother this way?" she whispered. "Her life must have been hell."

He looked for a minute as if he would strangle her. She

stood her ground, pale and frightened, until he relented suddenly and turned his profile to her, looking out the window. "Your mother," he said painfully, "was my wife. I adored her."

Laura was absolutely unable to answer him. She sat down weakly in the stuffed chair by the dresser and put her face in her hands. Her father—her enormous gruff harsh father—had never spoken such a tender word in her presence in all her life.

"I could never marry again, when she died," he said. Laura felt frightened as she always did when her mother's death was mentioned. She expected him to turn on her unreasonably as he had so often before. "I never struck her."

"Then why me?" she implored out of a dry throat.

He turned and looked at her, his mouth twisted a little, running a distraught hand through his hair. "You needed it," was all he would say.

"What for?"

"You *needed* it, that's what for!" And she was afraid to push him further. After some minutes he said, "Laura, you're coming back to Chicago with me."

"No Father, I can't. I won't."

"That's why I waited for you," he went on, as if she had said nothing.

"I won't go to Chicago or anywhere else with you. I'm through with you."

"You could look for work with a radiologist, if you like it so well. I won't insist on journalism. You have a flair for it, it's a waste to leave the field, but I won't insist. You see, Laura, I can be human enough."

She stared at him. She had never heard him talk like this. He glanced at her, annoyed by the look on her face. "I've made reservations," he said, "for June first. That's Saturday. I could probably get earlier ones."

"Father." She stood up. "I can't come with you."

"Don't say that!" he commanded her, so sharply that she started.

"I can't," she whispered.

"You can, and you will. That's all I want to hear on the subject." As she started once again to protest he held his hands up for silence. "No more discipline Laura. I promise you that. I was a fool. You were too, but never mind that now. I was too hard on you, it's true. I see that. Well, you're more or less grown up by this time. I guess we can dispense with spanking."

"Spanking! It was more than that and you know it!"

"Don't argue with me, Laura." He turned on her, his voice low and fierce. Then, making a visible effort to calm himself, he said, "Get your things together and I'll see about the reservations."

"No."

"Don't fight me, Laura."

"Father, there's something you don't know about me." *I have to tell him. I'll never be free from him till I tell him. Till he knows what he's made of his only child.* "There's something you don't know about me," she whispered.

"I don't doubt it. Now hurry up, we've wasted enough time."

"Father . . . listen to me." It was almost too hard to say. Her legs were trembling and her heart was wild.

"Well, out with it, for God's sake! Jesus, Laura, you go through more agony . . . Well? What is it?" He frowned at her tense face.

"I—I'm a—homosexual."

His mouth dropped open and his whole body went rigid. Laura shut her eyes and prayed. She held her lower lip in her teeth, ready for the blow, and felt the humiliating tears begin to squeeze through her shut lids. She moaned a little.

He made up his mind fast and his voice cracked out like a lash. "Nonsense!" he snarled.

"It's true!" Her eyes flew open and she cried again, passionately, "It's true!" It was her bid for freedom; she had to show this courage, this awful truth to him, or she would never walk away from him. She would spend all her life in a panic of fear lest he find her out. "I'm in love with my roommate. I've made love—"

"All right, all right, all right!" he shouted. His voice was rough and his face contorted. He turned away from her and put his hands over his face. She watched him, every muscle tight and aching.

At last he let his hands drop and said quietly, "Did I do that to you, Laura?"

Without hesitating, without even certain knowledge, but only the huge need to hurt him, she said, "Yes."

He turned slowly around and faced her and she had never seen his face like that before. It was pained and full of gentleness. Perhaps it looked that way to her mother now and then. "I did that to you," he said again, to himself. "Oh, Laura. Oh, Laura." His heavy brow creased deeply over his eyes. He walked to her and put his hands on her shoulders and felt her jerk with fear. "Laura," he said, "have you ever loved a man?"

She shook her head, unable to speak.

"Have you ever wanted a man?"

Again she shook her head.

"Do you know what it's like to want a man?"

"No," she whispered.

"Do you want to know?" His eyes were wide and intense, his grip on her shoulders was very hard.

"I'm so afraid of them, Father. I don't want to know."

He seemed to be in another world. Laura was utterly mystified by his strange behavior, blindly grateful for his sudden warmth, and she let herself weep softly.

"Laura," he said, as if he derived some private pleasure from saying her name over and over. "Your mother —you look so much like your mother. You never looked like me at all. Every time I look at you I see her face. Her fragile delicate face. Her eyes, her hair." He put his arms around her. "Come back to Chicago with me," he said gently. "You don't have to love a man, Laura. I don't want you to. I don't want you to be like other girls, I don't want you to go off with some young ass and give him your youth and your beauty. I don't mind if you're different from the rest. I can take that if you are able to."

Laura clung to him, astonished, fearful, grateful, anxious, a whirlwind of confused feelings churning inside her.

"I want you to stay with me," he said. "I always did. I won't let you go."

"You made me go, Father. You punished me so."

"No, no Laura! Don't you see, it was myself." He was holding her so hard now, as if to make up for years of avoiding her, that she ached with it. She began to cry on his shoulder.

"Oh, Father, Father," she wept. "You never told me you wanted me to stay with you. You made me believe you hated me."

"No," he said. "I never hated you." He spoke in a rush, as if he couldn't help himself, as if it were suddenly forcing its way out of him after years of suppression. "Never, Laura, it was just that I was so lonely, so terribly lonely; I wanted her so much and she was gone. And there was only you, and you tormented me."

"I?" She tried to see his face, but he held her too close.

"You were so much like her, even when you were a child. Every time I looked at you, I—oh, Laura, it's myself I should have punished all this time. I *was* punished. I've suffered. Believe me. Laura, please believe me."

Laura was suddenly shocked rigid to feel his lips on her neck. He put his hand in her hair and jerked her head back and kissed her full on the mouth with such agonized intensity that he electrified her. He released her just as suddenly and turned away with a kind of sob. "Ellie! Ellie!" he cried, his hands over his face.

Laura was shaking almost convulsively. At the sound of her mother's name she grabbed the thick and heavy glass ashtray from the dresser, picking it up with both hands. She rushed at him, unable to think or reason, and brought the ashtray down on the crown of his head with all the revolted force in her body. He slumped to the floor without a sound.

Laura gaped at him for a sick second and then she turned and fled. She left the door wide open and ran in a terrible panic to the elevators. She sobbed frantically for a few moments, and then she pushed the down button. She jabbed it over and over again hysterically, unable to stop until an elevator arrived and the doors opened. She stumbled in and pressed into a back corner, helpless in the grip of the sickness in her. The operator and his two other passengers stared at her, but she paid them no heed, even when one asked if he could help her. At the ground floor the operator had to tell her, "Everybody out."

She turned a wild flushed face to him and he said, "Are

you all right, Miss?" And she glared at him, violently offended by his manner, his uniform, his question.

"Don't you know those pants won't make a man of
you?" she exclaimed acidly. And rushed out, leaving him
gaping open-mouthed after her.

Chapter Fifteen

MARCIE called Jack late that night. "I haven't heard from her. I wouldn't bother you, but I don't know where she is, and I'm worried," she said. "Is she with you?"

"No. What's the matter, Marcie? It's only ten-fifteen."

"She said she'd be home tonight. She promised."

"Did you call the office?"

"Yes. She wasn't there today."

"Was she sick?"

"No." Marcie was almost physically sick with shame and the fear that Laura would do herself violence. She knew well how passionately Laura could respond, how intensely she could feel. She had been truly alarmed when she called the office in the afternoon and Sarah told her they hadn't seen Laura all day. And they'd damn well like to know where she was themselves.

"She left the house this morning to catch the subway to work. She said she'd be back tonight, but she didn't go to work. And she isn't back," Marcie told Jack.

Jack's first thought was Merrill Landon. "Out with it, Marcie. Tell Uncle Jack everything."

"Jack, I can't—" Jack of all people! Jack, who had a crush on Laura. Marcie would have slit her throat before she would have betrayed Laura to him. She was in no madcap mood any longer. She had wounded Laura with a callousness that shocked even herself when she thought back on it. She had no yen to hurt any more.

"Come on, doll, we've known each other for years," Jack said. "Spill the beans."

"Jack, I won't hurt her. Not even—"

"Not even if she drops dead because you won't tell me the truth."

"Oh! But she won't!"

"Oh, but she might! Now let's have it."

"Jack, I don't want you to think—"

"I think all the time. It's a congenital defect."

393

"Yes, but this—"

"Oh, for Chrissake, Marcie! *Say* it. Did you quarrel?"

"I—yes. We quarreled."

"What about?"

"I can't say."

"Now you listen to me, God damn it, I'm getting worried."

"About love." She whispered it.

And Jack knew at once what was the matter. But why hadn't Laura come to him? Why hadn't she told him? She couldn't be that ashamed. She knew he wouldn't hurt her with the knowledge. He would be kind, with the kindness of deep sympathy. Something was wrong—more wrong than Marcie admitted, or more wrong than she knew. Or both.

"I can't explain, Jack," Marcie moaned.

"You don't have to, Marcie. I get the message."

"Should I call the police?"

"No," he said quickly. Jack had an inborn aversion to cops. "I think I have an idea. I'll call you back later. And call me the minute you hear anything."

"I will, I promise!"

Jack called Beebo. "Marcie's straight," he said.

"So what, Jackson?"

"So Laura just found out—the hard way, apparently— and now she's disappeared."

"I couldn't care less."

"I don't believe you."

"Look, Jack, I don't even want to talk about the kid. I don't want to hear her name mentioned. She can go to hell as far as I'm concerned."

"I've got to find her, Beebo, and you've got to help me."

"The hell I do."

"I want you to check the Lessie joints. They won't let me in. I busted the mirror in the Colophon last month and they all hate me."

"That's your problem."

"Beebo, for God's sake. I know how bitchy she was. I'm not asking you to forget it. I'm asking you to help me find her. I think she went to see her father. From what she's told me of him, she might be dead before we find her."

There was a shocked silence and finally Beebo said, "Don't play around with me, Jack. Tell me the truth."

"That *is* the truth. He's a real bastard. God knows what he might have done to her. He has the Devil's own temper and he's been beating hell out of her since she was five years old."

There was a reluctant pause at Beebo's end and finally she said, "All right, damn it. All right. I'll go look for her. If she's with her father I don't know what good it'll do to check the bars down here."

"You never know. Besides, there's not much time."

"Okay, Jack. I'll get going."

"Call me as soon as you get back. Whether you find her or not."

"Right. Where are you going?"

"The McAlton. To check with her old man."

"What about Terry? Can you trust him alone?" she asked with slight sarcasm.

"No," he said matter-of-factly, looking at Terry as he spoke, in a voice that betrayed none of his passion for the boy. "I'm counting on the smoked oysters to keep him out of trouble."

Terry grinned a little but his eyes didn't leave the television set.

Beebo laughed. "Okay, doll, I'll help you out, but don't expect me to welcome Laura back and send her flowers. I'm through with that little bitch. If I find her I'll drag her home by the scruff of the neck and dump her."

"That's good enough, Beebo. Thanks."

Beebo scoured the Village. She knew it inside and out and backwards: all the gay bars, the favorite coffee shops, the side streets; the markets, the boutiques, the stalls and the brownstones; the parks, the alleys, the bookshops. Some were closed, some stayed open half the night. Wherever people collected down there, sooner or later Beebo investigated the spot.

The hours stretched out. Every hour or so she called Jack's apartment and talked to Terry. He simply said, "Jack's not back yet. He hasn't called in. Okay, I'll tell him." And as Beebo walked she began to feel a real fear for Laura's safety, a tender concern that welled up in her and aroused her own contempt. At three in the morning she muttered, "Oh, the hell with it. Nobody can cover the whole damn Village in one night." She called the penthouse.

Marcie, wide awake and alarmed, answered, hoping it would be Laura. She wasn't sure if she had a boy or a girl on the phone; she only knew it wasn't Laura.

"Marcie?" Beebo said.

"Yes. Who's this?"

"A friend of Laura's. Is she there?"

"No. Do you know where she is?"

"I wish I did."

"Who *is* this?"

"I'll call you back."

Marcie sat holding the receiver and staring perplexed at the phone some minutes after Beebo hung up.

Jack got back in the first light of dawn to find Terry asleep. He sat down without taking his jacket off, and called Beebo. No answer. Terry rolled over and looked at him. He was a medium-sized well-built boy, bright and handsome and easily bored, affectionate by nature, but spoiled, quick with his temper and quick with his generosity. He was not quite sure, being young and desirable, if he was in love with Jack. He liked being admired by a lot of people. But he was not the money grubber Jack had painted for Laura. He liked to be dominated and he was waiting for Jack to make a move in that direction.

"Where the hell have you been?" he asked Jack.

"Where's Beebo?"

"How should I know? You're the one who knows it all."

"Just this once, don't get smart with me, lover. I gotta find her." Jack was too worried to coddle him.

"She'll call back on the hour. She's been calling in every God damn hour since you went out. I can't get any sleep around here. Who's this Laura, anyway? She must be a living doll."

"I've told you a dozen times. She's a friend."

"You act like she was a lover."

Jack stared at his handsome arrogant young face. "So what?" he said. "You have your affairs. I have mine." And he turned around and walked into the bathroom and left Terry staring after him. Jack never talked that way to him, not even when he caught him *in flagrante delicto*. He never showed an erotic interest in girls, either.

The phone rang fifteen minutes later. It was Beebo. Terry answered and handed Jack the phone, listening to the conversation with his eyes half open.

"Absolutely no soap," Beebo said. "I've been all over the damn Village. Nobody's seen her."

"She saw Landon earlier this evening," Jack said.

"She did? Does he know where she is?"

"He doesn't know from nothing, doll. She gave him a first class concussion. Walloped him with a glass ashtray. On the back of his head. Must have snuck up on him when he had his back turned."

"God!" Beebo exclaimed.

"And then took off, hysterical, according to the elevator boy. She screamed all kinds of stuff at him. He says. Half of it's crap, of course. But he did tell me one thing—"

"What's that?"

"She told him those pants he was wearing would never make a man of him."

After a surprised silence Beebo gave a wry tired little laugh. "Jesus," she said. "She must have been screwy."

"The elevator boy thought so. It sounds kind of bad. I'd better call Marcie."

"I called her at three."

"God, Beebo, don't make it any worse than it is!"

"Relax. I didn't leave my name. Just asked for Laura and Marcie said she wasn't there. Well, Jackson? Now what? We call the cops?"

"You want us all to get thrown in the jug? They'd love to run in a bunch of queers. No, let's wait a day. She's a sensible girl underneath it all. She'll come to her senses and I'm the first one she'll call." Terry, on the bed beside him, gave a contemptuous snort.

"I wish I felt so confident," Beebo said.

"Yeah," Jack said. "I do too," he admitted.

"Okay, boy, keep in touch."

Jack hung up and sat drooping on the bed, the fatigue showing in his face.

"God, you look old," Terry said with a characteristic lack of tact. "How old are you? You never told me."

"Eighty-two," Jack said.

Terry grinned. "I don't believe you."

"You're not supposed to."

"How old? Tell me."

Jack stood up and turned to face him, in no mood for jokes. "Terry, don't bug me. I've had enough of you today." Terry gaped at him. Jack had never talked harshly to him and now he was doing it every time he opened his mouth. "I love this girl," Jack told him. "I don't know why, but I do know that for once I've found a decent sweet kid who isn't out for every damn thing she can get from me. She can give a little, she doesn't have to take all the time."

"Oh, you love her!" Terry said sarcastically, propping himself up on his elbows. "That's swell. Just swell! Thanks for letting me in on it."

"And I'll probably love her long after you've climbed out of this bed for the last time, you little bastard. You and a dozen other guys. It's a kind of love you don't know much about, Terry." He was too tired, too worried, to take much heed of what he said or how. His resentment spilled out and it felt good to let go with it and he did.

Terry wasn't used to being disciplined. He had managed, in eighteen crafty years, to avoid it. So he was surprised at himself when he reacted to Jack's tongue lashing with a renewal of interest in him. He lay back on the bed and watched Jack strip to his underwear. Jack was not a beautiful man physically; tough and wiry, but not beautiful. Yet Terry watched him with enjoyment, wondering what to expect from him next.

Jack stretched out on the bed next to Terry. There was an hour or so when he could sleep before he had to get to the office. He turned his head a little and saw Terry watching him. "You still here?" he said. "I thought I told you to go."

"I think I'll stay," Terry said, smiling. "I'm a glutton for punishment." He was intrigued by this new side of Jack.

Jack turned over and looked at him, surprised. "You're a brat," he said finally. "A beautiful, unbearable, stuck-up, silly, irresistible brat."

Terry laughed. "That's why you love me, Superman," he said, poking Jack in the ribs.

"Who says I love you?" Jack said wearily and turned away from him.

"Jack, be nice to me."

"I'm worried ·sick and he wants me to be nice to him. Ha!" Jack told the walls.

"Damn it, I think you *do* love this girl."

"She bought your oysters, lover. You can spare her a little good will yourself."

Terry dropped back on his pillow in silent surprise. It was the first hint he had had of the state of Jack's finances.

Jack went to work. There was nothing to be accomplished sitting around the apartment quarreling with Terry. It wouldn't bring Laura back any sooner, and there was not much he could do to find her now. Except call in the police and he gagged on that idea. He would wait at least until the next morning.

But at the end of the day things were getting black. Laura was still gone; Marcie was panicky and agitating for a call to the police; Beebo was glowering, furious at herself for caring what happened to Laura and yet caring anyway in spite of herself; and a thunderstorm was brewing.

They waited alone, Jack and Marcie and Beebo, in the gathering dark: each with his own peculiar fears and hopes. Jack drank. Marcie paced around the roof, praying God that Laura hadn't killed herself. Beebo came over after a while and talked to Jack.

They talked, they drank, the phone rang. Terry wandered around the apartment in a pet because nobody was paying any attention to him. In another part of town Burr cursed silently because Marcie would pay no attention to *him*. And still elsewhere Merrill Landon lay with an aching head and heart and peppered the detective agency he had hired with evil-tempered calls while they labored to locate his daughter.

Finally Terry exploded at Jack, "If you don't talk to me I'm going to get out of here!" He gave the nearest chair a petulant kick. "I don't have to hang around here till I drop dead from boredom."

"Go," said Jack. "You're driving me nuts anyway with that damn pacing the floor."

"I wish I *was* driving you nuts," Terry retorted. "I just seem to be in your way."

"You are, lover. Shut up and eat something. You'll feel better."

"I just ate!"

"Then just shut up."

"God! This place is a mausoleum. I've had enough!" He went to the bedroom and grabbed a sweater, but when he reached the front door he turned and found that Jack wasn't even looking at him. He was talking to Beebo. He was saying, "By God, it's worth a try. I'm going over there. Nothing could be worse than sitting here wondering if she's drowned in the damn river or swinging from a rope somewhere."

"Oh, for Chrissake, Jack!" Beebo snapped. "Have mercy. I'm not made of stone."

Jack got up and headed for the door. Terry stood uncertainly and watched him approach. "Make up your mind," Jack said to him. "In or out?" His anxiety over Laura made this attitude of impatience with Terry perfectly genuine. Yet Jack was not without a small sudden pleasure at Terry's reactions.

"How about you?" Terry said.

"Out."

"I'll go with you."

"I'll be back in an hour."

"I want to go with you."

Jack stared at him, again pleased and surprised. "You can't," was all he said, putting his cigarette in his mouth while he pulled his jacket on.

"Why the hell not?"

Jack took him by the shoulders. "Terry, you want to do something for me?"

Terry eyed him like a suspicious five-year-old. "I don't know. You're so bitchy tonight." He sighed. "All right, all right. What do I have to do?"

"Stay here. And if she shows up, hang on to her. I'll be back at—" He looked at his watch. "—at ten. No later."

Terry threw himself in an armchair with a huge sigh of disgust. "Oh, this Laura!" he groaned. "She must be the most fabulous female in the whole goddam world."

"She is," Beebo said briefly. She dinched her cigarette and walked out ahead of Jack. "I'll be at home, Terry," she called back. "If she shows up."

"Yeah, yeah, I know. I'll hogtie her and call all the newspapers. I'll notify the President. Christ!"

Jack and Beebo went down the stairs together and out into the lowering night. The first drops were coming down. "What'd you give him, Jackson?" Beebo smiled. "He's learning how to mind. He doesn't like it very much, but he's learning."

Jack shrugged. "He does like it, doll. That's the secret. He likes to be shoved around a little. I wish to hell I'd known before I bought all those stinking oysters."

Chapter Sixteen

IT was five past ten and the rain was fairly heavy outside. Terry was curled up in the armchair watching television, eating peanuts and drinking a beer. He was irritated with Jack for being late. He tried to get interested in the film and sat for a quarter of an hour with his eyes on the set, wiggling restlessly, like a child in need of a comfort station. He jumped when a knock on the door disturbed him.

"Come in, you know it's not locked," he said without looking up. "Where the hell were you? At least I tell you where I'm going. Well talk, damn it." And he turned around to see a tall slim girl standing five feet from him, her long hair streaming wet and her clothes clinging to her body. He was conscious of nothing in her face but her eyes; huge, blue and heavy, dominating, agonized.

Terry stood up suddenly, stammering a little. "You must be Laura," he said finally. "I was beginning to think you weren't real." He took another look at her, pale as a wraith, her eyes the only warmth in the cold oval of her face. "Are you?" he asked. And then smiled a little sheepishly. "Well, don't just stand there. Come in and sit down."

She moved as if she were dreaming, one hand to her forehead, and he guided her to the sofa where she half sat and half collapsed, letting her head fall back against the cushions. She looked utterly exhausted.

Terry stood hovering uncertainly over her, staring at her. At last he said, "Jack says I've got to keep you here." She shut her eyes. "He's supposed to be home at ten. He should be right along. I'm Terry. Terry Fleming. Jack says he told you about me. He certainly talks a lot about you. He thinks the world of you." She gave no sign that she had heard or cared to hear.

At last in some consternation he said, "Would you like something to eat, Laura? You look like you could do

402

with something." No answer. He went out to the kitchen and opened a can of soup. He fixed up the plate with crackers and cheese and, as a second thought, smoked oysters, and poured a glass of milk. Every two or three minutes he interrupted his task to go to the doorway and check on her. He thought she might vanish, like a ghost. But she didn't move. She looked dead. She scared him.

He put the food on a tray and brought it into the living room and sat down on the sofa next to her. He put the soup and milk on the coffee table in front of her and then he said, "Wake up. Wake up, Laura." She didn't stir. Terry put an oyster on a cracker. "Here," he said, shaking her a little. "Here, for God's sake, eat it. It's your oyster."

Laura stirred and opened her eyes, took one look at the smoked oyster, and turned away with a grimace. Terry was offended. "So what's wrong with smoked oysters?" he said. "Here. It's yours."

She looked at him then. Really saw him. And then sat up a little, rubbing her eyes. "Mine?" she repeated dimly.

"Jack says you bought 'em." Terry looked at her with bright eyes, curious now. "You might as well enjoy them."

Laura sighed and then saw the soup. Terry handed her a spoon and she ate it all without a pause or a word. It seemed to give her strength, to bring her back to life. "I haven't eaten." she apologized. "I can't remember . . ."

"Want some more?" he asked quickly.

"No. No thanks. Maybe later." She looked around the apartment, recognition and sense coming back to her face. "Where's Jack?" she said, and suddenly clutched Terry's sleeve. "Where's Jack?" She sounded frightened.

"He'll be back any minute," Terry said.

Laura stared at him then. "Oh, you're Terry," she said.

"You're Laura." He grinned. "I saw you first."

She blinked at him, unable to joke with him. Dead serious, she asked, "Did the oysters help?"

"Help?" he said. "Oh. You mean Jack and me."

"He says you love them."

Terry studied her, frowning over his smile, and then looked away in embarrassment. "Not the oysters so much," he said. "But you helped, in a roundabout way. By getting lost."

"I'm glad," she said, confused. "He loves you terribly."
She seemed to have no sense that this might startle him
or be the wrong thing to say. She hadn't the physical
strength to censor herself. She spoke the necessary truths
and no more. But Terry was strongly affected. He walked
to the other side of the room and refused to look at her
for a while, letting his feelings whirl around inside him.
When he did look back, she was stretched out on the sofa,
sleeping the sleep of complete exhaustion.

Laura woke up to find Jack sitting in the armchair sipping gingerly at a steaming cup of coffee. His eyes showed
over the rim of the cup, heavy, anxious, and old. He lowered the cup when she wakened, putting it on the coffee
table by the sofa and lighting a cigarette.

"It's a nice day," he said cautiously.

She sat up halfway. "What time is it?"

"Seven-thirty."

Laura dropped back and shut her eyes. She found a
blanket over herself and her shoes were on the floor beside the sofa.

"Well," said Jack, "are you going to tell me where
the hell you've been? Or am I going to ask?"

Laura turned her face suddenly to the back of the sofa
and wept. "Oh, Jack," she moaned. "I killed him. I killed
him. Oh, God help me." And she began to sob.

"Killed who?"

"My father."

"Your father," he said with friendly sharpness in his
voice "has a prize concussion. But he's very much alive."

She turned her head slowly to look at him, her eyes
enormous and her heart stopped in her chest. "Alive?"
Her voice was a startled whisper. She sat up suddenly and
said it out loud. "Alive?" She grabbed Jack's arms with
the strength of shock. "How do you know? How do you
know? Tell me quickly."

"I will, give me half a chance." He pushed her back
down and told her of his trip to the McAlton. "I just went
up to the fourteenth floor," he said. "It was easy. There
were a lot of people standing around outside his room and
the elevator boy told me about it. Incidentally, you made
a real friend. He thinks you're the original Goof Nut."

"But my father, Jack, my father?"

"There was a doctor with him. He's okay, Mother."

Laura half fainted and it was some minutes before Jack could bring her around. Terry sat on the floor by the sofa, watching her with interest while Jack propped her feet up on pillows. "That better?" he said.

"I hit him so hard," she murmured the moment she was able to talk. "I was sure I killed him. Maybe he died of the concussion." Her eyes went wide again with fear and she looked at Jack, but he shook his head with a little smile.

"No such luck," he said. "I talked to him last night."

She gasped. "What did you say? Is he all right? Did you tell him who you were?" The fears tumbled out of her.

"I called him on the house phone. Relax, Laura, you're among friends. I asked him if he knew where you were. He said no."

"What else?" Laura had clutched his arms with trembling hands.

"He was pretty curious about *me*, naturally. But I didn't give him my name and phone number. Now calm down, will you? You're giving me the screaming mimis."

"What did he say?" She was crying again. "What? Tell me!"

"He tried to get me to talk but I didn't tell him anything, except that I was your best friend. Finally he said he was afraid he had hurt you." Laura shut her eyes and covered her face with a groan. "He wanted a chance to explain. He said if I found you to tell him right away. He has an agency trying to track you down. He said to tell you he's sorry." Jack looked curiously at her.

"He's sorry," she repeated, staring. "He's sorry!"

"Did he hurt you, honey?" Jack said gently.

It was too enormous to describe, too torturous to explain; her own private agony. Not even Jack could share it with her. "Yes," she whispered. "He hurt me." She looked at Jack and he could see in her face how much more there was to it than the simple words told him.

Jack crushed out his cigarette angrily. "I wish I could break his head for him," he said.

"No, no," Laura said. "I thought I had killed him. I

never meant to. I was sick. I've been so sick, Jack, you wouldn't believe—Oh, thank God he's alive. Thank God. I wanted to hurt him and I did. I never wanted anything more. Just a chance to get even with him."

"What the hell happened between you two?"

"I can't talk about it."

"You can to me."

"No. I can't. Not to anybody."

"Did he beat you?"

She shook her head. "Don't ask me, Jack," she said. "It's my own personal sickness. And his. It's between us, and nobody else."

Jack lighted a cigarette, watching her closely through the blue smoke. "Why did you go to him in the first place? Didn't you know it would be bad?"

"I had to," she said, her face drawn and intense. "I've been running away from him all my life. I had to quit running and save myself. I had to tell him face to face what I am."

Jack's brows drew together heavily. "You told him you were gay?" he asked.

"Yes. I told him."

"What did he do?"

She turned her deep eyes, accentuated by the thinness of her face, to Jack. "He hurt me, Jack. And I hurt him. But it's all over. Oh, my God, I'm so grateful I didn't kill him. Have you ever thought you killed somebody, and tried to go on living with it? It eats you up, it corrodes your brain and your body, it makes you sick, oh, so horribly sick. Oh, Jack . . ." And he put his arms around her while she wept and Terry watched them in silence.

"That bastard," Jack murmured, comforting her. "That damn bastard. I think I hate him as much as you do, honey."

"No, no, I don't hate him," she whispered. "I can't any more. I never will again. I understand now, so much. Nothing ever made sense before, but now I understand. He was weaker than I was, Jack." She spoke with wonderment. "He was more afraid of me than I was of him." It was a strange new feeling this knowledge gave her. "I don't know quite how I feel about him now. I won't know for a long time, I guess. But I still love him. I always

loved him, even when I hated him the most. I only hope
we never meet again. I can stand it if I never have to see
him again."

Terry fixed her a breakfast, and she ate ravenously.
She discovered they had stripped her wet clothes off and
put a robe on her the night before while she slept. She
pulled the robe close around her while Jack tried to make
her tell him where she had been, but he got little satisfaction.

"I don't know," was all she would say, and when he
protested, skeptically, she turned to him, her face earnest,
and said, "I don't know."

"Ahhh, don't tell *me*," he said.

"I just walked, I guess. It all seems like a nightmare.
The first thing I remember after I left Father is eating
a bowl of soup. And then I fell asleep."

"Don't you remember me?" Terry said. "We had a nice
little talk last night."

"We did?" She was surprised.

"Sure." He smiled, and made her blush with embarrassment. "I'll tell you all about it sometime." He grinned at
Jack who gave him a quizzical smile.

"So you don't know where you were?" he prodded
Laura.

"I swear, Jack."

"Well, we didn't know either," he said. "And we damn
near lost our minds. We pictured you—well, never mind
what we pictured. You had us frantic, I can tell you."

Laura smiled at him a little. "Jack," she said, and put
a hand on his arm. "You've been so good to me. I
wouldn't have caused you any worry, only—only—oh, my
God. Marcie! I forgot about Marcie. And Beebo." She
turned to him, but he calmed her with a glance, holding
her down in her chair.

"I called them," he said. "I called everybody. Even
Papa Landon. I told them you were all right, and that's
all. Your father doesn't know where you are."

Laura hung her head. "Jack, I didn't have a chance to
tell you about Marcie."

"I know. You don't have to tell me. Marcie did."

"Marcie did?" She looked up amazed.

"Not in so many words, Mother. She just said you quarreled, and I got the idea. She sounds pretty unhappy about things."

Laura covered her face, her elbows resting on the table. "She knew, Jack. She knew all along that I was gay," she whispered brokenly. "She and Burr had a bet that she could make me make a pass at her."

After a long silence Jack squeezed her arm and said gently, "You had to learn. Now you know. We all go through it sooner or later." He looked up at Terry and found the boy staring at him, his eyes full. He looked away, confused, turning his attention back to Laura. "She wants to see you. She means it."

"I know. But I couldn't stand to see her. Even talk to her. It would be hell."

"I know what you mean." Jack got up and poured himself another cup of coffee, saving himself a half inch in the cup for a jigger of whiskey.

"It's not even ten o'clock yet," Terry reproached him.

"Shut up and drink your milk," Jack said and smiled at him.

"I'd better call the office," Laura ventured quietly.

"I did," Jack told her. "You're fired. They were damn nice about it, though. Dr. Hollingsworth wants you to come in and talk to him. Sarah gave me the pitch. It seems they admire your brains but they figure your nerves are loused up. I suggest, Mother, that you see my analyst."

"I can't afford it."

"Neither can I." Jack laughed. "Let's put Terry to work," he said to Laura. "It's time he earned his own way."

"Doing what?" Terry said.

"I don't know. What are you good for? Anything?"

"I can cook." Terry grinned.

"Good. I know a Greasy Spoon two blocks from here."

"Oh, hell!"

"Jack," Laura said suddenly. "Does Beth know I'm all right?"

"Beth?" Jack frowned at her. "You mean Beebo, doll."

"I mean Beebo," Laura said quickly, growing hot.

"She knows."

"Did you tell her when I disappeared?"

"She looked all over the Village for you. She was worried."

"Do you think she'd talk to me?"

"No."

"Oh, Jack." She turned an unhappy face to him, pleading for a chance to hope.

"She might say 'goodby' to you. Or 'go to hell'. Don't expect miracles."

"I guess I haven't any right to her friendship any more." But it suddenly seemed terribly important; the most important thing in the world.

"Not as long as you get her mixed up with Beth."

"Oh, that was just a slip of the tongue."

Jack stood up and paced across the kitchen. He turned, resting his rump on the counter by the sink, and parked his coffee cup next to him. "Laura," he said seriously. "You fell in love with a girl named Beth once. You told me that. Then you and Beth broke up and Beth married somebody and quit school. And then you ran away from home. And you came to New York, and every damn female you met reminded you of Beth."

"Oh, no—" Laura began, but he held up a hand to silence her.

"Now listen to me, damn it! I'm beginning to wonder if you were running away from your father or from Beth."

"Jack!" Laura stood up and faced him, her temper rising.

"Marcie and Beebo look about as much alike as Laurel and Hardy. Yet they both remind you of Beth."

"But that doesn't mean—"

"And you fell for both of them. And don't tell me they were the only ones." His eyes were hard to meet. Laura looked down.

She shook her head. "No," she whispered, confused, rubbing her eyes. "No."

"Beth must have been a great girl, Mother. But you can't stay in love with her all of your life. Even if she *was* the first one." Laura's face flushed.

"I won't talk about this, Jack!" she exclaimed.

"You don't have to. I will."

"It's *my* private life."

"You've pulled me into it. What's the matter, are you afraid to hear me talk about it?"

She sat down, angry. "No," she said sharply. "I'm not afraid."

Jack took a sip of his café royale. "Okay," he said in a business-like voice. "I'm going to tell you something you won't like. But I think you ought to know it. You were never in love with Marcie, Laura."

They looked at each other and finally Laura exploded, "You're cracked! I thought you understood. I thought you—*you*, of all people—understood how I felt about her!"

"I did."

"I don't want to hear any more!"

"I don't doubt it," he said. She rose again and faced him, defiant and hurt. "You loved Beth," he said, more gently. "You loved love. It showed in all you said to me, when we first met. You needed love and you went looking for it. You went looking for another Beth. You were bound to find her. You found her in every female face that appealed to you.

"Laura," Jack said slowly. "Marcie doesn't look like Beth. Neither does Beebo. Nobody looks like Beth but Beth. And Beth is gone. She isn't yours any more. She belongs to a man."

Laura covered her face suddenly with a groan. "Jack, don't! Please," she whimpered. Then, gathering her anger around her, she said, "They *do* look like her! I swear they do!"

Jack shook his head. "They just looked like love, Mother."

Laura gave a little sob. "Jack, don't torture me."

"You know why I'm doing it. You know I don't want to hurt you. Now listen to me, Laura. You can't stay in love with Beth all your life."

Laura put her hands down and looked at him again. "Jack, you don't know how wonderful she was. You never knew her, you can't talk about her. She was so beautiful, she was so good to me. She made me understand what I was, when I was so ignorant and scared that you wouldn't believe it! And she made me understand without hurting me. She made it beautiful. I owe her so much. I loved her so."

"But she's married, Laura. You told me that yourself. You'll never even see her again. No matter how good she was."

"She never hurt me!" Laura flared. "Marcie hurt me, Beebo hurt me, but never Beth."

"Oh, balls!" Jack said. "Never hurt you, hell! She left you, didn't she! She slept with a guy and married him. What do you want, Mother, a silk-lined accident-proof guaranteed romance? Good for six months with lotsa kicks and no pain? Or your money back? They don't come that way. Ask anybody. Ask me. Ask Terry." And then his face softened. "She's gone, Laura," he said quietly, significantly. "And you can't go back to Marcie."

Laura sat down and let the tears roll down her face, and her mouth trembled. "And I can't go back to Beebo," she whispered.

Jack walked over to her and leaned on the table, one arm on either side of her. He put his head against hers and said into her ear, almost in a whisper, "Beebo loves you, honey. She's no Beth. No Marcie. She's herself, and for all you know, that may be even better."

Laura covered her face then and cried.

Fifteen minutes later Jack, who had gone into the bedroom to dress, came back to the kitchen and said, "I'm going to the office for the rest of the day. Somebody has to pay the rent." He looked at Terry with a wry smile.

Laura looked up quickly. "I've *got* to talk to her, Jack. Where can I find her?"

"Beebo? She's working. Stick around till I get home, Mother. Sleep. You look like hell. Get Terry to read you a story or something. You can see her tonight."

"Thanks." She looked at him with wet eyes and then she smiled. "Thanks, Jack. For everything."

He grinned. "It's those damn oysters," he said. "I'm a new man." He winked at Terry and left.

Chapter Seventeen

THE CELLAR was not very crowded when Laura walked in at eight o'clock. By a quarter to nine, when Beebo got there, the place had filled up a little and the juke box was going. Dutton, the sketch artist, was making a few bucks with the tourists. There was a tableful of them in one corner that he was working on. Beebo sat down at the bar and began to josh the bartender. She didn't see Laura, and Laura's heart was pounding so high in her chest that she was afraid to go near Beebo. She didn't know what to say. She was sickeningly afraid of a rebuff, and she hung back in a sweat. She deserved a rebuttal, but she was afraid she couldn't take it.

She watched Beebo for a while, her face shaded slightly as she leaned away from the bar lights. She let the heads of the people next to her serve as a sort of cover behind which she could dodge when Beebo glanced her way.

For a while she was tortured to see Beebo chatting with other women; young pretty girls, like the two high-schoolers Laura had met with her one night.

Beebo was tired. She had two drinks and then she meant to go home. But she was detained by a boy who ran an antique shop a block from her apartment, who was a friend. They talked about nothing in particular, just glad to talk with somebody for a while. Beebo was slightly surprised when Dutton came up and handed her one of his sheets of drawing paper. Beebo took it with a wry little grin. "I knew you'd get around to me sooner or later, Dutton," she said. "I'm part of the décor in this joint. Let's see." She studied the caricature. "I hate to admit it, but it's good. Does my chin stick out like that?"

Dutton grinned. "Take it from me," he said.

Beebo eyed him. "You don't think you're going to get a buck out of me for this, do you?" she said, waving it under his nose.

"I've got my buck, friend," Dutton said, holding a folded bill up between his thumb and index finger. He smiled and pushed the sketch back at her. "It's yours," he said. "Keep it."

Beebo studied him a moment, frowning, and then she looked up and down the bar.

"If you don't like it," Laura said softly in her ear, "just tear it up. I can't complain."

Beebo turned on the bar stool to find Laura standing close behind her. They gazed at each other in silence for a moment. Then Beebo tore the sketch once across the long way and once the short, still watching Laura. And dropped the pieces on the floor. Laura looked at her, trembling. Beebo turned back to the bar and finished her drink at once swallow. Then she said to the boy beside her, "See you, Daisy." And she got up and left the bar.

For a moment, Laura thought she would die where she stood. And then she followed Beebo, walking twenty feet behind her, her heart working hard and making her gasp a little. Beebo walked out into the night, and Laura followed her, coming just a little closer, until she was about five feet behind her. Beebo walked on, slowly, without glancing back, without hurrying her pace. They walked for two full blocks like this, and across the street into a third.

And then Beebo stopped. Startled and scared, Laura stopped where she was, on the curb, with the street light illuminating her silver blonde hair and leaving her face in the shadow.

Slowly Beebo turned around. She looked at Laura. She dropped the cigarette in her hand and crushed it under her heel. For some moments they just stood there and gazed at each other. A man walked by, and then a couple. Then the street was empty.

Finally Laura said, in a whisper that carried clearly to Beebo's heart, "I love you, Beebo. Darling, I love you."

Beebo walked over to her, still moving very slowly, until they stood together in the pool of light just inches from each other. The dawn of a smile showed on her face.

"Little bitch," she said softly. "Laura . . . Laura . . ." She leaned down then, tipping Laura's face up to hers. "I can't hate you any more," she said. "I've given up.

There's nothing left but love." And she kissed her. Their arms went around each other suddenly, hard, and they stood there in the lamplight, kissing.

Then they turned and walked into the night toward Cordelia Street.

THE END

WOMEN IN
THE SHADOWS

1

JUNE 8: *God help me. God help me to stand it. Today was our second anniversary. If I have to go on living with her I'll go crazy. But if I leave her—? I'm afraid to think what will happen. Sometimes she's not rational. But what can I do? Where can I turn?*

That damn party was awful. Anniversaries are supposed to be happy affairs, but this one was more like a wake. Everybody got drunk and sang songs, but there was always that corpse there in the middle of the room . . . the corpse of that romance. Jack got terribly drunk, as usual. There's another one. If he doesn't crack up it won't be because he hasn't tried. What's wrong with us all, anyway? What's the use of living when things are like this all the time?

Laura shut her diary with a sudden furtive gesture, her pen still poised, and strained her ears at a sound. She thought she heard the front door open. It would be Beebo coming back. But it was only the dachshund, Nix, scratching himself on a stool in the kitchen. Laura sighed in relief and turned back to the diary. She ordinarily kept it locked in a little steel strong-box on the closet floor, and she wrote in it only when she was alone, in the evenings before Beebo got home from work.

Beebo had never read it—or seen it, in fact. It was Laura's own, Laura's aches and pains verbalized, Laura's heart dissected and wept over, in washable blue ink. If Beebo ever saw it she would tear it up in a frenzy. She would make Laura swallow it, because it did not say very nice things about Beebo. And Beebo always did things in a big way, the good along with the bad.

417

Laura opened the notebook once more and wrote a last brief entry: *Jack asked me to marry him again . . . but I could never marry a man, not even him. Never.*

Then she closed it quickly and took it back to the closet and locked it in the strongbox. She sat down from sheer inertia on the closet floor and picked up a shoe. It was one of her pumps, rather long and narrow—too large to be really fashionable. But it had the proper shape and the newest styled heel. Beebo liked to see her smartly dressed. She cared more about that than Laura did herself. Laura had worn these shoes to the unfortunate anniversary party two nights before.

Beebo was still hung-over from that long night of dreary festivity. Jack was always hung-over, so he didn't count. As for Laura, she had learned from Beebo to drink too much herself, and she was learning at the same time how it feels the next day. *Bad. Plain bad.*

It had been a strange night, with moments of wild hilarity and stretches of gloom when everybody drank as if they made their living at it. Laura remembered Jack arriving ahead of everybody else with a couple of bottles under his arm. "Thought I'd better bring my own," he explained.

"Jack, you're not going to drink two fifths all by yourself!" Laura had exclaimed. She always took things at face value at first, a little too seriously.

"I'm going to try, Mother," he said, laughing, his eyes behind horn-rimmed glasses sparkling cynically at her.

Beebo had been in a sweat of preparation all day, and the apartment ended up looking almost new. A fever seemed to have gotten hold of her. This had to be a big party, a good party, a loud, drunk, and very gay party. Because this party was going to prove that Beebo and Laura had lived together for two whole years, and in Greenwich Village that is a pretty good record.

Friends were invited, to admire and congratulate. Oh, to get drunk and live it up a little too, on Beebo and Laura. But mostly to stand witness to the fact that the girls had been together two whole years. Or rather, Beebo had hung on to Laura for two whole years.

Maybe that's a hard way to say it. Maybe it isn't fair. After all, Laura stuck with Beebo, too. But Laura stuck because she didn't have the courage to let go; because her life was empty and without a purpose, and living with somebody and loving —or pretending to love—seemed to bring some sanity into her world. But for a long time she had begun to squirm and struggle under Beebo's jealous scrutiny.

Laura let Beebo make most of the arrangements for the party. She felt almost no enthusiam for it. The whole thing had been Beebo's idea in the first place. Laura felt almost as outside of it as a late-arriving guest. She ran a few errands, but it was Beebo who planned and organized, who put up streamers and cleaned the apartment, who called everybody, picked up the liquor and the ice cubes, and even made hors d'oeuvres.

She treated Laura with unwonted gentleness and attention all day. She wanted her in a good mood for the party. They had quarreled so much and so bitterly lately that they were both a little sick over it. Beebo wanted to have a good day behind them, a day full of good will and even tenderness.

There wasn't much time to foster tenderness, though, with the vacuum going, the kitchen upside down with food in various stages of readiness, the dog barking, and the phone ringing in an endless hysterical serenade. But still, Beebo tried. She touched Laura's hair softly when she passed her or brushed her hands over Laura's face. And once she stopped to kiss her, so carefully that Laura was touched in spite of herself and submitted, though without returning the kiss. Beebo went away flushed with success. Laura had not suffered herself to be kissed for nearly a week.

So when the guests finally started arriving, Beebo greeted them with high color in her cheeks and almost too much heartiness. Everything had started out so well, it had to end well.

It was a weird group that assembled to fete the anniverary. Beebo had wanted a big party. "Jesus, honey," she complained. "How many people down here stick it out this long? We have something to be proud of, for God's sake. Let's advertise it."

"What have we got to be proud of?" Laura said sarcastically. "We're just a couple of suckers for punishment. We just happen to enjoy beating each other's heads in."

Beebo had risen to the occasion with her quick and awful temper and left Laura crying. And she had had her way. They invited just about everybody in the neighborhood: the ones they knew, the ones they knew by sight only, and the ones they didn't know at all, male and female. Beebo did all the calling, so it came as a shock to Laura to see two of Beebo's old flames among the guests. But she said nothing about it. There would be time to shout about it afterwards. And shout they no doubt would.

Jack came early because he liked the chance to talk to Laura by himself now and then. He liked to be with her lately since his own life had taken a sickening dip into loneliness and frustration. They were old friends; sometimes they thought of one another as each other's *only* friend. They were very close. It could never be a question of physical love between them; only deep affection, a mutual problem, a sort of harmony that sprang from sympathy and long acquaintance.

They were both homosexual. And if Laura could never understand why a man would desire another man, she at least knew, very well, how it was to love another woman. And so she could build a bridge of empathy on that knowledge and comfort Jack when some lovely boy was giving him hell. And he could do the same when Beebo raked her over the coals.

The party went along well enough for the first hour or so. Every time Beebo came near Laura she pinched her or bussed her. It was a part of her advertising campaign—a way to say, "She's still mine. And it's been two years. Hands off, the rest of you!" And she would look around at the guests a little defiantly.

But for Laura it was tedious. It scared her and bored her all at once. The fierce passion for Beebo that had boiled when they first knew each other flared up rarely now. And when there was no love there was nothing but fighting between them. She hated to be put on exhibit like this. And yet she kept her peace and let Beebo kiss her when she felt like it. After all, it was a party. Have a good time. If you can. Forget. If you can. Everybody drink up and laugh. Laugh, damn you all! If you can.

It was when Lili (she *would* spell it that way; she was born plain Louise) was well plastered that the party took a downward curve from which it never recovered. Lili was a former amour of Beebo's; Lili of the ash blonde hair and carefully blackened lashes; Lili of the lush, silk-draped body; Lili with the lack of inhibitions. Laura hated her with a good healthy female jealousy. It had been intolerable at first when she was still in love with Beebo and Lili had tried to manage their lives for them. Now it was just an exasperation to Laura to have her around.

Lili got high in a hurry. She believed in getting things done efficiently, and getting drunk was one of the things. She began to saunter from group to group around the small apartment, flirting, feeding sips from her martini to interested parties, telling tales. She came upon Beebo in the kitchen, getting more sandwiches from the refrigerator. The kitchen was crowded with people waving empty glasses and looking for refills. Jack was pouring them as fast as he could and sampling them all.

"Important to get it just right," he said. "Takes a good concentration of alcohol or you don't get fried till three in the morning. Terrible waste of time."

Lili wriggled through the crowd to Beebo and stood in front of her, weaving slightly, her underlip thrust out.

"I want something from you," she pouted. Beebo offered her a sandwich, but she shook her head murmuring, "No, no, no, no, *no!*"

"Jack's handling the concession," Beebo said a little nervously, jerking her head toward him.

"I don't want liquor," Lili said. "I want you. How come you never come to see me anymore, Beebo? You're enough to drive a girl frantic."

It was typical cocktail party drivel and Beebo was impatient with her. "You know why, Lili," she said. "Now scram."

But Lili was pugnacious. "If it's because of that bitchy little Laura out there, everybody knows you're all washed up. It's been obvious for weeks. You do nothing but fight. In fact, I was saying to Irene just five minutes ago that I can't imagine why you wanted to give this party in the first place and—" She stopped. Beebo's face had gone pale and dangerous.

"You say that once more and I'll kick you out of here on your fat can," Beebo snapped.

Lili drew herself up. "Okay, lie to yourself, I don't give a damn," she said. "Only it's perfectly clear—"

"Damn you, Lili, don't you understand English?" She said it loud enough to make heads turn.

Lili smiled. She generally performed better with an audience. "I understand," she cooed. "I understand you prefer a button-breasted bad-tempered little prude to a real woman."

Beebo took her roughly by the arms and pushed her out of the kitchen to the front door, causing a stir of curiosity in her wake. "Now get out of here and stay out!" she said.

"You never *could* handle me right," Lili smiled. Suddenly she took hold of her dress at the neckline and pulled it—soft, unresisting knit—down far enough to disclose that she wore nothing underneath. Two creamy, full breasts were bared. "All right, you fool—suffer!" Lili cried dramatically and burst out laughing. Beebo stared and then slammed the door.

There was some confusion among the guests. It was funny. And yet there was Laura, watching the whole thing. Everybody was uncomfortable. There was uncertain laughter. Jack, who took it all in from the kitchen door, said simply, "Don't worry about it, it's nothing new. She did it to Kitty Jackson last week."

After that there was obvious tension between Laura and Beebo. Beebo didn't kiss her anymore and Laura had nothing to say to Beebo. She eyed her coolly from across the room, and moved away if Beebo drew near. The guests absorbed the mood.

Jack took it with quiet cynicism, the way he took most things. He saw and he understood but he said very little. It was not his affair. No matter that he had brought Beebo and Laura together once, a couple of years ago. He hadn't forced them to fall in love. That was their idea and he took no credit. And no blame.

Laura came suddenly into the kitchen where he was lounging by the liquor bottles, waiting for customers and watching the company through the door.

"She's impossible!" Laura cried. "God, I can't stand it any more!" She covered her face with her hands, and her usually ivory skin crimsoned under her own harsh fingers.

"Take it easy, Mother," he said mildly, crossing his arms over his chest. "She may be impossible, but she loves you."

"That doesn't excuse the way she's acting—"

"She loves you a hell of a lot, Laura. She wouldn't hang on to you like this if she didn't."

"I don't want to be hung on to. I hate it! Jack, help me get out of here."

"I can't, honey, it's your mess. I wish to God I could. If I were young and female I'd lure her away from you. But I'm middle-aged and male. And short on allure."

Laura took advantage of the momentary seclusion of the kitchen to speak confidentially. She went to Jack and stood beside him, facing the sink, while he watched the door for intruders.

"She's in there showing off with that damn dog again," Laura said.

"Nix is a nice dog."

"Jack, we can't go to bed without that animal." She turned away to blow her nose. "Sure, he's a nice dog. But he eats more than I do, and he isn't housebroken when he's excited—which is right now. I swear Beebo loves that dog more than she loves me." Nix gave a volley of excited barks from the living room and they heard Beebo's throaty laugh. "Do it again," she was saying. "Come on, Nix, do it again."

"He will, too." Laura sighed. "He'll do anything she tells him to. And wet the rug like a happy idiot. Do you know what that rug cost me? Seventy-seven bucks. And I paid for it myself. Beebo didn't even have a rug in this place before I moved in."

"Okay," Jack said slowly. "The dog isn't housebroken and Beebo's old mistresses are a pain in the neck. Still, she loves you, Mother. So much that it astonishes me. I never thought I'd see that girl fall for anybody. Maybe you don't want her love, but you have to respect it. Real love isn't cheap, Laura. When you give it up once you sometimes never find it again."

"If it has to be like this, I don't ever want it again."

Jack finished his drink quickly, put it down on the kitchen counter, and turned Laura around to face him. He was the same height as she was but Laura looked up to him with her mind and heart.

"Mother," he said gently. "Don't ever say that. Don't ever throw love away. If it gets so you can't stand it, move out. But don't degrade it and don't disdain it. You can't stop her from loving you, Laura."

"I wish I still loved her. That's an odd way to feel but it would solve everything."

"You do love her, in a way. Only she exasperates you."

"No. It's all over, Jack. The only problem is how to get out without hurting her too much."

"No, the problem is to realize what your own feelings are and then have the courage to live with them."

"What you're trying to say is, you don't believe me. You think I still love her."

"Yes," he said.

"Why?"

"It's true."

"It's not!" she cried, grasping his arms, and then she heard Beebo laugh again and looked up to see her standing in the other room against the far wall. She was strikingly handsome and for a moment Laura felt the old feeling for her, but the love left almost as fast as it had come.

Beebo was a big girl, big-boned and good looking, like a boy in early adolescence. Her black hair was short and wavy and her eyes were an off-blue, wide, well spaced. She had come to New York from a small town near Milwaukee before she was twenty, and she had had a sort of heartiness then, a rosy-cheeked health that had faded too fast in the hot-house atmosphere of Greenwich Village. She took odd jobs where she could; anything that would let her wear pants. And she ended up running an elevator and wearing a blue uniform with gold trim. She had been there for over ten years.

The manager took her for "one of those queers, but perfectly harmless." But he meant a *male* homosexual, to Beebo's endless hilarity. She was fond of remarking, "I'm the world's oldest adolescent. I'm a professional teen-ager." It was funny enough the first time, but Laura was sick of it.

Now she stood in the living room of their small apartment playing with Nix, and her merriment brought color to her cheeks. She had begun to wear clothes that made her look sportier and healthier than she was: men's jackets and slacks, men's shirts. And even, to Laura's dismay, a sort of riding habit, with modified jodhpurs, a slightly fitted coat, and boots. She had a pair of high black boots in butter-smooth leather with little ankle straps, boots made to fit the finely shaped feet that she was proud of. It made her one of the sights of the village.

"You look like a freak!" Laura had exploded when Beebo first tried them on, and succeeded in offending Beebo royally. But the older girl stuck stubbornly to her outfit.

"I'm no man. Okay. But I'm sure as hell no woman, either. I don't look good in anything. At least these things fit me," she defended herself.

"Your underwear fits you, too, darling," Laura said acidly. "Why don't you parade around in that if you want to cause a sensation?" But though she needled her, Laura couldn't make her change.

Now Beebo stood in the living room, visible to Laura through the kitchen door, dressed in the riding clothes. She did not look mannish like some Lesbians. She simply looked like a boy. But she was thirty-three years old, and there were very faint lines around her eyes and mouth.

Laura's little flash of desire faded almost before it bloomed. And when she found that Nix had wet the floor, that Beebo had kissed Frankie Koehne and Jean Bettman, and that the police had appeared saying they had two complaints and the party would have to simmer down, Laura gave up.

She stormed into the bathroom and locked the door—the one lockable door in the apartment. The guests took the hint and filed out, leaving the apartment a quiet shambles.

When Laura came out, only Jack and Beebo were still there. They were sitting in the kitchen where they had collected most of the glasses, and were finishing up whatever liquor was left in them.

Beebo looked up when Laura came in. She was quite drunk and through the mists she saw Laura, with her long blond hair and pale face, as a sort of lovely vision. "Hi, sweetie," she murmured. "You sure got rid of the company in a hurry." She grinned.

Laura glanced disapprovingly at the used glasses Beebo was drinking from. "You'll get trench mouth," she predicted.

"Will you make love to me when I've got trench mouth?"

"NO!"

Beebo laughed. "You won't anyway, so it doesn't matter," she said dryly. "Come sit on my lap."

Laura leaned against the kitchen counter near Jack. "No," she said.

"Be nice to me, baby."

"Nix is nice to you. You don't need me. Nix ruins the rug for you. He barks loud enough to wake the dead. He even sleeps with you."

But Beebo felt too much desire for her to be jockeyed so fast into an argument. "Please, baby," she said softly. "I love you so."

And Jack, watching her, felt a pang of sympathy and regret go through him. She sounded too much as he sounded himself a couple of months ago. And Terry had left him anyway and wrecked his life. It was all so sad and wrong; unbearable when you're mismated and desperately in love.

"Go to her, Mother," he said suddenly. "She needs you."

Laura was miffed at his interference. But she knew what was bothering him, and to soften it for him, she went. Once she was on Beebo's lap, everything seemed to relax a little. Beebo held her, leaning back against the wall and pulling Laura's head down on her shoulder, and Jack watched them enviously. He knew, as Laura knew, and even Beebo must have known in her secret heart, that the affair was doomed, that the party had celebrated an ending, not a new beginning. And yet for a moment things were serene. Beebo held Laura and whispered to her and stroked her hair, and Jack listened to it as if it were a lullaby, a lullaby he had heard somewhere before and had sung once himself. But it was a mournful lullaby and it turned into the blues—a dirge for love gone wrong.

Beebo nuzzled Laura and Laura lay quietly in her arms and endured it. She relaxed, and that made it better. She didn't want Beebo to excite her; she didn't want to give her that satisfaction. So she shifted suddenly and asked Jack, "Do you think they had a good time?"

"Lili did. She loves to promote her bosom," he said.

"Laura, baby." Beebo turned Laura's face to hers and tickled her cheeks with tne tip of her tongue. "You taste so sweet," she whispered. "I want to lick you all over like a new puppy."

Laura couldn't stand it. The once-welcome intimacy sickened her now that she no longer loved Beebo. She got up abruptly and walked over to the stove. "Anybody want some coffee?" she said.

"You and your goddam coffee," Beebo said irritably.

"You could use a little," Laura said, "both of you."

"I'd be delighted," Jack said, speaking with deliberate care as he always did when he was drunk.

Laura made the instant coffee and passed the cups around. Jack doctored his with a double shot of scotch and took a cautious first sip. "Delicious," he said, looking up to find a storm brewing. Beebo was glowering at Laura.

"I said I didn't want coffee," she said. "Nobody around here understands English tonight."

"If you're referring to Lili, I don't like to be classed with your old whores," Laura said.

"Why not? You're in good company, baby. You don't think

you're any better than they are, do you?"

"You should have told me you asked Lili! You should have told me, Beebo! And Frankie, too. God, don't you think I have feeling?"

"Good." Beebo grinned. "I didn't think you could get jealous any more."

"Oh, grow up, Beebo!" Laura cried, exasperated. "I càn be humiliated. I can be embarrassed and hurt."

Beebo poured her coffee into an empty highball glass, which cracked from the heat with a loud snap. Her eyes looked up slyly at Laura, expecting a reprimand, but Laura ignored it, too angry to do anything. Beebo laughed and poured herself a watery drink from another glass. "Did I hurt you, Laura, baby? Did I really? How did it feel? Tell me how you liked it."

Laura didn't like the way she laughed. "Does that strike you funny?" she said sharply.

Beebo began to chuckle, a low helpless sort of laugh that she couldn't control; the miserable sort of laugh that comes on after too much to drink and too little to be happy about. "Yes," she drawled, still laughing. "Everything strikes me funny. Even you. Even you, my lovely, solemn, angry, gorgeous Laura. Even me. Even Jackson here. Jack, you doll, how come you're so handsome?"

Jack grinned wryly, twisting his ugly intelligent face. "The Good Fairy," he explained. "The Good Fairy is an old buddy of mine. Gives me anything I want. You want to be handsome like me? I'll talk to him. No charge."

Beebo kept laughing while he talked. She sounded a little hysterical. "No, I don't want to be handsome," she said. "I just want Laura. Tell your damn fairy to talk to Laura. Tell him I need help. Laura won't let me kiss her any more." She stopped laughing suddenly. "Will you, baby?"

"Beebo, please don't talk about it. Not now."

"Not now, not ever. Every time I bring it up, same damn thing. 'Not now, Beebo. Please, Beebo. Not now.' You're nothing but a busted record, my love. A beautiful busted record. Kiss me, little Bo-peep." Laura turned away, biting her underlip, embarrassed and defiant. "Please kiss me, Laura. That better? *Please*." She dragged the word out till it ended in a soft growl.

Laura hated Beebo's begging almost more than her swaggering. "If you didn't get so drunk all the time, you'd be a lot more appealing," Laura said.

Beebo got up and lurched across the room in one giant step and took Laura's arms roughly. She turned her around and forced a kiss on her mouth. They were both silent afterwards for a moment, Laura looking hot-faced at the floor and Beebo, her eyes shut, holding the love she was losing with awful stubbornness. Jack watched them in a confusion of pity.

He liked them both, but he loved Laura as well. In his own private way he loved her, and if it ever came to a showdown it was Laura he would side with.

At last Beebo said softly, "Don't shut me out, Laura."

Laura disengaged herself slightly. "If you didn't drink so much I wouldn't shut you out."

"If you didn't shut me out I wouldn't drink so much!" Beebo shouted, suddenly. "I wouldn't have to."

"Beebo, you drink because you like to get drunk. You were drunk the night I met you and you've been more or less drunk ever since. I didn't do it to you, you did it to yourself. You like the taste of whiskey, that's all. So don't give me a sob story about my driving you to drink."

"There you go, getting holy on me again. Who says you don't like whiskey?"

"I have a drink now and then," Laura flashed at her. "There are so many damn whiskey bottles in this apartment I'd have to be blind to avoid them."

Jack laughed. "I'm blind," he said, "most of the time. But I can always find the booze. In fact, the blinder I am the better I find it." He chuckled at his own nonsense and swirled the spiked coffee in his cup.

"Laura, you lie," Beebo said. "You lie in your teeth. You just like the way it tastes, like me."

Laura had been drinking too much lately. Not as much as Beebo, but still too much. She didn't know exactly why. She blamed it on a multiplicity of bad breaks, but never on herself. "If you wouldn't drag me around to the bars all night," she said. "If you wouldn't continually ask me to drink with you. . . ."

"I *ask* you, Bo-peep. I don't twist your arm." She eyed Laura foggily.

Laura turned to Jack. "Do I drink as much as Beebo?" she demanded. "Am I an alcoholic?"

Beebo gave a snort. "Jack," she mimicked, "am *I* an alcoholic?"

"Do you have beer for breakfast?" he asked her.
"No."
"Do you take a bottle to bed?"
"No."
"Do you get soused for weeks at a time?"
"No."
"Do you . . . have a cocktail now and then?"
"Yes."
"You're an alcoholic."
Beebo threw a wet dishcloth at him.
"I'm going to bed," Laura announced abruptly.
"What's the matter, baby, can't you take it?"
"Enough is too much, that's all."
"Enough of what?"
"Of you!"
Beebo turned a cynical face to Jack. "That means I can sleep
on the couch tonight," she said. "Too bad. I was just getting
used to the bed again. . . ." She hiccuped, and smiled sadly.
"Don't you think we make an ideal couple, Laura and me?"
"Inspirational," Jack said. "They should serialize you in all
the women's magazines. Give you a free honeymoon in
Jersey City."
"Knowing us as well as you do, Doctor," Beebo said, and
Laura, her teeth clenched, stood waiting in the doorway to
hear what she was going to say, "what would you recom-
mend in our case?"
"Nothing. It's hopeless. Go home and die, you'll feel better,"
he said.
"Don't say that." Suddenly Beebo wasn't kidding.
"All right. I won't say it. I retract my statement."
"Revise it?"
"God, in my condition?" he said doubtfully. "Well . . .
I'll try. Let's see . . . My friends, the patient is dead of the
wrong disease. The operation was a success. There is only
one remedy."
"What's that?" Laura asked him.
"Bury the doctor. Oops, I got that one wrong too. Excuse
me, ladies. I mean, *marry* the doctor. Laura, will you marry
me?"
"No." She smiled at him.
"I'm an alcoholic," he offered, as if that might persuade her.
"You're damn near as irresistible as I am, Jackson," Beebo

said. She said it bitterly, and the tone of her voice turned Laura on her heel and sent her out of the room to bed. Beebo went to the open kitchen door and leaned unsteadily on it.

"Laura, you're a bitch!" she called after her. "Laura, baby, I hate you! I hate you! Listen to me!" She waited while Laura slammed the door behind her and then stood with her head bowed. Finally she looked up and whispered, "I love you, baby."

She turned back to Jack, who had finished the coffee and was now drinking out of the whiskey bottle without bothering with a glass. "What do you do with a girl like that?" she asked.

Jack shrugged. "Take the lock off the bedroom door."

"I already did."

"Didn't work?"

"Worked swell. She made me sleep on the couch for five days."

"Why do you put up with it?"

"Why did you? It was your turn not so long ago, friend."

"Because you're crazy blind in love." He looked toward her out of unfocused eyes. Jack's body got very intoxicated when he drank heavily, but his mind did not. It was a curious situation and it produced bitter wisdom, sometimes witty and more often painful.

Beebo slumped in a chair and put her hands tight over her face. Some moments passed in silence before Jack realized she was crying. "I'm a fool," she whispered. "I drink too much, she's right. I always did. And now I've got her doing it."

"Don't be a martyr, Beebo. It's unbecoming."

"I'm no martyr, damn it. I just see how unhappy she is, how she is dying to get away from me, and then I see her brighten up when she's had a couple, and I can only think one thing: I'm doing it to her. That's my contribution to Laura's life. And I love her so. I love her so." And the tears spilled over her cheeks again.

Jack took one last drink and then left the bottle sitting in the sink. He said, "I love her too. I wish I could help."

"You can. Quit proposing to her."

"You think I should?"

"Never mind what I think. It's unprintable. I'm just telling you, quit proposing to her."

"She'll never say yes," he said mournfully. "So I don't see

that it matters."

"That's not the point, Jackson. I don't like it."

"I'm sorry, I can't help it."

"Jack, you don't want to get married."

"I know. It's ridiculous, isn't it?"

"What would you do if she did say yes?"

"Marry her."

"Why?"

"I love her."

"Drivel! You love me. Marry me."

"I could live with her, but not with you," he said. "I love her very much. I love her terribly."

"That's not the reason you want to marry her. You can love her unmarried as well as not. So what's the real reason? Come on."

If he had not been so drunk he would probably never have said it.

"I want a child," he admitted suddenly, quietly.

Beebo was too startled to answer him for a moment. Then she began to laugh. "You!" she exclaimed. "*You!* Jack Mann, the homosexual's homosexual. Dandling a fat rosy baby on his knee. Father Jack. Oh, God!" And she doubled up in laughter.

Jack stood in front of her, the faintest sad smile on his face. "It would be a girl," he mused. "She'd have long pale hair, like Laura."

"And horn-rimmed glasses like her old man."

"And she'd be bright and sweet and loving."

"With *dames,* anyway."

"With me."

"Oh, God! All this and incest, too!" And Beebo's laughter, cruel and helpless, silenced him suddenly. He couldn't be angry, she meant no harm. She was writhing in a net of misery and it eased the pain when she could tease. But the lovely child of his dreams went back to hide in the secret places of his heart.

After a while Beebo stopped laughing and asked, "Why a girl?"

"Why not?"

"You're gay. Don't you want a pretty little boy to play with?"

"I'm afraid of boys. I'd ruin him. I'd be afraid to love him. Every time I kissed him or stroked his hair I'd be thinking,

'I can't do this any more, he'll take it wrong. He'll end up as queer as his old man.' "

"That's not how little boys get queer, doll. Or didn't your mama tell you?"

"She never told me anything." He smiled at her. "You know, Beebo, I think I'm going mad," he said pleasantly.

"That makes two of us."

"I'm serious. I'm even bored with liquor. By Jesus, I think I'll go on the wagon."

"When you go on the wagon, boy, I'll believe you're going mad for sure. But not before." She put her own glass down as if it suddenly frightened her. "Why do we all drink so much, Jackson? Is it something in the air down here? Does the Village contaminate us?"

"I wish to God it did. I'd move out tomorrow."

"Are we all bad for each other?"

"Poisonous. But that's not the reason."

"It's contagious, then. One person gets hooked on booze and he hooks everybody else."

"Guess again."

"Because we're queer?"

"No, doll. Come with me." He took her by the hand and led her on a weaving course through the living room to the bathroom. The dachshund, Nix, followed them, bustling with non-alcoholic energy. Jack aimed Beebo at the mirror over the washbowl. "There, sweetheart," he said. "There's your answer."

Beebo looked at herself with distaste. "My face?" she asked.

Jack chuckled. "Yourself," he said. "You drink to suit yourself. As Laura said, you drink because you like the taste."

"I hate the taste. Tastes lousy."

"Beebo, I love you but you are the goddam stubbornest female alive. You don't drink because anybody asks you to, or infects you, or forces you. You're like me. You need to or you wouldn't! Ask that babe in the mirror there."

"I can't live with that, Jack," she whispered.

"Okay, don't. I can't either. I just made up my mind: I'm quitting."

She turned and looked at him. "I don't believe you."

He smiled at her. "You don't have to," he said.

"And what if you do? How does that help me?"

He shook his head. "You have to help yourself, Beebo.

That's the hell of it." He turned and walked toward the front door and Beebo followed him, scooping Nix off the floor and carrying him with her. "Don't go, Jack," she said. "I need somebody to talk to."

"Talk to Laura."

"Sure. Like talking to a wall."

"Talk anyway. Talk to Nix."

"I do. All the time." She held the little dog tight and turned a taut face to it. "Why doesn't she love me any more, Nix? What did I do wrong? Tell me. Tell me . . ." She glanced up at Jack. "I apologize," she said.

"What for?"

"For laughing about your kid. Your little girl." She stroked Nix. "I know how it feels. To want one. You just have to make do with what you've got," she added, squeezing Nix.

Jack stared a little at her. "You know, it comes to me as a shock now and then that you're a female," he said.

"Yeah. Comes as a shock to me too."

He saw tears starting in her eyes again and put a kind hand on her arm. "Beebo, you're trying too damn hard with Laura. Relax. Ignore her for a couple of days."

"Ignore her! I adore her! I die inside when she slams that door at me." She dropped Nix suddenly and threw her arms around Jack, nearly smothering him. "Jack, you've been through it, you know what to do. Help me. Tell me. Help me!" And her arms loosened and she slumped to the floor and rolled over on her stomach and wept. Nix licked her face and whimpered.

Jack stood looking over her, still smiling sadly. Nothing surprised him now. He had lived with the heartbreaks of the homosexual world too long.

"Sure, I know what to do," he said softly. "Just keep living. Whatever else turns rotten and dies, never mind. Just keep living. Till it's worse than dying. Then it's time to quit."

"Ohhhh," she groaned. "What shall I do?"

"Stop loving her," he said.

Beebo turned over and gaped at him. Jack shrugged and there was sympathy in his face and fate in his voice. "That would straighten things out, wouldn't it?"

Beebo shook her head and whispered, "I can't. You know I can't."

"I know," Jack repeated. "Goodnight, Beebo."

2

THE BEDROOM DOOR opened and Beebo surprised Laura sitting on the closet floor fingering her shoes and dreaming. The party was two days past, the hang-overs were still with them, but love was seven days behind them. Beebo didn't know how much longer she could take it. She had tried, since Jack's advice about relaxing, to keep her distance from Laura. It had not worked miracles, but it had helped.

However, Laura resented the love she could no longer return. Perhaps it was anger at her own failing, her own empty heart. Laura felt a sort of shame when Beebo embraced her. She blamed herself secretly for her fading affection. Beebo's love had been the strongest and Beebo's words, when she spoke of it, the truest. And yet Laura had said those same words and felt those same passions and believed, as Beebo had believed, that it would last.

She could not be sure where she had gone wrong or when that lovely flush of desire had begun to wane in her. She only knew one day that she did not want Beebo to touch her. When Beebo had protested, Laura had lost her temper and they had had their first terrible fight. Not a spat or an argument or a disagreement, as before. A fight—a physical struggle as well as a verbal one. An ugly and humiliating thing from which they could not rise and make love and reassure each other. That had been almost a year ago. Others had followed it and the breach became serious, and still they clung to each other.

Only now Laura's need was weakening and it was Beebo who held them together almost by herself. It was Beebo who gave in when a quarrel loomed, who took the lead to make peace afterwards, to try to soothe and spoil Laura. Beebo had the terrible fear that one of these days the quarrel would be too vicious and Laura would leave her. Or that she would go beyond the point of rational suffering and kill Laura.

Once or twice she had dreamed of this, and when she had wakened in sweat and panic she had gone to the living room

434

and turned the light on and spent the time until dawn staring at it, repeating the jingles of popular tunes in her mind as a sort of desperate gesture at sanity.

Now Beebo stood looking down at Laura and at Nix, who was chewing on a pair of slippers, and she felt a wrenching in her heart. It just wasn't possible for her to ignore Laura any longer. She had kept hands off since the party and her talk with Jack. There had been no begging, no shouting, no furious tears. Now she felt she deserved tenderness and she knelt down and took Laura's chin in her hand and kissed her mouth.

"I love you," she said almost shyly.

And Laura, who wanted only to leave her, not to hurt her, lowered her eyes and looked away. She could not say it any more. *I love you, Beebo.* It wasn't true. And Beebo knew it and the knowledge almost killed her, and yet she didn't insist. "Laura," she said humbly. "Kiss me."

And Laura did. And in a little wave of compassion she said into Beebo's ear, "I don't want to hurt you any more."

Beebo took it the wrong way, the way that hurt her least. She took it to mean that Laura was apologizing and wanted her love again. But Laura meant only that Beebo had been dear to her once and that it was awful to see her so unhappy. "It's my fault," she said. "Only—"

"Only nothing," Beebo said quickly. "Don't say it. Say sweet things to me."

"Oh, Beebo, I can't. Don't ask me. I've forgotten the sweet things." Suddenly she felt like crying. She had never meant to wound Beebo. She had had the best intentions of loving her faithfully for the rest of her life. And yet now every pretty face she saw on the streets caught her eye, every new set of eyes or curving lips at the lunch counter.

Laura was afraid and ashamed. She had always protested hotly when somebody accused Lesbians of promiscuity. And yet here she was refuting her own argument, at least in her thoughts and desires. It was still true that in the whole time they had lived together, she had never betrayed Beebo with another woman.

Knowing how Beebo felt only made Laura's conscience worse. It made her resentful and gentle by fits. Either way it was nerve-wracking and left her exhausted.

Suddenly Beebo picked her up and put her on the bed. She sat down beside her and slipped her arms around her and began to kiss her with a yearning that gradually brought little darts of desire to Laura. She didn't want it until it happened. And then, inexplicably, she did. It was good, very good. And she heard Beebo whisper, "Oh, if it could always be like this. Laura, Laura, love me. Love me!"

Laura turned her head away and shut her eyes and tried not to hear the words. Gradually the world faded out of her consciousness and there was only the ritual rhythm, the wonderful press of Beebo's body against hers. It hadn't been like this for Laura for months, and she was both grateful and annoyed.

Beebo made wonderful love. She knew how, she did it naturally, as other people eat or walk. Her hands flowed over Laura like fine silk in the wind, her lips bit and teased and murmured, all with a knowing touch that amounted to witchery. In the early days of their love Laura had not been able to resist her, and Beebo had loved her lavishly.

Often Laura had felt an ache for those days, when everything was sure and safe and certain in the fortress of passion. She had taken passion for love itself, and she had been secure in Beebo's warm arms. Now it seemed that Beebo had been just a harbor where she could rest and renew herself at a time when her life was most shattered and unhappy. She didn't need the safe harbor now. She was grateful, but she needed to move on. It was time to face life again and fight again and feel alive again. For Beebo the time of searching was over. It ended when she met Laura.

She had a small ten-watt bulb in a little bedstand lamp that shed a peachy glow around them, and she always had it on when they went to bed. Laura had loved it at first, when just the sight of Beebo's big firm body and marvelous limbs would set her trembling. But later, when she was afraid her slackening interest would show in her face, she asked Beebo to turn it out. It had been one more in a series of harsh arguments, for Beebo had known what prompted her request.

Now they lay beside one another, their hearts slipping back into a normal rhythm, their bodies limp and relaxed. Laura wanted only to sleep; she dreaded long intimate talks with Beebo. But Beebo wanted reassurance. She wanted Laura's soft voice in her ears.

"Talk to me, Bo-peep," Beebo said.

"Too sleepy," Laura murmured, yawning.

"What did you do today?"

"Nothing."

"Shall I tell you what I did?"

"No."

"I got a new shirt at Davis's," Beebo said, ignoring her. "Blue with little checks. And guess who rode in my elevator today?"

Laura didn't answer.

"Ed Sullivan," Beebo said. "He had to see one of the ad agency people on the eighth floor." Still no response. "Looks just like he does on TV," Beebo said.

Laura rolled over on her side and pulled the covers up over her ears. For some moments Beebo remained quiet and then she said softly, "You've been calling me 'Beth' again."

Laura woke up suddenly and completely. Beth . . . the name, the girl, the love that wound through her life like a theme. The tender first love that was born in her college days and died with them less than a year later. The love she never could forget or forgive or wholly renounce. She had called Beebo "Beth" when they first met, and now and then when passion got the best of her, or whiskey, or nostalgia, Beth's name would come to her lips like an old song. Beebo had grown to hate it. It was the only rival she knew for certain she had and it put her in the unreasonable position of being helplessly jealous of a girl she didn't know and never would. Whenever she mentioned her, Laura knew there was a storm coming.

"If I could only *see* that goddam girl sometime and know what I was up against!" she would shout, and Laura would have to pacify her one way or another. She would have to protest that after all, it was all over, Beth was married, and Beth had never even loved her. Not really. But when Laura grew the most unhappy with Beebo, the most restless and frustrated, she would start to call her Beth again when they made love. So Beebo feared the name as much as she disliked it. It was an evil omen in her life, as it was a love theme in Laura's.

Laura turned back to face Beebo now, nervous and tensed for a fight. "Beebo, darling—I'm sorry. I didn't mean to."

"Sure, I know. *Darling.*" She lampooned Laura's soothing love word sarcastically. "You just pick that name out of a hat. For some screwy reason it just happens to be the same name all the time."

"If you're going to be like that I won't apologize next time."

"Next time! Are you planning on next time already? God!"

"Beebo, you know that's all over—"

"I swear, Laura, sometimes I think you must have a girl somewhere." Laura gasped indignantly, but Beebo went on, "I do! You talk about Beth, Beth, Beth so much I'm beginning to think she's real. She's my demon. She lives around the corner on Seventh Avenue somewhere and you sneak off and see her in the evenings when I work late. And her husband is out." Her voice was sharp and probing, like a needle in the hands of a nervous nurse.

"Beebo, I've never betrayed you! Never!"

Beebo didn't really believe she had. But Laura had hurt her enough without betraying her and Beebo, who was not blind, could see that Laura would not go on forever in beautiful blamelessness.

"You will," Beebo said briefly. They were the words of near despair.

Laura was suddenly full of pity. "Beebo, don't *make* me hurt you," she begged. She got on her knees and bent over Beebo. "I swear I've never touched another girl while we've lived together, and I never will."

"You mean when you stumble on a tempting female one of these days you'll just move out. You can always say, 'I never cheated on Beebo while we lived together. I just got the hell out when I had a chance.' "

"Beebo, damn you, you're impossible! *You're* the one who's saying all this! I don't want to cheat, I don't want to hurt you, I *hate* these ugly scenes!" She began to weep while she talked. "God, if you're going to accuse me of something, accuse me of something real. Sometimes I think you're getting a little crazy."

Beebo clasped her around the waist then, her strong fingers digging painfully into Laura's smooth flesh, and sobbed. They were hard sobs, painful as if each one were twisting her throat.

"Forgive me, forgive me," she groaned. "Why do I do it? *Why?* Laura, my darling, my only love, tell me just once— you aren't in love with anybody else, are you?"

"No!" said Laura with the force of truth, resenting Beebo's arms around her. She wanted to comfort her, yet she feared that Beebo would pounce on the gesture as a proof of love

and force her into more love-making. Her hands rested awkwardly on Beebo's shoulders.

"If you ever fall for anybody, Bo-peep, tell me. Tell me
first, don't spare me. Don't wait till the breach is too wide to
heal. Give me a chance. Let me know who it is, let me know
how it happened. Don't keep me wondering and agonizing
over it. Anything would be better than lies and wondering.
Promise you'll tell me. *Promise, love.*"

She looked up at Laura now, shaking her so hard that Laura
gasped. "Promise!" she said fiercely.

"All right," Laura whispered, afraid of her.

"Say it."

"I promise—to tell you—if I—oh, Beebo, please—"

"Go on, damn you!"

"If I ever fall—for somebody else." Her voice was almost
too weak to hear.

Beebo released her then and they both fell back on the bed,
worn out. For a long time they lay awake, but neither would
make a move toward the other or utter a word.

The next day Beebo awoke feeling that they had come closer
to the edge of breaking up than ever before, and she could
feel herself trembling all over. She got up before Laura was
awake and, taking Nix with her into the kitchen, she poured
herself a shot. She was ashamed of this new little habit she
was acquiring. She hadn't told anybody about it, not even
Jack. Just one drink in the morning. Just one. Never more.
It made her hands steady. It made the day look brighter and
not quite so endless. It made her situation with Laura look
hopeful.

She took the hot and satisfying amber liquid straight, letting
it burn her tight throat and ease her. Then she washed out
the shot glass and returned it to the shelf with the bottle.

"Nix," she said softly to the little dog, "I'm a bad girl.
Your Beebo is a wicked bitch, Nix. Do you think anybody
cares? Do you think it matters? What the hell good is it to
be a bad little girl if nobody notices you? What fun is it then?
Shall I have another shot, Nix? Nobody's looking."

He whimpered a little, watching her with puddle-bright
eyes, and made her laugh. "*You* care, don't you, little dog?"
She leaned down and picked him up. "You care, anyway.
You're telling me not to be an ass and let myself in for a lot

of trouble. And you're right. Absolutely."

She sat down on a kitchen chair and sighed. "You know, if she loved me, Nix, I wouldn't have to do it. You know that, don't you? Sure you do. You're the only one who does. Every-body else thinks I'm just turning into an old souse. But it's not true. It's because of Laura, you know that as well as I do. She makes me so miserable. She has my life in her hands, Nix." She laughed a little. "You know, that's kind of fright-ening. I wish I knew if she was on my side or not."

There was a moment when she thought she would cry and she dumped Nix off her lap and quickly poured herself one more shot. It went down easier than number one, but she washed the shot glass out as before and put it and the bottle back on the shelf as if to tell herself: *That's all, that's enough.*

Beebo turned and smiled at Nix. "Now look at me," she said. "I'm more sober than when I'm really sober. My hands have quit shaking. And I'm not going to quarrel with her when she gets up. I'm going to say something nice. Come here, dog. Help me think of something. . . .

"I'd sell my soul to be an honest-to-god male. I could marry Laura! I could marry her. Give her my name. Give her kids . . . oh, wouldn't that be lovely? So lovely. . . ." Jack's desire for a child didn't seem grotesque to her at all any more.

"But Nix," she went on, and her face fell, "she wouldn't have me. My baby is gay, like me. She wants a woman. Would God she wanted me. But a woman, all the same. She'd never take a man for a mate."

She felt the vile tears sneaking up on her again and shook her head hard. "She couldn't take that, Nix. It'd be even worse than—than living with me." And she gave a hard laugh.

Beebo heard the bedroom door open and she dropped Nix and went to the icebox. Within moments Laura entered the kitchen.

" 'Morning," she said.

"Good morning, Madam Queen. What'll it be?"

"Soft boiled egg, please. Have to hurry, I'll be late to work." She had a job in a tourist trap over on Greenwich Avenue, where they sold sandals and earrings and trinkets.

Beebo busied herself with the eggs and Laura poured orange juice and opened the paper. She buried herself in it, moving just a little to let Beebo put her plate down in front of her. Beebo sat down opposite her and ate in silence for a minute, eating very little. She lighted a cigarette after a few minutes and sipped cautiously at her hot coffee.

"Laura?" she said.

"Hm?"

"Even in the morning, with your hair up and your nose in the paper and your eyes looking everywhere but at me . . . I love you, Laura." She said it slowly, composing it as she went and smiling a little at the effect. The liquor had loosened her up.

"What?" said Laura, her eyes following a story and her ears deaf.

"I have a surprise for you, Bo-peep," Beebo tried again.

"Oh. Says here it's going up to ninety today . . . A surprise?" She lowered the paper a bit to look at Beebo.

"Um-hm. I didn't get you an anniversary present. I thought we might get you a new dress tonight. Stores are open."

Laura was embarrassed. It still upset her to have to accept gifts from Beebo. She felt as if each one was a bid for her love, a sort of investment Beebo was making in Laura's good will. It made her resent the gifts and resist them. And still Beebo came home with things she couldn't afford and forced them on Laura and made her almost frantic between the need to be grateful, the pity she felt, and the exasperation that was the result of it all.

"I don't need a dress, honey," Laura said.

"I want you to have one."

"God, Beebo, if I bought all the clothes you want me to have we wouldn't have money to eat on. We'd be broke. We'd be in hock for everything we own."

"Please, baby. All I want to do is buy you an anniversary present."

"Beebo, I—" What could she say? *I don't want the damn dress?*

"I know," Beebo said abruptly. "I embarrass you. You don't like to be seen in the nice stores with me. I look so damn queer. Don't argue, Bo-peep, I know it," she said, waving Laura's protests to silence. "I'll wear a skirt tonight. Okay? I look pretty good in a skirt."

It was true that Laura was ashamed to go anywhere out of Greenwich Village with her . . . Beebo, nearly six feet of her, with her hair cropped short and her strange clothes and her gruff voice. And when she flirted with the clerks!

Laura had been afraid more than once that they would call
the police and drag Beebo off to jail. But it had never happened. Still, there was always a first time. And if she had a
couple of drinks before they went, Laura wasn't at all sure
she could handle her.

"Why don't you let me find something for myself?" Laura
asked, pleading. "I know you hate to put a skirt on. You don't
have to come. I'll pick out something pretty." But she knew,
and so did Beebo, that unless Beebo went along Laura would
buy nothing. She would come home and say, "They just didn't
have a thing." And Beebo would have to face the fact that
Laura resented her little tributes.

So she said, "No, I don't trust your taste. Besides, I like
to see you try on all the different things."

So it was that Laura met her at Lord and Taylor's on Fifth
Avenue after work. It had to be a really good store and Beebo
had to pay more than they could afford, or she wasn't satisfied.
Laura anticipated it with dread, but at least it was better than
another awful quarrel. If Beebo would just be quiet. If she
would just keep her eyes—and her hands—off the cute little
clerks in the dress departments. Laura always tried to find a
stolid middle-aged clerk, but the shops seemed to abound in
sleek young ones.

Still, Beebo, subdued perhaps by her plain black dress and
by Laura's nervous concern, kept quiet. Laura noticed a little
whiskey on her breath when they met outside the store, but
nothing in her behavior betrayed it.

"Do I stink?" she had asked, and when Laura wrinkled her
nose Beebo took a mint out and sucked on it. "I won't disgrace you," she said. She was making a real effort.

They zigzagged around the Avenue, finding nothing that
both looked right and could be had for less than a fortune.
At Peck and Peck, near nine o'clock, Laura said, "Beebo, I've
had it. This is positively the last place. I don't want you to
dress me like a damn princess. I'd much rather have one of
those big enamel-ware pots—"

"Oh, goddamn the pots! Don't talk to me of pots!" Beebo
exclaimed and Laura answered, "All right, all right, all right!"
in a quick irritated whisper.

She went up to the first girl she saw, determined to waste
as little time as possible. "Excuse me," she said. "Could you

show me something in a twelve?"

The girl turned around and looked at her out of jade green eyes. Laura stared at her. She was black-haired and her skin was the color of three parts cream and one part coffee. In such a setting her green eyes were amazing. There was a tiny red dot between them on her brow, Indian fashion, but she was dressed in Occidental clothes. She gazed at Laura with exquisite contempt.

"Something in a twelve?" she repeated, and her voice had a careful, educated sort of pronunciation. Laura was enchanted with her, pleased just to look at her marvelous smooth face. Her skin was incredibly pure and her color luminous.

"Yes, please," Laura said.

With a light monosyllable, unintelligible to Laura, the girl shrugged at a row of dresses. "Help yourself," she said in clipped English. "I cannot help you."

Laura was surprised at her effrontery. "Well, I—I would like a little help, if you don't mind," she said pointedly.

"Not from me. Go look at the dresses. If you see one you like, buy it."

Laura stared at her, her dander up. "You just don't care if I buy a dress or not, do you?" she prodded. The girl, who had begun to turn away, looked back at her in annoyance.

"Can you think of one good reason why I should?" she asked.

"You're a clerk and I'm a customer," Laura shot back.

"Thank you for the compliment," she said icily. "But I am no clerk. And if I were, I wouldn't wait on you."

It was so royal, so precise, that Laura blushed crimson. "Oh," she said in confusion. "Please forgive me. I—I just saw you standing there and I—"

"And you took it for granted that I must be a clerk? How flattering." She stared at Laura for a minute and then she smiled slightly and turned away.

Laura was too interested in her just to let her fade away like that. She started after her with no idea of what to say, feeling idiotic and yet fascinated with the girl. She touched her sleeve and that lovely beige face swiveled toward her, this time plainly irritated. But before either of them could speak Beebo came toward them. She had a couple of dresses over one arm and she sauntered up with typical long strides, a cigarette drooping from one corner of her mouth. Laura saw her coming with a sinking feeling.

"I found these, Laura. Try them on," she said, looking at the Indian girl. There was a small awkward silence. "Well?" Beebo said suddenly, smiling at the strange girl. "Friend of yours, Bo-peep?"

Laura could have slapped her. She hated that pet name. It was bad enough in private, but in public it was intolerable.

"No, I—I mistook her for a clerk," Laura said. Her cheeks were still glowing and the girl looked from her to Beebo and back as if they were both dangerous. Laura's hand fell from her arm and she stepped backwards, still watching them, as if she half-feared they would follow her.

"Don't mind her," Beebo told her, thumbing at Laura. "She thinks her best friends are clerks. She's just being friendly." Laura heard the edge in her voice and became uneasy.

But the Indian girl, if she was an Indian girl, unexpectedly relented a little and smiled. "It's all right," she said. She looked at Laura. "I'm not a clerk," she said. "I'm a dancer."

"Oh!" Suddenly an unwelcome little thrill flew through Laura. She couldn't have explained it logically. The girl was very demure and distant. But she was also very lovely, and Laura had a brief vision of all that creamy tan skin unveiled and undulating to the rhythm of muffled gongs and bells and wailing reeds.

She must have looked incredulous for the girl said suddenly, "I can prove it."

"Oh, no! No, that's all right," Laura protested, but the girl handed her a little card with a name printed on it, and Laura took it eagerly. "I did not mean I would demonstrate," the girl said carefully.

Beebo laughed. "Go ahead," she said. "We're dance lovers. I don't think Laura'd mind a bit, would you, baby?" She was mad at Laura for flirting and Laura knew it.

The little card read, *Tris Robischon* and underneath, *Dance Studio* and an address in the Village. "I just didn't want you to think I was lying," the girl said, somewhat haughtily. And before Laura or Beebo could answer her she turned and left them standing, staring after her.

Beebo turned to frown at Laura. "You made a hit, it seems," she said acidly. "Let's see her card." She snatched it from Laura's reluctant fingers.

"Take it. I don't want it!" Laura said angrily, for she did want it very much. She turned away sharply, giving her attention to a row of dresses, but she knew Beebo wouldn't let her off the hook so easily. There would be more nastiness and soon.

"You got her name out of her, at least. Pretty smooth." Beebo's voice was hard and hurt. "Tris Robischon. Doesn't sound very Indian to me."

"How would you know, swami?" Laura snapped. "If you throw a jealous scene in here I'll leave you tonight and I'll never come back, I'm warning you!" she added in a furious hiss, and Beebo glared at her. But she didn't answer.

Finally Laura dragged some dresses off the rack and turned to her. "I'll try these," she said. Beebo followed her to the dressing room and watched her change into one and then another in angry silence.

At last Laura burst out, "I didn't ask her for the damn card. I don't know *why* she gave it to me."

"It's obvious. You're irresistible."

Laura took two handfuls of Beebo's hair and shook her head till Beebo stopped her roughly and forced her to her knees. Fury paralyzed them both for a moment and they stared at each other helplessly, trembling.

Laura wanted that card. She wanted it enough to soften suddenly and play games for it. "Beebo, be gentle with me," she pleaded, her tense body relaxing. "Don't hurt me," she whispered. "I don't know who the girl is and I don't care."

Beebo stared at her suspiciously till Laura reminded her, "We came to get a dress, remember? Let's not spoil it. Please, Beebo."

Beebo released her and sat staring at the floor. Laura tried on dresses for her, but Beebo wouldn't look at them. No tender words, no coaxing, no teasing that would have been so welcome any other time worked with her tonight. When Beebo got jealous she was a bitch—irrational, unreasonable, unkind.

"I'm going to take this one," Laura said finally, a little desperate. "Whether you like it or not."

Beebo looked up slowly. "I like it," she said flatly, but she would have said, "I hate it," in the same voice.

Laura went over to her and took her face in both hands, stooped down, and kissed her petulant mouth. "Beebo," she murmured. "You love me. Act like it." It was so foolishly selfish, so unexpected, and so almost affectionate that it was funny, and Beebo smiled wryly at her. She took Laura's shoulders and pulled her down for another kiss just as a clerk—a genuine clerk—stuck her face in and said, "Need any help in here?"

"No thanks!" Laura blurted, looking up in alarm. Beebo put her head back and laughed and the clerk stared, pop-eyed. Then she shut the door and sped away. Beebo stood up and swept Laura into her arms and kissed her over and over, all over her face and shoulders and ears and throat until Laura had to beg her to stop. "Let's get out of here before that clerk makes trouble!" she implored.

When they left the dressing room Laura noticed that Beebo had put Tris Robischon's card in the sand pail for cigarettes. It stuck out like a little white flag. Laura risked her purse—with $15.87, all they had for the next week—to get the card back. She left the purse on the chair as she followed Beebo out. And so it was that she was able to make an excuse to go back and retrieve them both, purse and card, while Beebo paid for the dress.

3

It's an awful thing about Jack, Laura wrote in her diary, sitting on the floor by the closet door. *Such a nice guy, so bright and so—this will sound corny—so <u>fine</u>. But ever since Terry left him he's been a little crazy. I was really afraid of how much he was drinking until tonight when we had a beer at Julian's. Or rather, I had a beer. Jack's on the wagon. Maybe that will straighten him out. If he can stick with it. If he'd been straight I think he would have done something wonderful with his life. But is it fair to blame the failures on homosexuality? Is it, really? I'm selling junk here in the Village because Beebo wants me near her. She runs an elevator so she can wear pants all day. And Jack's a draughtsman so he can be in an office full of virile engineers. What's the matter with us? We don't <u>have</u> to spend our lives doing it. So why do we?*

She had asked Jack the same question at Julian's little bar just off Seventh Avenue, earlier that evening. "Why do we do it, Jack? Throw our lives away?" she said.

"We like to," he shrugged. "We all have martyr complexes."

"We give away the best part of ourselves—our youth and our health are all just given away. Free."

"What sort of profit did you expect to make on them?" he said. "You want to get paid for being young and healthy?"

Laura glared at him. "That's not what I mean—"

"If you're not giving, you're not living, doll," he said. "I quote the sob columns. Give yourself away, what the hell. What's youth for? And health? And beauty, and the rest of it. Keep it and it turns putrid like everything else. Give it away and at least somebody enjoys it."

"Jack, you know damn well I mean *wasting* it. Wasting it all day long on costume jewelry or a push-button elevator or a slide rule. God, when I think of what you—"

"Don't think of all the fine things I could have done with my life, Mother," he pleaded. "You give me the shudders. I'm

447

not happy, but I'd be worse off trying to live straight. I like men. My office is full of them."

"You hate your work."

"I never have to think about it. Purely mechanical. I just sit there and flip that little slip stick and I say, 'Evens, Johnson is straight. Odds, he's queer. If Johnson is queer on Tuesday —according to the slide rule—I make it a point to give him a kind word.'"

"Johnson is straight and you know it. Every man in your office is straight. Why do you torture yourself?"

"No torture, Mother. When the whole world is black, pretend it's rosy. Somewhere, in some little corner. If everybody's straight, pretend somebody's gay."

"That's a short cut to the bug house."

"I wouldn't mind the bug house. If they'd let me keep my slip stick." He laughed to himself and leaned over the bar to order. "One whiskey and water," he said.

"How about you, Mann?" Julian asked.

"Nothing."

"Are you on the wagon?" Laura was stunned. When he nodded she said, "Just a beer for me. I'm drinking too much anyway." Then she smiled. "You'll never last, Jack. You know what you need?"

"Do I know? Are you serious?" He grinned at her, but it was a pained smile.

"You need a real man," Laura said softly. "Not a bunch of daydreams at the office. That's enough to drive anybody nuts. You worry me, Jack."

"Good." He smiled and squeezed her arm. "Now I'll tell you what I really need." He looked at her through his sharp eyes set in that plain face Laura had come to love and find attractive. "I don't need a man, Laura," he said. "I'm too damn old to run after pretty boys any more. I look like a middle-aged fool, which is exactly what I am. When Terry left me, I was through."

"Do you still love him? Even after what he did?"

"I won't talk about him," he said simply. "I can't. But he was the last one. The end. I want a woman now. I want you, Laura." He turned away abruptly, embarrassed, but his hand remained on her arm.

Laura was touched. "Jack," she said very gently. "I'm a Lesbian. Even if you renounce men, I can't renounce women.

I won't even try."

"There was a time when you were willing to try.".

"That was a million years ago. I wasn't the same Laura I am now. I said that before I even met Beebo—when another girl was giving me hell, and I was new to the game and to New York and so afraid of everything."

"So now you know the ropes and you're absolutely sure you'd rather give your life away to the goddam tourists and a woman you don't love than come and live with a man you do love."

"Jack, darling, I love you, but I don't love you with my body. I love you with my heart and soul but I could never let you make love to me."

"I could never do it, either," he said quietly "You're no gayer than I am, Laura. If we married it would never be a physical union, you know that." Somewhere far back in his mind the sweet shadow of that little dream child hovered, but he suppressed it, lighting a cigarette quickly. His fingers shook.

"If it wasn't a physical union, what would it be?" Laura asked. "Just small talk and community property and family-plan fares?"

He smiled. "Sounds a little empty, doesn't it?"

"Jack," Laura said, speaking with care so as not to hurt him, "you're forty-five and life looks a little different to you now. I'm only twenty-three and I can't give up my body so casually. I could never make you promises I couldn't keep."

"I wouldn't ask that promise of you, Laura," he said.

"You mean I could bring girls home? To our home, yours and mine? Any girls, any time? And it would be all right?"

"Let's put it this way," he said. "If you fell in love with somebody, I'd be understanding. I'd welcome her to the house, and I'd get the hell out when you wanted a little privacy. I'd keep strict hands off and just one shoulder for you to cry on. As long as you really loved her and it wasn't cheap or loud or dirty, I'd respect it."

He knocked the ashes off the tip of his cigarette thoughtfully. ". . . only," he said, "you'd be my wife. And you'd come home at night and tuck me in and you'd be there in the morning to see me off." He sounded so peculiarly gentle and yearning that she was convinced that he meant it. But she was not ready to give in.

Laura smiled at him. "What would there be in all this for

you, Jack?" she said. "Just getting tucked in at night? Is that enough compensation?"

"Nobody ever tucked me in before." He said it with a grin but she sensed that it was true.

"And breakfast in the morning?"

"Wonderful! You don't know what a difference it would make."

"That's nothing, Jack, compared to what you'd be giving me."

"You'd be my wife, Laura, my honest-to-God lawful legal wife. You'd give me a home. You don't know what that would mean to me. I've been living in rented rooms since I was out of diapers. You'd give me a place to rest in and be proud of, and a purpose in life. What the hell good am I to myself? What use is an aging fag with a letch for hopelessly bored, hopelessly handsome boys? Christ, I give myself the creeps. I give the boys the creeps. And you know something? They're beginning to give *me* the creeps. I'm so low I can't go any place but up. If you'll say yes."

"What if I did? What about Beebo?" Laura said softly, as if the name might suddenly conjure up her lover, jealous and vengeful.

"It would solve everything," he said positively. "She could still see you, but you wouldn't be her property any more. It's bad for her to have the idea she owns you, but that's the way she treats you. If you were my wife she'd have to respect the situation. It would be a kind way to break with her," he added slyly. He was feeling too selfish to waste sympathy on Beebo now.

Laura thought it over. There was no one she respected more than Jack, and her love for him, born of gratitude and affection, was real. But it was not the love of a normal woman for a normal man she felt for him, and the idea of marrying him frightened her.

"Do you think, if we married, we could keep our love for each other intact, Jack?" she asked.

"Yes," he said.

"Even if I were having an affair?" She was thinking at that moment of Tris Robischon, the lovely, lithe Indian girl.

"Yes. I told you 'yes.'"

Laura finished her beer in silence, gazing into the mirror over the bar and pondering. She knew she would say no. But she didn't quite know how. "I can't, Jack," she said at last, in a small voice.

"Not now, maybe?" He wouldn't give up.

"Never."

"Never say never, Mother. Say 'not now' or something."

She did, obediently. But she added, "We'd quarrel and we'd end up destroying our love for each other."

"We'd quarrel, hell yes. I wouldn't feel properly married if we didn't."

"And there's always the chance that you'd fall in love. And regret that you married me."

He turned to her with a little smile and shook his head. "Never," he said. "And this once it's the right word." He took her hands. "Say yes."

"No."

"Say maybe."

"No."

"Say you'll think about it, Laura. Say it, honey."

And out of love and reluctance to hurt him, she whispered, "I'll think about it."

Laura was walking up Greenwich Avenue, searching for number 251. She had a small white card in her hand to which she referred occasionally, although she had memorized the address. It was a hot day, late in the afternoon, and she had just come from work, wilted and worn and bored. The idea of going home right away depressed her and she had decided to walk a little.

She hadn't gone two blocks before she was daydreaming of Tris Robischon and suddenly shivering with the thought of seeing her again.

Beebo wouldn't be home until nine o'clock that evening, and Tris's studio address was only a short distance from the shop where Laura worked. All at once she was walking fast.

She found the address with no trouble at all. In fact it was almost too easy and before she knew it she was standing in the first floor hallway of the modest building reading the names on the mail boxes. TRIS ROBISCHON. There it was. Third floor, Apartment C. Laura climbed the stairs.

What will I say to her! she asked herself. *How in God's name will I explain this visit? Ask her for a dance lesson? Me?* She had to smile at herself. Her long slim legs would never yield to the fluid grace and discipline of dancing.

Laura stood uncertainly before the door of Apartment C, a little afraid to knock. She could hear the sounds of music inside—rather sharp, tormented music. Laura glanced at the card once again. It had been almost three weeks since the Indian girl had given it to her. Perhaps she wouldn't even remember Laura. It might be embarrassing for them both. But then Laura envisioned that remarkable face, and she didn't care how embarrassed she had to be to see it once again. She knocked.

There was no response. She knocked again, hard. This time there was a scampering of feet and the music was abruptly shut off. Laura heard voices and realized with a sinking feeling that Tris wasn't alone.

Suddenly the door swung open. Laura was confronted with a young girl of twelve or so in a blue leotard. "Yes?" said the little girl. There were three or four others in the room in attitudes of relaxation, and then Tris appeared around a corner, wiping her wonderful face on a towel and coming quickly and smoothly toward the door. It was almost a self-conscious walk, as if she expected any caller to be a prospective pupil and had to demonstrate her talent even before she opened her mouth to speak.

She stopped behind the young girl and looked up. Laura waited, speechless and awkward, until Tris smiled at her, without having said a word. "Come in," she said.

"I hope I'm not interrupting a class," Laura said, hesitating.

"It does not matter. You are welcome. Please come in." Laura followed her into the room and Tris waved her to a seat. It was only a bench, set in a far corner of the room, but Laura went to it gratefully and sat there while Tris collected her charges and put them through a five-minute routine. It looked very pretty to Laura, although the Indian girl seemed dissatisfied.

"You can do much better than that for our visitor, girls," she said in her dainty English that Laura had nearly forgotten. It was a strange accent, like none Laura had ever heard; very precise and softly spoken, but not noticeably British or anything else. Laura puzzled over it, watching Tris move and demonstrate things to her students. She had on black tights and a small cotton knit bandeau that covered her breasts and shoulders but left her long supple midriff exposed. She was the same luscious tan from waist to bosom, and Laura, sitting there watching her, was helplessly fascinated by it; almost more by what she could see than by what she couldn't.

Tris gave two sharp claps with her hands suddenly. "That is all for today, girls," she said, and they broke up quickly, running into another room to change their clothes. Tris turned to look at Laura. She simply looked at her without saying anything, a stare so frank and unabashed that Laura lowered her eyes in confusion, feeling the red blood come to her cheeks.

"What is your name?" Tris asked her then, and Laura answered, surprised, "Laura." *Of course, I'd forgotten. She doesn't even know my name!*

Laura looked up to find Tris studying her with a little smile. The girls began to file past saying goodnight to her. She smiled at one or another, touched their heads and shoulders, and spoke to some. In between little girls she watched Laura who felt rather like a specimen on exhibit.

The studio was bare except for the bench, a record player next to it on the floor by Laura's feet, and mirrors. The mirrors were everywhere, long and short, all over the walls. Most gave a full view of you to yourself. The room where the children dressed was furnished as a bedroom. Laura could see parts of it, and there were more mirrors in there. There was a swinging door, shut now, which apparently led to a kitchen. Laura gazed around her, trying to appear interested in it, so she wouldn't have to look at Tris.

The front door shut finally, rather conspicuously, and a small silence fell. They were alone.

"You like my little studio, then?" said Tris.

Laura dared to look at her then and found that the last child was certainly gone and the studio was empty. Awfully empty.

"Yes, I like it," she said. She felt the need to excuse her presence and she began hurriedly, "I hope you won't think I—"

But Tris never let her finish. "Shall I dance for you?" she said suddenly with such a luminous smile that Laura felt her whole body go warm with appreciation. She returned the smile. "Yes, please. If you would."

Tris walked to the record changer beside Laura, knelt, and slipped a record into place. Then she looked up at Laura, her eyes larger and greener than Laura remembered, and infinitely

lovelier seen so close. She waited there, looking at her visitor,
until the music began to flow. It was not harsh like the music
Laura had heard through the door, but languid and rhyth-
mical, perhaps even sentimental.

Tris began to move so slowly at first that Laura was hardly
aware that she was dancing. Her arms, long and tender and
graceful, began to ripple subtly toward Laura, and then her
head and body began to sway, and finally her strong legs,
deceptively slim, moved under her and brought her, whirling
slowly, to her feet.

It was a strange dance that flowed and undulated. This
marvelous body seemed to float and then to sink like mist, and
at one point Laura had to shut her eyes for a minute, too
thrilled to bear it. She wanted terribly to reach out, put her
hands on Tris's hips, and feel the rhythm move through her
own body.

The music stopped. Tris stood poised over Laura, looking
down at her, and for a moment she remained there, balanced
delicately and smiling. Laura felt a familiar surge of desire
and she watched Tris like a cat watching a twitching string,
ready to pounce if Tris made a sudden move. And yet afraid
Tris might touch her and startle her passion into the open.

But Tris relaxed as the needle began its monotonous scratch,
and she turned off the machine. She sat on the floor then,
grasping her black-sheathed knees in her arms, one hand holding the wrist of the other.

"Did you like it?" she said, glancing up, and she seemed
for a moment to be unsure and distant, as she had been in the
dress shop.

"I thought it was wonderful," Laura said, herself a little
shy. "I didn't know dancing could be like that."

"Like what?" Tris demanded suspiciously.

"Well—like—I don't know. It was like nothing I've ever
seen . . . as if you were floating. It was beautiful."

Tris softened a little. "Thank you, Laura," she said. And
Laura felt a wild confusion of delight at the sound of her own
name. "I dance very well," Tris went on oddly. "There is no
point in false modesty. I hate that sort of thing, don't you?
It's so hypocritical. If you dance well, or do anything else
well, say so. Be frank. I think men like a girl who is frank.
Don't you?"

Laura was taken aback. "Oh, yes," she affirmed quickly.

But she stared. *She can't be straight!* she thought to herself, in a sudden agony of doubt. From the first she had taken it for granted that the lovely Indian girl was a Lesbian. It seemed so right, perhaps only because Laura wanted it that way. And too, Laura always prided herself on being able to tell if a girl were homosexual or not. She was sick at the thought that Tris might love men.

Tris watched her, interested. "What are you thinking of?" she said.

"Nothing," Laura protested uneasily.

"All right. I will not pry." Tris smiled. "Will you have some tea with me?"

"Thank you." Laura was glad to ease the tension a little. Tris got up and she followed her through the swinging door into the kitchen.

Tris made the tea while Laura watched her in a rapture of pleasure. "You moved so beautifully," she blurted, and then blushed. "I—I mean, it shows in all your movements. Dancing, or walking, or just getting down the teacups." She laughed. "I feel like a clumsy ox, watching you."

"You are wrong," Tris said. "I have been watching you, too. You move well, Laura. You could learn to dance. Would you like to learn?"

Laura looked away, confused and delighted but scared. "I'd be your worst pupil," she said.

"I find that hard to believe."

"It's—probably very expensive."

"For you . . . ," Tris shrugged and smiled, "nothing," she said.

Laura turned to look at her, surprised. "Nothing?" she repeated.

"Or perhaps your friend . . . the big one," Tris added softly. "Perhaps she would be interested?"

"Beebo?" Laura exclaimed. "Oh God no!"

Tris handed her a cup quickly, as if to make her forget the suggestion. "Do you like me, Laura?" she said, her green eyes too close and her sweet skin redolent of jasmine.

"Yes, Tris," Laura said, saying her name for the first time and feeling the fine shivering return to her limbs.

"Good." Tris grinned at her. "That is payment enough." Laura felt suddenly like she had better sit down or she would fall down. "You say my name now, that means you feel closer to me, hm?" Tris asked.

"Yes. A little." Laura gazed at her, completely confused, afraid to move, until Tris gave a little laugh.

"Come, we'll sit in the other room," she said, and Laura once again followed her across the bare studio into the bed-room.

The room was fitted up Indian fashion with rich red silk drapes on the bed. The bed itself was actually more of a low couch, very capacious, and covered with tumbled silk cushions. There were books and records scattered around, a couple of pillows on the floor to take the place of chairs, and a number of ashtrays.

"This is my bedroom, my living room, my den, my play-room—whatever you want," Tris said smiling, and sat down on the bed. "Come, don't stand there looking afraid of me," she said, "sit down." And she patted the bed beside her.

Laura came and sat there and as she did Tris lay back on the cushions and watched her. She put her tea on the floor while Laura held hers carefully, anxious about spilling it on the lush red silk.

"Are you—are you Indian, Tris?" she asked awkwardly, turning to look at her.

Tris crossed her black-sheathed legs. "Yes," she said. "Half Indian, at least. My mother was Indian but my father was French."

"Did you grow up in India?"

"Yes. In New Delhi. Have you been there?" Her clear eyes looked sharply at Laura.

"No. I've never been anywhere," Laura said. "Except New York and Chicago. I was born in Chicago."

"Is your family there?"

"Just my father. He's all the family I have."

"Do you see him often?"

"I never see him." She looked away, suddenly overwhelmed with the thought of her father. She had not seen him for two years. Not since she had gone to live with Beebo and admitted to him that she was a Lesbian. There had been a terrible scene. And then Laura had fled and Merrill Landon, for all she knew, had gone back to Chicago.

"Is that where your roommate is from? Chicago?" Tris asked slowly.

"No. Milwaukee." Laura turned to frown at her and Tris,

sensing her reticence, changed the subject. "Would you like to see my scrapbook?" she said. Before Laura could answer she was off the bed and searching for it among some books and papers across the room. She came back and sat next to Laura, spreading the green leather book open over their knees and putting an arm around Laura's waist.

"These were all taken six months ago," she said. "This boy is German. Isn't he handsome? I love blond hair. He's wonderful looking."

He was indeed. Jack would have appreciated the view more than Laura, for he was young and muscular and nearly naked. His body had been oiled so that every smooth ripple on arms and back and tight hips and long legs was highlighted. He had a shock of rich blond hair and particularly handsome features, and he was shown in a number of poses: some that looked like Muscle Beach shots and others that seemed like dance positions.

"He does dance," Tris said, anticipating Laura's question. "With me. He's named Paul Cate. We have a lot of routines together. We are a sort of—*team*."

"Are you engaged?" Laura asked. It sounded ridiculous once it was said, but she found herself unreasonably jealous of the boy.

Tris threw her head back and laughed. "Engaged!" she exclaimed. "He is a homosexual, Laura."

"A homosexual?" It sounded like fake innocence, even to Laura.

But Tris was too amused to notice. "Yes, of course," she said, still laughing. "Can you imagine two homosexuals getting married? Could anything be sillier? What would they do with each other?" And her laughter was too hard.

Laura was shocked at her crude dismissal of the possibility of a homosexual marriage, which made her feel instantly protective and tender about Jack. But she had said, "Two homosexuals," and Laura's heart rose. "Are you gay, Tris?" she asked, almost in a whisper, afraid to look at her.

"Not really." Tris flipped the words at her casually, turning pages in the scrapbook and concentrating on them. Laura sensed embarrassment in her concentration.

"Either you are or you aren't," Laura said, more boldly.

"Then I'm not," said Tris and startled her visitor. "If you force me to choose between black and white, *i*'m white," she explained, and Laura thought she heard a double emphasis on the word "white." "I like men. More than women." Laura was cowed into bewildered silence.

There were many enticing photographs of Tris. "The photographer is a friend of mine," she told Laura with a smile. "He always makes me look good." There was a series of her with the German boy, in dance poses. Tris was so lovely that Laura felt the gooseflesh rise up on her with Tris's breathing in her ear and her warmth touching Laura's arms.

"You would think we were madly in love," Tris said with a little laugh. "Oh, look at this one. This is my former husband."

Laura did look, hard. "You were married?" she said, unwilling to believe it.

"Yes. To him. He is handsome, no?"

"Yes." He was pictured lying on his side, very much of a young athlete, with curly hair and an honest sort of face, a little like Jack's long-lost Terry. He looked Irish. "Was he gay, Tris?"

"Yes," she said and the annoyance was plain in her voice. "It was an ugly mistake. We hated each other after we got married. Before that, we were the best of friends. So you see, I know what I am saying when I tell you gay marriages are hell."

Laura considered this in silence while Tris turned pages.

"Have some dinner with me," Tris said, piling the pictures on the floor at the foot of the bed.

Laura looked at her watch. It was only seven. Beebo wouldn't be home for another two hours.

"I never cook," Tris said, going across the room to pick up the phone. She began to order sandwiches, glancing at Laura for suggestions. "They bring them up from the corner shop," she said when she hung up. Laura looked up at her from her seat on the bed, and Tris began to move slowly, undulating, as if she were musing on a dance.

"Where did you learn to dance, Tris?" Laura asked her.

"England. Where do you live?"

"Cordelia Street. One-twenty-nine."

"With the big one? What did you say her name is?"

Laura felt uncomfortable at the mention of her lover, and resentful of Tris's curiosity about her. "Her name is Beebo," she said rather sullenly.

"Oh, yes—Beebo!" Tris laughed. "It almost sounds Indian," she said. "Is she nice?"

Laura shrugged. "I guess she is."

"You aren't sure, hm?" Tris seemed amused. "Are you in love with her?"

Laura was reluctant to say no, but determined not to say yes. "I—I was," she admitted finally.

"It is all over, then?"

Laura didn't like her bright-eyed interest. "We still live together," she said defensively.

"Does she still love you?"

"Yes. Yes, she does," Laura said sharply, looking Tris square in the eye.

"I'm sorry," Tris said softly, her gaze dropping. "I shouldn't pry."

"There are better things to talk about than Beebo," Laura said.

The food came and they were both relieved to turn to something else.

When the food was gone a quiet little interlude fell when Tris simply sat on the bed and watched Laura and Laura wandered idly around the room.

There was a terrible growing excitement in Laura. She felt she must run, escape somehow, get out of the studio before she made a fool of herself and an enemy of Tris. She turned at last and looked down at Tris. There was only one lamp lit in the room, and in the pale pink light Tris looked even riper and lovelier than she did in bright daylight.

"Tris, I—I have to go," Laura said. "It's getting late. I had a lovely time . . ."

"Then why go?"

"I must. I shouldn't have come, really."

"Will Beebo be angry with you?"

"She isn't home yet."

"Then you don't have to go yet. I'll bet she has a fine temper." She waited for an answer, but Laura ignored her remark. She was thinking only of the possibility of staying longer. Her heart fluttered with the temptation. She was afraid of Beebo and yet, in another way, even more afraid of Tris.

"Come sit beside me," Tris urged her, whispering. And Laura, unable to refuse her, came slowly toward the bed, as if she were in a trance, and sat down. Tris leaned back into the pillows, her hand on Laura's arm, and pulled Laura after her.

Laura lay on her back next to Tris for a while, breathing softly, nervously aware of the sound of her breath. She held herself in as if she expected to explode. She was tense and the sweat rolled down her body, and yet she was happy, very happy.

They lay that way for some time, silent, gazing at the ceiling, neither one speaking, yet neither able to relax. At last Tris took Laura's hand in her own warm brown one and said, "You're afraid of me, aren't you, Laura?"

There was a slight pause, almost a panic, while Laura tried to collect herself. "Yes," she mumbled at last.

"Why?"

"You're so beautiful . . ." Laura fumbled.

"Does beauty frighten you?"

"Yes. I don't know why. Maybe because I never had it."

Tris chuckled, a sweet throaty sound, and said, "Who ever told you that?" And it occurred to Laura, strangely, that Tris spoke without any accent at all. It sounded clear and plain, like Laura's own English. But it was only a quick impression and it passed. She thought Tris was teasing her, imitating her.

"Don't kid me," she said.

"Take your hair down, Laura," Tris said, her fingers playing with the prim bun at the back of Laura's head. Her hair had grown so long—Beebo wouldn't let her cut it—that she was obliged to roll it up one way or another in the back. It hung nearly to her waist when it was loose. She took the pins out of it now, raising herself on one elbow to accomplish the job. Tris helped her and the roll of hair came free suddenly and fell around Laura's shoulders like silk streamers, pale gold and scented. Tris took a handful of it, pressing it to her face.

"How lovely!" she exclaimed. "Lovely blond hair . . ."

She put her hands on Laura's shoulders and pushed her down into the pillows, bending over her to study her face. "I think you're very pretty," she said, and made Laura smile.

"I don't believe you," she said.

"I'll bet Beebo thinks you're very pretty, too."

"Please, Tris. Let's not talk about Beebo."

Tris leaned down and kissed her forehead very softly. "Now do you believe me?" she asked.

Laura stared at her, her heart suddenly pounding. "No," she said in a whisper.

Tris kissed her cheeks, so lightly that Laura could hardly feel it. "Now?" she said.

"No," Laura breathed.

And Tris kissed her lips. Laura lay beneath her, too thrilled to move, only letting the lovely shock flow through her body and closing her eyes to feel it better. At last Tris moved away —only a breath away—and she said, "Now?"

"Tris . . ." she murmured and all the melody of suppressed passion sang in the name. Her hands went up to Tris's bare arms, over the bandeau and down that silky midriff, and then they went around Tris's waist and pulled her close and kissed her.

It was a long kiss, so leisurely, so lovely, that Laura never wanted it to end. And when it did she followed Tris, laughing, all over the bed, kissing her wherever she could reach her, feeling Tris's fine body move beneath her hands and the fire of her own longing bursting in her bosom.

Suddenly Tris got off the bed and stood looking at Laura and trying to catch her breath. "No," she said. "No! That's enough! It's late."

Laura stared at her, amazed. "What do you mean?" she asked. "Tris, come here. Come to me. Don't do this to me. Tris!"

But Tris pulled her off the bed with sudden strength.

"Tris, it's only nine-thirty," Laura said.

"Nine-thirty? Is it that late? Laura, you must excuse me." She was transformed. All the play and warmth had gone out of her.

"But—" Laura began, but Tris interrupted sharply, "Time for you to go home to Beebo." There was no smile on her face.

Laura looked at her incredulously a minute longer, her cheeks burning, and then she smoothed her clothes out with lowered eyes. She was too proud and too hurt to speak. She walked noiselessly to one of the mirrors, taking her purse with her, and ran a comb through her long hair.

She stared at herself—her flushed face and trembling fingers, her body so ready for love only moments ago and now weak with denial and outraged nerves. Two feet of unpinned hair hung down her back to remind her of Tris's admiration. But it would take five minutes to get it up again properly.

Laura looked into the mirror over her own shoulder at Tris, who was standing on one foot and then the other, bent forward slightly and obviously waiting for Laura to get out of her way. What secret activities would occupy her as soon as she got rid of Laura? Her impatience was audible in her sharp breathing. Laura dared not risk her displeasure by taking the time to wind up her hair. She simply turned and walked out of the bedroom without a backward glance, without a word.

At the front door her heart jumped when Tris called after her. Laura turned to find her running lightly across the bare studio and she waited, holding her feelings in warily.

Tris stopped at the door. "I'm sorry," she said self-consciously. "I didn't know it was so late. I have something to do tonight, it slipped my mind."

Laura looked at her haughtily. "Goodnight, Tris," was all she said. When she turned to walk down the stairs Tris added, "Say hello to your bad-tempered roommate for me."

Incensed, Laura almost ran out the door below.

4

LAURA WALKED HOME as full of hope as of frustration and anger. Tris had treated her badly but she had treated her beautifully too. With a little start of alarm, Laura knew she was falling in love. Maybe it was worse than that already.

It was a dark soft night with no moon, only the dozens of quiet yellow streetlights. Her heels rang against the cement sidewalk as she turned down Cordelia Street and she left the world outside with regret when she opened her apartment door.

She knew Beebo would be there by now. *If she's only not drunk,* she thought to herself. "Beebo?" she called aloud. She heard a little groan from the bedroom and went toward it with a sinking feeling. *She couldn't be drunk already. She'd only been home forty-five minutes. Unless she cut work again. God forbid!*

Laura walked across the living room slowly, in no hurry to face the argument that would result if Beebo was full of whiskey and had been sitting there fuming because Laura was late. Beebo would have been phoning all over the neighborhood for her—a practice Laura abhorred but couldn't break her of. She touched her long loose hair nervously, wondering what Beebo would say when she saw it.

Laura pushed open the bedroom door. The first thing she saw was Nix—Nix, lying on the floor with his belly slit open from jaws to tail. Beside him was a crimson chef's-knife. Laura recognized it from the kitchen.

She stared at him for a full ten seconds in a paralysis of horror. Then she screamed with a force she had never suspected in herself. She turned back to the wall with her hands over her face and sobbed with all her strength. And while her face was hidden she heard another groan and knew it was Beebo, and she was too terrified even to open her eyes and look.

"Beebo?" she whispered, and her voice was rough with fear. "Beebo?"

Another sickening groan, and suddenly Beebo's voice saying confusedly, "Laura? Baby, where are you? Laura . . ." It faded out and Laura brought her hands away from her face quickly and looked around the room, carefully avoiding Nix. Beebo was on the bed.

Her clothes were torn—what few she still had on. Her shirt was in shreds and the jacket appeared to be ripped down the back, though she was lying on most of it and Laura couldn't be sure. She had nothing on from the waist down and there were several ugly bruises on her body. Laura felt nausea well in her. Beebo's face was not so badly hurt. There was a cut over one eye that was beginning to swell but that seemed to be all. Laura clapped her hands over her mouth and stood weaving by the bed, afraid to leave and afraid to stay, feeling the sandwiches she had just shared with Tris like a load of poison in her stomach. Until Beebo opened her eyes and looked at her.

"Laura!" she said, with such passionate relief that Laura went to her instantly and threw her arms around her and wept.

She could feel Beebo's tears on her face and she hugged her tight in a frenzy of sympathy and sorrow and whispered over and over, "Beebo, darling. Beebo, darling."

It was a long time before either of them made sense; a long time before either could speak. Laura finally raised herself on one elbow so she could see Beebo better.

"What's the matter with me?" she said softly. "I should be taking care of you. Crying isn't going to do you any good." She started to get up but Beebo caught her, and Laura was heartened to feel the strength in her arms.

"Stay with me, baby," she said, almost fiercely.

"Let me clean you up, Beebo. Let me make you comfortable. Please, sweetheart."

"Laura, I don't need anything but you. Just let me feel you lying beside me and I'll get over it somehow. I won't lose my mind. If you'll just stay with me. Please."

There were tears in her voice and rather than make her more miserable, Laura obeyed. She put her arms around Beebo and cuddled against her in a way she had almost forgotten.

"Beebo, can you talk about it, darling? Can you tell me what happened?"

"Not now. Not yet."

"I think you ought to see a doctor. You've got some awful-looking bruises."

"You're my doctor."

"Beebo, I'm scared. I don't even know what happened to you. I want to call a doctor," she said urgently.

"I don't *need* a doctor," Beebo declared.

"Please tell me what happened," Laura pleaded. She lay at the edge of the bed, her face away from the floor and the grisly spectacle of the little dog she had never liked very well and now felt such a horrified pity for.

"It's an old story," Beebo said, her voice tired and bitter, but curiously resigned. "I don't know why it didn't happen to me years sooner. Nearly every butch I know gets it one way or another. Sooner or later they catch up with you."

"Who catches up with you?"

"The goddam sonofabitch toughs who think it's smart to pick fights with Lesbians. They ask you who the hell do you think you are, going around in pants all the time. They say if you're going to wear pants and act like a man you can damn well fight like a man. And they jump you for laughs . . . God."

Her hand went up to her face which was contorted with remembered pain and fury. After a silence of several minutes while she composed herself a little she resumed briefly, "So they jumped me. They followed me home, hollering all the way. I hollered back. I—I was pretty tight and it was pretty noisy. I should have been more careful. I shouldn't have brought them here, but I knew you wouldn't be home so soon . . . I didn't work today, baby." She said it guiltily, and Laura knew it meant she had spend the day at Julian's or the Cellar or one of the other homosexual bars. But she didn't condemn her or shout, "You'll lose your job!" as she would have another time. She only listened in silence.

"So anyway," Beebo said, after an awkward pause, "I came home early. About four-thirty, I guess. They just followed me in. Oh, I got in the apartment all right and slammed the door and locked it. But one of them came up the fire escape and he let the others in. Gave me this." She pointed to the cut under her eye, and Laura kissed it. "I thought I'd gotten rid of them, baby, but those bastards followed me right up here and tried to prove what men they are." She spat the words out as if they had a bad taste and then she stopped, looking at Laura to see how she was taking it. And Laura, lying next to her and holding her tight, was overwhelmed with helpless anger and pity and even a sort of love for Beebo.

Beebo felt Laura clinging to her and the flow of sympathy warmed and encouraged her. Finally she said, softly, as if the whole thing had been her fault and she was ashamed of it, "I'm not a virgin any more, Laura. Don't ever let a man touch you." She said it vehemently, her fingers digging into the submissive girl at her side and her hurt face turned to Laura's. Laura let out a little sob and pulled closer to her.

"Beebo, darling," she said in a broken voice, "I can't stand to think of it. I can't stand to think of how it must have hurt. I know I'm a coward, I can't help it." And then, in her anxiety to heal the bitter misery of it, she blurted, "I love you, Beebo."

Beebo pulled her very close and lifted her face and kissed it delicately, almost reverently, for a very long time. At last she whispered, her lips against Laura's lips, "I adore you, Laura. You're my life. Stay with me, stay with me, don't ever leave me. I can stand this, I can stand anything, if you're with me. Swear you'll stay with me, darling."

Laura's voice stuck in her throat. She couldn't refuse. And yet she knew full well she would be swearing to a lie. It made her hide her face in painful indecision for a moment.

"Swear," Beebo demanded imperiously. "Swear, Laura!"

"I swear," Laura sobbed. She felt Beebo relax then with a sigh, running her hands through Laura's hair.

Beebo gave a faint little laugh. "I never thought anything so rotten ugly could have a good side," she murmured. "But if it's brought us back together, I'm glad it happened. It was worth it."

Laura was shocked. Beebo sounded a little unbalanced. "You can't be grateful for anything that horrible, Beebo," she protested. "You *can't*, not if you're in your right mind."

"You can if you're as much in love as I am!" Beebo said, looking at her. Laura was shamed into silence.

After a little while, Laura raised herself on an elbow. "Beebo, I'm going to call a doctor."

"You're going to do no such goddam silly thing."

Laura lost her patience. "Now you listen to me, you stubborn idiot!" she exclaimed. "You've been badly hurt. It's just madness not to have medical help, Beebo. You know that as well as I do. Don't argue with me!" She cut Beebo off as she was about to protest. "Besides," Laura went on, "you might want to prosecute them. How could you prove anything without medical evidence?"

"*Prosecute?*" Beebo stared at her and then she gave a short, sharp laugh. "Are you kidding? Who's going to mourn for the lost virtue of a Lesbian? What lawyer is going to make a case for a poor queer gone wrong? Everybody will think I got what I deserved."

Laura stared at her, disbelieving. "Beebo," she said finally, as if she were explaining a simple fact to a slow beginner, "you don't go into court and say, 'I am a Lesbian.' You don't go to a lawyer and say it. You don't say it to *anybody*, you nut! You say, 'I'm a poor innocent girl and I was criminally assaulted and hurt and raped and I have medical proof of it and I can identify the man who did it!' "

Beebo turned on her side and laughed, and her laughter made Laura want to weep. "Not man, Bo-peep," she said when she got her breath. "*Men*. Bastards, every last one. There were four of them."

Laura moaned, an involuntary sound of revulsion.

"No thanks, baby," Beebo said, her voice suddenly tired. "I've got enough trouble in the world without advertising that I'm gay. I always knew this would happen and I always knew what I'd do about it . . . just exactly nothing. Because there's nothing I *can* do. It's part of the crazy life I live. A sort of occupational hazard, you might say."

Laura pleaded with her. "I just want to be sure they didn't do you some awful harm you don't know about, darling!" she said. "I'm no doctor, I can't give you anything but bandaids and sponge baths and love."

"That's all in the world I want, baby," Beebo smiled. "I'll get well in no time."

But Laura was too genuinely frightened to let it go at that. "What if they come back?" she asked. "Then they'd get us both."

"No, they wouldn't," Beebo said and her face became hard. "Because I'd kill any man who laid a hand on you. Any man. I don't care how. I wouldn't ask any questions. I'd do it with whatever was handy—a knife or my own hands." Laura started, staring at her. "No man will ever touch you, Laura, and live. I swear."

Laura went pale, wondering how Beebo would react to a

marriage between herself and Jack; wondering how much violence she was capable of. "All right, Beebo," she said. "Will you—just tell me one thing? Why won't you see a doctor?"

Beebo turned away from her then, petulant as a child. "I haven't seen a doctor in twenty years, Bo-peep," she said.

"Why?"

Beebo sighed. "Because they might find out I'm a woman," she said quietly.

Laura covered her face with her hands and cried in silence. It was futile. Beebo *was* a woman, no matter how many pairs of pants hung in her closet, no matter how she swaggered or swore. And while she could fool some people into thinking she was a boy, there were a lot more she couldn't fool, and to them she looked foolish and rather pathetic. But Beebo was too sick to argue with. Laura was afraid of the way she talked, of the harsh way she laughed.

"We'll talk about it in the morning," she said.

"We won't talk about it at all," Beebo said, facing the wall, her back to Laura. "Where were you tonight, Laura?"

Laura swallowed convulsively before she could answer. "I was at the movies," she said.

She waited for Beebo to question her further, but there was no questioning.

"I guess I'd better wash," Beebo said. She rolled over and looked at Laura. "Do you really love me, baby?" she asked, and her eyes were deep and clouded.

"Yes," said Laura with a sad little smile, afraid to say anything else.

Beebo gazed at her for a while, returning the smile. "Thank God," she whispered, her hand caressing Laura's shoulder. And then she said, "Where's Nix?" She started to get out of bed but Laura stopped her.

"They hurt him, Beebo," she stammered.

"Hurt him? How?"

"They—darling, I don't know how to tell you—please, Beebo!" she cried in sudden fear as Beebo pushed past her. She stopped at the edge of the bed, staring with huge eyes at her little pet.

"I didn't realize—it was so bad," Beebo blurted inanely.

"He's dead," Laura whispered.

"Oh. Oh, that was too much. Too much . . ." Beebo stared

at him, her face almost stupid with sorrow. She didn't scream as Laura had, or turn away sick. She just gaped at him for a while with Laura clinging to her and murmuring, "It's all right, darling, it's all right," because she didn't know what else to say.

Beebo got off the bed and went to him, kneeling beside the ruined little body, and picked him up in her arms.

Beebo looked at Laura with the blood running all over her and there was grief on her face. "He was just a dog," she moaned. "Such a little dog. There was nothing queer about him! . . . And he could talk, too." She almost shouted it and Laura waited, trembling, for her to move.

"He was so sweet, Laura," she said with tears coursing down her face. "You never liked him much, but he was such a good dog."

"I loved him, Beebo, he was a part of your life," Laura protested anxiously.

But Beebo ignored it. It was half a lie, spoken in affection, but still a lie. "I could always talk to him and it seemed as if he understood," Beebo said. "I know you thought I was crazy. But there were times when I had to talk to somebody and there wasn't anybody. Only Nix. I had him for seven years . . . since he was six weeks old." And she clutched him to her and wept and Laura looked at her, all bloodied and heart-broken, and thought, *She feels worse about the dog than about herself.*

"Now that he's gone . . . at least we'll have one less thing to fight about." Beebo looked very pale and odd. "Won't we, baby?" she said.

"I—I guess so," Laura said. *She's cracked!* she thought. She went into the living room then, leaving Beebo alone for a few minutes, and called Jack. He was alone.

"Jack, I don't know how to tell you. I—they raped Beebo." Her voice was low and shaky.

Jack wasn't sure whether she was kidding or not. He wasn't even sure he heard her right. "Lucky bitch," he said. "I wish they'd rape me instead. I'm never in the right place at the right time."

"I'm serious, Jack."

And when he heard the catch in her throat he believed her. "*Who* raped her, sweetheart?" he said, and the levity was dead gone from him.

"She doesn't know. Some hoods. God knows who they were."

"Did you call a doctor?"

"She won't let me!" Laura's voice rose with indignation. "Of all the nonsense I ever heard in my life! She's afraid the doctor will find out she's a female. I think we're all going crazy—" But she felt Beebo's hand then taking the phone from her, and she surrendered it without arguing and went to the couch and collapsed.

"Jack?" Beebo said. "I'm all right. It looks worse than it really is. I'll live." The front of her was sticky with Nix's blood.

"You talk like it happens all the time," Jack said with scolding sympathy. "Like getting you teeth drilled, or something."

Beebo smiled wryly. "How is it you always know just what to say to a girl, Jackson? Make her feel real swell?"

"How is it that you're such a goddam prude you won't let a doctor examine you? The doctor doesn't give a damn what sex you are."

"They killed Nix." She threw it at him unexpectedly, silencing him about the doctor. And she described him with such detail that Laura didn't want to listen. She got up and went into the bedroom to escape the conversation.

Beebo joined Laura on the bed ten minutes later, wearing her men's cotton pajamas. Laura was too tired and weak to move. Beebo undressed her where she lay on the bed and dragged her under the covers naked.

"I don't know what to do with Nix," she said. "I'll have to figure something out in the morning."

They lay in each other's arms, absorbed in their own thoughts. Laura's mind was a potpourri of vivid impressions. She would never forget the bloody little dog, nor the fragrant skin of the Indian dancer, nor Beebo's misery, nor those sinfully sweet kisses she stole from Tris. . . .

"Jack's coming over tomorrow," Beebo said in her ear.

"Good."

"Why 'good'?"

"He'll help us. He'll make you see a doctor and he'll do something about Nix. I don't know, I just feel better with him around."

"If I didn't know for goddam sure how gay you are, baby,

I'd hate that guy."

Laura had to laugh. "Beebo, if you get jealous of Jack I'll send you to a head shrinker."

"Okay, okay, I know it's nuts. But you talk about him all the time."

"I'm very fond of Jack. You know that. He brought us together, darling." And she said it so gently that Beebo clasped her tighter and was reassured.

Laura slept, finally. But Beebo could not. She spent the night with her arms around Laura, taking her only comfort in Laura's nearness and the sudden apparent return of her affection.

Jack came at eight-thirty. It was a Saturday morning and he had the day to spend. With his usual detachment he wrapped Nix up while Beebo was dressing. He carted him down the stairs in a garbage pail and left him for the morning pickup in a trash bin, well hidden in a shroud of papers. When Beebo came into the kitchen a few minutes later he just said, "He's gone. Don't ask me about it, Beebo. It's all over." He found it almost as hard to talk about as she did.

"Damn you, Jack," Beebo said feebly. But she was glad he had done it for her. She felt lousy. All the excitement and anger that had sustained her the night before were gone, leaving a lassitude and nausea that swept over her in waves. Laura made her go back to bed and fed her breakfast from a tray.

"Don't leave me, baby," Beebo begged and Laura promised to stay near by. But as soon as Beebo had swallowed a little food and kept it down, she fell asleep, and Jack pulled Laura to her feet and dragged her, whispering protests, into the kitchen.

"How can I talk to you in there?" he demanded and fixed them both some coffee.

Laura drank in silence, listening to his rambling talk with one ear, gratefully. She thought of Tris and wondered whether to confess to Jack about the dancer or keep it a secret. She knew he wouldn't like it.

"Beebo acted kind of crazy last night," Laura said. "I think she felt worse about Nix than about herself."

"No doubt she did. But pretty soon she'll feel her own aches and pains. Maybe I can find her another hound somewhere. I just hope to God she doesn't use this thing to make a prisoner of you, Mother."

"A prisoner?"

"She was getting pretty desperate about you, you know. I think that has a lot to do with all the drinking."

Laura realized then that he didn't put a shot of booze in his coffee. "You're still on the wagon!" she said.

He swirled his coffee reflectively. "I remember," he said, "when Terry was giving me the works a few months back. I nearly drank myself to extinction. Beebo's not above trying it herself."

"Oh, God, that was awful!" Laura said, remembering Terry.

Terry had been enough to drive a strong man mad. If he had been nasty about it Jack could have stood it better. He could have preserved his self-respect and he might have had the strength to kick Terry out sooner than he did. But Terry was nice. He was delightful and cooperative. He was unfaithful, he was taking every cent Jack made as Jack made it, and he was hardly ever home.

But Jack was in love with him; angrily in love with the wrong person, sticking to a doomed attachment as if every new shock and every unexpected pain only strengthened his need for the boy.

Jack knew it was hopeless. He knew it was draining his strength and making a coward of him. In his mind the whole sad farce of the thing was perfectly clear. But he acted on his emotions in spite of himself, and as long as Terry loved him he couldn't let him go.

Curiously enough, Terry did love him. Jack was home base to him; Jack was security. Jack paid the bills and bolstered him when he was low, and no matter how rough and rotten the rest of the world might get, good old Jack was always there, always the same.

But the end had to come. There was never enough money, there was never enough understanding, there was never enough of the right kind of love. It took just one sharp explosion of acid resentment one night, when Jack caught Terry cheating after two years of bitter suspicions, to blow them apart. It was almost too painful to think about afterwards.

It was over now, of course. Terry was gone. But the ache

for him and the loneliness, even the desire to be tormented remained.

"You never heard from Terry, did you?" Laura asked.

"No. He took his things and left and I haven't heard from him since. Makes me think he must have left New York."

"Do you still want him?" She asked it not to hurt him but because she knew he had to say it now and then or die of it.

"Of course I want him," he said briefly. "Drink your coffee. Your patient is howling for attention."

5

Three weeks, Laura wrote in her diary, sitting in the living room while Beebo slept. *Three weeks of this, and if it goes on much longer I'll end up hating her. I felt so sorry for her at first. It was such a cruel thing and it hurt her terribly. But she's well now—I know she is. She's lying around getting fat and drinking like a fish and not working. If she doesn't get back to work soon I'll lose my mind. And she'll lose her job for sure. They've been calling all week.*

Laura hadn't minded being a nurse at first. She tended Beebo gently and made her rest and, being unsure herself and hounded by her patient to forget it, she never did call a doctor. But Beebo seemed to come out of it fast. Physically the scars healed quickly. At the end of a week she was up and around. She hadn't had a drink since the day it happened, and she talked about going back to work the next Monday.

But then Laura came home late one evening and she found Beebo drunk.

"Where the hell have you been?" Beebo shouted at her when Laura came in and found her in the kitchen. "I'm sick and miserable, I've just been through hell, and you can't even come home from work to make my dinner for me."

Confronted with such a bombardment of nonsense, Laura wouldn't even answer her. She undressed and took a shower, but Beebo followed her into the bathroom and went right on yelling. Laura had pulled the shower curtain but Beebo opened it and watched her bathe.

"Laura," she said, "where were you?" No answer. "Tell me. *Tell* me, damn it!" It was an order.

"Ask me like a civilized human being, then," Laura said, turning around to rinse her soapy back.

"I'll ask you any way I goddam please. I have a right to know."

Laura turned the water off and eyed her coldly. "I had dinner with Jack," she said. "He dropped in after work."

"I don't believe you."

474

"Call him." She stepped out of her bath, cool and dripping and haughty as a princess, and Beebo burned for her.

"I don't believe a word he says. He always lies for you. No matter what I ask him he's always got an answer. I used to like the guy, but Jesus, it's gotten so I can't trust him any more. He's always on your side."

Laura wrapped herself in a towel and began to rub herself, but Beebo suddenly put her whiskey down and clasped her in a bear hug.

"Laura, darling, I felt so rotten today. And I looked forward so much to having you home. It's so quiet and lonesome around here all day without Nix. I nearly go mad. Baby, I know I've taken up a lot of your time, but I couldn't help it. I didn't ask those bastards to rape me."

Laura relaxed slightly in the embrace, since she couldn't squirm out of it. "You felt better today, not worse, Beebo. You told me so this morning."

"That was this morning. I got worse this afternoon," she said petulantly.

"You got worse at exactly five thirty when I was fifteen minutes late."

"Where were you?"

"With Jack. Beebo, you've been drinking. You promised me you wouldn't."

"If you'd been home I wouldn't have to!" Beebo released her abruptly, picked up the whiskey glass with a swoop of her hand, and defiantly finished what was in it.

Laura cinched the towel around herself and approached Beebo. "Do you know what you're saying, you nut?" she said. "You big fool? Beebo, answer me!" But Beebo turned her back and watched Laura with glittering eyes in the mirror on the medicine chest.

"You're saying that you can't stay sober without me, Beebo. Do you realize that?"

"I can't stay sober if you don't love me, Laura."

"Oh, damn you, Beebo!" Laura almost wept with frustration. "You're only saying that to make me feel guilty. To put the blame on me instead of on yourself where it belongs! I didn't give you your first drink, God knows. I don't ply you with liquor. You've fixed it with your conscience so no matter when you get drunk it's my fault. No matter how much you drink, you're only drinking because Laura is such a bitch.

Well, I won't buy it! It's a damn plot to make a prisoner of
me!"

"A prisoner! Now where did little Bo-peep get that fancy
idea?" Beebo's eyes were narrow and sharp in spite of the
whiskey. Her anger brought clarity with it. "That sounds like
the kind of propaganda Jack would spout."

"No—" Laura began, but Beebo silenced her with a menacing wave of her hand. Laura found herself trapped against
the bathroom door.

Beebo put a hand up on the door on either side of Laura
and looked down at her. "Now, suppose you just tell me what
Jack said," she said.

"What makes you think Jack said it? I can think for myself
and you know it. And I *am* a prisoner here!"

"You can't think for yourself when Jack's around. That
bastard is the Pied Piper of Greenwich Village. He opens his
yap and all the little fairies listen popeyed to whatever he
has to say. Including you."

Laura looked at her and found herself caught by Beebo's
spell again. Beebo was born to lose her temper. She looked
wonderful when she did. It exasperated Laura to feel a bare
animal desire for her at times like this.

"Jack said it. Come on. Jack said it, didn't he?" Beebo
insisted.

"All right!" Laura almost screamed. "Jack said it!"

She looked up at Beebo with embarrassed desire and to
make her shame complete, Beebo saw it. And she knew she
was in command again, even if only for an hour or so. Beebo
was learning to live for those hours. The rest of the time
nothing much mattered.

Beebo shifted support of her leaning body from her arms
to Laura, lifted up Laura's angry helpless face and kissed it.
"Why aren't you like this all the time?" she asked. And Laura
startled her when she echoed, "Why aren't *you* like this all
the time?"

"Like what, baby? Drunk?"

"No . . . ," Laura hesitated. She didn't quite understand
what she meant herself.

"Mad?" Beebo asked.

"I don't know."

Beebo laughed. "If it'll help I'll get mad and stay mad,
Bo-peep. I'll get drunk and stay drunk. Would you like that?"

She interspersed her words with kisses.

"No. I just—I hate it when you act like a spoiled brat, Beebo."

"I never act like a spoiled brat." Her voice was little more than a whisper now.

They sank to the floor where they were and made love then.

And even after Laura had finally fallen asleep, in her arms, Beebo felt a tide of renewed passion. She caressed Laura's hair and back with her hands and thought, *If it can be this good it's not over.*

Laura had left work meaning to go straight home. But as before she hadn't gone far when she knew she was headed for Tris's little studio.

Tris opened the door herself. She had evidently been prac-ticing for she was dressed in tights and breathing hard. Her black hair was smoothed over her head, caught in back with a clasp and braided. The braid, heavy and shining, hung half-way down her back and swung like a whip when she whirled.

Tris paused for a moment when she saw Laura on her threshold and for an awful second Laura thought she might turn her away. But Tris smiled suddenly and said, "Laura. How nice. Please come in."

"I just dropped by to say hello," Laura apologized.

"That is not all, I hope?" Tris said, looking at her.

Laura felt an odd little twist of excitement. "Well . . . I shouldn't stay. I don't want to interrupt your work."

"Of course you do. That's why you came," Tris said, spin-ning reflectively in place, her weight shifting delicately to pull her around and around.

Laura didn't know if she was being scolded or teased, if she should leave or stay. Tris stopped twirling and said, "I'm glad you came. I didn't want to work any more anyway."

Laura hesitated, wondering whether to believe her. But when Tris walked across the room to her and kissed her cheek she melted suddenly with pleasure. She stood quietly and let herself be kissed, afraid to return the compliment. She was very unsure of herself with Tris. Even the gentlest gesture seemed to irritate the dancer sometimes. Laura could only let her take the lead.

Tris turned away abruptly, her mood shifting. "Well, now you are here," she said in her careful English. "What would you like to do?" It was a sort of challenge.

"I—I'd like to see you dance, Tris. Would you dance for me?"

"No." She was pouting. "You are my excuse for not dancing any more today, Laura."

"Maybe we could just talk for a little while, then."

"We could . . . but we won't."

Laura was at a loss for words. She stammered a little and finally she blurted, "I think you'd rather have me go home."

"I think Beebo would like you home more than I would. She doesn't let you out very often, does she?"

Laura colored. "She's not my jailkeeper," she said.

"I don't like this—this interference you force me to make in your love affair, Laura," Tris said and surprised her guest. "I don't know your Beebo, but I have nothing against her. Still, I do not imagine she will like *me* very well if she finds out you are my guest now and then."

"What do you care whether Beebo likes you or not?" Laura demanded, startled.

Tris broke into a charming smile then, as if to placate her visitor. "I want everybody to like me," she said. "I suppose it is a compulsion left from my childhood." And, as if she had made a guilty admission, she turned away abruptly saying, "Let's go into the kitchen. If I stand in here I will feel obliged to dance."

Laura followed her and sat down self-consciously. Tris fixed a plate of cookies and gave her a glass of milk. She smiled.

"I am hard to know, Laura. I am not very gracious. But I like your company." Her smile was as warm and luscious as ripe fruit in the sun.

They finished the food over small talk about men. Laura was lost, silent. She just nodded agreement and listened with dismay. *She's trying to tell me she doesn't like girls,* she thought. *But it's a lie!*

Tris rinsed the plates, watching herself all the while in one mirror or another. It was as if she felt herself on exhibition all the time, as if all those mirrors were scattered around to remind her of her own beauty.

Tris dried her hands and turned to face Laura. There was an awkward pause and Laura realized suddenly that she was supposed to get up and leave. They had had their small talk. She had been served food. That was all she could reasonably expect from her hostess, especially since she was an uninvited guest. She felt her heart contract a little in disappointment, and she thought with a flash of yearning of the intimacies of her last visit.

But she was too proud to overstay her welcome, especially after the way Tris had shown her the door last time. So she got up and said, "Thanks Tris. I have to go."

"Oh?" It was merely polite.

"Beebo's expecting me."

"I see." No protest. Tris followed her toward the front door. "Ask me over to your apartment sometime, Laura. You would make a much nicer hostess than I. Besides, I should like to see how your big roommate looks in pants. She does wear pants?"

"Yes, she does." Laura turned to look at her curiously. "But she's a jealous hellion."

Tris leaned on the wall by the door, crossing her feet at the ankles.

"Does she know you have been here to visit me?" Her smile was sly, interested.

"No. I don't think she even remembers you," Laura said shortly.

"Ah! Flattering. Do you think it's wise to make a secret of our friendship, Laura?"

"It's either that or get my neck broken," Laura said.

Tris laughed a little, as if the idea of such hard play amused her. "Laura . . . would you like to stay a little longer?" she said. Her voice made it sound very inviting.

"I can't." Laura was upset by all the talk of Beebo.

"As long as you leave by eight it would be all right," Tris said. "I have a date at eight."

"With a man?"

"Certainly with a man. I have no secrets, Laura. I do not like to cheat, like you. You cheat with your Beebo by seeing me. But still—" she hunched her shoulders and smiled—"I like you. You like me. Perhaps it is worth the risk. You are the one who will get your neck broken, not me. I have no right to deny you your pain."

Laura frowned at her. It was an odd thing to say. Tris put her hands on Laura's arms and they stood that way, silent, for a moment.

At last Tris said, "Dance with me."

"I don't know how," Laura said shyly.

"I am a teacher. I teach you. Come on."

"I'm so clumsy, Tris."

But Tris pulled her to the middle of the studio and put a record on. She stood for a minute in front of Laura as if trying to make up her mind where to grasp her, how to start. Laura felt impossibly awkward. But Tris made up her mind quickly and slipped her arms around Laura's neck. Laura was two inches taller than she and Tris was obliged to look up at her when she spoke.

"We will just do it like the teen-agers!" she said. "There is nothing to it really. Stand in one place and shift your weight from one foot to the other, with the beat. That's it. You've got it. That's a good beginning."

Laura couldn't help laughing. "Even I can do that much," she said.

"Ah. Then there is hope. Next year at this time you will do the *tour jeté.*"

Laura had her arms around Tris at the waist and they swayed gently to the music, and suddenly all her suspicion and embarrassment faded. She became conscious of the tanta-lizing jasmine that emanated from Tris—from her throat and her hair and her breasts, barely covered by the bandeau. The black braid moved softly against Laura's bare arms in back and Tris put her cheek against Laura's, tilting her face up. Her lips were near Laura's ear and she whispered, "You know, Laura, I must tell you something. You are a homosexual. Yes?"

Laura swallowed. "Yes," she said.

"You should know then . . . I am not. Not like you. I like the company of girls, yes. My dance pupils. Friends. But I love men. I love them. Do you understand?"

"No." Laura shut her eyes and pulled Tris a little tighter.

"Well, then, I will explain. Men excite me. All men, I mean. The idea of men . . . It is hard to say. But I would rather be with a man than with a woman. But now and then I meet a woman who interests me. And sometimes the interest goes beyond just talk. You see?"

"No."

"Sometimes I want to kiss her. Or be close to her. But that is all. Now do you see?"

"No."

Tris gave an impatient little sigh. "I am telling you I am not

queer like you!" she said sharply and Laura winced with
sudden pain. Tris felt it and she amended quickly, "That is
an unkind word. You people call it gay. All right. I am not
gay. I like you, I like to talk to you and watch you move
and sometimes I am moved myself to kiss you or be close to
you, like this. Our bodies like this, all up and down. You see?
But I don't like to go any farther. Not with a girl. You are
only the third girl I have felt this for. It will not happen again
for a long time. Perhaps I will marry soon, and then it will
never happen again."

"Marry! Who? An Indian?"

"No!" she exclaimed almost contemptuously. "Another.
He is *white*."

"You're full of contradictions, Tris," Laura said, looking
down at her in bewilderment. "You said you were gay and
you married a gay boy."

"Oh, yes. I did, didn't I?" She looked trapped. "Well, I
thought I was then. But I know now—positively—I am not."

"But you said—"

"Such wonderful blond hair you have, Laura. I would give
anything for such hair. Why do you always wear it wound up
like that?" And she began to slip pins out of the bun, letting
them drop to the polished floor, until the coil of gold came
loose and Tris gave a delighted, "Ah!"

Laura felt the thrill go through her hard. She forgot her
protests about Tris's sex drive and pulled the dancer very close
to kiss her full on the mouth. Tris yielded. With one accord
they stopped dancing and just clung and kissed, swaying
slightly. It lasted for long minutes—just kisses, soft and exploratory, but careful. Laura wondered vaguely, through the
fog of lovely sensations, what miserable devil prompted this
delectable girl to deny her Lesbian impulses. For Laura could
tell that Tris enjoyed this love play as much as she. She encouraged it, even when Laura tried to stop, and pulled her
back for more.

By eight o'clock they were lying on the big red silk couch
in the bedroom, murmuring inanities to each other, discovering one another's bodies and emotions through twin shields of
clothes and caution.

"Will you come and see me again?" Tris asked.

"Are you inviting me?"

"Of course."

"When would it be convenient?" She said it in clipped English, like the English Tris spoke, to tease her.

"It is never convenient. But come anyway."

Laura laughed. "When?"

"Tomorrow."

"No date tomorrow?"

"Yes. Every night."

"Save a night for me, Tris."

Tris gazed at her for a moment before she answered, "No."

"Why not?"

"We do too much in these few short hours. What would we do with a whole night? I do not like to think."

"I think of it all the time. I can't think of anything else."

"Ah, that is a very bad sign. I am sorry to hear you say that. You must not fall in love with me, Laura."

"I'll try to remember," she said sarcastically.

"I am serious," Tris said.

Laura didn't answer her. She lay on her back and looked up at the small skylight directly over the bed. It was a square of violet—the last shade of fading day.

"I do not want you to fall in love with me, Laura," Tris persisted.

"I hear you," Laura said quietly.

"Well, why don't you answer?"

"I don't know how to answer, Tris," she said, turning to look at her in the semi-gloom of the bedroom.

"What are your feelings for me?"

"Do you want a blue print?" Laura said, hurt. "I can't spell them out for you. I don't understand them myself." But she understood them all too well. She had felt these pangs before for other girls—only two or three, including Beebo, but enough to make them familiar and unwelcome. But still exciting and irresistible.

Tris lay beside her, quiet for a while, and finally she said, "Do you know why I was not very glad to see you at first today?"

"No." Laura reached across the bed to put a hand on Tris's breasts, to feel what she could not see in the gathering darkness.

"I was afraid," Tris whispered. "Of my own feelings. I do not like to become involved with women. It has always been unpleasant for me."

"Do you still want me to come back and see you?"

"Yes." She paused and Laura sensed a smile. "As long as I ask you to come back, Laura, you will know you are safe with me."

"Safe?"

"I will put it another way. If a day comes when I do *not* want to see you, it will be because I am in love with you. And that will be the end. From that day on we will never meet again, until I am cured."

Laura had to smile. Who could take such a charming speech seriously? "All right," she murmured and embraced the lovely dancer.

"Now you must go," Tris told her. "My date will be here soon. He is always prompt."

Laura got up without protest. But it was sweet to take the time to wind up her hair and know she was welcome. "Did you kick me out for the same boy last time?" she asked.

Tris had turned a light on and they watched each other in the mirror before which Laura was combing her hair.

"No. Another."

"I hate him," Laura said with a little smile. "And the rest of them."

Tris gazed at her coolly. "How very foolish," she said. And made Laura laugh.

They parted with a chaste kiss, and for the first time since they had met Laura felt as if she had a slim chance with this odd and irresistible girl who was still so much a stranger to her. She went home to her angry Beebo, her body tense with need. And later, when Beebo demanded her body, Laura surrendered promptly and helplessly.

Beebo, since the night of her attack, had become unbear-ably suspicious. Everything Laura did, everywhere she went, had to be reported in detail. She called Tris once or twice from work and Tris had bawled her out for not showing up. Laura was more pleased than sorry when Tris sounded jealous—while she bridled angrily at Beebo's jealousy, she was thrilled with Tris's.

Laura had strong doubts about Beebo's illness now. She could have gone to work weeks ago. The bruises were nearly invisible; only a pale yellow shadow stained the spot where the worst had been. Beebo was using it an as excuse to sit

around another week and take it easy and drink and bitch
over the phone to Lili about her problems.

"I always hated that damn elevator," she declared with her
feet up on the coffee table in the living room and a drink in
her hand.

"You make me sick!" Laura told her. "You're *well*. Get up
and go to work."

Beebo looked at her watch. "At six-thirty in the evening?"
she said, and laughed.

"I'm not going to support us both, Beebo," Laura said. "And
I'm sick and tired of playing nursemaid."

To her diary Laura confided, *I am in love. I'm sure of it.*
The more I'm with Beebo the more I want Tris. Oh, God, how
much I want her!

Laura was desperate after two more weeks of Beebo. Beebo
drove her frantic when they were cooped up together in the
small apartment, as they were every night. And Beebo was
wild for the love Laura denied her. The attack she had endured
seemed to have touched off a burning core of violence in her
that never went out.

When Beebo found the small steel strongbox on the closet
floor with Laura's diary inside, she pounded it with a stone
to get it open but the lock didn't break. When Laura got home
from work and found the battered box on the coffee table in
the living room she went pale with alarm, and Beebo, who
was lying in wait for her reaction, exclaimed, "Damn it, I
knew it. You sure as hell look guilty, Laura. What's in it?"
She kicked the box.

"Nothing." Laura walked across the room but her legs felt
weak.

"Open it, then."

"No."

"Where's the key?"

"I don't know."

"It's your box, goddam it. You know where the key is!
Why did you hide it from me? What are you ashamed of?"

"I'm under no obligation to show you everything I own!"
Laura said frostily. "I'll hide what I please."

"You tell me what's in it," Beebo threatened, "or I'll choke
you. I swear I'll choke you, you bitch." She slammed Laura
against the wall with one hand to her throat.

Laura gasped in panic. There was only one thing to do with Beebo in these moods and that was go along with her, stall, anything but resist her. That was too painful and Laura even feared that one of these days, with Beebo as crazy as she was, it might be fatal.

"All right," Laura said through a tight throat. "Let me go."

She rummaged for the key for ten minutes, knowing all the while that it was in the wallet in her purse.

"Don't tell me you can't find it," Beebo said, watching her through narrowed eyes.

"I almost never use the thing," Laura said as calmly as she could.

"You find it," Beebo said. And something in the tone of her voice made Laura very frightened. *I'm getting out of here,* she thought to herself suddenly. *If I can just get out of this somehow I'll leave her tonight and I won't come back. I'll go to Jack's.*

She turned and faced Beebo, desperate. "Beebo, it's just some personal papers. It's nothing you'd be interested in."

"It's exactly what I'd be interested in. I'd be even more interested in why you went white as a sheet when you saw I had it. Explain *that* to me, Bo-peep."

Laura pressed her teeth together in a small grimace of exasperation. "It's my birth certificate and my baptism certificate and two insurance policies and some old love letters." she said.

"Love letters from who?" Beebo demanded.

"Beth."

Beebo put her head back and laughed. "Oh!" she said. "Beth! Good old Beth. Your college flame. I'm getting so I *know* that goddam girl."

"She was a lot more—" Laura began, her cheeks hot. She couldn't bear to hear Beth laughed at, to hear that perfect love ridiculed.

"I know what she was," Beebo said acidly. "She was beautiful. She was bright. She was a queen on the campus and a devil in bed. She was a success. She even liked men, the traitorous bitch. She was so gorgeous and so intelligent and so everything that she could do whatever she damn well pleased— even dump you like a sack of bricks. She loved you so much she got you kicked out of school and got married. To a *man*." Beebo grinned at her, waiting for Laura to explode. But Laura only glared, too proud to spoil that memory with an ugly spat.

"Queen Beth was everything Beebo is not," Beebo said. "You'll never learn, will you? Love isn't pure roses and ro-mance, Laura. You can't live with a girl, however much you love her, and still faint with joy every time she looks your way. It's a shame you never lived with Beth like you have with me. You'd find out fast enought she is a human being, not a god-dess . . . Now, show me the letters."

"Why do you want to read a bunch of miserable old let-ters?" Laura said, angry that she had to beg. "That's all over, Beebo. It can't do anything but hurt you."

"I'm used to that, Laura. Anybody who lives with you has to be."

"You lie!" Laura flared suddenly. They gazed at each other in electric silence for a minute. Then Laura said quietly, in a move to restore her safety, "Let me fill your glass." She came to take it from her but Beebo held it away. "What are you trying to do, baby, get me drunk? Let's see the letters."

Laura sat down on the bed beside her. Maybe she could sweet-talk her out of the box. "Beebo," she said. "There's nothing in there you could possibly want to see or be inter-ested in. Will you believe me?"

Beebo looked at her coldly and didn't move. "The letters," she said and held out a hand.

Laura sighed. "After dinner," she begged. "Let's at least eat in peace." And before Beebo could answer she leaned over and kissed her lips. "I love you, Beebo," she said, very softly and hopefully. And there were still times when she wondered if she might not speak the truth. But this wasn't one of them. She spoke out of the need to save her skin.

Beebo swallowed the last of the drink. "Yeah," she said. "The letters."

Laura kissed her again. Beebo submitted to it without re-turning the kiss. "You're not very subtle, Bo-peep," she said.

"I just want a stay of execution," Laura said with a wry smile. "If we have to yell at each other, let's save it till after dinner. Please, darling. The box won't walk away." And Beebo, in spite of the obviousness of it, in spite of her own better sense and Laura's flagrant flattery, weakened.

"Are they that bad?" she asked. "The goddam letters from Beth the Beautiful?"

"They're just love letters. They're old and stale and the

affair is old and stale. It's over and done with."

"Like our affair?" And Beebo said it so simply, without the histrionics and the swearing and the noisy misery she usually showered on Laura, that Laura was touched. She put her forehead down on Beebo's shoulder and whispered, "I don't know, Beebo. You scare me so sometimes I swear I'll move out of here and run like hell and never come back. Sometimes I really think you mean to kill me."

"Sometimes I really do," Beebo said and her voice was rough. "If I did, I'd kill myself right afterwards, darling."

"A lot of good that would do me!" Laura exploded. But she softened when Beebo's face went dark. "You don't mean that, Beebo. You'd never really do it . . . would you?"

"I don't know," Beebo said, staring at her. "I've come close to it, baby. I've come close . . ."

"If you really love me, you couldn't."

"I really love you. But there are times when I don't think I could stop myself." Her eyes filled suddenly with tears and she looked away, at the wall. "Things that would hurt too much."

"Like what?"

"Like finding out you were cheating on me."

Laura shut her eyes and felt the sweat break out on her face. But I haven't really cheated with Tris, she told herself. We never went all the way. I don't think we ever will. "Don't be silly," she told Beebo. "Who is there for me to cheat on you with? Nobody."

"Jack."

"Jack?" Laura straightened up, astonished. "He's a man!"

"Sure he's a man. I know what he is."

Laura took Beebo's face in her hands and said, "I promise you I have never cheated wtih Jack or anybody else. I swear, Beebo. You think I have but I haven't. You just make it up."

"Do I just make it up that I love you more than you love me?"

Laura hung her head. "Let's shout about it after dinner," she said.

"Okay." Unexpectedly Beebo surrendered and Laura escaped to the kitchen with an audible sigh of relief.

They ate in near-silence, Laura concentrating on her plate and Beebo concentrating on Laura. They were almost finished with the gloomy little meal when there came a ring of the doorbell and Laura, without knowing why, felt a sudden start of fear.

"Who's that?" Beebo demanded.

"I don't know." Laura didn't even want to look at her. "Probably Jack. Or your darling Lili."

"Oh, Christ, I couldn't stand to see either of them right now. Lili would love to hear us quarrel."

"Let's disappoint her, then," Laura said and they smiled a little at each other. Laura was surprised at the strength of her relief. But when Beebo got up to ring the buzzer that opened the door below, the strange fear returned.

Far away downstairs she heard the front door open. Laura sat in uneasy silence in the kitchen, listening to the steps coming up the stairs out in the hall. She could picture Beebo leaning against the door jamb, waiting for the knock. More than once she had begged Beebo to be cautious opening that door. She had nightmares about the hoodlums that raped Beebo coming back to try it again—and getting Laura too this time. But Beebo shrugged it off.

"They won't be back," she had said.

"How do *you* know?"

"I know," was the cryptic answer, and that was all Laura could get out of her.

Laura found herself staring into her milk glass and whispering a prayer: *Let it be Jack. Please, dear God. I need him.*

The knock came. Beebo opened the door. There was a moment of silence and then the sound of a sweet feminine voice using a very dainty English. It was Tris!

Laura froze in a panic. For one frightened second she thought of climbing down the fire escape. And then she put her glass down with trembling hands and poised herself, tense with the near-hysterical force piling up inside her.

Suddenly Beebo said, "Well, I'll be goddamned. Hey, Laura! It's our little Indian buddy. From Peck and Peck. Come on in, sweetheart."

"Thank you," Tris said.

Laura held her breath. Beebo's friendliness would last just as long as it took her to start wondering what Tris was doing there and how she found the place. Laura could have slapped Tris. She hardly dared go in the living room and face them both.

Beebo called her. "Get in here, baby. Make like a hostess,

for God's sake. How'd you find us?" she said, her voice low-ering as she turned to Tris.

"I ran into Laura at the Hobby Shop," Tris said. "I was looking for a gift."

"Find one?" Beebo settled down on the couch, appraising Tris's slim smooth body with a cool and practiced eye. Laura saw the glance as she stood in the kitchen doorway. She disliked the way Tris let herself be admired.

"Hello, Laura," Tris said, almost shyly.

"Hello, Tris." Laura wanted Beebo to stop looking at that warm brown body, lightly sheathed in silk. Her eyes snapped angrily at Tris, and Tris saw it. "Sit down," Laura said.

"So . . . ," Beebo mused, her eyes half-closed and calcu-lating. "You discovered Laura in the Hobby Shop and got chummy, hm?"

"She told me where you live," Tris said, turning to her with an ingratiating smile. "It's not far from me. She said to come over sometime, so here I am. Perhaps I come at a bad time?" She looked from one to the other.

"Any time is a bad time in this little love nest," Beebo said. She thumbed at Laura. "We hate each other," she explained. "We only live together so we can fight."

"Oh." Tris looked uncomfortable.

Beebo grinned at the two girls, pleased to have embarrassed them both, her mind simmering with suspicions. Laura, stony-faced, refused to say anything to Tris to put her at ease. She was furious with her for coming in the first place.

"What's your name, honey?" Beebo said to Tris. "I've forgotten."

"Tris Robischon."

"Didn't you say you were Indian or something?"

"Yes."

Beebo laughed and shook her head. "Yeah . . . ," she said. "Indian."

Tris began to squirm under her gaze. She was no longer so pleased to be looked at as she had been when she entered. Beebo stared so hard, in fact, that Tris finally said coldly, "Perhaps you object to dark skins."

"So what if I do?" Beebo said casually, grinning.

Tris gasped. "Some people," she said sharply, "think all non-whites are inferior. Perhaps you are one of those?"

"Now what gives you a dumb idea like that?" Beebo

said. "Do I look unfriendly?"

"You stare at me as if I were not welcome."

"I stare at you as if you were a damn pretty girl. Which you are. You're also too sensitive, but you're welcome. I like that color." She waved at Tris's shapely legs, crossed at the knees and poised on high-heeled shoes. "On you it looks good." And she grinned. There was an awkward pause and Laura saw, with great irritation, that Tris was simply returning Beebo's gaze now, bashfully but rather eagerly.

"Have some coffee, Tris?" Laura said.

"Yes, please." Tris looked at her swiftly, as if she knew Laura didn't like her interest in Beebo.

"What do you do with yourself all day, Tris?" Beebo said. Laura was afraid of the way her voice sounded now.

"I dance."

"Where?"

"My studio. I teach."

"That all?"

"I—I have done professional work."

They talked for a few minutes until Laura brought the coffee in. She gave Tris a cup and placed one in front of Beebo. But Beebo reached out and collared her with one long arm and pulled her down on the couch beside her.

"Let go!" Laura snapped, but Beebo only held her harder.

"So you . . . just ran into Laura in the Hobby Shop," Beebo said to Tris. "Fancy that." She smiled a dangerous smile.

"Yes. It's not so surprising. I mean I—I live so close by."

Laura felt her fear rising in her throat and sweat bursting from her and she was desperately impatient to get rid of Tris.

"You know something, little Indian girl?" Beebo said.

"What?"

"I don't believe you."

The atmosphere became tense and ominous. "I apologize for her, Tris," Laura said with a show of casualness. "She doesn't believe anything."

"Now tell me, Tris," Beebo said, ignoring her, "how did you and Laura really meet?"

Tris looked squarely at her and said, "You know how. I have told the truth." She lied very gracefully. Laura wondered how many lies she had been fed herself. "But I see I am not welcome here," Tris went on. She stood up and replaced her coffee cup carefully in the saucer on the table. "Thank you for the coffee," she said regally and headed for the front door.

Beebo sprang up from the couch suddenly and Laura, frightened, followed her with almost the same movement. Beebo caught Tris at the door and turned her around and without even a pause for breath kissed her harshly on the mouth. It was a long and physically painful kiss, and Laura's furious exclamations did nothing to help. She pounded ineffectually on Beebo's back. "Beebo, stop it!" she cried.

But Beebo stopped in her own good time, and that was not until she had bruised Tris's mouth enough to make her cry. She cried softly, without a sound, her eyes shut and her head back against the door, still lifted toward Beebo.

Laura was shaken. "Tris—Tris—" she said, trying to get near her, but Beebo shouldered her out of the way.

"That's for being such a good friend of Laura's," Beebo said. "And that's all you get, too, my little Indian. Now get the hell out and don't come back."

"Beebo, please!" Laura felt her own angry tears start up, and it was unbearable to have Tris turn and leave so quickly, so quietly, without giving her a gesture of comfort or apology. "Tris, I'm so sorry!" she called after her, but it sounded trite and insincere.

Beebo shut the door and stood for a moment with her back to Laura. Laura, shaking, moved away from her.

"Where did you meet her?" Beebo asked, still not looking at her. "Tell the truth, Laura."

"At work."

Beebo whirled around. "How long are you going to lie to me!" she said.

"This is the last time!" Laura exploded, throwing her caution out with her patience. "I'm leaving you, Beebo. I've had it. You make me sick. You're ruining my life. I'm so damn scared and so damn miserable that nothing is any fun, nothing helps. Life isn't worth living, not like this!"

"Where did you meet her?" Beebo said, with single-minded jealous fury.

"I went to her apartment!" Laura blazed at her. "I went back for her card and I went to her apartment."

"And made love to her."

"No!" She shouted it angrily at first, but then she repeated it, frightened, "No, Beebo! I swear!"

But Beebo came across the room in one sudden leap of rage and threw her down hard on the floor, her big hands on Laura's slim shoulders, holding her cruelly and banging her head down again and again until Laura screamed with pain and terror. And then Beebo dropped her and slapped her and all the time she kept repeating like a mad woman, "You made love to her, love to her. Where's that key? The *key*, damn it!"

"I'll give it to you," Laura sobbed at last. "Oh, God, Beebo, don't kill me! I'll give it to you."

Beebo let her up then, or rather, dragged her to her feet. Laura stood beside her, swaying and dizzy, her eyes blurred by tears and her head aching. She went into the bedroom, shoving Beebo's hands away from her with sharp gestures of hatred, her teeth clenched. And she opened her purse and pulled out her wallet and gave Beebo the key.

Beebo snatched it from her and picked up the box like a miser going after a cache of gold. And Laura, seeing her chance, grabbed the purse and a sweater that hung on the back of a chair and backed silently out of the bedroom. She fled, on feet made feather-light with fear, to the front door. She ran down the stairs with all the speed her fear could muster and ran all the way—two blocks—to Seventh Avenue.

After a few frantic moments of scanning the street and looking back over her shoulder she hailed a cab and climbed in, crying audibly. "Drive uptown," she told the man. "Just drive uptown for a few minutes."

"Okay," he said, giving her a quick, cynical onceover.

Laura looked up and saw Beebo rush into Fourth Street as the cab turned around and headed north, and she sank down in the back seat, her hands over her face. She let him drive her almost to Times Square before she could control her sobs and give him Jack's address.

What if Beebo's already there? she wondered suddenly. *Oh, God!* She would be, of course. But Jack would save her somehow. Better to be with him, even if it meant facing Beebo again.

6

LAURA WAS RIGHT. Beebo went straight to Jack's apartment. She stormed in and beat noisily on his door until he opened it.

"Christ in the foothills!" he exclaimed, pulling on the door and looking into her wild furious face. She entered and slammed it behind her.

"She'll be over here in a few minutes," Beebo said wildly, waving the diary at him. "I haven't read much of this but I've read enough to know what a bitch she is. And you—you—" For once in her life Beebo was at a loss for words. "You lousy crawling scum sonofabitch, you've been egging her on! You've been putting ideas into her head—about leaving me."

She ranted hysterically at him, and Jack, although Laura had never described her diary to him, began to get the idea in a hurry.

"Where is she now?" he said quietly when he could get a word in edgewise.

"I don't know, but she'll be here before long. Whenever we have a quarrel she drags her can over here as fast as she can move. You're her father confessor, her lover by proxy. She tells you everything. She only lives with me." She spat it at him enviously. "I'm her lover for good and real but I'm not good enough to know what she thinks or what she does. She saves that for you. I'll kill her! By God, I will."

"Scram, Beebo," Jack said. His low voice was in sharp contrast to her own, loud and hard with wrath.

"What's the matter, isn't my company good enough for you?" She turned on him suddenly. He would have to take her threats till Laura got there; she couldn't hold them back.

"It's just that I don't like prospective murderers," Jack said. "They make me nervous."

"You bastard! You holier-than-thou bastard! You think you're so damn superior because you're still on the wagon. You *are* on the wagon, I can tell. You look so goddam sober it's repulsive. Repulsive!"

"That's the word for it, all right," Jack agreed. His compliant attitude only goaded her further.

"You hate me because Laura only comes to see you when she feels bad. She *lives* with me. But she doesn't give a damn about you until she feels bad. Then she comes running to good old Jack!"

"Beebo," he said and did not raise his voice. "When I lost Terry I did a hell of a lot of drinking and hollering. I came and drank your whiskey and told you my troubles and you listened to me. And it helped. Now you're welcome to my whiskey—there's still a little in the kitchen—and you're welcome to cry on my shoulder. But you're not going to murder anybody, here or anywhere else."

"Only Laura," Beebo said, and her voice was low now, too.

"Nobody," Jack said. "Now scram, or I'll throw you out."

Beebo grabbed the lapels of his sport jacket. "She cheated on me, Jack. You gave her the idea so don't try to squirm out of it."

"Cheated on you with who?"

"An Indian!" Her eyes were so big and her face so con' torted that Jack came very near laughter.

"What tribe?" he asked carefully.

"Not an *American* Indian, you owl'eyed idiot! An *Indian* Indian. A dancer! Jesus!" And she lifted her eyes to the ceil' ing. "A *dancer!*"

"Classical or belly?"

"Oh, shut up! You think it's funny!" She gave him a hard shove, but Jack didn't shove easily. He just stood his ground and surprised her. "It doesn't matter who she is, anyway," she said and ran a distraught hand through her close'cropped dark hair that waved and rolled around her head and used to delight Laura. "What matters is, they've been sleeping together and that cheeky little bitch—"

"Which one?"

"Jack, goddam you, quit interrupting me!" She paused to glare at him and then said, "Tris. The dancer. She had the nerve to come over to the apartment. Tried to tell me they met at the Hobby Shop. Oh, God!" And she gave a despairing laugh.

"Maybe they did." He offered it unobtrusively.

"Who're you kidding?" Beebo snapped. "Laura *admitted* she went to the girl's apartment."

"After you pounded it out of her."

Beebo held the diary out to him. "Read this, Jack. It's all in here," she said.

"Does it say they slept together?"

"Damn right!"

"Did you read it?"

"No, but it's in here," she said positively, in the grip of the spiraling violence that possessed her. "Jack Mann, college graduate, engineer, former gay boy, former whiskey drinker, former human being. Current know-it-all and champion bastard of Greenwich Village. *Read* it!"

He shook his head without even glancing at it.

"Are you too proper? Too moral? Don't tell me you've suddenly developed a conscience! After all these years," she said.

He shrugged. "Why read it? You've told me what's in it."

"Maybe you'd like to know what she says about me." He saw her face color up again and a shivering clearly visible in her hands and he said, "No." But Beebo opened the diary, leafing through it for the worst slander she could find.

Jack took the book from her hands so suddenly that she let it slip before she knew what he was up to, and then he socked her when she reached for it, catching her on the chin. She reeled backwards and sank to the floor. Jack leaned down and picked her up, hoisting her over his shoulder. He carried her that way, head dangling in back and feet in front, down the hall and out the door to the apartment building.

There he set her dizzily on her feet. She hardly knew where she was and let him hold her up. He found a taxi for her on the corner of Fourth and Seventh Avenue and told the driver, "She's drunk. It's only a couple of blocks, but I can't take her home," and handed him five dollars. "Take her upstairs," he said, giving him the address. "Apartment 2B."

He was headed up the steps to his apartment again when he heard Laura's voice calling him, and he turned around to see her running up the sidewalk, hair awry and face like chalk.

"Laura!" he exclaimed and caught her. She began to sob the moment she felt his arms around her, as if she had only been waiting to feel him for the tears to start.

"Is she here?" she asked, and he could feel her quivering.

"She left," he said. "I just put her in a cab. Your timing is faultless, Mother."

Laura looked at him out of big amazed eyes. "She's gone? How did you do it?" she asked. "What happened?"

"Come on inside," he said. He led her down the hall and in his kitchen at last, with the front door locked and no Beebo anywhere around and a comforting drink to brace her, she heaved a long sigh of relief.

"Now," said Jack, making himself some coffee. "Who is Tris?"

Laura clasped her glass in both hands and looked into the whiskey for an answer. "She's a dancer—"

"I know that part. I mean, are you sleeping with her?"

"No!" Laura flashed.

"Do you want to?"

And after a pause she whispered honestly, "Yes."

"So Beebo's not imagining things."

"She doesn't have to," Laura cried bitterly. "She's got my diary."

"I saw it."

"Did you read it?"

"No, but Beebo did."

"What did she say?" Laura's throat had gone dry all of a sudden at the idea of Beebo perusing those private pages, and she took a sip of her whiskey.

"She wants to solve the whole thing by murdering you."

"I think she would, too," Laura said, unsurprised. "Oh, Jack, help me. I'm scared to death."

"All right." He came over, pulling his chair, and sat down beside her. "Marry me."

Laura covered her face with her hands and gave a little moan. "Is that all you can think of? Is that all you can say?" she said, and she sounded a little desperate. "I'm in love with Tris, and Beebo wants to *murder* me and you want to *marry* me. What good will that do? I might as well be dead as married!" And she said it so emphatically that Jack was stung.

But he never let personal hurts show.

"Mother, you're in a mess," he said. "Nobody has a perfect solution for you. And you have none at all for yourself. So listen to one from an old friend who loves you and don't stomp on it out of sheer spite."

"I'm sorry," she murmured, sipping the drink again. She let the tears flow unchecked, without really crying. Her face was motionless, but still the tears rolled down her cheeks, as if they had business of their own unrelated to her emotion.

"Tell me something," Jack said gently, putting an arm over

the back of her chair and leaning close to her. And as always with him, she didn't mind. She liked his nearness and the fact that he was male and strong and full off affection for her. Perhaps it was because she knew he would never demand of her what a normal man would; because she felt so safe with him and so able to trust him. "Tell me why you went to live with Beebo two years ago," he said.

"I thought I loved her."

"Why did you think you loved her?" he asked.

"Because she—well, she was so—I don't know, Jack. She excited me."

He lighted a cigarette with a sigh. "And that's love," he said. "Excitement. As long as you're excited you're in love. When it turns flat you're not in love. Lord, what a way to live."

Laura was taken aback by the selfishness she betrayed. "I didn't mean it that way," she said. It had never seemed so cheap to her before.

"Are you in love with Tris?" he asked.

"I—I—" She was afraid to answer now.

"Sure you are," he said. "Just like Beebo. Fascinating girl. More excitement. Beebo's worn out now, let's try Tris. And when we wear Tris out, let's find another—"

"Stop it!" Laura begged.

"Where's your life going, Laura?" he asked her. "What have you done with it so far? Does it matter a damn, really? To anybody but you . . . and me?"

"And Beebo."

"Beebo's more worried about where her next drink is com' ing from than she is about you." He knew it wasn't true. He knew if it ever came to a choice, Beebo loved Laura desper' ately enough to give up drinking. But Jack was fighting for Laura now.

Laura began to cry now, her face concealed behind her hands. "Please, Jack," she whispered, but he knew what he was doing. He had to make her see it his way so clearly, feel the hurt so hard, that she would turn away from the whole discouraging mess of homosexual life and come to live with him far from it all.

"Look at me, Laura," he said and lifted her face. "We can't think straight because we always think gay," he said. "We don't know anything about a love that lasts or a life that means something. We spend all our time on our knees singing hosannas to the queers. Trying to make ourselves look good. Trying to forget we aren't wholesome and healthy like other people."

"Some of the other people aren't so damn wholesome either," Laura said.

Jack put his arms around her suddenly and pulled her tight against him and said, "Let's get out of it, Laura. Let's run like hell while we have a chance. We could get away, just the two of us. But we can't do it alone; we need each other. We could move uptown and get a nice apartment and you wouldn't have to work. We could get married, honey."

"But—"

"Please, Laura, please," he begged her. "Maybe we could even . . . adopt a child. Would you like that? Would you?" He sounded a little breathless and he leaned back to see her face.

Laura was startled. "I don't know anything about kids. They scare me to death."

"You'd get over it in a hurry," he said. "You're female. You have instinct on your side."

"Do *you* like kids?"

"I love them."

"*I* don't. You're more female than I am," she said.

He laughed. "Flattery will get you nowhere," he said. "Seriously, Laura—would you like a child? A daughter?"

"Why not a son?" she asked him, sharp-eyed.

"Okay." He shrugged warily. "A son."

Laura slid back in her chair and looked at the ceiling. "I never even thought about it before," she said. "I just never dreamed I'd ever have anything to do with a child of my own . . . with *any* child."

"Do you want one?" He seemed so eager that she was reluctant to hurt him. But she couldn't lie to him.

"No," she said. And when his face hardened, she added, "Because I'd be a terrible mother, Jack. I'd be afraid of it. And jealous, I think. I'd be all thumbs. I'd stick it full of pins and never be sure if I did it on purpose or by mistake."

"You won't always feel that way," he said, and she knew from the tone of his voice that there was no arguing with him.

"Maybe not," she said. "But if I marry you, Jack—" And they were both startled to hear the words, as if neither had really expected Laura to consider it seriously. "If I marry you, I wouldn't dare adopt a child for years. Not till I was sure we were safe together and the marriage would last."

"It would. It will. Say yes."

"I can't," she said and drove him to his feet in a fit of temper.

"Goddam it, Laura, do you want to grow old here in the Village?" he said. "Have you seen the pitiful old women in their men's oxfords and chopped-off hair, stumping around like lost souls, wandering from bar to bar and staring at the pretty kids and weeping because they can't have them any more? Or living together, two of them, ugly and fat and wrinkled, with nothing to do and nothing to care about but the good old days that are no more? Is that what you want? Because if you stay here, that's what you'll get.

"Pretty soon you won't know any other way of life. You won't know how to live in the big world. You don't care a goddam about that world now when you're young. So when you're old you won't *know* a goddam about it. You'll be afraid of it and of normal people and you'll hide in a cheap walk-up with a dowdy old friend or a stinking cat and you'll yammer about lost loves. Tempting, huh?" And he leaned on the kitchen table, his eyes so bright with urgency that she couldn't look at them and only watched his mouth.

"Horrible," she said.

He straightened up and shoved his hands in his pockets, and when he started to speak again he was gazing out the window. "I want to get so far away from here," he said, "that—"

"That Terry will never find you again," she guessed.

He dropped his head a little. "Yes," he said. "That, too. Terry and Joe and Archie and John and God knows who. We'd go way uptown and leave no forwarding address . . . nothing. Just fade out of the Village forever. No Beebo, no Terry . . ."

"No Tris," Laura whispered.

"I told you, Mother . . . I'm no bluebeard. If you want affairs, have them. You're young, you need a few. Only keep them out of the Village and keep them very quiet."

"Do you think Terry would really come looking for you again?" she asked. "After the way you threw him out?"

"There aren't many men stupid enough to put up with his

antics as I did," he said. "I think he might try to put the touch on me between affairs."

"Damn him!" Laura cried indignantly.

"Yes, he might try to find me. And Beebo would pace the city looking for you. But let them. We'd be through with them forever."

And Laura felt a very queer unwelcome pang for Beebo, for all that wealth of misdirected love. Jack was standing behind her now, his hands on her shoulders. "Well?" he said quietly. "Will you marry me?"

"Could I—answer you in the morning?" she asked.

"What the hell will you do tonight?"

"See Tris."

"Oh. And if she's nice, it's no to old Jack. If she's bitchy, it's yes. Right?" He said it lightly but she knew he was hurt.

"Not quite," she said. "I want to test myself, I guess. Jack, for the first time I feel almost—almost like saying yes. But I want to see her first. Please let me."

"You don't need my permission, Mother."

"Maybe Beebo's found her already."

"Beebo's in bad shape. I lay odds she sleeps it off for a while. Even if she's found Tris she won't be in condition to do either of you much harm. Just call a cop and say she's molesting you."

Laura got up and turned to face him and they gazed at each other for some minutes in silence. "Okay, Mother," he said. "Go. And come back *mine*."

She smiled and then she walked past him to the door.

Tris was at home giving lessons when Laura got there. She had evening classes twice a week, for adults. She didn't slam the door in Laura's face, but she gave her a black look and directed her curtly to sit down and be quiet. Her delicate mouth was ever so slightly swollen.

Tris went back to work and danced with her pupils for another forty minutes without a word or a glance at Laura. It was lovely to watch. There were only two students—a man and a girl—and they were learning an intricate duet at Tris's direction. They would execute what looked to Laura like a perfect step and suddenly Tris would swoop down on them, shouting temperamental criticisms. She finally made the man dance with her, to give the girl the idea.

Laura watched her fascinated as she leaped into his arms, straight and smooth and beautifully sure of herself. And Laura realized slowly that only when she danced with the man did Tris look over at her to see her expression.

She's trying to make me jealous, Laura thought, and she was suddenly weary; weary of all the envy and ill feeling and violence. She wanted nothing more than to lie down quietly by Tris's side, when the couple had gone, and gently, without explanations or apologies, make love till they both fell asleep. She knew if it happened like that—naturally and easily and without pain—that she would stay with Tris. But she was afraid that even if it were bitter and unhappy, she would stay anyway.

And still, an angry core of resentment smoldered in her, resentment at Tris for having the effrontery to walk in on Laura and Beebo and cause the bitter outburst that had separated them. She was brooding about this when Tris suddenly dismissed her dancers.

The two went into her bedroom to change and Laura waited for Tris to speak to her. But Tris only glared, performing a few indolent turns until her students returned. Then she unexpectedly introduced them all. She was curt, almost unpleasant about it.

The young man smiled at Laura and said, "Never mind her, she's bad company tonight. Thanks, Tris." And he gave her a strange look and left, following the girl.

Tris shut the door after them and turned to Laura. "The girl is insufferable," she said. "She can't dance, and she is a vixen besides."

"The boy can dance," Laura said, not without a jealous twitch.

"Yes, he can. He can make love, too. And he does—when I don't have company."

She said it pointedly and Laura felt her whole face go a hot red. She stood up without speaking and made for the door, her head swimming, but Tris stopped her there by embracing her. Laura was in no mood for Tris's sudden turnabouts.

"God damn you, let me go," she exclaimed.

"Tonight, I am grateful for the company," Tris said. "He bores me."

"I've had all I can take from you, Tris. You split me and Beebo up tonight—"

"Ah, then I did you a favor, no?" and she smiled.

"You damn near got me killed!"

"She is not gentle, is she?" Tris said, releasing Laura to touch her bruised mouth, but she was still smiling a little.

"Gentle?" Laura exploded. "Beebo? Gentle like a tornado. Why did you do it, Tris? *Why?*"

Tris shrugged, walking away from her. "I felt like it. I don't know why. I wanted to see you. I wanted to see—well, I wondered what she was like . . . Beebo."

"You're incredible," Laura breathed, furious, watching her saunter suggestively toward her bedroom.

"Are you coming with me?" Tris asked.

And Laura felt her legs weaken and her heart jump, and she hated herself for it. "No," she said.

"Of course you are. That is why you are here. Come."

And Laura, helpless, went to her. Tris took her hands and led her, walking backwards herself, into the room and onto the low couch. She began to kiss her and Laura felt her fury rise and change into passion. Tris had never been so close to her, so tantalizing.

Somehow her anger made her passion sharper and wilder. She wanted to hurt Tris with it. Beebo believed they had made love, did she? Well, Laura would give truth to her fantasies.

Laura could feel Tris's body begin to respond. A surging feeling of triumph flashed through her. She felt the familiar, wonderful insanity come over her and she relinquished herself wholly to feeling. It took her a few moments to understand that Tris was fighting her. And suddenly she came to herself with a shock and felt Tris slip away from her and saw her standing a few feet from the bed.

Tris gave her a look—almost of pity—and then turned and raced from the room. By the time Laura reached the door, it was locked. At first she was stunned, motionless. And then she began to throw her weight against it. "Tris! Tris, let me out!" she cried in a panic.

"Stay where you are till you cool off," Tris said. Her voice was very near, just on the other side of the door, and Laura was wild to join her.

"Please, Tris!" she implored and her voice was low with coming tears. "Tris, don't do this to me!" Her whole body ached and after a moment more of futile beating on the door she slumped to the floor, moaning.

A long time later she dragged herself off the floor and back to the bed and lay there, sleepless, until early dawn. She was sick with the need to hurt and the need for love all scrambled inside her; she was imprisoned in her homosexuality and thinking . . . thinking hard of Jack.

The first daylight was coming in the window when Laura heard the door open and saw Tris glide across the floor toward her. Laura smothered a first harsh impulse to jump at her. Tris came on tiptoe, thinking Laura would be asleep, and when she saw Laura's blue eyes staring at her, she was startled.

Then she came and sat in silence on the edge of the bed and looked at Laura for a while, until Laura, who was restraining herself tightly, saw that Tris was crying. And the crying became suddenly audible and made Tris cover her face with her hands. Laura lay beside her, refusing to touch her, feeling her spite and misery soften a little, feeling even a shade of pity. She wanted to beat the girl and at the same time stroke her shaking shoulders.

Tris turned her back to Laura and finally spoke with considerable effort. "I'm going out on the Island tomorrow," she said. "For two weeks, a vacation. Come with me."

Laura stared at her back, frowning in disbelief. "What?" she said.

"I want you to come with me," Tris whispered. Her voice sounded, as once before, quite American.

"You must enjoy torturing me," Laura said.

There was a long pause while Tris snatched a piece of face tissue from a box by the bed and blew her nose. Finally she said, "It was torture for me, too. But still, it was inexcusable, what I did to you. I was a beast. I—I can't talk about it," and she gave a quick sob. "But I promise it will never happen again —if you promise never to mention it. Promise?" And she turned and looked at Laura.

"Why did you do it?" Laura asked.

"I had to! I *had* to! I wanted to hurt you—last night—you made me feel—" and her speech was clipped again and careful —"you made me want you so much, Laura. And I hate it! I *hate* it!" She was almost shrieking.

"Why?" Laura asked.

"Because I'm not really a Lesbian. Not like you. It's men I love, Laura. Really," she added desperately.

And Laura felt compassion for her. "You're sick, Tris," she

said, but she said it kindly.

"Sick?" And Tris went a strange ashy color that scared Laura. "How do you mean?"

Laura realized then that she couldn't destroy Tris's illusion without destroying Tris. She raised herself to one elbow and brushed away the tears on Tris's cheek. "Let's put it this way," she said. "If you feel like this about me, we shouldn't be together any more. In two weeks we'd drive each other wild. I know you feel terrible about last night, Tris, I can see it. I know I can't forget you, or forgive what you did. If we were living together, I'd want you and you'd hate me for it. And pretty soon I'd hate you too, for denying me."

"I won't deny you, Laura," Tris whispered, without looking at her. "I promise you. If you'd just let me do it my way. Don't let it be like last night. When I feel as if I'm losing control, it's as if I were drowning, as if I were losing my sanity along with my will. It's as if—if I let it happen—I—I'll lose my mind." She spoke so painfully, with such evident anxiety, that Laura was touched.

"Poor Tris," she murmured, and smoothed her hair. "I thought I'd be pulling your hair out this morning, not playing with it," she said, running her long fingers over the sleek black braid.

"Come with me," Tris pleaded. "Let me make it up to you."

"Where are you going? Fire Island?"

"God, no!" Tris flared. "*That* place! It's crawling with queers. I wouldn't go near it."

"Tris . . . ," Laura said, a little hesitantly. Her ear did not betray her. Tris's accent fluctuated strangely and roused her curiosity. She asked cautiously, "What part of India do you come from?"

"Why do you ask?" And Tris's eyes narrowed.

Laura lifted her shoulders casually. "You never told me."

"I said New Delhi."

"Oh, yes."

"Besides, it has nothing to do with the vacation. I'm going to a place on Long Island. Stone Harbor. It's not far from Montauk, on the north side. I have a cottage there for two weeks. It's very secluded. No one will bother us. I was there last year and it's really lovely. You'd like it, Laura, I know you would. You can swim every day—we're only two blocks from the beach and—"

"Tris?" Laura stopped the almost compulsive flow of speech

and startled the dancer.

"Yes?"

"Why won't you tell me about India?"

"You wouldn't be interested."

"I'd be fascinated. Everything about you fascinates me. For instance, what are you doing in this country?"

"Dancing."

"Where are your parents?"

"Dead."

"How did you get here?"

"Scholarship."

"Are you a citizen?"

"Laura, stop it! Why do you ask me such things? What has this to do with our vacation? I refuse to be quizzed like a criminal. We'll leave tomorrow at eight. Can you be packed by then? I've rented a car."

"I can't even get into my own apartment," Laura admitted. "You fixed me up just fine."

"Of course you can. Call the police." Her odd green eyes flashed.

"No. Maybe Jack could get my things. I'll call him."

"Who's Jack?"

"Jack? He's a—sort of—fiancé. A permanent fiancé." She smiled slightly.

Tris snorted. "Does he know you are gay?"

"Of course." She would tell her no more. If Tris were going to seal her private life behind a wall of secrets, Laura could play it that way, too. "Can I use your phone," she asked.

"Yes. In the kitchen." Tris followed her across the empty studio into the sunny blue and yellow kitchen and while Laura was dialing she asked, "You will come, of course?"

"I'll tell you in a minute," Laura said. ". . . Jack?"

"Good morning, Mother."

"Jack, I wonder if you could—if you'd mind going over to the apartment and getting my clothes. Do you think you could? I hate to ask you, but I don't dare go near her."

"Sure," he said. "Did you pass your test?"

"My test? Oh." She glanced at Tris. "I—I flunked," she said and felt a tidal wave of pity and shame all at once. "Jack —I'm sorry. Oh, I'm so sorry. Let me come over—"

"Come get your clothes at five," he said. "I'll leave the door open." And he hung up.

Laura surprised Tris by dropping into a chair and sobbing.

Tris sat down opposite her and waited in silence till she caught her breath, expecting an explanation. But Laura only dried her eyes and asked for some coffee.

Jack wasn't home when she went to pick up her clothes. She had known he wouldn't be there, and still it made her want to weep. She was in a blue mood, and even the sight of Tris, waiting for her outside at the wheel of a rented convertible, didn't cheer her up. She made several trips with the clothes, leaving most of her other possessions behind, and on the last trip she wrote him a note. It said, in part:

You're the only man I would ever marry, Jack. Maybe it will still work out. Tris wants me to spend two weeks with her on Long Island. I'll call you the minute I get back. I'm crazy about her, but she's a sick girl and I've had enough of wild scenes wtih sick lovers. I don't know what to expect so am leaving most of my things here. Hope they won't be too much in the way. I quit my job, by the way. Will find something else when I get back. Thank you so much for everything, Jack darling. Hope Beebo didn't give you any trouble. Don't start drinking, I'm not worth it. I love you. Laura.

The cabin had two bedrooms, a kitchen and a living room, and a bathroom. It was furnished à la 1935, full of sand and ants, but comfortable. The walk to the beach was short and just enough to get you pleasantly warm before you soaked in the salt water.

There were a lot of other vacationers living all around them —young couples with dozens of hollering kids, mostly. Laura watched them romping on the sand, the little ones screaming and giggling and pouring water on each other. She wondered if she could ever want a child.

She lay on the beach with Tris, the day after they arrived, and luxuriated in the sun. Tris had lathered herself lovingly with rich sun cream and was sitting under a huge beach umbrella that she had erected with the help of a young man they discovered while they looked for a place to lie down. He was not very subtle about his admiration, which he confined to Tris. And Laura was not very pleased to see her prance for him. But she said nothing.

"You'll burn to a crisp, Laura," Tris warned her.

"I put some stuff on," Laura said lazily, wiggling a little and feeling the hot rays toast the backs of her legs.

"Not enough for one so fair," Tris maintained. "Such fair

skin you have." And Laura heard the yearning in her voice.
"If mine were that light I would never expose it like you do.
I'd do everything to keep it as light as I could. Even bleach it.
They say buttermilk works wonders."

Laura looked up at her through eyes squinted against the
sun "Your skin is beautiful, Tris."

"Oh, not like yours," Tris said, embarrassed.

"How can you say that? You're the prettiest color I ever
saw."

"And you're a dirty hypocrite!" Tris snapped.

Laura started at her, dumbfounded, for some seconds, before she answered softly, "No, I mean it." She was afraid to
say more. "You think I only say it to flatter you, don't you?"
she asked finally. "I won't say it, then. I'd rather you turned
your temper on yourself than on me."

After an elaborately casual pause, full of much smoothing
lotion and gazing around, Tris said, "Do you really like my
color?" The little-girl pleading in her voice touched Laura.

"If I say yes, you call me a liar. If I say no you call me a
bigot."

"Say yes."

"Yes." And Laura smiled at her and Tris smiled back and
gave Laura the feeling of false but sweet security.

Tris said, "Did you ever notice, when we lie on the bed
together, how we look?"

Laura finished, "Yes, I noticed." She looked at Tris in surprise. It wasn't like her to mention such things. "Me so white
and you so brown. It looks like poetry, Tris. Like music, if
you could see music. Your body looks so warm and mine looks
so cool. And inside, we're just the other way around. Isn't it
funny? I'm the one who's always on fire. And you're the ice-
berg." She laughed a little. "Maybe I can melt you," she said.

"Better not. The brown comes off," Tris said cynically, but
her strange thought excited Laura.

"God, what a queer idea!" Laura said. "You'd have to
touch me everywhere then, every corner of me, till we were
both the same color. Then you'd be almost white and I'd be
almost tan—and yet we'd be the same." She looked at Tris
with her squinty eyes that sparkled in the glancing sun. And
Tris, struck herself by the strangeness of it, murmured, "I
never thought of it that way."

Laura hoped Tris would look at it that way for the rest
of the vacation.

JACK WALKED INTO his apartment at five-thirty in the afternoon, tired and thirsty but dolefully sober. He was a stubborn
man and he had dedicated all his resistance to fighting liquor.
He meant to head for the kitchen and consume a pint of
cider and fix himself some dinner. Since Laura had left five
days ago he had not had much appetite. He did not admit that
she would ever come back or that he had lost a battle. It was
only a temporary setback. But it rocked him a little and it
hurt him a lot.

He came wearily down the hall, stuck his key belligerently
into the lock and kicked his front door open. He dumped a
paper bag full of light bulbs, cigarettes, and Scotch tape on a
chair, switched on a light and started toward his kitchen. It
came as a distinct shock to find Laura sitting on his sofa.

He stared at her. She had her legs up, crossed, on the cocktail table, and her head back, gazing at the ceiling. She knew
he was there, of course; she heard him come in. She turned
and looked at him finally, and something in her face dispelled
his melancholy. He felt elated. But he checked it carefully.
He slipped his coat off without a word, dropped in on the
chair with his package, and walked over to her, standing in
front of her with his hands in his pockets.

"Run out of suntan lotion?" he said.

"No. But you're out of whiskey."

"I gave it to Beebo. Traded it for your clothes."

"Take the clothes back and get the whiskey."

"Later," he said, and smiled. Then he added, "Was it bad?"

"Very bad," Laura said and for a moment they both feared
she would start crying. But she didn't.

"Want to tell me?"

"Jack," she said with an ironic little smile. "You'll have to
write a book about me someday. I tell you everything."

He grinned. "I'll leave that to somebody else. But I'm saving
my notes, just in case." He sat down beside her. "Well, it
could only be one of three things, seeing that she's gay," he

said. "She's a whore."

"No."

"A junkie."

"No."

"—or she's married."

"She's married."

He lighted a cigarette with a long sigh, his eyes bright on her.

"How did you know?" she asked.

"I didn't. But it had to be something that would shock you. And you seem pretty damn nervous about the idea of gay people being married." He paused and she had to drop her glance. "Does she hate him?" he asked returning to Tris.

"Most of the time. God, Jack, I need a drink."

"Steady, Mother. My neighbor always has a supply. I'll fix you up." He came back in less than three minutes with a bottle of sparkling burgundy.

"Ugh!" Laura said. But she took it gratefully.

"Now," he said, settling down on the cocktail table with a cup of instant coffee, "begin at the beginning."

Laura rubbed her forehead and then sipped the prickly drink. "It started . . . beautifully," she said. "Like a dream. It was all hot sand and cool water and kisses. We held hands in the movie, we sat up till all hours in front of the fireplace with a bottle of Riesling and sang, and danced. We traded secrets and we made plans. We made a boat trip to the point—"

"Did you make love?"

"You just can't wait, can you?" she said, half teasing, half irritated.

"My future may depend on it," he said and shrugged.

There was a long reflective pause and finally Laura said, sadly, "Yes. We made love. Only once."

"And that was the end?"

"It wasn't that simple. You see, she—well, she flirted. She flirted with men until I thought I couldn't stand it. Till I wanted to flirt myself to get even, if only I weren't so damn awkward with men. She's not. She's a genius with them. She didn't give a damn if they were married to not. She had them all proposing to her.

"After the first couple of days it got intolerable. She had been making me sleep on one bed and she took the other. And after she turned the lights out she made a rule—no bed hopping."

"And you obeyed her little rule?"

"I had to, Jack," she defended herself. "We had a sort of agreement before we left the Village . . . It was supposed to be up to her to choose the time and place."

"That's the lousiest agreement *you* ever made, Mother," he commented.

"No. She's sick, you see. Really. She thinks she's straight. And if you hint she's not, she gets terrified. Almost hysterical She can't accept it."

"Why do you always fall for these well adjusted ladies?" he asked.

"Beth was well adjusted."

"Beth is dead. As far as you're concerned." Laura glared at him while he smiled slightly, lighting another cigarette from the one he was finishing. "So Tris is a queer queer," he said. "And she flirts wtih the opposite sex. Very subversive. So what came next?"

"Well, they followed us home—"

"Who?"

"Men!" she flashed peevishly. "They followed us at the beach, in the bars, in the stores. They followed *Tris*, I should say. I was cold as hell with him. I tried to keep quiet about it, but after three days of it I blew up. We had a miserable quar-rel, and I was ready to pack up and leave right then. But she relented suddenly. I don't know why. I think she really likes me, Jack. Anyway, she got drunk. Just enough so that she wouldn't have to watch what I did to her. . . or hear what I said to her . . . or care too much . . ."

"That's pretty drunk," Jack said. He knew from the way she spoke that it had hurt her to make love like that, wanting so much herself, and herself so unwanted. "I know, Laura honey, I know the feeling," he said and the words comforted her.

"Jack, I hope I always love you this much," she said softly.

He looked up from his coffee cup with a little smile. "So do I," he said. And they looked at each other without speaking for a minute before she went on.

"Well," she said, "it was torture. I didn't want it any more than she did, if it had to be so cold and sad, and at the same time I *had* to have her. I was on fire for her. I have to give her credit, Jack, she tried. But it didn't mean anything to her."

"It's a lonesome job," Jack said. "And it's never worth it."

"I cried all night," Laura said. "Afterwards . . . I just got in my own bed and cried. And she was awake all night too, but she didn't come to me or try to comfort me. I think she was embarrassed. I think she just wished she'd never gotten mixed up with me.

"The next night—around dinner time—her husband arrived. I don't know whether she got sick of me or just scared and called him, or if they got their dates scrambled and he came too soon. You see, it turned out she had planned to meet him out there all along, after I left. But maybe I got to be too much for her and she told him to come and chase me out . . . I don't know. There wasn't time to go into the fine points. But I think myself she needed a man just then, to make herself feel normal. And protected."

"What was he like?"

"A nice guy. He really is. I know I sound—Tris would say —hypocritical. But I liked him. I understood right away, the minute I saw him, an awful lot of things about Tris."

"How?"

Laura paused, gazing seriously at Jack. At last she explained, "He's a Negro. And so is she. Only he's much darker than Tris. Very handsome, but he'd never pass as an Indian. And right away he humiliated her, without meaning to." She smiled sadly. "She's from New York, Jack. She was born right here and her name is Patsy Robinson. She's only seventeen but they've been married two years. She makes him keep out of sight because she thinks he'd be a drag on her career. That's why she tells everybody she's Indian, too—because she wants to get ahead and she thinks it makes it easier."

Jack shook his head. "I feel for her," he said.

"And I weep for her," Laura said. "You should have seen her, Jack. She was wild when Milo talked about her fake Indian past. I think it made him pretty damn mad. That, and all the flirting, and having to live apart. And her gay and him straight! Lord, what a mess. He's in love with her; she's his wife. And she denies him, and hides him."

Laura stopped talking then for a little while, sipping the burgundy and staring at her feet. "I took the bus back," she said at last. "She screamed at me to leave. Milo apologized for her. That poor guy."

"Do you still think you love her?" Jack asked.

"I don't know." She sighed. "She fascinates me. I feel sick about it, about the way things happened. If I thought I could stand it I'd go back to her. But I know I couldn't. What is love, anyway, Jack?"

" 'If you have to ask you never get to know,' " he quoted. "More?" He reached for her glass and she relinquished it with an unsteady hand. She felt completely lost, completely frustrated.

"What's Beebo doing?" she asked.

He picked up the bottle and poured some more wine into her glass. "All kinds of things," he said. "She got fired, of course. Hadn't showed up for weeks."

"Of course," Laura repeated, bowing her head.

"She's shacking up with Lili at the moment."

"Ohhh," Laura groaned, and it made her feel dismal to think of it. She felt a spasm of possessiveness for Beebo. "Lili is a terrible influence on her," she said irritably.

"So are you." He handed her her drink. "The worst."

"Not *that* bad."

"Life with you," he reminded her, "damn near killed the girl."

"And me," Laura replied. "Did she leave the apartment?"

"No, she gets over there from time to time."

"I wonder how she pays the rent."

"It isn't due yet," he said. "Besides, I imagine Lili can help out."

Laura shut her eyes suddenly, overwhelmed wtih a maddening tenderness for Beebo. "I hate her!" she said emphatically to Jack. And he, with his uncanny ear for emotion, didn't like the emphasis.

After a slight pause he said, "I got her a dog. Another dachshund pup."

"That was nice of you," she said to him in the tone mothers use when someone has done a kindly favor for their children.

"Beebo didn't think so. She didn't know whether to kiss it or throw it at me," he said. "She finally kissed it. But the poor thing died two days later . . . yesterday, it was."

"It died?"

"Yes." He looked at her sharply. "I think she . . . shall we say—put it to sleep?"

"Oh, Jack!" she breathed, shocked. "Why? Did it remind

her of Nix?"

"I don't know. It didn't cheer her up, that's for damn sure."

Laura sat there for a while, letting him fill her glass a couple of times and listening to the FM radio and trying not to feel sorry for Beebo. "She doesn't really need me any more, Jack," she told him.

"I do," he said, and she smiled.

"You didn't fall off the wagon," she said. "I'm so glad. I was afraid you might."

"I never get drunk over the women in my life," he said sardonically. "Only over the boys. And there are no more boys in my life. Now or ever."

Laura swirled the royal purple liquid in her long-stemmed glass and whispered into it, "Do you think I could make you happy, Jack?"

"Are you proposing, Mother?"

She swallowed and looked up at him with butterflies in her stomach. "Yes," she said.

He sat quite still and smiled slowly at her. And then he got up and came to her and kissed her cheeks, one after the other, holding her head tenderly in his hands.

"I accept," he said.

The day was hot and muggy, one of those insufferably humid August days in New York. Laura and Jack waited together outside the office of Judge Sterling Webster with half a dozen other sweating, hand-clasping couples.

Jack wasted no time when Laura said yes. As fast as arrangements could be made, they were made. Laura stayed with him in the Village apartment a few days while they hunted for another apartment, cooking for him and getting the feel of living with him. During the days, when he was out, she went uptown. This was Jack's idea. He had no intention of making his bride a sitting duck for Beebo. It was only for four days, anyway, and much to Laura's surprise, Beebo made no attempt to reach her.

They had found the apartment on the east side two days after Laura got back from the disillusioning sojourn with Tris. It was too expensive, but it was newly renovated, lustrous with new paint, elegant with a new elevator, and bursting with chic tenants.

"We can't afford it," was Laura's first comment, to which

Jack replied, smiling, "You're beginning to sound like a wife already."

And now, here they were, waiting on yellow oak chairs in the hall, while one couple after another passed in and out of the judge's office wtih the classic stars in their eyes.

Laura, who was sitting quietly in her chair, said, "They all look so happy," and drew courage from the fact.

"They're scared witless," Jack said, pacing up and down in front of her.

"Jack!" Laura exclaimed, appalled. "They'll hear you."

"Ours will be a happier marriage than any of these," he said with a contemptuous wave of his hand. He sat down suddenly beside her. "Ours could be damn near perfect, Laura, if we work at it a little. You know that? We won't have to face the usual pitfalls. Ours will be different . . . better."

"I hope so, Jack," she said in a near whisper, and a little thrill of passionate hope went through her.

"Will you try, honey?" he asked.

"I will. With all my heart I will." She gave him a tremulous smile. "I want this to work, Jack, as much as you do. I'll give it all I've got. I want terribly for it to be right." And she meant it.

"Then it will," he said and his smile gave her a needed shot of confidence.

Laura had had some bad nights since she said yes to him. Awful hours of yearning for Tris had tormented her. Stray unwelcome thoughts of Beebo had hurt her even more.

There were the lonely times when she thought about her-self and Jack, so different, so dear to each other, and won-dered if marital intimacy might not ruin it all with its inno-cent vulgarity. She tried to imagine Jack shaving in the morn-ing . . . the toilet flushing . . . his wrinkled pajamas, still warm from sleep, tossed on the floor . . . his naked loneli-ness mutely reproaching her. The idea of living with a man . . . a *man* . . . made her think of her father, her huge heavy domineering father, with his aggressive maleness stamped all over his body.

But for the most part, Laura tried not to think at all. She let Jack do her thinking. She let Jack make the plans. She let Jack take her by the hand and lead her where he deemed it best for her to go. And, trusting him, she went.

So here they were outside Judge Sterling Webster's door

with its glass window and neatly stenciled name, and they were next in line. Their predecessors in the marriage mill were slower than the rest, or so it seemed. And by the time they came out Jack was very nervous.

He herded her in ahead of him, and Judge Webster, as dignified and antique as his name, stood to greet them with an extended hand.

In less than five minutes he pronounced them man and wife and they signed the certificate of marriage. Jack turned to Laura and kissed his tall and trembling young wife on her cheek. He gave the Judge ten dollars, and then he took Laura's arm and steered her out again to let the next impatient couple take over.

Laura had to sit down for a minute on one of the limed oak chairs and cover her face with her hands. Jack leaned over her and said, "You're setting a lousy example, Mother. Every female here is watching you and figuring me for a wife-beater. Come on, Mrs. Mann."

She looked up and saw him grinning at her, and it gave her a lift. She grasped his hand and let him pull her to her feet. He was beaming, and Laura had to smile at all the nervous cynicism of half an hour ago.

They went straight to the apartment to rest for a while before they went out to dinner. Jack had made reservations for them at the Stork Club.

"We'll have a proper honeymoon at Christmastime," he said, when they reached the house on East Fifty-third. "I'll take a month off then. I have it coming."

Ignoring Laura's protests, he insisted on carrying her across the threshold. He swung her up easily, to their mutual pleasure.

"Jack, I think you're the world's worst sentimentalist," she teased him when he set her down, but he denied it at once.

"God forbid!" he said. "I just don't want anything to go wrong. We're going to do it all right, right from the start."

"And you're superstitious."

He laughed with delight. "Laura," he said and came to take her hands. "I'm so happy. You've made me so happy."

"I haven't done a thing, yet," she said, wondering a little at him, at his uncontainable good spirits.

"You've married me. That's something," he said. "I'm a married man. God Almighty, think of it!"

"If you were any prouder you'd explode," she giggled.

"I just may," he said. And they gazed at each other with a huge, wordless approval and relief.

"This calls for a celebration," he said suddenly. "I got a little something—"

"Oh, Jack, no drinking," she said. "I don't have to have a drink, really. I don't want you to get started."

"No nagging on our wedding day," he said and produced a bottle of champagne from the refrigerator. He poured her a glassful and himself a swallow. "Medicinal," he explained, and they toasted each other. He made her drink all of hers and kept pace with her with ginger ale. "I feel so good, by God, I don't even need it," he said, and laughed.

Laura watched him affectionately. She had never seen him so animated, so happy. He glowed with it. He was almost handsome, with his brilliant eyes and his proud smile. It made her feel a little like crying, and she stopped him in the middle of a delirious tirade of compliments to say, "Jack, please. You embarrass me. I'm afraid I won't live up to it all."

"Oh, but you will. I'll beat you if you don't," he said, laughing, and kissed her cheek. And she caught his hands and kissed them.

"You'd think we were a couple of normal people," she said.

He sobered a little, sitting down on the floor in front of her. "They have no monopoly on happiness, Mother. We have a right to our share. We have a chance now. We can make something beautiful of it together." He stopped and chuckled at himself. "I sound like a bad poem," he said. "But I mean it. I have so many wonderful plans, so many hopes." And the thought of that bright-eyed little girl he had cherished for so long danced into his head.

Laura couldn't look at his face. She got up and went to lie on her bed.

They stayed up very late and Laura had too much champagne and Jack had too much ginger ale, and they talked endlessly and held one another's hands tightly. And the next day they slept until four in the afternoon and got up smiling to treat Laura's hangover and make the beds and shop for groceries together. And Jack introduced her to the butcher with, "Meet my wife. She's a doll."

Laura blushed crimson and the butcher laughed at them and tried to sell them some oysters. "You want kids? Buy oysters," he advised. "Never fails. I know, I got eight."

It was smooth and sweet the first few months; smoother than either of them had dared to hope. Laura was naturally mild and yielding; Jack, efficient and good-humored and terribly proud of her. As soon as they had enough chairs and crates collected to seat a fair number of guests, they threw a party and Jack's office staff came to wish them well.

None of them knew he was a homosexual. Jack was a past master at deception. "You have to be if you're going to survive in the world," he said to her once. "It's either that or retire into a rotten little prison with the rest of the gay people and spend your life feeling sorry for yourself. No thanks, not for me. Sex rules my nights. But by God, as far as the world knows, I'm a normal man from dawn to dusk. And there isn't one guy in that office who'd question it."

She admired him for it. Her own vagrant sensuality had dominated her ever since the fatal day she first recognized it, and her efforts to hide it or deny it had always backfired sooner or later. Jack filled her with determination to make herself a part of what he called "the real world," the *straight* world. He made it seem very desirable to her for the first time.

Jack's office buddies brought their wives, except for two dauntless bachelors who spent the evening berating Jack for treason.

"Are they gay?" Laura asked him in a whisper. "The unmarried ones?"

"Not gay, just scared," he said. "Winslow is, though. That one over there with the gorgeous wife. Poor guy, I don't think he knows it. They aren't very happy." And he nodded at the suave young man in his early thirties with a stunning and rather bored young woman beside him. Laura looked at the girl without a trace of desire and felt a quiet little spark of triumph. The future looked bright if she could be around so lovely a woman without even a hungry glance.

The autumn months passed uneventfully, and they got used to each other, and most of their worst fears abated. Jack never wandered around the apartment naked, out of instinctive respect for Laura. He did drop his socks all over the floor and leave his dresser drawers open. But he never lost his temper. He took her out to dinner once or twice a week, and he brought her flowers and books and pretty things that caught his eye in the windows of the stores he passed.

And he loved her. It sustained Laura through her low hours

of doubt and confusion. She was the weak one of the two, and they both knew it. There were times when Jack had to be strong enough for both of them; times when Laura would cling to him weeping and tell him it was all a horrible mistake and she couldn't live without Tris, no matter how godawful it would be.

And then he didn't argue with her. He only said, "If you have to go, go, but come back. I want you here tonight at dinner time. I want you here in the morning when I get up. There'll be women in your life, I'm prepared for that, honey. Tris won't be the last. But there's only one man, and there will only be one man and don't you ever forget it."

He sounded so sensible and firm to her that her unrest would disappear. Now and then, when she was not in a passion for Tris, they talked about it. And she would say, "I know it'll happen one of these days, but I won't let it hurt us, Jack. When I can think about it like this, rationally and without fear, I know I can handle it. I won't panic when the time comes. I'll just accept it as quietly as I can. I won't let it touch our marriage."

"Good girl," he said and squeezed her arm.

There was no sex between them. Neither of them wanted it, and that was the way they planned it. Jack would make her take his arm when they went anywhere because he was proud of her. And he gave her a friendly peck when he left in the morning and when he came back at night. When she was frightened or depressed he held her and stroked her hair and talked to her the way she had always prayed her father would. And he liked to lie with his head in her lap and have her read to him before they went to bed.

But that was the limit of their physical contact. It was affectionate and gentle but utterly sexless. After the first few weeks, Laura began to like it. She had been shy at first and reluctant. But he didn't force her, and after a while she welcomed his little gestures of love. They spelled security and reassurance to her. Suddenly it occurred to her that Jack was a man who was taking care of his woman. And she relaxed. She felt her nerves ease and her tension relax. The apartment was quiet and pretty, and Laura, who was lazy as a cat for the first time in her life, felt like a princess.

They felt a mutual gratitude toward each other. Jack came home for the first time in his life to a warm kitchen and a

charming young wife. And just the thought of Laura reminded him, with a deep fine thrill, that he was married; he
was truly a man. It was worth a lifetime of homosexual
adventures.

Laura went to pains to please him, to show him that she
cared and that she was working to make things right as she
had promised him. And they were, all things considered,
happy.

It wasn't until Terry's letter came, forwarded from Jack's
old address in the Village, that Laura felt even the slightest
apprehension that anything was to go wrong. And the note
was postmarked San Francisco and seemed so far away that
she recovered promptly from the first shock and sat in the
kitchen with the rest of the mail on the table in front of her,
wondering what to do.

Laura and Jack had made a strict rule never to open each
other's mail and never to ask prying questions. But Laura
hated to think of the turn it would give Jack to have this
ghost from his past rise up to haunt him.

She turned and looked out the window at the sparse snow,
falling that first day of December, and played with Terry's
letter, letting it slip from corner to corner through her fingers.
She burned with curiosity.

I could just steam it open, she mused. *He'd never know the
difference. Damn that Terry anyway! Who does he think he
is! After the hell he put Jack through, he has a lot of nerve.
I'll bet he wants some money.*

She could bear it no longer. She got up and went to the
stove, where she had a kettle full of hot water left over from
breakfast, and turned the heat on under it. The glued flap of
the envelope surrendered to the steam in a quiet curl. Laura
held the letter a moment longer before opening it, feeling very
guilty. But she loved Jack and she felt a fierce desire to spare
him more pain. Besides, her curiosity was smothering her. She
rationalized that Jack had told her himself he had given up
the gay life forever, and that included Terry. What if this
set him to drinking again?

She sat down and pulled the letter out with nervous hands.
It was rather a short note, folded twice, and she opened it
and read it quickly. It was not dated.

"Dear Jack. Have been out here in S.F. since September.

What a crazy town. You'd love it. Have a nice apartment on Telegraph Hill with a kid I met at a party a
month ago. (Not the same one you beat up the night you
kicked me out.)"

*God! He just has to rub it in. He's just the kind of guy to
mention such a thing,* Laura thought, hot with indignation.

"Don't know how long I'll be out here. I sort of miss
the Village. And you. Why don't you come out for a
visit? We've got lots of room."

He doesn't seem to realize it would damn near kill Jack,
Laura thought. *He's hopeless. It never occurs to him that Jack
would go crazy in a situation like that. Or does it?*

Laura was used to the idea of Terry as a good-natured
scatterbrained boy who hurt people, mostly Jack, with monotonous regularity—largely because he didn't think about what
he was doing. Usually, this was true enough. But the rest of
his letter made her wonder if he weren't deliberately needling
Jack, trying to get him to come out to the coast.

She continued to read the tidy blue ink script.

"I do miss you, lover. I was always so unsettled before
we met."

Before, after, and during, Laura fumed.

"And now it's worse than before. I used to feel so safe
and comfortable with you, like you'd always watch out
for me, no matter what. I guess that's a selfish way to
look at it, but I wish we were back together. If you by
any chance want it that way too, write to me. Write to
me anyway, I really want to hear from you. Love, Terry."

He signed his name with an elaborate flourish, like a fifth-
grade child drunk on the possibilities of fancy penmanship.

Laura folded the letter and stuck it back in the envelope
and wrote a brief sizzling note in answer. She said:

"Terry—Jack and I are married. You are not welcome
here, now or ever. Jack asked me to write and tell you
that he does not want to be bothered with any more
letters from you and he will not answer any if you do
write. Please leave us alone. Laura."

It sounded sharp and cold, and she had a momentary feeling of misgiving. Terry was a nice kid, in spite of it all. Everybody liked him, even Laura. But she couldn't risk having him
torment Jack. It had to sound mean or he wouldn't believe it.
She put the note in an envelope, sealed and stamped it, and

copied his San Francisco address on it. Then she burned Terry's letter over the stove.

When Jack came home that evening Laura's note was in the mail and Terry's was in ashes in the wastebasket.

"Any mail?" he asked her.

"Just a bill from the laundry," she said.

But it bothered her. It came to her at odd moments and it seemed ominous and frightening to her, like the first sign of a break-up. She had broken her promise to him, and it didn't help much to tell herself she did it only to protect him. *I'm not going to let anybody hurt what we've got, least of all Terry Fleming,* she thought.

The thought of having it all end between her and Jack, suddenly and cruelly, in one big drunk on Jack's part or wild romance on hers, scared and depressed her. It mustn't end that way. They needed each other too much. Their marriage had helped them think of each other as normal. They felt as if they knew where they were going now and life was much better.

Laura missed women. She missed them desperately sometimes. But she was sure now, deep within herself, that the time would come when she and Jack would be secure with each other for the rest of their lives; when they would be able to trust each other without reservation and trust the strength of their union. When they reached that point, it would be safe to satisfy her desires.

As for Jack, he was through with men forever. He had said it and she believed him. The thought that he might take a lover himself some day never occurred to her. It just wouldn't happen. Nor had she asked him about Terry. Jack was so determinedly happy with her that she was afraid to mention Terry.

It seemed strange to Laura, however, that Beebo didn't try to find her. She might have found them, one way or another. But there was no word from her. Laura couldn't help wanting to know what she was doing. She didn't feel the old, urgent, painful need for Tris, but there was a persistent want that was strong enough to make her wince now and then.

Jack told her once, "If anything bothers you, tell me about it. Don't sit around letting it eat you up. Better to talk about it and get it out of your system."

And when he saw that she was pensive he made her talk.

But when he didn't see it, she kept it to herself. There were times when Laura couldn't share her feelings, when she just hugged them to herself and brooded.

Several times she had nearly talked herself into going down to the Village to wander around. She wouldn't go near her old apartment. Or Tris's studio. Or even Lili's apartment. She wasn't a fool, she wouldn't risk being caught.

But she was tempted, sometimes almost hypnotized, by the idea.

8

It was Christmas Eve. They had a fine big tree, freshly green in a sea of lights and tinsel. No honeymoon, as they had hoped; the office couldn't spare Jack. So they had a party instead.

"I hate those damn pink trees," Jack had said when they picked theirs out. "Or gold, or white, or whatever-the-hell color they're making them this year. Give me a nice healthy green."

They celebrated at the party and Jack drank eggnog without whiskey and Laura was very pleased with him. There was a lovely girl there—unmarried and probably gay. Laura flirted with her in spite of herself.

Jack teased her about it when they met briefly in the kitchen—he to make drinks and she to get more hors d'oeuvres from the refrigerator. "Looks like you got a live one," he said.

Laura blushed. "Was I too obvious?" she asked, scared.

"No," he said. "I just have X-ray eyes, remember?"

"I shouldn't—"

"Oh, hell," he said with a good-natured wave of his hand. "Flirt, it's good for you. Just don't elope with her." He gave her a grin and went out, holding five highballs precariously. She felt a flush of love for him, watching him.

It was three a.m. Christmas day before they got rid of everybody. Laura threw herself in their expensive new sofa and surveyed the wreckage with a sigh.

"I'm not even going to pick it up," she said. "I'm not going to touch a thing till morning."

"That's the spirit," Jack said. He fixed them both a cup of coffee, settled down beside her in the rainbow glow of the Christmas tree and took her hand with a sigh of satisfaction.

"That's the first goddam Christmas tree I ever had," he said. And when she laughed he protested solemnly, "Honest. And this is the first Christmas that ever meant anything to me." He turned his head, resting against the back of the sofa, and smiled at her . . .

"You shouldn't swear at Christmas," Laura told him.

He gazed at her for a while and then asked, "Are you in love with Kristi? Wasn't that her name?"

"Yes, it was her name. No, I'm not in love. With anybody."

"Me?"

"Oh, you. That's different."

She smiled a little and sipped her coffee, and then she leaned back on the sofa beside him, absorbed in the soft sparkle of the tree.

Jack was still watching her. "Laura?" he said in an exploratory voice.

"Hm?"

"What would you think of adopting a child?"

She stared at a golden pine cone, her face suddenly a cautious blank. "I don't know," she said.

"Have you ever thought about it?"

"A little."

"What did you think?"

"I told you. Kids scare me."

He bit his underlip, frowning. "I want one," he said at last. "Would you be willing to—*have* one?"

"You mean—" She swallowed. "—get pregnant?"

"Yes," he said, smiling at her outraged face. "Oh, don't worry, Mother. We'd do it the easy way."

"There is no easy way!" she fired at him. "What way?"

He took a long drag on his cigarette and answered, "Artificial insemination." She gasped, but he went on quickly, "Now before you get your dander up let me explain. I've thought it all out. Either we could adopt one, or—and this would be much better—we could *have* one. Our own. We can tell the Doc we've had trouble and let him try the insemination. There's nothing to it, it doesn't take five minutes. It doesn't hurt. And if it worked . . . God! Our own kid. You wouldn't be afraid of your own, honey."

There was a long pause while Laura sweated in silent alarm. Why did he bring it up tonight? Why? When they were so contented and pleased with each other, and the world was such a place of glittering enchantment.

"Couldn't we wait and talk about it later?" she asked.

"Why not now?"

"Couldn't I have time to think about it?"

"Sure. Think," he said and she knew he meant, *I'll give you five minutes to make up your mind.*

"Jack, why do we have to do it right now? Why can't we wait? We've only been married five months."

"I can't wait very long, Mother," he said. "I'm forty-five. I don't want to be an old man on crutches when my kid is growing up."

"Maybe in the spring," she said. The idea of becoming a mother terrified her. She had visions of herself hurting the baby, doing everything wrong; visions of her old passion coming on her and shaming them all; selfish thoughts of her beautiful, new, leisurely laziness being ruined.

"What would I ever tell any child of mine if it caught me— with a woman?" she said awkwardly.

"Tell it for Chrissake to knock before entering a room," he said, and something in his voice and manner told her that he had set his heart on this long ago.

"Would you *insist* on having a baby, Jack?" she asked him defiantly.

He was looking at the ceiling and he expelled a cloud of blue smoke at it and answered softly, "I want you to be happy, Laura. This marriage is for both of us."

There was a long silence. "I think I would hate myself if I ever got pregnant," she said, ashamed of her vanity but clinging to it stubbornly. "God, how awful. All those aches and pains and months of looking like hell, and for what? What if the baby weren't normal? What if I couldn't be a good mother to it."

He shrugged and then he said, "All right. We'll adopt one. That way at least we can be sure of getting a girl."

Laura wrung her hands together in a nervous frenzy. The last thing she wanted to do was hurt Jack. And yet she could feel the dogged one-mindedness in him, feel his enormous desire.

"A man needs a child," he said softly. "So does a woman. That's the whole reason for life. There is no other." And he glanced up at her and all the Christmas lights reflected on the lenses of his glasses. "We can't live our lives just for ourselves," he said. "Or we live them for nothing. We die, monuments to selfishness . . . I want a child, Laura."

"Is that why you married me?" she asked with sudden sharpness, feeling as if he had cornered her.

"I married you because I love you," he said.

"Then why do you keep badgering me about a child?" she demanded.

"This is the first time I've mentioned it since we got married," he reminded her gently.

"You act as if just because *you* want one it's all settled," she said, and surprised herself by bursting into tears. He took her in his arms, abandoning his cigarette, and said, "No, honey, nothing's settled. But think about it, Laura. Think hard."

They sat that way, hugging each other and watching the Christmas tree, letting the cigarette slowly burn itself out, and they didn't mention it again. But from that moment on it was very big between them, unspoken but felt.

Jack did not mention a child to her again for a while. But as the weeks slipped by Laura began to feel a growing dissatisfaction. She didn't know where it came from or what it meant. At home, in the apartment, it was shapeless. Outside it took the shape of girls. When she went out for groceries or to shop or to have dinner with Jack, she found herself looking around hopefully, gazing a little too boldly, desiring. Jack saw it too before long, but he said nothing.

Laura felt selfish, and she didn't like the feeling. She blamed it on Jack. It made her want to get away from him for a bit. And soon the wish crystallized in her mind to a desire for the Village, and began to haunt her.

She knew she ought to tell Jack she wanted to go. He would never stand in her way, as long as she was there at night to cook his meals and be a fond companion to him. As long as she let him in on it and kept it clean.

But she was embarrassed. She didn't want to tell him and see his disappointment and know she was so much weaker than he. So she kept it secret and let it fester inside her until it had grown, by March, to a great, irritating problem.

Then, one fine, sunny morning in the first week of spring, the phone rang.

It'll be Ginny Winston, she thought. *One of their neighbors. She'll want to go shopping again. I guess we might as well, it'll keep me out of trouble.* Ginny was thirty-five, a widow, a nice girl but hopelessly man-happy.

Laura grabbed the receiver after the fourth ring. "Hello?" she said.

"Laura? How are you?"

"Fine, thanks. Who's this?"

"Terry."

"Terry who?" She gasped suddenly. "Terry! Terry Fleming?"

"Yes." He chuckled. "Guess how I found you?"

She hung up. She just slammed the phone down in place and stood there shaking. Then she sat down and cried, waiting for the thing to start ringing again. She had no doubt it would.

It did. She picked it up again, and before he could say anything she told him, "I don't care how you found us. I don't want you around here. Don't you come near this place Terry, or I'll—I don't know what I'll do. You can't, you mustn't. Do you hear me?"

"Yes," he said, astonished. "What's the matter?"

"Didn't you get my letter?" she asked him.

"Sure. You're married. Congratulations, I always thought it'd happen. You got a great guy there, Laur. I wish I had him." And he laughed pleasantly.

"Terry, you're incredible," she said. "I don't want you to come near Jack. That's final."

"Go on," he laughed. "I thought I'd come over this afternoon."

"You can't!" She felt as she did in nightmares when she tried to talk and no one could hear her. She felt as if all her words fell on deaf ears.

"Sure I can. I thought we'd—"

"Look, Terry, I'm not going to tell him you're in town," she said, fighting a nerve-rasping frustration with him. "I'm just going to let it go, and I'm telling you right now that if you show up over here it'll hurt him more than he can stand. You broke his heart and that should be enough for you. You won't get any more of him!" She felt fiercely protective and loving, now that their life together seemed threatened. She would fight Terry every way she knew. And yet she had to admit to herself that Terry had more to fight with than she if it ever came to a showdown. That was why it was so important to keep him away.

Jack was a very sensual man and he had been deeply in love with Terry. He still was, in spite of everything. His love for Laura was different; strong, she was sure, but could it stand up to a sudden white-hot blast of passion?

"You sound real bitter, Laura," Terry said reproachfully, "I thought you were sort of kidding in your letter."

"I've never been more serious, Terry. Stay away from us!" She hung up again. When she took her hand away there was a ring of wet on the black handle. She cried all day, feeling angry and helpless.

Jack got home at five, but she told him nothing. She was gentle and solicitous with him in a way he had missed for a couple of months. She read to him and she chatted with him, and underneath it all was a tremulous fear of disaster that made her feel a great tenderness for him. He seemed vulnerable to her. If she betrayed him she would embitter him more than she was able to imagine. The thought was terrifying.

"Mother, you need a change," he said when they had fin-ished dinner.

"I do?"

"Leave the dishes and scram."

She felt a little spark of fear. "Are you kicking me out?" she asked.

"I sure as hell am, you doll," he said. "Get thee hence."

"Where?" His laughter relieved her.

"The Village. Where else?" And when she stared at him, wordless, he added, "You need it, honey. You're nervous as a cat. Go on, have a ball."

"You're kidding!"

"I'll give you three minutes to get out of here," he said with a glance at his watch.

Laura hesitated for a few seconds until he looked at her over the top of the paper again and then she ran, heels ringing staccato on the polished wood floor of the hall, and got her coat and purse. On the way out she stooped to kiss his cheek.

"Jack, I adore you," she whispered, to which he only smiled. At the door she turned and said, "I'll be home early."

"No curfew," he said solemnly.

Laura went first to the Cellar, a favorite hangout in Green-wich Village. The tourists had begun to stop there by this time, but the gay crowd outnumbered them still and it wasn't pri-marily a trap. The prices were reasonable and the decor smoky.

Laura settled at the bar with a sigh of sheer pleasure. All she wanted to do was sit there quietly and look at them . . . those lovely girls, dozens of them, with ripe lips and rounded hips in tight pants or smooth skirts. And the big ones, the butches, who acted like men and expected to be treated as such. They were the ones who excited Laura the most, when it came right down to it. Women, women . . . she loved them all, especially the big girls with the firm strides and the cigarettes in their mouths. . . . She realized with chagrin that she was thinking of Beebo.

God, what if she's here? she thought with a wonderful scare running up her spine. She looked around, but Beebo was nowhere in sight.

I wonder if she has a job, poor darling. I wonder if Lili's still supporting her. I wonder if she's still drinking so much . . . if she thinks of me at all . . . Oh, what's the matter, with me? What do I care? She nearly drove me crazy!

She thought of Tris suddenly, of that marvelous fragrant tan skin. In fact she indulged in an orgy of suggestive thoughts that would have driven her crazy cooped up at home. But here, surrounded with people who felt and thought much as she did, it was all right. It was safe somehow. She could even spend the evening flirting with somebody, if anybody caught her eye, and it would come to no harm. Just a night's outing. Nothing more.

Tris . . . Tris . . . she would never show up in a place like this. She'd shun it like the plague. All the same it would be nice. So nice.

But the harder Laura concentrated on Tris the more insistently Beebo obsessed her. Laura shrugged her off and ordered another drink. She laughed a little to herself and said, *But I don't love her at all any more.* And she turned to talk to the girl beside her.

The girl was very charming: small and curly-headed and pretty, and she laughed a lot. And soon Laura was laughing with her and learned that Inga was her name. But that face, that damned face of Beebo's, strong and handsome and hard with too much living, kept looking at her through the haze of Inga's cigarette.

"Did you ever have somebody plague your thoughts, Inga?" she asked her abruptly. "Somebody you'd nearly forgotten and weren't in love with any more, and never really were in love with?"

"What's her name?" Inga asked sympathetically.

"Oh, nobody you'd know." She was fairly sure Inga *would*

know, if she frequented the Cellar. If she'd hung around the Village long enough she'd know most of the characters by sight, if not personally. Beebo was one of the characters. And she had been around here for fourteen years. "How long have you lived down here?" Laura asked the girl.

"Two years next month."

Long enough, Laura thought.

"I'll bet I know her. She ever come in here? Come on, tell me," Inga said.

"I can't."

"You're silly, then. I'll clue you in on something, Laura. If you can't get her off your mind it's because you can't get her out of your heart. That sounds corny but it's true. I found out the hard way. Believe me."

Laura shook her head. "I never loved her," she said positively.

"You're fooling yourself, sweetie."

Laura looked at her, bemused. "I'm in love with somebody else," she said, thinking of Tris.

"Me?" Inga grinned.

"No. No, an Indian girl."

"Indian? What's her name?"

"Tris."

"Tris! Gee, I *do* know her. She comes in here a lot."

Laura stared at her, too shocked to answer for a minute. Finally she said hoarsely, "Tris would never come in here. She hates gay bars. I know that for a fact."

"Well . . ." Inga looked as if she knew she had put her foot in her mouth and regretted it. "Maybe it's a different Tris."

"What's her last name?"

"Robischon, or something. Something Frenchy. I think she made it up myself. But she's a gorgeous girl. I was really smitten when I saw her."

Laura blanched a little and ordered another drink and drank it down fast, and Inga laid a hand on her arm. "Gee, I'm sorry, Laura," she said. "Me and my big mouth. I should learn to shut up. But I'm in here all the time. I come in after work and I see just about everybody—"

"I know, I know. It's okay, Inga." She ordered another drink. "I'd rather know than not," she said. "Besides, I haven't seen the girl for eight months. It'd be pretty strange if nobody found out about her in eight months. She's beautiful."

"That she is. Somebody's found out, all right. A lot of people, I hear."

"Does she come in here alone?" The whole thing seemed incredible to Laura. Tris! So aloof, so chilly, so much better than the rest of the gay crowd. Tris, who wouldn't go near Fire Island for a summer vacation because it was "crawling with queers." It just couldn't be. But Inga certainly wasn't describing anybody else.

"She comes with somebody else," Inga said reluctantly. "Look, sweetie, why don't you come over to my place and have a nightcap. We can't talk in here."

"I'd like to know, Inga. Tell me. Who does she come in with?" Laura turned and looked at her, swiveling slowly on her stool, a little tipsy and feeling suddenly as if the situation were something of a joke.

"Oh . . . a big gal. Been around the Village for years. You might know her. Beebo Brinker's her name."

Laura sat there frozen for nearly a minute. It *was* a joke—colossal, cruel, hilarious. She laughed uncertainly and ordered another drink.

"I knew you were going to say that," she told Inga. "Isn't that the damnedest thing? Isn't that the goddamnedest thing?" And she began to laugh again, repeating, when she could get her breath, "I knew you were going to say that." Inga had to slap her face to stop the shrieking, irrepressible giggles that were strangling her. Then Laura's laughter changed, in the space of a breath, to tears.

Inga talked to her quietly with that odd intimacy that springs up between homosexuals in trouble, and it helped. After five or six minutes Laura wiped her eyes and drank her drink and let Inga help her out of the Cellar. A few curious eyes followed them and Laura prayed again that nobody she knew had seen her.

The cold air braced her a little, and she stood on the corner weaving slightly and trying to get her bearings.

"Come on," Inga said. "Let's get some hot coffee into you. I live just a couple of blocks from here. Come on."

Laura let herself be led by the diminutive curly-head, but when she saw they were headed for Cordelia Street she began to get scared. "Beebo lives near here," she said, hanging back. "I mean—she used to."

"She still does," Inga said. "I see her now and then. I live right over there." She pointed.

Laura brushed the girl's hand from her sleeve and turned to her. "Thanks, Inga," she said. "Thanks anyway, but I think I'll . . ." And her eyes wandered back into Cordelia Street.

Inga followed her gaze, catching the idea. "I wouldn't if I were you," she said. "You'll be real sorry the minute you get there." When Laura didn't answer she asked, "Tell me, which one of them is it?"

"Which one?"

"That you just can't get off your mind?"

Laura looked back up the street where she used to live and said softly, "Beebo. It's crazy, isn't it? Beebo. And it's Tris I'm in love with."

"Yeah," said Inga with kindly skepticism. "Sure . . . Have some coffee with me?"

Laura leaned over on a whim and kissed her cheek. "That's for being a woman," she said. "You don't know what a help it's been."

Inga stood on the corner and watched Laura walk away from her. "Any time you want that coffee, Laura," she called. "I'm in the phone book."

Laura stood in front of the door into her old apartment building for a long while on trembling legs before she turned the knob and walked in.

What if they're together? she wondered. *They'll just grab me and wring my neck. God, all those questions Tris used to ask me about Beebo. And it never entered my love-sick head!*

She crossed the little inner court to the second door, opened it, and went to the row of mailboxes to press the buzzer. She found Beebo's name, with her own crossed out beneath it but no other added. And a weird, wonderful panic grabbed her throat at the thought of Beebo.

She left the buzzer without pressing it and walked up the flight of stairs to stand in front of the door that had once been her own, with Beebo still swimming before her eyes.

She could picture her more and more clearly: wearing pants and going barefoot, tired at the end of the day and maybe a little high; a cigarette in her mouth and a towel tied around her middle while she did dishes or cleaned up the apartment; the smooth skin on her face and the handsome features that

used to fire Laura's imagination and make her tingle; the tired
eyes, blue and brilliant and somehow a little sick of it all . . .
except when they focused on Laura.

Laura remembered how it had been and a sudden flash of
physical longing caught her heart and squeezed until she felt
her breath come short. She stared at the door, afraid to knock
and still hypnotized with curiosity. Her hand was raised, quivering, only inches from the green painted wood.

Tris will open it, she thought, *and together they'll strangle
me.* Oddly, she didn't care. She was too tight to care. She had
a vision of herself falling into their arms and succumbing without a struggle. Just letting them have her life, her mixed-up,
aimless, leftover life.

She knocked—a quick scared rap, sharp and clear. And
then stood there on one foot and the other, half panicky like
a grade-schooler nearly ready to wet her pants and flee.

Footsteps. High heels. From the kitchen, Beebo's voice.
"Who the hell could that be? After ten, isn't it?" *Oh, that
voice! That husky voice that used to whisper such things to
me that I can never forget.*

The door swung open all at once, ushering a flood of light
into the hall. Laura looked up slowly . . . at Lili! The two
of them stared at each other in mutual amazement for a moment. And while they stared, mute, Beebo called again, "Who
is it, Lili?"

Lili, her candy-box pretty face overlaid with too much
makeup, as usual, broke into a big smile. "It's Laura!" she
exclaimed. "I'll be goddamned. *Laura!*"

For a tense moment Laura could feel Beebo's shock across
the rooms and through the walls like a physical touch. Then
her courage melted—fizzled into nothing like water on a hot
skillet, and she turned and ran.

She heard Beebo at the door, before she got out into the
court, saying, "Let her go, Lili. If she thinks I'm going to
chase her twice—" And that was all Laura got of it. It shot
through her heart like a bullet.

Laura reached the door to the street, tore it open, and
rushed out. But once there, with the door shut behind her
and no sound of pursuing footsteps, she collapsed against the
wall and wept. Between sobs, when she could get her breath,
she listened . . . listened . . . for the running feet that
would mean Beebo had changed her mind. Laura had to be-

lieve, at least for a minute, that Beebo would come after her. Because it was all tied up in her mind with Beebo loving her. If Beebo loved her she'd chase her. It was that simple. And it didn't matter a damn what Laura might have done to Beebo in the past, or how she might have hurt her.

Tris! she thought. *I've got to see her!* She said this to herself very urgently, but curiously, at the same time, she felt no desire to go and find the lovely tormented dancer. She told herself it would be all fight and misery. But in her heart of hearts she knew that real love would brave that misery now, being so close and so starved for passion.

She stood there for fully fifteen minutes before she was able to pull herself together and walk to Seventh Avenue. She went straight home in a cab.

Laura walked slowly up the stairs to her apartment. It was after eleven now, and Jack would be in bed. She had had too much to drink, but she was sober, a tired, bewildered sort of sobriety that made her want to lie down and weep and rest.

In the morning she would tell it all to Jack. Wonderful Jack. He would coax her back to living, coax her with his wit and his compassion and his incredible patience with her. And she would lie in a welter of dejection and let him work on her until she felt like lifting her head from the pillow and raising the shade from the window and going on with life. It was one of the things she loved him for and needed him for the most— this ability to revive her when she was so low that only death was lower.

Tonight was perhaps not quite that bad. But it was bad enough to have exhausted her. And Tris and Beebo! That had been the cruelest blow; the one she should have foreseen clear as a beacon in a black sea. She shoved a trembling key into the lock and walked into the apartment.

It was warm and well-lighted. It was pretty and it was comfortable. It was home. And Laura felt a sort of gratitude to Jack that needed words. She went to find him. But he wasn't in the living room, nor in the bedroom.

She stood on the threshold of the bedroom and said, "Jack? Hey, Jack! Where are you?"

"Here," he said from the kitchen.

"Oh. It's me. I thought you'd be in bed." She slipped her coat off while she walked through the living room to find him. "Hi," she said. He was sitting on a kitchen chair and he answered, "Hi."

Laura stood in the doorway and looked at him. And he stared back at her, and she knew something was wrong but she didn't know what. Her long fine hair had come loose when she ran from Beebo and she reached up and pulled it down in a shimmering cascade, watching Jack all the while through narrowed eyes.

"Have fun?" he asked.

"Beebo and Tris . . . are . . . shacking up." She threw it at him point-blank. She wanted his sympathy.

Jack put his head back and laughed, that awful bitter laugh she hadn't heard for months, and she knew with a sudden start of fear and pity that he was drunk. "That makes everything perfect," he said, still laughing, his eyes wicked and sharp behind the horn rims.

"Jack . . . ," she said shakily, coming in to sit beside him and seeing now the whiskey bottle on the table in front of him, two-thirds empty. "Jack, darling." She took his hands and her eyes were big with alarm.

Jack took his hands back. Not roughly, but as if he simply didn't want to be touched. Not by Laura, anyway.

"Mother, you are a living doll. If I had known you could keep secrets so well I'd have told you a few," he said. He spoke, as always when he was drunk, with a slow precision, as if each word were a stepping stone.

"Secrets?" Laura said.

"You are the living picture of guilt, my dear," he said. "It is written all over your beautiful face."

Laura put her hands over that face suddenly with a gasp. "Terry!" she sobbed through clenched teeth. "*Terry!* If I hadn't gone out he wouldn't have come."

"He comes when the mood hits him," Jack said. "Which is most of the time, most anywhere. It had nothing to do with you going out, my little wifey."

Laura looked up, her delicate face mottled pink and white and wet from the eyes down. "He wrote—"

"Indeed he did. He told me the whole romantic story."

"Jack, darling, I only kept it secret because I was afraid you'd—you'd start drinking, or something—I—"

"You hit the nail on the head. I'm indebted to you. Your solicitude is exemplary." He waved the fast-emptying bottle at her.

"Oh, shut up! Shut up! I *love* you. I did it because I love you."

"You opened my mail because you love me?" He continued to drink while he talked . . . slowly, but steadily.

"I knew it was from him, Jack. I just had a feeling. The handwriting and everything."

He laughed ruefully. "Just think what you've spared me!" he said. "I can drink in peace now. My wife loves me. Thanks, wife." He saluted her.

Laura slid off her chair to her knees and put her arms around him, still crying. "Jack, Jack, please forgive me. I'll do anything, I couldn't bear to hurt you, I'd die first. Oh, please—"

"You're forgiven," he interrupted her. "Why not?" And he kept on laughing. But his pardon was so light, so biting, that she cringed from it. She lifted her face to him, streaming with tears, and he said, smiling at her, "You make a lovely picture, Mother. Sort of Madonna-like. If I could paint you, I'd paint you. Black, I think. From head to toe."

She put her head down on his knees and said softly, "You'll never forgive me, will you?"

"I already have."

"Never," she whispered, stricken.

"Oh, let's not get maudlin," he said. "I admit I would have been grateful for a little forewarning. But after all, it's a simple question of sex. Maybe I should get rid of mine. That would solve everything." And his soft, insane chuckling underlined everything he said.

Laura felt terror then. It rose and fell inside her like nausea. Whenever she looked at Jack it surged in her throat. It wasn't the sweet guilty thrill of coming near Beebo that had cost her such sensual pain earlier in the evening.

"Jack, darling," she said.

"Yes, Laura darling." And the sarcasm burned her. But she went on, determined, raising herself back into her chair again with effort.

"Tell me what happened. Tell me everything."

"Oh, it was dandy," he said. "You should have been here. Incidentally, he asked about your health." Laura couldn't watch him while he talked. She looked at her hands. And all the while he told her about it she kept thinking, *If only I hadn't gone out tonight. Every time I do something completely selfish I suffer for it. And so does he. Damn Terry! Damn him to hell! He won't ruin Jack, I won't let him. This is once he won't have his way.*

It had been so completely unexpected, so startling, that Jack would never forget it or recover from it. Terry was as far removed from his life as if he were dead. And his life, Jack felt, had become a good thing at last. He had Laura to live for, not a wild, irresistible, good-for-nothing boy who wore him out and broke his heart and his bankroll. He had a new stature in the world as a married man, a new security. And the sweet hope of a child someday . . .

When he heard the bell ring, almost an hour after Laura had gone out, he took it for a neighbor and stood with the front door open while the elevator ascended. But when Terry stepped out, Jack was speechless. He couldn't believe it, and he would have slammed the door and passed it off as a nightmare if he could have moved a little faster.

But Terry caught him and from then on it was as degrading and overwhelming as it had ever been. Jack put up the best fight he could, but it was little more than a gesture of protest. He was helplessly angry, helplessly infatuated. And all the while Terry prated to him of San Francisco and the Beats and the fog and the styles in clothes and the styles in love-making, Jack kept wondering, *How did he find me?* And the answer was, had to be, *Laura.* Laura had failed him. Betrayed him. It almost tore him apart.

Terry didn't leave until nearly eleven, and Jack saw him out, still with the feeling that it hadn't happened, that it was all an incredible dream. It wasn't until he got the bottle and began to drink that he believed in it at all. By the time Laura got home he wished the whole damned world to hell, with himself first in line.

"And that's all," Jack said. "Naturally, the only thing to do after he left was get drunk." He had nearly finished the bottle and it was all he could do to get the words out. They left his mouth slowly, discreetly, each one a pearl of over-articulation.

Laura took away what was left—a shot or two at the most—and he didn't even try to protest. She helped him up and half dragged, half carried him to the bedroom, where she dumped him on his bed. He was unconscious the minute she pushed his head down on the pillow. Laura undressed him, tears running down her face.

"Sleep," she said. "Sleep and forget it for a while. I'll make it up to you, darling. All I wanted tonight was to cry on your shoulder. And you can't even hold yourself up."

She dragged and shoved and pulled until she got him under the covers. "He won't get you, Jack," she whispered. "You'd fight for me if I were in trouble. And I'll fight for you."

In the morning, Laura got up, moving softly as a bird on the sand, and left him to himself in the bedroom, still noisily and miserably asleep with a full-blown, brutal hangover brewing under his closed eyes.

She had to make it up to him, redeem herself. And she could only think of one thing. So before noon she called Terry and asked him to dinner.

"Sounds great," he said in innocent surprise and pleasure. "I was counting on mooching from you," he admitted, laughing.

When Jack woke up she told him what she had done. She waited until he had had four cups of coffee and eight aspirins and some forced warm milk and raw egg. He said nothing but "No. No! *No!*" to whatever she was trying to get into him. He sat in the kitchen with his head in his hands, and Laura began to fear he was still a little drunk. She had thrown out the rest of the whiskey.

"Where's the bottle?" he asked her finally, around the middle of the afternoon.

"Gone. I tossed it."

He nodded painfully, resigned.

"Jack," she said softly. "Terry's coming to dinner."

He lifted his throbbing head to gape at her. "Are you trying to kill me, Mother? Or just drive me nuts?" he said.

"I'm going to save you. Save *us*," she said passionately. "We're at the crossroads, Jack. This is the first real crisis we've had. We can't just fall apart. We have too much to save, too much worth saving. We have love, too, and I'm not going to let him hurt you any more." Somehow in the strength she found to fight Jack's battle was the strength to fight her own. The downright shock and humiliation of finding that her two ex-lovers were romancing might have thrown her into a full-blown depression. But now she hadn't time. It was Jack's turn. She loved him, she was absolutely sure of that. She was not absolutely sure she loved Tris any more. Nor was she sure now that she *didn't* love Beebo. Jack was her security, her chosen life; he deserved her loyalty.

But to her chagrin, her noble speech had very little effect on him. He got out of his chair with much agonized effort, making a face, and headed for the coat closet.

"Where are you going?" she asked anxiously, running after him.

"For a bottle."

"Oh, Jack, no!"

He turned to face her, sliding awkwardly into his coat sleeves. "Do you want me to go through this sober?"

"Darling, you don't even have to *look* at him! You can lock yourself in the john and sing hymns if you want to. I just want to talk to him."

"About the weather?"

"I'll get him out of here, I swear I will!"

"How? With a can opener? TNT?" He was moving toward the door as he spoke with Laura clinging to his arm and trying to hold him back.

"Darling, trust me!" she begged. She was not at all sure that she could get Terry out again, once he got in, but she had to make Jack calm down. She was frantic to stop him.

"Trust you?" He turned and looked at her uncertainly, his hand on the front door knob, and gave a little snort. "That doesn't work. I tried it."

"Oh, you damn, fatuous idiot!" she cried in exasperation, dropping his arm to stamp to the middle of the room and face him from there as if from a podium. "I open *one* goddam letter—out of love and anxiety—to spare you pain. And the thing backfires. Do you have to crucify yourself? I said I was sorry and I am. I'm sorry. I'm sorry, I'm sorry, I'm sorry!" she yelled.

"Were you born that way?" he snapped.

"Shut up and listen!" she cried. "Jack, let me make it up to you, let me *try*. You have no right to call yourself my husband if you won't give me a chance, and I'm telling you right now, Jack Mann, if you won't I'll walk out of this house and your life forever." She paused, flushed and trembling, for breath, while Jack stared at her, surprised, half-convinced, and himself trembling slightly from the hangover.

Finally he went to the arm of the nearest chair and sat down and said, "All right, Wife. Read him the riot act while I sing hymns in the bathroom, if you think it'll do any good."

"Oh, Jack." She ran to him, all pity and tenderness, and kissed his frowning face. He put his head back and ignored her.

Terry arrived at seven, half an hour late, with a huge bouquet of roses for Laura. "For Mrs. Mann," he said, bowing, and then gave her a quick embrace. "You look great, honey."

"Thanks," she said with reserve. "I'll put them in water."

"Where's Jack? Oh, there you are." Terry made a running jump to the couch where Jack was lying in state, wearing his hangover like a royal robe.

Jack let out all his breath in a wail of anguish when Terry hit him.

"Where did you get the flowers?" Laura asked, coming back in with them arranged in a tall vase.

"Nick's. On the corner. I had to charge 'em to you, Laur. I hope you don't mind." He smiled charmingly. "Your credit's much better than mine around here."

Jack laughed softly. "You haven't changed a bit, have you?" he said to Terry.

Laura sat down and looked at Terry's bright young face, smiling happily around a mouthful of salted pecans, and wondered if her little trick would work. It had to. But it might not. She felt a little sick, seeing Jack so miserable.

"No drinks?" Terry said, suddenly conscious of the lack of alcohol.

"Milk," Laura offered.

"Milk punch?" he asked.

"Just bare milk," Jack drawled.

"What's the matter with you?" Terry said and laughed at him. "Have a nut." And he popped one in Jack's half open mouth. "You aren't on the wagon, are you?"

"I was," Jack said. "Till last night."

"No kidding. God. Amazing. Since when?"

"Since we got married last August. A little before."

"Laura, how'd you do it?" He grinned at her.

"I didn't have to," she said. "The day you walked out of his life all the good things walked in."

"Including you?" Terry asked.

"Including me," she shot back.

"Oh." He smiled ruefully. "I wasn't *that* bad, was I?" he asked Jack. He seemed to think it was comfortably funny, like everything else connected with Jack. "Did I drive you to drink, honey?" he said.

"Only on the bad days," Jack said. "Unfortunately, there weren't any good days."

Terry laughed and stuck another nut in Jack's mouth.

"That's all," Jack told him, wincing. "The damn pecans sound like depth charges when I chew." He stroked his head carefully.

There was a silence while Terry ate, Laura stared at him nervously, and Jack concentrated on his pains. Laura wanted to make Terry uncomfortable, self-conscious. But it was nearly a lost cause.

"What's for dinner?" he asked suddenly, unaware that he was supposed to notice the silence.

She told him.

"Great," he said. More silence. Laura was determined to embarrass him, and Jack was too ill to care about conversation. Slowly, Terry began to realize something was amiss. Rather than take the hint he tried to lighten the atmosphere with chatter.

"How do you like the married life, old man?" he asked.

"He liked it fine the day before yesterday," Laura said crisply. Jack groaned. Terry understood.

He sat up and leaned toward his hostess. "Laura, honey, I don't want to mess things up for you," he said. "I just love Jack, too, that's all. You know that. You always knew it, even before you got married."

"I know you nearly killed him," she said quietly.

"No fair exaggerating."

"No fair, hell. It's true!" she exclaimed.

"It's not either!" he said with good-humored indignation, as if they were playing parlor games. "Is it, Jack?"

But Jack, his eyes on Laura now, kept silent.

"Well," Terry admitted, "I was pretty bitchy sometimes. But so was he. And no matter what, we loved each other. Even at the end, when he kicked me out."

"If he hadn't kicked you out that night he might have killed himself with liquor."

"I don't believe it."

Laura threw her hands up, exasperated. "What more do you *want* from Jack, Terry?" she said. "What do you want from *me*?"

Terry grinned. "Equal time," he said, nodding at the bedroom.

Jack laughed weakly and Laura got up and stamped her foot. "Terry, Jack loves you. I know that and I'll have to live with it. But that love is destructive, and I'm asking you now to get out of our lives forever and never come back to hurt us again." She said it with quiet intensity.

"Before dinner?" he asked.

"Oh, God!" Laura spluttered at the ceiling.

Terry lighted a cigarette for Jack, who had fumbled one from the box on the cocktail table, and told Laura, "I can't go away forever. Any more than you could desert Beebo forever. I love him. I'm stuck with him."

"I've *left* Beebo," she said.

"You'll go back," he told her serenely. "It was that kind of affair."

Laura held on to her self control as her last and dearest possession. She didn't dare to lose it. "Take me seriously, Terry," she begged, almost in a whisper. "Please let us live together in peace."

Terry shrugged. He didn't like to get serious. "What are you going to do the rest of your lives?" he asked them. "Live like a couple of old maids in your fancy little apartment? Pretend you're both straight? What a kick!" He said it sarcastically but without malice. "A kick like that won't last long, you know."

"It's not a kick. It's something we both need and want," Laura said earnestly.

"Nuts," Terry said amiably. "What you both need and want is a few parties. Get out and camp. Do you good."

"Sure," Laura said sharply. "So you make love to Jack and he goes out and drinks a fifth of whiskey, after *eight months* on the wagon. Was that what you had in mind?"

Terry made a little grimace of perplexity. "That was pretty silly," he told Jack. "Now she won't let me see you at all."

"He needs me more than he needs you, Terry," Laura said.

"Yeah? But he *wants* me more." He grinned at her. "You've got to admit that counts for something," he told her. "I can give him something you can't give him." He looked so smug, so sure of himself, that Laura, with her heart in her throat, decided to pull her rabbit out of the hat. If it didn't work, she would have to give up.

"And I can give him something *you* can't give him," she said, her voice low and tense. "A child."

There was a long stunned silence. Jack and Terry both stared at her—Jack with a slight smile of amazement and Terry with open-mouthed dismay.

"A child!" Terry blurted finally. "Don't tell *me!* I wasn't born yesterday."

"It's true," Laura spat at him. "And I'm not going to have any empty-headed, pretty-faced queers hanging around my baby! Not even *you*, Terry Fleming."

Terry turned to gape at Jack, his mouth still ajar. "She's kidding!" he exclaimed. "Isn't she?"

Jack paused slightly and then shook his head, and the strange little smile on his face widened. It was brilliant, he thought. Cruel, to himself even more than to Terry, because it wasn't true. But clever.

Terry stood up, bewildered, and walked around the living room. Laura watched him, her face flushed, sweating with expectation. Finally Terry turned to look at them. Jack, raising himself on one elbow, watched him.

"Do you still want me to have dinner with you?" he asked wryly, and Laura saw hesitation in his look and felt a first small hope.

She didn't know what to say. But she was thinking, *I've made Jack a man in his eyes now. He's thinking, Jack can do what he could never do himself. He's thinking, at least if I was wrong about him ruining Jack's life, I'm right about ruining a baby's. He knows damn well he could do that. Or does he?*

But at least he *was* thinking. His lovely young face was screwed up with the effort.

Suddenly he said to Laura, as if expecting to trip her up, "When's it due? The kid?"

"November," she said. She had anticipated him.

"Well!" His face brightened. "If it isn't due till November, we've got a long time to play around." And it was Jack he looked at now.

But Laura jumped at him, bristling. "I don't want an alco-

544

holic for a husband!" she said. "I don't want my baby to have
an alcoholic for a father. A drunken, miserable, tormented
man who doesn't know which sex he is, who has to chase
around after a thoughtless character like you all night. I don't
want to lose my husband, Terry. Not to you or any other
gay boy in the world. You'd ruin his health and make him
wild inside of a month."

She was crying, though she didn't realize it, and her cheeks
were flaming. Terry stared at her for some moments in surprised silence. And then he looked at Jack, who was still
propped on one arm, taking it all in with an inscrutable smile.

"Well . . . ," Terry said again, almost diffidently. Apparently he believed they were having a child. He looked to
Jack for moral support. "Is that the way you feel too, honey?"
he asked.

"Why certainly," Jack said cheerfully, incongruously.
"Can't you tell? Whatever she says, goes." A soft note of
hysteria sounded in his voice.

"I guess you don't want me to stay for dinner now," Terry
said, glancing at Laura. For answer she only turned away and
began to cry. Terry walked over to Jack and knelt before him
on the floor, putting his hands on Jack's shoulders. "I do love
you, Jack. I never lied about that. I didn't know it was so
bad. For you, I mean. I still don't see how it could have been.
But I don't want to mess things up for the kid. Shall I go? You
tell me." He waited, watching Jack's face.

"I told you to leave me once, Terry. I haven't the strength
to say it again. It's up to you."

Terry leaned forward and kissed him on the lips. "If you
haven't the strength to say it, I haven't the strength to do it.
No matter what she says," he said.

Laura came at him suddenly from across the room. "Go!"
she flashed. "Go, damn you, and never come back!"

Terry looked uncertainly from Laura to Jack, and Jack
covered his face abruptly with a noise rather like a sob.

Terry stood up. "All right," he said in a husky voice. "I'll
go. I'll go for the baby's sake. But not forever, Laura. Not
forever."

At the front door he turned to her. "You say you love him,"
he said. "Then you must understand why I can't leave him
forever. I love him too." He said it sadly but matter-of-factly.
And Laura, staring at him through tear-blurred eyes, realized

that he never would understand what he had done to Jack or
how. He thought it was a simple matter of giving a kid a
break. And because he loved Jack enough he was able to do it.

"Enjoy your flowers," he said with a rueful grin, and then
Terry went out the front door and shut it carefully behind
him. Neither Jack nor Laura stirred nor made a sound until
they heard the elevator arrive, the doors open, shut again, and
the elevator leave.

"He's gone," she whispered. "Dear God, don't let him ever
come back."

Jack rolled over, his back to her, and wept briefly and painfully with desperate longing. There was a moment of silence
while she watched him fearfully. And then he stood up and
headed for the door. Laura threw herself against it.

"No! Don't follow him, Jack!" she implored, her voice
rising.

"I won't," he said, trying to reach past her to open the door,
but she threw her arms around him and begged him to stay
with her.

"I got him to leave, Jack. He won't dare come back for a
long time. Maybe he'll find somebody new. Maybe we'll be
lucky and he'll never come back."

"I should be so lucky," he said acidly.

She looked at him, dismayed. "Isn't that what you wanted?"
she asked.

He stopped trying to grab the doorknob for a minute to
look at her. "Yes," he said, with effort. And after a pause,
"You were masterful, Mother. You really played your scene."

She looked at the floor confusedly, hearing all the sarcasm
and the hurt and the grudging admiration in his voice. "Do
you hate me for it?" she asked.

"No. I'm grateful."

"Do you still love me?" she whispered.

"Yes. But don't ask me to prove it now." He got the door
open in a sudden deft gesture, but Laura was still clutching
him.

"Where are you going?" she asked fearfully.

"For a bottle."

"Oh, God!" she gasped. "Then it's all been for nothing,"
she said despairingly.

"No," he said. "I'm not drinking this for Terry. I'm drinking it for the baby."

"The baby?" she said tremulously.

"The little kid who wasn't there."

He turned to go and she followed him into the hall.

"But Jack—" she protested as he rang for the elevator. "Jack, I—I—" She looked up and saw the long bronze needle moving swiftly toward "three" as the elevator ascended, having barely emptied Terry into the first floor. It seemed to be measuring off the last seconds of their marriage. She had to do something. Trembling and scared, she caught his lapels and said, with great difficulty, "I meant it, Jack."

"Meant what?"

"About the baby."

He stared at her, one hand holding back the door of the just-arrived elevator.

"I'll have a baby," she said. "If you still want one."

For a while they stood in the dim little hall and gazed at each other. And then Jack let his hand slip from the elevator door and, circling her waist with his arm, led her back into the apartment.

"He'll be back, you know," he said, stopping to look at her.

"I know. But by that time he'll know we aren't kidding," she said, looking dubiously at her tight, flat stomach. "By that time you'll be strong again. And ready for him. You'll know he's coming and you'll be able to take it. It won't be like now."

He kissed her. "Goddam it," he whispered, grateful and amazed. "I *do* love you."

9

THE DOCTOR'S WAITING ROOM was crowded, heavy with the eager boredom of people waiting to talk about themselves. It was the fourth doctor they had been to see within a week. Jack, as Laura might have expected, was in a hurry. But he had to find the right man, too—a man he genuinely liked. Not just any bone-picker was going to perform the wizardry to bring *his* child into being.

Laura had simply sat in red-faced silence through Jack's expositions of their supposed marital troubles, both unwilling and unable to contribute a word. And the whole thing had been lengthy and bewildering and not a little tiring.

But when they finally got into Dr. Belden's plush, paneled office, it went well. And she knew, suddenly paying attention to the words of the men, that it was going to be settled. And it was.

She answered the standard questions, her voice low with embarrassment. They always bothered her excessively, like so many spiders crawling over her tender shame. Other girls might not mind, or even liked to yammer to doctors about their intimate selves, but not Laura.

Jack bolstered her up as they were leaving. "You were heroic, Mother," he assured her. "I know you hate it—yes you do, don't lie," he added impatiently when she tried to protest. "It's all right, honey, it's all in a good cause."

"Don't call me honey."

"Why?"

"Terry calls everybody honey." She was in a grumpy mood; he saw it and let her be for a while. "When do I have to go back?" she asked as they rode home in a taxi.

"A week from Thursday." He looked at her somewhat anxiously as if wishing that Thursday had already come. "You won't change your mind, of course," he said to comfort himself. His voice was calm but his eyes were worried.

"No," she sighed. She looked at her gloved hands until his anxious gaze moved her to give him one and make him smile.

He looked strangely different, almost young. Jack had the kind of a face that must have made him look forty when he was twenty. In a sense it was an ageless face because it had hardly changed at all. Laura supposed that when he was sixty, he would still look forty. But for the few weeks after Terry disappeared it looked young. And Laura thought with an ache of how much of that was due to her. How much she had forced him to depend on her. She was deeply committed now. There was no retreating.

Laura saw Doctor Belden three days in a row, and it was unspeakably humiliating for her. But she endured it. By the time her appointment came due, she was too afraid for Jack not to go. But she prayed when she was alone, with big wild angry sobs, that the artificial insemination wouldn't work; that she was barren or Jack was sterile or the timing was off; any-thing. And she felt a huge, breathtaking need for a woman that absolutely tortured her at night.

After her first examination with Belden she went out of the office to meet Jack and told him she was going to the Village.

"I don't know why I need to. I just do," she said.

"Sure, sweetheart," he said at last, standing facing her on the pavement outside the doctor's office. "Go. Only, come back."

"I will," she said, near tears, and turned and almost ran from him. She couldn't bear to touch him, and it was painful even to look at him.

It was mid-day in the Village and mothers walked their babies in the park. Laura hurried past them. Old ladies strolled about in the unusually warm weather, dogs barked, and a few hardy would-be artists had set up shop in the empty pool at the center of Washington Square. A small crowd of students had gathered to offer encouragement and argue.

Laura walked quickly through the park to Fourth Street, and then she turned and walked west, not sure why. On the other side of Sixth Avenue she stopped and found a drug-store and went in for coffee.

I can't see Tris, she told herself, playing nervously with her hands. *I won't see Beebo. Or rather, Beebo won't see me. That's for sure.* She tried to think of anything but what she had just been through, but it didn't work. It never does.

Just so it's normal, she thought angrily. *I won't hate it but I couldn't stand an abnormal child.* God, *I've got to talk to somebody, somebody who doesn't know, who'll put it out of my mind.* She thought of Inga then, but she couldn't remember her last name and she wasn't too sure where the girl lived. She had been too drunk that night.

And then, for no apparent reason, she thought of Lili. Beautiful, brazen Lili. At least Lili would talk. Laura wouldn't have to open her mouth. Maybe it would be better that way. She wouldn't betray any secrets to Beebo's old lover about her marriage. But Lili would be only too happy to tell Laura what had gone on between Beebo and Tris if only to see her squirm, and Laura was burning to know.

She went to the phone booth at the back of the store and looked up Lili. She was still listed, still in the same apartment on Greenwich Avenue. It was late afternoon by the time Laura got there. Lili would just be getting out of bed, if she followed the same habits she used to have.

Laura felt very tired and reluctant when she finally found the right building and the right button to press; afraid and a little ashamed. But she rang anyway, as if she had no will to stop herself. And when the answering ring came she went inside and walked up the stairs.

Lili, hanging over the bannister to see who was waking her up so early, saw her coming. Laura stopped on the first landing at her amazed, "Laura! Again! Are you a ghost?"

Laura gazed up, her long pale hair hanging defiantly free and her eyes blue-shadowed the way they were when she was tired or scared. Now she was a little of both.

"No, no ghost," she said.

"I don't believe you. But come in anyway. I have the most divine friend who's a Medium. Where the hell have you been? I thought sure you'd come back, after you saw Beebo a couple of weeks ago." She watched Laura mount the stairs as she spoke and took her by the arm when Laura reached her. "You look worn out, poor lamb," she said. "I'll give you a drink. What do you want?"

"Nothing."

"Nothing!" It was an explosion, not a question. "God. Next you'll be telling me you've gone straight."

"I came to ask about Beebo," Laura said.

"Oh," said Lili knowledgeably. "I thought so." She went

about fixing Laura and herself a drink in spite of Laura's objections. "Well, lamb, what about her?"

"Are she and Tris living together?"

"Mercy, who told you *that*?" Lili turned to stare at her.

"A friend of mine."

"Your friend lies. They aren't living together and they never did. Oh, Tris spent the night with her a few times. You know how it is." She laughed sociably, coming toward Laura with two filled glasses. "Here, lamb, I insist. It'll revive you. My doctor says—"

"Tell me about Tris and Beebo."

"Well," Lili said, confidentially. "It was just an affair."

"What does that mean?" she said.

"It means when you can't get what you want you take what you can get," Lili said archly.

"They saw each other all the time. Beebo even had Tris going into the gay bars. I know this, Lili, don't hide it," Laura said.

"All right, all right," Lili said soothingly. "Tris had to go to the gay bars to find Beebo, that's all. Beebo's never home. You know how she is. And she didn't chase Tris so Tris had to chase her."

Laura felt an ineffable lightening of the heart. Somehow, if it had to happen, that was the best way.

"Tris was nuts about her," Lili said juicily. "She came over when she got back from Long Island last summer . . . without *you*, if you recall."

"I recall."

"Yes. Well! Beebo was pretty low. You may remember that, too." She looked at Laura sharply, and Laura looked at the floor and refused to answer. "Anyway, Tris fell into her arms and Beebo just caught her. I wish I could say that Beebo fell for her. I think it would have spared her some of the agony you inflicted on her." So now it was out in the open. Lili spoke dramatically, but it wasn't all play-acting. She had loved Beebo once, and she didn't like to see her hurt as Laura had hurt her.

The two females eyed each other, wary but curious, each eager to know what the other could tell her. Lili was ready to hurt Laura to find out. She had seen what happened to Beebo when Laura left her, and it was shocking. Laura didn't know about it, and to Lili it seemed as if she was nothing but a spoiled, headstrong little bitch who didn't care whom she hurt . . . a little like Lili herself ten years before, and that made Lili even more critical.

If Laura were told how hard Beebo had taken it—how intensely she had suffered and torched for her—maybe it would touch her and make her sorry. Lili enjoyed the idea of Laura on her knees to Beebo, and Beebo kicking her out. For she knew what Laura did not—that Beebo was a different girl now. And to Lili's way of thinking it meant that Beebo would never take Laura back.

So they were agreed, without having said a word about it, that Lili would talk and Laura would listen to her; Lili because she had to hurt and Laura because she had to know.

Lili lighted a cigarette and stuck it carefully into an ebony holder with a water filter, a rather bulky conversation piece. Everything she did was staged.

"I'm going to talk turkey to you, lamb," she informed her guest. "Now that I have you in my clutches." She smiled slightly, a warning smile.

"Talk," Laura said. "But I'd appreciate it if you'd spare me the sermon."

"I'm sure you would." Lili gazed at her. "But, unfortunately, you *need* a sermon. Oh, just a little one, of course. I won't be crude about it."

Laura ignored her, picking up the drink she didn't think she wanted and sipping at it.

"Well," Lili began. "You almost killed her. I suppose you could have guessed that."

"I knew it would be hard for her," Laura said, "but not that bad." Her voice said she thought Lili was exaggerating, but in her heart she was afraid . . . afraid it was true.

"It was bad enough to send her to the hospital with a stomachful of sleeping pills. I know. I took her over." She said this with her green eyes flaring and her voice low enough to make Laura strain a little to hear her.

"Oh, damn it, Lili, don't make up a melodrama for me!" Laura cried.

"I thought I was stating it rather plainly. But I'll try again."

"Beebo wouldn't take sleeping pills!" Laura said contemptuously, and this she really believed. "It's not like her. It's too —I don't know—phony. It's more like something *you'd* do than Beebo."

"Luckily I'm not in love with you, pet," Lili countered. They glared at each other. "You don't know her at all, do you?" Lili went on. "You lived with her for more than two years, and you just don't know her at all."

"I know her better than anybody! What do you mean?"

"All right, lamb, we won't argue the point. Anyway, when she got back from the hospital she was terribly despondent. I kept telling her you'd come back. Everybody did. I didn't believe it, of course, but I was afraid if I told her you were gone for good she'd try something worse than sleeping pills."

"Did she drink awfully hard?"

"Are you kidding? She drank like a fish, naturally," Lili said. "As if you had to ask. Then she got a job. But I'm getting ahead of myself. You wanted to hear about Tris."

Again she smiled, and Laura hated her smile. "Just tell me, Lili," she said. "Without the dramatics."

"Certainly, darling . . . Well, Tris came back and the first thing she did was come looking for you to tell you she was sorry. I don't know for what. But I was there when she arrived. I couldn't leave Beebo alone for five minutes, it was that bad. So anyway, we were having dinner when Tris came and she looked very surprised not to see you, but if you ask me, she was thrilled to death. She's been on the make for Beebo ever since you met at the dress shop. She strung you along for a contact with Beebo."

"I don't believe you," Laura lied bravely. "Go on."

"Well, darling, that makes it slightly awkward. It's essential to the narrative that you believe it." But Laura's cold white face discouraged her sarcasm and she went on. "Well, Tris was nuts for her. That time she burst in on you and Beebo got so mad—yes, she told me about it—she came to see Beebo, not you. She didn't care a damn if it got you in trouble. The only thing she cared about was seeing Beebo. She wasn't very happy about the way Beebo treated her then, but she's had better luck since . . .

"Well, Beebo didn't even try to fight her off. She just let her in and they spent a couple of weeks together. And the whole time that awful Milo—Tris's husband—I think you've met?—yes. That must have been jolly." She grinned maliciously. "Well, Milo was over there all the time, just mad as hell. It's a wonder he didn't kill Beebo, the way Tris carried on about her. It took him four whole months to drag her away, and Tris still comes over whenever she can sneak out. But Beebo and Milo get along better now. Since he realized Beebo's not in love with his wife.

"For some strange reason she can't seem to fall in love with anybody. I think she's crazy myself. I mean, after all, you're not *that* irresistible." She paused and Laura took advantage of it to switch the subject, fast.

"What about the job? You said she had a job."

"Oh, yes, I did, didn't I? Well, she's waiting on tables at the Colophon. Oh, don't look so disappointed, lamb, she *likes* it. Besides, she can wear pants." Lili knew how Laura hated Beebo's elevator uniform, and it pleased her to point out that Beebo hadn't reformed. "She works from five to eleven," Lili went on. "Really very good hours. And then of course she's free to get soused till dawn."

"Does she?"

"Sometimes."

"Is it very bad?" Laura asked, her voice a little shaky with fatigue.

"Sometimes."

"God, Lili, is that all you can say? Sometimes? *Tell* me about her, I haven't heard anything for eight months!"

"That's the way you wanted it, darling."

"No. No, it isn't," she whispered. "That's the way it had to be."

"I would say—judging strictly from your very interesting diary—that you were glad to get rid of Beebo. Maybe you're just here to ease your conscience, hm? Be sure she hasn't done anything messy you'd have to blame yourself for?"

Laura had to look away for a minute. The shame was too plain on her face. "That was a stupid thing, that diary," she mumbled. She started crying softly, helplessly. "Lili, cut out the sarcasm," she pleaded, knowing it would do no good.

"Why, don't be silly!" Lili exclaimed, enjoying the scene. "I haven't an ounce of sarcasm in me. I'm just a reporter giving you the facts."

"You're a lousy gossip columnist!" Laura said. "You're all dirty digs and snide cracks, and about a tenth of what you say is true. Tris Robischon was shy and neurotic. She hated gay bars. She wouldn't have gone in if she hadn't been forced. She hated gay people so much that she wouldn't associate with them."

"Like hell," Lili said elegantly. "She lived in the Village, didn't she? Who do you think her ballet pupils were, any-way?"

"Children! Men! Little girls!"

"*And* big girls, darling."

"She never had affairs with them. She might have slept with one or two of the men, but not with the girls. I'm sure of it."

"Have you talked to Milo about that?"

"No . . . not about that. But I *know* Tris!"

"Must be wonderful to be so sure of yourself, pet," Lili drawled. "The fact is, your little pseudo-Indian slept with dozens of her pupils. She went to the Lessie bars because Beebo did, and Beebo's not the first girl she's done it with. You can check it. Go ask the bartender at the Cellar. Ask the lovelies at the Colophon. At Julian's. Go on. Scared?"

Laura stood up suddenly and headed for the door. "I've had enough, Lili. Thanks. Thanks a lot." She spoke briefly, afraid of more tears, and grabbed her coat as she went. But Lili got up and ran after her.

"But darling, I want to know where you've been all this time!"

"It's no business of yours."

"Oh, tell me, Laura. Don't be difficult," she said. "Beebo would be interested," she wheedled.

"Oh, I doubt it. After what you've told me. But just for the record, I've been living uptown."

"Where uptown?"

But Laura shook her head.

"Alone?" Lili said.

"No." Laura didn't know why she said it. It just seemed easier than arguing. Besides, she didn't want Lili to think she was friendless and despised everywhere.

"You know, Jack Mann disappeared from the Village the same time you did," Lili said, her voice vibrant with curiosity.

"Yes."

"Do you knew where he is?"

"I see him now and then." She slipped her coat on and opened the front door, not bothering to look back at Lili. Her face was streaked with tears and torment and she wanted to go, to get out, to hide somewhere.

"Where are you going, pet? Why in such a hurry?"

"I'm a little sick, Lili, thanks to you. You have that effect on me," Laura said.

Lili laughed charmingly. "Imagine!" she said. "It's an even trade, then. Well, just so you don't go near Beebo, I guess it's safe to let you loose."

"I have no intention of going near Beebo," Laura said coldly, turning to look at her.

"Good," Lili said. "She'd kill you for sure."

Laura felt a red fury come up in her and she stepped back into the living room, her face so strange and tense that Lili, for the first time since Laura had come, became rather alarmed.

"Lili, goddamn you to hell, quit telling lies! Quit exaggerating!" Laura cried. "I hurt Beebo, but not *that* much. I didn't ruin her life, for God's sake! Or cripple her or kill her or drive her crazy! And I won't stand here and be accused of something I didn't do. Beebo's no angel, you know. Beebo damn near drove *me* out of my mind when we lived together. She hurt me more than once—I mean *really* hurt, and I've got scars to prove it. I know she loved me, but that doesn't make her perfect and me a double-damned bitch. Love affairs have broken up before. The world keeps on spinning!" She spoke fiercely to bolster up her words. For the truth was that Laura remembered only too well the night Beebo had told her she might kill her someday, and then herself.

But she couldn't let Lili see that, or suspect it, or think that Laura feared it. She hated Lili with all the force of her own fear and uncertainty and resentment at that moment, and her wild hair and hot face actually did scare Lili.

"All right," Lili said finally, putting her drink down on a dainty Empire drawer table near the door. "All right, Laura Landon, I'll tell you something." And Laura saw now that Lili had to defend the things she had said with a good serving of bitter anger: the *pièce de résistance*. "You think Beebo would welcome you back with loving arms? You think she'd forgive you?"

"I didn't say that!"

"You think I've been kidding about how hard she took it when you broke up? When you left her? Sure you do. You make yourself think it. Because you don't want to feel guilty about it. But you listen to this. Listen!" she cried suddenly as Laura made a sudden move to leave.

Lili threw herself against the door, panting with the exaltation of mingled fear and pleasure at hurting Laura. "Remember Nix? Remember that nice little dog you hated so much? Oh, you hated him all right. Beebo didn't have to tell me, I saw it with my own eyes. Everybody did. You did everything but kick him. And I wouldn't be surprised if you did even *that* when nobody was looking. Well, what happened to poor Nix?"

"You know damn well!" Laura flashed, feeling trapped and desperate. "You know as well as I do. Let me out of here, Lili!"

"He died, didn't he? Rather messily. Let's say, horribly. Such a nice little dog. You know how he died, Laura?"

"If you're trying to say I did it—"

"Beebo killed him. Sliced him in half with that big chef's knife you had in the kitchen table drawer."

For a horrified second, Laura was silent, paralyzed. She almost fainted. She actually staggered backwards and lost her balance. Lili grabbed her to break the fall and left her lying on the floor, her face buried in the plush carpet, sobbing, wailing with shock and horror. Even Lili, finally, was worried about her. She tried to snap her out of it with sarcasm.

"You could have shown a little concern when it happened," she said, "instead of saving it all for now. It's a little late now. Those are crocodile tears, Laura." But they weren't, and Lili couldn't get much conviction into her voice. She bent over Laura and said, "Stop it! Really, Laura! Don't make a scene. Oh!" she exclaimed in exasperation and alarm. "And she accuses *me* of theatrics!" she cried to the ceiling, her hands to her temples.

After a long while Laura rolled over, her breath tumbling uncontrollably in and out of her, her face blotched and stricken.

"It isn't true, is it?" she whispered. "You just wanted to hurt me. Lili?"

Lili, sitting on the edge of her velvet couch, with her elbows on her knees and her chin in her hands, said, "It's true." She gazed at Laura and there was no pose, no elegance in her. It wasn't worth the effort now. Laura was beyond noticing or caring. With her face relaxed, the lines of thirty-seven years showed around Lili's mouth and eyes. She was wondering if the startling effect her words had had was worth it.

Laura looked sick. What a bother to have to call a doctor! She shouldn't have told her. She had had a good time roasting her. She should have let her go. But there was Laura, her bosom heaving, her face a strange color, her eyes enormous. *Odd, I never noticed how big they are,* Lili thought idly.

"Did anyone . . . really . . . beat her up?" Laura said, her breath betraying her and making her gasp. "Or did she make up the hoodlums, too—like Nix?" And she covered her face to cry while Lili answered her.

"She did that to herself. After she killed Nix. I don't know why she did it. I hate to admit it, but I guess she did it out of frustrated love. I tried to make her explain it when she told me about it—and believe me, she wouldn't have if she hadn't been fried—and she just said, 'Laura hated him. I thought she might stay with me longer if he was gone.' After she did it she beat herself. I don't know how. I don't know with what. She didn't say. Maybe she just whacked at herself with her fists. Maybe she used something heavy. Anyway, she did it while she was hysterical. At least, that's what I think. I don't see how she could have hurt herself that much if she hadn't been half crazy. She was mourning for Nix and she was afraid of losing you."

Lili stopped talking, and Laura realized dimly that there had been no cutting edge in her voice for the past few minutes.

After a little while of silence Laura got up dizzily from the floor and dried her eyes. Her face had gone very white and she sat down for a minute in a chair.

"Did you ever love her?" Lili asked. "Really?"

Laura turned to look at her, and her eyes seemed remarkably deep and different, as if she had seen something for the first time. She didn't seem to have heard Lili.

"Did you ever love her, Laura?" Lili asked again.

"Not until now," Laura said, and Lili stared at her.

When Laura got home, all she wanted was to go in the bedroom, turn out all the lights, and crawl half dressed into her bed. And try to make sense of her awful knowledge, try to live with it. She couldn't think of Beebo without pain.

Jack followed her into the bedroom where she sprawled on the bed sobbing. He went to her and said worriedly, "Jesus, honey. Tell me about it." He sat down beside her, his hands on her shoulders trying to ease her. "Did the stock market crash?"

She wept on as if he weren't there.

"You got a bad pickle in your hamburger?"

No response.

"Your girdle split?"

She rolled over and looked at him with mournful eyes. "Jack, this is no time to be stupid."

"I can't say anything very bright till you tell me what's the matter," he said.

Laura blew her nose hard. He made her feel ludicrous and she resented it. "Beebo," she said finally. "Beebo. Oh, Jack." She looked at him with red eyes. "She *must* have killed your little dog. The one you gave her after Nix died."

"*Must* have?"

"She killed Nix. Nobody beat her up. She did it to herself."

They stared at each other, Jack beginning to share her feelings.

He heaped his scorn on Beebo. "Damn!" he said. "Damn silly hysterical female. I thought Beebo had more sense than most women."

"Just because she's not *like* most women?" Laura cried. "Jack, you make me furious! The more mannish a woman is, the more sense you think she's got! God! Beebo's *sick!* She's sick or she wouldn't have done it. When I think what she must have gone through, I—oh . . ." And she wept again, silently and hard. "She's no damn silly female. You damn silly *man!*"

"What *is* she, then?" he asked, smiling a little.

Laura turned back to the bed and muttered, "I don't know. She's mixed up and unhappy and maybe she's still in love with me. She's miserable because of me, anyway. I know that much."

"Isn't that touching," Jack commented acidly. "You have a desirable woman walloping herself and bisecting dachs-hunds out of love for you. It must do wonders for your ego."

Laura didn't even answer. She just flew at him, nails first, and took a wild swipe at his face. She missed; Jack was fast, and prepared. But she struggled desperately with him with her knees, her elbows, teeth and nails, until she was exhausted. She didn't last long. Lili had taken the fight out of her.

He laid her back down on the bed when she was gulping for air and went to get her some coffee.

"Now, tell me where you learned about Beebo," he said when he returned.

After a long, reluctant pause she answered him. Her basic trust in him persuaded her, but she promised herself that if he got sarcastic again she would stop speaking to him. Permanently.

"I saw Lili this afternoon," she whispered.

He gave a snort. "For old times' sake?" he asked.

"To ask about Beebo," she said haughtily.

"And she told you that romantic little tale? About carving up Nix?"

"Yes."

"And you believed her?"

"Yes. She wasn't kidding."

"Oh, she never does," he said with false agreement.

Laura flipped over to face him, her face red, but he interrupted her before she could get a word out. "Okay, she told the truth, we'll say." He moved her coffee gently toward her as he spoke. "And if she did it's pretty awful and it's pretty sad. And I wish like hell that it hadn't happened to Beebo, because she's a damn nice kid and I always liked her. I'm sorry about it, Laura—"

"Sorry!" she exploded. "What a stinking little word that is for what she must have gone through!"

"What's in a word, honey?" Jack shrugged, frowning. "You want a eulogy? I'm sorry, if Beebo really did it. That's not fancy but it's true. I can't put Nix back together. I can't order you to love Beebo the way she loves you."

There was a long silence then while Laura considered what he said. Her feelings for Beebo seemed to have undergone a transformation that afternoon. It was as if she saw clearly, and for the first time, into Beebo's secret heart, into her pain and frustration and passion. And Laura's own heart melted, touched, awed, a little exalted even to think that she could have inspired such a wonderful, terrible, mad, single-minded love in anybody. All of a sudden it seemed very valuable to her. She wanted it back, just the way it had been. She would know how to respect it now.

She lay there looking at Jack and felt a small fear licking at her heart like a flame. What if her love for Beebo became more precious to her than her love for Jack?

She said pensively, "I felt so bad about everything. I've been so selfish."

"Not with me, honey."

There was a long pause. At last she said, "You mean—going to the doctor, and everything?"

"That's only part of it." He got up and went to her.

Laura was standing in her bare feet, leaning against a wall and looking out at the East River. Her eyes were fastened on the night lights of the city. Jack touched her shoulder.

"Laura, darling, I've loved you for a long time . . . ever since we met, I think. I've never loved you less than I did at the start. And now I love you much much more. Just the fact that you were willing to try for a child means the whole world to me. Even if it never works out. I can't love you with my body. You wouldn't want it even if I could. But I don't think I've ever loved anyone as much as you, honey. Not even the lovely boys I could never resist. Not even Terry, and there never was a lovelier one. When all the sweat and passion are over with there's nothing but ashes and melancholy. Nothing's deader than a gay love that's burned out. But with you . . . I don't know, it just goes on and on. It's steady and comforting. It won't fail me, no matter what. It gives me a little faith —not much, but a little—in myself. In people. In you."

Laura turned her head away so he wouldn't see the tears.

"Laura, you can say what you please but you'll never convince me that I did a cowardly thing marrying you. A selfish thing, yes. A hell of a selfish thing. I think I would have gone to pieces without you. But I wasn't running away from my old life as much as I was running to a new one."

Suddenly Laura felt a big ugly need to fight. Maybe it was just to let off steam after a nerve-wracking afternoon. Maybe it was to make her forget how guilty she felt about Beebo. Probably it was both.

Laura turned and walked away from him, feeling his hand slip from her shoulder, unwanted and unsure. "Well, I don't know why *you* left the Village but I think I know why *I* did. Finally," she said. Her voice was hard and she knew she was going to hurt him and she cringed from it almost as much as he did. And still she spoke, compulsively. "I left because it was the only way I could see out of my problems. You were my escape hatch, Jack. You were just too damn convenient."

"That's my charm," he said harshly. "Ask Terry."

"It isn't the first time I've run away from my problems. I ran away from Beth in college. I ran away from my father. From Marcie—remember her? She was straight. I didn't find out till I tried to make love to her."

"I remember. You ran straight to me. And if you hadn't you'd be enjoying a protracted vacation in a mental institution at this moment."

"You helped, I admit it. I don't know what I would have done. But that's not the point. The point is, that here I am doing it again. Running away. Not *to* you this time, but *with* you."

"So?" he said. "So we run away. So what the hell? Let's run. Who gives a damn? What's *eating* you, Laura?"

"It's wrong, that's what! You told me when we left the Village I'd get over it and Beebo didn't matter . . . she'd survive. And I believed you. Until today."

"And now you think she won't survive?" he asked bitingly. "Because of something she did ten months ago while you were still living with her?"

Laura was swallowed up for a moment in a sob. "I want her!" she gasped finally. "Oh, God and Heaven, I want her!" And she stamped her foot like a furious child.

When she was quiet enough so he could talk without shouting, Jack said, "Sure. I want Terry. But we're poison together. So are you and Beebo. If you go to her you'll come running back to Uncle Jack before the month is out. Fed up all over again. Only this time there'll be a difference. This time Beebo really will commit mayhem. Or murder. Or both. And if you don't run fast enough, Mother, it may be you she murders. I wouldn't put it past her."

"I want her back!" Laura amazed herself with her own words, words she never meant to say. Jack stared at her, his face pale and determined.

"You can't have her."

"Jack," she said, suddenly pleading, "let me go to her. Just for a week or two. Please. Please let me." She walked toward him as she spoke, her arms extended.

"No," he said flatly. "Two weeks, hell." He was afraid she wouldn't ever come back.

"Jack, I wouldn't stay. I'd come back to you."

"No!" It was absolute. He couldn't take the chance. "We've had all this out. We agreed to it before we got married."

"Jack, darling—"

"I won't talk about it, Laura. You can't go back to her and that's final."

"But only for a week or two, just a few days . . ."

"You're my wife," he blazed so fiercely that she stopped in her tracks, startled. "You're my wife and you're not going to live with any Lesbian in any Village! Not while I live!"

She tried once more. "Jack, don't you understand? For the first time I'm beginning to realize how I feel about her, how I always felt. Tris made me realize it a little. And now Lili. And even living with you—"

"Living with me has made you lonesome for women, that's all. And Beebo's a handy woman. Goddam it, Laura, I never denied you women. I've encouraged you. Admit it, go on! I've *asked* you to chase a few broads. It's not my fault if you've developed an itch. Go out and have yourself a fling; you should have done it long ago. I don't give a damn, only don't go to Beebo. And come back. Come back here, you understand? If you don't I'll come after you! And I'm capable of mayhem myself!"

She looked at his big burning eyes and trembled. "I just want to see her," she whispered.

"What makes you think she wants to see *you?*" he demanded. "What makes you think she won't greet you at the door with the same knife she used on Nix?"

"That's what Lili said."

"Well, for once Lili is right. I know Beebo; she's crazy. You catch her on a wrong day in a wrong mood and she won't even think about it. She'll just operate on you as she did on the dogs." He gazed unblinking at her. "That would kill me, Laura, as sure as it would you. Besides, I can't take any chances. You might be carrying my child."

This struck fury into Laura. She had nearly managed to forget the child, in the press of other things, but no longer. She picked up a pair of his shoes, sprawled near the closet, and flung them at him, one after the other. One flew through the window, splattering glass in its wake, and the other struck his arm.

"Why do you torment me?" she shouted. "Why do you talk about nothing but baby, baby, baby? I never wanted the damn thing! I hope I never have a baby! I hope I never have *your* baby! I hope it's born a boy! I hope it's born blind! I hope it's never born at all!" She was screaming at him, and he came to her carefully, coaxing her.

"You're all wrought up, Mother," he said. He could see

that she was hysterical.

"Don't call me Mother!" she shrieked, her voice strained so that she could hardly articulate.

"Laura, for God's sake," he said, trying to brush it off, trying to keep calm, help her. "I call you 'Mother' in honor of my Oedipus complex. Purely a formality. It has nothing to do with babies. Come lie down, honey. Come on. I'll get you something to quiet you down. Come on," he wheedled gently, but she looked at him like he meant to murder her then and there, backing away from him. When he made a quick move to grab her, she sprang away, picking up the stool to her dressing table. She threw it at him with all her strength. While he dodged she grabbed her shoes and coat and ran from the room.

At the front door she paused briefly to stare at him with desperate eyes and then she heaved an ashtray at him and fled. It cut his hand, which he threw up to protect his face.

Laura ran down the stairs. There was no time to wait for the elevator. She could hear Jack behind her, running and calling her name. At the front door she turned swiftly toward the river and climbed a chain link fence, ripping the flesh here and there along her limbs and tearing her blouse. She dropped, torn and gasping, to the other side just as Jack burst from the door and looked wildly in all directions for her. She rolled soundlessly some feet down the long slope that ended in chill black water.

There she waited, sobbing quietly, clinging to handfuls of greasy mud and roots and embedded rocks. She heard his footsteps going toward First Avenue. He thought she would run for a taxi or hide in a doorway. Laura scrambled and stumbled south along the embankment, not waiting for him to come back looking for her. There was a suffocating panic in her. She didn't question it or wonder where it came from. She just did as it bid her, struggling through the dirt on the incline.

There was no looking back, no stopping for rest. She moved forward doggedly, tripping and sinking to her knees and clambering up again and going on, trying to stay near the fence in case she lost her footing. The going was slippery and rough and her breath rasped in and out with a fast whining sound. She had gone nearly three blocks when a jutting stone, invisible in the semi-dark, threw her, and she felt herself begin to skid and roll. She made a wild grab for the fence but it was already fifteen feet above her and receding fast. The wind was bumped out of her and she could not even scream. She had no idea how far she had fallen before she stopped.

Laura lay gasping and moaning for a few minutes, trying to get her breath back. She knew she was crying but she made no effort to stop. She moved herself gently to see if anything was broken, but the ground was not hard and she had missed the bad stones. She had no idea how long she had been there. It might have been minutes, it might have been hours. She thought vaguely it must have been hours when she finally stirred, chilled through, and opened her eyes. Beside her, on the ground, sat a man.

Laura screamed, a weak shuddering noise, and fell back, covering her face with her hands.

"Don't mind me," he said. "I won't hurt you."

Laura felt herself trembling with fear. She tried to pull her torn clothes straight, but it was so dark she could hardly see what she was doing. When he turned his face toward her she could see a little of it. It was very indeterminate; there was no way to guess his age or anything about him.

She stood up quickly and started to scramble up the hill, but he said, "There's an easier way."

She gave him one quick scared glance and then went on, but he stood up and said, "There's steps about a half block on."

Again she turned, very wary but willing to listen now. It looked a million miles to the top.

"I'll show you," he offered. His voice was not menacing and he stood facing her with his hands in his back pockets, a black statue with silver edges. "Come on, I'll walk ahead."

He turned then and went southward, agile and sure. After a moment Laura began to follow him, moving clumsily and with great effort, trying to copy his movements and praying that he wouldn't suddenly attack her. She stooped and grabbed a sharp stone glinting at her feet and held it tight in a sweating hand, just in case.

He heard her panting behind him and stopped, bringing Laura up sharp with a gasp. "You're tired," he said. "Want to sit down a minute?"

She shook her head at him.

"You can talk to me, I'm no devil," he said. And she had the idea he was grinning at her. But when she maintained her tense silence he shrugged and turned back. Now and then he glanced at her to see how she was doing. "Want some help?" he asked when she stumbled once, leaning toward her, but she drew back fast and he said, "Okay. Just trying to help."

They walked for a few moments and Laura was almost ready to bolt from him when she realized that the lights ahead she had taken for far distant were in reality small bulbs strung up to illuminate a row of steps.

"Maybe you're wondering who I am," he said almost hope-fully as they neared the steps, as if he had a story to tell and was looking for a listener.

He turned, one hand on the iron rail that ran alongside the steps, and held out a hand to her. "Here y'are. Help you?"

She ignored him, turning her back to him to swing a leg over the low railing.

"Don't you wonder who I am?" he said. "I don't help just anybody, little girl." He spoke sharply. "Don't you want to know my name?"

"No!" she cried suddenly, angrily, startling herself. "You're just a man and all men are alike. No matter what their names are!" He gaped at her, astonished. "You don't really care about me, only about yourself. You don't want to know *my* name, you only want me to know *yours*." She spoke breath-lessly at breakneck speed. "You can't suffer like a woman can. You aren't made to take it, you men. You're just made big enough and brute enough to hurt us. But we can't hurt you. We can't hurt you, do you hear?" And she stopped abruptly, putting her hand over her mouth in a storm of self-pity and shame and revulsion. It was Jack she was screaming at, not this stranger. She couldn't believe she had hurt Jack as she had hurt Beebo or it would destroy her. She screamed to make herself believe she couldn't really hurt him, no matter what she did.

The tears burst from her eyes when she saw it all for a lie. A lie shouted to spare her own tortured feelings. The man looked at her, patient now and unamazed. He was over his first surprise. And hers was not the first desperate speech he had heard on the shores of the East River.

Laura began to run up the steps.

"You won't get far, looking like that," he called after her.

Momentarily Laura stopped and looked at herself in dis-may. She turned and glanced back at her guide. He was standing on the steps some twenty feet below her, smiling at her consternation. He was a large man, big-boned, and she thought, *My God, he could break me in two. Like my father.*

"Cat got your tongue?" he said.

She started up again on shaky legs and he called, "Is that all the thanks I get?"

At this Laura began to run, but to her alarm he ran after her. She felt her heart balloon in her chest, beating frantically, and when he caught her, only a few steps from the top, she yelled in fear. She would have screamed without stopping until somebody heard her if he had not wrapped a big hand around her mouth and forced her against the gate.

"I won't hurt you," he said. "I told you that. I never hurt anyone. I'm harmless." He grinned, and Laura, squirming under his big hand, was dizzy with panic.

He held her quietly for a few minutes as if to assure her that he spoke in good faith. Finally he asked her, "Where are you going?" and released her mouth. When she tried to holler at once he covered it again.

"I'll ask you again," he said. "But don't yell. Where are you going?"

When he freed her mouth this time she murmured, "Home. I'm going home. Let me go."

"How you getting home?"

"I—I'll walk. It's not far. Just a block."

"You know what block this is?" He smiled with superior knowledge.

"It can't be far," she said.

He shook his head quizzically. "I don't get it. You're not even drunk. You're tore up but you're no tramp neither. Mostly the ones I find down here are hitting the bottle. Or they wouldn't be down here. Or kids, exploring. Not pretty girls." He smiled and Laura's one intense hope was that she not faint and fall into his clutches.

"Let me go," she said, trying to sound controlled. But her big eyes and urgent breathing gave her away.

"Okay." He took his hands away from her altogether, and said, "Go. But I'll bet you need a dime to telephone with."

She turned, dragging on the gate behind her until he said, "Here. Let me." He opened it for her. And when she saw that he was really going to let her go, she allowed herself to turn and look at him. See him. He was holding out a dime.

"Take it," he said. "At least you can call somebody to come get you."

Laura stared at him. He was big and ugly, seamy-faced, and wearing dirty clothes with a worn cap tilted over his ear. But he had a nice honest grin. And he looked, for all his dirt and size, rather childish. Laura stood poised at the gate, wavering between flight and the dime. At last she took it, her face reddening. She had to drop her sharp stone to get it.

"Didn't need that, didya?" he said with a smile, watching it fall.

She shook her head and whispered, "Thanks."

"That's all I want to hear," he said and let her go. She ran halfway down the block, and then turned, overwhelmed with curiosity, to see what had happened to him. He was standing there behind the closed gate gazing after her, smiling. *He's nuts,* she thought. *An idiot. A damn man! That's probably all he does, save people from the river. But even that . . . even that pitiful life is worth more than mine. All I've ever done is hurt the people I love the most.*

At the end of the block she stopped running and looked once more. He was gone.

10

LAURA HID HERSELF for a minute in a shadowed doorway and tried to make sense of things. She was a mess, with mud on her torn clothes and on her face, tangled hair and dried blood.

She made an effort to smooth her hair down. There was some Kleenex in her pocket and she wiped her face off carefully, reaching every corner of it and rubbing till the skin turned pink. She brushed at her disheveled clothes rather hopelessly. Maybe it was late enough so nobody would notice her.

She began to walk, holding her arms together in front of her as if to keep herself warm, but in fact to keep the worst rips from showing. And she kept her head down. *If only the police don't stop me*, she thought. *I must look like a whore.*

Laura walked straight west on Forty-first Street, for it was Forty-first, past Lexington Avenue and Park and Fifth and Broadway and over to Seventh. No cops stopped her, although more than one passerby stared.

It was cold, a raw March night with the sting of coming storm in the air. Laura went south on Seventh Avenue, walking almost mechanically. When she thought of it she realized it was cold. But she hardly thought of it. There was too much else on her mind.

She was very surprised to reach Fourth Street so quickly. She had known, without thinking, that that was where she was going. In less than five minutes she had entered the little court in front of Beebo's apartment building and the old familiar trembling had begun.

She sat down on a bench in the court to gather her strength. At last she looked up the wall of dark windows behind her, twisting on the bench to see, and saw lights in Beebo's living room, and began to shiver.

Ten or a dozen times she looked up anxiously at the lights on the second floor. They were faint, as if only one small light were on. With a sudden rush of desire that eliminated the need to make a decision, she pulled open the inside door and raced up the stairs.

At the top she stood trying desperately to get her breath. But she knew after a moment that her whole body would shake and sweat and wear itself out with unbearable anticipation if she didn't get the door open. She reached for the knob, but it was locked.

She rattled the knob hard and then she knocked.

When the door swung open a moment later she gasped in amazement. It was Milo Robinson—Tris's husband.

"Milo!" she exclaimed.

He stared at her.

"Don't you remember me? I'm Laura. Laura Landon."

"I remember," he said quietly. "I just never saw you fresh out of the gutter before."

She looked down at herself and her cheeks went scarlet. "I look awful, don't I?"

"Somebody after you?" Milo asked.

"Yes. No. I don't know. Can I come in?"

"I guess you can," he said, stepping back. "You've got as much right to be here as me, that's for sure."

Laura walked into the living room and just the sight of it, warm and comfortable and a little raggy, made her want to weep. She sank down on the couch, exhausted.

"Want some coffee?" Milo said, staring at her.

"No, thanks. I've had too much tonight."

"Milk?"

"I guess so. Thanks."

"You look real bad, Laura. You'd better get to bed," he said frowning at her.

"Where's Beebo?"

"Tell me that and I'll tell you where my wife is," he said sharply.

"You coming back to Beebo?" he asked her.

"If she'll have me."

"From what I know of it, she won't. But I'm on your side, Laura. I'd do anything to pry Patsy loose."

It startled her to hear him call Tris by her real name. "Is Beebo in love with her?" she asked cautiously.

"Naw," he said with leisurely disgust. "She puts up with her but she's not in love with her." He ambled out to the kitchen to pour her some milk. "I should be so lucky," he called. "I'd dump her. Right now."

"How about Tris? How does she feel?"

He answered her while he poured the milk. "I don't know, Laura. I never could figure that kid. Living with her only makes it more confusing." He sounded very tired, like a man defeated. "I wish I could forget her, forget the whole thing."

He came back and handed her the milk and sat down in a chair near her.

They looked at each other. He was a tall young man in his early twenties, handsome and well educated. His skin was dark and satiny in the pink lamplight.

"Does she love you?" Laura asked gently.

He shrugged and gave a little laugh. "Who knows?" he said. "She says so now and then. But that's only when I lay down the law on the Lessie stuff."

"What's the law?" Laura said.

"Well, goddam it, enough's enough!" he exclaimed. "I like to see her once in a while myself. She's my wife."

Laura thought of Jack and felt the tears start quietly down again. "Excuse me," she sniffled. "I'm running like a sieve tonight. I don't know why. Did Jack Mann come over here tonight?"

"I wouldn't know," Milo said. "I've only been here since midnight."

"Did he call?"

"Nobody called."

"Nobody?" She had been so certain Jack would follow her here. "When does Beebo get in?"

"You tell me, then we'll both know." He sighed.

"What will you do with Tris, Milo?" She spoke softly, sympathetically, in a raspy tired voice.

"Take her home again."

"Do you understand her? What makes her so contrary?"

"No." He turned and gave her a doleful grin, lighting another cigarette from the first. "We've been married almost two years but I don't know her at all, to tell the truth. But I sure won't let her go."

"Does she want you to?"

"I don't think she does," he said. "Sound screwy? Well, not so very. She needs me. Because I'm a man." There was a pause and Laura mopped up the useless tears and tried to think of Milo's troubles, not her own.

"How long are you going to stay?" she asked him finally.

"I guess till they get back," he said.

"Are you sure they're together?"

"More or less. Patsy has a big thing on her."

"Milo? Would you stay here till they get back, then? I'm afraid—I'm afraid of Beebo. She might hurt me."

He looked at her thoughtfully. "Yeah. Okay," he said, studying her. "Say, haven't you been gone a while? Patsy doesn't tell me much, but I got the idea . . . I haven't seen you around or anything."

"Yes. I've been gone awhile," she said, getting up. "I'm going to take a shower and get cleaned up. Don't tell her I'm here if she comes."

"Patsy?"

"Beebo! Either of them."

"Who shall I say is in the shower?"

"Santa Claus," she said. She looked at him sitting glumly slumped in the chair. "Why do you put up with it?" she said. "She's too much. Tris is too much for anybody."

"Don't call her Tris. She's been Patsy ever since she was six years old and skinned her knees in front of my house. Tris. Christ! It's too affected."

"Did she . . . every really love me, Milo?" Laura asked it with a catch in her throat.

"Did she ever love any of us? I don't know."

"Why do you keep coming back for more?"

He shrugged. "Same reason you do. You love Beebo. You know it's a mess and you're in for a lot of hell. It'll never be right. But you love her. So you take it." He gave another sad little chuckle. "I wish I knew what it is about you girls. What makes you love each other?" Laura stared at him. "If I knew there's one thing sure—I'd put a stop to it. What makes you queer, Laura? You tell me."

"What makes you normal, Milo?"

"I was born that way. Don't tell me you were *born* queer! Ha!" And he was sarcastic now.

"I was made that way," she said calmly.

"By who?" he asked skeptically.

"A lot of people. My father. A girl named Beth. Myself. Fate."

He snorted. "Why don't you give up women?"

"Why don't *you!*" she flashed.

He blinked at her, beginning to feel her stormy intensity.

572

"Is it *that* bad?" he asked.

"*Sure*, it's that bad! Do you think I live this way because I like it? Would you live like you do if you could live like a white man?"

After a moment he shook his head, looking curiously at her.

"Neither would Tris. *Patsy*. So don't be too hard on her, Milo. You damn men, you're all lousy selfish bastards."

And to his astonishment, she threw the dirty dime at him.

Laura was pulling on a pair of Beebo's big men's flannel pajamas when she heard the front door open, and her heart came to a sudden stop in her breast. It started again with a wild thump, and she stood with an ear to the door struggling to pull the roomy tops over her damp body and hear what was said.

"Where is she?" Milo demanded.

The front door shut and there was a pause. Laura heard the scrape of a match and the soft whistle of expelled breath.

"I sent her home," Beebo said. And her voice sent a sharp thrill of desire and recognition through Laura. She pressed her hands firmly over her breasts till the flesh nearly burst between her fingers, as if to still her own hard breathing.

"Where, the studio?" Milo said.

"Yeah. You entertaining, Milo?"

"What?"

"Who's the milk drinker?"

And Laura remembered suddenly the milk Milo had fixed her. She hadn't finished it; just left it sitting on the table.

"Santa Claus," Milo said.

"No kidding," Beebo said with a grin. "I used to leave Santa Claus a glass of milk. And cookies. When I was a little kid. But that was Christmas Eve. This isn't Christmas Eve, Milo."

"Check the shower," Milo said. "I didn't ask her over. You sure Patsy's home?"

"Hell, no," Beebo said and she was right by the bedroom door. Laura leaped backwards across the room, stumbling and catching herself on the bed. She straightened up, her heart in her throat, watching the door. Her long blond hair was still damp from the shower, and she had on only the long, striped tops of Beebo's pajamas. They reached to mid-thigh on her.

Beebo's hand twisted the knob. "Go home, friend," she said to Milo, pausing. "Your wife needs a man tonight."

Milo shrugged at her. "She asked me to stay."

"*Who* asked you to stay?"

He thumbed at the bedroom. "Says you might hurt her."

Beebo stared hard at him for only a second more before she threw the door open hard. It cracked like a shot against the wall and Laura opened her eyes slowly. Her arms were crossed at the wrists and clamped tight over her breasts, as if to ward off attack. She looked at Beebo and Beebo looked at her without a word for several amazed minutes. Laura felt such a flash of agonized desire for this big, handsome, passionate girl who had been her lover that she was unable to speak.

Finally Beebo walked slowly into the room, her hands shoved into the pockets of her pants, squinting through the smoke of the cigarette between her lips. "I thought Lili was kidding," she said softly. "Seeing things." And she gave a single short laugh. She walked to the bed and dropped her coat. "Relax, Laura, I'm not going to rape you," she said. She turned, with her weight on one foot and the other on the bed rung, and called to Milo, "You can go now, Sir Galahad."

"It's all right?" He came to the door and looked at Laura, who finally found the strength to nod at him. "Okay," he said. He looked her up and down, surprised to find how desirable she looked with a clean skin and no rags. "Lotsa luck, girls," he said with his rueful defeated smile, and he went out.

"Thank you, Milo," Laura called after him, but her voice was so low and husky with emotion that he did not hear her.

There followed a long strange silence while Beebo stared at her. Laura kept her eyes on her toes, afraid to meet that penetrating gaze.

At last Beebo crushed her cigarette and lay down on the bed, crossing her feet and stuffing her hands behind the pillow to raise her head.

"All right, Laura," she said calmly. "You're here. Tell me what you want."

Laura looked up then, slowly, still very afraid. She was prepared for any violence, any brutality. It no longer mattered if Beebo hurt her or not. She was ready to submit to anything if Beebo would only take her back.

"What do you want?" Beebo said.

"To stay," she whispered.

Beebo's eyes widened with surprise. "To stay? With me?" She looked away then at the wall. "You could have stayed last August."

"Last August I was miserably unhappy because of you. I had to get away. I found out I'm more unhappy without you than with you."

Beebo laughed outright then. "Doesn't give you much of a choice, does it?" she said and her voice was not kind. Her laughter made Laura realize that she was a little drunk. Laura walked over to the side of the bed and knelt beside it, with her heart working as if it had taken her up a stiff hill.

Beebo turned her head to watch her. "What's that for?" she said, catching a corner of her pajamas between thumb and forefinger. Her flesh was only inches away from Laura's for the first time in eight long months and there was a sudden current of feeling between them that leaped like a spark from Beebo's hand to Laura's breasts.

"I had to change. My clothes were filthy. I took a shower and borrowed your pajamas. . . . I've been walking all night. All the way from midtown."

"What the hell did you do that for? Don't they still have taxis in this town?" She was cold. Her hand dropped away from Laura.

"I didn't have any money. And I had to see you."

"Why?"

Laura put her head down on the bed on her clasped hands and began to cry. "I love you," she wept. And it was the first time since they had met that Beebo had heard her say it that way.

She got up on one elbow and leaned toward Laura. Her face was impassive, but shrewd. "Not Tris?" she said.

"Not Tris."

"Anybody else?"

"Nobody else." Laura lifted her tearful face. "Oh, Beebo, I've done you so wrong, darling. I didn't know how bad it was. Lili told me—"

"I know she did, the miserable bitch. God damn her soul. The only secret she can keep is her age."

"Beebo, I'll do anything for you—anything—if you'll have me back. Oh, darling, it took me months to figure out what was wrong with me. I've been so confused. And lately I've been thinking of you all the time. I don't think I ever stopped loving you, Beebo. I thought when you saw me here you'd beat the hell out of me. If you want to . . . do it . . . if it'll help." She looked at her out of large frightened eyes, half expecting

Beebo to jump her.

But Beebo sat up then, grasping her ankles with her hands. "No, Laura, it's too late for that. What good would that do?" She made a face, frowning. "There was a time when I would have. If you had come back last fall instead of now. I would have loved you enough then to hate you. But I've changed, Laura . . . It doesn't seem to matter so much any more."

There was a shocked silence from Laura. "You mean," she ventured finally, "you don't love me any more? Oh, Beebo! Oh, Beebo! No!" She covered her mouth with both hands, pressed so tight they turned white.

Beebo looked at her curiously. "I love you, Laura," she said, but it was impersonal, detached, as if it were just another fact in her life like her job or her black hair. "I'll always love you. But I'll never love you again the way I did before you ran out on me last summer. That was too much. When it happened it was a question of either dying of it . . . or living with something else, changing myself. Becoming a different person. That's what happened."

Laura, in her desperation, found the courage to touch Beebo then. She reached out for her, and Beebo unexpectedly turned to help her. She dragged Laura up on the bed with her two strong arms, and Laura gave a long groan of need and fear and gratitude, all mixed up together. Beebo held her in both arms, her back pressed against the wall, watching Laura struggle to control her tears and trembling. She was kind, she was patient. And it scared Laura, who suddenly discovered that she missed the old stormy fury and passion. Beebo seemed odd to her, and it was true that she had changed.

"Laura," she said. "I've been doing some thinking. I want to tell you something. Maybe you won't want to come back to me so much any more."

"Let me tell you something first," Laura begged. "If I don't tell you, Beebo, I haven't any right to touch you. I haven't any right to be here. Maybe I don't anyway. Darling, I—I'm married." Beebo gasped a little, and Laura said quickly, "To Jack."

Beebo simply gaped at her for a second and then she burst out laughing. "Good God! *That's* what happened!" she exclaimed. "You and Jack. Oh, God!"

"It wasn't exactly—ridiculous," Laura whispered, hurt. "We loved each other." But Beebo went on laughing.

"I'm sorry, baby, but it sounds so damn—goofy," she said. And when she called her baby, Laura felt a small glow of warmth and hope. Maybe it wasn't hopeless; maybe things could work out. She clung to Beebo and found herself half laughing with her, and half weeping to hear Jack's name.

"Where is he now? Does he know you're here?" Beebo asked her.

"He knows," Laura said, for there could be no doubt that he did.

"Did he send you? Married life got him down?"

"No, I ran away. I—I hurt him. It meant so much to him to have a wife and all. . . ." She couldn't say any more about it; it broke her up to think of it.

Beebo sobered a little. "You have a talent for that, Laura—hurting people. Sometimes I think that's your only real ability."

"I know," Laura murmured, shame-faced. "And the trouble is, I never want to. I never mean to. I'd give anything to undo it, once it's done. But I begin to feel like I'm smothering. Like I'd die of it if I can't get away."

"Is that the way I made you feel?" Beebo said.

Laura hung her head. "Yes," she whispered. "I won't lie about it."

"You can't very well. I read the damn diary—every word of it."

Laura flushed at the thought of the thing. "Beebo, I—I didn't understand before how you felt. Or how I felt myself. But I know now I love you." She said it quivering with hope.

But Beebo only answered, "Do you, Laura? How do you know?" There was a little smile on Beebo's face. She asked the question gently as if she were talking to a bewildered child, brushing Laura's hair from her forehead.

"Because I want so terribly to be with you," Laura said, shaking her head to emphasize her words. "I can't bear it like this, being apart from you."

"I've changed so much," Beebo said, wondering at it, "and you haven't changed at all. Have you? I think you're just tired of being a wife, honey."

"No. I love Jack. But it's different. I don't *need* him like I need you."

"How about Jack? Doesn't he need you?"

Laura covered her face again with her hands to stifle the

sudden sobs. "A lot, I'm afraid. I'd be better off dead, Beebo, I swear I would. I've caused so much heart ache. And most of all to myself. I'm no good to anybody. I wish to God you'd get that big knife and do to me what you did to Nix. I wish you'd beat me the way you beat yourself—"

"Laura! God, spare me!" And for a second the latent fire in her flared and gave Laura a curious thrill.

"I thought you would," Laura cried. "I was prepared for anything, even that, when I came here. I still can't believe you —I mean, you seem so funny. I thought you'd hurt me, and you're so calm, so quiet—"

Beebo shook her head, looking at Laura with her disillu-sioned eyes. "I won't hurt you, baby," she said.

"You said once you'd kill me," Laura said wildly, as if she were asking for it, as if it would be proof of Beebo's huge need for her.

"I know. I meant it then, too. I was nearly crazy. But things have changed, Laura. I don't throw my threats around so easily any more. There was a time when I could have done it, but no more. No more. Stop crying, baby. Stop, honey." She began to stroke Laura's long hair.

Laura looked up at her through pink eyes, her chest heaving in Beebo's warm embrace, and they gazed at each other for some time before Beebo told her, kindly, trying to ease it for her, "I said I loved you, Laura. But it's not the same for me, now. I don't love you the way I used to. I couldn't and go on living. You were my whole life for two years. I thought I couldn't exist without you. I thought it would be better to kill you and die with you than go on without you. So what did I do?" She smiled in contempt for herself. And pity. A bitter smile. "I chickened out. I slaughtered a poor innocent pup instead. In the fury I should have saved for you. And what did it prove? Nothing. How did it help? It didn't. It was a wasted gesture, Laura. A stupid, senseless thing.

"But you see, I was out of my mind in love with you at the time. Now all the madness has gone out of me, Laura. There's not much fire left." And she bent suddenly to touch Laura's brow with her lips. Laura felt the sweet touch flow through her to her toes and she nestled close against Beebo, weeping at her words. "It's not wild and wonderful and tormenting any more."

"How did it happen?" Laura begged her, cruelly disappointed. "Maybe it'll change." She felt almost betrayed, as if she were in the arms of a stranger.

"No. I wouldn't want it to change, now. It happened be-cause if it hadn't I would have died, Laura. I was so sick, so lost without you, that I would have gone to pieces. I'd have used the damn cleaver on myself."

"Oh!" Laura breathed, horrified.

"I changed to save my life . . . and my sanity. It took all my strength, but I did it. And strangely enough, it was a relief. I felt as if I'd laid down a killing burden." She looked down at Laura, pulling her so tight that they could feel one another's hearts beating, and Laura, her eyes shut, was saying to herself, "No, no, no . . ."

"I love you still, baby," Beebo told her. "I know I should be proud and angry with you. I should kick you out or beat you up or both. But if I did it wouldn't mean anything. It would only hurt, like I hurt Nix, for no purpose. I know Lili and the rest of them will bitch at me for taking you back—"

"Oh, will you, Beebo? Darling, darling, will you?"

"If you want it that way. . . ." She stopped, looking into Laura's tear-bright eyes.

"I want it that way," Laura gasped.

But at the same time she had to realize that this was not her Beebo any more; that things had changed irreparably and forever between them; that the love they had left now was only good and tender, not the exalted, shivering passions of the past. It had to be so, because Beebo could never have for-given her, let alone taken her back, otherwise. *And it's my fault—all my fault. It's the price I have to pay to get her back,* Laura told herself.

"If you had been like this last summer . . . so calm, so casual," she whispered humbly, "I would have stayed."

"And now that I've calmed down, you want me wild again, don't you?" Beebo laughed a little, a sad, wise laugh. "Crazy, isn't it? Ironic and crazy. And there's not a goddamn thing we can do about it, Bo-peep. Either of us . . . baby. . . ." She lifted Laura's face and kissed it.

"I won't tell you how I missed you. I won't tell you what I went through. I wouldn't even know how. It took a lot out of me. Too much. But you're welcome to what's left. If you want it."

"I want it," Laura said passionately. "I want *you,* Beebo."

She hung her head. "Unless . . . unless you still want Tris?"

"I never did. I never wanted anybody else. I've been trying to give Tris back to Milo since she walked in on me the first time," Beebo said. "She'll give up on me when she finds out you're home. She won't want to make it a threesome."

"Home," Laura repeated. "Oh, Beebo . . ."

And suddenly her arms were locked around Beebo's neck and they were lost in kisses and thrilling, half-forgotten caresses and the warm satin touch of each other's bodies. The pajama top Laura had pulled on so frantically slipped off with no trouble, and she stretched out on the white spread beneath the girl she had loved so much, in spite of so much, and surrendered with a groan of delight tempered with sorrow. And perhaps the beginning of understanding at last.

It was only a matter of hours the next day before Laura knew that the feeling of strangeness she felt would not wear off. It was another two days before she could bring herself to give up hope that Beebo might change, that being together again would reawaken their crazy, beautiful, love affair.

But it was two whole weeks, two very long weeks full of wondering and self-pity and struggle and doubt, before Laura could tell herself that she had made a mistake.

Beebo was drained of feeling. She was tired, tired of love and even tired of life. Perhaps time and innate toughness would revive her, but she had nothing to give Laura now. Laura realized with chagrin how little she had to give Beebo. She had never given much, always taking, taking, taking, from the older girl, who seemed to have so much to offer. It had been too easy to help herself to that wealth of love and she understood now, painfully, that she had come back to Beebo to be worshipped again.

She had turned tail and run at the moment when her problems with Jack seemed too much for her, and she had run to the one person who had adored her spectacularly in the past. She needed her ego bolstered, she needed flattery and passion and reassurance from a woman. So it had come to her as an eye-opening blow to find her tempestuous lover subdued, transformed, almost a different person.

It never was right, Laura thought, watching Beebo over the dinner table. *She had to give beyond her strength and I took it all with no return. At least she was generous with her-*

self. *I was the selfish one. I always have been the selfish one.
I thought the world was giving me a bum deal, but I was too
selfish to see the good side. Even with Jack . . . Oh my God,
Jack. My poor darling. With him most of all.*

"What are you thinking about?" Beebo asked her, seeing
her absorption.

"I—I have to go back, Beebo," Laura said and her own
words startled her. "I have to see Jack once more." Once expressed, these feelings so long in the making made her feel
like crying. She looked apprehensively at Beebo, expecting her
sarcasm.

But Beebo only said, "I thought you would. Well, go on,
baby. Go tell him you're sorry, it was all a nasty misunderstanding." She spoke mildly.

"Don't make it sound cheap, Beebo," Laura pleaded.

"It won't be anything *but* cheap unless you go back to stay,"
Beebo told her. "Otherwise there's no point in going back
at all."

"But—but I'm going to live with you now," Laura faltered.
"I just have to see him once more. Explain to him—"

"You're his wife. Either go home to him and grow up or
don't go back. What do you think you'd accomplish with a
quickie visit, Bo-peep? Just pep him up a little? Make it all
bearable? You'd be lucky if he didn't run you out with a rifle.
If you haven't learned anything else in all this time, you *must*
have learned that you can't play around with love as if it were
a bargain basement special. Real love isn't a production line
thing, it isn't waiting for you in any old shop window. Haven't
you learned that yet, baby?"

Laura nodded, putting her head back against the chair and
letting the soothing tears flow quietly. "I've learned it. But
it's so hard to live by what you learn. I needed you so much
when I came back two weeks ago. But I needed you the way
you used to be." It was a difficult admission, but Beebo understood it.

"Sure," she said gently. "Now you've seen me. Now you
know what I couldn't find the words to tell you. It's over,
Laura. I'll always be here, I guess we'll always need each other
a little. Maybe we'll see each other now and then. But there's
no point in our living together."

Shame colored Laura's cheeks pink and she said warmly,
"I'm not a child, Beebo, and I didn't come back here just to

run off and leave you again. I gave up too much to come back."

"Yes, baby, I think you did. You gave up too much. It wasn't worth the price, and you see that now. Admit it. Don't be a stubborn idiot."

Laura was appalled at the apathy in her voice. "What would you do if I insisted on staying with you?" she asked.

Beebo shrugged. "I'd let you stay, of course. I haven't the ambition to kick you out. Besides, I love you still, in my way. I meant it when I said it."

Laura stood up, unable to look at her any more. "I'm going back to the apartment, and I'm going to talk to Jack," she said. "I'll be back in a couple of hours."

"I doubt it." Beebo did not even leave her chair. She lighted a cigarette slowly, watching Laura's back.

Finally Laura turned around and faced her. "Please, Beebo, don't talk to me as if nothing in the world mattered any more. I can't stand it, I can't stand to think I did it to you."

"Jack still matters, baby. Don't do it to him, too."

Laura went and got her coat and purse from the bedroom, and then she looked into the kitchen. Beebo sat with her back to the door, still smoking thoughtfully. "I'm leaving," Laura told her. "I should be back around nine."

"Sure, sweetheart. Tell old Jack I said hello."

"I will." Laura looked at her dark curly head, not sure if the frosting on her curls came from the kitchen light above or from the first gray hairs. She walked over to Beebo and kissed her cheek, leaning over her chair from behind. Beebo smiled though she did not turn her head.

And then Laura walked out, knowing somehow, deep within herself, that it was for the last time.

11

LAURA APPROACHED the apartment building with her legs trembling. It was all she could do to keep from turning around and running. It was hard to imagine what she might find. She left Jack a desperate man, and her absence for two weeks would not have made things any easier for him.

She stopped at the front door to marshal her strength, and the chain link fence at the end of the street caught her eye. She marvelled that she had been able to climb it the night she ran away. It looked almost insurmountable now with the long shadows creeping along the ground beneath it. She touched one of the cuts on her arm, still healing, and wondered where her shabby guide with his friendly dime was now. All unaware, he had taught her a valuable lesson about herself and turned a spotlight on the lies until even Laura had been forced to see them and confess the truth. She loved Jack too much to hurt him, and she had come back now to heal him if she could.

That thought gave her the most strength as she pushed open the lacquer red front door with its brass knocker. *If he didn't need me so desperately, I couldn't do this,* she told herself. *And if I didn't love him so much, I couldn't do it, either.* She pushed the button for the elevator and felt a thrill of shame and fear that almost made her sick. And then, out of habit, she glanced at her mailbox. It was so full that it could not be locked and the door hung open. Laura went to it and pulled the bundle of mail out with a sudden premonition.

The box had not been emptied for days, perhaps weeks; perhaps not since the night she ran away.

Is Jack—is he gone, then? she wondered. For a second her weakness and humiliation overwhelmed her and she hoped he was. She hoped she would never have to face him. For she dreaded what she had done to this man who loved her, in his own odd way, more than he loved, or ever had loved, anyone else on earth.

And then, suddenly, she whispered aloud, "No! Oh, no!

He's *got* to be here!"

She took the elevator to the third floor in a frenzy of impatience and crossed the carpeted hall to her apartment door swiftly. Like the mailbox, the door was unlocked, and that gave her hope. He wouldn't go out and leave it open for any stranger to wander into. It wasn't like him.

Silent and tremulous, Laura entered the living room. "Jack?" she said softly, knowing already there would be no answer. "Jack? Be here. Darling, please be here," she murmured. Slowly and fearfully she entered each room, saying his name as she did so, and silently, each room revealed nothing but his absence. Never had a home seemed so empty. Never had her own voice awed and saddened her so.

She had been through all the rooms a couple of times, half-heartedly picking up a thing or two and looking with frightened eyes into the dark corners, before she spotted the note. It was rolled into the top of a whisky bottle, one of several sitting on the kitchen table. She picked it up with trembling fingers and read:

> "*Laura darling.* I'm with Terry. I guess you've gone back to Beebo. Maybe that's fate, but I still think we could have made a go of it. You're my wife, Laura—that's the difference between life and death to me, even now. If you ever read these words, remember, I love you, Mrs. Mann. And remember it too if you ever want to come home. Jack."

Laura wept silently, her throat and chest painfully tight with it, crushing the letter against her neck.

She walked dazedly into the living room, still holding the letter, and stared around through her tears. She thought of Beebo and the warm, slightly worn rooms she lived in and the worn-out love she had left. And she thought of Jack. There had been none of his usual piercing sarcasm in the note. Nothing but gentleness, nothing but love.

After a long moment Laura pulled herself together. She sank down on the sofa by the table and picked up the mail. She felt weak, and she shuffled listlessly through the pile of bills and ads and notes and papers. Near the end she almost passed up one with Dr. Belden's name in the return address spot. His name registered suddenly in her mind, and she tore his letter open with hands newly sprung to life.

She read only the first half of the first sentence:

"Dear Mrs. Mann. I am delighted to inform you that next November, if all goes well, you and Mr. Mann will be parents, and . . ."
She fainted.

When Laura awoke she was lying on the couch with her head back and her mouth open and uncomfortably dry. Carefully she lifted her head on a stiff neck, turning it gingerly, and sat up straight. On the floor at her feet was the doctor's letter. She picked it up and found her hands shaking so that she had to grab at it three times before she caught it between her fingers.

For some moments she sat there, her cornflower eyes enormous with shock. Finally she whispered, "I'm going to have a child. *Me.*" A first hysterical thought of abortion flew through her mind, but she dismissed it almost before it formed.

"I'm going to be a woman. I have eight months to get ready and I've got to *be* ready when it comes. I've got to love it and take care of it."

Cautiously she stood up, and unsteadily walked toward the bedroom, one hand warm across her stomach. "Now that I know, it's not so bad," she said, speaking aloud as if to reassure herself. "I don't resent it so much any more. Strange . . . I'm not afraid of it. I don't know why, exactly. Yes, I guess I do . . . It's Jack's. It's a part of him. It's a way to make it up to him for what I've done."

She reached her bed and raised her eyes to the windows, and the darkness and sparkle of the city outside. It looked very beautiful. Jack was out there somewhere. He had to be; he couldn't have gone away, not this soon. His note sounded too much as if he were going to look for her, as if he knew he and Terry couldn't last, and he would have to search her out and make her try again.

Laura swept some pajamas and shoes off her bed and sat down with a curious feeling of elation and exhaustion. She stretched out, still fully dressed, and gazed at the ceiling.

I'll find him, she thought. *Terry was staying at the Bell Towers. I heard him say so. Somebody'll know where they are.* She felt very tired and she was surprised to find that she was crying again. There seemed to be no reason for it, except that she was having a baby. And it belonged to Jack too, and that made her smile through the tears.

A little later, when she dimly realized she was falling asleep, she thought of Beebo, and the thought twisted in her heart like a pain and almost brought her awake again. But it was over for Beebo now. Her life lay in another direction. Laura had to save Jack, and somehow, in the saving of him, would come her own life and strength. She knew it now, and it gave her the first peace she had known in all the years since she had first realized that she was a Lesbian.

Only the lightest rustle of air awakened her. She opened her eyes. It was still deep night; the room was dark except for the small bedlamp she had switched on when she lay down. And yet she was wide awake, and she knew he was there.

Laura turned and saw him standing in the doorway to the bedroom, disheveled, his hands in his pockets, his round horn rims sliding down his nose. She came up suddenly on her elbow, so fast that her head swam a little.

They looked at each other in silence for a minute; first startled, then embarrassed.

"Jack?" Laura said timidly, the way she had whispered it to the empty rooms earlier in the evening. And again her own voice awed her into silence.

He straightened and walked slowly toward her bed. At the foot, he stopped, his hands still in his pockets, his tie loosened, his shirt a little gray. His face was serious and tense, as if he were quite ready to believe she was a mirage.

At last he spoke to her softly. "I've been coming back every night. I was hoping . . . I thought you might . . ." He stopped, shutting his eyes for a minute as if to search for composure.

Laura sprang up to her knees on the bed and put her arms around him. "I'm here," she cried. "I'm home, I love you, I won't leave again, Jack."

But he loosened her arms gently. "I don't believe you," he said. "I'm afraid to."

"Believe me," she exclaimed passionately. "Jack darling, please believe me."

"We were going to leave for San Francisco Thursday," he said, still slightly incredulous. "Terry and I. I promised him, if you didn't come back."

"When did he ever keep a promise to *you?*"

"I love him, Laura," he reminded her.

That stopped her for a minute. She bowed her head and cast about desperately for something to say, something to convince him forevermore, as she herself was now convinced, that it was their only hope to make this marriage work.

"Jack, I'd have gone anywhere in the world to find you," she said, unable to look at him while she talked for fear the sight of his face would make her cry again. "I've had to hurt so many people—too many—to learn my lessons. And I was hurt as badly as the others. I've made mistakes, ugly ones, and I've been selfish and silly. But I've been trying, I have, Jack! And I've been learning. I—I—love you." She looked up at him now and for the very first time, in all their long acquaintance, she felt a pleasant flush in her cheeks at the sight of him. Him . . . a man. She felt flustered suddenly, unable to go on speaking.

Jack saw it too after a moment, disbelieving it at first and then accepting it slowly, with wonderment. "Laura," he said. "Do you still believe we're just a couple of scared kids? Do you still believe we're running away from the world by marrying each other? Do you think we're going to spend our whole lives running after a love that doesn't exist?"

"No," she whispered.

"You're still my wife," he said softly, and put his arms around her now, at last, and made her tingle with awkward new feelings and unbearable tenderness. "Do you want to live with me again? As my wife?"

"Yes, Jack." It wasn't the passionate unreasoning yes she had flung at Beebo in desperation two weeks ago. It was quiet and intensely felt. It was a recognized necessity, but a beautiful one.

"For how long?" he asked skeptically.

"I'm your wife," she repeated gently to him. "I'll stay with you now." There was a new sound, a new tone in her voice that caught in his heart. As for Laura she was once more bewildered by an unexpected tide of emotion that made it impossible for her to look at him. "Say yes, Jack," she whispered. "Say it's all right. Please, before I start crying again."

He took her head in his hands and kissed her forehead and said, "It's all right. It's all right honey," and suddenly they clung hard to each other and Laura began to sob with relief and joy. She could hardly articulate, trying to spill her lovely secret to him. "Jack, Jack, it worked. We're going to have a baby! Darling, we're going to have a baby!'"

She felt his arms tighten till she lost her breath and when she looked up at him this time, with her face blotched and her eyes red and her lips curved into a smile, he found himself crying happily with her.

When he could talk, he murmured into her neck, "I saw the letter in the box. It came two days after you left. The damn thing terrified me. I swear, Laura, I couldn't open it, I couldn't even touch it. I wouldn't even *look* at the damn mailbox. I was hoping so much it would be true—and so damn afraid if it was you wouldn't come back. That I'd lost you and you might have to have it alone and you wouldn't want it or love it—"

"Oh, stop," she begged. "Jack, darling, stop."

And they fell back on the bed together, crying and laughing and touching each other's faces.

"My God!" Jack exclaimed suddenly, aware of his weight on her. "Did I hurt you? You ought to take it easy, honey." But she chuckled at him.

"If you knew what this poor baby has been through already you wouldn't have a single qualm about it," she said, smiling.

He stroked her face with such an expression of love that she had to shut her eyes again. "I love you, Jack. I keep telling you that. I don't know why, it just seems like I have to. Like I really believe it myself now, for the first time. I love you."

And he kissed her mouth then. It had never happened before but it was right and wonderful.

They lay in each other's arms and talked and made plans. They talked about Beebo and Terry, about themselves, about their baby, about life and how good it was when you were brave enough to face it.

Laura was afraid of Terry still. "Where is he?" she asked.

"God only knows," Jack shrugged. "I left him in his room at the Towers. I've been doing this every night since you left. No drinking, no cruising, until I've checked the apartment to make sure you haven't come back. I just told him, 'If I don't make it back some night you'll know she came home. Don't wait for me.' I don't suppose he waited very long, either. He's not the type." He looked down at her, his face serious again and frowning. "What about Beebo?" he said.

"It's over. She knew it long ago. I finally realized it, too."
She raised her eyes to his. "I'm not in love with her now.
Maybe I never was. But I respect her and admire her. She's
amazing. And much stronger than I ever gave her credit for.
I wish to God I could change some things—"

"Don't play that game, darling," he said quickly. "That's
the surest way to break your heart and lose your mind. Save
yourself for now. And for later. Save yourself for me and
the baby." He leaned down and kissed her again and, silent
and amazed at herself, she returned his kiss with warmth.

"Besides," he added, whispering into her ear, "Somebody's
got to clean up the apartment."

"I'll take the living room. You can have the kitchen," she
offered.

"Thanks." He grinned and pulled her close in his arms,
and she didn't resist him; just nestled against his warm body
and relaxed in the circle of his strength, a real strength, a
man's strength. It felt very good to her.

"After all, we aren't expecting any visitors today, are we?"
he said sleepily into her long light hair.

"Not a soul," she murmured. She wondered, in that violet
twilight before sleep, how long it would take her to get used
to this closeness with him. She was so comfortable . . . more
comfortable, it seemed, and more safe than she had ever been.

And they fell asleep together with the sigh of relief and
hope that only the lost, who have found themselves, can feel.

BEEBO BRINKER

JACK MANN had seen enough in his life to swear off surprise forever. He had seen the ports of the Pacific from the deck of a Navy hospital ship during World War II. He had helped patch the endless cut and bloodied bodies, torn every which way, some irreparably. He had seen the sensuous Melanesian girls, the bronzed bare-chested surfers on Hawaiian beaches, the sly stinking misery of the caves of Iwo Jima.

A medical corpsman gets an eyeful—and a noseful—of human wretchedness during a war. When it was over, Jack left the service with a vow to lead a quiet uncomplicated life, and never to hurt anybody by so much as a pinprick. It shot the bottom out of his plans to enter medical school, but he let them go without undue regret. He'd be well along in his thirties by the time he finished, and it didn't seem worth it any more.

So he completed the course he started before the war: engineering. And after he got his degree he took a job in the New York office of a big Chicago construction firm as head of drafting.

During those war years, when Jack was holding heaving sailors over the head and labeling countless blood samples, he had fallen in love. It was a lousy affair, unhappy and violent. But peculiarly good now and then. Good enough to sell him on Love for a long time.

He organized his life around it. He earned his money to pamper whatever passion came his way. That was the only real value his bank account held for him; that, and helping stray people out of trouble, the way others help stray cats.

But by the time Jack reached his thirties, there had been too many who took advantage of his generosity to swindle him; his confidence to cuckold him; his affection to torment him. He turned cynic. There was hope in him still, but he buttoned it down under his skepticism.

He wanted to stabilize his life, settle down with one person

and live out a long rewarding love. But Jack Mann could
only love other men: boys, to be exact. Volatile, charming,
will-o-the-wisp boys, who looked him up Friday, loved him
Saturday, and left him Sunday. They couldn't even spell
"stabilize."

His emotional differentness had given Jack a good eye for
people, a knack for sizing them up fast. He usually knew
what to expect from a boy after talking to him twenty or
thirty minutes, and he had learned not to give in to the type
who brought certain suffering—the type who couldn't spell.

But Jack had also learned that he couldn't live his life only
for love. The less romantic he got about it, the clearer his
view of life became. It didn't make him happy, this cynicism.
But it protected him from too much hurt, and gave him a
sort of sour wit and wisdom.

Jack Mann was thirty-three years old, short in height, tall
in mentality. He was slight but tough: big-shouldered for his
size and deep-chested. His far-sighted eyes watched the world
through a pair of magnifying lenses, set in tortoise shell
frames.

They were seeing sharply these days, for Jack was between
lovers: bored and restless, but also healthy, wealthy, and on
the wagon. When the new love came along—and it would—he
would stay up most nights, blow his bankroll, and hit the
bottle. It was nuts, but it happened every time. It seemed
to preserve his lost illusions for a while, till the new "love"
vanished and joined the countless old ones in his memory.

Jack lived in Greenwich Village, near the bottom of Manhattan. It was filled with aspiring young artists. Filled, too,
with ambitious businessmen with wives and families, who
played hob with the local bohemia. A rash of raids was in
progress on the homosexual bar hangouts at the moment, with
cops rousting respectable beards-and-sandals off their favorite
park benches; hustling old dykes, who were Village fixtures
for eons, off the streets so they wouldn't offend the deodor-
ized young middle-class wives.

Jack was pondering the problem one May evening as he
came up the subway steps at 14th Street. At six o'clock the
air was still violet-light. It was a good time for ambling
through the winding streets he had come to know so well.

He tacked neatly in and out through the spring mixture
of tourists and natives: young girls with new jobs and timid
eyes; older girls with no jobs and knowing eyes; quiet sensitive boys having intimate beers together in small boites.

Shops, clubs, shoebox theaters. It always delighted him to see them, people and buildings both, blooming with the weather.

Jack stopped to buy some knockwurst and sauerkraut in a German delicatessen, eating them at the counter with an ale.

When he left, feeling sage and prosperous, he saw a handsome girl passing the shop, carrying a wicker suitcase in one hand. Her strong face and bewildered eyes contradicted each other. Jack followed a few feet behind her, intrigued. He had done this many a time, sometimes meeting the appealing person behind the face, sometimes losing the face forever in the swirling crowds.

The girl he was tailing appeared to be in her late teens, big-tall, with dark curly hair and blue eyes: Irish coloring, but not an Irish face. She walked with long firm strides, yet clearly did not know where she was. In her pocket was a yellow "Guide to Greenwich Village" with creased pages. Twice she stopped to consult it, comparing what she read to the unfamiliar milieu surrounding her.

A sitting duck for fast operators, Jack thought. But something wary in the way she held herself and eyed the crowd told him she knew that much herself. She was trying to defend herself against them by suspecting every passerby of ulterior motives.

At the first street corner she nearly collided with a small crop-haired butch, who said, "Hi, friend," to her. The big girl stared for a moment, surprised and uncertain, afraid to answer. She moved on, crossing the street and detouring widely around a Beat with a fierce beard who sat guarding his gouaches, watching her pass with a curious who-are-you? look.

Jack was amused at the girl's odd air of authority, the set of her chin, the strong rhythm of her walking. And yet, despite her efforts to look self-assured, she was clearly no native New Yorker. Her face, when he glimpsed it, was a map of confusion.

Rather abruptly, as if suddenly tired, she stopped, and Jack waited discreetly behind her, leaning against a railing and lighting a cigarette, watching her with a casual air.

She searched with travel-grimy hands for a cigarette in her

pocket, but found only tobacco crumbs. Wearily she let herself sag against a shop window, evidently convinced it was silly to keep marching in the same direction, just because she had started out in it. Better to rest, to think a minute. Her gaze fell on Jack, who was studying her with a little smile. She looked square at him, and then her eyes dropped. He sensed something of her reaction: he was a strange man; she was a girl, forlorn and alone in a city she didn't know. And probably too damn poor to squander money on cigarettes.

Jack strolled over to her, pulling a pack from his pocket and extending it with one cigarette bounced forward for her to take. She looked up, startled. She was four inches taller than Jack. There was a small pause and then she shook her head and looked away, afraid of him.

"You'd take it if I were somebody's grandmother," he kidded her. "Don't hold it against me that I'm a man."

She gave him a tentative smile.

"Come on, take it," he urged.

She accepted one cigarette, but still he held the pack toward her. "Take 'em all. I have plenty. You look like you could use these."

She obviously wanted to, but she said shyly in a round low voice, "Thanks, but I can't pay you."

Jack chuckled. "You're a nice girl from a nice family," he said. "Know how I know? Oh, it's not because you want to pay for the pack." She looked at him with guarded interest. "It's because you're afraid of me. No, it's true. That's the mark of a nice girl, sad to say. Men scare her. I can hear your mother telling you, 'Dear, never take presents from a strange man.' Right?"

She smiled at him. "Close enough," she said softly, and inhaled some smoke with a look of relief.

"Well, consider this a loan," he said, gesturing toward the cigarettes, and then he tucked them in her pocket next to the "Guide." She jumped at the touch of his hand. He felt it but did not say anything. "You're pretty new, aren't you?" he said.

"I'm pretty used, if you want to know," she said ruefully.

Jack laughed. "How old? Seventeen?"

"Do I look *that* young?" she asked, dismayed. There was intelligence in her regular features, but a pleasant country innocence, too. And she was uncommonly handsome with her black wavy hair and restless blue eyes.

"Do you have a name?" he asked.

"Do you?" she countered, instantly defensive.

He held out his hand affably and said, "I'm Jack Mann. Does that make you feel any better?"

She took his hand, cautiously at first, then gave it a firm shake. "Should it?" she said.

"Only if you live down here," he answered. "Everybody knows I'm harmless."

She seemed reassured. "I'm going to live here. I'm looking for a place now." She paused as if embarrassed. "I do have a name: Beebo Brinker."

He blinked. "Beebo?" he said.

"It used to be Betty Jean. But I couldn't say it right when I was little."

They smoked a moment in silence and then Beebo said, "I guess I'd better get going. I have to spend the night somewhere." And she turned a sudden pink, realizing the inference Jack might draw from her remark. "Everybody" might know Jack down here, but Beebo wasn't everybody. For all she knew he was harmless as a shark. The mere fact that he had a name wasn't all *that* reassuring.

"Looks to me like you need some food first," he said lightly. "There's always a sack somewhere."

"I don't have much money."

"Better to spend it on food," he said. "Anyway, what the hell, I'll treat you. There's some good Wiener schnitzel about a block back." He tried to take her wicker case to carry it for her, but she pulled away, offended as if his offer were a comment on her ability to take care of herself.

Jack stopped and laughed a little. "Look, my little friend," he said kindly. "When I first hit New York I was as pea-green as you are. Somebody did this for me and let me save my few bucks for a room and job hunting. This is my way of paying him back. Ten years from now, you'll do the same thing for the next guy. Fair?"

It was hard for her to resist. She was almost shaky hungry; she was worn out; she was lost. And Jack looked as kind as he was. It was a part of his success in salvaging people: they liked his face. It was homely, but in the good-humored amiable way that made him seem like an old friend in a matter of minutes.

Finally Beebo smiled at him. "Fair," she said. "But I'll pay you back, Jack. I will."

They walked back to the German delicatessen, Beebo with a firm grip on her suitcase.

She finished her meal in ten minutes. Jack ordered another for her, over her protests, kidding her about her appetite.

"Jesus," he said. "When did you eat last?"

"Fort Worth."

"*Indiana?*" Jack stared.

"Yes. I ate three sandwiches in the rest room, on the train. That was yesterday." Beebo drained her milk glass and put it on the table. The pneumatic little blonde waitress brought the second plateful. Jack, watching Beebo who was watching the waitress, saw her wide blue eyes glide up and down the plump pink-uniformed body with curious interest. Beebo pulled back, holding her breath as the waitress leaned over her to set a basket of bread on the table, and there was a look of fear on her face.

Jack thought to himself, she's afraid of her. Afraid of that bouncy little bitch. Afraid of . . . women?

When she had finished eating, Beebo glanced up at him. For all her physical sturdiness and arresting face, she was not a forward or a confident girl.

"You eat like a farm hand," he chuckled.

"I should. I was raised in farm country," she said, looking away from him. Her shyness beguiled him. "Thank you for the food."

"My pleasure." He observed her through a scrim of cigarette smoke. "If I weren't afraid of scaring hell out of you, I'd ask you over to my place for a drink," he said. She blanched. "I mean, a drink of milk," he said.

"I don't drink," she told him apologetically, as if teetotaling were something hick-town and unsophisticated.

"Not even milk?"

"Not with strange men."

"Am I really that strange?" he grinned, laughing at her again.

"Am I really that funny?" she demanded.

"No." He reached over the table top unexpectedly and pressed her hand. She tried to jerk it away but he held it tight, surprising her with his strength. "You're a lovely girl," he said. It wasn't suggestive or even romantic. He didn't mean it to be. "You're a sweet young kid and you're lost and tired and frightened. You need one thing right now, Beebo, and the rest will take care of itself."

"What's that?" She retrieved her hand and tucked it behind her.

"A friend."

She gazed at him, sizing him up, and then began to move from the booth.

"I'm no wolf," Jack said, sliding after her. "Can't you tell? I just like to help lost girls. I collect them." And when she turned back with a frown of disbelief, he shrugged. "Everybody's got to have a hobby."

He bought some Dutch beer and sausage, paid the cashier, and walked with Beebo out the front door. On the pavement she stopped, swinging her wicker case around in front of her like a piece of fragile armor. Jack saw the defensive glint in her eyes.

"Okay, little lost friend," he said. "You're under no obligation to me. If this bothers you, the hell with it. Find yourself a hotel room, a park bench. I don't care. Well ... I care, but I don't want to scare you any more."

Beebo hesitated a moment, then held out her hand and shook his. "Thanks anyway, Jack. I'll find you some day and pay you back," she said. She looked as much afraid to leave him as to stay with him.

"So long, Beebo," he said, dropping her hand. She walked away from him backwards a few steps so she could keep an eye on him; turned around and then turned back.

Jack smiled at her. "I'm afraid I'm just about your safest bet," he said kindly. "If you knew how safe, you'd come along without a qualm."

And when he smiled she had to answer him. "All right," she said, still clutching her wicker bag in both hands. "But just so you'll know: my father taught me how to fight."

"Beebo, my dear," he said as they began to walk toward his apartment, "you could probably throw me twenty feet through the air if you had to but you won't have to. I have no designs on you. Honest to God. I don't even have a bunch of etchings to show you in my pad. Nothing but good talk and cold beer. And a bed."

Beebo stopped in her tracks.

"Well, the bed is good and cold too," he said. "God, you're a scary one."

"Did you go home to bed with the first stranger you met in New York?" she demanded.

"Sure," he said. "Doesn't everybody?"

She laughed at last, a full country sound that must have carried across the hay fields, and followed him again. He walked, hands in pockets, letting her curb her long stride to keep from getting ahead of him. But when he tried to take her arm at a corner, she shied away, determined to rely only on herself.

Jack unlocked the door of his small apartment, holding it with his foot while Beebo went in. The corridor outside was littered with buckets, planks, and ladders. "They're redecorating the hall," he explained. "We like to put on a good front in this rattrap."

He headed for the kitchen with the bag of sausage and the beer, set them on the counter, and sprang himself a can of cold brew. "What do you want, Beebo? One of these?" He lifted the can. When she hesitated, he said, "You don't really want that milk, do you?"

"Have you got something—weak?"

"Well, I've got something colorful," he said. "I don't know how weak it is." He went down on his haunches in front of a small liquor chest and foraged in it for a minute. "Somebody gave me this stuff for Christmas and I've been trying to give it away ever since. Here we are."

He took out an ornate bottle, broke the seal and pulled the cork, and got down a liqueur glass. When he up-ended the bottle, a rich green liquid came out, moving at about the speed of cod-liver oil and looking like some dollar-an-ounce shampoo for Park Avenue lovelies. The pungent fumes of peppermint penetrated every crack in the wall.

"What is it?" Beebo said, intimidated by the looks of it.

"Peppermint schnapps," Jack said. "God. It's even worse than I thought. Want to chicken out?"

"I grew up in a town full of German farmers," she said. "I should take to schnapps like a kid to candy."

Jack handed over the glass. "Okay, it's your stomach. Just don't get tanked on the stuff."

"I just want a taste. You make me feel babyish about the milk."

He picked up his beer and the schnapps bottle, and she followed him into the living room. "You can drink all the milk you want, honey," he said, settling into a leather arm chair, "before the sun goes over the yardarm. After that, we switch to spirits."

He turned on a phonograph nearby and turned the sound low. Beebo sat down a few feet from him on the floor,

pulling her skirt primly over her knees. She seemed awkward
in it, like a girl reared in jeans or jodhpurs. Jack studied her
while she took a sip of the schnapps, and returned her smile
when she looked up at him. "Good," she said. "Like the
sundaes we used to get after the Saturday afternoon movie."

She was a strangely winning girl. Despite her size, her
pink cheeks and firm-muscled limbs, she seemed to need caring for. At one moment she seemed wise and sad beyond
her years, like a girl who has been forced to grow up in a
hothouse hurry. At the next, she was a picture of rural naïveté
that moved Jack; made him like her and want to help her.

She wore a sporty jacket, the kind with a gold thread
emblem on the breast pocket; a man's white shirt, open at
the throat, tieless and gray with travel dust; a straight tan
cotton skirt that hugged her small hips; white socks and tennis
shoes. Her short hair had been combed without the manufactured curls and varnished waves that marked so many
teen-agers. It was neat, but the natural curl was slowly fighting free of the imposed order.

Her eyes were an off-blue, and that was where the sadness
showed. They darted around the room, moving constantly,
searching the shadows, trying to assure her, visually at least,
that there was nothing to fear.

"What are you doing here in New York, Beebo?" Jack
asked her.

She looked into her glass and emptied it before she answered him. "Looking for a job," she said. "Me and everybody else, I guess."

"What kind of job?"

"I don't know," she said softly. "Could I have a little more
of that stuff?" He handed the bottle down to her. "It's not
half as bad as it looks."

"Did you have a job back home?" he asked.

"No. I—I just finished high school."

"In the middle of May?" His brow puckered. "When I
was in school they used to keep us there till June, at least."

"Well, I—you see—it's farm country," she stammered
"They let kids out early for spring planting."

"Jesus, honey, they gave that up in the last century."

"Not the little towns," she said, suddenly on guard.

Jack looked at his shoes, unwilling to distress her. "Your
dad's a farmer, then?" he said.

"No, a vet." She was proud of it. "An animal doctor."

"Oh. What was he planting in the middle of May—chickens?"

Beebo clamped her jaws together. He could see the muscles knot under her skin. "If they let the farmer's kids out early, they have to let the vet's kids out, too," she said, trying to be calm. "Everyone at the same time."

"Okay, don't get mad," he said and offered her a cigarette. She took it after a pause that verged on a sulk, but insisted on lighting it for herself. It evidently bothered her to let him perform the small masculine courtesies for her, as if they were an encroachment on her independence.

"So what did they teach you in high school? Typing? Shorthand?" Jack said. "What can you *do?*"

Beebo blew smoke through her nose and finally gave him a woeful smile. "I can castrate a hog," she said. "I can deliver a calf. I can jump a horse and I can run like hell." She made a small sardonic laugh deep in her throat. "God knows they need me in New York City."

Jack patted her shoulder. "You'll go straight to the top, honey," he said. "But not here. Out west somewhere."

"It has to be here, even if I have to dig ditches," she said, and the wry amusement had left her. "I'm not going home."

"Where's home?"

"Wisconsin. A little farming town west of Milwaukee. Juniper Hill."

"Lots of cheese, beer, and German burghers?" he said.

"Lots of mean-minded puritans," she said bitterly. "Lots of hard hearts and empty heads. For me . . . lots of heartache and not much more."

"Why?" he said gently.

She looked away, pouring some more schnapps for herself. Jack was glad she had a small glass.

"Why did you ditch Juniper Hill, Beebo?" he persisted.

"I—just got into some trouble and ran away. Old story."

"And your parents disowned you?"

"No. I only have my father—my mother died years ago. My father wanted me to stay. But I'd had it."

Jack saw her chin tremble and he got up and brought her a box of tissues. "Hell, I'm sorry," he said. "I'm too nosy. I thought it might help to talk it out a little."

"It might," she conceded, "but not now." She sat rigidly, trying to check her emotion. Jack admired her dignity. After a moment she added, "My father—is a damn good man.

He loves me and he tries to understand me. He's the only one who does."

"You mean the only one in Juniper Hill," Jack said. "I'm doing my damnedest to understand you too, Beebo."

She relented a little from her stiff reserve and said, "I don't know why you should, but—thanks."

"There must be other people in your life who tried to help, honey," he said. "Friends, sisters, brothers—"

"One brother," she said acidly. "Everything I ever did was inside-out, ass-backwards, and dead wrong as far as Jim was concerned. I humiliated him and he hated me for it. Oh, I was no dreamboat. I know that. I deserved a wallop now and then. But not when I was down."

"That's the way things go between brothers and sisters," Jack said. "They're supposed to fight."

"You don't understand the *reason*."

"Explain it to me, then." Jack saw the tremor in her hand when she ditched her cigarette. He let her finish another glassful of schnapps, hoping it might relax her. Then he said, "Tell me the real reason why you left Juniper Hill."

She answered at last in a dull voice, as if it didn't matter any more who knew the truth. "I was kicked out of school."

Jack studied her, perplexed. He would have been gently amused if she hadn't seemed so stricken by it all. "Well, honey, it only happens to the best and the worst," he said. "The worst get canned for being too stupid and the best for being too smart. They damn near kicked me out once...I was one of the best." He grinned.

"Best, worst, or—or different," Beebo said. "I was different. I mean, I just didn't fit in. I wasn't like the rest. They didn't want me around. I guess they felt threatened, as if I were a nudist or a vegetarian, or something. People don't like you to be different. It scares them. They think maybe some of it will rub off on them, and they can't imagine anything worse."

"Than becoming a vegetarian?" he said and downed the rest of his beer to drown a chuckle. He set the glass on the floor by the leg of his chair. "Are you a vegetarian, Beebo?" She shook her head. "A nudist?"

"I'm just trying to make you understand," she said, almost pleading, and there was a real beacon of fear shining through her troubled eyes.

Jack reached out his hand and held it toward her until she gave him one of hers. "Are you afraid to tell me,

Beebo?" he said. "Are you ashamed of something? Something you did? Something you *are?*"

She reclaimed her hand and pulled a piece of tissue from her bag, trying to keep her back straight, her head high. But she folded suddenly around a sob, bending over to hold herself, comfort herself. Jack took her shoulders in his firm hands and said, "Whatever it is, you'll lick it, honey. I'll help you if you'll let me. I'm an old hand at this sort of thing. I've been saving people from themselves for years. Sort of a sidewalk Dorothy Dix. I don't know why, exactly. It just makes me feel good. I like to see somebody I like, learn to like himself. You're a big clean, healthy girl, Beebo. You're handsome as hell. You're bright and sensitive. I like you, and I'm pretty particular."

She murmured inarticulately into her hands, trying to thank him, but he shushed her.

"Why don't you like yourself?" he asked.

After a moment she stopped crying and wiped her face. She threw Jack a quick cautious look, wondering how much of her story she could risk with him. Perversely enough, his very kindness and patience scared her off. She was afraid that the truth would sicken him, alienate him from her. And at this forlorn low point in her life, she needed his friendship more than a bed or a cigarette or even food.

Jack caught something of the conflict going on within her. "Tell me what you can," he said.

"My dad is a veterinarian," she began in her low voice. "Everybody in Juniper Hill loved him. Till he started—drinking too much. But that wasn't for a long time. In the beginning we were all very happy. Even after my mother died, we got along. My brother Jim and I were friends back in grade school.

"Dad taught us about animals. There wasn't a job he couldn't trust me with when it came to caring for a sick animal. And the past few years when he's been—well, drunk so much of the time—I've done a lot of the surgery, too. I'm twice the vet my brother'll ever be. Jim never did like it much. He went along because he was ashamed of his squeamishness. But whenever things got bloody or tough, he ducked out.

"But I got along fine with Dad. The one thing I always wanted was to live a good life for his sake. Be a credit to him. Be something wonderful. Be—a doctor. He was so proud of that. He understood, he helped me all he could." She drained her glass again. "Some doctor I'll be now," she said. "A witch doctor, maybe." She filled the glass and Jack said anxiously, "Whoa, easy there. You're a milk drinker, remember?"

She ignored him. "At least I won't be around to see Dad's face when he realizes I'll never make it to medical school," Beebo said, the corners of her mouth turned down. "I hated to leave him, but I had to do it. It's one thing to stick it out in a place where they don't like you. It's another to let yourself be destroyed."

"So you think you've solved your problems by coming to the big city?" Jack asked her.

"Not all of them!" she retorted. "I'll have to get work, I'll have to find a place to live and all that. But I've solved the worst one, Jack."

"Maybe you brought some of them with you," he said. "You didn't run as far away from Juniper Hill as you think. People are still people, no matter what the town. And Beebo is still Beebo. Do you think New Yorkers are wiser and better than the people in Juniper Hill, honey? Hell no. They're probably worse. The only difference is that here, you have a chance to be anonymous. Back home everybody knew who you were."

Beebo threw him a sudden smile. "I don't think there's a single Jack Mann in all of Juniper Hill," she said. "It was worth the trip to meet you."

"Well, I'd like to think I'm that fascinating," he said. "But you didn't come to New York City to find Jack Mann, after all. You came to find Beebo Brinker. Yourself. Or are you one of those rare lucky ones who knows all there is to know about themselves by the time they're seventeen?"

"Eighteen," she corrected. "No, I'm not one of the lucky ones. Just one of the rare ones." Inexplicably, it struck both of them funny and they laughed at each other. Beebo felt herself loose and pliable under the influence of the liqueur. It was exhilarating, a floating release that shrouded the pain and confusion of her flight from home and arrival in this cold new place. She was glad for Jack's company, for his warmth and humor. "You must be good for me," she told him. "Either you or the schnapps."

"You're going pretty heavy on that stuff, friend," he warned her nodding at the glass. "There's more in it than peppermint, you know."

"But it tastes so good going down," she said, surprised to find herself still laughing.

"Well, it doesn't taste so good when it comes back up."

"I haven't had that much," she said and poured herself some more. Jack rolled his eyes to heaven and made her laugh again.

"You know I could take advantage of you in your condition," he said, thinking it might sober her up a little. But his fundamental compassion and intelligence had put her at ease, led her to trust him. She was actually enjoying herself a little now, trying to forget whatever it was that drove her into this new life, and Jack hadn't the heart to stir up her fears again. He wondered if she had left a scandal or a tragedy behind her in Juniper Hill.

"I was going to be a doctor once myself," he said.

She looked at him with a sort of cockeyed interest. "What happened?"

"Would have taken too long. I wanted to get that degree and get out. And I wanted love. But you can't make love to anybody after a long day over a hot cadaver. You're too pooped and the sight of human flesh gives you goose pimples instead of pleasant shivers. Besides, I spent four years in the Navy in the Second World War, and I'd had it with blood and suffering."

Beebo drank the schnapps in her glass. "That's as good a reason as any for quitting, I guess," she said.

"You could still finish up high school and go on to college," he said, trying not to sound pushy.

"No. I've lost it, Jack. That ambition, that will to do well. I left it behind when I left my father. I just don't give a double damn about medicine, for the first time in my life."

"Because a bunch of small-minded provincials asked you to leave their little high school? You make it sound like you were just squirming to be asked."

"You're saying I didn't have the guts to fight them," she said, speaking without resentment. "It isn't that, Jack. I did fight them, with all I've got. I'm tired of it, that's all. You can't fight everybody all the time and still have room in your life to study and think and learn."

"Was it that bad, Beebo?"

"*I* was that bad—to the people in Juniper Hill."

Jack shook his head in bewilderment and laughed a little. "You don't happen to carry the bubonic plague, do you?" he said.

She knew how curious she had made him about herself, and she hadn't the courage to expose the truth to him yet. So she merely said, "That's over now. My life is going to be different."

"Different, but not necessarily better," he said. "I wish to hell you'd come clean with me, honey. I can't help you this way. I don't know what you're running away from."

"I'm not running away from, I'm running *to*," she said. "To this city, this chance for a new start."

"And a new Beebo?" he asked. "Do you think being in a new place will make you better and braver somehow?"

"I'm not chicken, Jack," she said firmly. "I left for Dad's sake as much as my own."

"I didn't say you were, honey," he told her gently. "I don't think a chicken would have come so far to face so much all alone. I think you're a decent, intelligent girl. I think you're a good-looking girl, too, just for the record. That much is plain as the schnapps on your face."

Beebo frowned at him, self-conscious and surprised. "You're the first man who ever called me 'good-looking'," she said.

"No, the second. My father always thought..." Her voice went very soft. "You know, it kills me to go off and—and abandon him like this." She got up from the floor and walked a little unsteadily to the front window.

"Why don't you write to him?" Jack suggested. "If he was so good to you—if you were so close—he deserves to know where you are."

"That was the whole point of leaving," she said, shaking her head. "To keep it secret. To relieve him."

"Of what?"

"Of myself. I was a burden to him. He did too much for me. He tried to be father and mother both. He indulged me when he should have been stern. He never could bear to punish me."

She stood looking out his front window in silence, crying quietly. Her face was still, with the only movement the rhythmic swell and spill of tears from her eyes.

"My father," she said, "is no angel. Much as I love him, I know *that* much." Jack sensed a whole raft of sad secrets behind that brief phrase.

He stood up, crushed his cigarette, and looked at her for a moment. She stood with her legs apart and well-defined by her narrow cotton skirt. Her hair was tousled and damp with sweat, and there was a shine in her wet eyes reflected from the lamplight that intensified the blue. She had left her schnapps glass on the floor and her empty hands hung limp against her thighs. She lifted them now and then to brush away tears. Her head inclined slightly, like that of a youngster who has grown too tall too fast and doesn't want to tower over her classmates.

Her face, sensitive and striped with tears, was in many ways the face of a boy. Her stance was boyish and her low voice too was like a boy's, balanced on the brink of maturity. And there it would stay all her life, never to plumb the true depth of a man's.

She became aware of Jack's eyes on her and turned to pick up her glass, but bumped against a corner of a table and nearly fell. Jack reached her in two big steps and pulled her straight again while she put both hands to her temples. "I feel as if I'm dreaming," she murmured. "Am I?" She looked quizzically at him.

"You're not, but I am," he said, taking her elbow and steering her toward the bedroom. "I'm a dream walking. I'm dreaming and you're in my dream. When I wake up, you'll cease to exist."

"That would solve everything, wouldn't it?" she said, leaning on him more than she realized. She tried to stop him in the center of the room to get her liqueur, but he kept pushing till she gave up.

"Come on, let Uncle Jack bed you down," he said. He took one of her arms across his shoulder, the better to balance them both, pulled her into the bedroom, and unloaded her on his double bed. Beebo spread-eagled herself into all four corners with a sigh, and it wasn't till Jack had all her clothes off but the underwear that she came to and tried to protest. Jack removed her socks with a yank.

"Why, you lousy man," she said, staring at him. But when he smelled the socks, she laughed.

"God, what an exciting creature you are," he grimaced, surveying her muscular angles with all the ardor of an old hen.

"So I'm not your type," she said, getting to her feet. "I can still take off my own underwear." She tried it, lost her balance and sat down summarily on the bed.

Jack tossed her a nightshirt from his dresser. It was scarlet and orange cotton flannel. "I like flashy sleepers," he explained.

She put it on while he washed in the bathroom. But

when he returned he found her leaning on the dresser, dizzily close to losing the schnapps.

Jack guided her into the bathroom and got her to the washbowl before it came up.

"I had no idea there was so much in the bottle," Jack said when she had gotten the last of it out. At last she straightened up to look in the mirror. "By God, Beebo, you were the same color as the schnapps for a minute there."

He made her rinse her mouth and then dragged her back to bed, where he washed her unconscious face and hands. He sat and gazed at her before he turned out the light, speculating about her. Asleep, she looked younger, adolescent: still a child, with a child's purity; soon an adult with adult desires. Did she know already what those desires would be? And was that why she fled from Juniper Hill? The knowledge that her desires and her adult self would shock the town, shock her father, shock even herself?

Jack thought so. He thought she knew what it was that troubled her so deeply, even though she might not know the name for it. It wasn't just being "different" that she hated. It was the kind of differentness. Jack wanted to comfort her, to explain that she wasn't alone in the world, that other people were different in the same way she was. But he couldn't speak of it to her until she admitted it first to him.

He smoothed the hair off her forehead, admiring her features and her flawless skin without the least taint of physicality. He felt sorry for her, and scoffed at himself for wishing she were the boy she so resembled at that moment. Then he lay down beside her and went to sleep.

Beebo slept for fourteen hours. She wakened with a glaring square of sunshine astride her face. When she rolled over to escape it, she felt a new sensation: the beginning beat of the long rhythm of a hangover—her first.

The thought of the peppermint liqueur nauseated her for a few moments. She looked around the room to forget it and clear her head, and found a note pinned to the pillow next to hers. It gave her a start to realize Jack had spent the night in bed with her. And then it made her laugh and the laugh sent aching echoes through her head.

The note said, "I'm at work. Home around 5:30. Plenty
of feed in refrig. You don't want it but you NEED it. White
pills in medicine chest for head. Take two and LIVE.
You're a devil in bed. Jack."

She smiled, and lifted herself with gingerly care from the
bed. It was two-thirty in the afternoon.

When Jack came home with a brown bag full of groceries, she was smoking quietly and reading the paper in
his kitchen.

"How are you?" he said, smiling.

"Fine."

"I don't believe it."

"Well, I'm clean, and you can believe *that*. I took a
bath."

"On you it looks good," he said, putting food away.

Beebo shook her head a little. "I was just thinking...
you're about the only friend I have, Jack. I've been kicking
myself all day for not thanking you. I mean, you listened
to me for hours. You've been damn nice about my problems."

"That's my style," he said, but he was flattered. "Besides, us frustrated doctors have to -stick together. It's nice
to come home to a welcoming committee that thinks I'm the
greatest guy in the world."

"You must have a lot of friends down here," she said,
curious about him. Beebo had done all the talking since they
met. But who was Jack Mann, the guy who did all the
listening? Just a goodhearted young man in a strange town
who gave her a drink and a bed, and was about to give
her some dinner.

"Oh, plenty of friends," he said, lighting the oven.

"You made me feel safe and—and *human* last night,
Jack. If that doesn't sound too silly."

"Did you think you weren't?" He put the ready-cooked
food in the stove to warm.

"I'm grateful. I wanted you to know."

"Marry me and prove it," he said.

She looked at him with her mouth open, astonished.
"You're kidding!" she said.

"Nope. I always wanted a dozen kids."

Beebo began to laugh. "I'd make a lousy mother, I'm afraid," she said.

"You'd make a dandy mother, honey. Nice girls always like kids."

"Is that why you want to get married? Just to have kids?"

"When I was in the Navy, I was always the sucker who put on the whiskers and passed out the popsicles on Christmas Day in the Islands. Hot? Mamma mia! I nearly passed out myself. Melted almost as fast as the goo I was giving away. But I loved those kids."

"Then why aren't you married? Why don't you have some kids of your own?" she prodded. It seemed peculiar to her that so affable a man, especially one who liked children, should be single.

"Beebo, my ravishing love, why don't *you* get married and have some kids?" he countered, disconcerting her.

"A woman has to do the having," she said. "All a man has to do is get her pregnant."

"*All*," Jack repeated, rolling his eyes.

"Besides, I don't want to get married," she added, her eyes veiled and troubled.

"Hell, everybody gets married," Jack said, watching her closely. Maybe she would open up a bit now and talk about what really mattered.

"Everybody but *you*," she said.

He hunched his shoulders and grinned. "Touché," he said. Then he opened the oven door to squint at the bubbling ravioli, and drew it out with a potholder, spooning in onto their plates.

They sat down at the table and Jack told her, "This is the greatest Italian food you'll ever eat. Pasquini on Thompson Street makes it up." He glanced up and found Beebo studying him. "What's the matter? Don't like pasta?"

"Jack, have you ever been in love?" she said.

Jack smiled and swallowed a forkful of food before he answered. She was asking him, as circuitously as possible, to tell her about life. She didn't want him to guess it, but that was what she wanted.

"I fall in love twice a year," he said. "Once in the fall and once in the spring. In the fall the kids come back to school, a few blocks from here. There are plenty of newcomers waiting to be loved the wrong way in September. They call me Wrong Way Mann." He glanced up at her, but instead of taking the hint, she was puzzled by it.

"I didn't know there was a wrong way," she said earnestly.

"In love, as in everything else," he said. "I just—well, let's say I have a talent for goofing things up." He wondered if he ought to be frank with her about himself. It might relieve her, might make it possible for her to talk about herself then. But, looking at her face again, he decided against it. The whole subject scared her still. She wanted to learn and yet she feared that what she learned might be ugly, or more frightening than her ignorance.

He would have to go slowly with her, teach her gently what she was, and teach her not to hate the word for it: Lesbian. Such a soft word, mellifluous on the tongue; such a stab in the heart to someone very young, unsure and afraid.

"And in the spring?" she was asking. "You fall in love then, too?"

"That's just the weather, I guess. I fall in love with everybody in the spring. The butcher, the baker, the candlestickmaker." He smiled at her face. She was amused and startled by the male catalog, and afraid to let her amusement show. Jack took her off the hook. "Good, hm?" He nodded at the food.

Beebo took a bite without answering. "What's it like to live down here? I mean—" She cleared her throat. "In the Village?"

"Just one mad passionate fling after another," he said. "Try the cheese." He passed it to her.

"With the butcher and the baker?" she said humorously and made him laugh.

At last he said, "Well honey, it's like everyplace else. You eat three squares a day, you sleep eight hours a night, you work and earn money and obey the laws ... well, *most* of the laws. The only difference between here and Juniper Hill is, we stay open all night."

She laughed. And suddenly she said, "You know, this *is* good," and began to eat with an appetite.

"So's the salad." He pushed the bowl toward her. "Now you tell me something, Little Girl Lost," he said. "Were *you* ever in love?"

She looked down at her plate, uncomfortably self-conscious.

"Oh, come on," he teased. "I'm not going to blackmail you."

"Not real love," she said. "Puppy love, I guess."

"That kind can hurt as much as the other," Jack said, and Beebo was grateful for his perception. "But it ought to be fun now and then, too."

"Maybe it ought to be, but it never was," she said. "I guess I'm like you, Jack. I goof everything up."

He pointed his fork at her plate. "You've stopped eating again," he said. "I want you to taste your future employer's cooking."

"My what?" she exclaimed.

"Pasquini needs a delivery boy. Can you drive?"

"I can drive, but can I be a boy?" she said with such a rueful face that he laughed aloud.

"You can wear slacks," he said. "That's the best I could do. The rest is up to you."

His laughter embarrassed her, as if perhaps she had gone too far with her remark, and she said as seriously as possible, "I learned to drive on a truck with six forward gears."

"This is a panel truck."

"Duck soup. God, I hope he'll take me, Jack. I have exactly ten bucks between me and the poorhouse. I didn't know what I was going to do with myself."

"Well, you haven't got the job yet, honey. But I told Pasquini you had lots of experience and you'd do him the favor of dropping by in the morning."

"Some favor!" she grinned. "Me, who couldn't find Times Square if my life depended on it, making deliveries in this tangled-up part of town."

"You'll catch on."

"What are the Pasquinis like?" she said.

"You'll like Marie. She's Pete's wife. Does all the cooking. It's her business, really. It was just a spaghetti joint when Pete's dad ran it. After he died Pete took over and damn near went bankrupt. Then he married Marie. She cooks *and* keeps the books—like nobody can. She used to be a pretty girl, too, till she had too many kids and too much pizza."

"What about Pete?"

"I don't know what to tell you about that guy. I've known him slightly for the past ten years, but no one knows him very well. As far as Marie's concerned, he's her number one delivery boy. As a husband and a father, he's her idea of a bust."

"You mean he cheats?"

"He's out every night of the week with weird girls on his

arm. As if he were proud of it. He picks out the oddballs—you know, the ones who haven't cut their hair since they were four years old, and wear dead-white make-up and cotton lisle stockings."

"Lousy taste," Beebo said, but when Jack smiled she looked away. She wasn't going to give him the chance to ask what her own taste might be.

Jack paused, sensing her reticence, and then he went on, "Pete used to run a gang when he was in his teens. He was our local color."

"You mean he's a juvenile delinquent?" Beebo asked naively. "Are you sending me to work for a crook?"

"He's an *ex*-j.d.," Jack chuckled. "He went on to better things the day they broke his zip gun."

"My God! Is he a criminal, Jack?"

"No, honey, don't panic. He's just a kook. He's more of a loner now. It comes naturally to him to skulk around. But as far as I can tell, he only skulks after dark. And after Beat broads. He hasn't been arrested since he was nineteen, and that's been ten years."

"He sounds like the ideal employer," Beebo cracked.

"You could do worse; you with ten bucks in your pocket," Jack reminded her. "Besides, he's lived here all his life. He may be odd but you get used to him."

"Just how 'odd' is he?"

"Honey, you've *got* to be a little odd down here, or you lose your membership card," he said. "Besides, I'm not asking you to cut your veins and mingle blood with him. Just pass out the pizzas and take his money once a week."

Beebo shook her head and laughed. "Well, if you say so," she said. "I guess I'm safe as long as I don't wear cotton lisle stockings."

She got the job. Pete Pasquini had more deliveries than he could handle alone. Marie's sauces, salads, preserves, and pastas were making a name and making a pile. The orders were going up so fast that it would take a second driver to deliver them all.

Beebo, dressed in a clean white shirt, sweater, and tan slacks, faced Pete at eight in the morning. She was somewhat intimidated by the looks of him and by Jack's thumb sketch of the night before. He was a dour-faced young Italian-American with blue jowls and a down-turned mouth. If he ever smiled—Beebo doubted it—he would have been almost handsome, for his teeth were straight and white, and he had a peculiarly sensual mouth beneath his plum-dark eyes. He looked mean and sexy—a combination that instantly threw Beebo high on her guard.

"You're Beebo?" he said, looking up at her with an order pad and pencil poised in his hands.

"Yes," she said. "Jack Mann sent me. I—he—said you needed a driver."

He smirked a little. Probably his smile for the day, she thought. "You're as tall as I am," he observed, as if pleased about it; pleased at least to make her self-conscious about it.

"Would you like to see me drive? I'm a good driver," she said resentfully.

"How come you're so tall, Beebo? Girls ain't supposed to be so tall." He put the paper and pencil down and turned to look her over, leaning jauntily on a linoleum-covered counter as he did so.

Beebo folded her arms over her chest in a gesture that told him to slow down, back off; a very unfeminine gesture that ordinarily offended a man's ideals. "I can drive. You want a driver," she said curtly. "Let's talk business." She had learned long ago to stand her ground when someone taunted her. Otherwise the taunting grew intolerable.

To her amazement, she made Pete Pasquini laugh. It was not a reassuring sound. "You're a feisty one, ain't you?" he grinned. "You—are—a—*feisty*—one." He separated each word with slow relish, enjoying her discomfiture. For though she stood tall and bold in front of him, her hot face betrayed her embarrassment. She gave him a withering look and then turned and strode toward the door till she heard his voice behind her, accompanied by his footsteps.

"No offense, Beebo," he said. "I'm gonna be your boss. I wanta be your friend, too. I don't want people workin' for me don't like me. Shake hands?"

She turned around slowly, unconvinced. Maybe he really thought he was ingratiating himself with her. But she didn't like his method much. It was the thought of her nearly empty wallet that finally prompted her to offer him her hand. He took it with a rather light loose grasp, surprising Beebo who was used to the hearty grip of the farmers in her home county. But when he lifted her hand up and

said, "Hey, that's big, too!" she snatched it away as if he
had burned her.

"Okay, okay, all you got to do is drive, you don't have
to shake hands with me all day," he said, amused by her
reaction. "I can see it ain't your favorite game."

It seemed peculiar enough to Beebo that they shake hands
at all. They were not officially employer and employee yet,
and even if they were, they were still man and girl. It
made her feel creepy. She assumed that Pete had to get his
wife's approval before he could hire her. Marie was supposed to run the business.

"Well, come on, I'll show you where things is," Pete
said.

"You mean it's settled?" She hesitated. "I'm hired?"

"Why not?" He turned back to look at her.

"Well, I thought your wife? I mean—?" She stopped, not
wishing to anger him. His face had turned very dark.

"My wife *what?*" he said. "You never mind my wife.
If I say you're hired, you're hired. I don't want no back
talk about the wife. You dig?"

She nodded, startled by the force of his spite. She made
a mental note not to press that sore spot again. He apparently needed and wanted the money Marie's succulent
concoctions brought in, but he hated surrendering control of
the shop to her. Yet it was the price of their success. She
knew what she was doing, in the kitchen and in the ac-
counts, and he was afraid to interfere.

Beebo stood frowning at the sawdust floor.

"What's the matter, kid? Something bugging you?" Pete
asked.

She glanced up at him. It was strange that he should hire
her on the spot without the slightest idea if she could drive
worth a damn. "Do you want me to start deliveries this
morning?" she said.

"I'll take you around, show you the route," he said.
"First we got to make up the orders."

He walked toward the back of the store with Beebo behind him. "Mr. Pasquini, there's just one thing," she said.

"It's Pete. Yeah, what thing?" He handed her a large
cardboard carton to pack a grocery order in.

"How much will it pay?" Beebo asked, standing there with
the box, unwilling to start working till she knew what she
was worth.

"Fifty a week to start," he said, without looking up. He

lifted some bottled olive oil down from a nearby shelf. "Things work out good, I'll raise you. You want it, don't you?" He looked at her then.

There was a barely noticeable pause before she answered, "I want it." But she spoke with a sliver of misgiving stuck in the back of her mind.

Pete accompanied her on the delivery route that morning and again in the afternoon, watching her handle the truck, showing her where the customers lived. She had spent the night before with Jack studying a map of New York City and Greenwich Village, but what had seemed fairly logical on paper bogged down in colorful confusion when she took to the streets.

Pete swung an arm up on the seat behind her, his knees jutting toward her legs, and now and then when she missed a direction he would grab the wheel and start the turn for her. She disliked his closeness extremely, and throughout the day she was aware of his eyes on her face and body. It almost made her feel as if she had a figure, for the first time in her life, and the idea shocked her.

Beebo had broad shoulders and hardly a hint of a bosom. No man had ever looked at her appreciatively before, not even Jack Mann, who obviously liked her and enjoyed her company. She was not sure whether Pete admired her or was merely interested because she was so different from other girls.

He can't possibly like me, she thought. Not the way men like women. The notion was so preposterous that it made her smile and reassured her. Till Pete noticed the smile and said, "What's so funny, kid?" He looked too eager to know and she brushed it off. He let it go, but watched her more attentively, making her squirm a little.

It was a relief to climb down from the truck that afternoon—and a blow to feel the heavy clap of a masculine hand on her shoulder. "You did real good, Beebo," Pete said, and the hand lay there until she spun away from him and walked inside to meet his wife.

Marie Pasquini was twenty-six, the overweight and overworked mother of five little Pasquinis. She did most of the cooking while Pete's mother tended her kids, and the two women fell into several pan-rattling arguments per day. Beebo could hear the soprano squeals of young children upstairs in the apartment above the store, and a periodic disciplinary squawk from Grandma Pasquini.

Marie greeted Beebo with a big smile, revealing the
shadow of the pretty face concealed beneath the fat.

"Your accent is French, isn't it?" Beebo said.

"You got it," Marie beamed. "Smart girl." She moved
about the kitchen while they got acquainted, eating, working,
and talking incessantly. Pete slouched against the kitchen
door chewing a wooden matchstick and watching Beebo.

Marie worked hard and she ate hard and she was going
all to hips. But she was friendly and cheerful, and Beebo
liked her.

"That's a good boy, that Jack," Marie said. "He comes
in here two, three times a week, buys my food. Tells his
friends, 'Eat Pasquini's stuff,' and by God, they eat."

"He gave me some last night," Beebo said. "It's good."

"You bet." Marie stirred her sauce and glanced at Beebo.
"You live with him now?"

"Well—temporarily," Beebo said, taken aback both by
the question and by Pete's silent laughter.

"About time he got a girl," Marie said briskly. "Even one
in pants." And she glanced humorously at Beebo's tan
chinos.

Beebo colored up. "Well, it's not quite like that," she
protested.

"Oh, don't tell me," Marie said, holding up two spattered
hands. "A boy and a girl . . . well . . . !" and she gave a
Gallic chuckle.

"What you want to do, embarrass the kid?" Pete demanded suddenly with mock anger. "She don't sleep with
no lousy fag."

"Shut that big mouth, Pete," Marie said sharply, without
bothering to look at him. "She don't want to hear dirty
talk, neither."

Beebo was burning to ask what a fag was, but she didn't
dare. She could hear in her imagination the cackling it
would provoke from Pete.

Marie stirred in silence for a moment. "I never saw a
boy put up with so much," she said finally. "He got people
in and out, in and out, every damn day, eating him out
of house and home." Beebo squirmed guiltily. "His only
trouble, he got too big a heart. Don't never take advantage
of him like the others, Beebo."

"What others?"

"You don't know?" Marie looked at her, puzzled.

"Well, I've only known Jack a little while. I mean—"

"Oh." Marie nodded sagely. "Well, he got too many fair-weather friends. Know they can have whatever he got they want. So they take. And he lets them. Can't stand to see people go without. He's a good boy. Too good."

"He ain't all *that* good, Marie," Pete drawled, grinning at Beebo. "You just like him because he comes in here and gives you that swishy talk about what a good-looking dame you are. All that proves is, he got bad eyes. Now, Beebo here might have trouble with him, you never know. If I was her, I wouldn't climb in his bed."

"Pete, you got a mind even dirtier than your mouth," Marie said. "Get out of my kitchen, I don't want the food dirtied up too. Out, *salaud!*"

Beebo was amused by her accent, comically mismated with the ungrammatical English she had learned from Pete.

Marie threw a potlid at her husband. "See?" Pete shrugged at Beebo, catching the lid. "I try to say a few words and what do I get? Pots and pans. And she wonders why I go out at night."

"Out!" Marie stamped her foot and he left them, disappearing bizarrely like a wraith into the gloom of the darkened store. After nearly a full minute had elapsed Beebo became aware with a silent start that the fingers of his left hand were curled around the door frame: five orphaned earthworms searching for the dirt.

Beebo stared at them with something very near loathing. She wondered if she was supposed to see them, and if he thought they would please her for some obscure reason. Or was he hiding, thinking the fingers out of sight? No, he knew damn well she could see them, and would. They were his gesture of invitation, unheard and unseen by his wife.

Beebo began to sweat with alarm and revulsion. She chatted determinedly with Marie for almost fifteen minutes before those five pale fingers retreated from their post. Maybe it was supposed to be a gag, Beebo told herself. She didn't want to mention it to Marie. It would make her look a fool, perhaps even hysterical if the whole thing was only a joke.

That's what it is, Beebo told herself firmly. That's what it has to be. She stood up and thanked Marie, accepting a bag of hot fresh-cooked chicken to take home for dinner, and walked through the front of the shop. She held herself together tightly, and if she had seen the least movement, heard the least whisper, she would have lashed out in abrupt terror.

She had the uncanny feeling that Pete was somewhere waiting with those loathsome hands. But she couldn't see him, she didn't hear him, and she reached the door and the outside with a gasp of relief.

The relief was so deep that it turned into a laugh, soothing her and making her a little ashamed of herself. Away from Pete she could scold herself for her aversion to him. Maybe it wasn't fair. He was just a guy, not a ghost, not a snake. He was spooky, but Marie seemed as healthy and normal as her good foods.

Beebo was disturbed by the strangeness of Pete's manner, but she could never believe that any man would truly desire her, no matter how creepy he was. Not even a nut like Pete Pasquini. For his own reasons he was making a study of her, but beyond that he would never go. She began to feel safe and comfortable again as she rounded the corner to Jack's street. She felt unassailable in the fortress of her flatchested, muscular young body. It was not the stuff that male dreams are made of.

As Jack explained to her later, it was himself and others like him who had talked the Pasquinis' shop into a financial success. Rather abruptly, Pete and Marie found themselves making money, and Pete, after an adolescence full of alley wars and hock-shop heists, found himself taking a belated interest in the dough: not the flour kind, the folding kind.

He had married Marie overseas when he was in the service and brought her back to his inheritance: the foundering grocery shop his father had left him. Undismayed, Marie set out to bear his kids and learn his mother's recipes. By a combination of luck, sense, and skill, Marie pulled them out of the dumps.

It was still nominally Pete's business, yet he did little more that run his wife's errands and pocket all the money Marie would let him have. He always demanded more, but he respected her French thrift. The money she refused to give him went back into the business and made it possible for him to insist on more gradually as time went on.

This arrangement galled Pete but he preferred it to poverty. Still, he had to get even with her. So he did it by openly sniffing up skirts around Greenwich Village. He would even flaunt a girl at Marie now and then and she, stung, would call him half a man who played with other girls because he didn't have what it took to keep one good woman satisfied. Or else she ignored him entirely, which enraged him. It was not a quiet cozy family. Pete did not know or like his children very well. He got on famously with his mother, but his mother and his wife were lifelong enemies. Beebo began to learn about them as she worked near them in the shop.

Pete watched Beebo move around during the first week, making her feel clumsy as a young colt; getting in her way deliberately (she was sure) to make her dodge around him; turning up in out-of-the-way corners where she didn't expect to see him. Her antipathy to him was lively, but fortunately she didn't see much of him. Filling orders took less time than delivering them and she was out of the shop most of the day. In the truck she was disposed to be pleased with her job. She liked to drive. She liked to talk to people, and the customers were friendly. She even liked the chore of carrying the heavy cartons up and down all day. It pleased her to feel strong, equal to the task.

A week ago all her hopes had been crashing around her. She had retreated in disgrace from a cruel predicament. Then she found Jack Mann, a friend; a job, and some self-respect, one right after the other. She was grateful, full of the resilient optimism of youth.

Without any specific words on the subject, Beebo and Jack came to an understanding that she would live with him for a while, till she could afford a place for herself. "You'll be better off with a roommate," Jack advised her casually. "I'll have to introduce you to some of my upper-class female friends."

"Sure," she grinned. " 'Pamela, this is my lower-class female friend, Beebo Brinker.' And she'll say, 'Dahling, you're absolutely crashing, but I can't possibly share my apartment with those pants.' " She made Jack laugh at her. "Besides, Jackson," Beebo added rather shyly, "I've already got a roommate. He only has one fault—he won't let me pay my half of the rent."

"I like to pay bills," Jack said. "Gives me a sense of power."

"Marie says you've got too big a heart," Beebo told him. "And she's right."

"Marie's a good girl," he said. "How are you getting along with Peter the Wolf?"

"Fine, as long as he's out of my sight."

Jack grinned. "You can handle him, honey. Just keep a can of corn beef in your pocket. If he tries to lift your wallet, clobber him."

"It's not my wallet I'm worried about," she said. "There's nothing in it, anyway. It's just that he's always under my feet when he should be on the other side of the store."

"I suspect it's for Marie's benefit," Jack said. "Every female who comes into the store gets the once-over from Pete—provided Marie is looking. And most of the time, she is. She likes to keep score, I guess."

"There was a girl today," Beebo said. "She came in the shop about noon, when Marie was fixing lunch. I waited on her." Her face became intent, as she summoned the girl's image in her mind's eye.

"What about her?" Jack said curiously.

But Beebo, coming to herself at the sound of his voice, said, "Oh, nothing. But she was moré Pete's type . . . *any* man's type."

"What was she like?"

"She had long black hair," Beebo said, as if it were very special. "People don't let their hair grow like that any more. It was lovely. She let it hang free down her back. And her face. . ." She was gone again, seeing it in her imagination.

"She must have been a looker," Jack said, frustrated by the reticence between himself and Beebo. He knew what hundreds of questions she needed to ask, what a wealth of help she would be wanting soon. But she didn't dare start asking and because she didn't, Jack dared not force the answers on her yet.

"She was absolutely gorgeous," Beebo said with a certain wonderment and innocence that touched him. "I never saw such a girl in my life before." There was a small silence. Beebo's words hung in the air like a neon sign and reduced her abruptly to confusion. To cover up, she said, "She wasn't a very nice girl, though. Not by your standards."

"My standards?"

"She's not afraid of boys," Beebo grinned. "At least, she

wasn't afraid of Pete. But I think they knew each other from somewhere. He called her . . . Mona." She spoke the name self-consciously. "It sounds old-fashioned, doesn't it?"

"I wonder if it's Mona Petry," Jack said. "She has black hair, but I didn't think it was that long. Still, I haven't seen her for a while."

"Who's Mona Petry?" Beebo asked, her eyes intent on Jack.

"Old flame of Pete's," Jack said. "She used to come into the store a lot three or four years ago. She and Pete got quite a charge out of putting poor Marie on. Mona isn't the charitable type. She likes to land a man who belongs to some other woman—more to spite the other woman than because she wants the man. As soon as she won Pete, she dumped him like a sack of meal. For some reason, Pete never fought back. Makes me think she really meant something to him. God knows, none of the other broads do."

"Is she one of those man-hungry girls that can't get enough?" Beebo said. "I forget what they're called, but there's a name for it."

"The name is nymphomaniac," Jack said. "But Mona doesn't love men. She just plays around with them. They're good ego builders." He lighted a cigarette, seeing without seeming to, the concentration on Beebo's face. The question was there on her tongue, in her mind, but she couldn't get it out. *If Mona doesn't love men,* she was thinking . . . *then who?*

"There's another word for Mona," Jack said. Beebo tensed up. "Bitch." He threw her a grin and made her laugh with nervous relief. "Actually, Mona loves girls," Jack went on, speaking in a smooth casual flow, a conversational tone that bespoke no shock, no disapproval, nothing but ordinary interest. He deliberately looked at the front page of the evening paper as he spoke.

Beebo answered huskily, "What do you mean? What girls?"

"Lesbians," He said. "Want to freshen this up for me, pal?" He handed her his highball glass. She took it with astonishment still plain on her face. When she returned from the kitchen with the new drink, she asked him, "Aren't they sort of—*immoral?* I heard the word once before. I thought you weren't supposed to say it."

At that, Jack looked up. "Lesbian? You mean you thought it was a dirty word?" he exclaimed, and laughed in spite of himself. Beebo was momentarily offended until he cleared his throat and said, "Forgive me, honey, but that's the bloodiest nonsense I've heard in a long time. Whoever in the hell told you it was dirty?"

"Doesn't it mean loose women?" Beebo asked.

He shook his head. "It means *gay* women," he said. "It means homosexual women. It means women, Beebo, who love other women. The way heterosexual women love men."

His words put a focus on Beebo's fascination. She stared at him from the sofa with her lips parted and her eyes fixed steadily on his. "You said Mona was a bitch," she said finally, softly. "And then you said she was a Lesbian. Doesn't that make her cheap? Q.E.D.?"

"Some of the staunchest Puritan ladies I know are double-dyed bitches," Jack said briskly. "And just because Mona is a bad apple doesn't mean all the gay girls in the world are full of worms. Mona would be bitchy anyway, gay *or* straight."

"What's 'straight'?"

"Heterosexual," Jack said.

"Where did you learn all those words?" Beebo said, bewildered.

"I'm a native. I speak the lingo," he said, but instead of catching his implication, she thought he meant only that he lived in Greenwich Village so long he had picked it up, like everyone else.

"Does it ever happen that a nice girl is a Lesbian?" she asked him shyly.

"All the time," he said, opening up the paper and gazing through the ball scores.

"Did you ever meet any?"

"I've met most of them," he chuckled. "They're just as friendly and pleasant as other girls. Why not?"

"But can't you tell by looking at them that they're—" She rubbed a hand over her mouth as if to warn herself not to speak the word, and then said it anyway: "—Lesbian?"

"You mean, do they all wear army boots and Levis?" Jack said with a smile. "Does Mona Petry look like a buck private?"

Beebo shook her head. "That's why it's so hard to believe she's what you say she is."

"Gay? Why hell, she's slept with more girls than she has men. And let me tell you, that's damn near enough girls to elect a lady president."

Beebo laughed with him, and yet she felt a strange obsession with the whole idea. She half resented Jack's merriment on the subject, although she was relieved that he displayed no contempt for Lesbians as a group. Only for Mona Petry. She was surprised to find herself wanting to defend Mona, whom she knew so little. And yet she trusted Jack's judgment. Still, what a pity to think a girl that pretty was that hard.

Jack sipped his drink and picked up his cigarette, still with his eyes on the paper. "There are some nice little gay bars around the neighborhood," he said. "We'll have to take some of them in. Maybe this weekend, hm?" He didn't look at her. His cigarette waggled between his lips as he talked.

"Is it all right to go there?" Beebo asked. "Don't the police make raids on those places?"

"Now and then!" he conceded. "Of course, if you'd rather not..."

"Oh, I'd like to go," she said, so quickly that he smiled into the newsprint. "But aren't they just for men—the gay bars?"

"Men, girls, and everything in between," he assured her.

"Do you ever go there, Jack?"

Again he was tempted to be honest with her, and still again he restrained himself. "I go when the mood is on me," he said. Beebo became silent at once, as if she suspected she was trying to learn too much too fast. But she spent the remaining weekdays waiting impatiently for a tour of the bars with Jack.

Jack took her to three or four of his favorite places, and to one strictly Lesbian bar where they admitted only the faces they recognized, through a window in the door. Beebo followed him around quietly, watching, listening, almost breathing in the atmosphere. She said little, and most of what she did say was interrogatory.

Jack answered her calmly while he sipped one beer after another. He would order one for her and let her work at it, but he usually ended up finishing it himself. In every bar he was kept busy greeting people, trading jokes, laughing. Beebo trailed along in his wake, smiling and shaking hands with the strangers who were Jack's friends, and promptly forgetting their names.

But not their faces. Toward the end of the evening she began to feel that she had seen more faces in one night than she had seen in a lifetime in Juniper Hill. And these faces seemed different to her: rare and beautiful, sharers of a special knowledge. They had bright eyes and young smiles, no matter how old they were.

"They make a big thing of keeping young down here," Jack told her. "The men are worse than the girls. Nobody loves an old queen."

It was almost one in the morning when they left the last co-ed bar and Jack asked if she was game for one more. "This one is just for Lesbians," he said.

She nodded, and a few minutes later they were being admitted to a basement bar saturated with pink light, paneled with mirrors, and filled with girls. More girls, more sizes, types, and ages, than Beebo had ever seen collected together in one place. The place was called the Colophon and it was decorated with the emblems of various famous publishing houses.

Jack fought his way through the crush at the bar, absorbing a lot of pointed merriment directed at his masculinity.

"Sour grapes," he cried good-naturedly and inspired a chorus of laughter and catcalls. Beebo, pushing in behind him, became aware suddenly that she was the object of mass curiosity. She could look over the heads of most of the girls and her height made her visible from all directions.

Abashed, she closed in on Jack, who was hollering an order to the bartender. "Maybe we ought to go. I—I mean—" She didn't know how to explain herself to him. He was looking at her with a startled frown. "They don't seem to like having a man in here," she said lamely.

Jack began to laugh. "You want me to go, honey? Okay. Just give me two bits to see a movie."

She gasped. "That's not what I meant!" she objected. "I don't want to be in here alone!"

"Why not?" He reached between two girls at the bar to grab his beer. "You'll make out. I might cramp your style."

"Jack, damn it, if you go, *I* go."

"Okay, pal, I won't ditch you," he said, glimpsing her anxious face. "Relax. We'll have one more and then cut out."

She had had quite a bit of beer already, even with Jack finishing them for her. But she couldn't stand there with all

those eyes on her and do nothing. Better to drink a beer than
gape back at the gapers. She poured some into her glass and
drank it. And then drained the glass and poured some more.

Jack took her elbow. "I see some friends over there," he
said, guiding her toward a table near the back. There were
introductions all around, but to Beebo, things seemed different. The other bars had been all male or mixed. In this
one, Jack Mann and the two bartenders, and a small
scattering of "Johns," were the only men in a big room
solidly packed with women. It excited Beebo intensely—all
that femininity. She was silent, studying the girls at the table
while Jack talked with them. When she shook hands with
them, a new feeling gripped her. For the first time in her
life she was proud of her size, proud of her strength, even
proud of her oddly boyish face. She could see interest, even
admiration on the faces of many of the girls. She was not
used to that kind of reaction in people, and it exhilarated
her. But she didn't talk much, only answering direct questions when she had to; smiling at them when they smiled at
her; looking away in confusion when one or another tried to
stare her down.

They had been there half an hour when somebody came
over from another table and asked her to dance. Beebo
turned around, her stomach in a knot. "Are they dancing?"
she asked.

"Sure," said the girl. "By the jukebox."

Beebo had heard music without looking to see where it
came from. She got up from the table and went to the
back room, realizing as she stood up how much beer she
had drunk. At the back of the crowd surrounding the dance
floor, there was room to stand and watch.

The music was rhythmic and popular. The floor was
jammed with a mass of couples . . . a mass of girls, dancing,
arms locked around each other, bodies pressed close and
warm. Their cheeks were touching. Quick light kisses were
exchanged. And they were all girls, every one of them:
young and lovely and infatuated with each other. They
touched one another with gentle caresses, they kissed, they
smiled and laughed and whispered while they turned and
moved together.

There was no shame, no shock, no self-consciousness
about it at all. They were enjoying themselves. They were
having fun in the most natural way imaginable. They were

all in love, or so it seemed. They were—what did Jack call it?—gay.

Beebo watched them for less than a minute, all told; but a minute that was transfixed like a living picture in her mind for the rest of her life. She was startled by it, afraid of it. And yet so passionately moved that she caught her breath and held it till her heart began to pound in protest. Her fists closed hard with the nails biting into her palms and she was obsessed momentarily by the desire to grab the girl nearest her and kiss her.

At that point she murmured, "Oh, God!" and turned to flee. She felt the way she had in childhood dreams when she was being chased by some vague terrible menace, and she had to move slowly and tortuously, with great effort, as through a wall of water, while the monster gained on her from behind.

She caught Jack's shoulders in her big hands and squeezed them hard. "Let's go, let's go," she said urgently.

He looked at her as if she had lost her senses. "I just ordered another round," he said.

"Jack, please!" She pulled him to his feet.

"Jesus, can't you wait a little while, honey?" he said, and triggered an outburst of merriment at the table. But she meant it, and he was not too high to see her panic. He picked his jacket off the back of his chair, apologizing to his friends. "When she wants it, she wants it now," he grinned, shrugging.

"Who are you kidding?" they laughed.

Beebo was already pushing her way to the exit and Jack had a battle to catch her. He found her waiting for him outside by the door.

"Hey," he said, and put a friendly hand on her shoulder as they started to walk toward his apartment. "What happened?"

"I don't want to go back there, Jack," she blurted.

"What's the matter with it? Too much fun?"

"It was awful," she said, not even knowing why she said it.

"You liked the other places."

She wouldn't answer, only striding along so fast in her haste to leave the Colophon behind that Jack had to run to keep up.

"Was it the dancing?" he said.

She whirled to answer him, her face flushed with emotion. "I suppose you've seen it so many times you think nothing of it," she cried. "Well, it's—it's *wrong!*"

"Who the hell do you think you are to call it wrong?" Jack demanded. "Those are damn nice girls. If they want to dance with each other, let them dance. You don't have to watch."

Beebo listened, her anger fading, to be replaced by a fearful desire.

"Did it make you feel... that way, Beebo?" he said gently.

"It made me feel..." She turned away, unable to face him. "Funny inside. As if it was wrong. Or too right. I don't know."

"It's not wrong, pal," he said, speaking to her back. "You've been brought up to think so. Most of us have. But who are they hurting? Nobody. They're just making each other happy. And you want their heads to roll because it makes you feel funny."

She covered her face with her hands and rubbed her eyes roughly. Through her fingers she said, "I don't want to hurt them. I just don't want to stand there and watch them."

"Well, why didn't you dance?" he said. "Hell, I don't like being a wallflower, either."

"Jack, I can't dance like that," she said in a hushed voice. "Why can't you?" She refused to answer, so he answered for her. "You can. You just won't. But you know something, my little friend? One of these days, you will."

"You're no prophet, Jack. Don't predict *my* future." She started walking again.

He followed her, throwing up his hands. "Okay, okay. It shook you. But not because it was vulgar and indecent. Because it was beautiful and exciting. Besides, you envied those kids on the dance floor. Didn't you?"

Her confession never came. They walked in silence the rest of the way to Jack's apartment. He closed and locked the front door and turned on the living room light, tossing his jacket into a chair.

"Beebo," he said, lighting a cigarette. "You've been living with me almost a month now—"

"If you want me to move, I'll move." She was surly and defensive.

"I want you to stay. When you move, it'll be because you want to," he said. "Besides, that's not what I want to talk about. In the past month, you have never once told me the most important thing about yourself, Beebo."

She felt a flash of fear, piercing as sudden light in darkness. "I don't know what you mean," she said.

Jack gave her the freshly lighted cigarette and she hid gratefully behind a smoke screen. "You know," he said. "But I'm not going to insist on it. I think you want to talk to me, but you're afraid. I'm trying every way I know to show you that it won't offend me, Beebo. You think about that. You think about the people who are my friends—people I enjoy and respect—and then you ask yourself what you have to fear."

There was a long pause. At last she said. "It isn't that easy, Jack. I should know what I am. But I don't know myself at all. Especially here in this new place. Back in Juniper Hill, I could only see what other people saw, and I was afraid and ashamed. But here, I look all different. I even feel different." She looked at her hands. "Don't push me, Jackson." And she rushed past him suddenly, to cry in the privacy of the bathroom; to wonder why the girls she had seen that night had moved her so dramatically.

She did not fall asleep until very late. And when she did, she dreamed of sweet, supple, smiling-faced girls, dancing sensuously in each others' arms; glancing at her with wide curious eyes; beckoning to her. She saw herself glide slowly, almost reluctantly, over the floor with a girl whose long black hair hung halfway down her back; a girl with an old-fashioned name: Mona. Beebo touched the hair, the long dipping curve of the back till her hands rested on Mona's hips.

The next thing she knew, Jack was shaking her awake. "Wake up! Jesus!" he said, grinning at her in the early light. "You're beating hell out of the mattress."

Her eyes flew wide open and she stared at him, stuttering.

"Funny thing about dreams," he said softly. "They let you be yourself in the dark. When you can be yourself in the morning, too, you'll be cured."

"Cured of what?" she said in a disgruntled whisper.

Jack chuckled. "Dreams," he said. "You won't need 'em."

Beebo was relieved when he went back to sleep. There was no escaping now what she was. The dancing lovers in the

Colophon had impressed it indelibly on her. And yet Jack wanted her to confirm it in so many words, and the idea terrified her. It would be like accepting a label for the rest of her life—a label she didn't even understand yet.

And there was no one to tell her that the time would come when the label wouldn't frighten her; when she would be happy simply to be what she was.

They went a while longer without discussing it. Jack was on the verge of confronting Beebo a dozen times with his own homosexuality. But she would catch the look in his eye and warn him with tacit signs to keep still. He began to wonder if she understood about him at all. He had tried to make it obvious the night they went barhopping. He wanted to say to her, "Okay, I'm gay. But that doesn't make me less human, less moral, less *normal* than other men. You've got the same bug, Beebo; only with you, it's girls. Look at me: I'm proof you can live with it. You don't need to hate yourself or the people you're attracted to."

But if she saw it she kept it to herself. *She's too wrapped up in discovering herself to discover me too,* he thought. He tried to kid her. "You think it's all right for the other girls but not for Beebo," he said, but she wouldn't give him a smile. He felt stumped in front of her stubborn silence; aching to help her, afraid of scaring her into an emotional crack-up.

She was very tense. And then one evening, about a week after her night out with Jack, over dinner she said, "Mona was in the shop again. I talked to her."

Jack looked up in surprise. "What about?"

"I asked if she was Mona Petry. She is." She seemed afraid to elaborate.

"Is that all?" he smiled.

"You were right about her—she's gay." She looked up to catch the smile.

"Did she say so?" he asked.

"No, Pete said so after she left. He said he used to date her but he dropped her when he found out."

"Well, he's got it backwards, but never mind. The point is, Mona's a slippery little bitch. She's good to look at but she isn't any fun. She's out to screw the whole damn world. If I were you—"

"Jackson, I don't give a damn what you think of Mona Petry," Beebo said.

"Then why bring her up?"

She colored, and put down a few more bites of the dinner they were eating. Finally, slowly, with her face still pink, she said, "Do you think it would be all right if I went out tonight? I mean—alone?"

"If you eat all your spinach."

"I am asking you," she said hotly, "because I value your judgment. Not because I'm an addlepated child."

"All right," he said, smiling into his napkin. "Where do you want to go?"

She looked at her plate. "The Colophon," she said, making him strain to hear it.

"Why? Want to drop a bomb on the dance floor?"

She sighed. "Pete says Mona hangs out there."

"In that case, I don't think it's safe," he said flatly. "But it should be educational."

She said, "Jack, I'm scared. I don't think I've ever been so scared of anything in my life."

"It's no disgrace to be scared, Beebo. Only to act like it."

"I feel as if that damn silly bar—the people in it—are a sort of challenge," she said, fumbling to express it justly. "As if I have to go back or I'll never know. . ." She shook her head with a self-conscious smile. "That's a hell of a place to go looking for yourself."

"Hell of a place to go looking for Mona," he said. "I don't know though, pal. It has to come sooner or later. It's time you learned a thing or two. You're naive, but you're no fool. Go on—but go slow."

Mona was not at the Colophon that night, nor for many nights afterward. In a way, Beebo was relieved. She wanted to meet her, but she wanted time to meet other people too, to see other places, and cruise around the Village without any pressure on her to prove things to herself. Or to a worldly girl like Mona Petry. Beebo was still a stranger in a strange town, unsure, and grateful for a chance to learn unobserved.

She would sit and gaze for hours at the girls in the bars

or passing in the streets. She wanted to talk to them, see what they were like. She was often drawn to one enough to daydream about her, but she never mentioned it to Jack. Still, she was eagerly curious about the Lesbian mores and social codes. The gay girls seemed so smooth and easy with each other; talking about shared experiences in a special slang, like members of an exclusive sorority.

Beebo, watching them as the days and weeks passed, became slowly aware how much she envied them. She wanted to join the in-group. And she would watch them longingly and wonder if their talk was ever about her. It was.

A few of Jack's friends, who had met her in his company, would come up and talk with her, and knowing for certain that they were Lesbians gave Beebo a vibrant pleasure, whether or not the girls themselves were exciting. Looking at one she would think, *She knows how it feels to want what I want. I could make her happy. I know it.* Even the word "Lesbian," that had offended her before, began to sound wonderful in her ears.

She shocked herself with such candid thoughts, but that was only at first. Little by little, it began to seem beautiful to her that two women could come together with passion and intelligence and make a life with and for each other; make a marriage. She dreamed of lovely, sophisticated women at her feet, aware even as she dreamed that she hadn't yet the *savoir faire* to win such a woman. But she was afire with ambition to acquire it.

She would walk into a bar, order a beer, and sit alone and silent through an evening. In her solitude, she seemed mysterious to the laughing chattering people around her. They began to point her out when she came in.

At first, ignorance and inexperience kept Beebo aloof. But she quickly understood that her refusal to be sociable made her the target of a lot of smiling speculation. When she got over being afraid of the situation, it amused her. The fact that she attracted girls, even ones she knew she would never pursue, was almost supernaturally strange and exciting to her. She submitted to their teasing questions with an enigmatic smile until she realized that one or two had worked themselves up to infatuation pitch over her.

There followed a period of elation when she walked into Julian's or the Cellar and saw the eyes she knew had waited all night to look into hers turn and flash in her direction. She always passed them by and went to a seat at the bar. But

each time she came closer to stopping and answering a smile
or asking someone to join her in a beer. And still, she
couldn't find Mona.

The only wrong note in the tune was a boy, slight and
fine-featured, who watched her and seemed to have persuaded himself that he loved her. He fell for her with an
awkward crush that embarrassed them both. Often, at the
end of an evening when he was pretty high, he would
approach her and timidly offer to buy her a drink.

Beebo kept turning him down, kindly but firmly. He always flinched when she said no, and she pitied him. He had
a gentle appealing face, fair in the way of extreme youth.
She guessed he must be a couple of years younger than she,
and wondered how he could buy drinks in a bar.

"I'm sorry, I'm just leaving," she would tell him.

And he would watch her go, wistfully. He looked tired
and malnourished, and she wondered once if it would offend
him to be offered a free sandwich. She never quite got up
the nerve to find out.

At home, Jack did not press her. But her silence regarding
her activities at night worried him and put a strain between
them. She knew that Jack was waiting for her to talk about it,
and she wanted to be honest with him more than ever.
He had been patient, humorously tolerant with her. And she
knew that he was a man of the world. He had made it clear
that he enjoyed the friendship of many delightful gay
women, that he approved of them and that he thought she
might enjoy their company.

But he had not said, "Oh, come on, Beebo. You're gay.
Admit it. We both know it." He had, however, come closer
than she knew to saying it. And it was hard for Jack himself to realize that his hints and jokes were couched in a
language still foreign to her in many ways. Often they went
over her head or were taken at face value; saved and worried over, but never fathomed.

So she found herself hung up on a dilemma: she was
sure of his friendship as long as she was an observer of the
gay scene, not a sister-in-the-bonds. But what would he say if
she told him she had a desperate crush on Mona Petry with
the long black hair? Or that she got dizzy with the joy of

being in a crowd of gay girls; near enough to touch, to overhear, to look and look and look until they whirled through her dreams at night.

Would he say, *You can play with the matches but don't get burned?* Would he pity her? Turn on his wit? Would he —could he—take it with the easy calm he showed in other circumstances?

She thought he could. She felt closer to him now that she had spent nearly two months under his roof. She knew his heart was big, and she had seen him in a Lesbian bar talking with his friends there. He was not being condescending. He valued them.

Perhaps more than anything, she was persuaded by the need to talk it out; the need for help and comfort. And that was Jack's forte.

Beebo and Jack were watching a TV show one evening when he asked her, during the commercial, why she wasn't going out that night. "Don't tell me you gave up on Mona," he teased.

Instead of answering, she told him about the boy who was in love with her. "His name is Pat," she said. "The bartender told me. He looks hungry, as if he needed to be cared for." She laughed. "I was never much for maternal instincts— but he seems to bring them out."

"I'd like to meet him. He might bring mine out, too," Jack said.

"Why don't you come with me Friday? He's always at Julian's."

Jack looked away. "I've been trying to give you a free rein," he said. "You don't want me along. I'll find him myself."

"I do want you along," she said. "I like your company."

"More than the girls'?" he grinned.

She felt herself tense all over. There had been so many chances lately to talk to him, and she had run away from them all. Now, she felt a surge of defiance, a will to have it out. He had a right to know at least as much about her as she knew about herself. He had earned it through his generosity and affection.

"I read a book once," she said clumsily. "Under my

covers at night—when I was fifteen. It was about two girls who loved each other. One of them committed suicide. It hit me so hard I wanted to die, too. That's about as close as I've come to reality in my life, Jack. Until now."

He leaned over and switched off the television. The room was so quiet they could hear themselves breathing.

"I was kicked out of school," she went on hesitantly, "because I looked so much like a boy, they thought I must be acting like one. Chasing girls. Molesting them. Everything I ever did to a girl, or wanted to do or dreamed of doing, happened in my imagination. The trouble was, everybody else in Juniper Hill had an imagination, too. And they had me doing all these things for real." She shut her eyes and tried to force her heart to slow down, just by thinking about it.

"And you never did?" he said. "You never tried? There must have been girls, Beebo—"

"There were, but all I had to do was talk to one and her name was mud. I wouldn't do that to anybody I cared for."

Jack stared at her, wondering what geyser of emotion must be waiting to erupt someone so intense, so yearning, and so rigidly denied all her life.

"My father tried to teach me not to hate myself because I looked like hell in gingham frills," she said. "But when you see people turn away and laugh behind their hands. . . . It makes you wonder what you really are." She looked at him anxiously, and then she said it. "I've never touched a girl I liked. Never made a pass or spoken a word of love to a single living girl. Does that make me normal, Jack? . . . . And yet I know I could, and I think now I will, and God knows I want to desperately. Does that make me gay?" She spoke rapidly, stopping abruptly as if her voice had gone dead in her throat at the word "gay."

"Well, first," he said kindly, "you're Beebo Brinker, human being. If you *are* gay, that's second. Some girls like you are gay, some aren't. Your body is boyish, but there's nothing *wrong* with it." His voice was reassuring.

"Nothing, except there's a boy inside it," she said. "And he has to live without all the masculine trimmings other boys take for granted. Jack, long before I knew anything about sex, I knew I wanted to be tall and strong and wear pants and ride horses and have a career. . . and never marry a man or learn to cook or raise babies. Never."

"That's still no proof you're gay," he said, going slowly, letting her convince herself.

"I'm not even built like a girl. Girls are knock-elbowed and big-hipped. They can't throw or run or—look at my arm, Jack. I was the best pitcher on the team whenever they let me play." She rolled her sleeve back and showed him a well-muscled arm, browned and veined and straight as a boy's.

"I see," he murmured.

"It was the parents who gave me the worst of it," she said. "The kids weren't too bad till I got to high school. But you know what happens then. You get hairy and you get pimples and you have to start using a deodorant."

Jack laughed silently behind his cigarette.

"And the boys get big and hot and anxious, like a stallion servicing a mare."

Jack swallowed, feeling himself move. "And the girls?"

"The girls," she sighed, "get round and soft and snippy."

"And instead of round and soft, you got hot and anxious?"

"All of a sudden, I was Poison Ivy Brinker," she confirmed. "Nobody wanted whatever it was I had. My brother Jim said I wasn't a boy and I wasn't a girl, and I had damn well better be one or the other or he'd hound me out of school himself."

"What did you do?"

"I tried to be like the rest. But not to please *that* horse's ass." Her farmer's profanity tickled him. "I did it for Dad. He thought I was adjusting pretty well, and that was his consolation. I never told him how bad it was."

"So now you want to find Mona Petry," Jack said, after a small pause, "and ask her if you're gay."

"Not *ask* her. Just get to know her and see if it could happen. She makes me wonder so . . . Jack, what makes a feminine girl like that gay? Why does she love other girls, when she's just as womanly and perfumed as the girl who goes for men? I used to think that all homosexual girls were three-quarters boy." She hung her head. "Like me, I guess. And that they were all doomed to love feminine girls who could never love them back. It seemes like a miracle that a girl like Mona could love a—" she stopped, embarrassed.

"Could love a girl like you," he finished for her. "Take it on faith, honey. She doesn't have to look like a Ram tackle to know that her happiness lies with other women. The girls you see around town aren't all boyish, are they?"

"They're not all gay, either."

He ground out his cigarette. "Tell me why they ran you out

of Juniper Hill. The whole story. Was it really just a nasty rumor about you and the Jones girl?"

Beebo lay down, stretched out on the sofa, and answered without looking at him. "They'd been hoping for an excuse for years," she said. "It was in April, last spring. I went to the livestock exhibition in Chicago with Dad and Jim. I was in the stalls with them most of the time, handling some of the steers from our county. Sweaty and gritty, and not thinking about much but the job. And then one night—I'll never know why—I took it into my head to wear Jim's good clothes.

"I knew it was dangerous, but suddenly it was also irresistible. Maybe I just wanted to get away with it. Maybe it was the feel of a man's clothes on my back, or a simple case of jealousy. Anyway, I played sick at dinnertime, and stayed in the hotel till they left.

"Jack, it was as though I had a fever. The minute I was alone I put Jim's things on. I slung Dad's German camera over my shoulder and took his Farm Journal press pass. On the way over, I stopped for a real man's haircut. The barber never said a word. Just took my money and stared.

"I looked older than Jim. I felt wonderful." She stopped, her chin trembling. "A blonde usher showed me to the press section. She was small and pretty and she asked me if I was from the 'working press.' I said yes because it sounded important. She gave me a seat in the front row with a type-writer. It was screwed down to a stand. God, imagine!" She almost laughed.

"I really blitzed them," she said, remembering the good part with a throb of regret. "Everybody else was writing on their machines to beat hell, but I didn't even put a piece of paper in mine. After a while I took out the camera and made some pictures. The girl came back and said I could work in the arena if I wanted to, and I did. It was hotter than hades but I wouldn't have taken that tweed jacket off for a fortune.

"I guess I took pictures for almost three hours . . . just wandered around, kidding the girls on horseback and keeping clear of the Wisconsin people." She hesitated and Jack said, "What happened then?"

"I got sick," she whispered. "My stomach. I thought it was bad food. Or that damn heat. Awful stomach cramps. In half an hour I was so miserable I could hardly stand up and I was scared to death I might faint. If I'd had any sense I'd have gone back to my seat and rested. But not Beebo. I didn't want to waste my moment of glory. It would go away—it *had* to.

"Well, I was right about one thing—I fainted, right there in the arena. The next I knew, I was strangling on smelling salts and trying to sit up on a cot in the Red Cross station. The doctor asked how I felt and I said it was indigestion. He wanted to have a look.

"I was terrified. I tried to laugh it off. I said I was tired, I said it was the heat, I said it was something I ate. But that bastard had to look. He thought it might be appendicitis. There was nothing I could do but cover my face and curse, and cry," she said harshly. Jack handed her a newly-lighted cigarette, and she took it, still talking.

"The doctor saw the tears, and that was the tip-off. He opened my shirt so fast the buttons flew. And when he saw my chest, he opened the pants without a word. Just big bug-eyes." She gave Jack a look of sad disgust. "I had the curse," she muttered. "First time."

After a moment she went on, "I never meant to hurt anybody or cause a scene. But I hurt my father too much. He suffered over it. I had to wait till my hair grew out before I could go back to school, but I could have saved myself the bother. They let me know as soon as I got back I wasn't wanted. Before Chicago, they thought I was just a queer kid. But afterwards, I was really queer. There's a big difference."

Jack listened, bound to her by the story with an empathy born of his own emotional aberration.

"The principal of the high school said he hoped he could count on me to understand his position. *His* position. I wanted to ask him if he understood *mine*." There was hopeless bitterness in her voice.

"They never do," Jack said quietly. "Still, that's not the only high school in the world. You could finish up somewhere else and go on to pre-med, Beebo."

"You didn't," she reminded him. "You got fed up and quit. But me—I've been expelled. I'm not wanted anywhere."

"Do you think a job as a truck driver is worth sacking a medical career for?"

"What did you sack yours for?" He was making her defensive.

"My story's all over," he said. "But there's still time for you. Beebo, do you know what you're trying to do? Get *even* with the world. You're so mad at it, and everybody in it for the bum deal you got, you're going to deny it a good doctor some day."

"I'd be a rotten doctor, Jack. I'd be scared. I'd be running and hiding every day of my life."

"Hell, plenty of doctors are gay. They manage." He was surprised at the importance it was assuming in his own mind. He really cared about it. It depressed him to think of what she might be and what she was in a fair way now of becoming. "You're thinking that if people are going to reject you, by God you're going to reject them first. If they make it hard for you to be a doctor, you'll make damn sure they never *get* that doctor. You've been keeping score and now you're avenging yourself on the world because most of the people in it are straight. You keep it up and you'll turn into a joyless old dyke without a shred of love in her heart for anyone."

Beebo sat up and frowned at him, surprised but not riled. "Are you telling me to go to hell because I—I think I'm gay?" she asked.

"I'm telling you to go to college," he said seriously.

"Jack, you goofed your chance for an M.D. for reasons a lot flimsier than mine. What are you trying to do? Push me into school so you can make peace with your conscience? You're the one who wants to give that good doctor to humanity. If it can't be yourself, better it should be Beebo than nobody. And Jack Mann will have made a gift to his fellow men. Jack, the Great Humanitarian. And you won't even have to crack a book." She spoke wryly, but without rancor.

Jack was stunned into silence by her flash of insight.

"I hit it, didn't I?" she said. "Jack, you don't know what you're asking me to do: wear a skirt for the rest of my life. Forget about love till my heart dries up. Go back and face the father I destroyed and the brother who hates me . . . well, I can't. I'm no martyr. I'm not brave enough to try to be a doctor now, just because you tried and failed. And feel bad about it."

He took her hands and rubbed them. "You hit it dead on, little pal, but only part of it," he said. "Sure, I'd like to see you with a medical degree and know I'd had something to do with it. But forget me. Be selfish about it. A degree would protect you, not expose you to more trouble. Knowledge, success, the respect of other doctors—that would be your defense against the world."

"There's no protection against myself. My feelings. I

didn't tell you about the girls back home, Jack, walking down country lanes after school with their arms around the boys, kissing and laughing. The girls I couldn't touch or talk to or even smile at. The girls I'd grown up with, suddenly filling out their sweaters and their nylons, smooth and sweet with scented hair and pink mouths. I didn't tell you how I ached for them."

He got up and crossed the room, looking out his front windows. "I don't want you to end up an old bull dyke in faded denims, letting some blowsy little fem take care of you," he said acidly. "You're not a bum."

"I don't want that, either. But Jack, I can't spend the rest of my life wondering!" She went to his side, speaking urgently, wanting him to root for her, not against her. "They call this life gay," she said softly, following his gaze out the windows. "I need a little gaiety."

"They call it gay out of a perverted sense of humor," he said.

Across the street two young women were walking slowly in the mild evening air, arms around each other's waists. "There," Beebo said, nodding at them. "That's what I want. I've wanted it ever since I knew girls did such things."

"You mean Mona?" he said.

Beebo shoved her hands into her pockets, self-conscious as always when that name came up. "You have to start somewhere," she said.

"You have quite a thing about her, don't you?" he said.

Beebo's cheeks flushed and she looked at the floor. "I never dared to admit that I wanted a girl before, Jack. Maybe I picked the wrong time. Or the wrong audience."

"Pal, you just picked the wrong girl."

"I don't want you to pity me. That's why I held out so long. I need you, Jack. You're the first friend—the first brother —I ever had."

Jack was touched and embarrassed. "I feel no pity for you, Beebo," he said. "You don't need pity. I feel friendship and. . . anxiety. If you've made up your mind to stay here, I'll do anything to help you, teach you, take you around. But, honey—not Mona. She doesn't believe in anything but kicks. She'll charm the pants off you and then leave you standing naked in front of your enemies."

"Are you trying to say you disapprove of Mona, but not of the fact that I'm—I *must* be—gay?" she said.

"Why would I disapprove of that?" he said and then he

laughed. "I swear to God, Beebo, you can be thicker than bean soup. I've done everything but sing it for you in C sharp."

"I know you've tried to be tolerant and all, introducing me to your friends. I thought it was because you suspected about me and you wanted to be a good sport."

"I'm trying to explain about *me,* not you," he said, throwing out his hands and still chuckling.

Beebo smiled back, mystified. "Let me in on the joke, will you?"

"The joke's on me this time," he said.

She studied him a moment, her smile yielding to perplexity. And then she said, "Oh!" suddenly and lifted a hand to her face. She went back to the sofa and sat down with her head in her hands.

"Well, you don't need to feel badly about it, pal," he said, joining her. "I don't. There are even days when I feel sorry for the straight people."

"Jesus, I should have seen it," she murmured.

"No, you shouldn't. I'm a genius at hiding it."

"Jack, I'm sure a fool. I've been up to my eyes in my own troubles."

He shook his head. "I couldn't believe you wouldn't figure it out. It's hard to realize the kind of life you've been leading up to now. How little you've been allowed to see or understand."

She looked up at him. "Thanks for being patient," she said. "I mean it. Jack, how long have you been gay? How did you find out about yourself?"

"I didn't. I was told. In the Navy, by a hairy little gob who kept climbing into my bunk at night and telling me fairy stories. When he got a rise out of me, he made the diagnosis. I told him to go to hell, but the next night, I was climbing into *his* bunk."

It made her smile. "Can you forgive me?" she said.

"Nothing to forgive. And I'll let you back into my good graces on one condition. Do you think your friend Pat will be in bloom tonight?"

"Probably," she said, seeing him through her new understanding as through a rainbow curtain. He was a new shape, a new color, a new man. She was vastly relieved, and just a little awed. And ashamed of her bean-soup intuition.

"Let's go look at him," Jack said.

The night was hot and damp, with a low black sky that had looked menacing in the daylight, but was soft and close as dark came down, floating over the neon merriment below.

Beebo was quiet as they walked, preoccupied with a new attitude toward Jack and an almost unbearable sense of anticipation. Pat was usually at Julian's. When they arrived, the bar was crowded but there was standing room at one end. They squeezed in and ordered drinks, and Beebo began to pick out the faces that searched for her.

"Is he here?" Jack asked, glancing around.

She discovered him right away. "Over there in the blue shirt," she said, nodding.

"They all have blue shirts," Jack said, squinting through the smoke.

"The blond one."

There was a pause and Jack's face puckered thoughtfully. "He looks pretty young," he said in a bemused voice.

"You mean, you like his face?" Beebo smiled at him.

"It's a face," he said noncommittally, and when she laughed he shrugged and added, "Okay. A nice face. Beebo, I think you're playing cupid."

"I wouldn't know how," she said. "Besides, you told me you only fell in love in the fall or the spring. This is midsummer." But she wondered suddenly what would happen if he broke his rule. It made her heart drop. Jack's apartment was small, with just one bed. Even if he didn't ask her to leave, how welcome would she be if he invited a third party to share it with them? She'd have to bow out, out of simple consideration. But where could she go? She had avoided making any friends, and the Pasquinis with their five kids were out of the question. She would have preferred a park bench anyway to a room with Pete Pasquini in it.

Beebo and Jack were both caught unaware by the sudden quiet interruption. There he was, Beebo's boy, standing behind and between them. He had come over in the moment it took them to discuss him and now they looked at him in surprise.

He paled a little and started to back away, but Jack put a

hand on his shoulder. "Don't panic. We're harmless when
we're drinking," he said. "What's your name?"

"Pat Kynaston," said the boy, staring into his beer. He
supposed Beebo had Jack with her this time to show him
she was taken, and he was crushed.

"Pat? That's a girl's name," Beebo kidded.

Pat swallowed some beer and moved the sawdust under his
shoes.

"Have a drink, honey," Jack said, and Beebo felt a stir of
strange interest in the endearment. And yet Pat seemed more
like a child than a man, and it was easy to call him fond
names. In spite of his light beard he had a child's face, full
of a child's hardy trust. He smiled at Jack, reassured.

"He looks as green as you did last May," Jack told
Beebo. "How long have you been here, Pat?"

"Oh, since seven-thirty, I guess."

"No, I mean in New York?" Jack grinned.

"Oh. January." Pat's eyes remained on Beebo while he
answered Jack. But when she returned the look, he glanced
down to her belt. "I left school then," he said.

"Sounds like the story of my life," said Beebo. "How old
are you?"

"Twenty-seven."

Jack cleared his throat and Beebo's mouth dropped open.
"With that face?" Jack protested. "You mean your *father*
is twenty-seven."

Pat laughed a little and shook his head.

"Besides, what is a twenty-seven-year-old child doing in
school? You should be through."

"I was working on a doctorate in entomology."

"Bugs? You don't look like a bug collector," Jack said with
a grimace, and they laughed while the drinks came up. Jack
pulled Pat between himself and Beebo and teased him for a
while, making him blush and answer questions. But when it
came out that Pat was working as a garbage-collector for the
New York City Department of Sanitation, Jack stopped laughing.

"God! A frail kid like you? You shouldn't do work like
that," he declared.

"It was all I could get. Nobody wants an entomologist
manqué," Pat said. "I guess that's why I'm skinny. I look at
those rotting scraps all day and when I get home the stuff in
my icebox looks just as bad."

Jack tapped Beebo on the shoulder. "Do we have any of Marie's chicken tetrazini in the refrigerator?"

"Plenty."

"Let's go." Jack threw a couple of bills on the counter and took Pat by the elbow. Beebo took the other and they walked him out of Julian's and down the street.

Beebo had been elated to learn that Jack, too, was gay. But now she felt the first twinge of misgiving. Jack was the older brother she never really had; one she could learn from, look up to, even love. It was a valuable feeling, new to her. For as fiercely as she resented Jim, she had always harbored a secret regret that they could not have been friends.

They walked toward Jack's place with Pat clinging in bewildered pleasure to Beebo, the object of what had seemed so long a futile attraction. But Beebo was lost in herself, wondering if she could make it yet in the city on her own. She was strong and handsome, and she walked, gestured, even swore with a boyish gusto that made her seem more experienced than she was. But she was still untutored in the ways of metropolitan gay life and that fact undermined her self-confidence.

They put Pat, who was high enough to be sleepy, on Jack's sofa and looked at him. He dozed a little, his fair face averted, and the two roommates were struck with the beauty of his features. Beebo was unnerved to find herself suddenly wanting a girl with blast-furnace intensity.

"I'll heat the bird," she offered to Jack, "if you'll mind the patient."

"You're on," he said.

But she was sorry to have to leave them alone together. Jack was entirely too taken with the boy. Beebo moved pensively around the kitchen, preparing the food with unaccustomed hands.

Jack brought Pat to the table when she called them. Pat looked so slender and peaked that she felt a good doctor's desire to stuff him full of nourishment.

He leaned against the door frame, gazing at Beebo. "Who are you, anyway?" he asked, drunk enough to be brave.

"Sit down, Hungry," Beebo said, smiling at him.

Abashed, but unappeased, he obeyed.

"You know what's wrong with you, Pat? Malnutrition," she said. "If you had any food under your belt, you wouldn't give two bits for me." He turned a baffled face to her. "Why hell, the damn bugs eat better than you do," she told him. "They get all the garbage that ruins your appetite."

She tried to feed him but he turned away. "I can't," he said. The excitement of coming home with this girl he had admired so fervently for a couple of months was too much; that, and all the beer he had drunk . . . and a new gentle feeling stirring in him for Jack Mann.

"Sure you can," Beebo said, and began to feed him as if he were a sick lamb, while Jack cut the chicken bits for her. When Pat tried to protest she popped a mess of spicy meat between his teeth and shushed him, wishing all the while that she were ministering to a lovely girl instead of a lost boy.

Beebo stole a look at Jack, afraid of what she might see. But he was regarding Pat with compassion, the same he had shown to her when he found her . . . and just a trace of desire, tightly controlled. Jack had kindly instincts. It was one of the things Beebo admired most in him. He took care of people because it made him happy. No one was to blame if, when the person was a beautiful young boy, it made him very happy indeed.

Beebo got the chicken down Pat and made him drink his milk, which he did out of pure infatuation for her. And then Jack filled the silence with one word: "Bedtime."

But Pat seemed to be in a sort of trance, brought on by fatigue, fascination, and a full stomach. "Are you conscious?" Jack asked him with a smile.

"I was just thinking," Pat murmured, blinking at Beebo. "Maybe I'm straight."

They laughed at him, till he got indignant and tried to explain that even Beebo's marginal femininity didn't discourage him.

"You need some sleep, buddy," Jack told him, and took him off to the sofa. "And no damn trash cans for you in the morning."

"What if I lose my job?" Pat said.

"That would be the best thing that could happen to you."

"I'll starve," Pat whispered.

"Not while I'm around," Jack said. Pat smiled at him sleepily, and then shut his eyes and turned on his side.

Beebo climbed into Jack's bed feeling like an impostor. But she was embarrassed to make an issue of it; more than that, afraid. If she offered to take the sofa herself, Jack might grab the chance to have Pat beside him all night.

Beebo felt no physical attraction to Pat; only sympathetic interest. But his puppy love had scorched her a little; just enough to keep her moving and twisting on the warm sheets for an hour, obsessed with the growing need for a girl. A girl to curl in her lap and kiss her and talk away her fears.

Pat's loneliness shocked her. She saw herself mirrored in his predicament. Who was more alone than a lost and defenseless soul, hungry for something it couldn't find? Couldn't even define? It was enough to warp the heart, deform the soul.

It was enough to get her out of bed at midnight that night, make her dress in silence and leave the apartment, undetected by Jack or Pat.

She was almost as surprised to find herself on the street as Jack would have been to see her there. And yet the cool night air washed gratefully over her face and cleared her thoughts. She wandered aimlessly a while, as if trying to ignore the one place she wanted to visit: the Colophon.

But her feet took her there anyway, and she found herself ringing the bell. The owner opened the peek-through in the door and nodded to her. She felt a momentary country-girl shame at being recognized in such a place. But she was glad enough to gain entrance. The glow inside was the color of fluorescent Merthiolate. It seemed almost antiseptic to Beebo, who had painted the undersides of countless cows and sows with disinfectants the same shade prior to a delivery.

She took a seat at the bar. "Scotch and water," she said.

While the barman got it, she gazed idly into the mirror behind him, picking out the interesting girls surrounding her.

She felt uncomfortable here in the pants she usually wore to work; in her hair that had just been cut and was too short again.

Do they think I'm funny? she wondered. *Or—exciting?* She drank in silence, and ordered another, thinking that the solitude and uncertainty she felt now were worse than those she felt with Jack. For a minute, almost anything seemed better than having to leave Jack, with only fifty bucks a week to spend, no friends, and no place to live.

The bartender brought her another drink while she searched for the last cigarette in her pack. It was empty. The girl sitting next to her immediately offered her one, but Beebo declined. It was partly her shyness, partly the knowledge that it was better to be hard-to-get in the Colophon.

"Do you have cigarettes?" she asked the bartender.

"Machine by the wall," he said.

She got up and sauntered over, ignoring the outrage on the face of the girl at the bar. The machine swallowed her coins and spit out a pack of filter-tips. Beebo noticed the jukebox, looked at her change, and fed it a quarter, good for three dances. She liked to watch the girls move around the floor together, now that the initial revolt had worn off.

But when she regained her seat, she found most of the patrons paying attention to her, not the tunes. She looked back at them, surprised and wary. The cigarettes in her hand were an excuse to look away for a minute and she did, lighting one while the general conversation died away like a weak breeze. She lowered her match slowly and glanced up again, her skin prickling. What in hell were they trying to do? Scare her out? Show her they didn't like her? Had she been too aloof with them, too remote and hard to know?

She had started the music, and it was an invitation to dance. They were waiting for her to show them. It wasn't hostility she saw on their faces so much as, "Show us, if you're so damn big and smart. We've been waiting for a chance to trap you. This is it."

She had to do something to humanize herself. There was an air of self-confidence and sensual promise about Beebo that she couldn't help. And when she felt neither confident nor sensual, she looked all the more as if she did: tall and strong and coolly sure of herself. She had turned the drawback of being young and ignorant into a deliberate defense.

It didn't matter to the sophisticated girls judging her now that she was a country girl fresh from the hayfields of Wis-

consin, or that she had never made love to a woman before
in her life. They didn't know that and wouldn't have believed
it anyway.

Beebo recognized quickly that she had to start acting the
way she looked. She had established a mood of expectation
about herself, and now it was time to come across. The
music played on. It was Beebo's turn.

The match she held was burning near her finger, and because she had to do something about *it* and all the eyes on
her, she turned to the girl beside her and held out the
match.

"Blow," she said simply, and the girl, with a smile, blew.

Beebo returned the smile. "Well," she said in her low
voice, that somehow carried even into the back room and
the dance floor, "I'm damned if I'm going to waste a good
quarter." She got up and walked across the room toward the
prettiest girl she could see, sitting at a table with her lover
and two other couples. It was exactly the way she would
have reacted to student-baiting at Juniper Hill High. The
worse it got, the taller she walked. Her heart was beating
so hard she wanted to squeeze it still. But she knew no one
could hear it through her chest.

She stopped in front of the pretty girl and looked at her
for a second in incredulous silence. Then she said quietly,
"Will you dance with me, Mona?"

Mona Petry smiled at her. Nobody else in Greenwich
Village would have flouted the social code that way: walked
between two lovers and taken one away for a dance. Mona
took a leisurely drag on her cigarette, letting her pleasure
show in a faint smile. Then she stood up and said, "Yes.
I will, Beebo." Her lover threw Beebo a keen, hard look
and then relapsed into a sullen stare.

Beebo and Mona walked to the floor single file, and Mona
turned when she got clear of the tables, lifting her arms to be
held. The movement was so easy and natural that it excited
Beebo and made her bold—she who knew nothing about
dancing. But she was not lacking in grace or rhythm. She
took Mona in a rather prim embrace at first, and began to
move her over the floor as the music directed.

Mona disturbed her by putting her head back and smiling up at her. At last she said, "How did you know my
name?"

"Pete Pasquini told me," Beebo said. "How did you know
mine?"

"Same answer," Mona laughed. "He gets around, doesn't he?"

"So they say," Beebo said.

"You mean you don't know from personal experience?"

"Me?" Beebo stared at her. "Should I?"

Mona chuckled. "No, you shouldn't," she said.

"Did I—take you away from something over there?" Beebo said.

"From *somebody*," Mona corrected her. "But it's all right. She's deadly dull. I've been waiting for you to come over."

Beebo felt her face get warm. "I didn't even see you until I stood up," she said.

"I saw you," Mona murmured. They danced a moment more, and Beebo pulled her closer, wondering if Mona could feel her heart, now bongoing under her ribs, or guess at the racing triumph in her veins.

"Did you ask Pete about me?" Mona prodded.

"A little," Beebo admitted. And was surprised to find that the admission felt good. "Yes," she whispered.

"What did he say?"

"He said you were a wonderful girl."

"Did you believe him?"

Beebo hesitated and finally said, huskily, "Yes."

"You're a good dancer, Beebo," Mona said, knowing, like an expert, just how far to go before she switched gears.

"I dance like a donkey," Beebo grinned, strong enough in her victory to laugh at herself.

"No, you're a natural," Mona insisted. "A natural dancer, I mean."

"I don't care what you mean, just keep dancing," Beebo said.

Mona put her head down against Beebo's shoulder and laughed, and Beebo felt the same elation as a man when he has impressed a desirable girl and she lets him know it with her flattery. Mona—so elusive, so pretty, so dominant in Beebo's dreams lately. Beebo was holding her tighter than she meant to, but when she tried to loosen her embrace, Mona put both arms about her neck and pulled her back again.

For the first time, Beebo had the nerve to look straight at her. It was a long hungry look that took in everything: the long dark square-cut hair and bangs; the big hazel eyes; the fine figure, slim and exaggeratedly tall in high heels. But it was still necessary for her to look up at Beebo.

"It's nice you're so tall," Mona told her.

"Who's the girl you're with?" Beebo said. "I think she wants to drown me."

"No doubt. Her name's Todd."

"Is she a friend?"

"She was, till you asked for this dance," Mona smiled. Beebo didn't want to make trouble. "I'm sorry," she said.

"Are you?" Mona was forward as only a world-weary girl with nothing to learn—or lose—could be. And yet she seemed too young for such ennui—still in her twenties. "Are you sorry about Todd?" she pressed Beebo.

"I'm not sorry I'm dancing with you, if that's what you mean," Beebo said.

"That's what I mean," Mona smiled. "Would you like to dance without an audience, Beebo?"

Beebo frowned at her. "You mean ditch your friends?"

Mona could see that Beebo was offended by such a suggestion of two-timing; and Mona was interested enough in this big, beautiful, strange girl, not to want her offended. "They aren't true friends," Mona said plaintively, "that you can count on, anyway. It's all over between Todd and me, too. We just came here to bury the corpse tonight. This is where we met five months ago."

"Five months? That's not very long to be in love with somebody," Beebo said.

"I wasn't," Mona said.

"Was she?" It seemed indescribably sad to Beebo that one partner be in love and the other feel nothing. She wanted everyone to be happy on this night full of sequin-lights and clouds of music: even Todd.

"I never meant much to Todd," Mona said. "Talk about ditching, Beebo. I'm the one who's getting ditched."

"You?" Beebo held her tightly, glad for the excuse. "How could anyone ever do that to you?"

Mona swayed against her, smiling with her eyes shut, and Beebo was too immersed in her to notice the look on Todd's face.

"She likes to torment her lovers," Mona whispered. "She uses them, as if they were things. When she gets tired of them, she puts them in a drawer and pulls them out to show off, like trophies. That's all she does—collect broken hearts."

"She sounds like a female dog," Beebo commented. And yet the little speech recalled disturbingly some of Jack's remarks about Mona; as if Mona were amusing herself by describing her own faults to Beebo and pretending they were Todd's.

The music ended and they stood on the floor a moment, arms still clasped about each other. "Wait at the bar," Mona whispered into Beebo's ear. "I'll get my coat." Beebo glanced doubtfully at the table, but Mona said, "It'll be better if I tell her alone. Go on."

Beebo released her reluctantly, went to her seat and sipped at her drink till Mona came up. She let Mona lead the way, feeling a sudden wild exhilaration as she followed, lighting a cigarette, holding the door for Mona, taking the street side when they reached the sidewalk.

"Was Todd angry?" she asked.

"No one wants to look the fool," Mona said lightly, with a smile.

"I'm sorry. I wouldn't like to get you up the creek, Mona," Beebo said. "I didn't want trouble."

"I make my own trouble, Beebo. I thrive on it. The way I see it—" she paused to give Beebo her arm, and Beebo took it smoothly with a sense of power and burgeoning desire "—life is flat and dreary without trouble." Mona dodged a puddle, then continued. "Good trouble. Exciting trouble. You can't just walk across the Flats forever, doing what's expected of you. Excitement. That's everything to me." Mona stopped in her tracks to look at Beebo with bright sly eyes. "Being good isn't exciting. Right?"

"I'm no philosopher," Beebo said.

"I'll prove it to you. You're a good person, aren't you? You felt bad about Todd. You've been good all your life. But are you happy?"

"I am right now. Are you telling me to be bad?" Beebo said, laughing.

"Would making love to me be bad?" Mona asked her, so directly that Beebo wondered if she were being made fun of. There was no respect in Mona for the innate privacy and mystery of every human soul. She saw them all as part of the Flats—unless they could make beautiful trouble with her. Then, she was interested. Then, she saw an individual.

"Making love to you," Beebo said slowly, "would have to be good."

"I'll make it better than good." Mona reached up for Beebo's shoulders, pulling her back into the dusk of a doorway. They stood there a moment, Beebo in a fever of need and fear, till Mona's hand slid up behind her head, cupped it downward, and brought their lips together.

Beebo came to life with a swift jerking movement. Mona's kiss had been light and brief, until Beebo caught her again in a violent embrace and imprisoned her mouth. She forgot everything for a few minutes, holding Mona there in her arms and kissing her lips, pressing her back against the doorway and feeling the whole length of her body against Beebo's own.

It wasn't till she became aware that Mona was protesting that she let her go. She stood in front of Mona, still trembling and weak-kneed, her breath coming fast and her head spinning, and she felt oddly apologetic. Mona had started it, but Beebo had carried it too far. "I'm sorry," she panted.

"Stop saying you're sorry all the time," Mona told her in a sulky voice. And, with a briskness that all but shattered the mood, she turned and started walking off, her heels snapping against the asphalt. Beebo stared after her, shocked. Was this the end of it?

But Mona turned back after a quarter of a block and called her. "You aren't going to spend the night there, are you?" she said crisply.

Beebo hurried after her, and they walked for two more blocks without exchanging a word. Beebo could only suppose she had done something wrong. Yet she didn't know what, or how to make amends.

Mona stopped at a brownstone house with six front steps. "I live here," she said.

Beebo glanced up at it. "Shall I leave?" she said.

"Do you want to?"

"Don't answer my questtions with more questions!" Beebo said, a tide of anger releasing her tongue. "Damn it, Mona, I don't like evasions."

"All right. Don't go," Mona said, and smiled at the outburst. She went up the steps with Beebo coming uneasily behind her, opened the door, and went to the first-floor apartment in the back. At her door she pulled out her key and waited. Beebo was looking around at the hall, old and modest, but cleanly kept. The apartments in a place like this could be astonishingly chic. She had seen some belonging to Jack's friends.

Mona let her take it in till Beebo became aware of the silence and turned to her quizzically.

"Approve?" Mona said.

Beebo nodded, and Mona, as if that were the signal, turned the key in the lock. She walked over the threshold, switched on a light, and abruptly backed out again, preventing Beebo from entering.

"What's wrong?" Beebo said, surprised.

"There's someone in there," Mona said.

Without thinking, Beebo made a lunge for the door. She had thrown prowlers out of her father's house before. A situation like this scared her far less than being in that room alone with Mona—much as she wanted it.

But Mona caught her arm. "It's a friend of mine!" she hissed. "Beebo, please!" Beebo stopped, irritated, waiting for an explanation. "It's a girl. I told her Todd and I were breaking up," Mona shrugged. "I guess she came over to cheer me up. We've been friends a long time. Oh, it's nothing romantic, Beebo."

"Well, send her home," Beebo said. It was one thing to be afraid of Mona; but another entirely to forfeit the whole night in honor of a hen party.

"I can't." Mona looked up at her in pretty distress. "She's my one real friend and I owe her a lot. She's had some bad times in her own life lately. Beebo, look—here's my phone number. Call me in an hour. Maybe we can still make it." She took a scratch pad from her purse and scribbled on it.

Beebo took it, feeling rebuffed and insulted. But Mona stood on tiptoes and kissed her lips again. And when Beebo refused to embrace her, Mona took her wrists and pulled them around her and gave Beebo a luxurious kiss. "Forgive me," she said. "It would be tough if she knew I'd brought someone home—it really would." She slipped out of Beebo's arms and put a hand on the doorknob. "Be sure to call me," she said. And then she disappeared inside her apartment.

Beebo stood in the hall a while, leaning on the dingy plaster and trying to make sense out of Mona. There was no sound from the apartment. Perhaps Mona and the girl had gone into a bedroom to talk. The idea made Beebo angry and jealous. She went slowly down the front hall. There was a pay phone by the entrance. Beebo went outside and sat on the front stoop for about forty-five minutes, and then went in to call.

She had lifted the telephone receiver and was about to

drop in a dime, when she heard a bang from the end of the hall, as if someone had dropped something heavy. It seemed to come from Mona's door, and Beebo rushed toward it. But at the threshold, she froze.

Mona's voice, muffled as if through the walls of several rooms, but discernible, penetrated the wood. "And you! You sneak in here like a rat with the plague! God damn, how many times do I have to say it? *Call* first. Are you deaf or just stupid?"

Beebo's mouth opened as she strained to hear the answer. It came after a slight pause: "Rats don't scare you, doll. You already got the plague."

Beebo whirled away from the door as if she had been burned, and stood with her knuckles pressed angrily against her temples.

The voice belonged to a man.

It was several days before anything happened. Beebo went back to work as usual. There were no calls, no notes, no effort on Mona's part to get in touch with her and explain. Or apologize.

Beebo worked dully, but gratefully. Keeping busy was a balm to her nerves. She took pleasure in driving, taking corners faster and making deliveries in better time as she learned the routes. During the morning she took out groceries. In the afternoon, it was fresh-cooked, hot Italian food in insulated cartons.

Mona and her male visitor were on Beebo's mind so constantly that she didn't even take time to worry about Jack, or the possibility he might fall in love with Pat. She saw them every evening, but said little and saw less.

She was full of a boiling bad temper; half-persuaded to go out on the town with as many girls as she could find, sure that Mona would hear about it; and half-toying with the idea of dating a man out of sheer spite. It would be nice irony—almost worth the embarrassment and social discomfort.

She was mad enough at Mona, in fact, to be nice to Pete. After all, Mona had stood him up too, long ago. He was still under her feet, and although he had never made any indecent proposals, he manged to always look as if he were just about to. Beebo was comforted to see that he gave the same look, and likely the same impression, to every woman in range of his sight, except his wife.

One day at noon, she went deliberately to the table in the kitchen where he was eating and pulled up a chair, while Marie served them. Pete looked at her with his somber eyes and stopped munching for a minute. She ordinarily managed her schedule so she could eat before or after he did. Marie noticed the change, as she noticed everything, but whatever she thought, she kept her own counsel.

"How is it with Jack and Pat?" Marie said conversationally.

Beebo straightened around. "How did you know about that?" she said, surprised.

"They was in earlier. Pat says he knows about bugs. Maybe he can stomp out my roaches . . . He is a nice boy? I never did trust blonds."

Beebo felt threatened, as if Marie had just announced the end of Beebo's life with Jack. "Sure. Very nice," she said, and swallowed her stew. She was conscious of Pete's piercing gaze on her face.

"So?" Marie said, nodding. "He got a friendly style."

Beebo recounted mentally her evenings in the past week. Since Jack and Pat had met they had been together every night. Pat was in the apartment all day—no matter what hour Beebo dropped in during her deliveries. What about his job? And Jack? Jack Mann was a charming and persuasive man, and the fact that his face was plain did not alter the fact that his strong body was clean and pleasing, nor that his wits were quick and could make you learn and laugh.

"What's the matter, Beebo? You don't like rabbit?"

She started at Pete's voice and pulled away. His face was too close. But she was glad for the diversion. He aimed a big spoon at her stew. "Maybe you like a cheese sandwich?"

"No, this is fine," she said, forcing a social smile . . . and then wishing it were possible to retract it. Pete was examining her curiously.

She ate with concentration for several moments, still seeing Pat and Jack in her mind's eye. Pat liked Jack already. He was afraid of the city, and he abominated his job. If he didn't get back to it fast, he wouldn't have it any more, and she knew he didn't give a damn—as long as somebody fed and loved him. He was like a pet: a big lovable goddamn poodle. She knew his liking for Jack would grow to fondness,

if not love. She could see it coming, especially at night
when Jack let him talk his heart out. Nobody listened or
comforted more intelligently than Jack.

*And when they fall in love—then where do I go? Shack
up with Mona and her stable of strange men?* she wondered.
Jack's remarks about Mona's past were haunting her days
and ruining her nights.

"Beebo," said a quiet male voice into her ear. "You want
the afternoon off?"

It was an indecent proposal, all right. His voice made it
one.

"No thanks," she said frostily.

"You look bad."

"I'm all right," she snapped.

"You could've fooled me," he said. And when she didn't
answer, he went on, unwilling to let the conversation die,
"The way you was acting, I thought you was sick."

"Maybe I am," she said sardonically. "I've got the plague."

"The plague?" He stopped eating, his teeth poised around
a bite, and grinned. "Plague, like the rats bring?"

"Yeah." Beebo frowned at him.

"I got a friend with an obsession about rats," he said.
"You seen her in here once or twice. Mona. You know?"
Beebo nodded, her eyes fixed on him. It was the longest
she had looked at him squarely. "She tells every man she
knows—and that's plenty—he's a rat. I asked her why once.
Want to know what she said?" He paused, building suspense,
while Beebo held her breath. "She says they're all hairy . . .
filthy . . . and stupid. And they'll sleep with anything ain't
already dead. You agree?" He grinned at her.

Beebo turned away. "I don't know any *men*," she said
pointedly.

Pete threw his hands out. "Is that nice to say?" he demanded. "Jack, I can understand. All he got of man is his
name. Your father, who knows? Another fag?" Beebo got
halfway out of her seat, but he protested elaborately at once.
When she simmered down, he added confidentially, "But *me*
. . . Even Marie will admit that much, when she's feeling
honest."

"Marie's in a position to have an opinion," Beebo said
acidly. "But I don't think that's *it*."

Pete folded his arms on the table and leaned on them,
unoffended. "You want to be in that position too, Beebo?"

"Not for a million bucks," she said, and drank down her milk in a gesture of scorn.

"I know a lot of good positions," he said cozily, laughing at her.

Beebo had enough sense not to get visibly angry; not to make a scene. It wasn't worth it and it would only tickle Pete. If it did no more than embarrass the two women, he would be satisfied.

She put her glass down. "What do you do with all your women, Pete?" she asked him, making no effort to keep her voice from Marie. "Line them up in half-hour shifts? It beats me how one mighty male can keep so many women happy."

She picked up her plate and took it to the sink.

Marie tossed her a grin. "You tell him, Beebo," she said. "To hear him talk, he's sold out till next March."

"I'm selling nothing, bitch," Pete told her sharply. "What I got, I give away."

"Listen to Robin Hood," Beebo cracked, and walked out of the kitchen toward the truck with a load of Marie's packaged foods. Pete followed her. Marie turned and took a step toward them, thought better of it, and returned to brood over the stove. Beebo could handle him. She didn't need any help.

In the parking area, Pete took some of the load from Beebo and helped her put it in the truck. "You think I brag a lot, Beebo?" he said.

"I think you're a creep," she said.

He waited a moment, chagrined but not about to show it. "That mean you don't like me?" he said finally.

"Let's drop it, Pete."

"You *do* like me?" he pestered her.

"What do you want, a friendship ring?" she demanded.

Pete shrugged, staring at the low clouds; taking out a toothpick to spear the food specks stuck in his white teeth. "Just an opinion," he said.

"I told you. That's Marie's department. Now, if you'll get out of my way, I have some deliveries to make."

He turned to her. "Everybody got an opinion, Beebo. You worked for me over two months now. So say it. Say the truth."

Beebo swallowed her aggravation. This was a game of wits, and the first man to blow off, lost. She put on the same casual cloak Pete was wearing. "You're my boss. You keep clear of me, I keep clear of you, and we get along."

"You make a big thing of keeping clear," he said. "I smell bad, or something?"

"I wouldn't know. I never get that close," Beebo said.

Something in his eyes made her swing up into the driver's seat with unusual speed. She started the motor, but he came around the truck and pulled her door open.

"You want to know where Mona hangs out?" he said.

Beebo set her jaw. "Not from you," she said tautly.

Pete grinned. "Why not? My information is as good as the next guy's."

It made Beebo wildly impatient. She gripped the steering wheel in hard hands. "You through now, Pete?" she said, gunning the motor.

But he stood there, angled into the truck doorway so that she couldn't move without bending some of his bones the wrong way.

"It's okay, Beebo, don't get sore," he said, and put a hand on her knee. She picked it up and dropped it like a knot of worms, and he laughed. "You know why I do that?" he asked. " 'Cause you put on such a good show. It really bugs you, don't it? When I touch you."

"You get the hell out of my truck or I'll roll you flat!"

He chuckled again. "Okay," he said. "I just got one piece of news for you, butch. Listen: 121 McDonald Street— Paula Ash. Tonight. For those as wants to locate Mona." He pulled away from the truck, and Beebo backed out in a rumble of dust and gravel.

It was nearly midnight before Beebo could bring herself to the McDonald Street address. She had debated it tempestuously throughout the evening, but without confiding in Jack. She could have gone to Mona's apartment instead, or called her and demanded an explanation. But something told her Pete Pasquini had an interesting motive for sending her here. She might get hurt; but she might also learn the truth, whatever that was, about Mona. So she took the chance.

She was in a don't-give-a-damn mood, expecting to find Mona with a man in the apartment, rented under an assumed name; or Mona making love to Paula Ash, whoever

the hell she was; or even—best joke of all—Mona waiting
for her alone, while Pete peeked through the keyhole.

She stood at 121 McDonald Street in a light drizzle,
partially sheltered by an inset doorway, her hands shoved
into the sleeves of her windbreaker, and tried to make up
her mind to call the jest.

At last the chill drove her into the foyer to look at mailboxes. There was a Paula Ash, all right. Apartment 103.
Beebo took a deep breath and pushed the buzzer.

The answer came after so long a wait that Beebo was
just leaving in disgust, and had to turn back quickly to open
the inner door. She had scarcely entered the hall when a
door opened ahead and a girl looked out.

"Yes?" she said. She appeared very sleepy, as if she had
been in bed for many hours already, even though it was not
quite midnight.

"May I come in?" Beebo said. She walked down the hall
looking Miss Ash over candidly. If Mona were going to
stand her up, and Pete play jokes on her, the least she
could do was fall into the pit with as much bravado as
possible—and perhaps, a pretty girl in her arms.

"I don't know," the girl said doubtfully, opening her eyes
very wide as if the stretch would keep the lids up a few
minutes more. "Who are you?"

"I'm Beebo." Beebo looked at her, standing about three
feet away in the door, wondering if her name would register.
The living room behind Paula looked inviting after the gray
rain outside.

"Beebo Who?" The girl was beginning to wake up, staring
at her visitor.

Beebo smiled. "Didn't Mona tell you?"

The girl gasped and rubbed her eyes open earnestly.
"Mona!" she said, her voice husky. "Did Mona send you
here?"

"Not exactly," Beebo said. "But I was made to think I'd
find her here." The girl was so distressed that Beebo began
to think Paula was the victim of whatever joke was afoot,
and not herself. She was moved to apologize. "I'm sorry,
Miss Ash," she said. "There must have been a mistake. I
came expecting some sort of practical joke. I guess nobody
let either one of us in on it."

"Will you come in, please," Paula Ash said unexpectedly.
She was shy and looked at Beebo's shoulder when she spoke.

"Thank you," Beebo said, walking past her into the living

room. "It's pretty cold outside." She took off her jacket and handed it to Paula, who hung it in her front closet.

"Will you have coffee?" Paula said.

"Thanks, that sounds good." Beebo watched her curiously while the girl busied herself in a small doorless kitchen. She had a delicately pretty face, different from Mona's slick good looks and more appealing to Beebo.

Paula ran an uneasy hand through her hair and bit her underlip as she stood by her stove, waiting for the water to boil. "Would you tell me," she asked timidly, "just what Mona told you?"

"I haven't seen Mona for a week," Beebo said. "A mutual acquaintance told me she'd be here tonight."

"Well, your mutual acquaintance has a queer sense of humor," Paula said. "Mona and I were never good friends. And lately we've been pretty good enemies."

"So that was it," Beebo said. "That's a hell of a note. I'm sorry, Miss Ash, I—"

"Paula, please. Oh, it wasn't your fault," Paula said. "Mona has done crazier things than meeting her new lovers in my living room. I've known her almost five years." She came back with two cups of hot coffee. She still seemed half-conscious, and when she stumbled a bit, Beebo got up and rescued the coffee.

Paula made a hissing sound of pain, pulling air between her teeth and looking at her left thumb.

"Did you scald it? Here. Under the cold water, quick." Beebo left the steaming cups on an end table and took Paula by the arm to the sink. She turned on the tap full force and held Paula's burn under the healing stream. Paula tried to pull away after a few seconds but Beebo held her securely. "Give it a good minute," she said.

And as they stood there, Beebo studied Paula at close range. She was a lovely looking girl, even though she seemed non compos at the moment. "Are you sick, Paula?" Beebo asked kindly.

"No, no. Really. I'm just terribly tired. And then I took some sleeping pills. Probably too many. I haven't been sleeping well."

"If you're so tired, why do you take sleeping pills?" Beebo asked.

Paula's dainty face contracted around a private pain. "The doctor gave them to me. It's harder to sleep when you're too tired than when you're just tired." She weaved a little, and Beebo put an arm around her.

"Are you supposed to take so many they send you into a coma?"

"No. But one pill doesn't work. Three or four don't work any more. I just keep swallowing them till I drop off."

"That's dangerous," Beebo said. "One of these days you'll drop too damn far." She turned the water off and reached for a paper towel, blotting the injured hand gently. Suddenly, to her dismay, Paula pulled her hands away and hid her face in them to cry. Beebo watched, frustrated with the wish to touch and comfort her.

Paula's sobs were short and hard, and she pulled herself together with a stout effort of will. All Beebo could see for a moment was the top of her head, covered with marvelous rich red hair. And, when she looked up, a trail of pale freckles across her cheeks and nose. Beebo handed her a tissue from her shirt pocket, and Paula blew her nose and wiped her eyes.

She was a fragile, very feminine and small girl, wearing a pair of outsized, plaid-print men's pajamas.

Beebo took a bit of sleeve between her fingers with a smile. "You always wear these?" she asked.

"Only lately. They aren't mine. A former roommate left them behind when she moved."

"Oh," Beebo said. "I didn't think they were your type."

"They're not. They're hers. And she's gone, and this is all I have left of her." Paula shook out her smoldering curls and cleared her throat. "I'm better now. Shall we have the coffee?" she said. It was obvious that she had humiliated herself with the unplanned personal admissions, and Beebo did her the courtesy of dropping the subject and joining her in the living room.

They drank the coffee in preoccupied silence a while. Beebo lighted a cigarette and offered it to Paula, who refused. Finally she said lightly, hoping to cheer Paula up, "Seems to me those pajamas are the answer to your insomnia."

"What? How?" Paula looked at her as if suddenly remembering her presence in a room where Paula had thought herself alone with a ghost.

"Switch to nighties—your own—and get some rest," Beebo said. "If I had to wear a plaid like that, I'd have nightmares all night."

Paula smiled wanly. "I know," she said. "They're silly. I

just needed somebody else to say it, I guess. It's hard to break away from a person you've been close to. You hang on to the stupidest things."

"Well, her old sleep gear won't bring her any closer," Beebo said. She pulled a sleeve out full length. "Did she play basketball?" Beebo said, and they both laughed.

"She wasn't a shorty," Paula admitted. Her laughter made her wonderfully pretty. She stopped it suddenly to say, "That's the first time I've laughed in a month." She gazed at Beebo with grateful astonishment.

"Looks like I got here just in time," Beebo said, not realizing till after she spoke what a hoary come-on that was. Paula's pink blush clarified things for her.

"I suppose you want to be getting home," Paula said shyly, rising from her chair. She was struck for the first time with Beebo's size. Stretched across the sofa with her long legs thrusting out from under the cocktail table, Beebo looked too big for a nine-by-twelve living room.

To her surprise, Beebo found she didn't want to be getting home at all; not even to run interference between Jack and Pat. And thinking of Pat brought a flash of recognition to her mind. "You remind me of a friend," she told Paula, sitting up to scrutinize her. "A boy named Pat. A lovable thing. Shy and just a little childish. In the nice way, I mean."

"I remind you of a *boy?*" Paula stared.

"More of a child than a boy."

Paula didn't know quite how to take it. "In the nice way?"

"Yes. Trusting, affectionate. Still curious about people and life. It's a very—endearing quality."

"And you think *I'm* like that?" Paula asked.

"You obviously don't," Beebo chuckled.

"I've been told I'm nasty and spoiled and selfish . . . childish in the bad way."

"Who told you that? Your friend with the plaid pajamas?"

"Yes."

"If you were that way with her, she must have done something to deserve it. You look like a natural-born angel to me," Beebo said, surprising them both with her frankness.

"That's a very nice thing for a stranger to say," Paula said. "Thank you."

"My pleasure," Beebo said, blanketing her sudden confusion with an offhand nod.

There was a pensive pause while Beebo tried to remember

the books she had read about Lesbian love. It wasn't always a question of sweeping girls off their feet and carrying them away to bed, as Mona had made it seem at first. How did you approach a sensitive, well-bred girl like this one? Mow her down with kisses? Certainly not.

Beebo began to wonder how to make herself welcome for the night. It seemed far better than going back to Jack's and stewing again until dawn about her future. She would be leaving Jack and Pat alone together all night for the first time, and yet it seemed less painful now than it had before. It would suffice Beebo if she and Paula did nothing but sit and talk all night.

"I suppose somebody's waiting for you?" Paula said.

"Nobody."

Paula frowned at her. "Your roommate?" she asked.

"My roommate is having an affair with a man," Beebo said and shocked Paula, until Beebo smiled at her and made her think she was kidding.

"Well . . . Mona?" she asked.

"Mona could be on the moon for all I know. I thought I'd find her here."

"And now you're disappointed," Paula said diffidently.

"Not at all. I'm relieved."

Paula drained her coffee cup and put it down with a nervous clink. "It must be—awkward—if your roommate is really in love with somebody else," she said, in a voice so soft it was its own apology for speaking.

"It is," Beebo said. "I hate to go home. I'm too long to sleep on the damn sofa."

"I'm afraid you're too long for mine, too," Paula said. There was a pause. "But I could sleep on it and you could take my bed, if you will."

It was such a completely disarming—almost quaint—invitation, that Beebo smiled at her, prickling with temptation. Paula's bashfulness was enough to make Beebo self-assured.

"At least you're not too long for the pajamas," Paula said.

"I can't put you out like that," Beebo said.

Paula was flustered. She looked at her hands. "I don't mind," she said. "It's long and I'm short. We're used to each other."

"You and the sofa?" Beebo said, and stood up. She went to the closet and found her jacket. You can't take somebody's bed away just because you told a lie about sleeping on your own sofa. She pulled the jacket on and zipped it.

"You're a sweet girl, Paula," she said, not looking at her. "Miss Plaid Pajamas must be nuts. Find somebody who deserves you, and she'll never make you sleep alone on the sofa."

She started for the door but Paula, recovering suddenly, jumped up and put a restraining hand on her arm. Beebo turned around, a shiver of sharp excitement radiating through her. She was not—she was *never*—as sure of herself as she seemed.

"Beebo," Paula said, whispering so that Beebo had to bend her head to hear her. "I'd like you to stay. Make yourself welcome. Please."

Beebo was afraid to believe her ears. It had seemed almost easy, in retrospect, to storm the Colophon. She was not unaware that Mona was something of a catch, and when she went over the events of that night, she was satisfied at the way she had acted. Nobody, not Mona herself, knew how inexperienced and uncertain Beebo was, and nothing she had done gave her away. Unless it was her exuberance when Mona kissed her.

But now it seemed incredible that this exquisite stranger should reach out for her from the middle of nowhere. "Paula," she said, "I think we're both just lonely. I think it would be best if I go. You don't want to wake up tomorrow and hate yourself." She was still hedging about the ultimate test with a girl.

"I *was* lonely. I will be again if you go."

"Maybe you'd be better off lonely than sorry."

"Beebo, do I have to beg you?" Paula pleaded, her voice coming up stronger with her emotion.

Beebo reached for her in one instinctive motion, suddenly very warm inside her jacket. "No, Paula, you don't have to beg me to do anything. Just ask me."

"I did. And you didn't want to stay."

"I didn't want to scare you. I didn't understand."

"I thought it was Mona. She can make herself so—so tempting."

"I can't even remember what she looks like."

"Aren't you in love with her?"

Beebo's hands, with a will of their own, closed around Paula's warm slim arms. "I met her last week for the first time. You can't be in love with someone you just met."

"You can't?" Paula demurred cautiously, looking down at her big pajamas.

"I never was," Beebo said, feeling sweat break out on her forehead. She pulled gently on Paula and was almost dismayed when Paula moved docilely toward her. Beebo became feverishly aware that the plaid pajamas did not conceal all of Paula Ash. The sweeping curve of her breasts held the cotton tops out far enough to brush Beebo's chest with a feather touch. Beebo felt it through the layers of her clothes with a tremor so hard and real it tumbled eighteen years of daydreams out of her head.

She held Paula at arm's length a moment, looking at this lovely little redheaded princess with a mixture of misgivings and want too powerful to pretend away. Paula took her hands and held them with quivering strength, returning Beebo's gaze. Beebo saw her own doubts reflected in Paula's eyes. But she saw desire there, too; desire so big that it had to be brave: it hadn't any place to hide.

Paula kissed Beebo's hands with a quick press of her mouth that electrified Beebo. She stood there while Paula kissed them over and over again and a passionate frenzy mounted in them both. Paula's lips, at first so chaste, almost reverent, warmed against Beebo's palms ... and then her kitten-tongue slipped between Beebo's fingers and over the backs of her broad hands until those hands trembled perceptibly and Paula stopped, clutching them to her face.

Beebo reclaimed them, but only to caress Paula's face, bringing it close to her and seeing it with amazement.

"I never guessed I'd feel love for the first time through my hands," she murmured. "Paula, Paula, I would have done this all wrong if you hadn't had the guts to start it for me. I would have manhandled you, I—"

Paula stilled her with a finger over Beebo's mouth. "Don't talk now," she said.

And Beebo, who had never done more than dream before, slipped her arms around Paula and pulled her tight. It was a marvel the way their bodies fitted together; the way Paula's head tipped back naturally at so beckoning an angle, and rested on Beebo's arm; the way her eyes closed and her lips parted and her hair scattered like garnet petals around her flower-face.

Beebo kissed her mouth and kissed her mouth again, holding her against the wall with the pressure of her body. Paula submitted with a sort of wistful abandonment. Everywhere Beebo touched this sweet girl, she found thrilling

surprises. And Paula, coming to life beneath Beebo's searching hands, found them with her.

It was no news to Beebo that she was tall and strong and
male-inclined. But her voluptuous reaction to Paula shocked
her speechless. Paula began to undress her and Beebo felt
herself half-fainting backwards on the sofa into a whirlpool
of sensual delight. The merest touch, the merest flutter of a
finger, and Beebo went under, hearing her own moans like
the whistle of a distant wind. Paula had only to undo a belt
buckle or pull off a shoe, and Beebo responded with a beautiful helpless fury of desire.

It was no longer a question of proceeding with caution, of
"learning how." The whole night passed like an ecstatic
dream, punctuated with a few dead-asleep time-outs, when
they were both too exhausted to move, even to make themselves comfortable.

Beebo had only a vague idea of what she was doing, beyond the overwhelming fact that she was making ardent love
to Paula. She seemed to have no mind at all, nor need of
one. She was aware only that Paula was beautiful, she was
gay, she was warmly loving, and she was there in Beebo's
arms: fragrant and soft and auburn-topped as a bouquet of
tiger lilies.

Beebo couldn't let her go. And when fatigue forced her to
stop she would pull Paula close and stroke her, her heavy
breath stirring Paula's glowing hair, and think about all the
girls she had wanted and been denied. She was making up,
this night, for every last one of them.

Paula whispered, "Do you still believe you can't love
someone you just met?"

"I don't know what I believe any more."

And Paula said, "I love you, Beebo. Do you believe that?"

Beebo lifted Paula's fine face and covered it with kisses
while Paula kept repeating, "I love you, I love you," until
the words—the unadorned words—brought Beebo crashing
to a climax, rolling over on Paula, embracing her with those
long strong legs.

She felt Paula sobbing in the early dawn and raised
up on an elbow to look at her. "Darling, did I hurt you?"
she asked anxiously, not stopping to think that she had never
called a girl "darling" before, either.

"No," Paula said. "It's just—I've been so unhappy, so
confused. I thought the world had ended a month ago, and

tonight it's just beginning. It's brand new. I'm so happy it scares me."

Beebo held her tenderly and brushed the tears off her cheeks. Paula put her head in the crook of Beebo's arm and gazed at her. "You must have been born making love, Beebo."

"How do you know?" Beebo had no intention of setting the record straight just then.

"I don't, really. It's just that I never reacted to anybody the way I have to you. I never did this with anybody before."

"Never made love?" Beebo said, surprised almost into laughter. *The blind leading the blind,* she thought.

"No, I've made love before," Paula said thoughtfully. "With men, too. It's just that I never ... You'll think I'm making this up, but it's the truth. I never—oh, God help me, I'm frigid. I mean, I was, till tonight."

Beebo lay there in the dark, holding her, torn between the wish to accept it and the suspicion that she was fibbing.

"You don't believe me," Paula said resignedly. "I shouldn't have told you. It's enough that it happened."

Beebo petted her, smoothing her hair and letting her hands glide over Paula's silky body. "Okay, you never came before," she said. "Now I'll tell you a fish story. I never made love before."

Paula laughed good-naturedly. "All right, we're even," she said. "That's a real whopper. Mine was the truth."

Beebo laughed with her, and it didn't matter any more whether she had been lied to or not. It was the truth in spirit, and only Paula knew if it was the truth in fact. Her attraction to Beebo was so real that it took shape in the night, surrounding her like the aura of her perfume. Beebo kissed her while she was still laughing. "You have such a mouth, Paula. Such a mouth..."

"Does it please you?"

"You please me. All of you," Beebo said, and she meant it. Paula was wholly feminine, soft and submissive. She was finely constructed, looking somehow as breakable, as valuable—and as durable—as Limoges china. Beebo wanted to protect her, accomplish things for her.

She kept touching her admiringly. "You're so tiny," she said. "I'm going to feed you lasagna and put some meat on your bones."

"Will you buy me a new wardrobe when I get too fat for my old one?"

"I'll buy you anything. Mink coats. Meals at the Ritz. New York City," Beebo said.

"All of it?"

"Just the good parts."

Paula clutched at her suddenly, first laughing, then trembling. "Beebo, don't leave me," she said. "I do love you." She seemed dumfounded. "It frightens me, it makes me believe all over again in my childhood dreams. Did you ever feel like that?"

"Only on the bad days. My childhood wasn't that pretty," Beebo said.

"When are the bad days?"

"Never any more. Not with Paula around."

They got up at noon the next day, and it was some time before Beebo could think rationally about her job. She should call Marie, she should call Jack and tell him where she was. But it was impossible to get out of the bed while Paula was in it. And every time Paula sat up, Beebo pulled her down.

"Let me make breakfast," Paula smiled, and after wrestling a moment, pulled free and scampered halfway across the bedroom, pulling a sheet after her. She stood with her dazzling naked back, delicately sugared with freckles, to Beebo, who admired it in infatuated silence.

Paula ruffled through her closet looking for a negligee until Beebo said, "Paula, are you in love with me or that sheet?"

"I don't want you to see me," Paula confessed. "You said I was too thin."

"I said 'tiny.' And beautiful. Honey, I felt you all over; I know you with my hands. Would it be so awful if I know you with my eyes, too?" When Paula hesitated, Beebo threw the covers off and stood by the bed.

Paula studied her in silence. "You're wonderful," she breathed at last.

"I'm homely," Beebo answered. "But I'm not ashamed of it."

"You are many things, Beebo, but homely isn't one of them," Paula declared. She faced Beebo sheet-first, like a highborn Roman girl in her wedding chiton. "How many girls have admired you like this?"

"Never a one," Beebo said. She crossed the room toward Paula and saw her flinch. "Are you afraid of me?" she said, surprised.

"A little."

"No, Paula." Beebo reached her, touching her with gentle hands. "I'd never hurt you. Don't you know that?"

"Not with your hands, maybe," Paula said, bending her graceful neck to kiss one. "But I'm so in love ... it would take so little. And scores of other girls must want you, Beebo. It would hurt me awfully if you ever wanted *them*."

"What girls?" Beebo scoffed.

"Well, for a starter—Mona."

"Paula, I kissed Mona twice. She stood me up twice. That's the end of that," Beebo said flatly. Abruptly, she pulled Paula's sheet off and gazed delightedly on the fresh fair curves beneath. And before Paula had time to blush, Beebo picked her up, grateful at last for the uncomely strength in her arms, and placed her on the bed.

"Beebo," Paula whispered, her arms locked tightly around Beebo's neck. "How old are you?"

Beebo couldn't blurt idiotically, "Eighteen." Instead she asked, "How old do I look?"

"Like a college kid," Paula sighed. "Which makes me older than you. I'm twenty-five, Beebo."

"An ancient ruin." Beebo kissed her nonchalantly, but she was secretly surprised. Nonetheless it pleased her to have won an older girl.

They made love again, lazily now. There was no wild rush, no fear on Beebo's part that it would hurt and disillusion her. They rolled in caresses like millionaires in blue chips ... ran their fingers over each other, and kissed and tickled and laughed and blew in each other's ears.

And all the while Paula kept repeating, with the transparent affection that is the crown of feminity, "I love you, Beebo. I love you so much."

Beebo couldn't answer. She couldn't have been happier, or hotter, or more rapturously charmed with the girl. She could hardly believe she had found one so lovely, so generous, so responsive, so single.

But there was a lot of roaming restless curiosity in Beebo, and while she was willing and eager to make love to and romanticize Paula, she was not willing to fall in love with her.

It wasn't Paula's fault, though Paula, with a woman's quick awareness of emotions, sensed the situation. It was just that Beebo wasn't ready for it. Paula had come too early in

Beebo's life. And that fact alone made Paula realize how young Beebo must be.

Beebo had caught Paula in a vulnerable state, on the re-bound from an unhappy love affair with the girl in the plaid pajamas. But it was the culmination of a lot of bad affairs with both sexes that had left Paula drained and skeptical; hopeless about her future and unable to cope with her present. She had nearly taken the whole bottle of sleeping pills the night before, instead of the four that knocked her out.

Beebo was too good to be true, too young to know herself, too masculine to be faithful. But how strong she was, how sensual and sure; in some ways, wise beyond her years with that hard-won maturity Jack had perceived months before.

Paula tried to tell herself, as she lay in Beebo's embrace, that she had nothing more than a hot crush that would end as suddenly as it began, and make her laugh to think she had called it love. She wanted very much to believe it, be-cause it would have spared her the pain of losing Beebo Brinker to another girl—a pain she was in no condition to take safely then.

They ate together in Paula's kitchen, and Paula obligingly sat on Beebo's lap and let Beebo feed her. They were en-chanted with each other. It was the kind of day everybody ought to have once in a while; if you knew it was coming, you could bear the boredom and solitude in the interim.

Paula told Beebo about her young years in Washington, D.C., and the shock that accompanied her suspicions that she was a Lesbian. Because it was Paula speaking, and be-cause Beebo had never talked heart-to-heart with another Lesbian, the story seemed remarkable. She held Paula on her knees, answering with sympathy and affection, troubled and touched by it . . . and stirred by the warmth of Paula's close, firm bottom.

They were startled when the phone cut in on them late in the afternoon.

Paula answered it over Beebo's protests. "Hello?" she said, and as she listened her eyes went to Beebo in surprise. Finally she held out the receiver. "It's for you," she said. "Jack Mann."

Beebo stood up, concerned. "How did he know I was here?"

"You're his roommate, he says. Roommates ought to keep track of each other," Paula said, teasing but with just a trace of chill in her voice. "Why didn't you tell me you were straight, Beebo?"

Beebo took the phone with a comical grimace. "You would have guessed, anyway," she said. "Hey—do you know Jack?"

"Everybody knows Jack," said Paula.

Into the receiver Beebo said, "Jackson?"

"I hear you've been out stupefying the female population of Greenwich Village," Jack said. "You must have something. Paula's usually a deep freeze."

"How did you know I was here?" Beebo said.

"My spies are everywhere. And a damn good thing, too. I would have given you up for dead. Listen, pal, I just got an s.o.s. from Marie. There's a very large customer on Park Avenue who wants a very large pizza right now. Marie is whipping it up and Beebo will whip it over to said customer."

"Park Avenue is Pete's territory," Beebo said. "He won't like it."

"He's out somewhere, as usual. Marie can't find him and besides, she's afraid to look."

"You want me to leave now?" Disappointment growled in her voice.

"I know Paula, honey; she's a good girl. If she likes you enough to sleep with you, she likes you enough to wait for you."

"You mean you knew this beautiful girl all along and didn't tell me about her?" Beebo said, grinning at Paula.

"Well, hell, you waited two months to tell me you *wanted* one. Come on, Marie's in a hurry. Show her what you're made of."

"I'm made of sugar and spice, like the rest of the girls," Beebo said sourly. "It doesn't mix with cheese and anchovies."

"Get your ass over there, Beebo," Jack said. "This order goes to Venus Bogardus."

The name rang in Beebo's head. "The actress?" she said, frowning. "She's not one of our customers."

"She is now."

"But Jack, my God. Venus Bogardus!"

"The original. The girl with the bosom that just won't stop. Can you take it?"

"It's worth it just for a look," Beebo grinned. "Okay, call Marie and tell her I'm coming. And Jack—I know I should have called you. I'm sorry."

Beebo hung up and walked to Paula, expecting to embrace her and explain. But Paula was quite pale. "What's all this about Pete and Marie? Do you mean the Pasquinis?"

"Yes. I work for them. Marie wants me to deliver a pizza to—"

"—to Venus Bogardus. I heard. Beebo, why didn't you tell me about Pete?"

"There's nothing to tell," Beebo said, mystified. "Honey, are you mad at me? Why?"

"Pete and Mona are thick as thieves. What Mona does, Pete does; what Mona thinks, Pete thinks—unless they're quarreling. If they don't like you, they'd as soon exterminate you. They wouldn't cut you down if you were hanging."

Beebo laughed a little at this explosion. "I know you don't like Mona, honey. But Pete's just a twerp. He's the one who sent me over here last night. I'll admit it wasn't exactly ethical—"

"Then Mona knows you're here. How charming," Paula said sourly.

"So what's Mona, the Wicked Witch?" Paula scowled and Beebo said, "Okay, Pete's a slob; and my opinion of Mona is slipping fast. But I can't be mad at anybody who sent me to you, Paula, no matter what their motives were."

"Now they'll do everything to take you away from me," Paula said, looking fearfully at Beebo.

"There's no way they could do that, sweetheart," Beebo said, pulling Paula down beside her on the bed. "Paula, I'll be back in an hour. I won't do anything but deliver the pizza."

Paula clung to her. "Promise," she said. "And if Milady Bogardus walks into the room, you have to shut your eyes and run."

"At the same time?"

"Yes."

"You want me to break my neck?" Beebo laughed.

"Better your neck than my heart," Paula whispered.

At the door Beebo took Paula's hands and kissed them

the way Paula had first kissed hers. "I never liked Venus Bogardus," she said. "I read somewhere that her curves are built into her clothes. She's about as sexy as a hatrack under the finery—and a cool forty-eight years old."

"Come back," Paula said seriously. "That's all I ask."

They parted and Beebo left the building with a soaring pride and satisfaction that seemed to lift her clear of the pavement.

Marie Pasquini was waiting in the shop when Beebo arrived. She had just argued with her mother-in-law and it made her visage long and dark.

"Thank God, a happy face," she said when she saw Beebo.

"Maybe we ought to find Pete, Marie," Beebo said. "He considers Park his street."

"*His* street!" Marie spat. "It's too good for him. An alley full of donkey-do is too good for him."

"Too bad for you there ain't no such alleys handy," said Pete's voice from the front of the shop, approaching the kitchen. "You'd be right at home in one. Like the one where I found you in Bordeaux." He appeared in the kitchen doorway, making Beebo wonder how long he had been lurking there. Unaccountably, he gave her a case of gooseflesh.

"Here he comes," said Marie to Beebo. "Captain Marvel. Okay, Captain, here's an order. You want to deliver?"

"That depends on Beebo," Pete said, meandering unsteadily toward her. "Where were you today, butch? I had to make all the deliveries myself." His grin made her want to hit him.

"I was indisposed," she said.

"Indisposed," he mimicked in a fussy voice. "Well, ain't that a shame. I understand Paula Ash was indisposed today, too." His breath smelled of zinfandel.

Beebo stared at him with cold-eyed loathing and then stalked toward the back door.

"Wait a minute!" Pete called.

"Not for you," Beebo said.

"Beebo!" It was Marie's voice this time. "He's full of dry red. He can't drive. Please, I don't want to lose Venus

Bogardus. Nor the truck, neither," she added, with a significant glance at Pete.

At the sound of that famous name, Pete burst into winy laughter. "Go on, Beebo, go on. Maybe she'll fall for you, too," he said. "How you gonna keep two of 'em happy at the same time? You want a few lessons?"

Beebo took the wrapped pizza from Marie and stormed out of the kitchen. She could hear the opening blast of a real wingding behind her.

Beebo drove through a light rain that was quickly slicking down the city streets. It was Midwestern weather. Her father's face crossed her mind, obscuring some of her revulsion against Pete. *I wonder where Dad thinks I am now?* she mused despondently.

She punished herself by picturing her father: a tall solid man, with the lines of worry and weather on his face, delivering a foal to its snorting, laboring mother; stooping with the burdens of alcohol and anxiety over his strange young daughter.

Beebo felt a surge of guilty love for him as she neared the address Marie had given her. She almost drove past. It was a big chilly building that looked loftily down on the summer sprinkle.

Beebo went up on the service elevator, her head full of whirling images: Paula, of the glorious red hair and sweet mouth. The big kindly father whose love had made her strong and himself weak. The people who had lately come to matter in her life in the city.

She knocked on the back door, becoming aware as she did so of strident voices within: a woman's, bright and soprano with anger; a boy's breaking with resentment; another woman, refereeing timidly for the first two.

"All right, all right, answer the goddamn door!" cried the soprano.

"Mother, do you have to swear like a whore?" the boy cried. "In front of delivery boys?"

"What do you care what I do with delivery boys, darling?"

Beebo recognized the celebrated voice, just as the door opened. "Are you the pizza?" asked a gray dumpling of a woman.

"No, but I have one with me," Beebo grinned. Her voice
stilled the argument momentarily. "Five bucks," Beebo told
the Dumpling, who wore a white uniform like a nurse, or
nanny. Beebo waited for the money, suddenly full of springy
laughter that might go off any second like a string of fire-
crackers.

"Five bucks?" said Venus Bogardus. "I haven't got a damn
dime."

With a thrill of recognition, Beebo suddenly saw her. She
was wearing a scarlet, silk-jersey dress. When she moved,
she proved there was nothing beneath it. The hatrack story
lay down and died. But Beebo was still so full of Paula that
the sight of Venus Borgardus was little more than an entertainment.

Toby, the boy, turned his pockets inside out. "I gave you
all my money yesterday," he said, glum and embarrassed.
To Beebo he said, "I'm sorry," with the pathetic air of a
child who is struggling to assume the responsibilities of dissipated parents. He was a good-looking boy; in his early
teens, Beebo guessed, and finding life with a movie-star
mother a stormy combination of high excitement and humiliation. He was not the type to take it lightly.

"Toby, don't you have something in your piggy bank,
dear?" Venus persisted, aware of Beebo now.

"You threw my piggy bank down the incinerator shaft,"
he mumbled.

"I did?" She blinked at him with incredible blue eyes,
encircled by long black lashes.

"A year ago," Toby said wearily.

"God, that was careless. Was there anything in it?" Venus
said.

"Two-fifty in pennies. I was saving up for a catcher's
mitt."

"Well, that wouldn't be enough anyway. For the pizza,
I mean."

"Excuse me—why don't you charge it?" Beebo said. She
was somewhat abashed to have walked in on a Love
Queen in the midst of a common little argument.

"Do you think they'd let me?" Venus said, turning to
Beebo at last, her voice melting off her tongue like buck-
wheat honey. Toby slammed out of the kitchen in utter disgust.

"I think so," Beebo said, smiling.

Venus came to take the pizza from her, opening the container for a taste. "Somebody said it was 'peerless pasta.' Is it *that* bad?"

"It's good."

Venus put it on the breakfast table and tore off a bite. "You're right," she said. "Want some?"

"No thanks," Beebo said, staring at her. Perhaps now was the time to back out and run, as Paula suggested.

"Don't be shy," Venus said. "Toby, come back and eat, dear," she called through the kitchen door. "We have a guest." Toby shuffled in while Venus explained to Beebo, still hesitating at the back door, "No cook tonight. She just quit for the hundredth time. Bring some plates, Mrs. Sack. I'll get the milk for these growing children."

"Miss Bogardus, I can't possibly stay; I—" Beebo said, but Venus interrupted her, as if she hadn't heard her, with a stream of cordial inanities.

Toby's face colored. "Mother, will you listen?" he said in an angry hiss. "She doesn't *want* to stay."

"I know, darling. Now shut up and sit down, all of you."

They did. It seemed to be the thing to do. But Beebo had a tingling feeling that the whole building would fold under her as soon as she touched down on the seat.

Venus opened the refrigerator and a loud smell came out. "God, look at the mess!" she cried. "I'll bet that bitch hasn't cleaned it for weeks."

"If you'd come home long enough to look at it once in a while, she would have," Toby said.

"Darling, I look at it every day, when I put the champagne in to cool."

She joined them, passing the milk around, and badgered Beebo to eat more than Beebo wanted. Toby couldn't stand it.

"Leave her alone, Mother!" he said, rising from his seat.

"Don't behave like a nervous girl, Toby," Venus reproved him breezily.

"I'm not a girl," he said in real anguish.

"Of course not, dear. Boys wear pants and girls wear skirts. That's how I've always known you were a boy."

Beebo became abruptly conscious of her chino slacks and found it hard to keep eating naturally.

"I'm sorry," Toby said again to Beebo. "My mother's a little cracked. It comes from getting her own way all the time."

"God, how dreadful to be fourteen," Venus said, gazing at

her son pityingly. "I don't know how I lived through it myself." She ate for a minute quietly while Beebo plotted an
escape. "I'll have to tell Leo about this; it's really marvelous," Venus said, cutting another bite.

"Leo's her husband," Toby said, making a face.

"You'd think they loathed each other," Venus said, glancing at Beebo. "Actually, Toby gets along better with Leo
than with any of the others."

"It's a good thing *I* get along with him, because *you* sure
don't," Toby flared, to the accompaniment of horrified shush-
ings from Mrs. Sack.

"One more crack like that and you can leave the table,"
Venus said sharply. "God! What do you do with children
that age?"

"I don't know. What do they do with you?" Beebo said.

Toby turned to her with an amazed grin.

"And how old are *you*, darling?" Venus asked Beebo,
her eyes shining through their black fringe like hard chips of
sapphire.

"Fourteen," Beebo said, and evoked a chuckle of relief
from Toby. Beebo smiled at him, and suddenly they were in
league; two friendly conspirators subverting Venus's authority.

"I'd have said twelve, to judge from your table manners,"
Venus cooed.

And unruffled, she continued eating, giving Beebo a chance
to study her surreptitiously. Her face had been called the
most perfect in the world when she was a starlet twenty years
before. And still she was very lovely, even without make-up
on her face. The lines about her eyes and mouth were faint
and fine. You had to look for them, and somehow they
made her beauty the more poignant, emphasizing as they did
the perishability of human loveliness. She was probably in
her late thirties, Beebo guessed.

"Tell me, darling," Venus said unexpectedly, startling Beebo. "Do you live in town somewhere with your mommy and
daddy? I mean, surely a fourteen-year-old child isn't out
delivering pizzas for a living."

"I live in town," Beebo said. "My father lives back in
Wisconsin."

"How primitive," Venus said, with a smile that told Beebo
she was aware of her own oversophisticated nonsense. She
made it rather charming. "Just one father?" she said. "Toby
has six."

"That must be a record," Beebo said quietly, trying to focus on her food.

"It's Mother's record, not mine," Toby said. "As far as I'm concerned, you can throw all six in the East River. All but Leo, anyway."

"Darling!" his mother cried, more amused this time than angry, perhaps because she shared his view. "After all the lovely presents they've given you, too."

Beebo watched her curiously. Venus was not dense or callow. But her glamour and her fortune obviously hadn't spared her the problems of raising a pubescent boy. Most mothers approached their kids with a mixture of love, common-sense, and frazzled tempers. Venus approached hers with all the gorgeous razzle-dazzle, passion, and impatience that made obedient slaves of the older men in her life.

Toby, at fourteen, was supposed to react with the fascination of an adult male three times his age for a beautiful and tempestuous woman.

If he ever does, Venus will get the shock of her life, Beebo thought with amusement.

Instead, of course, Toby lashed out at her in frightened confusion. He loved her very much, but he was afraid and overawed, and bitter about the life she made him lead.

He wanted a mother comfortably middle-aged and unpretentious, like other people's mothers. Instead, he had what other people thought they wanted: a glittering courtesan who couldn't kiss him at night for fear of smudging her mouth, who took him on vacation trips with her lovers while her husband—and Toby's friend, Leo—stayed behind in Hollywood.

Beebo sensed much of this in the pointed wordplay between mother and son. Their mutual love stood aside, forlorn and unexpressed, while they took out their grievances against one another.

Beebo stood up to leave as soon as she decently could.

"Heavens, you're not going!" Venus protested.

"I have a heavy date," Beebo smiled. "Thanks very much, Miss Bogardus."

"You're welcome. Who's the lucky boy?"

Beebo frowned uncomprehendingly at first, till she realized Venus meant her date. "Oh," she said, humiliated to know she was blushing. "Just an old friend."

"Bring him around."

Beebo began to stammer excuses and Toby came to her

rescue. "Let her go, Mom," he said, ashamed of Venus, as usual. He liked Beebo for taking his side; for making him laugh and getting one up on his mother. And it galled him to see Venus tease her. He was not too young to see how uncomfortable Beebo was. When Venus turned to him with a dangerous smile, he said, "I just wish you'd act like a mother now and then."

"Why, I act like a mother twenty-four hours a day," she said innocently. "I *am* a mother. There sits the proof, eating his pizza like an absolute boor." She turned elegantly to Beebo, who had just noticed her dainty bare feet under the table. "All right, darling, go. But do come again some time," Venus said.

Beebo smiled her thanks and got as far as the door before Venus called her again. Her voice, even though Beebo half expected it, sent a wave of shivers down her back.

"I forgot to ask," Venus said. "What's your name? I mean, so we'll know when we order peerless pasta again."

Toby had had it. Venus was practically flirting with Beebo. He clambered over Mrs. Sack and started out of the kitchen. Venus turned in her seat and said, "Damn it, Toby, you come back here!" Her eyes sparkled.

"What for?" he said blackly.

"To finish your dinner."

"I've lost my appetite, Mother." He glanced at Beebo and added, "I apologize for my mother. I hope you don't have a rotten impression of us."

"Not at all," Beebo said, moved by his distress, his anxious efforts to protect her opinion of them. She wondered if he had any friends at all up here in his gilded cage. A Manhattan apartment isn't the ideal place to raise a spirited boy.

Mrs. Sack rose to her feet clucking, but Venus waved her down. "Oh, the hell with him, Mrs. Sack," she said. "He'll be right back . . . He's a lovely boy," she told Beebo. "He'll outgrow this rebellious stuff in another year or so." She spoke confidently but Beebo knew it was a cover-up for deep concern. "Now—what did you say your name was?"

Beebo answered in a low voice, "Beebo Brinker."

"You're kidding," said Venus.

"No." Beebo smiled.

"Lord, that's even worse than mine. Did your press agent dream it up? Or don't you delivery boys—excuse me, girls— have press agents?"

"I have dozens, but they're all starving," Beebo said.

"Mercy, we'll have to find you a job," Venus said. "Are you literate, by any chance?"

"No, I'm perfectly normal," Beebo said. She had learned not to get mad at the wild assortment of jibes people tossed at her. It was better to catch and toss back than to fall and lie as if dead; make a sideshow of your strangeness.

Venus put her head back and laughed, and Beebo felt suddenly very warm and nervous, looking at her. From across the room her face looked flawless. "Poor Beebo," Venus said, enjoying the name. "Came all the way up here in the rain to bring me a pizza, and I didn't even pay her for it."

"You fed me part of it," Beebo said.

"Well, I'll order spaghetti next time. When the sun is shining and I have a few nickels in my jeans," Venus promised. "I suppose you're in a mighty rush to get home to your heavy date?"

"If you don't mind," Beebo said politely.

"Of course I mind, but go anyway. I'll see you on spaghetti day," Venus smiled, and Beebo slipped out the back door with her spine still prickling.

Beebo wondered, all the way downtown in the truck, what sort of kicks Venus got out of inviting a strange delivery girl in for an unpaid-for dinner. *She had a bad day and I amused her,* Beebo thought. *The cook cut out, Toby bugged her, and all six husbands are out of town.*

She approached Pasquini's wishing she could leave the truck somewhere else for the night, just to avoid seeing Pete. But he was out of sight, if not off the premises, and she parked and left without incident.

Under a streetlight she looked at her watch. She had been away three hours instead of one and she was anxious about the trusting girl she had left behind. She ran most of the way to Paula's place.

It surprised her when Paula left her waiting in the entry almost four minutes before she buzzed to open the door.

No one was in the living room when Beebo came in. She called, feeling her heart quicken with alarm.

"Paula, where are you? Are you all right?"

"In here." Paula's voice was faint and Beebo rushed

into the bathroom to find her, standing quiet and sad in front of the mirror. A bottle full of pills, with the cap off, rested on the bowl. Paula had an empty glass in her hand.

Beebo looked at her face in the mirror and then saw the bottle.

"Sleeping pills?" she said, picking it up. Her eyes went dark and she grabbed Paula by the shoulders. "You didn't!" she said. "Good God, Paula!"

"No, I didn't," Paula murmured. "The bottle's still full."

Beebo emptied it into the toilet and flushed the pills away. She turned to Paula, trying to comfort her, but Paula averted her face and broke into tears. She flung her arms around Beebo. "Where have you *been?* You've been gone for hours," she wept.

"She wanted me to eat the damn pizza with them," Beebo said clumsily. "Come on, honey, lie down on the bed." She pulled a protesting and white-faced Paula toward the bedroom. "What's the matter?" Beebo said as Paula's resistance stiffened.

"I think she's afraid of a scene," came a cool, unexpected voice. Beebo whirled and saw Mona Petry sitting on Paula's bed, smoking calmly. "But she needn't worry. Will you please tell her I don't plan to stay more than a minute? I tried to tell her myelf, but we don't seem to speak the same language."

Beebo looked back at Paula, who had covered her mouth and cheeks with tight-pressed hands while tears spilled out of her eyes. Beebo stood between the two jealous girls; one frightened and hurt, the other pleased to have her so. It was up to Beebo to restore peace.

Beebo walked into the bedroom, leaving Paula in the hall behind her. "All right, Mona, I'm sorry," she said briefly. "If you're angry about it, remember you're the one who stood me up." Her voice was sharper than she intended. She wanted to get it over with.

"I didn't stand you up at all, Beebo," Mona said. "I told you to call in one hour. If you had, we could have spent the night together. Instead, you walked out and disappeared.

"I called too soon," Beebo said, recalling the man's voice through Mona's door.

"Not on the phone," Mona said, and through her disdain, Beebo could see the flash of real anger. "Do you mean you eavesdropped?"

"I didn't have to, Mona. I went in to use the phone in

the front hall, and you were throwing things and arguing with some guy. So I left. I just figured you had a taste for men that night."

"Did you really?" Mona said acidulously. "After the way I acted with you? Knowing that any man in my apartment must be an uninvited guest?"

"An uninvited guest doesn't get in with his own key," Beebo shot back. "I didn't like the idea of sharing you with a man, Mona."

"I fought with the man," Mona said, standing up. "I wouldn't have fought with you, ever. Now, it can't be helped." She crushed her cigarette on the floor under her shoe as a gesture of contempt for Paula's tidy bedroom, and smiled. "Or did you think we could all be buddies? We three?"

Beebo colored up with anger. "Three's a crowd, Mona. You make such a thing of it. Why didn't you call *me?* I waited for days. I wanted you to call."

"Wanted. Past tense," Mona said, looking at Paula. "Besides, Beebo, I was wronged, not you. The least you could have done was let me explain. Now you don't give a damn. Well, just know that I don't either. I wouldn't dream of taking you away from Paula. She needs somebody to count the sleeping pills for her." She hooked her sweater on her index finger, and swung it over her shoulder with an air of satisfac n. Paula was distracted and Beebo was exasperated with .   This was Trouble and it exhilarated her.

"Is that what you came here to say?" Beebo demanded.

"That's most of it," Mona said. "It's only fair to warn you, though ... I may drop some more bricks before I'm through. You turn such a nice color when you're burned, Beebo." She sauntered deliberately through the hall, past Paula, who shrank from her, and to the front door, where she turned for one last shot.

Beebo had followed her and stood in the middle of the living room with her arms folded over her chest, the way she faced Pete when he crowded her.

Mona looked her over and then blew a poisonous kiss toward Paula. "I hope you two will be happy," she said. "It's obviously one of those marriages made in hell." She pulled the door shut very slowly till Beebo reached over and gave it a hard shove to.

Mona thumped against it on the outside, laughing at the show of temper.

Beebo turned to Paula, mystified. "What in hell was all that about?" she said.

Paula was leaning against the wall, still pale and quite exhausted. "You've heard of jealousy," she said tiredly.

"She had something more than that on her mind," Beebo said. "She looked like she wanted blood. You can be jealous without being plain mean."

"Mona can't. That's how she makes her life interesting. It's funny. You think of a *man* being sadistic, coldhearted, capable of evil just for kicks. But when a woman's that way, it shocks you. Mona just—enjoys it, I guess."

"Enjoys tormenting people?" Beebo said. She had known people like that back in Juniper Hill, but it was hard to believe about someone you had so recently admired.

Paula nodded. "I think she came here tonight because she's mad at Pete and she can't find him to give him hell. Pete sent you over to bug Mona, and it worked. And you and I went right along with his game and fell for each other. Mona likes to think she's a femme fatale, and I guess to Pete, she is. She jilted him once and he never got over it. She's always telling me I'm a 'goddamn milkmaid' and nobody wants a milkmaid these days. She must have really wanted you, Beebo, or she wouldn't have been so hurt to lose you."

"Pete told me he dumped Mona when he found out she was a Lesbian," Beebo frowned.

"He's lying, as usual. He only falls for gay girls," Paula said. She had gone to Beebo's side and put her arms around her for consolation. Beebo, reviewing Pete's behavior toward her in a new light, felt faintly nauseated. "And I thought he was just trying to get my goat," she said, returning Paula's embrace.

"Darling," Paula said, and Beebo thought how much warmer and truer the word was when Paula spoke it than when it bloomed on Venus's perfect lips like a gaudy rose.

"Beebo, I want to explain—about myself—" Paula said haltingly.

"You don't have to, I understand."

"No, you don't. I didn't myself. Beebo I've always been such a steady, sensible girl. Even when I discovered I was gay. I didn't go all to pieces like so many kids. It shook me up, yes, but I did the reasonable thing. I went out and learned all I could about it. I'd never had special prejudices against other peoples' problems, and I hadn't any against my own.

"I tried to accept the fact, and after a while I got used to it. But all the time I was waiting for somebody wonderful to come along; for a beautiful love affair to make it all right. We'd live quietly together, we'd cherish each other, and life would be rosy.

"I didn't think it would be simple, but I thought it would be satisfying—and permanent. That's the kind of girl I am, Beebo.

"I found other girls while I was waiting so trustingly for this perfect love," she said, speaking with the disillusioned realism of hindsight. "And they taught me a lot. I thought this was necessary. You have to know the different kinds of love before you can recognize the kind you need. I met Mona during this period. She's mean as an old crow, but she's sharp and I learned a lot from her.

"And then the girl in the plaid pajamas came along. It wasn't beautiful, Beebo. Nothing I had learned before prepared me for what I went through.

"I lost my self-respect . . . my ideals. My efforts to please her rubbed her the wrong way. I did everything I thought would draw us close, even when it seemed like madness. I moved to the Village, I went with her fast crowd, I quit my job. I drank too much and played too hard, for fear if I didn't she'd think I was square. I did things that were downright degrading."

Beebo embraced her tightly. "Honey, you're the sweetest girl I ever knew," she said. "I won't believe anything bad about you." She guided her back to the bedroom.

"What I want you to know is," Paula whispered, lying down on the bed, "that I'm not a kook. I don't usually fly off the handle emotionally. I never did it before my affair with the girl in the pajamas. I live an orderly life, I work hard, I care about people. Only, Beebo, you just couldn't have happened. You walked in here asking for Mona last night—was it only last night!—and I realized that all I'd suffered before was the dark before the dawn. Maybe it was a sort of price I had to pay for being gay. I paid it, and Heaven dropped you in my lap. I want to deserve you, Beebo."

Beebo was nonplused. She kissed Paula's white throat, holding her and frowning into the dim light where Paula couldn't see her face. It was disturbing to have such a strong emotion centered on her. She desired Paula passionately. Every endearment Beebo had spoken to her, she had spoken truthfully, but without once repeating, "I love you."

Paula had brought her out; something Paula herself couldn't believe. And no matter what other women might figure in Beebo's life, Paula would always be dear to her for that alone.

But Beebo was afraid of hurting her. There was more than a humble excuse in Paula's explanations; there was also that weapon of amorous women, a plea for sympathy. It was a hint to Beebo: *Don't hurt me like the girl in the plaid pajamas did, or you'll destroy me.* Beebo caught it and fretted over it in silence.

Paula began to worry that she had said too much. She raised up on one elbow, pressed her mouth against Beebo's cheek, and said, "I want you to know I'm as surprised as you are by this love-at-first-sight thing. I thought it was all rot till I met you. Darling, I'm well aware it didn't hit you as hard as it did me. I promise I won't be a nuisance. I'll love you very quietly like a good sensible girl. I won't shriek and weep in public, or chase you, or take pills. I'll just love you. So much and so well you'll have to love me back . . . someday. You will, won't you?"

Beebo felt suddenly cornered and couldn't answer. But when she finally glanced at Paula, Paula had found the courage to smile at her, to tuck her dismay out of sight. It gave Beebo an odd sort of pride in her, as if a child of hers had performed bravely in the face of a hard disappointment. It made Paula still sweeter and more attractive.

"Doesn't everybody love you, little Paula?"

"Almost everybody . . . except Miss Plaid Pajamas and Beebo Brinker." Paula gave her a wry grin that let Beebo relax. "But they don't count. All the intelligent, rich, beautiful people are insanely in love with me."

Beebo laughed and pulled her down on the bed. "Not hard to see why," she said. "You're adorable." She was still full of wonderment and fascination over the new role she was playing with Paula: lover, friend, protector. It felt so good, it fit so well, it rather astounded her. It was like picking up a violin for the first time and finding you could play a lilting tune with no practice at all.

Beebo's good humor rescued Paula from the dumps. She began to feel affectionate again. For Beebo, it was a delirious pleasure to act out on a real girl in a real bed all the intense love play that had filled her solitude. She fell asleep very late, very tired. with Paula in her arms.

Beebo got up early the next morning. She was in no hurry to face Pete Pasquini, knowing what she now knew about him, but she didn't want to lose her job till she could scout down another. She was not in a financial position to get hard-nosed with him yet, and besides she was confident that she could handle whatever he could dish out. They were nearly of a size, and he had never shown himself more than a brash nuisance. And anyway, a man who could fall in love with the likes of Mona Petry was not likely to find himself erotically interested in Beebo Brinker.

Paula was pensive throughout breakfast and when Beebo demanded to know why, she admitted, "It's Mona."

Beebo laughed, but Paula was serious. "She's one of those people with nothing to do. She has to make trouble to keep from going mad with the 'Flats'—that's what she calls it. She doesn't work—her men give her enough money to live on. She doesn't do a thing but amuse herself. If you know her at all, you have to be a lover or a hater. There's no middle ground with her."

"Shall I hire a bodyguard?" Beebo kidded.

"She'll try to punish you somehow. She's been stood up by you and tricked by Pete. She's not the kind who can tolerate being made a fool of. Pete doesn't count, he's only a man, and she can twist him around her finger if she's in the mood. But *you* . . ."

"What can Mona do to me?" Beebo said, still smiling.

"Mona is very inventive. She'll think of something," Paula said.

"Do you mean she'd hurt *you?*" Beebo's smile faded.

"Oh, I doubt it," Paula said. "It wouldn't be half as much fun as making an effigy of Beebo and sticking pins in it. If she does, you'll squirm, too. For heaven's sake, darling, don't do anything she could blackmail you for."

Beebo laughed and reassured her. Mona's jealousy seemed more silly to her than dangerous.

Beebo didn't see Pete Pasquini at work all day, and Marie
had no idea where he was. "Out making babies with the
filles," she said with offhand contempt.

Beebo had no wish to confront him and she finished out
the day's work in relief. But when she got home that night,
there was a new surprise for her.

Jack let her in, taking the bags of groceries from her.
"Haven't seen you for two nights," he said. "Paula must
have attractions I can't match."

"Oh, you're not bad," Beebo smiled. "For a man."

He started stowing things in the refrigerator, and Beebo
became aware of Pat, who had followed them into the
kitchen. "Good news," Jack said. "Celebration tonight." He
pulled a bottle of sparkling burgundy from the shelf.

Beebo glanced from one to the other. "Did you boys finally
tie the knot?" she said, trying to make it sound light.

"Nothing formal yet," Jack grinned. "I believe in long en-
gagements. No, little pal, we are festive tonight because
Pat is no longer with the Sanitary Department."

"It was too unsanitary," Pat chuckled.

"I thought you were taking your vacation," Beebo said.
Suddenly, her precarious place in this still-new city was men-
aced. The time to move out was coming fast.

"Vacation, hell. He quit," Jack said. "I asked him to."
"How come?"

"I don't want my betrothed to work," Jack said, pouring
the champagne. It exploded into tiny fountains of fizz, and
they each took a glass.

Jack lifted his. "Long life and health," he said, and added
significantly, "and love all around."

They drank. Beebo nodded to Pat. "All I can say, Pat, is
what they said to me when I left Juniper Hill: good
riddance to bad rubbish."

"Beebo, you should have been a poet," Jack said.

She finished her drink and stood up. "I guess you two
want to celebrate by yourselves," she said.

"Not at all. Have dinner with us," Jack said.

"I think Paula's waiting for me," Beebo said. After an
awkward pause she added, "She asked me to move in with
her."

"She doesn't waste time does she?" said Jack. "Do you want to?"

"I don't know. It would give her the right to expect me to be faithful. I can't imagine a lovelier girl. But I hardly know her. And there are so damn many girls in the world."

"Which reminds me. How was La Bogardus?"

"If you mean the bosom, it's authentic."

Jack laughed. "You must have been a big hit, if you got that far."

"No. I just have good eyes. And she's allergic to underwear, which makes it pretty obvious." She sat down heavily for a moment on a kitchen chair across the table from Pat.

"You look tired, honey," Jack said concernedly.

"I haven't had much sleep the last two nights," she said and let them chortle at her, smiling a little.

"She's a doll, that Paula," Jack said. "If I were you, I'd keep a close eye on her." He waited a moment. "You don't have to go as far as moving in with her, though. Not if you're not ready."

Beebo looked up at him and reached out to squeeze his arm. "You're too damn good to me, Jack," she said. "I know it's getting crowded here."

"Nobody's complaining!" Jack said. "Besides, if you move out, Pat will probably go, too. You're still my biggest asset."

Pat smiled and Beebo laughed, but there was just enough truth in it to make them all a little uncomfortable.

"If only you could get your elbow in your ear," Pat said to her wistfully, making Jack hilarious. But despite the bantering tone, Pat had found a serious new interest in himself. He was staring and wondering at the many handsome, mannish, and somewhat authoritative girls around Greenwich Village. His crush on Beebo had the effect of opening his eyes to a new and quite fascinating possibility. But so far it was nothing to threaten his affection for Jack, and he said nothing.

Beebo lighted a cigarette, watching as Jack refilled her wine glass. "If I ask a hard question, will you boys tell me the truth?" she said at last. They nodded at her curiously in silent assent.

"When you want me to move out, will you, for God's sake, please say so? I feel bad enough about mooching from Jack as it is."

"Forget it," Jack said. "Stay as long as you want to, pal."

She sipped the drink. "It's not that I don't want Paula," she said. "I just don't want her enough to cut loose from all the rest of the women in the world yet. And I'm not earning enough to live alone."

"You should have met her five years from now," Jack said sagely. "You would have been ready then."

"Maybe we can make it together after a few months," Beebo said. She was musing guiltily about somebody else; someone who had nothing to do with Paula, and yet who affected Beebo's decision not to go live with the pretty little redhead. Beebo had been eager to stay with Paula, eager to be asked, throughout the first night and day of their acquaintance. It would have solved so many problems, economic and emotional.

Then she got away from Paula for a few hours. She met a woman of provocative beauty who stuck in her imagination, almost without her realizing it at first, and who roused her desire for variety: Venus. When she got back to Paula, she was made to see that Paula was urgently in love with her, and it scared her. She was flattered but afraid of the responsibility. And not at all sure she could return the love in full measure.

So she dodged the decision temporarily by volunteering to take Jack's sofa and leave the bed to the men. And for a while it worked out. Beebo spent most of her evenings with Paula—and sometimes the entire night—and Paula wisely refrained from pushing her any more on moving in.

There was a complete—and, Paula thought, ominous— silence from Mona. And another odd development was the disappearance of Pete Pasquini. For almost two weeks, nobody saw him. Marie kept saying she hoped to God he had deserted her at last. She was massively uninterested in finding him.

When he finally made a startling appearance, he touched off a howling family feud, with Marie vowing to drown him in spaghetti sauce and his mother promising to throw Marie in after him. The children lined up on the narrow stairs leading up from the kitchen and shrieked approval of the melee.

Beebo walked in on it at eight-thirty in the morning and brought a sudden stillness to the room. She stood there uncertainly with all eyes on her and finally said, "Don't let me stop you." Pete smiled at her.

Marie came to life, striding toward Beebo to plead her case with feminine ardor. "We find out this morning. He gets back last night, without telling nobody," she said, waving a steaming red spoon at her husband. The coating of sauce underlined her threats to drown him.

"We're all asleep, it's late. The phone rings twice and stops. We go back to sleep—they must've hung up. What we don't know," she hollered in a rising voice, "this piece of dung is in the shop and *he* answers it. Why is he in the shop in the middle of the night? It's dark, no customers, nothing to do. Nothing but tin cans and dry pasta. Is he making love to the tomato paste? Who knows what a crazy dago goes for?"

Pete laughed, and all the while his brilliant black eyes were fixed on Beebo, who refused to meet them, concentrating instead on Marie's theatrics.

"So who's on the phone? *Bogardus,*" Marie said.

Beebo gasped.

"Yeah, that's right," Marie said, hands on her hips, spoon dripping bloody sauce. "She wants spaghetti this time. It's the middle of the night—never mind. She got a taste for spaghetti. 'Send me that one with the funny name,' she says. And she don't mean Pasquini." She threw Pete a look of ferocious scorn. "So Hot Pants here, he says sure, he bring it right up, the stupid sonofabitch. No spaghetti, never mind, he makes up a leftover pizza." She rolled her eyes to Heaven for vengeance.

"What happened?" Beebo said, her mind suddenly full of the star's vivid face and sensual body.

"So I make the delivery," Pete said languidly, seating himself on a table amid the crunchy bread crumbs. "Bogardus opens the door herself and says, 'Where's Beebo?' Well, I'm surprised, I don't realize how popular you are with these actress types." He grinned and picked his teeth with neat nonchalance, while Beebo began to sweat nervously.

"So I tell her, you're sick, you can't make it, but it's okay, I got her spaghetti. She says, 'Thank you, darling—' " He rolled the endearment interminably off his tongue, always smiling directly at Beebo. "—and opens it. I'm waiting for her to hand me some money, minding my own business—"

"For the first time in two weeks!" Marie interpolated. "Where was your hands all this time, Pete?"

"In my pockets," he replied coolly. "She wasn't in a mood for no man last night."

Beebo's whole face flushed a high red. She wanted to turn

and rush out of the place, but the thought of his raucous laughter alone prevented her.

"So instead of the money," he went on leisurely, "she hands me back the pizza. In the face."

"I begin to respect this woman," Marie commented.

Pete continued, "She says, 'What do you mean spaghetti? This ain't spaghetti. And *you* ain't no Beebo Brinker, neither.' How do you like that, butch? You can write your own ticket with that one. Only you better make it a round trip. I understand you got a good reason for visiting back on McDonald Street these days."

"She got a good reason to spit in your face, you damn wop!" Marie declared, siding with Beebo.

Pete ignored her. "That Paula, she's a looker, hm? I wouldn't mind cracking that little nut myself," he said to Beebo, folding his arms and enjoying her alarm.

"I'll crack yours one of these days," Beebo said in a sudden fury. "Don't talk about Paula, you dirty her name."

"Don't mind him, Beebo," Marie said, sensing trouble. "It ain't just Paula, anyway. It ain't enough he runs after skirts all the time. He wants the girls who want other girls. Figure *that* one out. After all his big talk about fags."

"Fags go for other fags. I go for girls," Pete said, but Marie had finally rattled him. Any challenge to his manhood threw him into a panic. It was clear he drew a fine distinction between his own sexual preferences—"normal"—and everybody else's.

"You go for Lesbians," Marie said, silencing him with a wave of her gory spoon. She did him further insult by describing his desires to Beebo, as if Pete were not even in the room. "He's three-fourths fag and the rest sadist," she said. "That's why he don't chase real women. He has to hurt a girl—a girl who don't *want* it—before he can get it up." She glared at him like a cannibal.

Pete looked back with cold wrath. "I got five kids on those stairs says you're a liar," he said. "Or are you saying *you* ain't a real woman?"

"Don't fake with me, Pasquini. I know what you pretend in bed," Marie shouted. "You married me to prove you was a man, and once we left the church, you figure you próved it. Well, it ain't that simple."

Pete walked toward her and Marie paled and stiffened, ready for a blow. But he passed her and went to Beebo, who could only stand her ground like Marie and hope he'd go on by. But he stopped, putting a hand on her shoulder, and pulled her aside.

"Don't listen to her, she's cracked," he said softly. "I told Bogardus you'd be up with the spaghetti this afternoon. Does that make me your friend?"

"After your cracks about Paula?" she said, shaking his hand off roughly.

"I told you where to find Paula, too," he reminded her, and his eyes glittered. "I always say nice things about that one. She's a nice girl."

Beebo looked at him with revulsion. "You sent me there to even some secret score of yours with Mona. Don't act noble about it."

He chuckled. "Still, I sent you, butch. And you went. You tell me if you're sorry. You tell me if I ever done one thing you want to complain about."

"We'd be here all day," Beebo snapped. She turned to start working on the morning's orders, but he followed her into the store, leaving Marie and the others to understand he was through fighting. Beebo heard Marie say wearily to Mrs. Pasquini, "So how come your son looks so good in Bordeaux and so lousy in New York? Okay, don't yell, go see about the kids."

Pete and Beebo worked in silence but whenever she glanced at him he seemed to have glanced at her first and was waiting for her eyes with a smile. He got his orders packed ahead of her and loped out the back door at a jaunty pace. Beebo watched his retreating back with relief. Before he drove away he leaned in and called to her.

"Don't forget—Bogardus wants her pasta at five-thirty," he said. She straightened up and glowered at him till he laughed and withdrew.

Beebo finished the orders quickly, her mind teeming with ideas for another job. Anything would be preferable to Pete's endless leering. It was one thing for him to chase pretty Lesbians like Mona. But that he might desire Beebo—big and rangy, almost more boy than girl—seemed as utterly perverse and unnatural to her as that she might desire him.

She was surprised when the front bell rang and Pat Kynaston walked in. She was just ready to leave.

"What are you doing here!" she exclaimed.

"I brought Marie some goodies for her cockroaches," he said, shaking a colored cylinder full of powder. "The Last Supper. Going to make some deliveries?"

Beebo nodded.

"Take me along," he said pleasantly. "I haven't anything to do, and the heat in that apartment is godawful."

She relented after a moment's indecision, and gave him a smile. "Okay, bring those boxes and follow me," she said. "You can take my mind off things."

Late in the afternoon they arrived at Venus Bogardus's apartment on Park Avenue. Beebo parked in the service entrance, letting her hands drop between her knees with a sigh. Pat lighted her cigarette and they sat and smoked a minute.

"Kind of a stuck-up looking dump, isn't it?" she said, squinting up at the glistening windows, stacked with parallel nicety clear to the clouds. "Well, let's go do it."

She got the hot spaghetti and on a sudden inspiration, included a jar of kosher dills intended for a different customer.

"Who are we going to see this time?" Pat yawned on the way up.

"Probably another maid," Beebo said.

"Whose?"

"Venus Bogardus's."

Pat straightened up and stared at her.

But it was Toby, Venus's problem child, who let them in. "Hi, Beebo," he said, pleased to see her.

"Hi, buddy. Where's your mama?" She was sorry at once she had asked. There was a cook by the stove this time— apparently the one who ditched Venus periodically, but always came back. She was thin and sticky with butter, and she looked inhospitable.

"I hear Venus threw some food around last night," Beebo smiled at Toby. "I brought her a peace offering. Sweets to the sweet," and she handed Toby the pickles. "This is a friend of mine, Toby—Pat Kynaston." They shook hands and a silence ensued. All Beebo had to do now was wait for her money and leave. But she heard herself asking again, "Is Venus here?"

"Come on in. I'll go see," Toby said unwillingly.

He left the kitchen briefly and returned, his hands jammed nervously in his pockets. "She's in her room," he reported. "In a goddamn peignoir. She only wants to see you, Beebo. I told her about Pat and she said she didn't want any peace offerings. She wouldn't even listen about the pickles."

"Oh, God," Pat whispered to Beebo. "I suppose I go to the cook as a consolation prize."

Toby walked over to them. "I have a good collection of records," he said diffidently. "And guns. That's one thing all those fathers are good for. I didn't go for the guns at first, but I've gotten kind of interested. If you'd like to see them ... I mean, I think Mom is busy for a few minutes."

Beebo was touched by his loneliness, his eagerness for company. She had the feeling that he was choosy about his friends, and living a life where he could hardly meet any anyway. It made her seem quite important to him.

He grinned at her. "You're still on my side, aren't you?" he said.

"All the way," she laughed. "I just want to apologize to your mother for our delivery boy. I guess he got fresh."

"No," Toby said, his face lengthening. "She did."

The cook absorbed all this with silent disapproval. She was the type who disapproved of everything—even food.

"I wish you wouldn't see my mother," Toby confessed unexpectedly.

Beebo's mouth dropped open a little. "I thought somebody ought to ask her pardon for last night," she said, embarrassed. "The Pasquini's don't want to lose her."

"They don't need her," he said, looking at the floor.

"Hmp," said the cook to the spinach during the shocked pause that followed.

"That's no way to talk about your mother, Toby," Beebo said.

"You heard how she talks about me," he countered. "What am I supposed to do? Pretend I'm deaf?"

Beebo listened, full of compassion, but afraid of the big-eared cook. Toby spoke as if she were no more than another kitchen appliance, like her stove.

But he saw Beebo's glance, and pushed the kitchen door wide. "Come on in my room," he said. "We can talk there."

Beebo put the spaghetti on the counter and followed him, with Pat behind her. The apartment was richly decorated and unkempt.

In his room, Toby sat on the bed, and Beebo and Pat found places on chairs. He had his guns in two glass cases hung on the wall, and the rest of the room was a jumble of phonograph records, books, and school mementos.

Toby wanted to talk frankly to Beebo, and yet they were more strangers than friends. But he needed to talk, to melt the strangeness away and find the friend. At last he began, rather abruptly, "I just don't want my mother to turn you against me. I mean, you're a good kid and I want you to know me the way I am. Then you won't think I'm such a dumb baby when she starts talking about what a 'lovely child' I am, but she can hardly wait till I outgrow it."

Beebo heard this awkward speech with an ache of recognition. How it hurt to be so young, so at the mercy of your elders, and, often, lessers. So full of rainbows and music and romantic love... yet always cracking your head against the walls of reality.

"I know she says some silly things, Toby," she said seriously. "But you love her anyway, don't you?"

"I guess so. But I've seen her with so many guys it just about makes me sick," he said tiredly. "Until this year. Now, she says they all bore her and she's sworn off men forever. I hope she means it. It's been three months since she had a date. She's terrible to men. They make such fools of themselves for her. I don't know what she does to them, honest. And I'm not stupid!" he added quickly. "I mean, I know what she does—*technically.*" It was a toss-up whether his contempt was greater for his mother or her men.

Pat cleared his throat to camouflage a smile. Toby was conversant with sophisticated sex beyond his years; yet it was difficult and embarrassing for him to talk with friends his own age. Venus could take the blame for it, and Beebo felt a swell of righteous anger at her.

"You know what I think?" Toby said thoughtfully. "I think she's bored with me, too. Well, after all, I'm a male." He said it with pride and resentment, as if it were a fact not always respected in his family. "She needs somebody new to hurt and tease. If you make yourself available, I'll bet she picks on you. It's no fun, either."

"Me?" Beebo said incredulously.

"You see her today and *you'll* find out," he warned.

Beebo, conditioned by Venus's flirting and by the mood of her night with Paula, said incautiously, "You mean— she's interested in me? I mean..." Her voice trailed off, giving her meaning away, and Toby's cheeks turned crimson. She realized she had shocked him, but he thought it was his fault for making the wrong implication.

"Not *that* way," he explained hastily. "She's not *sick.*"

"Oh," Beebo said. "Excuse me."

Pat frowned at her, and she looked at her knees.

"She wants somebody around to admire her and say yes to her," Toby said. "Somebody whose feelings she can hurt. You have to be tough as Leo to get along with her. Leo doesn't have any feelings . . . at least, they never show."

"Leo—her husband?"

"Yes. He's the only man in her life who won't get down on his knees to her. But I think he's the only one who really loves her, too. The others love the glamour, but Leo knows her through and through, and he loves her." He shook his head as if it were incomprehensible.

"You love her too, Toby," Beebo said.

He hunched his shoulders. "She's my mother. What can you do?" he said with heartbreaking, youthful cynicism. "Even if the old bag did raise me."

"Who's the old bag?"

"Mrs. Sack. She's my—well, you might say, my nurse . . . she's been around so long, she's part of the family, even if I am too old for her now." The blush on his face deepened, but he needed terribly to share his burdens, and he felt safe with Beebo. She was a girl, so she couldn't fall in love with his mother. And she had spirit and humor, which she had used to defend him. Besides, his solitude weighed desperately on him.

"Mrs. Sack was there when Mom brought me home from the hospital, and she's done everything for me since then. Mom just sat around and blew kisses at me between lovers."

"She must have done more than that or you'd hate her," Beebo said.

"I do hate her!" he flared. "Leo hates her, too. That doesn't mean we don't love her, but she makes it awful hard." In a knowing voice he added, "There are two things in this world my mother really loves, and one of them is not *men.*" Pat and Beebo stared at him. "She loves herself and money. Mostly herself. She'll tell you that if you ask her. She'll tell the whole damn world. That's how full of shit she is."

"Toby," Beebo said gently. "Mabe you just see all the bad things now. Maybe when you grow up and get away from her, you'll see her good side."

"If she *has* one," he said. "She calls me 'darling' all the time, and five minutes later she's calling a complete stranger 'darling.' I mean about as much to her as the stranger."

"I think it's just a habit with her," Beebo guessed. "Like some people calling everybody 'honey.' "

"And secretly hating them all," Toby said. "I wish just once in my life she'd call me Toby—when she wasn't mad at me, I mean. That *is* my name. She gave it to me."

Beebo wanted to pat him on the back, wanted to smile and say, "She will—I guarantee it." He was a perceptive boy and very appealing. But she had nothing to comfort him with. "Well, if it's any consolation, *I'll* call you Toby," she grinned, and was pleased to see him answer her smile.

There was a difficult silence until Pat said, getting to his feet, "That's quite a bunch of guns. Who gave you the Japanese bayonet?"

Toby followed him to the case and began an animated conversation. Beebo sat pensively listening. Evidently it never occurred to Toby that Beebo could be sexually attracted to his mother. All his precocious knowledge of sex was confined strictly to his mother's—admittedly free-wheeling—activities. And while Venus had done many things with many people, she had not, to Toby's knowledge, done everything.

Beebo was surprised to feel so concerned about the boy. She was better acquainted with him now. His descriptions of his mother's character were so youthfully lopsided they revealed more about him than they did about her. But it seemed certain that one thing he said was true: he did honestly both hate and love her very much.

The three of them were startled when Toby's bedroom door swung open and Venus stood in the hallway. "Well, darling, why didn't you send my visitor to me?" she demanded of her son.

Toby turned around, his chin jutting forward, ready for a tilt with her. But she merely inclined graciously all around, her smile flitting over Pat as though he were just another gun and settling on Beebo.

"Come in and talk with me," she told Beebo. "I had a dreadful experience last night and it's all your fault."

"I'm sorry, Miss Bogardus," Beebo said, standing up and feeling like a bumpkin dripping hayseeds in front of her.

"Don't go, Beebo, it's a trap," Toby said sardonically.

"Darling, what a lyrical sentiment," Venus fired at him. "Come on, Beebo." She turned and sailed down the hall, and Beebo felt angrily like a toy dog, expected to jump when Venus snapped her fingers.

Pat went to her and whispered, "If you feel yourself getting friendly, scream for help."

"Big help you'd be," Beebo said.

"Well, at least I won't be tempted to sin," he said. "I don't go for peignoirs."

"I hope you don't go for guns, either," she warned him in a whisper. And aloud, she said to Toby, "Don't worry, I won't turn traitor."

Then, with a sense of exasperation, shame and excitement, she followed Venus to her room.

It was a real boudoir; a luxurious old-fashioned bower, a glamorous retreat where a coveted woman makes herself irresistible in perfumed privacy; receives the gifts of rich and handsome men, and strikes them helpless with adoration. At least, that was the general idea.

The rug was white, the walls pale blue, and the dressing table wore six silk chiffon petticoats.

"Well, darling?" Venus said. "Do you like my little nest?"

Beebo began to laugh in spite of herself. "If you'll forgive me, Miss Bogardus," she said. "It's one great big gorgoeus cliché."

"Of course it is," Venus smiled. "I planned it that way to offend Leo ... You know, you sound like you've made it in more boudoirs than Errol Flynn."

"Oh, no," Beebo said, taken aback. "I've just read more bad novels. The sirens always have a boudoir like this."

Venus turned around and studied her with amusement in the oval mirror above her dressing table. "Come over here and tell me why they sent that ghastly man over with the pizza, when I asked for you with spaghetti."

Beebo stood her ground, suddenly aware that there was nothing under the "goddamn peignoir" but naked Venus. "That ghastly man owns the place," she said. "He sent himself."

You couldn't look at Venus Bogardus without admiring her form. Even in her late thirties, it was fine: the kind men hope and dream all women will have, especially their wives. She was small-waisted, full-breasted, with a firmly swelling hipline and long shapely legs; the whole package wrapped up in mathematically right proportions that hadn't changed since Venus was a bouncing daisy of sixteen.

Venus scratched something on a piece of paper and swept across the room with it in a cloud of cologne and blue silk. "Here you are, darling," she said. It was her autograph. "Take this to your boss and tell him I hope he gets the sauce out of his ears."

"He'll be overcome, I'm sure," Beebo said, tucking it in her shirt pocket.

Venus stood a few feet from her, watching her and making up her mind to open a difficult subject. "You know, poor Toby is absolutely terrified we're going to like each other," she said restrainedly. "He's quite ashamed of me."

Beebo was far more embarrassed by Venus's admissions than by Toby's. Toby was still a child you could pity and help. But who could pity someone with the blinding assets of his mother? Who had enough crust to offer her any help?

"Miss Bogardus, I'm sorry about the pizza thing. I—" She hesitated, wanting only to duck out and avoid facing the new feelings taking shape inside her.

"I only threw it at him because he wasn't you," Venus said, and Beebo allowed herself one quick startled look at That Face. She felt perspiration under her arms and knew her face was damp, too.

"Sit down, darling, you look feverish," Venus said. And when Beebo stuttered something about going home, Venus laughed. "Why Beebo, I think I've got you going," she said. "I'll bet I'm not the first girl who ever did that to you." It was said in a light friendly tone intended to tease, but it made Beebo so intensely uncomfortable that she began to tremble. It became acutely clear to her that she desired that remote and laughing goddess very much; so much she suddenly lost her voice.

"You were full of beans the last time you were here," Venus said. "Don't be a square now. Tell me all the nice things you know about me. I promise not to take any of them seriously."

Beebo got her voice out finally by blasting on it like an auto horn. "I only know what everybody knows," she blurted.

"The gossip columns?" Venus said. "You can't be so naive that you believe that crap, darling. I'll bet Toby's been talking to you. Telling you stories about his wicked mama."

From the look on Beebo's face, she concluded he had. Beebo didn't want to insult her. "Why should he?" she said, wishing all the while that she could open a window somewhere for fresh air.

"Oh, he thinks I'm dreadful. And of course I am. But I'm kind of sorry he realizes it already."

Beebo saw a real regret shadow her face, and all at once it seemed possible—almost—to feel sorry for her.

"If you don't want him to know it, you'll have to put blinkers on him," Beebo said quietly. "I was fourteen a few years ago. You don't miss seeing much at that age."

"When he was born," Venus said, "I was much too young and ambitious to give a damn about him. Now, when he matters, I find I've done everything wrong...everything I've bothered to do for him, that is. I haven't bothered to do very much."

"You don't need to tell me these things, Miss Bogardus," Beebo said, amazed to hear Venus speak such damaging truths about herself, to see the steel surface of her go-to-hell gaiety buckle and crack.

"He likes you," Venus said, somewhat self-conscious now. She lighted a cigarette and shrugged. "He's such a baby. I love him awfully, but he makes me so damn mad."

"He's a nice kid, Miss Bogardus," Beebo said. "Maybe if you could see his side now and then...It's so easy to ruin a kid that age."

"I'm a nice kid, too, darling," Venus flashed, and Beebo realized from her anger that she had spoken too bluntly. "And I'll do whatever I damn please with Toby. That includes ruining him if I feel like it." She sat down suddenly on a satin-topped stool, tired. "I—I ruined him anyway, and I never felt like it at all," she said, as if too weary to repress the truth.

"I don't want to bore you, Beebo. But I do want to know what he's been saying about me. I know he's been talking to you the last half hour." She looked across the room at Beebo. "Please," she said. Her voice was rough with fatigue.

Beebo shifted her weight and her legs felt almost boneless. "Well," she said uneasily. "I don't suppose it's anything he hasn't already said to you." Venus looked directly at her, and Beebo wondered if it might not impress her more to hear these things from somebody other than Toby. "He loves you very much, Miss Bogardus," she said. "But I don't think he likes you."

Venus merely nodded. "That's no news," she said. "He's like all the other men I know." She looked disgusted.

"He said you didn't like men," Beebo said.

"I beg your pardon!" Venus exclaimed. "I absolutely *adore* men. All but Leo, anyway." She stood up and walked briskly back and forth for a moment, as if she intended to hear no more—at least not till her feathers settled.

"Tell me about yourself, Beebo," she said, and again Beebo was miffed by the offhand order.

"I'd bore you to tears," she said. "You don't want to hear about my daddy's cows and chickens down on the farm."

"I think I do," Venus said sincerely. "I never had a daddy. Or a chicken." Beebo began to protest about leaving again and Venus waved at her impatiently. "All right, all right, but before you go, tell me the rest about Toby."

Beebo didn't know what to make of her. Hadn't she heard it all from him herself? Venus glanced at her. "He's been chattering about you since you brought that pizza over," she explained. "He *likes* you. That means he'll talk to you. He only shouts at me . . . Sit down, Beebo."

Beebo obeyed her out of growing curiosity. It seemed clear to her now that she had inadvertently become a line of communication between mother and son; that perhaps Toby did say things to Beebo he refused to mention to Venus—or at least, said them more candidly.

"There isn't much to tell," Beebo said, trying to squirm out of it. Venus looked very worried. "He just seems lonesome. I think it was a relief to him to spout off at me." She smiled.

Venus sighed. "He's a bewildering little devil," she said, "but I guess he's the only human being I've ever loved. Or ever will love. I loathed him when I was carrying him. I thought he'd ruin my waist. I scarcely looked at him till he was nine or ten. Mrs. Sack brought him up. He grumbles about her, but there are times when I'd give anything if he'd grumble about me the same way . . . times when I actually hate that woman!" Beebo watched her blow her nose on a tissue on the dressing table and realized with a twinge that she was crying.

"He calls her 'the old bag'," Beebo said kindly.

"And I'm 'the old bitch'," Venus said. Her voice was unsteady. "I should never have let him slip away from me. But he scared me, to tell the truth. Not just that he was a baby, and I resented him and didn't know where to begin caring for him. But he ... he had convulsions and things. Terrifying things that absolutely paralyzed me. And Mrs. Sack was so efficient and reassuring. Oh, hell, it's no excuse. But it seemed like one then."

"Convulsions?" Beebo repeated, surprised.

"Yes. He has epilepsy. The *grand mal* kind. Big stuff." There was a shocked silence and Venus added sharply, "Well, it's not a oneway pass to the bughouse."

"No, no, I know," Beebo replied. "I—I'm just so sorry."

"Well, I'm sorry, too," Venus said, and she had control of herself now. The tears had stopped. "Most of the time he's perfectly normal—whatever *that* is for boys of fourteen. But every so often, when he's especially tired or nervous, he gets these... seizures. He gets rigid as a post." She faced Beebo. "Have you ever seen it?" she said.

Beebo shook her head. "But I've heard about such things. It's like a muscle spasm, isn't it?"

Venus's eyes drifted away, seeing it in her mind. "He shoots up from a chair like a jack-in-the-box, and falls straight and stiff as a pole. His saliva foams. We have to be careful that he doesn't swallow his tongue." She took a breath. "It's frightening to see your own child like that ... Well, then he goes to sleep, a stone-dead sleep, and when he wakes up he usually can't even remember it. He just wants to be quiet for a while, by himself. Read books and stare out the window, sometimes for a couple of days."

"What do you do for it?" Beebo said. "Is there anything?"

"There are treatments," Venus said. "Shock therapy, chemotherapy. He hates it but it helps. He hates to talk to me about it. Mrs. Sack always rescued him while I ran screaming from the room. He thinks it makes him repulsive to me. I've tried and tried to explain—I'm just a coward!—but he's so jittery about it now, I don't dare bring it up."

Beebo sat looking at her linked fingers, young enough to wonder why the fair and fortunate of this world are afflicted with sorrows as humbling and frustrating as those of the poor. Venus, whom men feared and worshipped, women feared and disliked, and children simply feared; Venus, herself afraid.

"Toby said some hard things about you, Miss Bogardus," she said at last, "but he also said he loved you, and you don't get that kind of mush out of fourteen-year-old boys unless they mean it."

"I wish he'd say it to me!" Venus cried. "I love him so terribly, but all I do is drive him nuts. I can't talk to him and he clams up with me." She came and put a perfumed hand on Beebo's shoulder. "He hasn't made a new friend in years," she said. Her hand was tight and warm and busy, twisting Beebo's cotton shirt. "I haven't made much sense, I'm afraid," she said. "I'm trying to be honest and I'm not used to it." She gave a clumsy little laugh. "He seems so impressed with you. That was half the reason I wanted you to come back. I thought if you could draw him out somehow . . . Did he say anything else?"

Beebo was worried about that expensive and beautiful hand on her shoulder. About that "half the reason I wanted you back"—what was the other half? About Toby's opinion of his mother's beaux?

Venus guessed the last part. "My admirers?" she said. "I know he can't stand them. Neither can I."

"He thinks you're too fond of . . . " Beebo stopped and cleared her throat.

"Don't get scared off all of a sudden," Venus pleaded "I couldn't take it. I'm too fond of *what?*"

"Money. And yourself."

"He's wrong," Venus said, frowning. "I know it looks that way. And I do like money. But myself I hate. I hate, hate, hate!" Her voice broke and her hand held tight to Beebo's shoulder, steadying her. "Money and my career. That's all I have in the world. That's why I hang on so hard to them both."

"You have Toby," Beebo ventured, wishing she dared to look up at Venus's face, knowing it was kinder not to.

"Toby isn't mine," Venus whispered bitterly. "He just lives here. He won't let himself be loved. I gave birth to him, but Mrs. Sack is his mother." She was weeping again.

Beebo reached up and touched her hand, her eyes still down. The whole mess was so sad and ugly; sadder still for having been preventable. Beebo was moved and hurt by Venus's words because she was moved by Toby: his loneliness, his hopeful trust in her, and now the revelation of his illness.

"You've reached him, Beebo," Venus said. "He wants to be friends with you. You could help me." She came around the divan and sat down next to Beebo. The swift drum-bump of her heart was visible under the gauzy blue silk and it made Beebo want to touch her there; hold her and say something wise and therapeutic. But she hadn't the wisdom to manage her own life yet, let alone someone else's.

"I don't know much about love, Miss Bogardus," she said shyly. "I just know if you love somebody, he can't stop you. All you have to do is keep loving him till he believes in it, I guess."

"That's not enough, or he'd be happy," Venus said.

"Maybe if you did things with him," Beebo said. "My dad used to spend a lot of time with me. We walked, we talked things over, we played chess."

"I don't know the black from the white," Venus said miserably.

"Toby's pretty big on guns right now."

"I don't even know which end the bullet's supposed to come out," Venus said. But after a pause full of self-examination she added, "But I guess I could learn... guns. God."

"It might make all the difference," Beebo said.

"Will you come back and see him?" Venus said. "That would help."

"Sure," Beebo said, but she looked away. Venus had touched her arm again. "He could drive around with me while I make the deliveries tomorrow. Would he like that?"

"He'd probably die of joy. Anything with a motor in it sends him into rhapsodies."

Beebo stood up, her own heart beating so fast now that she felt near suffocating. "It's getting late," she said. Venus followed her to the door.

"He might resent it if I start sticking my nose into his guns all of a sudden," she mused.

"Not if you're really interested," Beebo said. "He won't hold it against you, Venus... beautiful Venus." It was an unpremeditated explosion of admiration. Beebo clamped her mouth shut suddenly, mortified.

But Venus was restored by the slip to good humor. She laughed, and this time it was a pretty sound, a charming answer to a compliment.

"Maybe Toby will turn out all right," Venus said. "You're bound to be a good influence."

Beebo smiled in embarrassment. "He'll probably disgrace you by turning into a model citizen," she said.

"I hope he does." Venus walked the rest of the short distance between them and put her hands on Beebo's shoulders.

She looked very solemn and a bit surprised at herself. "Thanks," she said.

"For nothing." Beebo shook her head. She had a wild impulse to pull Venus's hands off and run.

"Beebo," Venus said thoughtfully. "Do you want to kiss me?"

In the electrified pause that followed, Beebo heard Toby's voice echoing in her ears: "Not *that* way. She's not *sick.*" It pounded through her like a pulse and she knew the answer was obvious to Venus. She reached down and touched Venus's waist. "Yes," she murmured. Venus seemed reassured, almost pleased. She was on home ground again. She lifted her face and gave Beebo her lovely mouth.

It was an astonishing kiss, long and warm. And after it, they stood with their arms around each other a while, faces averted. Beebo didn't realize how hard her embrace was until Venus began to giggle. "Darling, you're crushing me," she said. Beebo released her and backed off hastily, mumbling apologies.

"Here," Venus said, handing her a hanky. "Take the lipstick off, or Toby will think I've perverted you and come after me with one of those damn guns." She watched Beebo dab at her chin ineffectually, and then did it for her. Beebo stood still and let her work, watching her face intently. It was classically beautiful still, though lacking the pearly perfection of a twenty-year-old's. But the bone structure beneath was superb. Beebo admired her ardently. "Think of all the poor girls who have to go homely in the world to make one Venus Bogardus," she said.

Venus smiled. "I don't think it works that way, darling," she said. "Besides, a face is a temporary thing. After a while you find it doesn't work the same old spell any more." She spoke soberly. "Then you have to depend on what's behind it ... if anything. Know who told me that?"

Beebo shook her head.

"Leo. My louse of a spouse," Venus said, blinking. "He told me that when I was seventeen, and I didn't believe him. I do now." She stepped back and transformed the mood with a smile. "There, you look completely innocent."

"Thank you," Beebo said.

"What for? The mop-up? Or the kiss?"

Beebo swallowed. "Both," she said.

"Do you have to go, Beebo? Really?" Venus swirled away a few steps, making Beebo want to dash after her. But she stood resolutely with her hand on the door, still too unnerved to know how to behave. "Another heavy date?" Venus asked.

"You might say," Beebo said.

"Tell me the truth," Venus said, looking at Beebo over her shoulder. "Was it an 'old friend' last time? Or was it a girl?"

Beebo looked up at her slowly, her hand so hot and damp it slipped on the knob. "A girl," she said finally.

Venus took this shattering intelligence with serenity. "I thought so," she said. "I warn you, darling, I'm going to order spaghetti all week. You'd better teach her to play solitaire."

Beebo bridled at the teasing certainty of Venus's attitude. "Then Pasquini will have to make the deliveries," she said flatly.

"All I can do is invite you," Venus said. "I can't make you come."

The double meaning was not lost on Beebo. "I don't think it would be the best approach to Toby if you and I got involved," she said edgily. She was seeing more than Toby, however; she was seeing Paula. Gentle, sympathetic, pretty Paula, so in love with her. Paula for whom she felt such affection and desire. Paula, who told her to run from Milady Bogardus. She wanted to be safe in Paula's arms, not here in this silk-lined trap where so many lovers were so neatly netted.

Beebo was deeply suspicious of Venus, anyway. What could such a woman want but transient amusement? Was she gay at all, or just bored and curious?

"Toby is the only human being I'll ever love." Venus said it. It would be madness for Beebo to fall in love with her, knowing that. But she had already learned from Paula that falling in love is not a deliberate act at all. Sometimes the only way to fight it is to do as Paula said: run.

"I wish you'd stay a while," Venus said.

Beebo gazed steadily at her, and then she opened the door and strode out.

❦

The boys looked up from the living-room TV, Toby catching Beebo with worried eyes and wondering what humili-

ations Venus had invented for her. But the sight of his
beautiful mother swishing after Beebo with her face screwed
into a scowl consoled him and his heart rose. He wanted
Beebo to teach him nonchalance; teach him to laugh and
take Venus less seriously, before Venus scared her off.

"Are you going already?" Toby said.

"How would you like to drive the route with me tomorrow, Toby?" Beebo asked with a smile.

Toby threw his mother an uncertain glance, but she said,
"Go on, darling. Learn something about the mysterious pasta
business."

Toby grinned at her. He hadn't smiled at her in so long
that Venus merely gazed at him with her mouth open, unable to answer until he had turned back to Beebo.

"I'll pick you up after lunch," Beebo said. "Come on,
Pat."

"Just a moment," Venus said. She caught Pat and put her
arms around him, boarding him like an empress her barge,
and kissed him soundly on the mouth. "There, darling," she
said alluringly. "Don't wash your mouth for days. Everybody will die of envy."

Pat touched his lips and said a startled, "Thank you."

"Mother, that's repulsive," Tony muttered.

"Just wait a year, dear, and it will all come crystal clear,"
Venus told him.

Beebo took Pat by the arm and propelled him into the
kitchen. She was dismayed at the effort of will it took to
leave Venus behind.

"What a spectacular female," Pat said, scrambling
through the door with her. "If I weren't already in love with
you, I'd fall for her."

"And Jack would be best man," Beebo quipped.

"You know, something tells me I *could* fall for a girl," he
said, hoping Beebo would pay attention.

But she only said, "Well, fall outside will you?" She
was afraid if she didn't get out fast, inertia would set in.
The back door latch eluded her skittery fingers.

"Turn it all the way right," said a crisp female voice.

They saw the cook, still stirring her witch's brew.

"Thanks," Beebo said, and they got out at last with a
grateful gasp. Pat began to laugh, until he saw Beebo put
her head in her hands while they waited for an elevator.

"What's the matter, honey?" he said. "Was Venus bitchy?
I'll go back and throw something at her."

"After the bussing you got?" Beebo said.

"How about you?" Pat asked softly. And when she didn't answer, he put his arms around her, enjoying the contact, standing with her till the elevator arrived.

The wicked witch peered at them through the glass in the kitchen door.

Beebo was gloomy all the way home, answering Pat laconically.

"I didn't even leave a note," Pat lamented. "Jack will snatch me bald-headed."

"Never. He's too fond of those blond curls."

"Not so fond he won't clobber me when we get home. It's late."

"You've got Jack and I've got Paula," Beebo said, and they brooded about it.

Beebo parked in front of Jack's apartment. Pat looked up at his windows. "The lights are blazing," he reported. "And so is Jack, you can bet on it."

"I never saw him mad before," Beebo said, looking at him quizzically. Pat's apprehension seemed silly to her.

"He's not in love with you, my friend," Pat said, and made her wonder at the distortions—some good, some bad— that love could work in the lover.

"He probably called Marie. She'll tell him you're with me," she said.

"That'll only make him frantic. He thinks we're a couple of lambs in the lion's den."

"Maybe he's right," Beebo said. She had never felt so exhilarated and confused and afraid and eager for God-knew-what in her life.

They hesitated with a common reluctance before the apartment door. "You go first," Pat said. "You're the bravest. If he throws anything, so help me, I'm going to run for it."

Beebo chuckled at him, and then turned the cold brass handle. She opened the door with a quick swing that revealed only the empty living room. They walked in. "Jack?" they said together, and a pile of newspapers on the sofa rolled over and sat up. Jack was very drunk.

"Hello, you two beautiful dolls," he said. They looked at one another. "Paula was here," he told Beebo. "We got loaded together. If you don't want her, I'm going to marry her."

Beebo picked up Jack's empty glass and the bottle on the coffee table and poured herself a shot. She gave the Scotch to Pat. "Have some. Jack won't mind, will you, *darling?*" She imitated the famous Bogardus inflection.

"Why should I?" he said, eyes on Pat. "Did you run into Venus while you were lunching at 21?"

"We went up to her apartment. She threw a pizza at Pasquini last night."

"I heard all about it. Marie was celebrating when I dropped in. Well, it must have been a jolly reunion." He saw the smudge on Pat's lips. "Looks like the goddess and the gay boy are starting a new trend. You're solid lipstick from the nose down."

Pat reproached Beebo instantly. "My God, why didn't you tell me?" he demanded.

"I wasn't looking at you. I'm sorry."

"Where's yours?" Jack said, turning to her. "Or wasn't this ladies' day?"

"I wiped it off," Beebo said touchingly, and Jack didn't know whether to believe her or not.

"Something for everyone," he said. "She must be a Democrat. And what was Patrick doing while you and Venus occupied the loveseat? Taking notes?"

"Watching TV," Pat said casually. "With Toby. Her son."

"I hope he was friendly," Jack said.

"Very," Pat replied, irritated by Jack's jealousy.

"I'll bet. Especially if you curled up in his lap."

"He's a nice little kid, Jackson," Beebo said, surprised at him. Jack was usually so patient and gentle and funny. "He's just fourteen, very mixed-up and very straight." Jack's spite amused her a bit and made her sorry for him. She had never seen him hurt before. He was comical, but the pain showed too and roused her affection for him.

"He's a baby, and I don't go for babies," Pat said. "It's illicit."

"Oh, let's be licit, by all means," Jack said. "I can see the both of you, sitting there watching Captain Kangaroo together. Just a pair of Babes in Boyland."

"Honest to God, Mann, you just bug the hell out of me!" Pat exploded in sudden wrath.

"With pleasure. Till you scream for mercy," Jack snapped.

"Jack, it was your idea that Pat give up his job," Beebo

said. "I took him with me today for fun. It's better than having him cruise the streets all day. Admit it."

After a pause, Jack said, "Okay. You're a pair of worms . . . but I'm a dirty bird. I'm sorry. Call Paula, she's frantic."

Beebo hesitated so long that Jack looked at her and added, "In case you've forgotten, the phone's in the kitchen."

"I know where it is . . . I can't call her. I don't know what to say," Beebo said, and took down another shot like cough medicine.

Jack noticed her unsteady hands and brooding eyes. "Say, 'Hello, Paula. It's me, Beebo. I'm home,' " he suggested. While his attention was on Beebo, Pat went over and sat down quietly beside him on the couch. He took care not to touch him.

Beebo folded dejectedly onto the floor. "I'm just not sure how I feel, all of a sudden," she said, letting her forehead drop into her hand.

"You didn't fall for Toby, did you?" Jack said, ignoring the tentative hand Pat put on his knee. "This seems to be the night to go straight."

"Don't make lousy jokes, Jack."

"All right, pal. What happened with Venus? Did she really kiss you? Was it that great?" True to form, he pushed his own chagrin aside a while to worry about her.

"She hates everybody but Toby. She can't even like herself, and Toby's the only human being she'll ever love. How can such a lovely woman be so messed up?" Beebo mourned.

"I see she's messed you up a bit, too. Beebo, was it you who was cheating tonight, and not Pat? Are you falling for Venus? Because if you're not, you'd go call Paula and laugh this off with her. You wouldn't care who Venus loved or why."

"I don't know. Don't ask me," Beebo said, crushed almost to despair by the shame of it—of being a pushover for a professional temptress, and too mesmerized by her even to phone Paula, whose love for her had become a torment to them both.

Pat leaned against Jack cautiously and said, "Toby has seven yo-yos. We watched the Lone Ranger."

"Okay," Jack said, smiling into space. "Hey, Beebo. Hey!"

She had rolled over suddenly on her stomach to cry, her face in the scratchy rug. She shook her head to show she heard him but couldn't stop.

Pat clucked softly at her. "She couldn't have cared less

about that woman till she checked out the boudoir. They were in there an hour. Beebo came out transformed."

Beebo wept into the stiff wool pile. "I thought I wanted to apologize. But I really wanted . . . Oh, God help me, I'm wild for her. She's fabulous."

Jack lighted a cigarette and blew a stream of smoke over Beebo's back. "Well, that's two nuts in the family: you and me. We fall in love with the wrong ones as if it were in the by-laws."

Pat turned to stare at him. "Who's in love?" he said.

"I am. With you."

Pat began to smile. "Why the hell didn't you *say* so?" he exclaimed. "You never said so."

"I was waiting for Beebo to go first. Misery loves company."

"Come on, you nut, you know I'm crazy about you," Pat said, smiling at him. He leaned over. "Stick out your tongue," he said. Jack obeyed. "It's black. You're lying, you don't love me at all."

Jack began to laugh. Suddenly they forgot Beebo. It was the wonderful selfishness of love that swept them out of her world into their own; the selfishness that friends can only envy and forgive.

Beebo stood up after a while and wandered into the bedroom, wanting to give them some privacy and herself some relief from their pleasure. She lay down on the bed and saw Venus on the ceiling; shut her eyes and saw Paula and felt the tears start again. She stuffed her face into the pillow, beating it and crying Paula's name. But when the fit passed, it was still Venus for whom her limbs ached and body burned; Venus whose face flamed in her brain and made her heart race.

Before she slept she thought of Jack and Pat, facing up to their love at last, and knew she had to move out. Yesterday she could have gone to Paula, even if it was premature. To-day, there was again no place to go.

Beebo drove the truck to work with a thundering headache. She felt cut off from home and help; cut out—halfway at least—from Jack's life. Venus wanted her to come back but only, Beebo was sure, to entertain herself. Paula wanted her, but to smother her with a love she couldn't honestly accept, much as she respected and even wanted it.

At the shop she handed Venus's autograph to Pete Pasquini. "Something for your memory book," she said darkly.

He looked at it disinterestedly. "So how come you're so cheerful this morning? Didn't she throw nothing at you last night? She got a good right hand, that one."

"She said to tell you she's sorry," Beebo said, refusing to look at him while she worked.

"Yeah? I think you're the one who's sorry. You didn't do so good, hm?"

Beebo lifted a heavy can of peeled tomatoes, almost persuaded to heave it, when Marie's voice broke in. "Beebo— a visitor. A young lady."

Beebo put the can down, and a hand to her head. *Paula. Holy God! I can't face her.* But she had to. She walked slowly to the front of the store, aware that Pete was trailing her at a discreet distance.

A tall dark-haired girl wheeled around and took off a pair of showy sunglasses. "Hello, Beebo," she said. It was Mona.

Beebo could find nothing to say. Even "hello" was too much of a courtesy.

"I want some groceries. Over there on the counter—I've got most of them. I'm taking them to Paula. She didn't feel much like going out today . . . for some reason."

The thought of Paula, defenseless against Mona, was enough to crowd Beebo's reluctance to see her little redhead right out of her mind. "I'll take them over. I was going to see her at lunchtime anyway," she said.

"I'm sure it'll come as a surprise to Paula," Mona observed, smiling at a display of spinach noodles.

Pete heard it and laughed his oily mirth to the canned fruits in the next aisle. Beebo wanted to strangle him. She shoved Mona's five-dollar bill back at her and put the food for Paula on a shelf behind the counter. Mona had that high color on her face brought up by the excitement of willful malevolence. "I hear you and Pete are getting to be regular cronies," she said in a syrupy voice. "Isn't he a ray of sunshine, though?"

"You ought to know. He's your sunshine, not mine," Beebo said briefly.

"Pretty noble of you to pay for the groceries," Mona said, sliding the bill back into her purse. "On your salary." She gave Beebo a provocative stare that reminded them both of the night they met at the Colophon. A warm feeling arose in Beebo that was strictly physical and angered her.

Mona slunk down Pete's aisle and Beebo heard them murmuring together. From the back of the shop she could see Pete making animated gestures as he told Mona something. Marie came out of the kitchen a minute to glance at them. "Ain't that a pretty sight?" she said in a caustic whisper to Beebo. "The 'Happiness Kids' Jack calls 'em. They was made for each other, them two."

Beebo had to grin at the spunky little Frenchwoman.

Pete didn't let Mona leave till he heard the motor of Beebo's truck starting in the delivery yard. Beebo was backing out when he caught her. He put his head in the cab, forcing her to stop.

"Well?" she said impatiently.

"Bogardus just calls in," he said. "For tonight—lasagna. You can deliver; I want no more in the face." He waited for her reply, but she was gazing through the windshield, seeing nothing but that face, that face. So fair. So unfair! Pete slapped her knee and made her start. "You alive?" he said.

"I hear you."

Pete squeezed her knee—the kind of grip known as a horse bite. It hurts and it tickles at the same time. Beebo wrenched her leg away and the truck lurched backward. Pete leaped agilely out of the way, laughing at her disgusted curse.

She drove off fuming, wondering what it was about him that made her think, when they met, that he never laughed. She would damn well quit, whether she had another job or not. But then she saw herself, jobless and homeless at one stroke. Everything had seemed so right and easy just a few weeks ago. Everything now seemed bewilderingly bleak.

She spent an hour with Paula at lunchtime, trying to explain by fits and starts how she had made friends with Toby, talked to Venus about him, and got home late, too tired to call.

"I'm sorry," Beebo said, her voice soft with embarrassment. "That was plain selfishness. Please eat, honey; I brought you all this good food."

"Because Mona Petry told you I was staying at home today." Paula put a bite in her mouth as if it were a ball of cotton. There was little more said, and the silences between words became unbearable. They did not make love, they didn't laugh. Beebo's lapse of the previous night hung between them like a fog. She was almost too inhibited when it was time to go to kiss Paula. At last she leaned over and gave her a shy peck on the cheek. Paula accepted it with solemn dignity, but would not return it.

"May I see you tonight?" Beebo said.

"If you think you can put up with my mood."

"I'm afraid the mood is my fault. Let me come over, please, Paula."

Paula gave her a faint smile. "I won't be very nice to you," she said.

It was the first of many quiet cool nights, when Paula's intense desire for Beebo, and Beebo's unadmitted desire for Venus, kept them restranied and doubtful with each other.

Beebo picked Toby up the next day and spent the afternoon with him. He turned into a handy helper, carrying orders with her and keeping her busy with his talk. He was interested, as a child five years younger might have been, in the panorama of the city, especially the areas that were new to him. Though he lived there much of the time, he saw very little of New York.

He would fire a broadside of questions at Beebo and leave her wallowing in his wake, searching for answers, while he hurried on to set up the next bunch. Fortunately, it seemed more important to him to be able to ask than to get answers. Beebo didn't want to disappoint him with her ignorance.

They became quite good friends in the following few weeks, and to Beebo's surprise, they accomplished it without any sideline coaching from Venus. Venus, in fact, stayed out of sight, though she kept on ordering from Marie Pasquini. And Beebo, knowing as Toby did not, that Venus was sacrificing her pleasure for his sake, was grateful to her.

Beebo dreaded facing her, even though it seemed inevitable sooner or later. And when it happened, Beebo foresaw her relationship with Paula going down the drain; her friendship with Toby smashed; and her self-respect, already slipping, destroyed completely.

It was something to be spared the encounter for a while. Everything in Beebo's life felt very temporary and precarious to her. But at least she had a breathing space, a time to test her feelings before they were exposed to others.

Alone, she was miserable with the problems of where to live, who to live with, how to control her urgent new emotions. But with Toby, she forgot a little and studied his troubles instead. They kidded each other and they laughed a lot. And they talked. At first it was mostly about guns— Toby's forte; or horses—Beebo's. Boy talk. Getting-to-know-you talk. The necessary preliminaries to a heart-to-heart. And it did Beebo as much good as it did Toby.

When they first met, Toby had blurted some awkward and ugly things to Beebo about his life with Venus. He seized upon her empathy for him and used it brashly because for all he knew he would see her once and never again. And it might be years before somebody else came along who seemed able to understand it. It had to be someone Toby instinctively liked and respected or it wouldn't ease his troubled young heart to bare it. So Beebo was special and he had grabbed her and said too much too fast.

So he back-pedaled into gun-talk, horse-talk, horseplay, and finally friendship, now that he could approach it more slowly. A little at a time, he unbent with her. He told her about the girls he knew in Bel-Air, California, where they lived when Venus was working in a film.

"I love it out there," he said. "We have five horses. Leo rides with me. You'd love it. Say, maybe you could come out and take care of them for us. You know all about it from your dad. It's too bad other girls are so square. You know, I took one riding once, and she was scared to death."

"You just got the wrong one," Beebo said. "Lots of girls like to ride."

"Not the ones I know," he said. "Or if they like to ride, they don't like me."

"You haven't looked around enough."

"It's embarrassing," Toby said. "The dumb ones can't talk to you about anything. And if you find a decent one, you can't talk to *her*. It's awful." He smiled ruefully while Beebo laughed at him, and then added, "Why can a guy talk to other guys but not to girls?"

"You talk to me," she said.

"You're different," Toby said, with no inkling that he might have scraped a sore spot. He meant it as a compliment and she took it that way. "I don't think I'll ever love a girl, Beebo. You can't trust them."

"You think they're all like your mother," Beebo told him.

"They are."

"No more than all men are the same."

"According to my mother, all men are dirty dogs. That includes me. Sometimes I think the reason she named me Toby was because it makes me sound like an alley cat. Toby the Cat, and Leo the Lion. What a zoo she lives with. I wonder why she didn't name me Fido. She treats me like a hound most of the time."

"Hey, buddy," Beebo said. "Maybe she's mixed up but she's still your mother. You know what we talked about that day when I was there? How much she loves you. She cried because you don't believe her."

Toby pressed his lips together, unwilling to concede a single virtue to Venus. "My name isn't Bogardus," he said finally. "It's Henderson."

"Your mother loves you, Toby Henderson."

"My father lives in Chicago. Were you ever there? He runs a dairy processing plant in Gary, Indiana. I've never met him and I never want to."

Beebo was shocked. After a moment she said, "Well, maybe you can't love somebody you don't know, even if he is your father. But aren't you curious?"

"Oh, he's probably a dirty dog like the rest of us. At least if I never meet him, I can pretend he's something better."

Beebo felt a stinging sympathy for him. "My father means a lot to me," she said.

"How come you don't live with him, then? You said he lived in Wisconsin. Did you run away, Beebo? You're awful young to be on your own here. How come?"

He had scored a bull's eye. She wondered how many years of lonely introspection it had cost Toby to become that perceptive; that quick to see the truth beneath the social tricks.

"I had some tough problems, Toby," she said. She was suddenly so grave that he retreated from the subject, afraid of hurting her. Beebo was thinking what it would do to him to know that she was a Lesbian; how desperately he would worry about her and his mother.

"I'm not the dope Mom thinks I am," he declared. "You can talk to me."

"No, you're no dope, but I am, for running away. And I'll tell you something, buddy. Fathers are something special. Even yours."

"Sure. He and Mom got together and manufactured me. Something special. A gorilla could have done the job better, Mom says. Or a test tube. Sometimes I think that'd be okay —a test tube. Then I'd never even have to know his name."

Beebo felt a little like crying. But it would ruin her prestige with him. She swallowed and said, "He must write to you. Send you brithday presents, and things."

"The only present he ever gave me was epilepsy," Toby said in a flinty voice. "Mom says it came from his side of the family. So I haven't much to thank him for. Do you know what that is—epilepsy?" He had said the word so many times there was no longer any drama in it for him.

"Your Mom told me," Beebo said. "Does it . . . make things rough for you? Like at school, with the other kids?"

"Not too bad," he said. But she looked at his face and thought differently. It had made him shy and apologetic about himself, and consequently, fiercely defensive. At any time, he might become a major source of inconvenience or even panic to his schoolmates, though the seizures hit him infrequently in their presence. Still, it was those times he remembered better than any others.

"Leo is good about it," Toby said. "He's a pretty good guy. I'd rather have him around than Mrs. Sack, even."

"What's Leo like?" Beebo said, suddenly afire to know.

"He stands up to Mom, if that's what you mean. She hates him, naturally, but she respects him. Leo gave her her name. He knew her before anybody else in Hollywood. He was her agent, and he got her started."

"What's her real name?"

"Jean Jacoby."

"That's pretty . . . why won't Leo divorce her?"

"He really loves her, I guess. Boy, what a glutton for punishment," Toby marveled.

"If she hates him, why did she marry him?"

"Oh, she talked herself into a crush on all her husbands," Toby said, and Beebo wondered who had explained it all to him with such authority . . . Leo? Mrs. Sack? "They were all rich and good looking and married to somebody else till she came along. I think it was sort of a challenge."

Beebo absorbed this in silence, disapproving and yet oddly amused. "What does Leo do?" She pictured him as a sort of legitimatized gigolo for his stunning wife.

"He's a director now. He directs all her films. That's why people think she's an actress. He can get a performance out of her nobody else can. She hates to admit it, but she loves her reviews. If they ever did get divorced, she'd have to let him keep on directing." His words made Leo Bogardus seem like more of a man than Beebo would have liked. She lighted a cigarette.

"Hey, can I have one too?" Toby said, with the light of friendly collusion in his eyes. "It's okay, I've smoked before."

She handed him her pack. "I'm contributing to the delinquency of a minor, you know," she grinned. "It's your fault, buddy. You'd better kick the habit before they haul me in."

He did not inhale the smoke, but he was very pleased with himself, and with Beebo. He held the cigarette in a self-conscious imitation of a man's gesture, taking a cautious mouthful occasionally and blowing it out with dreamy satisfaction.

"Do you get along with Leo, Toby?" Beebo asked.

"He's been real decent to me. He does things with me, even when they're things I don't want to do. It's nice of him ... you know? And sometimes I end up liking the things I didn't think I would. It's funny ... he tries to make them interesting. I guess you could say I like him."

Beebo grinned at him, impressed by his adolescent acuity; and aware, despite his wary phrasing, that Leo was quite an influence in his life. "You're pretty grown up for your age, aren't you?" she said seriously, and made him smile at the flattery.

But his answer startled her. "I had to grow up," he said, "with men climbing in and out of Mom's bed while I played on the floor with my blocks."

"God! Was it that bad?" Beebo said.

"They all thought I'd be the best adjusted kid for miles around," he said with psychological detachment into a cloud of very grown-up smoke. "I don't know why all that stuff should embarrass me now that I'm nearly fifteen. I used to sit there and watch the whole show when I was little." His face lengthened. "It never got to me then."

Beebo saw the resentment on his face flash and alternate with confusion, even love, for Venus. She wondered how much Venus was trying to show her love for him these days, and if it was making Toby all the more suspicious of her.

"Toby," Beebo said. "Do you know that Venus is kind of afraid of you?"

He turned his face away.

"She wants you to know she loves you, but she's afraid you'll think she's kidding after all these years."

"She's right."

"Maybe now that she's trying to say it, you could listen," Beebo suggested casually.

Toby gave a deep sigh. "I guess that's what she's been doing all week," he said. "She keeps saying she has something to say but she never says anything." He returned Beebo's gaze, his blue eyes, so like his mother's, pained and puzzled. "I don't care how she says it, if only she means it. I was lousy to her because whenever I try to tell her something, she's lousy to me. I wanted to get back at her."

"You've only got one mother, Toby. You've got to make the best of her. I wouldn't care so much what my mother was like, if I'd only known her. She died when I was young."

Toby pondered this a while, and then said, "If you ever run away again, I'll go with you." It was not an offer, it was a request—a plea.

"You're welcome aboard," she smiled.

Venus was waiting for them outside the elevator door in the service entrance, one early evening in the first week of September. Strangely, Beebo wasn't surprised. It had been coming for weeks, and now she had to face it.

Toby grimaced at his mother, and Beebo handed her the carton of home-cooked food. "Here's your dinner," she said. "Mrs. Pasquini appreciates all the orders."

"You might as well keep it, she never eats it," Toby revealed. "She just orders it to keep you coming over."

"Sh!" Venus exclaimed at him. She was wearing a bright-blue knit dress, into which her famous frame was smoothly slipped; a glowing target for the eyes.

"Toby says you're a good driver," Venus said. "Now I suppose he'll pester Leo to teach him when we get home."

"You know I can't drive, Mom," he said wearily. "They don't give licences to epileptics."

"Well, we'll talk to the governor, darling," she said.

"Besides, what do you mean 'home?' California?" He looked at her suddenly, brightening. "I thought we were going to be here all winter."

Beebo felt almost dizzy at the thought of losing Venus before she had won her. It was too much to bear. Everything went wrong in bunches. "Home?" she repeated, frowning at Venus.

"Well, you both look as if I had dropped a bomb," Venus declared. "I just thought, with Toby's friends in California, and all those miserable horses and sunshine and ocean ... I guess I can put up with the smog."

"Mom, that's great," he said, surprise all over his face. "Are you doing a new picture?"

"No, darling. I'm turning over a new leaf," she said.

They looked at each other and Beebo sensed an awkward rapport between them. After a decent pause she said, "Well —have a good trip, you two. I guess I won't be seeing you again, Toby."

He turned to her in consternation, and Venus said, "Don't be silly, darling. I have some lovely martinis all ready upstairs and a perfectly irresistible business proposition for you."

"Business?" Beebo said.

Toby made a face. "Monkey business," he said. "Can you walk on your hands, Beebo?"

"Hush, darling," Venus said, pulling them both into the elevator. "Not until she's had her martini."

Toby had a distant look on his face on the way up. "I'll have to write to everybody," he said. "So they'll know I'm coming."

Beebo let herself be led into the living room, full of sharp doubts that made her jumpy. Venus watched Toby go with a smile. "He'll be busy for hours," she told Beebo. "He rewrites all his letters two or three times. You'd think he was going to publish them someday."

Beebo sat down on a long white sofa and accepted a martini with an unsteady hand. The trembling had started already, and it seemed impossible to talk or act like a normal human being.

But Venus, who was more of a sorceress than a goddess,

talked softly to her for half an hour, letting the drinks and her own silvery charm relax her guest. Even then, Beebo looked so gloomy that Venus began to chuckle at her. She refilled their glasses and asked her, "Do you hate yourself for coming up tonight?"

"Not as much as I hate you for asking me," Beebo said.

"Be fair now, darling," Venus chided. "I'm not responsible for your weakness, am I?"

"You know damn well you are," Beebo said. And in the pause that followed she felt that if she didn't escape now, she never would. "I'm sorry, it's not your fault," she said, trying to sound matter-of-fact. "I guess you were born with —all that." She couldn't look at "all that" while she spoke of it.

"No, I had to grow it, darling. Took me 15 years, and it was a hell of a wait."

Beebo moved to the edge of the sofa when Venus joined her. "Were you a poor proud orphan till some movie scout discovered you?"

"Oh, God no!" Venus laughed. "My family was solid apple pie. The trouble was, I was always so damn beautiful I never had a chance to be normal." She spoke dispassionately, as if she were analyzing a friend. It wasn't snobbish. "I was supposed to be fast and loose because I looked it. At first the attention spoiled me. I was cocky. A candybox valentine brat with corkscrew curls—my mother's pride and joy. Until I drove her frantic, and my friends out of my life. Nobody could stand me. *Honestly.* You laugh, but I cried when it happened. I couldn't understand why I was alone all of a sudden.

"I got shy and scared. Went my own way and told the world to go to hell. After a while, when my figure caught up with my face, I made some new friends: boys. It was so easy to give in. So hard to be anything but what people thought you were," she said, and Beebo responded with a startled swell of sympathy. "Well, in a phrase, they made me what I am today: a conniving bitch." Venus spoke defiantly . . . and regretfully.

"I'm not proud of it, but I want to be truthful with you. You're a sweetheart, Beebo. And very young, and maybe not too experienced. Tell me why you've made Toby come up alone with the food all these weeks. Did you think I'd throw spaghetti at you?"

Beebo took a swallow of her drink. "I don't want to

crawl, Venus. I don't want to be hurt," she said harshly, defending herself with painful honesty in lieu of a worldly white lie.

"Nobody does," Venus said. "Were you expecting to be?"

"Isn't that what you want?" Beebo said, looking deep into her ice cubes. "To play games?"

Venus touched a finger to Beebo's cheek. "You're not crawling," she said. "You're being difficult. That's new for me."

"Is playing around with girls new for you, too?" Beebo asked, afraid to know the answer.

"Depends on how you mean it," Venus said. "You don't trust me, do you?" She smiled.

Beebo caught Venus's hand as it caressed her cheek and kissed it warmly. And remembered with sudden sadness the way Paula had done that to her when they met. She put Venus's hand down gingerly on the sofa.

Venus let her sit and stew for a minute and then slipped across the cushion toward her. Their faces were very near and Venus put her rejected hand on Beebo's leg. "I'm trying to give myself to you and you won't have me," she said. "Now who's crawling?" She let her other hand, cool and questing, touch Beebo's neck and slip over her shoulder, drawing fire with it.

"You're putting me on," Beebo said, determinedly suspicious as only the young and uncertain can be. She took a deep breath. "But I don't care," she cried suddenly. "I don't care. I'll have you any way I can." She put her head down and kissed Venus's throat, putting her arms around her and grasping her firmly. Venus leaned against her, warm and willow-supple.

"You want to know how it feels, don't you?" Beebo said, trying to hurt her feelings, so sure Venus would hurt Beebo first if she could. "You want to know what it's like for a girl to hold you instead of a man. Any time you get bored, let me know." She bent to kiss her again but Venus stopped her. She was dismayed, and Beebo was ashamed to see it.

"You really *do* hate me, don't you?" Venus said.

Beebo closed her eyes for a minute. "I'm sorry," she whispered. She felt Venus moving in her arms. "I thought you were bored and frigid. Taking me like a prescription, or something. The way you talked—"

"The way I talked about *men*, not women. Beebo, do you

know something? I was scared to death you'd take one look at this face of mine, panic, and run out." Her hands slid around Beebo's back and into her short dark hair.

Beebo's face turned hot while those hands trailed softly through her hair and over her eyes. "You're superb, Beebo," Venus said. "I think I'm the one who's afraid. I wouldn't be if I knew you better. And myself."

"You know more than I know," Beebo said. "Is this all a joke, Venus?"

Venus hushed her by pulling her down and kissing her mouth, and her tenderness was no pleasantry. Beebo kissed back: Venus's face, her ears, her pale throat, till Venus made her stop, shaking her curls to be let loose, and laughing.

"Who the hell am I," Beebo exclaimed, "that you should kiss me like this?"

Venus caught her breath. "You talk to me as if I were a woman, she said at last, gratefully. "Not a goddess, or a bitch. It hurts a little, but it feels good to hurt like that. Like when you're awfully young and you have a beautiful dreamy pain to cry over."

Beebo rubbed her head back and forth in the cradle of Venus's shoulder. "Did you cry over your dreams like other girls, Venus?"

"I cried, but not like other girls. I never did anything like other girls. I never even looked like them."

"Would you rather be plain?" Beebo asked.

Venus looked away and found the dignity to be honest. "No," she said. "It's a funny thing about women and me. Half the time I want to make them weep with despair over my beauty. And the other half I ache to be friends with them. Accepted. All the things I wasn't when I was growing up. My whole world is men. They're the only friends I have, and they aren't really friends at all. Not with a woman like me. The women close to me are either fat and old, like Mrs. Sack, or homely and heartless, like Miss Pinch."

"The cook? Is that her name?" Beebo gave in to laughter that relieved her tenseness a little.

"I know, it's too good to be true," Venus said. "Leo started calling her that, and it caught on. I fire her regularly but she comes back like a bad dream. She's devoted to Leo."

Beebo put her head down so she could talk without exposing her emotions to Venus's eyes. "Do you miss having a woman in your life?" she asked.

"Yes. The right kind. Somebody cultured and intelligent

and well-educated. Somebody to teach me things. I'm so damned stupid."

Beebo gave a short wry laugh. "Venus? I think there's something you should know."

"What?"

"I didn't finish high school."

Venus laughed, a charming sound, full of pleasure. "I thought you meant, did I want a secretary, or something," she said.

"I'll bet you did." Beebo sat up and lowered herself to the floor, where she leaned back on the sofa, locking her fingers around her knees. She felt Venus's hand come down to play with her ear.

"Did I say something wrong, darling?" Venus said.

"Not a thing. Just that for a girl who likes girls, you did a damn queer thing marrying six men," Beebo said.

Venus answered pensively. "I kept thinking one of the six would set me straight somehow," she said.

Beebo felt those lovely hands in her hair, and she looked over at the kitchen door. It was about thirty feet away ... thirty miles, it seemed.

"You've got such soft hair, Beebo," Venus said, and she leaned down and kissed the crown of Beebo's head, and then lifted her face and kissed everything upside-down from her perch on the couch. "You kiss me so gently," she said. "I never knew a lover so gentle before. There isn't a man alive who could come near you." And she kissed Beebo again till Beebo reached up from the floor and caught Venus's breasts in her hands, returning the kiss with a young warmth that struck sparks in Venus. Beebo held her hard and groaned, "Don't, don't, you don't know what it's doing to me. Oh, God ... oh, please ..."

"Do you still think I don't know?" Venus said. "Don't you understand by now I'm not doing this for kicks? Or to hurt you? Or God knows what other medieval torments you imagined? I think you're amazing. Exciting. Adorable. Did you think I'd never tried it before with a woman? I've tried everything, darling. Everything but corpses, anyway."

"Oh, Venus, Venus—"

"Hush, I'll explain. You see, it was always so rotten with men. It was as good as it ever got with a girl. But never this good." Her directness threw Beebo emotionally offstride. "I kept thinking it should be. If men were so bad there had to be something else worth living for. So I kept looking. But I have to be so damn careful. Whatever I do is news."

Beebo looked at her and saw tears on her cheeks. "My daydreams were always better than my life," Venus whispered, "and when you reach that point, you're in trouble. All the money in the world can't make those dreams real." She brushed lightly at the tears, embarrassed by them.

"I was wild when that dreadful Pasquini came up here," she said. "I'd been looking forward to seeing you all day. After he left, I began to think maybe his coming was a sign that I should give you up while I still could. An affair between us would seem like the world's worst cliché: the jaded vamp seducing the innocent girl for the sake of a few cheap kicks." She sat silent a moment and then she smiled at Beebo.

"Do you know what Miss Pinch said after you left? She came marching in and announced that you were a dyke and Pat was a queen."

"Miss *Pinch* said that?" Beebo said, and laughed at the incongruity of it.

"Well, she put it a little differently. She said, 'The dark young gentleman was a female and the blond young gentleman was a lady, if you know what I mean, ma'am.'"

They laughed together and Beebo felt suddenly close to Venus; her fear had vanished. "The only thing I worry about is, Miss Pinch might tell Leo," Venus said. "It makes him simply wild when I take up with a girl."

"Do you take them up often?" Beebo asked, looking down.

Venus shook her head without answering. It was a wordless admission of her loneliness and frustration; as great, in its way, as Toby's. Beebo got up on her knees and encircled Venus's waist. "Venus, darling," she said softly, hesitantly. "I love you so much. I can't understand this thing. I thought you were—all glittery and cold. I thought we'd finally climb into bed, and you'd kill me with your laughter. And then to have you like this! God, I don't know what I'm doing. It's so crazy. Venus, Venus, I adore you." She began to kiss her again and Venus let herself be pulled off the sofa and into Beebo's arms, giving in a bit at a time, so that Beebo was trembling and wild-eyed one moment, and overwhelming Venus the next.

She had just enough sense to pick Venus up moments later and carry her to the bedroom, through the overstated boudoir, and out of the sight of Toby and the women. She laid Venus down on the blue silk coverlet of her bed, leaning over her with her fists planted in the mattress.

"This is where I do my dreaming," Venus told her. "I take off my clothes and lie down here and tell myself beautiful crazy stories. I've been doing it for years."

"Who do you dream about?" Beebo asked.

"Who do you think?" Venus smiled. "God, you're so tall for a girl. So tanned and strong. Like a boy."

"I hate to think of you all alone on that blue silk, wanting me," Beebo said. "And me out delivering salami."

"And talking to Toby," Venus said.

"That means a lot to you, doesn't it?"

"Everything," Venus admitted. "I can't tell you how much. I can talk to him now without screaming at him. I owe that to you, Beebo."

Instead of accepting the compliment gracefully, Beebo stared moodily out the window. "Are you keeping me around so you won't lose Toby again? I don't want to find myself pounding on your locked door the day you learn you can talk to him without me."

"What does it take to make you trust a girl, Beebo?" Venus teased.

"I guess I never will trust you—quite," Beebo said truthfully. "You're too good to be true."

Venus pulled her head down on the pillow and asked seriously, "How many people know you have a crush on me? Don't fib, darling. I have a special reason for wanting to know."

Beebo gritted her teeth together a moment before she answered. "My roommate. His name is Jack Mann. He's gay, too. He's the best friend I ever had and I trust him more than I trust myself."

"Who else? Pasquini?"

"No," Beebo said, lying forcefully with the sudden knowledge that Venus was trying to decide how dangerous their affair could be. The safer it seemed to her, the better the chances she would keep Beebo with her... perhaps even take her to the West Coast.

"How about this girl who's in love with you?" Venus said.

"She's not in love with me. It's a crush," Beebo said, ashamed of the betrayal but unable to help herself. "She'll get over it."

"Do girls ever get over their crushes on you?" Venus said.

"Every day," Beebo protested. "Venus . . . would you ever lock me out . . . if people knew?"

Venus rolled away from her, sitting halfway up. Her face was dark. "I'd have to," she said. "For Toby, if for no other reason. And even without him, there's my career. It's my life, my anchor. I can't afford to jeopardize it, especially now that I'm thirty-eight." She glanced at Beebo. "Is that unforgivably selfish of me? Don't answer. It is, of course. I want you, and all the rest, too. And that means you're the one who'd have to sacrifice. It's just that . . . for some people a job is a job. For me, it's self-respect. Acting is about the only thing I've done in my life I'm not ashamed of. Is it too much to ask, Beebo—secrecy?"

"Is it possible?" Beebo said.

Venus nodded. "There are ways. I've had to learn them."

"With the other girls," Beebo said resentfully.

Venus stroked her shoulder. "You don't have to be jealous," she said. "I do."

"I'm jealous of all your husbands. All your lovers, male and female. Every slob who ever saw you in a movie."

Venus chuckled, letting her tripping voice twist her body back and forth on the blue silk, and Beebo suddenly forgot everything in her life that had preceded this moment. She lunged across the bed and caught Venus by the wrist, whirling her around just as Venus got to her feet.

For an instant they stayed as they were, breathless: Beebo stretched out the length of the bed, looking at Venus with her blue eyes shining like a cat's. Venus could feel the avalanche of passionate force trapped inside Beebo, ready to burst free at the flip of a finger. Already it was near exploding.

Venus stood there pulling against Beebo; warm, even hot to the point of perspiring. The light sweat excited Beebo far more than the perfume Venus usually wore. Her body was a soft pearly peach and between her breasts Beebo could see the quivering lift and fall of her sternum.

Beebo gave a swift tug on Venus's arm and brought her tumbling down on the bed, laughing. That laugh sprang the switch in Beebo. She stopped it with her mouth pressed on Venus's. And at last Venus submitted, all the twisting and teasing melting out of her. She let herself be kissed all over.

Beebo looked at her, stripped of the tinseled make-believe and the wisecracks; her lips parted and her eyes shut and her fine dark hair spilling pins over the pillow, coming down almost deliberately to work its witchery. Beebo kissed handfuls of it.

She fell asleep a long time later, still murmuring to Venus, still holding her possessively close, still wondering what she had done—or would have to do—to deserve it.

They were shaken out of sleep by the shrill ringing of the blue phone by Venus's bed. Venus answered sleepily, pulling the receiver onto the pillow by her ear where she lay across Beebo's chest.

But she came awake fast.

It was Leo Bogardus, calling from Hollywood. Beebo opened her eyes and watched while Venus flushed with wrath and suddenly burst into furious tears, threatening to hitchhike for Reno if she had to.

When she had slammed the phone down she told Beebo angrily that Leo had signed her to a television special series called, "Million Dollar Baby."

"I'm the Baby, but I'll never see the million bucks," she cried. "God, I hate TV! You get overexposed, underpaid, and worked to death. And all the lousy profit goes to the lousy sponsors."

Beebo stroked her and tried to calm her. After a while Venus sat still, her head in her hands. "Will you really go to Reno?" Beebo asked.

"No," she sighed. "He won't give me a divorce. I've tried everything . . . I'll go to Hollywood. I have no choice, Beebo. That's where they're going to film this little horror."

"Well, you were going anyway, for Toby."

"But not *this* soon! God damn that Leo! Well, at least I asked Toby first. I tried to do it right."

"How soon is *this* soon?" Beebo asked disconsolately.

"Tonight, if I can get reservations."

Beebo sat up in a mood of defiance. "Venus, you can't—"

"I have to, darling. Leo has ways of forcing me. Besides, I knew he'd been talking about this for months. But I didn't think it would come so soon." She glanced at Beebo and suddenly turned halfway around to kiss her mouth, startling Beebo.

"Is that goodby?" Beebo said, so coldly that Venus smiled at her.

"I told you I had a business proposition for you, you wicked child," she said. "And it's a damn good thing, or I could never explain to Toby why you spent the night. I'm going in right now and mess up the guest room. Bring your clothes."

Beebo pulled some of them on en route to the guest room. "What proposition?" she demanded, full of new hopes.

"Would you like to work for me?" Venus said, turning down the covers of the extra bed. She had thrown her negligee around herself.

"As what?" Beebo said. "Your companion?"

"No. Toby's. He says you know horses. Maybe you could work in the stables." She spiraled the sheets around on the bed and dumped a pillow on the floor. "That should do it. . . Well, don't stand there, darling, go home and pack," she said, glancing up at her astonished guest. "I want you back here before six tonight. There's a flight at eight I can usually get seats on. What's the matter, don't you want to go?"

"I—yes—I do," Beebo stammered.

"Well, go, darling. Go, go, go!" Venus said, clapping her hands under Beebo's nose and laughing. "And don't talk about it!" she hissed at Beebo's retreating back. "To *anybody!*"

***

Beebo drove downtown in a fog of confusion. After the first shock of flattered pleasure died away, she found herself preoccupied with Paula; so concerned, so anxious, that there were tears in her eyes she had to keep squeezing away, just to see the traffic ahead of her.

She would stop at Paula's apartment before she left. She had to. It was one thing to hurt somebody, but to do it like a snake, striking and slipping away before the victim knows what hit her—or who, or how—was beyond Beebo. She would tell Paula the truth herself, however much it cost them both in sorrow and resentment.

***

Beebo returned the Pasquini's truck, hoping to escape unnoticed. But Pete was lying in wait for her.

"So, you brought it back!" he said, grinning at her like a slick little fox. "We thought maybe you was taking a vacation in it."

"It's your truck," she said, getting down. "I don't want the damn thing." She turned to look at him. "I—uh . . . I'm quitting, Pete. I got another job."

"No kidding." He picked his teeth without disturbing the leer on his face. "Walking the dog for some swell lady?"

"I've had it with dogs," Beebo shot back. "I've been working for one all summer."

Pete left the pick in his teeth in order to fold his arms over his chest in imitation of Beebo when she was insulted. "So, Beebo," he said softly. "You don't like it here with us no more?"

"You tell Marie I'm sorry," Beebo said. "I like her fine."

"Sure you do, sweetheart. She wears a skirt," he said, rocking back and forth on his heels, needling her skillfully.

Beebo felt her temper expanding in her like hot air. It would have relieved her hugely to have punched him where it would hurt the worst. But that was no way to solve any problems—especially not with this covert, twisted young man who was trying to provoke the punch out of her on purpose.

"Marie is a friend of mine," Beebo said stiffly.

"Meaning I ain't? Ain't I been friendly to you, Beebo?" he said, sauntering toward her. "Well, I can fix that up right now." And with one abrupt movement he reached her side and threw her hard against the door of the truck, pulling her left arm up high in the back in a wrenchingly painful hammer lock. Beebo gave a gasp of shock and tried to break free. But for all her size and strength, she was still a girl, and no match for an angry, jealous man who had been wanting her and wanting to hurt her since he first saw her.

He forced his mouth on hers and when she struggled he bit her. She tried to knee him, and he pulled her arm up so hard they both thought for a moment he had broken it. Beebo went white with the pain, and leaned weakly against the door. Pete kissed her again, taking his time and not trying to unhinge her arm any more. The rough scratch of his whiskers, and smell of his winy breath, the push of his hard hips, almost made her faint.

"Now why do you make me hurt you, Beebo? Why do you do that?" he said in a tense whisper, as if it were all

her fault. "I don't want to hurt you. I want to be friends."
He kissed her again. "Don't that prove it?"

Beebo knew she was crying with pain and fury and sickness. "Let me go," she said hoarsely. She would have
screamed if she had had any strength, but her heart was
pounding and she was clammy pale, very near to toppling
over.

Pete released her suddenly, caught her as she stumbled,
and seated her on the running board. He shoved her head
down between her knees till the blood flow revived her.
"You don't got to put on a show," he said irritably. "I know
you don't want it from a man. I know you're gay, for
chrissakes. That's one thing I can spot a mile off. I like gay
girls, Beebo, in case you ain't noticed. I'm on your side.
Jesus God, you'd think I hated you, or something."

She looked at him sideways, when she thought she was
strong enough to stomach him. "Get out of my sight, you
rotten little creep," she said. "Go find Mona. She plays both
sides of the street."

"Ah, Mona's a drag," he said. "She's got this big thing
about putting you down on account of Paula. And you standing her up that night. I'm sorry about that, Beebo, it was
kind of my fault. It was me at her place that night."

"Oh, God," Beebo said, and let her head drop into her
hands again. "I should have known."

"Well, how am I supposed to know she's bringing somebody home? I know this girl for years. I drop in on her
when I feel like it."

"If you're so goddamn big with Mona, you call on *her*
when you feel like it, not me. Don't you come tomcatting
around to me, Pasquini." She stood up, weaving slightly,
and put a hand on the fender to steady herself.

He stood beside her, and she saw that her angry disgust
with him was beginning to annoy him. He wanted a fight—
that was part of the build-up for him. But he wanted an
eventual surrender, on his terms. Beebo showed no signs of
yielding and her revulsion for him was plain enough to
anger him.

"Maybe Mona was right," he said, his voice getting thin
and mean. "Maybe you need a lesson before you learn
what's good for you."

"I don't need any from you," Beebo spat at him. "I'm
getting out of here right now, and you'll never see me
again."

"I'll catch up with you one of these days," he said. "No matter where you go."

"The hell you will. You're not going to chase me all the way to California just to kick my can," Beebo said hotly. But when Pete began to smile, she rethought her words in sudden panic.

"California?" Pete grinned. "Well, that'd almost be worth the trip. I think I'd like it out there. Maybe get another autograph from Venus. Huh, butch? You could work it for me."

Beebo looked at him, her face a mask but her heart dismayed. "You believe it if you want to," she said. "If you think I'd work anything for you, you're more of a fool than a creep."

She turned and ran out of the delivery yard while he watched her. He didn't like to let her go. But at least she was leaving a trail behind her; one that shouldn't be hard to follow. Pete smiled.

Beebo and Pat drank a few parting shots while Beebo packed her strap-fastened wicker bag and waited for Jack to get home. She was ready to go and a little tight when he rolled in at five.

"Having a party?" he asked.

"A goodby party. I'm getting off your back, Jackson," Beebo said. "I'm going to Hollywood."

"They were bound to call you sooner or later," Jack said. "Anyone can see you've got talent."

Beebo looked at the floor. "I'm going with Venus," she said, humiliated by it. "I didn't know what else to do, Jack," she added vehemently. "I couldn't live with Paula. I couldn't live with you, not if I wanted to keep your friendship. I had to quit the Pasquini job—Pete's been helling after me since I started. And besides—besides . . ." She stopped, throwing her arms out and letting them drop against her sides.

"And besides, Venus asked you to go?" Jack said. Beebo nodded. Jack made no comment, but she knew he thought it was asinine of her. "Did you ever write to tell your father where you are?"

"I thought about it, but I didn't know what to say."

"Have you told Paula?"

"Not yet. I was waiting till you got home."

"Paula's more important."

"Jack, damn it, Paula doesn't own me!" she cried, angry because she knew he was right. "My father doesn't own me. I don't have to tell them every move I make, just because they—"

"They love you," he finished for her. "Listen to me, little pal. You came to this town to grow up and find yourself. You can do that without breaking hearts. And so help me, Beebo, the first one you're going to break is your own."

Beebo sat down on the bed. "Jack, I didn't ask Paula Ash to love me," she said. "I never said I loved *her.*"

"Well, that makes it all swell."

"She's a sweet, fine girl. I wouldn't hurt her for anything. But what can I do?"

"Shall I give her that message?" Jack asked

"I'll tell her myself!" Beebo said, stung. But she wished, with all the force of shame and indecision, that she didn't have to.

Jack lighted a cigarette thoughtfully. "I've gotten to know her a lot better the last few weeks. She was over last night, when you didn't show again. There's a new girl in her life, Beebo." He tossed his match in an ash tray, scrutinizing Beebo's startled face. "Miss Plaid Pajamas. You know her?"

Beebo was shaken. "I know about her," she said. "Oh, Paula . . ." She recalled the sleeping pills, the tears. Paula's red hair, her scent, her green eyes luminous with love. She pressed a hand over her mouth, half to control a sob, half in recollection of Paula's first gesture of love.

"Regrets?" Jack said gently.

Beebo took a deep breath. "It's Venus I love," she said softly, but it was strangely hard to say.

"Well, that's that," Jack said. "Off you go to follow your star."

"I can't help myself," Beebo said, and that, at least, was true. "I'd rather cut off my arm than hurt Paula, believe me."

Jack smiled and lifted a hand to show he would not sermonize. "I wish you well, pal. I wish you love," he said. "I only wish—"

The phone rang. They all looked at each other. Finally Pat answered it, while Jack and Beebo watched him. "It's for you, Beebo," Pat said, holding out the receiver. She took it, looking apprehensively at him, and he mouthed the word, "Paula."

She shut her eyes. "Hello?" she said.

"Hello, Beebo."

"Paula, I was just coming over. I—I wanted to tell you..." Her voice trailed off.

"I know. I called to wish you Godspeed."

"You what?" Beebo wheeled around to look at the two men.

"Pete called me," Paula said. "He likes to play town crier."

"God damn him!" Beebo exploded. "Paula, I'm so sorry. I wanted to tell you myself, at least. I—what did he say?"

"He said you were going to California with Venus Bogardus," Paula said simply.

"Is that all?"

"It doesn't matter about the rest, Beebo. Pete always exaggerates. I just wanted to tell you, it's all right. I think you should go. It'll be a great experience." Her voice faltered ever so slightly, and Beebo wanted desperately to hold her, to be able to say, "No, I'll stay with you," and somehow still be able to go with Venus. She felt as if she were being physically ripped in half.

"I'm not being melodramatic, honest!" Paula said and she managed a small laugh. "I'm a hopeless optimist. I think you'll be back. Or I couldn't be such a good sport. Mona says 'good sport' is just another word for 'sucker'. She's wrong, isn't she? Beebo?"

"Yes, Paula. She's wrong, honey." Beebo felt her own voice break and Paula said quickly, "Don't come over, there's no need. It's much easier on the phone. Write to me now and then."

"Paula? Is that girl in the plaid pajamas pestering you again?" Beebo said anxiously. "Jack said—"

"Jack is my knight in shining armor. If things get bad, he'll come rescue me. He has before." There was a pause. Beebo glanced gratefully at Jack and then she heard Paula saying, "Goodby, Beebo. Good luck. No, *bad* luck, and come home soon. I love you, you know. You worm."

"I know." Beebo swallowed. "Goodby, Paula." She let the receiver drop into its cradle and stood with her head against the wall for a minute.

"You look like you're set for a real pleasure cruise," Jack said, noting her wan face and full eyes.

Beebo picked up her bag in a brusque motion and strode to the door. But she couldn't turn the handle. "Thanks for everything, Jack," she said, full of fears at cutting loose from her only friend in the new world.

"Come back when Venus shows you out," he said kindly. "Our bunk is your bunk," and he put an arm over Pat's shoulder.

"She won't show me out," Beebo said with what pride she still had. "Jackson, take care of that Paula for me." She caught his shoulders in a hard grip. "I don't know if I can stand to do this to her."

"You're doing it," Jack commented.

Beebo looked at her bag, then grabbed it and ran down the hall and front steps without daring to look back.

Jack shut the door softly and gazed at Pat. "You're tanked," he said indulgently. His thoughts were elsewhere.

"You didn't tell her about Pete and Mona," Pat said. "Why?"

"She's going three thousand miles from here. Let's hope she doesn't need to worry about those two twerps any more."

"I've heard some of their sickening stories about Beebo around the bars lately," Pat brooded.

"Well, don't give Pete and Mona all the credit," Jack said shrewdly. "Not that they ever say anything nice about anybody. But it helps to have someone else feeding them information . . . Somebody whose initials are Pat Kynaston." It was as sharp a reproof as Jack had given him.

"I only say *good* things about Beebo!" Pat protested, instantly wounded. "I adore that girl!"

"I know. Good things. That's all they need. Somebody in the Cellar heard you carrying on Tuesday afternoon: Beebo's father, her home town, even that thing at the livestock exhibition. You want Pete to hear that, Pat? Think what he could do with it, if he wanted to."

Pat sank dismally to the living room floor. "Lord, I didn't realize. I thought I was telling them how great she is. I thought Pete and Mona were inventing their stuff."

"They are, but not all of it. The nearer the truth they can get, the louder they'll shout it—screwed around just enough to make Beebo look like the type of witch decent citizens should spend their Sundays burning."

Pat's chin trembled. "I could strike myself dumb," he said bitterly.

Jack sat down and put an arm around him. "Just watch it, lover. She's put herself in a spot to be crucified, if Pete has anything against her ... and Mona already has, or thinks she has. All that girl needs is a whim, anyway."

The Bogardus home was located in a lush and secluded area of Mandeville Canyon Road in Bel-Air._It was huge, elegant, well-staffed and maintained. The grounds were a glowing sweep of hand-tailored grass, tropical palms exploding against the sky like green rockets, swimming pools—two—and the noisy brilliance of equatorial blooms.

Toby showed Beebo around. They walked over the lawns in bare feet, and Beebo marveled at it. It dazzled her eyes enough to take her mind off her sore heart a while. "Every time you push a button, somebody runs up with a martini," she said. "It's fantastic, Toby."

"I wish it weren't," Toby said. "I wish I had an ordinary house to live in."

"Poor little rich boy," she grinned. "Wants an ordinary mama and papa, too, no doubt. Maybe when you're older you'll be glad you're different."

"How would you know? You didn't have to grow up this way."

"No, but I had to grow up," Beebo said. "I would have traded my problems for yours any day."

"That's what Leo says. His family didn't have a dime," Toby told her as they picked their way over the manufactured rustic rocks circling one of the pools.

"Where is that guy, anyway?" Beebo said. Leo worried her, like a family ghost: much was made of him, yet he was rarely seen.

"He's in S.F.," Toby said. "The servants expect him back the end of the week. He's talking to a sponsor for Mom's show."

"What's he like? How do you talk to him?" Beebo said.

"Oh, you don't have to worry. He likes kids. Beside, he's been talking about getting somebody to help with the horses for years." Beebo felt a sudden wave of relief. She had not brought up the reason for her presence here, and it seemed odd to her that Toby hadn't either—till she realized how Venus had explained it to him. "Besides," Toby added, "it'll be nice to have you around. You can help me with my homework. You ought to be good with the biology. For once, Mom didn't get a square for me."

Beebo wondered how many other young people had preceded her in this household; how many synthetic friendships with young tutors, horsemen, and valets Venus had tried to promote for Toby, hoping he would turn into the easy-mannered socialite she somehow pictured him when he was grown.

At least it was reassuring to have a job, something legitimate to do to explain her membership on the family staff.

Toby sat down at the pool's edge and put his legs in the cool water. He was well-developed for his age, though still only five-feet-six. Beebo looked at his young male body, so carelessly normal, and she envied him painfully.

"Leo's jealous, but he's tolerant, too," Toby said. "I mean, he's put up with so damn many men tailing Mom, he knows how to outsmart or outlast all of them. He doesn't like it much, but he knows she needs them. At least, that's what *she* says. I don't know why a woman can't be happy with one man ... especially if he's a good one."

"Some women can," Beebo said. But she was thinking that a man of Leo's knowledge and well-founded suspicions would doubtless take one look at Beebo and know good and damn well what his beautiful wife was up to There was nothing to do but wait till he got home for the showdown.

🝿

She confronted Venus with her misgivings about Leo. "He won't hurt you, darling," Venus said. "Don't offend him and don't defy ´him. He's nervous as hell with a girl around the house."

"If he puts up with your men, why not with your women?" Beebo said gloomily.

"I never cared much for the other girls," Venus said circuitously. "Only for you."

"Well, that ought to ingratiate me with Leo for good," Beebo said.

"Leo's afraid for my career. I guess that's the only thing we agree on. My 'normal' affairs have scandalized enough

people as it is. A gay love—if it got out—would finish me,
Beebo." She looked at her apologetically. "It's hard for me
to fight Leo. He—sort of—owns me. Economically, I mean,
like he owns this house."

"Do you really hate him, Venus?"

Venus picked at a nonexistent thread on her skirt. "I
guess he's a kindly man at heart. I think I've ruined his
temperament." She put her arms around Beebo as they
lounged on her private sun porch. "Bèebo, are you sorry
you're gay? Are you bitter about it?"

"Yes," Beebo said, and Venus frowned. "All day long,
when you go off to the studio, I'm sorry as hell. At night, I
get down on my knees and give thanks."

"There must have been bad times before I came along."

Beebo surfaced from a kiss on Venus's golden shoulder.
"When I was younger, I used to look out my bedroom window on summer nights," she said, "and the brightest star in
the sky was Venus. I wanted to reach out and take it in my
hand. Put it in a box and make it mine forever."

Venus chuckled. "I'm not in a box yet, thank God. And
I'm a lot handier than that dreadful planet."

Beebo settled closer to her and said with comfortable intimacy, "I want to share so many things with you, Venus. I
want to see you sparkling at parties . . . take you shopping . . .
watch you at rehearsals . . ."

"You can't," Venus said, putting a finger on Beebo's nose.
Beebo brushed it off, protesting. "There won't be time, for
one thing," Venus explained. "Not while we're filming. And
besides, Leo won't let you. You're too young, you're too noticeable, and you're too—well, female. I'll have all I can do
to keep him from putting *you* in a box."

"Well, of all the goddamn nonsense!" Beebo said, cloud-
ing up. "I just want to drive you places and wait. Watch
you from a distance. I'm willing to be a servant, Venus,
but not a dog on a leash."

"Darling, use your head. What if we were seen together,
and it was common knowledge you lived here and went
everywhere with me and—oh, Beebo, don't look so crushed.
I don't like it either."

"You don't want me around where you have to look at
me all the time," Beebo sulked.

"Darling, I can't look at you enough!" Venus said, half-
amused and half-concerned at the outburst. "You're the hand-
somest thing I ever saw."

"Is that what I am? A thing?" Beebo said, swinging her legs to the ground. She was surprised at herself for being pettish. But the moment she questioned herself about it, her thoughts flew to Paula. *Paula would never talk to me this way.*

"That's not what I meant and you know it," Venus said. "You don't want your *things* following you around in public."

"Beebo!" Venus cried, hurt. "I love you!" Her words made Beebo turn back and take Venus in her arms.

"I'm sorry," she said, realizing all at once that Venus was crying.

"I adore you," Venus wept. "I feel so free with you. Able to do the things that used to terrify me. Able to *think* about them without shame. I never let go like this with anybody in my life, Beebo." She clung to her. "Darling, don't shout at me for the things we can't have. Be glad with me for the things we *can*. I'm trying to look at the world more charitably, Beebo—for you and for Toby. You try to look at me that way. Don't just love me, understand me. I need it so." She wiped her tears on Beebo's shirt and glanced up at her.

"You know something silly? I want to dress up for you. I want to sit and hear you talk. I don't care whether I say a word. I want to be a real actress, not an obedient puppet. I even want to mother my son. When you tell me to do a thing, I fret for the chance to try."

Beebo stared at her, amazed at this oddly touching admission. "I even got a bunch of pamphlets from the Department of Agriculture," Venus said, "on how to raise chickens and wean calves."

Beebo succumbed to laughter. "All you had to do was ask me," she said.

"I'll show them to you," Venus offered, trying to get up, but Beebo pulled her down again, her fit of pique soothed away.

"I'll take your word for it," she said. "Besides, I've got you half undressed. What would the servants say?"

"They'd say Venus is in love," Venus answered, letting Beebo hold her. "And they'd be right."

Beebo made love to her with a new tenderness. And yet, again, when they fell asleep, she dreamed restlessly of Paula Ash.

Venus began to spend all the daylight hours, and some of the night, with the production staff of *Million Dollar Baby*. Leo returned from San Francisco, but Beebo would not have known it if Toby hadn't pointed it out.

They had been all day riding Leo's horses in the boulder meadow surrounding the Bogardus estate, and when they got in, Toby announced, "Leo's back."

"How do you know?" Beebo asked, suddenly on her guard.

"Orange juice glass," Toby said, pointing to a brandy snifter with an orange puddle at the bottom, sitting on an end table. "That's all Leo ever drinks. He says we've got orange trees in the yard and the juice is free. He likes things that are free. Besides, he's always on a health kick. Right now it's citric acid. When he's home there's always a mess of sticky glasses around."

"He's not going to like seeing *me* around," Beebo said glumly.

"Why not?" Toby looked at her curiously. "The stables are cleaned up for the first time in a year. And Mom is getting so nice to be around...Gee, Beebo, he'll probably hang a medal on you."

Beebo understood from his answer how little aware he was of his mother's relationship with her. He had grown to trust Beebo, as well as like her, and as far as he knew, she was there only to help out with the horses during the day and look over his homework at night. The fact that she had been able to encourage Venus and Toby to try to know and respect each other at last was the frosting on the cake.

But after he went to bed, Beebo would go to Venus's room. They were lovers at night, but during the day, if Venus was home, she had to be as breezy and casual with Beebo as she was with everybody else.

As for Leo, Beebo didn't meet him for nearly a week. He got up at six A.M. and left the house by seven, before Beebo was stirring. He looked in on her with Venus once. Beebo was awakened early by the click of the bedroom door shutting behind him. But when she asked Venus about it, Venus only said, "I told him you were a farm kid. He likes that. It makes you a sort of walking health exhibit."

"Does he like the fact that I'm a girl?"

"Not a bit," Venus said with a grin, refusing to spoil the moment by elaborating.

Beebo dodged around squads of empty orange-juice glasses for several days with the eerie feeling that the ghost who emptied them would come cackling out of the rafters at her before long.

The night they finally met, Beebo had been living under Leo's roof for over two weeks, using his hospitality without ever having seen or spoken to him.

She was sitting in the huge recreation room with Venus and Toby, watching TV and listening to Venus tell about the casting problems, wardrobe, scripts she had read.

Beebo commented quietly, "It takes up your whole life, doesn't it?"

Venus looked at her anxiously. "You're lonesome during the day, aren't you, darling?" She threw a guarded glance at Toby, but he spoke without taking his eyes off the TV screen: "What do you mean, lonesome, Mom? She's busy all day. Besides, I get home from school at four, and I'm better company than you are."

Venus smiled and reached out to hug him. She startled herself as much as Toby, but he endured the embrace with less embarrassment than he would have felt the month before in New York.

"When is that PTA thing at school?" Venus said. "I want to go with you, Toby." *Toby.* His name. The first time in memory she had called him that when she wasn't in a rage. Beebo saw the smile in his eyes.

"You can go if you promise not to call anybody 'darling' or wear a knit dress," he said.

Venus gasped and Beebo laughed at him, looking behind his back at Venus. "All right, darling, I promise," Venus said wryly. "If *you* promise not to ditch me this year, and tell lies to your friends about how I do the dishes every night, like all the other mothers."

Toby smiled without looking at her, and it was a bargain. Beebo felt her own satisfaction at this bashful honesty between mother and son. And then Venus surprised her by saying, "Beebo, I'm going to get you a car. It isn't fair to make you shovel manure all day."

"What would I do with a car?" Beebo said, mystified at the sudden generosity.

"You could ferry Toby around. Pick up the groceries for Miss Pinch. Maybe we'll get something to eat that isn't poisonous for a change."

"Miss Pinch doesn't use poison," said a gravelly voice. "Just too much paprika. It's her Hungarian heritage."

Beebo turned around with a start to see, at long last, Leo Bogardus coming down the wide steps to join them.

"Well, darling, you should know," Venus said. "You and Miss Pinch have such a beautiful thing together."

Leo strode across the room, a solid, rather squarely built man; gray hair and gray suit; neat and natty and silver-eyed behind his black French-framed glasses. He was about Beebo's height and attractive without being handsome.

Beebo stood up to greet him, somewhat subdued. "Mr. Bogardus? I'm Beebo," she said and held out her hand.

Leo put a just-drained orange-juice glass on a table. "I know," he said. "I hope you'll be comfortable with us, for as long as you stay, Beebo." He shook her hand briefly.

Beebo wasn't sure if he meant to be sarcastic or not. She let her hand drop awkwardly and sat down again as Bogardus settled in a chair, trying to size him up. His face was clean-lined and his manner decisive. She imagined him quick to anger, stubborn, and hard to handle when he was mad.

"You're picking them younger every year, Venus," Leo said five minutes later, without once having looked at Beebo in the meantime.

Venus grimaced a warning at him over Toby's head to shut up. Leo nodded wearily.

"I don't pick them, darling; they pick me, she said in a pointed whisper.

To Beebo's discomfiture, Leo gazed straight at her then and laughed with a honk of mirth. Moments later he got up and left as abruptly as he came, and Beebo spoke not another word to him for several more days. She had just begun to hope she wouldn't have to at all. It would have suited her, not because she disliked him—she didn't. Considering her position in his house, he was more than decent. But he scared her. He was no ghost, but he was still the unknown quantity.

Fortunately, the next few times they saw each other there was only time for small talk, and no more.

Venus got her the car before the end of the week—a silver sport coupé—and Beebo and Toby cruised around Hollywood and the coastal communities when he got home from school in the afternoons.

Toby kept on talking, confiding in her, and she began to see how much he respected and liked Leo; how strongly he sided with his step-father in any argument between Leo and Venus; what a source of strength Leo was to him. Here was no dirty dog like the rest of the boys. Here was a man to admire and emulate, and Toby did. Leo was good for him, and Beebo was glad they had each other.

Beebo felt conspicuous, even though they rarely stopped the car or got out. She was afraid somebody would recognize Toby, and she hated to be stared at, with her short hair and slacks and casual cotton shirts. Skirts looked wrong on her and men's pants looked fake.

She looked the best in riding wear: a formal tight-waisted jacket and white stock, hard velvet cap, smooth leather boots, jodhpurs. The kind of clothes she used to wear at shows around Juniper Hill, when she won ribbons for jumping other people's horses. She had a lithe elegance that the riding clothes dramatized.

But you can't walk into Schwab's drugstore in formal riding clothes. At least not if you have orders to make yourself invisible. Beebo began to feel hemmed in. The only safe place in the county of Los Angeles was the Bogardus estate, and even there she worried about guests and servants.

Miss Pinch disapproved sniffily of her, but she'd probably hold her tongue for Leo's sake. Mrs. Sack was as plump and amiable as a currant bun, and about as perceptive. The others were a shadowy and obsequious crew whom Beebo rarely saw, yet she distrusted them all.

In the evenings, when she was alone, Beebo started writing to Paula and Jack. They were short letters at first, though the ones to Jack were longer and franker. To Paula, she described the flash of October across the southern California landscape; the whipped-cream weather, the purple hills, the flowers.

To Jack she said, "Venus is wonderful. She's working so hard I hardly ever see her, though. But she says she'd spend every minute with me if she could. Nobody else exists but me. It's funny—that looks so made-up on paper. But she really said it, and I believe her.

"I almost never see Leo, either. When I run into him, I ask about his diet and he asks me about the horses. I think he's a good man—good for Toby—but I'd hate like hell to have him mad at me.

"I guess the one thing I don't like about it here is being alone so much. Even Toby's gone till late in the day. What a nice kid he is, underneath the shell. He wants to be somebody in his own right, and I'll bet he makes it.

"How is that doll you room with? Please write and tell me *everything* about Paula. Best—Beebo."

There was no trouble between Leo and Beebo until the day she and Toby picked Venus up at the studio in Television City. They knew she was coming home early to prepare for a party, and they talked one another into it like a pair of school boys ditching class for a day to have a ball. It seemed quite innocuous, and yet rather worldly and exciting when they discussed it, tooling around in the silver car.

But when they actually arrived in that principality of a parking lot, they were rather abashed.

"What if she doesn't see us?" Toby said.

"That'd probably be all for the best," Beebo said.

But Venus saw them plain and clear when she emerged from the building, surrounded by aides and admirers. She walked briskly to the car, surprising the crowd which began to straggle after her, opened the door, and pulled Toby out by his collar.

"Darling," she said smoothly, "I want you to meet Mr. Wilkins and Mr. Klein. Boys, will you introduce him around for me?" She smiled at one of the men who quickly obliged her.

Venus thrust her head into the car. "Beebo, what the hell!" she hissed.

"I'm sorry—we thought it would be fun," Beebo faltered.

"You thought—" Venus shut her eyes a minute and swallowed her temper. "Oh, balls. I'm not going to get mad at you. I can't, I'm too much in love with you. But oh! you fool, *Leo* can. I hope to God he doesn't hear about it." She withdrew, collared Toby again, and popped him into the front seat, sitting down beside him to wave and smile at the group of people so charmingly that no one but herself was likely to be noticed as they pulled away.

The sponsors for *Million Dollar Baby* were openhanded, despite long rehearsal hours and high rents and salaries, because they figured that with Venus in the show, it had to be a smash. So Leo, anxious to live up to their expectations, worked her unremittingly day and night throughout October.

Venus not only had to act, she had to dance and sing. The big number for the second show, then in production, was "I'm Putting My All On You."

"I never sang before in my life!" Venus yelled at Leo.

"Marilyn Monroe can do it," he said softly, infuriating her.

"Leo, *I can't sing!*" she cried, trying to explain fundamentals to him as if he were retarded.

"Well, don't," Beebo said, surprising both of them. She was watching the scene in the Bogardus rec room. Leo threw her an irritated look, and Beebo explained quickly, "*Talk* the song. Whisper and wiggle like Marlene Dietrich. Venus, Leo's right. You have to live up to the title. *Million Dollar Baby.* God, you ought to be able to do anything for that price, including grand opera."

Leo laughed, a clattering jangle of a sound, while Venus salved her wounds in prim silence, peeved at Beebo for backing up her husband.

"Now, you see?" Leo told her, waving at Beebo. "That's it. Beebo can see it. Why can't you? I tell you the same damn thing and you squawk at me like a fishwife. Okay, I'm not young and handsome, but I'm smart. That's how you got where we are today. You do this right, and you'll get more than that million."

Beebo watched him with interest as he directed Venus. He was electrically alive, cunning in the way he teased and bullied and loved the song out of her. Beebo could almost feel the tune, the words, Venus herself, coming to life. Leo was a good seat-of-the-pants psychologist.

After several run-throughs he turned to Beebo. "You're helping," he said laconically. "She sings better for you than for me. I show her what to do. You make her feel it." He scratched his head, then let his shirt-sleeved arms drop. "That's okay, as long as she doesn't lose it at the studio," he decided. "Maybe we'll let you watch some other scenes at home, Beebo."

Beebo grinned. It was a relief to participate at last in the paramount sphere of Venus's life.

"It helps to have her in love again," Leo observed candidly. "Makes her much more responsive."

"Don't talk about me as if I were a machine," Venus flashed at him. "And don't laugh at me. I know how silly you think it is. I *know* Beebo's too young."

Leo sat down on a leather-topped bar stool. "You're happy, Beebo?" he asked.

Beebo nodded, wondering where he was going.

"It's rough, isn't it? Venus isn't home much these days. And you have nothing to do but goof around in that car."

"I get along," Beebo said cautiously. "Are you against the car, Leo?"

"No, just the taxi service." There was a deadly pause, and Leo's face folded into a heavy frown. Beebo was lost for a moment, till Venus sighed and lighted a cigarette with angry movements. "Who squealed?" she said.

"It doesn't matter," Leo said crisply. "I don't like the idea of you two ladies consorting in public."

"Leo, don't pull that solemn face on me," Venus said. "She and Toby came together. They picked me up at work. Nobody saw her face—"

"Nobody had to," Leo said, taking a drag on his cigarette.

"Look, Leo, let's not fight over it," Beebo said. "Be reasonable. Things are working out all right. I'm discreet and I swear I'll never—"

"I know, you'll never do anything to hurt darling Venus," Leo said acidly. His eyes narrowed, and he began to pace the room. When either of the women tried to speak he silenced them with a gesture.

Finally Venus said, "That poor kid never goes anywhere. She deserves—"

"She deserves to torpedo your career, just to alleviate her ennui?"

"Well, damn it, Leo, if you turn her out, I'm going with her. I happen to be in love with Beebo and I don't give a damn what you think of it."

"Venus, go upstairs," Leo said. He lighted a cigar—a concession to his mental distress. When Venus objected he said, "Will you please go?" as if she were a naughty child. He was almost fatherly with her. "I can't talk to Beebo with such a distraction as you around." He made her hope he and Beebo would understand each other. She left slowly, telling Beebo not to believe a word Leo said.

Leo stopped his pacing and sat down to face Beebo. "There's too much at stake, Beebo," he said at once. "I can't tolerate even small slip-ups. Venus is silly, but that's no excuse for you. You're a sensible kid."

"But Leo, such a little thing—"

"Nothing is little, Beebo," he said. "Let's be frank with each other. It worries me enough that you're so young. At least her other lovers were nearer her own age. But to have you a girl..." He puffed rapidly on the cigar. "I won't disguise the fact that I find you rather... well, unsympathetic. I think most normal men would. Partly from masculine resentment, I guess. A natural revulsion for women who parade as poor imitations of men, but—"

"You liked me well enough when you got home and found Venus acting like a lovable human being," Beebo interrupted him heatedly. "I'm the same person now as then. I just happened to pick her up in a parking lot and drive her home."

"The guy who told me about it," Leo said thoughtfully, "said Venus was picked up by a good-looking boy. A friend of Toby's he supposed. Of course, you were hard to see inside the car. But Venus had told him, when she saw you pull up, that you were one of the servants. So he was a little surprised to see her jump in the front seat with you... and you didn't have a uniform on, either. He was giving me the old elbow-in-the-ribs treatment." He blew cigar smoke at the ceiling without looking at her.

Beebo cleared her throat. "It was so innocent," she said.

"Nothing is innocent," Leo said flatly. "Especially a classy young butch on the make."

"Damn it, Leo!" she said. "I'm clean, I'm healthy, I've worked hard all my life. And so help me God, I'm not ashamed of being what I can't *help* being. That's the road to madness." Her cheeks were crimson.

"Well said, Beebo," he acknowledged calmly. "You're right—but so am I. You might as well face up to the world's opinion. I speak for the ordinary prejudiced guy, too busy to learn tolerance, too uninformed to give a damn. We are in the majority. I admire your guts but not your person. As for the intolerance, it's mostly emotional and illogical. I can't help it and neither can most men. I apologize. I warn you that it's there. I add: it's beside the point.

"What I think of you is less important than what the people in Venus's world think. I don't care what you say, somebody in this world besides the Bogardus family knows you're living here and laying my wife. It's no secret from the servants, you know."

Beebo caught her breath and Leo looked at her piercingly. "I've heard them laughing about it," he said. "And our servants bat the breeze with the other stars' servants. They know more guff about us—what we eat, when we pee, who our lovers are—than all the gossip columnists rolled into one and stashed behind the keyhole. All I can say is, I pay them and most of them like me. Not Venus, not you. But *me*. I hope they respect my privacy, but I know human nature. Sooner or later they'll blab."

Beebo rubbed a hand over her eyes, angry and frightened. "Well, if it's so bad, why the hell did Venus bring me out here? She must have known how it would be."

"Venus isn't very big for denying herself what she wants," Leo said. "Besides, there's a lot to be said in your favor. Venus is more stable. She means it when she says she loves you. I believe that, Beebo, and I hope you do. Her love is a unique gift, and I tell you honestly that I envy you it. It has transformed her."

Beebo was flattered and surprised to hear this coming from Leo. She felt suddenly sorry for him. He seemed gray all over, from his damp shirt to his strained face.

"I struggled for years to win her love . . . my God, just to win her attention. I finally decided there was no love in her, not even for poor Toby. You proved me wrong, and in a way I'm grateful to you. Venus will never be an easy woman to live with, but she's improved measurably with you, and I think some of it will last long after you've left us."

"Left you?" Beebo opened her mouth to protest but was bull-dozed by his rush of words.

"Her tantrums now are kid stuff compared to the blasts we used to get. Now, I get a sort of half-assed cooperation. Toby gets some affection. The servants get some peace. And that's a lot when you're starting from zero."

Beebo was taken aback by it.

"I thank you for that, Beebo. I thank you for being discreet most of the time, when it's boring and humiliating. But I have to look at the other side of the coin. Venus has survived some potentially filthy scandals because she has the smartest director and press agent in the world: me. But it took all I've got and more to keep them out of the papers. Sometimes the only way was to jump in front of her and take the crap meant for Venus on my own kisser, just to keep her clean. I'd do it again if I had to, but I don't want to do it for you. If it gets out she's sleeping with a girl, we're dead. All of us.

"Venus makes a touching speech about walking out of here with you if anything goes wrong, but she won't, Beebo. Don't kid yourself. Don't get hurt worse than you have to be when the end comes."

Beebo was too mad at him and too proud to admit any such thing. "The end won't come, Leo," she flared. "She's in love with me and that makes her a different woman from the one you've always known. You can't make predictions about her."

"I can predict anything about that woman, Beebo," he said in a sad voice that mourned the passing of mystery in his love. "I wish there were something left in her for me to worship. You forget that there was a great love in her life before Beebo Brinker came along and that love will last to the end, long after Beebo falls by the wayside. That's self-love. She loves herself more than she loves you."

"You're unjust, Leo. She's told me—"

"Sure—that she only loves the money, the career. Why, Beebo? Because they glorify the *woman*. The woman she loves —herself."

Beebo stared at him, silenced.

"You flatter her, you kid her, you make a good try at understanding her, despite your blind spots. And you're also nuts about her, which she finds very ingratiating. Plus the

fact of your femininity... something I will never understand.
You know, she's tried this Lesbian stuff before."

"She said you objected pretty violently."

"Hell, yes. It's much more dangerous than a normal affair.
I'm no blue-stocking. I'm for falling in love and making it
work, as long as it doesn't hurt other people. It has nothing
to do with my emotional prejudices. Intellectually, I'm damned
fair. The only two people Venus hurts are me and Toby. I
give her hell about Toby; I try to protect him. But letting
Venus hurt me is the abiding condition of my life. The rock
on which our marriage is built."

Beebo listened, rooted with fascination, shock, pity, distaste. He was making an accomplice of her by revealing the
secrets of his life with Venus; putting her in a spot where she
would be virtually obligated to help him, if only to save all
their skins.

"But when I see disaster coming," Leo went on, "that will
crush our son, destroy her career, ruin all our lives—I have
to act. Beebo, you're eighteen. You're among the adults. I
lay this on the line to you. I'd ask you to leave of your own
free will, if I thought you had any left. But you're too infatuated for that. All I'll say now is, stay out of sight, watch
the servants, and do as I say."

"Look, Leo, I know you're bending over backwards for
me," Beebo said. "I appreciate it. Since I've been here you've
been just a face to me, but a kind enough face. Now I see
you're not just an operator—you're an intelligent and honest
man. And it's too bad Venus won't admit it. I think she
could have loved you if she had.

"But if you're working up to telling me that no matter
how good a kid I am, I'm going to have to pack up one
of these days and blow, I'm sorry. I can't go." *Unless,* she
thought, *I go for Paula. I'll never go because I'm pushed.*

"No," he said. "I'll tell you precisely what the situation is.
I should have talked to you about this before. You should
know where I stand. It must never—under any circumstances
—get out that you're queer, much less involved with Venus."
He spoke without self-consciousness, his voice coming sharp
and sure. Beebo wondered if his long experience with "ar-
tistic" types had made him a little wiser than other men.

"I found Venus when she was about your age: just plain
Jeanie Jacoby from Fostoria, Ohio," Leo said. "She wrote
me a letter saying she was beautiful, available, and hated
her family, and would I please make her a star. She enclosed

a snapshot. And she added that she was writing me because I was the biggest agent in Hollywood. It was pure guff, but her picture got me.

"Later I found out she wrote the same letter to twenty other guys. But I was the one who fell for it and sent her a ticket for L.A. I figured if only half of what I saw in the pic was for real, I could still sell her and make a fortune. Well, she came. I saw. She conquered. I named her Venus for the obvious reason, and Bogardus because I guessed I'd never have the chance to give her my own name any other way. I never thought we'd marry.

"I loved her the day we met, for all the wrong reasons, and I love her still. My reasons haven't improved any.

"I was just an agent, but I went out and worked my ass off and got her going. I launched her. She would have sunk after a couple of the flops she made if they hadn't let me direct her finally. I made an actress out of her and saved her career.

"When her star rose, so did mine. Her success was the only thing we loved together and cried over and cherished—together. I watched her run through five lousy marriages in ten years. And when she was weary and demoralized, I stepped in like Sir Galahad, thinking I could make her happy. I was delirious when she said yes, and I think even Venus was pleased. Till the honeymoon was over.

"I suppose she's told you what it was like. Things have been more peaceful with you around. But we've driven each other to mayhem in years past. She thinks she wants her freedom. But she'd come back to me, Beebo, even if she got it. She needs me as much as I need her. (Don't tell her that, she won't believe it.) I'll never divorce her. I love her enough to prefer the torment of living with her to the torment of living without her."

He stopped a moment, fixing Beebo with his silver eyes to impress his next words on her. "That is one hell of a terrible lot of love, Beebo," he said slowly. "I doubt if you could top it. There's one thing Venus and I agree on: I made her and I'm keeping her on top. If she didn't care about that, she wouldn't care about me, either.

"Listen, Beebo. I don't want her ever to love you more than herself. And if I see it coming, I'll fight you. I'll bring out every drop of self-love and self-pity and money-lust in her system—and she's got more of it than she has blood.

Because if she drops her career, she'll drop me with it." He
paused and they looked at each other.

"That's it, Beebo," Leo said at last. "I'm sorry if it sounds
egotistic to you. You just mind me, and maybe we'll make
it for a while. I don't know what you can do about Toby. He
doesn't get the picture about you and his mother yet, but he
will. He's a bright kid. But don't go out of your way to tell
him. It's going to stagger him. I'll try to explain when he
catches on.

"If anything comes up, deny it. I give you this chance
because of what you've done for Venus. Don't make me
regret it."

"I don't know whether to thank you or kick you in the
slats," Beebo said sourly. "You make it sound like a great
life."

"Did anyone tell you to expect something else?" Leo said.
"You've been living it the last two months. You should be
used to it."

"Used to it but not fond of it," she said.

"But fond of Venus . . . enough to put up with it? Because
if you aren't, say so. I've been honest enough with you to hurt
myself, Beebo. You be that honest with me."

Beebo's gaze fell. "I'll put up with it," she said, but her
voice was rough with resentment.

"I'm sorry, Beebo," Leo said, and though his masculine
aversion to her was as real as he declared, he was still capable of a restrained sympathy for her. "The world wasn't
made for dykes, you know."

"No," she flashed. "It was made for movie queens and
their tyrannical husbands."

Leo hunched his shoulders, unoffended. "The world was
made for normal people," he said. "The abnormal in this
world have a tough go. If they keep their abnormality
secret, they're damnably lonely. If they broadcast it, they're
damnably hurt. You were born with that, and you'll have to
live with it, the way I have to live with Venus's faults."

Beebo was impresssed with his sensitivity. But she answered
moodily, "I don't feel so damned abnormal, thanks. I feel
as normal as you do. I eat three meals a day, I pay my
bills, I respect the other guy."

"Well, I can tell you, society doesn't give a hoot in hell
how normal you *feel*, Beebo. You *look* queer, and that's
enough. People are waiting around to throw some crap your
way."

"What about the queers who look normal?" Beebo demanded.

"They have a chance," he said. "They can hide. You can't. And when the stuff hits the fan, I don't want Venus anywhere near you. You can have it all to yourself."

"You're a pretty goddamn infuriating individual, Leo," Beebo said.

"Sure," he agreed, getting up and stamping the cigar butt into the tile floor. "An honest man always is. I've said some harsh things to you, but they were true. And I've permitted you to stay on—conditionally. You know the conditions, my friend, and if you feel like ignoring them, you'd better feel like saying goodby, too. You dig?"

"I dig," Beebo said, glowering at him from the sofa.

She wrote to Jack that night, sitting in one of the unused spare rooms, where she was shunted when Venus was out. She recounted a little of what Leo had said.

"God, Jack, it makes you want to go out and convert the whole damn world to homosexuality," she told him. "Just so you can walk down the street with your head up.

"Maybe I grew up too fast, maybe that's my trouble. I feel so lost out here . . . hung up between two worlds; half-kid and half-adult, half-boy and half-girl. And sometimes it seems like I get the dirty side of both. Leo's whole life is one long compromise . . . maybe that's what he was trying to tell me about mine.

"I wanted Venus and I got her, but I'm not sure having her is worth the shame and secrecy of it. I'm strong and tall as a boy, but I'm not free as a man. I wanted to be gentle and loving with women, but I can't be feminine.

"Venus tries to make it better for me. She argues with Leo to let me out more. She gives me things all the time—money, clothes, anything—and it makes me realize how much she thinks about me when she's working. She's even been going to Toby's PTA meetings.

"And damn it, Jack, I know she loves me. She proves it to me whenever she's home. But that's the catch—that whenever. It gets later every day, and she's so tired. She never says no, but I feel like a dog.

"You know something? I wish all this had happend to me ten years from now. You said that about Paula, but you were wrong. Paula was just what I needed. I miss that girl, Jack. I sit here on these long empty days and dream about her. My letters to her are awful, I don't know what to say. Say I love her for me, will you?

"No—better not. Because I don't know how I can leave Venus, and I'm still not sure I want to. God, what a mess!"

Leo confronted her one morning two days later and said, "Lay off Venus a little, Beebo. She has circles under her eyes."

Beebo, still half-asleep by herself in Venus's bed, mumbled at him and sat up.

"Her eyes don't photograph well. She looks her age and that's no good," Leo said. "She gets home at midnight, pooped, and you light into her for another couple of hours. She's too crazy about you to say no, but she has to get up at six-thirty next day, while you lie around till noon."

Beebo rubbed her eyes. "Leo, I don't force her to make love to me," she said, trying to clear her head. "She *wants* to."

"Well, she can't. Not till next Tuesday. That's the pre-mière showing and we're all under a hell of a strain till then."

"My God," Beebo whispered, almost to herself. "I have to give that up, too? Leo, what else is there?" She turned to him, scowling.

"After Tuesday night, whether we sink or swim, the whole cast and crew get a week off, and you can make up for lost time," he said, gazing at her long form with curiosity; wondering how it could appeal to anybody, yet respecting his wife's intense admiration. "I'm sorry, Beebo. It's either con-tinence, or I take her to a hotel. You choose."

"I have so little of her, Leo. You're asking me to do with-out even the little I have." She put her head down on her knees.

"Just for a few days."

She lay down on the bed, turning her back to him, and Leo watched her a moment before he shut the door.

In the half week before *Million Dollar Baby* bowed, a one-liner appeared in a trade gossip column. It said, "Who's been picking Venus Bogardus up at TV City in a silver sport coupé these days?"

Leo spotted it, underlined it in red, and left it on Venus's dresser, where Beebo picked it up the next morning and read it with round-eyed shock.

The next day, another columnist asked, "What's this about Venus Bogardus taking a personal interest in her son's friends? Especially one near and dear to the family?" Leo under-lined that one, too. Beebo read it while she was sitting alone in the spare room again. She was sleeping there till Tuesday night.

Leo made no comments in the margins. He didn't have to. Beebo was scared enough at the unembellished print. She hadn't seen Venus for a couple of days. Venus was too busy and after the hints in the papers, she and Leo removed to a hotel. Beebo was afraid for Venus, afraid for their love affair, and afraid for herself. If only Jack were there to help her. If only it had been possible to tell all to her father long ago and run to him now.

Toby saw how blue she was later in the day and tried to cheer her up. "Hey, don't look so gloomy," he said. "What's got you down?"

Beebo looked at him. "Toby," she said, almost hoping he wouldn't hear. "Did you read the newspapers today?"

Toby's face reddened and she wished immediately that she hadn't brought it up. "I don't read them," he said. "I heard about it at school. Everybody wants to know which friend of mine they're talking about. But they all think it's a boy, naturally. I—I mean. . ." He paused, flustered, un-willing to hurt her "There was a thing like this once before, Beebo, and it just wasn't true. Leo proved it. He'll get Mom out of this, he always does. There's always some jerk waiting around to throw a scandal at the movie stars." He sneaked a look at her to see if he was helping any.

"I know it's not true Beebo, so don't worry," he said put-ting his hand on her arm "You know I don't believe that junk. You kid around, but you wouldn't do anything like that."

Beebo looked away from him. "I wouldn't hurt your mother—" she began.

"I know," he said, with surprising warmth and sympathy. "She'll be okay, don't worry. The thing that scares me is ... well I don't want you to leave us Beebo. You've done so much for us. Besides who'd help me with my biology? Honest—these gossipers—they'll say anything about anybody."

Beebo was touched by his anxiety. "I'm not going anywhere, Buddy," she said. But she meant, *Not right now. Tomorrow, I may have no choice.* And Toby realized it.

Beebo was a thin line away from despair. All the charmingly confessed selfishness, that had seemed adorable in Venus at first, had become Beebo's prison.

And having nothing else to do, Beebo studied Venus's faults as never before. The self-love, the endless clichés. Venus might laugh at them, but she couldn't abandon them. People said there was only one great glamour queen left in Hollywood: Venus Bogardus. And Venus thought they meant her trimmings—her velvet-paved boudoirs and flashy conceits; not her Self.

Beebo loved her with excited fascination still. And Venus loved Beebo as well and truly as she knew how. More, certainly, than anyone but Toby. And yet ... was that enough?

Beebo stood looking out the window of her room at twilight, taking in the grounds of the estate and the evening star. Venus. So high and bright and beautiful. And as far out of reach at that moment as ever it was when she was growing up back in Juniper Hill.

That night, when she tried to write to Jack again, she spoiled her page twice with tears and gave it up. She was trying not to admit that Venus had no room in her life for a gay lover; that theirs was a time-bomb romance, set to explode in their faces. The papers had lighted the fuse. And Beebo, looking at that perfect point of light in the black sky, knew in her heart that her days with Venus were numbered.

The morning of that crucial Tuesday, a nationally syndicated columnist who wielded huge power in Hollywood, said she was checking a New York source for verification of a

shocking news item about one of the town's greatest stars...
a woman, currently headlining a TV series.

Two other columnists pretended special information on the
same subject, but all refused to reveal their information or describe the scandal till it was authenticated.

Venus was on trial that night. One columnist had snickered,
"If Leo doesn't mind, I don't know why I should. After all,
he's been through this a dozen times."

Even at that they had let her off pretty easily. But the
atmosphere around her crackled. Fortunately, advance notices
on *Baby* were good. They had had a good schedule and an
extravagant budget. And Leo, with bench-coaching from
Beebo, had wheedled a radiant performance out of his wife.

Venus and Leo watched the broadcast on monitors at
Television City with the whole *Baby* company, and went on
afterwards to a baroque party on the famous Restaurant
Row of LaCienega Boulevard. They hit most of the eateries,
picking up celebrities en route, and capping the bash at the
home of a popular singer who had guest-starred on the
opener.

The party was noisy and crazy, and Venus, a show-
stopper in silver sequins, took Hollywood under her thumb,
with the subtly effective aid of her husband. She had her
arms around every man present at least once, as graceful
and captivating as any lovely woman aware of her success.
When she was twitted about the dark secrets mentioned in
the papers, she laughed and told everyone she was screwing
her cat, and the whole subject was swept away in the
laughter that followed. Only Leo remained grave, smiling
slightly and talking, but inwardly seething.

And Venus, if the truth were known, was even more disturbed than he.

Beebo saw the show in the Bogardus rec room with Toby.
The house was eerily quiet. All the servants had been given
the night off, except Venus's correspondence secretary, a
fussily officious young man; and Mrs. Sack, who never went
anywhere anyway.

The show had hardly started before the phone began to
ring: telegrams, roses at the front gate, long distance rhapsodies. The secretary took the calls, but Beebo and Toby

picked up the red wall-phone and listened in to some.

At the station break, the secretary put his head in and said, "Beebo? Telegram for you." He handed her the yellow envelope.

Beebo felt the bottom of her stomach sink southward. She was sure it couldn't be good news. Not when she had left so much angry confusion behind in New York.

The wire was from Jack: "Get home, pal. N.Y. safer than L.A. Couple of people want your scalp. Jack."

What does he want me to do, go back and give it to them? she wondered, taking her worry out on Jack.

"Was it bad news?" Toby said, looking at her face. Beebo pursed her lips and nodded.

"A friend in New York. He says my enemies want me dead."

Toby paled, started to ask about it, and suddenly turned back to the TV screen as if afraid to know the truth.

When the show was over, Toby and Beebo went for a walk on the lawn, meandering side by side and speaking little. Beebo was full of the shadow-image of Venus on the screen; glittering, gorgeous, inaccessible. Finally Toby stopped in a garden path, standing stiff-legged and staring back at the lighted windows of the empty living room. "Beebo," he said. "You're not going to leave, are you?" It was not just Beebo he feared to lose. It was his mother as well.

Beebo's hands curled into fists. "I don't know," she said, so softly it was hard to hear her. She knew she was going to have to, that she was way beyond herself here. And yet not even the discouragements of boredom, shame, and abstinence had completely crushed her. She kept thinking of how it might have been.

"I feel so bad about it all," Toby said. "They have no right to say those things about you. It makes me sick. Stay with us, Beebo. Leo will take care of you."

His faith in Leo moved her. She wished she could risk the truth with him, without destroying him. She wished he could know somehow what she was, and that the knowledge would not make him loathe her.

Beebo stood beside him, silent in the night, letting him rant against the cruel accusations in the papers with youthful outrage, protesting his trust and affection, and she felt a terrible sob coming up in her throat.

Leo had forbidden her to tell him she was his mother's lover. But it was the meanest sort of cowardice to let him stand there and thank her, and beg her to stay on, when all the while she was betraying his gratitude.

"Nobody in this world ever did so much for Mom and me," he was saying. "Honest, Beebo. If you go now, it would ruin everything. I don't see—"

"Toby, stop it! Please! Oh, God," Beebo cried. The sob broke and her voice went hoarse. "Stop it, stop it, stop it!" She covered her face with her hands for a few agonized moments. Toby stared at her as if she had taken leave of her senses, very much distressed at her sudden explosion. He tried clumsily to calm her.

"Did I say something wrong?" he asked apologetically.

"It's no use, Toby," Beebo cried, so brokenhearted that he was stunned. "I have to go."

"Go where?"

"New York."

"You said there were people back there who want to hurt you," he objected, turning white again. "Beebo, if that's true, you *can't* go. I won't let you."

"Anything would be better than here," she said, looking at him in torment. "They'll flay me alive out here—if not tomorrow, then the next day. Oh, Toby, I'm sorry, I'm so sorry." The sobs silenced her for a minute. "Please believe me. I wouldn't do this to you for the world, only—"

Toby turned and walked away.

She pursued him, calling anxiously, "Toby! Toby, wait!" She caught up as he was letting himself down gingerly on a stone bench, moving for all the world like an old man with bursitis. Beebo joined him, reaching out to touch him, then pulling back when he turned away.

"I don't understand," she heard him murmur. "I told you—Leo—don't you believe me? He can help—if it were true, but it's not—"

He frightened her. The words were so breathless and disjointed, the voice so small and hurt. He was rocking back and forth, as if shaken with sobs, but there was not the slightest sound audible now from his throat. "Toby? Are you all right?" Beebo said.

He moved around, again with that strange parody of crippled age, and seemed about to answer her, when all of a sudden he startled her by springing straight into the air with a weird howl. In the elapsed time of less than a second, Beebo realized he hadn't sprung at all; he had been thrown upright

by the abruptly powerful tensing of his entire muscular system.
He was having an epileptic seizure.

And before she could move to help, he had fallen forward, rigid as a cigar store Indian. He struck his head on a
decorative rock across the path when he hit the ground.
Beebo cried out, horrified, and then dashed to his side, lifting
him carefully off the gravel and onto the soft grass.

Her years of experience with sick animals and illness
steadied her a little. She knew he mustn't swallow his tongue
but it was too late to put anything between his teeth. His
jaws were locked shut. She rolled him gently on his side, thinking that he could breathe better and would be less likely to
choke on his own saliva, which came foaming out of his
clenched jaws. He was quivering like a vibrator machine
and groaning uncontrollably while the white suds oozed
from his mouth. It was a ghostly wail that made Beebo
shiver. And yet she knew that a seizure—even one as alarming to see as this one—shouldn't be a cause for panic.
Aside from his contortions, it was the blow on his head that
worried her, but she couldn't get a look at it.

Toby's feet were pointed downward, tight and hard as a
toe dancer's, and his arms were glued to his sides. Beebo
was relieved when finally she felt him go limp. But it was
then that she saw his forehead and gasped. There was a
gash in it, deep and ragged. She began to tremble with alarm.
Now that Toby was relaxed, the wound opened like a foun-
tain. Such quantities of blood flowed over his face and onto
Beebo and the ground beneath them that she felt almost sick.

She tried to pick him up, but her legs failed her momentarily and she collapsed beside him, sweating frantically.

"This won't help him, idiot!" she berated herself. "Get
up!" She tried again and made it, desperate to get him in
the house and clean the wound. She wanted help, anybody,
a doctor—Mrs. Sack. "Mrs. Sack!" she shouted suddenly, but
there was no sound from the house. Mrs Sack's room was on
the other side on the top floor and she would never hear
Beebo calling from the lawn below.

Beebo lifted Toby and carried him into the house. She put
him down on a satin-upholstered sofa, watching with pity
and fear as the red blood soaked into the pink silk. She pressed
her bare hand down hard on the wound and the flow
abated slightly. Nearby was one of the house intercom
phones, and Beebo reached it with her free hand.

"Mrs. Sack," she said breathlessly. "I'm in the living room

with Toby. He had an attack and hit his head. Call the
doctor and then get down here—fast!"

Mrs. Sack rushed into the living room moments later, armed
with rolls of gauze and tape and disinfectants. She stopped at
the sight of Toby, so limp and colorless, except for the
scarlet stains on his face and the sofa.

"I've been waiting for something like this all my life,"
she said grimly. Beebo was astonished to see how firm and
fearless she was; not at all the comfortable muffin she seemed
when all was well with her boy. "We've had some bad falls
before, but not like this."

"Is the doctor coming?" Beebo asked.

"Yes, in ten minutes." She knelt by Toby, washing the
wound while Beebo watched.

"Shall I call Venus?" Beebo said.

"No," said Mrs. Sack emphatically. "She's worse than
nothing in a crisis. She goes all to pieces. It doesn't help Toby
and it certainly doesn't help the doctor."

Beebo thought, *I should be grateful she's here—she knows
just what to do.* And yet she was distressed to think that
Venus should be playing goddess at a party while her son
lay hurt and bleeding—and no one was making a move to
tell her.

"She has to be told, Mrs. Sack," Beebo said.

"Go and tell her, if you must," Mrs. Sack said. "She can
meet us at the hospital. At least over there they can give
her a sedative."

Beebo stood uncertainly by the phone, trying to picture herself walking in on the fancy party in her bloody slacks; infinitely preferring to call .

Mrs. Sack looked around. "Beebo, this boy is more my
child than hers—she says so herself," she said unexpectedly.
"All his life he's come to me when he was hurt, and I'm the
one who knows how to care for him. Not her. It's my job.
My life." She was as proud and strong in her words as a
soldier bristling with defense.

To Beebo, staring at her, it became clear that Venus
didn't just give Toby up. Toby was deftly taken from her
by this plump, kindhearted woman who never had a child
of her own, but was obviously made to mother one. She
believed Toby was truly her child because Venus had for-
feited her right to him, even the right to be there to comfort him and patch his wounds.

"Mrs. Bogardus could have had him when he was born," Mrs. Sack went on, ministering to Toby. "But she practically threw him at me. And I was overjoyed to have a little son to raise and love. She can't walk in here like a queen and demand him back, just because he cuts himself and scares her."

Beebo went over and patted Mrs. Sack's shoulders. "I'm sorry," she said gently. "Nobody's criticizing you, Mrs. Sack. But Venus is his mother, no matter how much you've done for him or how much you love him."

"If you call that woman," Mrs. Sack said, turning around and standing up to italicize her words, *"I will not be responsible* for the condition of this boy. Beebo, you're a nice youngster and you're his friend. It'll be bad enough for Venus to see him at the hospital, but if she comes racing in here shrieking bloody murder, she's likely to make Toby believe it. Do you want a sick boy or a dead one on your conscience?"

Beebo ran a distraught hand through her hair. "But Mrs. Sack, I *can't* go get her."

"Nonsense. Just change your clothes and drive over. It should take you about half an hour, and by that time the doctor will be with us and Toby will be at the hospital."

"But the papers..." Beebo muttered.

"I don't read the papers, Beebo. but I'm quite sure they'll forgive you for getting the mother of a sick boy from a party." She had turned back to Toby. "It's an emergency and there's no one else to go."

"What about Rod—her secretary?"

"He doesn't drive. And besides, he overdramatizes everything. He'd really fix Mrs. Bogardus." Mrs. Sack didn't seem to care whether Beebo ever got there. But Beebo knew Venus had to be told at once. Venus herself had admitted to hysterical behavior in the face of Toby's attacks. Perhaps the only way then was to pick her up and drive her to the hospital, as Mrs. Sack suggested.

Beebo put on some clean clothes in her room, and as she ran down the stairs again, headed for her car, she heard the newly-arrived doctor saying on the phone, "Yes, a concussion. Get an ambulance over here." He looked up and saw Beebo.

"Are you Miss Brinker? Get his mother, will you? Tell her not to worry—I don't want two patients on my hands tonight. Better not say much about the wound. Just tell her

it's a bump. We're hospitalizing him till the risk of hemorrhage is passed."

"Yes, sir," Beebo said, and ran out to the garage.

She left her car directly in front of the main entrance to the
house where the party was, and went in.

"Excuse me, this is a private party—" said a doorman,
but Beebo, with that peculiar air of authority that came to
rescue her from various crises, interrupted him calmly.

"Where's Miss Bogardus?" she said, scanning the living
room. "It's an emergency."

The butler, who read the gossip columns like everyone
else, gazed at her with new interest. "I believe she's occupied," he said with a venal smile. Beebo gave him a twenty-
dollar bill, too worried even to begrudge it.

"You'll find her in the back gardens. Out the French
doors," he said, gesturing toward them.

Beebo strode through the champagne-stained living room.
Many a famous face glanced at her, and a columnist whispered to his scribe to take notes.

She slipped through the heavy shadows bordering the
spotlighted garden. Venus was at the farthest corner. Beebo
simply looked for the heaviest concentration of men. In the
center, slim and straight in her coruscating sequins, stood
Venus Bogardus: a silver exclamation point in the purple
dark.

Too much shivaree had followed Beebo out of the house
for Venus to be unaware of it. Leo alerted her at almost the
exact moment her eyes fell on her lover. There was a half-
second of undressed fury visible in her eyes, flashing brighter
than her dazzling gown. And then she pulled her pride
across her face like a veil.

Beebo walked toward her, her mission making her impossibly sure of herself. The two women eyed each other as
Beebo approached down an aisle of staring men, like an in-
fernal bridegroom passing through an honor guard of devils.
Luckily, neither Beebo nor Venus were people to collapse
in the face of public shock.

Silence fell, except from Leo who said clearly, "I'll tell
you just once, Beebo. *Leave.* You're fired, and I never want

to see you again." He spoke softly but in the hushed garden his voice carried to the audience of Hollywood topnotchers.

"Fired? I never worked for you, Leo," Beebo said.

"Venus, tell her to go," Lee ordered his wife.

But Venus, watching Beebo, loved her enough to feel instinctively that Beebo would not come to humiliate her in public without a drastic reason. With her characteristic public calm, so different from the histrionics she indulged in private, she walked boldly to Beebo and said, "All right, what is it?"

Beebo hadn't even time to take a breath before she heard Leo say, "By God, you get that kid out of here or I will."

Venus ignored him, walking toward the house with Beebo coming close in her wake. But this was once that Leo would not let himself be flouted in front of his friends. He had to bring Venus to heel as a matter of pride, and not only because he considered her action self-destructive. It seemed as if Venus were making a donkey of him before God and the world as payment for the years of tolerance and love and patience he had spent on her. It was too much for him. He caught up with her, spun her around, and brushed Beebo aside.

"Tell her to get out of our lives, or I'll take her apart," he said. He so rarely threatened Venus that he scared her. But Beebo faced him. "Leo, why in hell do you think I'm here? I came—"

He didn't let her finish. "You cocky little bitch, you want it all, don't you? Even her ruination! After all I told you."

"Let me explain!" Beebo said, alarmed now like Venus. But Leo reached out with icy rage and slapped her face. A red storm swirled up suddenly in Beebo, and she lit into him so hard that for several amazed seconds, he let himself be punched. But when he got his bearings he was after her with all the tornado fury of a cuckolded husband. Every man who had ever shared a bed with Venus Bogardus got a souvenir sock that night—and every girl. Only it was Beebo who took the blows.

She fought well enough, but Leo came on with a wild single-minded lust for vengeance that had her back in the grass before long, heaving for breath, cut and bruised. She would never surrender, and Leo, possessed by years of bitter grievances and pent-up vengeance, was in no mood to be merciful.

Beebo, sinking beneath his punishment, became aware at last that the blows had ceased. She heard Leo give a cry and opened her eyes to see Venus, shoe in hand, glaring at him. She turned to Beebo and her face softened. "Can you get up?" she asked. "I'll take you home."

Leo put a hand to the back of his head where the sharp heel had cut his scalp. He brought his fingers away, wet and red, and turned to look at his wife. But Venus, taking advantage of his brief confusion, had pulled Beebo to her feet and rushed her through the house toward the car.

The crowd surging after them deterred Leo's chase just enough to prevent him from catching them as they drove away. An uneasy silence settled on the party as the silver coupé sped off. Nobody knew what to say to Leo. But he left almost at once, making brusque apologies to his host.

"Well," said the smug voice of a Hollywood observer, who wrote for one of the trades, "I guess it's true, after all. I wasn't going to print it."

"Print what? What?" the crowd chorused eagerly.

"The tip I got from New York last week."

"I got it, too," a woman reporter piped up. "I thought it was sour grapes, but I have my people checking it."

The guests began to rumble for enlightenment, but the first gossipist said, "Read it in the morning paper, friends." And he left with several other members of the movie press, all chattering as they walked down the drive.

Beebo slumped in the front seat, her head against the window, mute with pain for several moments.

"We'll take you home and clean up those cuts, darling," Venus said, wincing at the sight of them when she stopped for a light.

Beebo shook her head. "Dr. Pitman has Toby at the hospital," she said. "That's what I came about."

"*What?*" Venus was so shaken she almost lost control of the car. Beebo had to grab the wheel from her. "It's okay, honey, he's going to be all right," she said quickly. "He had a seizure, that's all."

"God, I knew it was something awful the minute I saw your face," Venus cried as the car moved erratically down the street. "And that sonofabitch husband of mine had to pound you to pieces—"

"Don't blame Leo," Beebo said, her voice soft and drained. "I don't. It wasn't me he was hitting so much as all the people who came before me."

Venus was crying and Beebo tried to make her stop the car. "Toby's had dozens of seizures in his life, but they didn't put him in the hospital. What aren't you telling me?" Venus said.

"He fell," Beebo said. "We were walking in the garden after the show. He had a seizure and fell, and his head struck a rock. He has a cut on the forehead, but—"

"Oh, dear God!" Venus gasped, and Beebo said, "Stop the car. Damn it, Venus!"

"But we have to get to the hospital—"

"In one piece," Beebo said. "I'll drive."

"You're in no shape—" Venus began, but Beebo broke in, "I'm in better shape than you are." She made Venus slide over on the front seat while Beebo walked painfully around the car. Her wounds were the sharp residue of Leo's wrath— but her head was clear. She started the motor, and told Venus firmly, "Toby's going to live, and so am I."

Venus looked down at her sparkling knees, trying to control her weeping.

"Look, honey, if you have any ideas about running to Toby with tears streaming down your face, and carrying on as if the end were near, so help me, I'm going to join Mrs. Sack's team. She said that's exactly what you'd do."

"She's wrong," Venus said. It was just enough to prick her conscience into action, and she wiped her eyes while they were still flowing.

Neither of them said anything more about Toby or the coming storm with Leo and the papers till they reached the hospital. Venus insisted that Beebo accompany her inside, and Beebo acceded to keep her from getting frantic.

Toby had a concussion all right. They were making a spinal tap to determine the extent of pressure, if any, on the brain, and to relieve it surgically if necessary. It was urgent to do this as promptly as possible, to avoid brain damage.

"The blow was pretty hard," Dr. Pitman told them while a nurse dressed Beebo's wounds in Toby's room, at Venus's request. No one dared to question Beebo about them. Venus said imperiously, "She's hurt. Can you help her?" But her eyes were wild and her thoughts all with Toby.

"Fortunately," the doctor went on, while Venus bent over her son, peaked and scarcely conscious on the hospital bed, "the skull is thick and tough in the front, with heavier bone than in the back. A blow to the back, of the same force as the one Toby sustained, might have done serious damage. As it is, I'm as concerned about the blood loss as the concussion. We're preparing a transfusion. He'll feel a good deal stronger after that than he does now."

Dr. Pitman looked curiously at Venus. "I must say, Miss Bogardus, you're taking this better than I expected."

"Mama?" Toby whispered, and Venus clutched one of his hands in both of hers.

"Yes, Toby," she said.

"Am I going to be all right?" He looked at her. "I feel so punk."

"Yes, darling, you are," she said.

He shut his eyes, reassured, and Venus turned away to cover a sob. The doctor gave her an "I-should-have-known" look and helped her to the door.

"You're very tired," he said. "Do you still have some of those yellow pills I gave you at home? All right, I want you to take one and try to rest. You can do Toby more good in the morning, when both of you are feeling better."

Venus tried to object, but Pitman pulled Beebo aside and said hastily, "I've been treating her for years. I know how she can be. If she doesn't sleep tonight, we'll see real fireworks, and that will set Toby back if she gets at him."

Beebo looked at the boy, resting now as the nurses prepared his arm for the blood transfusion, his head neatly bandaged. "Is he really going to be okay, doctor?" she said.

"You convince me, and I'll convince Venus."

"I think so," Dr. Pitman said, but his concern was still plain on his face. "To be honest, there is always some risk with any head injury—especially with an epilepsy patient. He needs absolute peace and quiet and as little movement as possible, until the danger of internal hemorrhage is past . . . but he's young and sturdy, and we'll have a twenty-four-hour watch on him. I do believe, Miss Brinker, that his mother will only be in our way tonight. We'll call immediately if there's any change for the worse, but I don't anticipate one now."

Beebo took Venus out of the hospital in stages, letting her fold up and rest on chairs in the hall on their way, till she had her in the car and could drive her home.

Venus was forced to expend her frustrated maternal impulses on her hurt lover instead of her hurt child. She investigated and re-dressed all of Beebo's bruises, making small noises of reproof and pity.

"Thanks for braving that party, darling," Venus told her. "I'd have died of self-contempt if you hadn't let me know."

"Toby would have been all right."

"Maybe. But I wouldn't. It would have killed me to let Mrs. Sack do it all again. Especially now when Toby and I are getting so close."

"Where do you suppose Leo is?" Beebo said, touching a cut with careful fingers.

"I'll be damned if I know. Or care," Venus said harshly. "I thought for sure he'd be here, waiting to skin both of us alive. He'll be around sooner or later, you can bet on that." She sighed, leaving Beebo to turn on the radio by her bed. "I wish they had let me stay with Toby," she said. "I'm ashamed that they couldn't."

"You can see him first thing in the morning," Beebo comforted her.

Venus unzipped her sequins and dropped them in a starry heap on a chair. Fifteen-hundred dollars' worth of dress and she treated it like a dishcloth. There was nothing underneath it but her shoes, which she kicked off.

Beebo put a hand gently on Venus's neck, massaging it a little. "Maybe this is a poor time to bring it up," she said softly. "But we have to talk, Venus. I—I love you, but I can't stand living this way, honey. I realized something in front of those people at the party: I was on trial. My life, my love for you, my self. I can never love you openly, like a human being. They don't give me credit for being human."

"Beebo!" Venus said, looking at her with a shocked face. "Don't say such ugly things. You're talking about the girl I adore."

Beebo looked away. "I'm not the kind of person I want

to be, Venus. Not the kind I want you to love. I'd rather die than hurt you, but I feel as if I'm dying, anyway ... of shame and ... well, doubt about us. I want to love you somehow without it torturing us both. And I can't."

"I know," Venus said, and Beebo sensed their mutual hopelessness. She embraced her and Venus began to cry. "When I saw him beating you tonight, I could have killed him," she said, her voice rusty with tears. "It took all the meanness out of me. I just wanted to console you. Beebo, whatever happens to us, always believe that I loved you—I *love* you."

"I promise," Beebo said, but the past tense gave her a premonition of what was coming. "What do you mean, whatever happens?"

"I mean, the papers, and the rest of it. I have to deny everything, Beebo. I have to pretend you're nothing to me. Oh, darling, understand why!" It was a declaration of love that struck Beebo's heart.

"I understand," Beebo said, and thought she did. But she didn't get quite all of it. For Venus was saying goodby to her. Beebo didn't know that this loveliest night they would spend together would be the last. She had thought all along that when the end came, she would pick her own time and day to go; not that the whole thing would be out of her control.

Venus said nothing, did nothing, to spoil the night. She was silent about Toby, even though her heart contracted at the thought of him, and she ached to be beside him. She spoke only words of love to Beebo.

Beebo, surprised at Venus's ardor, gave in at first to humor her, and finally found herself forgetting even the bruises and cuts on her body.

The night was mild and the stars were sprinkled thick as spilled soapflakes across the sky. Venus pushed aside the sliding door to her patio, and they danced out there a while on a rug of cool grass, moving with the music and the air and the three o'clock mocking bird, arch-deep in the tickling soft grass.

Beebo felt as if she could have held and loved her fabulous lady forever. When she leaned down to kiss Venus's face, her cheek was wet.

"Oh, it's nothing, darling," Venus assured her. "I'm just a sentimental idiot. Say you love me and I'll recover."

"I love you," Beebo said. "I love you, Venus." And to

her surprise, her mind was with Paula Ash for a moment. It staggered her a little. Venus stopped dancing and looked up at her in the moonlight. "Do you? Really?" she asked. It wasn't just a woman's endless need to be told over and over. It was the knowledge that she wouldn't hear it again after this night had passed.

Venus loved her enough to hope that when she sent her away in the morning—for she would have to—Beebo's wounds would heal and she would be able to think back on their love without the regret that rots so many sweet memories.

"Beebo, promise me one last thing, darling, and then I'll shut up."

Beebo squeezed her, turning her tenderly to the rhythm of a waltz. "I'll promise you that moon on a platter if you want it."

"Promise me you'll remember this night as long as you live. Everything about it. The stars inches over our heads, and the music, and the grass, and . . ." The famous voice broke and she cried again.

Beebo picked her up and sat with her on a bamboo garden chair. "Darling, what's the matter?" she demanded.

"Oh, Toby and—the damn gossipists. I don't know. It'll never be the same for us, Beebo."

Beebo, full of apprehensions, had no comfort to offer her now, except to hold her tight. Then Venus slipped from her arms to the feathery grass and Beebo followed her down, and there were no more questions or tears or promises. Nothing but beautiful oblivion till the trespassing sun announced the morning.

Beebo awoke, a head-to-toe bouquet of blue bruises from the jolting Leo had given her. But it hardly bothered her. Venus had loved her so warmly all night that she was half-ready to hope they could work out some sort of compromise; half-ready to give in to more months of demoralizing secrecy, if it could be like that every night.

Venus called the hospital the moment she awakened, and they reassured her that Toby was no worse; in fact, seemed better.

She hung up, looking as blue as before her call. "Now we have to face Leo," she said.

"He won't eat you alive, honey," Beebo said.

Venus paled suddenly. "Look!" she said, pointing at her dresser. Beebo saw the telltale glass, still coated with orange juice. "He's already been in looking for trouble." Venus stole a glance at Beebo, so young and handsome, so vulnerable to the worst ostracism society could offer; and her heart swelled. *I can't hurt her,* she thought in anguish. *I've had twenty years of adulation and I've got more money than I'll ever use.* She began to wonder if she had the guts to go with Beebo after all. *What the hell, I've never loved anybody like this before. Am I afraid to stick to the one person who knows how to make me happy?*

It gave her the courage to try, at least, to defend Beebo against her formidable and stubborn husband.

While she was preoccupied with these thoughts the bedroom door opened. Beebo was just pulling her shoes on, sitting on the edge of the bed in her clothes of the night before. She stiffened, expecting Leo, but it was the corresponding secretary again. "Another telegram," he said to her. "For you."

"Thanks, Rod." Beebo got up to take it and was about to open it when she heard him say, "Good morning, Mr. Bogardus," and there was Leo. He dismissed Rod with a wave of his hand and Beebo stepped aside wordlessly to let him enter the bedroom. He had a lighted cigar—a bad sign—and another glass of orange juice in his hand. Beebo thrust the telegram in her pocket and followed him in, shutting the door.

"All right," Leo said. "We're adults, and we aren't going to scream at each other. Let me talk first if you please. Beebo, are you all right?"

His board-meeting tone, typical though it was of him, offended her more than an explosion of fury would have. "Relax, Leo, you won't have to pay any more doctor bills," she said. She was pleased to see that she had given him a shiner.

"I've been to the hospital. I was there all night. I can understand your concern at the party, Beebo. But let me remind you that this house is full of telephones, anyone of which would have got a call through to Venus."

"Leo, Mrs. Sack told me Venus would—"

"But you preferred to repay my kindness to you by shaming me in public."

"The doctor said it, too: Venus would get hysterical if she heard over the phone that Toby was hurt and had to be hospitalized."

"You know it's true, Leo," Venus said softly.

"I didn't go there to shame you, Leo," Beebo said. "It's bad enough being holed up in this fort like a prisoner of war, but not so bad I'd do that to you. I just want you to believe one thing: I was really scared about Toby, and I never thought of anything but getting you and Venus to him as fast as I could."

Leo finished his glass of juice while she talked. "I believe you," he said. "I also believe you could have sent somebody else and spared us what we're about to go through—all of us. I've been tolerant about Venus's lovers in the past because they were vital to her existence. But none of them ever treated me like a sucker."

"Beebo has always treated you respectfully, Leo," Venus interrupted heatedly. "It isn't you she's rebelling against; it's the way we've made her live."

"What other way is there? Did she think she'd be your escort at parties? Meet all your friends? I think I've had to put up with a hell of a lot more than Beebo has. All the worry of this queer situation has been on my shoulders. Christ, I never could understand why a woman would want anything to do with another woman that way, anyway. And if she did, why love a woman who does everything possible to make herself look like a boy? Why not love a real woman? Or a real man? If you want a lover in pants, Venus, I'm available. I have been for years, and I still love you, though God alone knows why.

"If you want to love a female, don't run after a mistake of Nature like Beebo Brinker."

"Leo, that's brutal!" Venus cried. "Beebo can't help how she was born. Good God, do you think any human being would deliberately choose to live with a problem like this? Leo, there are homosexuals in this world—I'm one myself—emotional strays of one kind or another, who at least have the comfort and privacy of an inconspicuous body to live in. The shelter of a normal sex on one side of the fence, or the other."

"Are you trying to stir my pity for her?" Leo said.

"I don't want your lousy pity!" Beebo said.

"I'm trying to make you see how it feels," Venus said urgently. "Leo, what if you'd been raised as a boy and learned to be a man, and had to do it all inside a female body? What if you had all your masculine feelings incarcerated under a pair of breasts? What would you do with yourself? How could you live? Who would be your lover?"

Leo nodded, answering slowly. "That's what I'm saying: it's not an easy life, nor a desirable one, no matter where Beebo lives it. And I know she didn't pick it out. But whether you two like it or not, she is a freak. And I am sorry for her. Now, Venus—do you want me to sit by and watch that kid wreck the career I've spent twenty years of my life to build? Yours, my dear—all yours!"

"I don't want it!" Venus shouted stridently, wanting to hurt and frighten Leo.

But Beebo was recalling Leo's words: "If you ever mean more to her than her career, I'll lose her. I won't let that happen. I'll fight you—I'm warning you, Beebo." When she thought of leaving Venus, she meant to leave a path open behind her for an occasional meeting, a correspondence, a night together now and then when Venus was in New York. But Leo was about to sabotage even that small hope. She looked at him and caught her own thoughts in his eyes.

"That shellacking I gave you was only the opening round, Beebo. Unless you're ready and willing right now to walk out of here and never come back. Never call, never write, never speak to Venus or see her again. *Never*."

"Leo, I love this girl!" Venus said. "If you insist on kicking her out of my home, you can kick me out with her." It was not what she had thought she would say when the time came. She felt a sort of amazed pride in her foolish bravery.

Beebo, too, was overcome with gratitude; yet wondering at the same time what recriminations Venus would vent on her as the weeks and months went by, if they did leave together. Where would they go, with Venus as notorious as she was? The thought of running away with her—of being tied to her for life—alarmed Beebo in spite of herself.

Leo walked to his wife and spoke straight in her face. "Fine," he said. "Go with her, Venus. Never mind losing your money, your name . . . and your son. Not to mention me. The things that have sustained you all these years. Ditch them all.

"What for? For your bargain, here: Beebo. She'll love and protect you better than I can, no doubt. You're thirty-eight

years old and you won't have that face of yours so damn
much longer. If you quit now, it'll go to hell in a hurry. By
the time Beebo's twenty-eight, you'll be nudging fifty. Probably a grandmother with a face full of charming crow's
feet. Every night you and Beebo will sit by the TV and watch
old Bogardus movies on the late late show."

Beebo and Venus stared at him.

"You won't have your face or your fortune or your home,
or me to fight your battles, or Toby to love and respect you
at last. You won't have Toby at all, for that matter. Do this,
Venus, and you've lost him forever. No state board in it's right
mind would give custody of a child to an infamous Lesbian
who'd surround him with scandal and expose him to homosexual obscenities—even if the child himself wanted to be
with her, which he damn well would not.

"And what do you trade Toby for? A big, overgrown
penniless butch with no job and no prospects for one, who'll
dump you the minute that face and body begin to sag."

"You bastard!" Beebo shot at him, appalled.

"Shut up, Beebo," he said coolly. "Do you have a job?"

"No, but—"

"Do you deny you're gay?"

"No, but—"

"Do you deny Venus would lose everything if she went
with you? Do you love her so much you can't wait to destroy
her?"

"Leo, for the love of God—"

"For the love of my wife I say these hard things!" he shouted at Beebo. "You were warned. You have no business standing there now with a slack jaw. What will you do, take a
cold-water flat in Greenwich Village and live on love till you
get hungry and cold? Do you think Venus Bogardus can go
anywhere in the world right now with the papers headlining
her lewd romance with another woman? 'Venus Bogardus,
queen of hearts, has found a queen of her own.'" He was
quoting, unknown to the two women, the morning's gossip
columns.

Venus, thinking he had made it up, turned all her famous
fury on him. "Get out of this house, you stinking dog!" she
cried. "I never want to see you or hear your filth again!"

"I'll be over at Sam's when you're ready to call me," Leo
said, referring to the friend who took him in whenever Venus
turned him out.

"I'll never call you!" she screamed at his retreating back. It was always her parting shot. Later in the day she would pick up the phone and tell him that even though he was a sonofabitch, she guessed he'd better come home. Miss Pinch had just squeezed a batch of fresh orange juice.

At the door Leo picked up a stack of newspaper columns, torn from the morning papers, and held them out to Venus. "These will pass the time while Beebo is packing," he said, but Venus refused to glance at them. Beebo, in the grip of a spiraling alarm, took them instead.

Leo looked at her. "I'm sorry I had to hurt you," he said. "If you weren't so young you might have handled things better. I got hurt too, Beebo. The most I can hope for now is to save Venus and Toby. It'll take all my ingenuity—and maybe all my money. And I have to start at once. Just like you have to get gone."

She didn't answer him, but she felt moved, realizing slowly that he needed her pity as much as she needed his. She could never forgive him for calling her a freak, and yet it had been a valuable lesson in the prevailing attitude toward mannish women.

Jack had been sympathetic and patient with her. Pat, himself quite feminine, had responded to her much the way that the Lesbians who liked her did. Even the people back in Juniper Hill had been pretty used to her most of her life. They watched her grow up and while they laughed unkindly and sometimes lied about her, still they had never said to her face the things Leo Bogardus had said. Beebo damned well had to stand up and fight back, or lose her self-respect forever.

Her gaze fell on the pile of columns in her hand, as Leo left them alone. Venus tried to throw them all in the wastebasket, till she saw the spreading shock on Beebo's face. She read over Beebo's shoulder, holding her breath:

"Venus Bogardus, ruler of the hearts of men the world over, is ruled herself it seems: by a WOMAN! Is this true, or just vicious gossip? Readers of my column know I never use any but the most carefully validated tips from reliable sources. This one has been double-checked and we can say positively: the handsome youngster sharing the Bogardus manse as companion to Venus's son, is really the apple of the movie star's eye. Is Venus Bogardus really one of those unfortunate misfits, a LESBIAN? Leo, do you know about this? Does your stepson know it? Our hearts are with you in this difficult situation.

"Readers who doubt me may ask themselves if I would dare to print such an accusation under the threat of legal action from Miss Bogardus, if it were false. No! I would never, etc., etc. . . ."

Beebo shuffled through the others quickly. It was the top story in all the trades and made full columns in the big L.A. dailies. She looked at Venus and saw such a pallor on her face that she was afraid Venus would drop where she stood. Beebo helped her to her satin-draped bed where Venus deflated in a heap.

Beebo stood beside her, her hands crammed into her pockets, afraid to touch her. At last she asked, "Does this mean I have to go right now? Alone?" She knew it did; she had known all along it was coming. Yet here they were, and the time was upon them, and it was abysmally hard to do. Strangely, she found herself picturing Paula again. It comforted her. Not that she had any illusions about a warm welcome from Paula. But even the thought of a fight with the little redhead was better than the thought of not seeing her at all.

Beebo touched Venus's long hair gently. "A few minutes ago you were telling Leo he'd have to kick you out, too, if he wanted me to go." It wasn't kind to remind Venus, and yet it was a relief in a way.

"Oh, darling, I'm such a coward," Venus said brokenly. "I can't bear it. Where in hell did they find out? Miss Pinch would never tell. The others don't like me, but they wouldn't do anything to ruin Leo. Besides, I was never around during the day and at night we were so careful. How in hell—?"

Beebo knew perfectly well how it got out. She touched the telegram in her pocket fearfully, and Venus saw her face change and guessed. "Your friends in New York?" she asked.

Beebo pulled out the wire. Jack had written: "Hope this catches you before the sky falls, pal. If not, chin up. We love you. I found out too late from Pat that Mona wired the Hollywood press. Come home and ride out the storm. This is a time for friends to help you, not lovers. Jack."

Beebo folded it with the meticulous care you give to the oddments of life that happen to be in your hands when pain strikes; each fold careful, straight, and neat—as tidy as her life was not. There is an obscure comfort in smoothing a small piece of paper to it's ultimate neatness. It seems a symbol of order and reason that must somehow rescue you from the chaos of suffering. It eases the misery that wants to pour out of your eyes and wail from your throat.

"My friends in New York," Beebo said huskily, "are still my friends. My enemies in New York did this to me. Venus, Venus . . ." She shook her head. "I don't know what to say. I've been trying to tell you, but I didn't know how. I thought we could part lovers and come together again, still lovers, some day."

Venus reached up for her, both of them admitting tacitly that it could never have lasted; neither willing to say the words outright.

But Beebo rejected her arms. "I have to confess something terrible to you," she said. "I—I brought on Toby's attack. I was telling him I thought I would have to leave here, so you wouldn't be hurt by the papers. He got more and more upset and strange . . . he tried to answer me . . . and then suddenly he shot up and fell over."

Venus looked away. "It might have happened anyway," she said. "We know so little . . . I'm going to lose him, Beebo. He'll never get over this."

"You're wrong. You've got to be! You can't lose all you worked for with him in one stroke like that," Beebo said.

"Maybe Leo can help me," Venus said, the dimmest spark of hope in her eye. "He always seems to put me back together. Maybe he can do it for Toby."

Beebo could see that she was floundering at the prospect of losing the props that had supported her for so long: Leo, Toby, her money, mass love.

"One thing you have I'll never have, darling," Venus told her quietly. "Courage. I'll bet you didn't know how much till now. Maybe you've got it because without it you'd have been destroyed long ago. Well . . . I hate to admit it, but Leo is my courage. I can't run away with you, even though my heart breaks to let you go." She stopped talking for a minute till her voice steadied a little. "I thought you'd given Toby to me at last, but I'm afraid you've lost him for me forever."

"I hope to God he has better sense than that," Beebo said, kneeling by the bed with her face near Venus's. "I hope he loves both of us more than that, and I think he does. He's brighter and steadier than you are, Venus. Besides, he's lived all his life with a condition that makes him different from ordinary people. Maybe that will help him understand me a little now."

Venus stopped crying and embraced Beebo. "Forgive me," she whispered. "All I want to say to you is, thank you. For the time I had with Toby, for the love you gave me."

For a moment Beebo wanted to stay so badly she was ready to sacrifice her life again—but only for a moment. It was easy to get carried away when you had your arms full of Venus.

"I love you, Beebo," Venus said seriously. "Some day you'll know how it feels when you're my age, and the girl you'll adore forever is yours. And you know it's going to end before long and you'll have to go on living somehow."

Beebo caressed her shoulders without looking at her face. "You'll never say you love me again, will you?" she murmured. "Will you say it to another girl?"

Venus's arms tightened around her. "Will you?" she countered.

"You'll say it to men as long as you live, won't you?" Suddenly it seemed unbearable to Beebo; bad enough to know that other girls would follow her, even if Venus never loved any of them. But intolerable that she would keep on climbing into bed with men, too. Her hands hardened on Venus's shoulders. "God, how I wish I could make you choose!" she said. "Be gay or be straight. Don't be both. The only other girl I know who's both is contemptible."

Venus answered quietly. "Beebo, you knew what you were early in life. Some of us don't find out till after we've committed ourselves to a man and children. You're one hundred per cent gay. You never doubt it. You breathe such easy contempt for me. But darling, believe me, you're the lucky one. You knew yourself in time to save yourself from housewifery and husbands—things the rest of us have to live with.

"But I didn't know till it was too late. It wasn't just all the men I've known that confused me. It was the way I was raised, too, and the girls I knew. It was having a man and a child and a career in my life to defend before I knew I wanted anything else. It was a paralyzing fear of the truth. I didn't have a body like yours that threw the truth at me whether I wanted to see it or not. I could pretend. I pretended with men and men and more men.

"And the more clearly I realized I was gay, the more terrified I was to admit it to myself, and the more I had to lose. Do you have to loathe me for it, Beebo? Am I sort of second-class Lesbian, is my love a second-class love, because I live with a man and I've borne a child?"

Beebo shut her eyes. "I'm your lover, not your judge," she said, pulling Venus's head down on her shoulder. "All I know is, I hate it—sharing you. If it were another girl, I could fight back on my own ground. But Leo confronts me with marriage and motherhood and morality and . . . God, what can I say? Tell all of society to go to hell?" She kissed Venus disconsolately. "If you'd known what you were when you were young, would you really have given up all this for the life of a Lesbian? The kind of life I'll lead?"

"If I'd known I could be as happy with a girl as I've been with you, Beebo . . . and I didn't have my son or a name to worry about . . . I could have given up anything to be with you."

Beebo couldn't hate her, in spite of the distressing knowledge that she had been used. Venus was no Mona Petry. Venus proved her love and did her utmost to go beyond her limitations for the sake of that love. But she had lived too long in the world of safety and social acceptance that is the normal woman's—a world Beebo would never know—to leave it now. She was imprisoned in the only security she knew, just as Beebo was imprisoned in her body and her strong emotional needs.

"You despise me a little for hiding behind my husband and child," Venus said, seeing it in Beebo's face. "What do you want me to do with them, darling? I love Toby and I need Leo. I can't wish them out of existence. They existed for me long before you did."

"Venus, I don't know what's right or wrong," Beebo said. "I only know I love you and it's made me miserable. God spare either of us another affair like this one." She caught Venus in an impassioned embrace, holding her hard enough to hurt her and crying soundlessly against her cheek.

Then she released her, walking swiftly too the door. Venus gave a small scream and rushed after her. "Oh, not like this! Wait, stay with me a while. There's no need to go just yet. I need you more than I ever did. Beebo!"

"Don't make it hurt any worse, Venus," she said. "Let's not cut it off an inch at a time." Beebo was the strongest and it was up to her to make the break physical and final.

"Say it one last time, then," Venus pleaded wildly. "I'll never see you again! Beebo, darling—say it!"

"I love you," Beebo said huskily. "Goodby, lover." She reached out and put her hands on Venus's shoulders to draw her near; kissed her ardently on the lips and then chastely on the brow.

Venus gazed at her, afraid to believe it for a minute, and then dropped her face into her hands with a sob. Beebo left her, running down the curving stairs to the front door. If she were to move at all, it had to be at top speed.

It was raining in New York when Beebo landed at Idlewild, a standard, sharp November rain: liquid ice tumbling out of a dirty sky. She reached Jack's familiar door early in the evening and rang his bell. The answer was immediate, as reassuring as a personal word.

She dashed up the stairs and saw him leaning in the open doorway, waiting for her. Neither of them said a word. Beebo went up and hugged him against her damp jacket. He fit neatly under her chin, letting himself be squashed in the name of friendship.

"Come in, pal," he said.

"I should have wired you. I left in such a damn hurry," she said. "Jack—you aren't even surprised to see me!"

"I read the garbage in this morning's paper," he said. "I didn't think Venus would keep you around long after that. But I have to admit I wasn't prepared for her phone call."

Beebo's mouth fell open. "Venus called *you?*" she said.

"About four hours ago. Said you were flying back. She remembered my name and had her secretary try every Jack, John, and J. Mann in the Manhattan directory," he chuckled. "She sounded very sweet and sad. I was impressed with her—I really was. She said to tell you she loves you."

Beebo leaned forward on the sofa. "Poor Venus," she said, too tired even to feel surprise at her compassion. "She's so afraid I won't believe her. You know something, Jackson? She does love me. That's the craziest part of it. She just isn't strong enough to snap her fingers at the world. And God knows she had more at stake than I had—mostly a son she's just beginning to know and love. I have no business condemning her. But oh my God, it hurts so much. She was so lovely."

Jack sat down beside her. "I know the feeling," he said. "I guess it's the one pain on earth you can always remember perfectly, down to the last mean twinge."

Beebo smiled a bit, putting her head back on the sofa and accepting gratefully a lighted cigarette from Jack.

"How about a peppermint schnapps?" he said. "Or would you prefer Scotch and water?"

"That's more like it."

"It'll warm you up a bit. What a rotten day for a homecoming." The rain pelted the roof and windows with an endless muted rattle. He handed her the drink, making one for himself.

"Thanks, Jack," she said. "You know, it was sunny in California. Eighty-two degrees and not a cloud in the sky."

"I was stationed there a while during World War II. I remember that weather."

The small talk comforted Beebo and the drink relaxed her. They had another, and it wasn't till Beebo had been there several hours and told Jack all the highlights of her life with Venus, that she became aware at last of a void in the room. She sat up. "Where's Pat?" she said.

Jack glanced down into his drink. "Pat left," he said simply.

"Left?" Beebo looked at him incredulously. "Jack, he couldn't just leave, he was so fond of you!" she said. "I'm so sorry."

"So am I. But it's winter, after all. Spring will bring somebody new. It always does."

Beebo's heart turned over for him. "But you . . . really loved him. Oh, Jackson," she sighed. "And you let me deluge you with my problems."

"Yours are worse than mine, pal," Jack said kindly. "And newer. Pat left me about four weeks after you did. First of October."

Beebo shook her head, still half-disbelieving. "Why?" she said.

"He found somebody else," Jack said, and when Beebo exclaimed in protest, he added, "A woman." Beebo stared at him. "I guess you put that bug in his ear," Jack said wryly. "He began to brood about being gay. He thought if he could be so attracted to you, maybe it would work with another aggressive girl. And he was a bit lost when you left, anyway. Then he met Sandra and got quite a crush on her. She took him on. It all happened in a few weeks' time. They're living upstate, running an antique shop. She's teaching him the business. And I guess he's exterminating her termites. Now and then he comes down to see me. We get along fine."

"And I thought he was so happy here," Beebo mourned.

"I think you meant more to him than we realized. He moped around after you left and wanted to follow you to L.A. I talked him out of it, but it seemed to relieve him to talk about you. Frankly, he talked too much. I warned him, and he really tried to stop, but he'd have a drink or two and open up. And he always got around to you. It was complimentary—what he said—but there was too much of it. Mona or Pete managed to get most of the dope.

"And when Pat realized he was hurting you, he began to blame himself for all your troubles. He felt guilty about living with me—'off me'—when he couldn't give me his whole love. He's a damn nice kid, Beebo. It's best for him that he look around a bit more."

"What's best for you, Jackson?" Beebo asked fondly.

"Somebody new, I guess."

"I hope you don't have to wait till the spring."

"I'd rather. It'll give me time to get over Pat. Besides, I'd rather fall in love in the sunshine than the rain."

He fixed another round while Beebo mused, "I hope Venus's son gets through this all right. It's tough enough on Leo and Venus . . . but Toby. I was his best friend. He thought if I ever left he'd lose his mother again."

"He didn't lose her," Jack said. "Venus said Leo explained things to him at the hospital. It shook him up pretty badly, but he came out of it on Venus's side. That Bogardus must be a wise man. Venus said he didn't say one bitter word about you. Anyway, Toby ended up wanting to comfort her. She said it saved her life. She couldn't have stood to lose you both in one day.

"Toby doesn't know what to think about you, and maybe he never will."

"That will draw him closer to Venus, at least," Beebo said. I don't like to think he'd ever hate me. But there's some comfort in knowing I brought him and his mother together. It's a funny thing . . . all of a sudden she seems as remote and inaccessible as—as the California sunshine. The end of the rainbow. Jack, I hate to give up the pot of gold."

She bent her head and shut her eyes a moment. When she looked up she asked, "How's Pasquini doing?"

"Got a new driver—a boy," Jack shrugged. "Marie can still cook. I don't know about Pete. He's a scared little man. I guess that's what makes him so vindictive. He feels brave hurting somebody who can't hurt back."

"He and Mona sent the scoop to Hollywood, didn't they?"

"They did. They called me about it later. They were that sure of themselves." He studied her face. "Venus told me about the boxing match with Leo. He must have given you those bruises."

"It's all right," Beebo said, touching her face. "I gave him some, too."

Jack lighted a cigarette. "There's one more thing, honey," he said. "Your brother." He spoke carefully in an effort to keep from alarming her.

"Jim?" Beebo said, grimacing. "God, I suppose he read about all this, too. Did he tell Dad?"

"No," Jack said. "Somebody sent your father the news, but he never saw it. I suppose it was Mona."

"Damn it, why does that girl enjoy persecuting me? All I ever did was get my wires crossed on a date with her once. I can't understand—"

"You will," Jack promised her. "Beebo, listen to me. Your father . . . never knew."

She looked at him, suddenly white-faced, and whispered, "Oh, Jesus. Oh, God. Jack? He's dead, isn't he?"

"I guess I shouldn't have told you tonight," Jack said. "Coming on top of the rest, maybe it's too much."

"No," she said, breaking down and crying a little. "Do you know, Jack, I'm almost glad. I'm sick that I wasn't with him at the end—if I'd known it was so close I'd have come back. But that poor unhappy man went through too much over me as it was. I think—I hope—that he knew why I left him. Maybe he seized the chance to lay his burdens down.

"Oh, I don't mean he'd kill himself. But he kept himself alive through sheer will power, to help me out of my scrapes. After I left, he was free to surrender. For all he ever knew, I ended up the doctor he hoped I'd be." She shook her head. "Such a good man. So kind, so humanly frail. I loved him, Jack."

"I got quite a biography of him from Jim," Jack said. "His drinking, his poverty, his tantrums. Jim's bitter as hell."

"I was the cause of most of it," Beebo said. "What happened to Jim?"

"He sent me a letter from the University of Wisconsin. He said your father didn't have any money, but you could have any of his belongings you wanted. If he doesn't hear from you before the end of this month he's going to sell what he can and throw out the rest."

"Is that all?"

"He said he was sorry for you but he never wants to lay eyes on you again."

She laughed sourly. "I'll bet," she said. "That's the nicest he's ever put it, too. I never loved him, Jack, but he's all the family I have, and he's no family at all. It's too bad... but he's right. We're poison together. I guess I'll let him sell Dad's things. I have his picture and my memories. They're worth more to me than some worn-out furniture."

She fell into bed soon after, lying in the familiar warmth and watching Jack move around the room. She envied the fullness and strength of his arms and chest.

When the lights were out she asked him softly, "Jack? How's Paula Ash?"

"Pretty lonesome."

"Do you see her at all?"

"All the time. We shore each other up."

"What do you do together?"

"Talk about Pat and Beebo."

Beebo smiled faintly in the dark. "Is that all? Does she hate me?"

"No, little pal."

"Does she...love me?"

"You'll have to ask Paula that one."

"Jack, is she living with anybody?"

"She was. The girl with the Plaid Pajamas moved in for a while."

Beebo felt an odd melancholy that had nothing to do with her father or Venus. "Have you met her? Plaid Pajamas?"

"Yes."

"Who is she?"

"Nobody you'd go for. Didn't Paula tell you about her?"

"Not much."

"Well, you'll meet her one of these days," he said.

That was all she could get out of him.

Beebo spent the next week resting and living quietly out of sight. She had no plans for wild revenge against Pete and

Mona; only the wish to forget, to learn to live with herself again.

Venus was often in her thoughts and would be for a long time. But more and more, as the hurt faded, she found herself preoccupied with Paula. Paula, so real and so faithful; so unlike the fairy-tale princess, Venus, who had vanished inevitably into Never-Never Land. Beebo had crashed back to earth, and she wanted a real girl in her arms.

The cackling in the papers about the Bogardus-Brinker affair made life awkward for her for a while, with reporters trying to scout her down and people whispering about her wherever she went. But the talk was slowly yielding at the other end of the country to Venus's surprising dignity. She appeared in public at Leo's side emphasizing the duration of their life together. Both of them swore that their marriage had never been stronger, and in a way, it was true. They needed each other extremely then.

The official story was that Beebo was a young woman who had taken a job on the household staff and subsequently became a close friend of Toby's. Nobody was aware that she was harboring a feverish crush on Venus. When the situation blew up in their faces, Venus and Leo were as startled and shocked as the rest of the movie colony. They expressed their sympathy for their unfortunate young friend and hoped she could find a happier life somewhere else.

"No one who knows me will believe that there was anything between this poor girl and myself except a friendly relationship based on her closeness to my son," Venus was quoted. And Beebo, reading the statement, could picture Leo writing and rewriting it at the desk in his library, with a cigar fuming in his mouth and a glass of orange juice nearby.

Somehow, Leo brought it off—partly by expending huge sums on public relations and partly by exploiting Toby's illness: he hinted broadly that unless the furor died down, the boy's health was in danger of permanent damage.

Beebo shed a few tears over it in private. But it was, after all, as merciful towards her as Leo and Venus dared to make it. Her picture was kept out of the papers. She still had some anonymity in this biggest of all big cities.

It had been two weeks since she returned to New York; weeks spent resting and job-hunting. Beebo was tense throughout the day, for that night the second segment of *Million Dollar Baby* was scheduled for showing. It was the one in which Venus sang, "I'm Putting My All On You"—the song Leo and Beebo had coaxed out of her that night in the recreation room.

Beebo tried all day to forget about it. But when she came home again that night without a job, Jack had to cheer her up with a cold martini. "When are you going to call Paula?" he said casually.

"Paula who?" she said with a little smile.

Jack pinched her amiably in the arm. "She wants to see you. This would be a dandy night not to watch television."

"How do you know Paula wants to see me?"

"Well, if she hadn't called to say so, I'd still know. I'm telepathic."

"You're psychopathic. What am I supposed to do, go over there and beat the daylights out of Miss Plaid Pajamas? You said they were living together."

"*Were*—past tense. I don't know what the situation is now, with you home. Anyway, pal, what's the matter with you? Afraid of a little fight? Or isn't Paula worth it?"

"What are you promoting it for, Jackson? Taking bets?"

"If the Pajamas are still hanging around, you can take her with one hand behind your back. Leo must have taught you *something*."

"And after I kayo her, then what do I do?"

"You claim the fair damsel, stupe," Jack said. "Jesus, you're thick sometimes, Beebo." He chuckled at her.

Beebo sobered slightly. "Jack, I'm not so sure. I mean, I hurt Paula. I was damned unfair and unfeeling with her."

"Really? *Unfeeling?*"

"I ditched her for what must seem like the cheapest kind of affair, when Paula needed me and Venus only wanted me."

"You're ashamed of yourself. Is that why you're stalling? Beebo, don't you know a girl in love is always ready to forgive her lover?"

Provided the lover's in love with her," Beebo said.

"Well, aren't you? Not one letter did I get from California that you didn't fret and worry over Paula Ash."

Beebo looked at him. "I've been thinking about just two people for the past two weeks: Venus and Paula. And every day, it's more Paula and less Venus. And yet I think if Venus were to call and say, 'Come back, I can't stand it without you'—I'd go."

"No, you wouldn't, pal. You've learned too much." Jack nodded at the phone. "Besides, she'll never call. Venus Bogardus isn't real any more. She's the doll millions of us will watch and covet tonight on TV. And you're just one of the millions now."

Beebo felt momentarily swamped with frustration. Gradually she became aware of Jack's voice saying, "Paula doesn't belong to the public or a bank or a one-track husband. She doesn't have any of those things. Paula can get up when the show is over and turn the set off, and come back to your side, ready for love. Venus will be gone forever with a turn of the knob."

Beebo lighted a cigarette to cover her emotion. "Maybe I should call Paula. The least I can do is apologize. But I don't want to see her till I'm sure—"

"Sure of what?" Jack said. "Loving her? Beebo, you can wait a lifetime trying to be sure of love. You didn't wait to be sure of Venus. I didn't wait to be sure of Pat."

"And look how those affairs turned out," she said.

"If we had waited, we wouldn't have known any happiness at all with them. I still love Pat. We're friends and I think we always will be. Venus loves you, Beebo, and the things you gave her are the most precious in her life. Because of her, you're growing up a little, at last. Would you rather it had never happened, just because it hurt?"

She glanced at him, puzzled. "No. But I don't want to hurt Paula any more. She doesn't deserve anything but my love, and I don't know if I can give her that yet."

"Well, she can give you hers. And right now, that makes her the strong one. You need love and it's her joy to give it. Maybe the gift will transform the recipient. That's what happened to Venus."

"God, if I could make myself love her, I would," Beebo said, but Jack laughed at her.

"Hell, honey, that's *her* job," he said. "Be honest with her and she'll take it from there. If she's willing to risk a love affair with you now, knowing all she knows, you have nothing to be ashamed of."

Beebo doused her cigarette. "Can you eat all that hamburger by yourself?" she said, pointing at it.

"Without the slightest strain." He smiled at her.

"Okay," she said, answering the smile reluctantly. "I'm going calling. But if I come back here tonight with two black

eyes and a broken heart, by God, Mann, you're going to pay
for it."

"I can't wait," he said.

Beebo threw a plastic saucer at him, which he fielded
deftly, and left with his laughter in her ears.

She walked through the night air, crisp and cold enough
to crack if you just knew how to grasp it, all the way to
McDonald Street. It was easy enough to find Paula's building.
Not so easy to go in and ring her bell.

Beebo looked at the small black button for several minutes
before she pressed it. When the answer sounded at once, she
wondered if Jack had called to forewarn Paula. She opened the
door and walked down the hall with the feeling of reliving in
life what she had once dreamed an eon ago.

Paula's door was open as it had been the night they
met. A slice of light lay across the hall. Beebo felt her heart
beating higher in her chest. Soon Paula would appear in a
pair of plaid pajamas that weren't hers, and say sleepily,
"Yes?"

But she didn't. Beebo stopped at her door and waited. She
could feel Paula's presence somewhere just inside the room.
Finally she glanced in, blinking at the light. Paula was leaning against the far wall, facing the door. Her hair had
grown quite long in the few months since they had seen each
other, and it washed over her pink silk shoulders in an auburn
tide.

Her eyes were enormous and there was a flush of love and
fear in her cheeks. She wasn't just pretty. She was so lovely
that Beebo's breath caught in her throat. Everything Paula felt
and feared and hoped for shone on her face.

Beebo stood in the doorway, her hands characteristically
shoved into her pockets, her bright blue eyes fixed on this
gentle girl who, incredibly, learned to love her in three days
and loved her still after three months.

"Paula," Beebo said. "Are you still my Paula?"

"Still yours," she answered.

"I don't see any plaid pajamas around," Beebo said, but it
was no wonder: she didn't see anything around that room
but Paula Ash.

"She left," Paula said. "The day you came home. I told

her to leave. Oh, Beebo." Paula shut her eyes, and when she opened them, Beebo was standing beside her, hesitating, absorbing the mystery of their attraction.

"Paula, I feel as if I'm seeing you for the first time," Beebo said. "I swear I do."

"I'm no match for the goddess," Paula said, smiling without any malice. She was prompted by an innocent little-girl need to be admired and loved, so transparent that it charmed Beebo completely.

"The goddess was no match for you." Strangely, all at once, it was true. "Jack was right—you're the real woman." She closed the small space between them, taking Paula's shoulders in her big hands and kissing her suddenly on the mouth. Paula put her arms around her, so hard Beebo could feel her quivering.

"Paula—darling—I want to know just one thing," Beebo said. "Where are your damn sleeping pills?"

"I gave them to Jack the day you left," Paula said. "Kiss me again, Beebo." Beebo obeyed her gladly, over and over, rediscovering with her all the things they had learned to need and love in each other months before.

When Paula took Beebo's hands and turned them palms up to kiss, Beebo groaned with the delight she couldn't hold back. "Paula," she said, "oh, Paula. I came here like the self-centered idiot I am, thinking I could pay you off for what you've been through with a few silly kisses. Honey, I'm the one who wants them. I'm the one who needs them. I just didn't have the sense to see it."

She was full of crazy joy that was part nostalgia, part relief, and mostly desire. The touch, the fragrance, the feel of this marvelous girl were beyond anything Beebo had remembered.

Beebo picked her up and carried her into the bedroom, bending over her on the bed, her hands supporting her weight on either side of Paula's face. "Oh, that hair, that mouth. Paula, I came so close to loving you before. And then ... Jesus, she dazzled me. Honey, I was helpless with her."

"Don't explain, Beebo. I got through it somehow, and it's over. Jack practically adopted me. We talked all night every night for a week after you left. He told me you'd be back, and he was so sure of it that I believed him. I knew you weren't in love with me, but I knew you wanted me. And because of Jack, I never despaired. I wasn't even afraid of Mona any more. She thought I was nuts, but—"

"Mona! Has she been after you, too?" Beebo flared. "Hasn't she hurt me enough? Does she have to take it out on you?"

"You stood her up for me, remember?"

"How could I forget?" Beebo leaned over to kiss her. "Unbutton me, Paula," she whispered.

Paula complied with a tremor. "Mona thought she owned me," she said softly. "She shucked me off months before, but I wasn't supposed to love anybody new for the rest of my life."

"Paula..." Beebo seized her hands and looked at her searchingly. "Are you trying to tell me—oh my God!—was *Mona* the girl in the plaid pajamas?"

Paula nodded, still opening buttons until Beebo's shirt slipped off. "She came back this fall when you left. She wanted information about you at first, but then she decided to live with me again. I let her do it. I supposed I was looking for a way to hurt you both. Make you jealous, and get even with Mona for the pain she gave me. She was astounded when I told her to get lost two weeks ago. She's still waiting for you to snub me, and then she'll come back to say, 'I told you so.' "

"That's one thing she'll never say," Beebo said emphatically. "She won't have the chance. How could you fall for a girl like that, darling? You so sweet all the way through, and Mona so sour?"

"It's you I love, Beebo. Let's not talk about Mona."

Beebo kicked her slacks off, lying down beside Paula. "Did you know Mona was going to send that smear to the gossipists?" she asked.

"Yes," Paula confessed and shocked Beebo. "I'll be truthful. This is the hardest thing I have to tell you, Beebo. I knew, and maybe I could have stopped her, I'm not sure. But I didn't even try. I knew it would separate you and Venus. It would have come sooner or later, but I wanted you so awfully and this was the fastest way to do it. I couldn't have done it to you myself. But when I found out what Mona and Pete were up to, I didn't have the guts to stop them."

There was a long silence. "Beebo, I forgive you everything. Can you forgive me this?" Paula's voice, slight and sweet as herself, hung close to tears. This was the test.

Beebo turned Paula's face up to hers finally and kissed it. "You have far more to forgive than I do," she said. "If you can, so can I."

Once again they held each other, immersed in the swell of love. Paula lay beneath Beebo, letting her work a while; letting the ardor slowly take fire inside her, until the urge to respond became irresistible.

Then, suddenly, her head went back in a beautiful arch, into a pool of auburn hair. Her body heaved against Beebo's, and one of her legs slipped between her lover's. Her hands began to wander through Beebo's close-cropped curls, over her broad back and trim hips, caressing her everywhere. Beebo answered her with gratitude, amazement, and the first warm thrill of real love. Not an infatuation that knocks the breath out of you and dislocates your life for a while. But the slow sure kind, strong and reassuring, that holds together. Honesty, trust, respect, all were growing between them.

When they had slept a little, Beebo raised herself up on one elbow to light a cigarette and talk. "You know something, Paula," she said. "I tried to tell you this our first night together, and you wouldn't believe it. But it's true, and it has a lot to do with the way I feel about you now."

"What, darling?" Her look of love, so womanly and so complete, moved Beebo warmly.

"You brought me out, Paula. You were the first. I spent my life back home saying no to everything but my daydreams. There wasn't a soul I could have touched without the whole town finding out. It would have killed my father. That's one of the reasons I had to leave. Paula, you precious girl. God, how lucky I was that it was you."

"It might have been Venus," Paula said.

"If it had, I'd have botched it. She would have laughed at me."

"Her show is on," Paula said, looking at the clock-radio by the bed. "Want to watch it?"

"No thanks."

"I think you should. Come on, I'll watch it with you." Paula got up smiling and pulled her halfway out of bed.

"Paula, honey, I don't give a damn—"

"No fibs!" Paula cautioned, throwing her pink silk wrapper around herself. "Come with me, Beebo." She stood at the bedroom door, waiting, and Beebo couldn't turn her down. She stood up, but not without misgivings.

The show had already started and the commercial was in progress. Beebo took Paula in her arms and together they settled back on the sofa.

"If you had refused to look, I would really have been scared," Paula admitted. "I would have thought you were still tied to Venus emotionally—too much to bear to see her, even on the screen." She twisted around in Beebo's arms to look at her face and kissed her swiftly a dozen times till Beebo was suddenly embracing her tightly and murmuring her name eagerly.

Paula was trembling with the immensity of her feeling, full of whirling thoughts hard to word. "I know you don't love me yet the way I love you, Beebo," she said at last. "But God, I hope you will. It's kept me going—that hope—all this time. You felt so right to me."

Beebo stroked her hair and gazed at her, unaware that Venus, in black satin, was singing, "I'm Putting My All On You."

"You've only seen the rough side of gay love," Paula told her. "People can be so cruelly selfish. Even the people who try to be good to you, and I guess Venus tried.

"Darling, Lesbian love doesn't have to be brief or heartbreaking, just because it's a love between two women. I want to teach you that. I want to live with you and do things for you and even let you do things for me.

"Oh, Beebo, don't you see it? Women have a special knack for loving. Even Venus, in her way, found that knack. There's a tenderness, an instinctive sympathy, between two women when their love is right . . . it's very rare in any kind of love. But it comes near perfection between women.

"You haven't known that tenderness yet. You've only known a hectic affair with a fantastically difficult actress. I want to give you a home. I want you to come back to me every night and know you'll be loved and cared for and spoiled. Beebo, darling, I want you to spoil me a little, too."

"Paula, it'll be a pleasure," Beebo smiled.

Paula relaxed in her lap and Beebo put her hand back on the cushions. They watched the end of the song as the camera closed in on the face of Venus Bogardus. She was talking the words the way Beebo had suggested, her head tilted to one side and her eyes full, glittering with a giveaway brilliance of real tears.

At the end, she let her head drop so that her gleaming hair swung around her face and hid her eyes. The tune— just a gimmicky little love song to begin with—had become a torch. And for just one moment, Venus was living flesh for Beebo again.

Beebo moved Paula off her lap and got up, going to the TV and turning it off. "It's not that I'm still close to her, Paula," she said, coming back to the sofa. "It's just that that was goodby. From her to me."

They looked at each other. "Did you really love her, Beebo?" Paula whispered.

Beebo sat down and took both of Paula's hands in hers and kissed them in a gesture that had become special to them both. And then she pulled Paula down on the couch in her arms and kissed her neck until she squirmed and laughed. "I won't know for sure what love is till I've spoiled you for a while, sweetheart," Beebo grinned.

ANN BANNON (a pseudonym) was born in 1932. In 1957, shortly after her marriage, Bannon's first novel, *Odd Girl Out*, was published and became a surprise bestseller. Five more of her lesbian novels were published in paperback, the last in 1962, but her work fell into obscurity until Naiad Press brought five of the books back into print in 1983. Bannon is now a college professor at a California university.